John Haynes

HILARY MANTEL is the author of fourteen books and is a two-time winner of the Man Booker Prize. In the 2014 Birthday Honors, she was appointed Dame Commander of the Order of the British Empire for services to literature and counts the David Cohen Prize, the Costa Book of the Year, the Costa Novel Award, the Walter Scott Prize, and the National Book Critics Circle Award among her honors. She lives on the coast of East Devon, England, with her husband and is at work on the third and final installment of the Thomas Cromwell trilogy.

Also by Hilary Mantel

FICTION

Beyond Black

Every Day Is Mother's Day

Vacant Possession

Eight Months on Ghazzah Street

Fludd

A Place of Greater Safety

A Change of Climate

An Experiment in Love

The Giant, O'Brien

Learning to Talk

Bring Up the Bodies

The Assassination of Margaret Thatcher

NONFICTION

Giving Up the Ghost

Praise for *Wolf Hall*

❖

A *Time* Magazine Top Ten Book of the Year
A *New York Times Book Review* Notable Book of the Year
A *Boston Globe* Best Book of the Year
A *Christian Science Monitor* Best Book of the Year
An *Economist* Best Book of the Year
A *Financial Times* Best Book of the Year
A *New Yorker* Favorite Book of the Year

"A brilliant historical novel . . . That Thomas Cromwell was a histori-
cally important figure is beyond doubt; that he should serve as the
sympathetic hero of a novel is more surprising. . . . *Wolf Hall* provides
a powerful hallucination of presence, the vivid sensation of lived life.
It sets the dead in motion and makes them speak."

—STEPHEN GREENBLATT, *The New York Review of Books*

"Reader, you're in excellent hands. . . . Mantel is as nimble as writers
come. . . . Part of the delight of the masterfully paced *Wolf Hall* is how
utterly modern it feels. It is political intrigue pulsing with energy and
peopled with historical figures who have never seemed more alive—
and more human. . . . From the few scraps known of Cromwell's life,
Mantel has woven a richly textured character. She writes with such
intimacy that the reader always feels what Cromwell feels. . . . Flinty,
funny, and always dead-on honest, Mantel is much like Cromwell.
Each is gifted with a quicksilver wit, a cool, uncanny ability to deci-
pher the world, and, despite all they know, a surprisingly compas-
sionate heart."

—ELLEN KANNER, *The Miami Herald*

"Mantel's an author as audacious as Anne Boleyn herself, imagining private conversations between public figures and making it read as if she had a glass to the wall."

—SUE CORBETT, *People* (four stars)

"Ms. Mantel has a knack for getting under the skin of her characters and capturing them (one feels) as they must have been, as readers will know who have read her wonderfully imaginative novel about the French Revolution, *A Place of Greater Safety*. So convincing is she with *Wolf Hall* that it is easy to feel that we are seeing the real Cromwell before us."

—MARTIN RUBIN, *The Wall Street Journal*

"With its excellent plotting and riveting dialogue, *Wolf Hall* is a gem of a novel that is both accurate and gripping."

—CODY CORLISS, *St. Louis Post-Dispatch*

"Mantel always goes for color, richness, music. She has read Shakespeare closely. One also hears the accents of the young James Joyce. . . . Mantel should be congratulated for creating suspense about matters whose outcome we've known since high school."

—JOAN ACOCELLA, *The New Yorker*

"Fans of historical fiction—or great writing—should howl with delight."

—DEIRDRE DONAHUE, *USA Today*

"Mantel's main characters are scorchingly well rendered. And their sharp-clawed machinations are presented with nonstop verve in a book that can compress a wealth of incisiveness into a very few well-chosen words."

—JANET MASLIN, *The New York Times*

"A brilliant portrait of a society in the throes of disorienting change, anchored by a penetrating character study of Henry VIII's formidable advisor, Thomas Cromwell. It's no wonder that her masterful book won [the] Booker Prize . . . only an exceedingly bold novelist could envision this odyssey. . . . *Wolf Hall* is uncompromising and unsentimental, though alert readers will detect an underlying strain of gruff tenderness. Similarly, Mantel's prose is as plain as her protagonist (who's sensitive about his looks), but also (like Cromwell) extraordinarily flexible, subtle, and shrewd. Enfolding cogent insights into the human soul within a lucid analysis of the social, economic, and personal interactions that drive political developments, Mantel has built on her previous impressive achievements."

—WENDY SMITH, *The Washington Post*

"Cromwell remains a controversial and mysterious figure [and] Mantel has filled in the blanks plausibly, brilliantly. . . . Its five-hundred-plus pages turn quickly, winged and falconlike."

—CHRISTOPHER BENFEY, *The New York Times Book Review*

"Mantel is at her best when turning her penetrating novelistic gaze to history. . . . She burrows down through the historical record to uncover the tiniest, most telling details, evoking the minutiae of history as vividly as its grand sweep. The dialogue is so convincing that she seems to have been, in another life, a stenographer taking notes in the taverns and palaces of Tudor England."

—ROSS KING, *Los Angeles Times*

"What is surprising is how *Wolf Hall* stitches new splendor into the rather worn cloth of kings, courtiers, plagues, and power. . . . An addictively rich window into a time both alien to and mirroring our own."

—SCOTT MUSKIN, *Star Tribune* (Minneapolis)

"Mantel has achieved a genuine voice for the time. . . . The story of Cromwell's rise shimmers in Ms. Mantel's spry, intelligent prose. . . . It is in capturing such twists and turns of fate—so common to the Tudors—that Ms. Mantel shines. She leaches out the bones of the story as it is traditionally known, and presents to us a phantasmagoric extravaganza of the characters' plans and ploys, toils and tactics. There is rich dialogue here, removed from its datedness and assigned a very contemporary charge. . . . The crackling energy of Mantel's narration, the eternal spark of her subject, and her assiduous determination to rescue the reputation of Thomas Cromwell—all these make *Wolf Hall* quite perfect an enterprise by itself."

—VIKRAM JOHRI, *The Washington Times*

"A darkly brilliant reimagining of life under Henry VIII . . . Instead of bringing the past to us, Mantel's writing, brilliant and black, launches us disconcertingly into the past. We are space-time travelers landed on an alien world. . . . She gives rich detail. She is able to powerfully advance the main line of the story, while conducting fascinating side excursions. . . . In Mantel's *Wolf Hall*, history is a feast whose various and vital excitements and intrigues make the book a long and complex pleasure. . . . A darkly magnificent novel."

—RICHARD EDER, *The Boston Globe*

"A rich, rounded portrait . . . provocative."

—LAURA DeMARCO, *The Plain Dealer* (Cleveland)

"A stark and unsentimental triumph . . . *Wolf Hall* depicts a Tudor England rife with realpolitik. Period detail is subtle, suggestive. . . . This masterwork is full of gems for the careful reader. . . . Plainspoken and occasionally brutal, *Wolf Hall* is both as complex and as powerful as its subject. . . . Fascinating."

—CLEA SIMON, *The Boston Phoenix*

"In all respects a superior work of fiction, peopled with appealing characters living through a period of tense high drama. . . . There will be few novels this year as good as this one."

—DAVID KEYMER, *Library Journal*

"*Wolf Hall* succeeds on its own terms and then some, both as a non-frothy historical novel and as a display of Mantel's extraordinary talent. Lyrically yet cleanly and tightly written, solidly imagined yet filled with spooky resonances, and very funny at times."

—*The Guardian* (UK)

"This is a beautiful and profoundly humane book, a dark mirror held up to our own world. . . . Hilary Mantel is one of our bravest as well as most brilliant writers."

—*The Observer* (UK)

"Spirited . . . Mantel has a solid grasp of court politics and a knack for sharp, cutting dialogue."

—*Entertainment Weekly*

"Dazzling . . . Historical fiction at its finest, *Wolf Hall* captures the character of a nation and its people. It exemplifies something that has lately seemed as mythical as [a] serpent princess: the great English novel."

—HEPHZIBAH ANDERSON, *Bloomberg.com*

"Mantel not only illuminates the era's religious revolutionary zeal and Henry VIII's utilization of it in pursuit of the male heir he needed to ensure the succession, she also makes it immediate, even suspenseful. . . . Her prose is clean and straightforward; she evokes the era without wielding archaic forms. Her research never protrudes, but the details paint pictures in the mind's eye. Dialogue drives much of the narrative, as words are meat and bread to Cromwell. . . . Beguiling, dense, colorful, and often funny."

—LYNN HARNETT, *Portsmouth Herald* (New Hampshire)

"Mantel quietly produces one excellent novel after another. . . . They all contain the essential Mantel element, which is a style—of writing *and* of thinking—that combines steely-eyed intelligence with intense yet wide-ranging sympathy. This style implies enormous respect for her readers, as if she believes that we are as intelligent and empathetic as she is, and one of the acute pleasures of reading her books is that we sometimes find ourselves living up to those expectations. . . . You will, I suspect, read each new piece of information about Tudor England with fresh and sharpened eyes. But none of this, however instructive, will make up for your feeling of loss, because none of this additional material will come clothed in the seductive, inimitable language of Mantel's great fiction."

—WENDY LESSER, *Bookforum.com*

WOLF
HALL

WOLF HALL

A Novel

Hilary Mantel

PICADOR

A John Macrae Book
Henry Holt and Company
New York

This is a work of fiction. All of the characters, organizations, and events portrayed in this novel are either products of the author's imagination or are used fictitiously.

WOLF HALL. Copyright © 2009 by Hilary Mantel. All rights reserved. Printed in the United States of America. For information, address Picador, 175 Fifth Avenue, New York, N.Y. 10010.

www.picadorusa.com
www.twitter.com/picadorusa • www.facebook.com/picadorusa
picadorbookroom.tumblr.com

Picador® is a U.S. registered trademark and is used by Henry Holt and Company under license from Pan Books Limited.

For book club information, please visit www.facebook.com/picadorbookclub or e-mail marketing@picadorusa.com.

Wolf Hall is available on Blu-ray and DVD. To purchase, visit shopPBS.org.

Masterpiece™ is a trademark of the WGBH Educational Foundation. Used with permission.

The PBS Logo is a registered trademark of the Public Broadcasting Service and used with permission.

Designed by Meryl Sussman Levavi

The Library of Congress has cataloged the Henry Holt edition as follows:

Mantel, Hilary, 1952–
    Wolf Hall : a novel / Hilary Mantel.—1st U.S. ed.
        p. cm.
    ISBN 978-0-8050-8068-1 (hardcover)
    ISBN 978-1-4299-4328-4 (e-book)
    1. Cromwell, Thomas, Earl of Essex, 1485?–1540—Fiction.   2. Great Britain—History—Henry VIII, 1509–1547—Fiction.   I. Title.
    PR6063.A438W65 2010
    823'.914—dc22

                                                                    2009019912

Picador Movie Tie-in ISBN 978-1-250-07758-5

Picador books may be purchased for educational, business, or promotional use. For information on bulk purchases, please contact the Macmillan Corporate and Premium Sales Department at 1-800-221-7945, extension 5442, or write to specialmarkets@macmillan.com.

Originally published in Great Britain by Fourth Estate, an imprint of HarperCollins Publishers

First published in the United States by John Macrae Books, an imprint of Henry Holt and Company, LLC

First Picador Edition: September 2010

First Picador Movie Tie-in Edition: March 2015

10 9 8 7 6 5 4 3 2 1

To my singular friend
Mary Robertson this be given.

"There are three kinds of scenes, one called the tragic, second the comic, third the satyric. Their decorations are different and unalike each other in scheme. Tragic scenes are delineated with columns, pediments, statues and other objects suited to kings; comic scenes exhibit private dwellings, with balconies and views representing rows of windows, after the manner of ordinary dwellings; satyric scenes are decorated with trees, caverns, mountains and other rustic objects delineated in landscape style."

VITRUVIUS, De Architectura, on the theater, c. 27 B.C.

❖

These be the names of the players:

Felicity	Cloaked Collusion
Liberty	Courtly Abusion
Measure	Folly
Magnificence	Adversity
Fancy	Poverty
Counterfeit Countenance	Despair
Crafty Conveyance	Mischief

Good Hope

Redress

Circumspection

Perseverance

Magnificence: An Interlude,
JOHN SKELTON, c. 1520

CONTENTS

❖

PART FOUR

PART FIVE

PART SIX

CAST OF CHARACTERS

❖

In Putney, 1500

Walter Cromwell, a blacksmith and brewer.

Thomas, his son.

Bet, his daughter.

Kat, his daughter.

Morgan Williams, Kat's husband.

At Austin Friars, from 1527

Thomas Cromwell, a lawyer.

Liz Wykys, his wife.

Gregory, their son.

Anne, their daughter.

Grace, their daughter.

Henry Wykys, Liz's father, a wool trader.

Mercy, his wife.

Johane Williamson, Liz's sister.

John Williamson, her husband.

Johane (Jo), their daughter.

Alice Wellyfed, Cromwell's niece, daughter of
    Bet Cromwell.

Richard Williams, later called Cromwell, son of Kat
    and Morgan.

Rafe Sadler, Cromwell's chief clerk, brought up at
    Austin Friars.

Thomas Avery, the household accountant.

Helen Barre, a poor woman taken in by the
    household.

Thurston, the cook.

Christophe, a servant.

Dick Purser, keeper of the guard dogs.

AT WESTMINSTER

Thomas Wolsey, Archbishop of York, cardinal, papal legate, Lord Chancellor: Thomas Cromwell's patron.

George Cavendish, Wolsey's gentleman usher and later biographer.

Stephen Gardiner, Master of Trinity Hall, the cardinal's secretary, later Master Secretary to Henry VIII: Cromwell's most devoted enemy.

Thomas Wriothesley, Clerk of the Signet, diplomat, protégé of both Cromwell and Gardiner.

Richard Riche, lawyer, later Solicitor General.

Thomas Audley, lawyer, Speaker of the House of Commons, Lord Chancellor after Thomas More's resignation.

AT CHELSEA

Thomas More, lawyer and scholar, Lord Chancellor after Wolsey's fall.

Alice, his wife.

Sir John More, his aged father.

Margaret Roper, his eldest daughter, married to Will Roper.

Anne Cresacre, his daughter-in-law.

Henry Pattinson, a servant.

IN THE CITY

Humphrey Monmouth, merchant, imprisoned for sheltering William Tyndale, translator of the Bible into English.

John Petyt, merchant, imprisoned on suspicion of
     heresy.

Lucy, his wife.

John Parnell, merchant, embroiled in long-running
     legal dispute with Thomas More.

Little Bilney, scholar burned for heresy.

John Frith, scholar burned for heresy.

Antonio Bonvisi, merchant, from Lucca.

Stephen Vaughan, merchant at Antwerp, friend of
     Cromwell.

AT COURT

Henry VIII.

Katherine of Aragon, his first wife, later known as
     Dowager Princess of Wales.

Mary, their daughter.

Anne Boleyn, his second wife.

Mary, her sister, widow of William Carey and
     Henry's ex-mistress.

Thomas Boleyn, her father, later Earl of Wiltshire
     and Lord Privy Seal: likes to be known as
     "Monseigneur."

George, her brother, later Lord Rochford.

Jane Rochford, George's wife.

Thomas Howard, Duke of Norfolk, Anne's uncle.

Mary Howard, his daughter.

Mary Shelton ⎫
                  ⎬ ladies-in-waiting.
Jane Seymour ⎭

Charles Brandon, Duke of Suffolk, old friend of
     Henry, married to his sister Mary.

Henry Norris
Francis Bryan
Francis Weston ⎱ gentlemen attending the king.
William Brereton
Nicholas Carew

Mark Smeaton, a musician.

Henry Wyatt, a courtier.

Thomas Wyatt, his son.

Henry Fitzroy, Duke of Richmond, the king's
    illegitimate son.

Henry Percy, Earl of Northumberland.

THE CLERGY

William Warham, aged Archbishop of Canterbury.

Cardinal Campeggio, papal envoy.

John Fisher, Bishop of Rochester, legal adviser to
    Katherine of Aragon.

Thomas Cranmer, Cambridge scholar, reforming
    Archbishop of Canterbury, succeeding Warham.

Hugh Latimer, reforming priest, later Bishop of
    Worcester.

Rowland Lee, friend of Cromwell, later Bishop of
    Coventry and Lichfield.

IN CALAIS

Lord Berners, the Governor, a scholar and translator.

Lord Lisle, the incoming Governor.

Honor, his wife.

William Stafford, attached to the garrison.

AT HATFIELD

Lady Bryan, mother of Francis, in charge of the
    infant princess, Elizabeth.

Lady Anne Shelton, Anne Boleyn's aunt, in charge of the former princess, Mary.

THE AMBASSADORS

Eustache Chapuys, career diplomat from Savoy, London ambassador of Emperor Charles V.

Jean de Dinteville, an ambassador from Francis I.

THE YORKIST CLAIMANTS
TO THE THRONE

Henry Courtenay, Marquis of Exeter, descended from a daughter of Edward IV.

Gertrude, his wife.

Margaret Pole, Countess of Salisbury, niece of Edward IV.

Lord Montague, her son.

Geoffrey Pole, her son.

Reginald Pole, her son.

THE SEYMOUR FAMILY
AT WOLF HALL

Old Sir John, who has an affair with the wife of his eldest son, Edward.

Edward Seymour, his son.

Thomas Seymour, his son.

Jane, his daughter: at court.

Lizzie, his daughter, married to the Governor of Jersey.

William Butts, a physician.

Nikolaus Kratzer, an astronomer.

Hans Holbein, an artist.

Sexton, Wolsey's fool.

Elizabeth Barton, a prophetess.

THE TUDORS

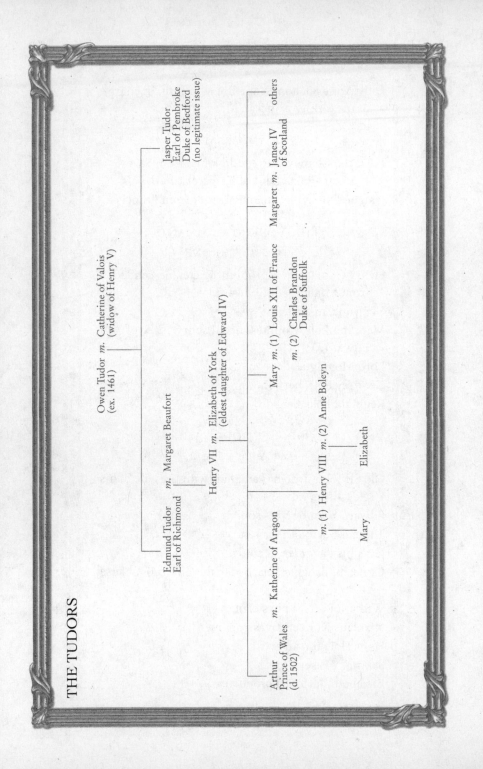

Owen Tudor *m.* Catherine of Valois
(ex. 1461)   (widow of Henry V)

Edmund Tudor   *m.*   Margaret Beaufort   Jasper Tudor
Earl of Richmond   Earl of Pembroke
                                                    Duke of Bedford
                                                    (no legitimate issue)

Henry VII   *m.*   Elizabeth of York
                   (eldest daughter of Edward IV)

Arthur   *m.* Katherine of Aragon   Mary *m.* (1) Louis XII of France   Margaret *m.* James IV   others
Prince of Wales   of Scotland
(d. 1502)   *m.* (2) Charles Brandon
                                                             Duke of Suffolk

          m. (1) Henry VIII *m.* (2) Anne Boleyn

          Mary   Elizabeth

THE YORKIST CLAIMANTS

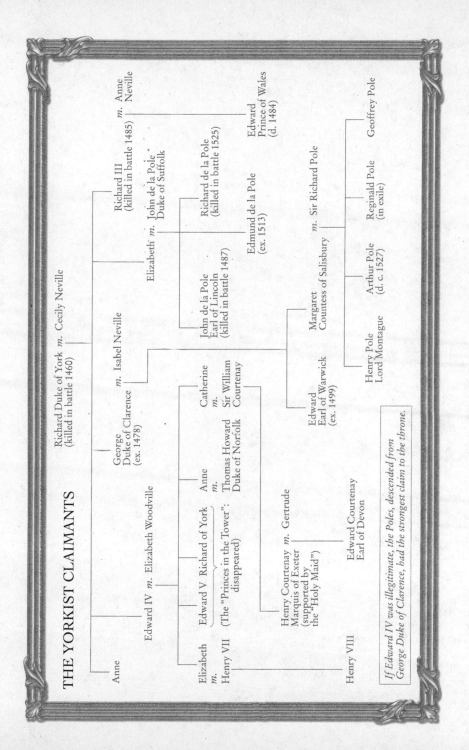

Richard Duke of York (killed in battle 1460) m. Cecily Neville

Anne

Edward IV m. Elizabeth Woodville

George Duke of Clarence (ex. 1478) m. Isabel Neville

Richard III (killed in battle 1485) m. Anne Neville

Edward Prince of Wales (d. 1484)

Elizabeth m. Henry VII

Edward V Richard of York (The "Princes in the Tower": disappeared)

Anne m. Thomas Howard Duke of Norfolk

Catherine m. Sir William Courtenay

Elizabeth m. John de la Pole Duke of Suffolk

John de la Pole Earl of Lincoln (killed in battle 1487)

Edmund de la Pole (ex. 1513)

Richard de la Pole (killed in battle 1525)

Edward Earl of Warwick (ex. 1499)

Margaret Countess of Salisbury m. Sir Richard Pole

Henry Courtenay m. Gertrude Marquis of Exeter (supported by the "Holy Maid")

Edward Courtenay Earl of Devon

Henry VIII

Henry Pole Lord Montague

Arthur Pole (d. c. 1527)

Reginald Pole (in exile)

Geoffrey Pole

If Edward IV was illegitimate, the Poles, descended from George Duke of Clarence, had the strongest claim to the throne.

WOLF
HALL

PART ONE

I

Across the Narrow Sea

PUTNEY, 1500

o now get up."

Felled, dazed, silent, he has fallen; knocked full length on the cobbles of the yard. His head turns sideways; his eyes are turned toward the gate, as if someone might arrive to help him out. One blow, properly placed, could kill him now.

Blood from the gash on his head—which was his father's first effort—is trickling across his face. Add to this, his left eye is blinded; but if he squints sideways, with his right eye he can see that the stitching of his father's boot is unraveling. The twine has sprung clear of the leather, and a hard knot in it has caught his eyebrow and opened another cut.

"So now get up!" Walter is roaring down at him, working out where to kick him next. He lifts his head an inch or two, and moves forward, on his belly, trying to do it without exposing his hands, on which Walter enjoys stamping. "What are you, an eel?" his parent asks. He trots backward, gathers pace, and aims another kick.

It knocks the last breath out of him; he thinks it may be his last. His forehead returns to the ground; he lies waiting, for Walter to jump on him. The dog, Bella, is barking, shut away in an outhouse. I'll miss my dog, he thinks. The yard smells of beer and blood. Someone is shouting, down on the riverbank. Nothing hurts, or perhaps it's that everything hurts, because there is no separate pain that he can pick out. But the cold strikes him, just in one place: just through his cheekbone as it rests on the cobbles.

"Look now, look now," Walter bellows. He hops on one foot, as if he's dancing. "Look what I've done. Burst my boot, kicking your head."

Inch by inch. Inch by inch forward. Never mind if he calls you an eel or a worm or a snake. Head down, don't provoke him. His nose is clotted with blood and he has to open his mouth to breathe. His father's momentary distraction at the loss of his good boot allows him the leisure to vomit. "That's right," Walter yells. "Spew everywhere." Spew everywhere, on my good cobbles. "Come on, boy, get up. Let's see you get up. By the blood of creeping Christ, stand on your feet."

Creeping Christ? he thinks. What does he mean? His head turns sideways, his hair rests in his own vomit, the dog barks, Walter roars, and bells peal out across the water. He feels a sensation of movement, as if the filthy ground has become the Thames. It gives and sways beneath him; he lets out his breath, one great final gasp. You've done it this time, a voice tells Walter. But he closes his ears, or God closes them for him. He is pulled downstream, on a deep black tide.

❖

The next thing he knows, it is almost noon, and he is propped in the doorway of Pegasus the Flying Horse. His sister Kat is coming from the kitchen with a rack of hot pies in her hands. When she sees him she almost drops them. Her mouth opens in astonishment. "Look at you!"

"Kat, don't shout, it hurts me."

She bawls for her husband: "Morgan Williams!" She rotates on the spot, eyes wild, face flushed from the oven's heat. "Take this tray, body of God, where are you all?"

He is shivering from head to foot, exactly like Bella did when she fell off the boat that time.

A girl runs in. "The master's gone to town."

"I know that, fool." The sight of her brother had panicked the knowledge out of her. She thrusts the tray at the girl. "If you leave them where the cats can get at them, I'll box your ears till you see stars." Her hands empty, she clasps them for a moment in violent prayer. "Fighting again, or was it your father?"

Yes, he says, vigorously nodding, making his nose drop gouts of blood: yes, he indicates himself, as if to say, Walter was here. Kat calls for a basin, for water, for water in a basin, for a cloth, for the devil to rise up, right now, and take away Walter his servant. "Sit down before you fall down." He tries to explain that he has just got up. Out of the yard. It could be an hour ago, it could even be a day, and for all he knows, today might be tomorrow; except that if he had lain there for a day, surely either Walter would have come and killed him, for being in the way, or his wounds would have clotted a bit, and by now he would be hurting all over and almost too stiff to move; from deep experience of Walter's fists and boots, he knows that the second day can be worse than the first. "Sit. Don't talk," Kat says.

When the basin comes, she stands over him and works away, dabbing at his closed eye, working in small circles round and round at his hairline. Her breathing is ragged and her free hand rests on his shoulder. She swears under her breath, and sometimes she cries, and rubs the back of his neck, whispering, "There, hush, there," as if it were he who were crying, though he isn't. He feels as if he is floating, and she is weighting him to earth; he would like to put his arms around her and his face in her apron, and rest there listening to her heartbeat. But he doesn't want to mess her up, get blood all down the front of her.

When Morgan Williams comes in, he is wearing his good town coat. He looks Welsh and pugnacious; it's clear he's heard the news. He stands by Kat, staring down, temporarily out of words; till he says, "See!" He makes a fist, and jerks it three times in the air. "That!" he says. "That's what he'd get. Walter. That's what he'd get. From me."

"Just stand back," Kat advises. "You don't want bits of Thomas on your London jacket."

No more does he. He backs off. "I wouldn't care, but look at you, boy. You could cripple the brute in a fair fight."

"It never is a fair fight," Kat says. "He comes up behind you, right, Thomas? With something in his hand."

"Looks like a glass bottle, in this case," Morgan Williams says. "Was it a bottle?"

He shakes his head. His nose bleeds again.

"Don't do that, brother," Kat says. It's all over her hand; she wipes the blood clots down herself. What a mess, on her apron; he might as well have put his head there after all.

"I don't suppose you saw?" Morgan says. "What he was wielding, exactly?"

"That's the value," says Kat, "of an approach from behind—you sorry loss to the magistrates' bench. Listen, Morgan, shall I tell you about my father? He'll pick up whatever's to hand. Which is sometimes a bottle, true. I've seen him do it to my mother. Even our little Bet, I've seen him hit her over the head. Also I've not seen him do it, which was worse, and that was because it was me about to be felled."

"I wonder what I've married into," Morgan Williams says.

But really, this is just something Morgan says; some men have a habitual sniffle, some women have a headache, and Morgan has this wonder. The boy doesn't listen to him; he thinks, if my father did that to my mother, so long dead, then maybe he killed her? No, surely he'd have been taken up for it; Putney's lawless, but you don't get away with murder. Kat's what he's got for a mother: crying for him, rubbing the back of his neck.

He shuts his eyes, to make the left eye equal with the right; he tries to open both. "Kat," he says, "I have got an eye under there, have I? Because it can't see anything." Yes, yes, yes, she says, while Morgan Williams continues his interrogation of the facts; settles on a hard, moderately heavy, sharp object, but possibly not a broken bottle, otherwise Thomas would have seen its jagged edge, prior to Walter splitting his eyebrow open and aiming to blind him. He hears Morgan forming up this theory and would like to speak about the boot, the knot, the knot in the twine, but the effort of moving his mouth seems disproportionate to the reward. By and large he agrees with Morgan's conclusion; he tries to shrug, but it hurts so much, and he feels so crushed and disjointed, that he wonders if his neck is broken.

"Anyway," Kat says, "what were you doing, Tom, to set him off? He usually won't start up till after dark, if it's for no cause at all."

"Yes," Morgan Williams says, "was there a cause?"

"Yesterday. I was fighting."

"You were fighting yesterday? Who in the holy name were you fighting?"

"I don't know." The name, along with the reason, has dropped out of his head; but it feels as if, in exiting, it has removed a jagged splinter of bone from his skull. He touches his scalp, carefully. Bottle? Possible.

"Oh," Kat says, "they're always fighting. Boys. Down by the river."

"So let me be sure I have this right," Morgan says. "He comes home yesterday with his clothes torn and his knuckles skinned, and the old man says, what's this, been fighting? He waits a day, then hits him with a bottle. Then he knocks him down in the yard, kicks him all over, beats up and down his length with a plank of wood that comes to hand . . ."

"Did he do that?"

"It's all over the parish! They were lining up on the wharf to tell me, they were shouting at me before the boat tied up. Morgan Williams, listen now, your wife's father has beaten Thomas and he's crawled dying to his sister's house, they've called the priest . . . Did you call the priest?"

"Oh, you Williamses!" Kat says. "You think you're such big people around here. People are lining up to tell you things. But why is that? It's because you believe anything."

"But it's right!" Morgan yells. "As good as right! Eh? If you leave out the priest. And that he's not dead yet."

"You'll make that magistrates' bench for sure," Kat says, "with your close study of the difference between a corpse and my brother."

"When I'm a magistrate, I'll have your father in the stocks. Fine him? You can't fine him enough. What's the point of fining a person who will only go and rob or swindle monies to the same value out of some innocent who crosses his path?"

He moans: tries to do it without intruding.

"There, there, there," Kat whispers.

"I'd say the magistrates have had their bellyful," Morgan says. "If he's not watering his ale he's running illegal beasts on the common, if he's not despoiling the common he's assaulting an officer of the peace, if he's not drunk he's dead drunk, and if he's not dead before his time there's no justice in this world."

"Finished?" Kat says. She turns back to him. "Tom, you'd better stay with us now. Morgan Williams, what do you say? He'll be good to do the heavy work, when he's healed up. He can do the figures for you, he can add and . . . what's the other thing? All right, don't laugh at me, how much time do you think I had for learning figures, with a father like that? If I can write my name, it's because Tom here taught me."

"He won't," he says, "like it." He can only manage like this: short, simple, declarative sentences.

"Like? He should be ashamed," Morgan says.

Kat says, "Shame was left out when God made my dad."

He says, "Because. Just a mile away. He can easily."

"Come after you? Just let him." Morgan demonstrates his fist again: his little nervy Welsh punch.

❖

After Kat had finished swabbing him and Morgan Williams had ceased boasting and reconstructing the assault, he lay up for an hour or two, to recover from it. During this time, Walter came to the door, with some of his acquaintance, and there was a certain amount of shouting and kicking of doors, though it came to him in a muffled way and he thought he might have dreamed it. The question in his mind is, what am I going to do, I can't stay in Putney. Partly this is because his memory is coming back, for the day before yesterday and the earlier fight, and he thinks there might have been a knife in it somewhere; and whoever it was stuck in, it wasn't him, so was it by him? All this is unclear in his mind. What is clear is his thought about Walter: I've had enough of this. If he gets after me again I'm going to kill him, and if I kill him they'll hang me, and if they're going to hang me I want a better reason.

Below, the rise and fall of their voices. He can't pick out every word. Morgan says he's burned his boats. Kat is repenting of her first offer, a post as pot-boy, general factotum and chucker-out; because, Morgan's saying, "Walter will always be coming round here, won't he? And 'Where's Tom, send him home, who paid the bloody priest to teach him to read and write, I did, and you're reaping the bloody benefit now, you leek-eating cunt.'"

He comes downstairs. Morgan says cheerily, "You're looking well, considering."

The truth is about Morgan Williams—and he doesn't like him any the less for it—the truth is, this idea he has that one day he'll beat up his father-in-law, it's solely in his mind. In fact, he's frightened of Walter, like a good many people in Putney—and, for that matter, Mortlake and Wimbledon.

He says, "I'm on my way, then."

Kat says, "You have to stay tonight. You know the second day is the worst."

"Who's he going to hit when I'm gone?"

"Not our affair," Kat says. "Bet is married and got out of it, thank God."

Morgan Williams says, "If Walter was my father, I tell you, I'd take to the road." He waits. "As it happens, we've gathered some ready money."

A pause.

"I'll pay you back."

Morgan says, laughing, relieved, "And how will you do that, Tom?"

He doesn't know. Breathing is difficult, but that doesn't mean anything, it's only because of the clotting inside his nose. It doesn't seem to be broken; he touches it, speculatively, and Kat says, careful, this is a clean apron. She's smiling a pained smile, she doesn't want him to go, and yet she's not going to contradict Morgan Williams, is she? The Williamses are big people, in Putney, in Wimbledon. Morgan dotes on her; he reminds her she's got girls to do the baking and mind the brewing, why doesn't she sit upstairs sewing like a lady, and praying for his success when he goes off to London to do a few deals in his town coat? Twice a day she could sweep through the Pegasus in a good dress and set in order anything that's wrong: that's his idea. And though as far as he can see she works as hard as ever she did when she was a child, he can see how she might like it, that Morgan would exhort her to sit down and be a lady.

"I'll pay you back," he says. "I might go and be a soldier. I could send you a fraction of my pay and I might get loot."

Morgan says, "But there isn't a war."

"There'll be one somewhere," Kat says.

"Or I could be a ship's boy. But, you know, Bella—do you think I should go back for her? She was screaming. He had her shut up."

"So she wouldn't nip his toes?" Morgan says. He's satirical about Bella.

"I'd like her to come away with me."

"I've heard of a ship's cat. Not of a ship's dog."

"She's very small."

"She'll not pass for a cat." Morgan laughs. "Anyway, you're too big all round for a ship's boy. They have to run up the rigging like little monkeys—have you ever seen a monkey, Tom? Soldier is more like it. Be honest, like father like son—you weren't last in line when God gave out fists."

"Right," Kat said. "Shall we see if we understand this? One day my brother Tom goes out fighting. As punishment, his father creeps up behind and hits him with a whatever, but heavy, and probably sharp, and then, when he falls down, almost takes out his eye, exerts himself to kick in his ribs, beats him with a plank of wood that stands ready to hand, knocks in his face so that if I were not his own sister I'd barely recognize him: and my husband says, the answer to this, Thomas, is go for a soldier, go and find somebody you don't know, take out his eye and kick in his ribs, actually kill him, I suppose, and get paid for it."

"May as well," Morgan says, "as go fighting by the river, without profit to anybody. Look at him—if it were up to me, I'd have a war just to employ him."

Morgan takes out his purse. He puts down coins: chink, chink, chink, with enticing slowness.

He touches his cheekbone. It is bruised, intact: but so cold.

"Listen," Kat says, "we grew up here, there's probably people that would help Tom out—"

Morgan gives her a look: which says, eloquently, do you mean there are a lot of people would like to be on the wrong side of Walter Cromwell? Have him breaking their doors down? And she says, as if hearing his thought out loud, "No. Maybe. Maybe, Tom, it would be for the best, do you think?"

He stands up. She says, "Morgan, look at him, he shouldn't go tonight."

"I should. An hour from now he'll have had a skinful and he'll be back. He'd set the place on fire if he thought I were in it."

Morgan says, "Have you got what you need for the road?"

He wants to turn to Kat and say, no.

But she's turned her face away and she's crying. She's not crying for him, because nobody, he thinks, will ever cry for him, God didn't cut him out that way. She's crying for her idea of what life should be like: Sunday after church, all the sisters, sisters-in-law, wives kissing and patting, swatting at each other's children and at the same time loving them and rubbing their little round heads, women comparing and swapping babies, and all the men gathering and talking business, wool, yarn, lengths, shipping, bloody Flemings, fishing rights, brewing, annual turnover, nice timely information, favor-for-favor, little sweeteners, little retainers, my attorney says . . . That's what it should be like, married to Morgan Williams, with the Williamses being a big family in Putney . . . But somehow it's not been like that. Walter has spoiled it all.

Carefully, stiffly, he straightens up. Every part of him hurts now. Not as badly as it will hurt tomorrow; on the third day the bruises come out and you have to start answering people's questions about why you've got them. By then he will be far from here, and presumably no one will hold him to account, because no one will know him or care. They'll think it's usual for him to have his face beaten in.

He picks up the money. He says, "*Hwyl*, Morgan Williams. *Diolch am yr arian.*" Thank you for the money. "*Gofalwch am Katheryn. Gofalwch am eich busnes. Wela i chi eto rhywbryd. Poblwc.*"

Look after my sister. Look after your business. See you again sometime.

Morgan Williams stares.

He almost grins; would do, if it wouldn't split his face open. All those days he'd spent hanging around the Williamses' households: did they think he'd just come for his dinner?

"*Poblwc,*" Morgan says slowly. Good luck.

He says, "If I follow the river, is that as good as anything?"

"Where are you trying to get?"

"To the sea."

For a moment, Morgan Williams looks sorry it has come to this. He says, "You'll be all right, Tom? I tell you, if Bella comes looking for you, I won't send her home hungry. Kat will give her a pie."

❖

He has to make the money last. He could work his way downriver; but he is afraid that if he is seen, Walter will catch him, through his contacts and his friends, those kinds of men who will do anything for a drink. What he thinks of, first, is slipping on to one of the smugglers' ships that go out of Barking, Tilbury. But then he thinks, France is where they have wars. A few people he talks to—he talks to strangers very easily—are of the same belief. Dover then. He gets on the road.

If you help load a cart you get a ride in it, as often as not. It gives him to think, how bad people are at loading carts. Men trying to walk straight ahead through a narrow gateway with a wide wooden chest. A simple rotation of the object solves a great many problems. And then horses, he's always been around horses, frightened horses too, because when in the morning Walter wasn't sleeping off the effects of the strong brew he kept for himself and his friends, he would turn to his second trade, farrier and blacksmith; and whether it was his sour breath, or his loud voice, or his general way of going on, even horses that were good to shoe would start to shake their heads and back away from the heat. Their hooves gripped in Walter's hands, they'd tremble; it was his job to hold their heads and talk to them, rubbing the velvet space between their ears, telling them how their mothers love them and talk about them still, and how Walter will soon be over.

❖

He doesn't eat for a day or so; it hurts too much. But by the time he reaches Dover the big gash on his scalp has closed, and the tender parts inside, he trusts, have mended themselves: kidneys, lungs and heart.

He knows by the way people look at him that his face is still bruised. Morgan Williams had done an inventory of him before he left: teeth (miraculously) still in his head, and two eyes, miraculously seeing. Two arms, two legs: what more do you want?

He walks around the docks saying to people, do you know where there's a war just now?

Each man he asks stares at his face, steps back and says, "You tell me!"

They are so pleased with this, they laugh at their own wit so much, that he continues asking, just to give people pleasure.

Surprisingly, he finds he will leave Dover richer than he arrived. He'd watched a man doing the three-card trick, and when he learned it he set up for himself. Because he's a boy, people stop to have a go. It's their loss.

He adds up what he's got and what he's spent. Deduct a small sum for a brief grapple with a lady of the night. Not the sort of thing you could do in Putney, Wimbledon or Mortlake. Not without the Williams family getting to know, and talking about you in Welsh.

He sees three elderly Lowlanders struggling with their bundles and moves to help them. The packages are soft and bulky, samples of woolen cloth. A port officer gives them trouble about their documents, shouting into their faces. He lounges behind the clerk, pretending to be a Lowland oaf, and tells the merchants by holding up his fingers what he thinks a fair bribe. "Please," says one of them, in effortful English to the clerk, "will you take care of these English coins for me? I find them surplus." Suddenly the clerk is all smiles. The Lowlanders are all smiles; they would have paid much more. When they board they say, "The boy is with us."

As they wait to cast off, they ask him his age. He says eighteen, but they laugh and say, child, you are never. He offers them fifteen, and they confer and decide that fifteen will do; they think he's younger, but they don't want to shame him. They ask what's happened to his face. There are several things he could say but he selects the truth. He doesn't want them to think he's some failed robber. They discuss it among themselves, and the one who can translate turns to him: "We are saying, the English are cruel to their children. And coldhearted. The child must stand if his father comes in the room. Always the child should say very correctly, 'my father, sir,' and 'madam, my mother.'"

He is surprised. Are there people in the world who are not cruel to their children? For the first time, the weight in his chest shifts a little; he thinks, there could be other places, better. He talks; he tells them about Bella, and they look sorry, and they don't say anything stupid like, you can get another dog. He tells them about the Pegasus, and about his father's brewhouse and how Walter gets fined for bad beer at least twice a year. He tells them about how he gets fines for stealing wood, cutting down other people's trees, and about the too-many sheep he runs on the common. They are interested in that; they show the woolen samples and discuss among themselves the weight and the weave, turning to him from time to time to include and instruct him. They don't think much of English finished cloth generally, though these samples can make them change their mind . . . He loses the thread of the conversation when they try to tell him their reasons for going to Calais, and different people they know there.

He tells them about his father's blacksmith business, and the English-speaker says, interested, can you make a horseshoe? He mimes to them what it's like, hot metal and a bad-tempered father in a small space. They laugh; they like to see him telling a story. Good talker, one of them says. Before they dock, the most silent of them will stand up and make an oddly formal speech, at which one will nod, and which the other will translate. "We are three brothers. This is our street. If ever you visit our town, there is a bed and hearth and food for you."

Goodbye, he will say to them. Goodbye and good luck with your lives. *Hwyl*, cloth men. *Golfalwch eich busnes*. He is not stopping till he gets to a war.

The weather is cold but the sea is flat. Kat has given him a holy medal to wear. He has slung it around his neck with a cord. It makes a chill against the skin of his throat. He unloops it. He touches it with his lips, for luck. He drops it; it whispers into the water. He will remember his first sight of the open sea: a gray wrinkled vastness, like the residue of a dream.

II

Paternity

1527

o: Stephen Gardiner. Going out, as he's coming in. It's wet, and for a night in April, unseasonably warm, but Gardiner wears furs, which look like oily and dense black feathers; he stands now, ruffling them, gathering his clothes about his tall straight person like black angel's wings.

"Late," Master Stephen says unpleasantly.

He is bland. "Me, or your good self?"

"You." He waits.

"Drunks on the river. The boatmen say it's the eve of one of their patron saints."

"Did you offer a prayer to her?"

"I'll pray to anyone, Stephen, till I'm on dry land."

"I'm surprised you didn't take an oar yourself. You must have done some river work, when you were a boy."

Stephen sings always on one note. Your reprobate father. Your low birth. Stephen is supposedly some sort of semi-royal by-blow: brought up for payment, discreetly, as their own, by discreet people in a small town. They are wool-trade people, whom Master Stephen resents and wishes to forget; and since he himself knows everybody in the wool trade, he knows too much about his past for Stephen's comfort. The poor orphan boy!

Master Stephen resents everything about his own situation. He resents that he's the king's unacknowledged cousin. He resents that he was put into the church, though the church has done well by him. He resents the fact that someone else has late-night talks with the cardinal, to whom he is confidential secretary. He resents the fact that he's one of those tall men who are hollow-chested, not much weight behind him; he resents his knowledge that if they met on a dark night, Master Thos. Cromwell would be the one who walked away dusting off his hands and smiling.

"God bless you," Gardiner says, passing into the night unseasonably warm.

Cromwell says, "Thanks."

❖

The cardinal, writing, says without looking up, "Thomas. Still raining? I expected you earlier."

Boatman. River. Saint. He's been traveling since early morning and in the saddle for the best part of two weeks on the cardinal's business, and has now come down by stages—and not easy stages—from Yorkshire. He's been to his clerks at Gray's Inn and borrowed a change of linen. He's been east to the city, to hear what ships have come in and to check the whereabouts of an off-the-books consignment he is expecting. But he hasn't eaten, and hasn't been home yet.

The cardinal rises. He opens a door, speaks to his hovering servants. "Cherries! What, no cherries? April, you say? Only April? We shall have sore work to placate my guest, then." He sighs. "Bring what you have. But it will never do, you know. Why am I so ill-served?"

Then the whole room is in motion: food, wine, fire built up. A man takes his wet outer garments with a solicitous murmur. All the cardinal's household servants are like this: comfortable, soft-footed, and kept permanently apologetic and teased. And all the cardinal's visitors are treated in the same way. If you had interrupted him every night for ten years, and sat sulking and scowling at him on each occasion, you would still be his honored guest.

The servants efface themselves, melting away toward the door. "What else would you like?" the cardinal says.

"The sun to come out?"

"So late? You tax my powers."

"Dawn would do."

The cardinal inclines his head to the servants. "I shall see to this request myself," he says gravely; and gravely they murmur, and withdraw.

The cardinal joins his hands. He makes a great, deep, smiling sigh, like a leopard settling in a warm spot. He regards his man of business; his man of business regards him. The cardinal, at fifty-five, is still as handsome as he was in his prime. Tonight he is dressed not in his everyday scarlet, but in blackish purple and fine white lace: like a humble bishop. His height impresses; his belly, which should in justice belong to a more sedentary man, is merely another princely aspect of his being, and on it, confidingly, he often rests a large, white, beringed hand. A large head—surely designed by God to support the papal tiara—is carried superbly on broad shoulders: shoulders upon which rest (though not at this moment) the great chain of Lord Chancellor of England. The head inclines; the cardinal says, in those honeyed tones, famous from here to Vienna, "So now, tell me, how was Yorkshire."

"Filthy." He sits down. "Weather. People. Manners. Morals."

"Well, I suppose this is the place to complain. Though I am already speaking to God about the weather."

"Oh, and the food. Five miles inland, and no fresh fish."

"And scant hope of a lemon, I suppose. What do they eat?"

"Londoners, when they can get them. You have never seen such heathens. They're so high, low foreheads. Live in caves, yet they pass for gentry in those parts." He ought to go and look for himself, the cardinal; he is Archbishop of York, but has never visited his see. "And as for Your Grace's business—"

"I am listening," the cardinal says. "Indeed, I go further. I am captivated."

As he listens, the cardinal's face creases into its affable, perpetually attentive folds. From time to time he notes down a figure that he is given. He sips from a glass of his very good wine and at length he says, "Thomas . . . what have you done, monstrous servant? An abbess is with child? Two, three abbesses? Or, let me see . . . Have you set fire to Whitby, on a whim?"

In the case of his man Cromwell, the cardinal has two jokes, which sometimes unite to form one. The first is that he walks in demanding cherries in April and lettuce in December. The other is that he goes about the countryside committing outrages, and charging them to the cardinal's accounts. And the cardinal has other jokes, from time to time: as he requires them.

It is about ten o'clock. The flames of the wax candles bow civilly to the cardinal, and stand straight again. The rain—it has been raining since last September—splashes against the glass window. "In Yorkshire," he says, "your project is disliked."

The cardinal's project: having obtained the Pope's permission, he means to amalgamate some thirty small, ill-run monastic foundations with larger ones, and to divert the income of these foundations— decayed, but often very ancient—into revenue for the two colleges he is founding: Cardinal College, at Oxford, and a college in his hometown of Ipswich, where he is well remembered as the scholar son of a prosperous and pious master butcher, a guildman, a man who also kept a large and well-regulated inn, of the type used by the best travelers. The difficulty is . . . No, in fact, there are several difficulties. The cardinal, a Bachelor of Arts at fifteen, a Bachelor of Theology by his mid-twenties, is learned in the law but does not like its delays; he cannot quite accept that real property cannot be changed into money with the same speed and ease with which he changes a wafer into the body of Christ. When he once, as a test, explained to the cardinal just a minor point of the land law concerning—well, never mind, it was a minor point—he saw the cardinal break into a sweat and say, Thomas, what can I give you, to persuade you never to mention this to me again? Find a way, just do it, he would say when obstacles were raised; and when he heard of some small person obstructing his grand design, he would say, Thomas, give them some money to make them go away.

He has the leisure to think about this, because the cardinal is staring down at his desk, at the letter he has half-written. He looks up. "Tom . . ." And then, "No, never mind. Tell me why you are scowling in that way."

"The people up there say they are going to kill me."

"Really?" the cardinal says. His face says, I am astonished and disappointed. "And will they kill you? Or what do you think?"

Behind the cardinal is a tapestry, hanging the length of the wall. King Solomon, his hands stretched into darkness, is greeting the Queen of Sheba.

"I think, if you're going to kill a man, do it. Don't write him a letter about it. Don't bluster and threaten and put him on his guard."

"If you ever plan to be off your guard, let me know. It is something I should like to see. Do you know who . . . But I suppose they don't sign their letters. I shall not give up my project. I have personally and carefully selected these institutions, and His Holiness has approved them under seal. Those who object misunderstand my intention. No one is proposing to put old monks out on the roads."

This is true. There can be relocation; there can be pensions, compensation. It can be negotiated, with goodwill on both sides. Bow to the inevitable, he urges. Deference to the lord cardinal. Regard his watchful and fatherly care; believe his keen eye is fixed on the ultimate good of the church. These are the phrases with which to negotiate. Poverty, chastity and obedience: these are what you stress when you tell some senile prior what to do. "They don't misunderstand," he says. "They just want the proceeds themselves."

"You will have to take an armed guard when next you go north."

The cardinal, who thinks upon a Christian's last end, has had his tomb designed already, by a sculptor from Florence. His corpse will lie beneath the outspread wings of angels, in a sarcophagus of porphyry. The veined stone will be his monument, when his own veins are drained by the embalmer; when his limbs are set like marble, an inscription of his virtues will be picked out in gold. But the colleges are to be his breathing monument, working and living long after he is gone: poor boys, poor scholars, carrying into the world the cardinal's wit, his sense of wonder and of beauty, his instinct for decorum and pleasure, his finesse. No wonder he shakes his head. You don't generally have to give an armed guard to a lawyer. The cardinal hates any show of force. He thinks it unsubtle. Sometimes one of his people— Stephen Gardiner, let's say—will come to him denouncing some nest of heretics in the city. He will say earnestly, poor benighted souls. You pray for them, Stephen, and I'll pray for them, and we'll see if between us we can't bring them to a better state of mind. And tell them, mend their manners, or Thomas More will get hold of them and shut them in his cellar. And all we will hear is the sound of screaming.

"Now, Thomas." He looks up. "Do you have any Spanish?"

"A little. Military, you know. Rough."

"You took service in the Spanish armies, I thought."

"French."

"Ah. Indeed. And no fraternizing?"

"Not past a point. I can insult people in Castilian."

"I shall bear that in mind," the cardinal says. "Your time may come. For now . . . I was thinking that it would be good to have more friends in the queen's household."

Spies, he means. To see how she will take the news. To see what Queen Catalina will say, in private and unleashed, when she has slipped the noose of the diplomatic Latin in which it will be broken to her that the king—after they have spent some twenty years together—would like to marry another lady. Any lady. Any well-connected princess whom he thinks might give him a son.

The cardinal's chin rests on his hand; with finger and thumb, he rubs his eyes. "The king called me this morning," he says, "exceptionally early."

"What did he want?"

"Pity. And at such an hour. I heard a dawn Mass with him, and he talked all through it. I love the king. God knows how I love him. But sometimes my faculty of commiseration is strained." He raises his glass, looks over the rim. "Picture to yourself, Tom. Imagine this. You are a man of some thirty-five years of age. You are in good health and of a hearty appetite, you have your bowels opened every day, your joints are supple, your bones support you, and in addition you are King of England. But." He shakes his head. "But! If only he wanted something simple. The Philosopher's Stone. The elixir of youth. One of those chests that occur in stories, full of gold pieces."

"And when you take some out, it just fills up again?"

"Exactly. Now the chest of gold I have hopes of, and the elixir, all the rest. But where shall I begin looking for a son to rule his country after him?"

Behind the cardinal, moving a little in the draft, King Solomon bows, his face obscured. The Queen of Sheba—smiling, light-footed—reminds him of the young widow he lodged with when he lived in Antwerp. Since they had shared a bed, should he have married her? In honor, yes. But if he had married Anselma he couldn't have married Liz; and his children would be different children from the ones he has now.

"If you cannot find him a son," he says, "you must find him a piece of scripture. To ease his mind."

The cardinal appears to be looking for it, on his desk. "Well, Deuteronomy. Which positively recommends that a man should marry his deceased brother's wife. As he did." The cardinal sighs. "But he doesn't like Deuteronomy."

Useless to say, why not? Useless to suggest that, if Deuteronomy orders you to marry your brother's relict, and Leviticus says don't, or you will not breed, you should try to live with the contradiction, and accept that the question of which takes priority was thrashed out in Rome, for a fat fee, by leading prelates, twenty years ago when the dispensations were issued, and delivered under papal seal.

"I don't see why he takes Leviticus to heart. He has a daughter living."

"But I think it is generally understood, in the scriptures, that 'children' means 'sons.'"

The cardinal justifies the text, referring to the Hebrew; his voice is mild, lulling. He loves to instruct, where there is the will to be instructed. They have known each other some years now, and though the cardinal is very grand, formality has faded between them. "I have a son," he says. "You know that, of course. God forgive me. A weakness of the flesh."

The cardinal's son—Thomas Winter, they call him—seems inclined to scholarship and a quiet life, though his father may have other ideas. The cardinal has a daughter too, a young girl whom no one has seen.

Rather pointedly, he has called her Dorothea, the gift of God; she is already placed in a convent, where she will pray for her parents.

"And you have a son," the cardinal says. "Or should I say, you have one son you give your name to. But I suspect there are some you don't know, running around on the banks of the Thames?"

"I hope not. I wasn't fifteen when I ran away."

It amuses Wolsey that he doesn't know his age. The cardinal peers down through the layers of society, to a stratum well below his own, as the butcher's beef-fed son; to a place where his servant is born, on a day unknown, in deep obscurity. His father was no doubt drunk at his birth; his mother, understandably, was preoccupied. Kat has assigned him a date; he is grateful for it.

"Well, fifteen . . ." the cardinal says. "But at fifteen I suppose you could do it? I know I could. Now I have a son, your boatman on the river has a son, your beggar on the street has a son, your would-be murderers in Yorkshire no doubt have sons who will be sworn to pursue you in the next generation, and you yourself, as we have agreed, have spawned a whole tribe of riverine brawlers—but the king, alone, has no son. Whose fault is that?"

"God's?"

"Nearer than God?"

"The queen?"

"More responsible for everything than the queen?"

He can't help a broad smile. "Yourself, Your Grace."

"Myself, My Grace. What am I going to do about it? I tell you what I might do. I might send Master Stephen to Rome to sound out the Curia. But then I need him here . . ."

Wolsey looks at his expression, and laughs. Squabbling underlings! He knows quite well that, dissatisfied with their original parentage, they are fighting to be his favorite son. "Whatever you think of Master Stephen, he is well grounded in canon law, and a very persuasive fellow, except when he tries to persuade you. I will tell you—" He breaks off; he leans forward, he puts his great lion's head in his hands, the head that would indeed have worn the papal tiara, if at the last election the right money had been paid out to the right people. "I have begged him," the cardinal says. "Thomas, I sank to my knees and from that humble posture I tried to dissuade him. Majesty, I said, be guided by me. Nothing will ensue, if you wish to be rid of your wife, but a great deal of trouble and expense."

"And he said . . . ?"

"He held up a finger. In warning. 'Never,' he said, 'call that dear lady my wife, until you can show me why she is, and how it can be so. Till then, call her my sister, my dear sister. Since she was quite certainly my brother's wife, before going through a form of marriage with me.'"

You will never draw from Wolsey a word that is disloyal to the king. "What it is," he says, "it's . . ." He hesitates over the word. "It's, in my opinion . . . preposterous. Though my opinion, of course, does not go out of this room. Oh, don't doubt it, there were those at the time who raised their eyebrows over the dispensation. And year by year there were persons who would murmur in the king's ear; he didn't listen, though now I must believe that he heard. But you know the king was the most uxorious of men. Any doubts were quashed." He places a hand, softly and firmly, down on his desk. "They were quashed and quashed."

But there is no doubt of what Henry wants now. An annulment. A declaration that his marriage never existed. "For eighteen years," the cardinal says, "he has been under a mistake. He has told his confessor that he has eighteen years' worth of sin to expiate."

He waits, for some gratifying small reaction. His servant simply looks back at him: taking it for granted that the seal of the confessional is broken at the cardinal's convenience.

"So if you send Master Stephen to Rome," he says, "it will give the king's whim, if I may—"

The cardinal nods: you may so term it.

"—an international airing?"

"Master Stephen may go discreetly. As it were, for a private papal blessing."

"You don't understand Rome."

Wolsey can't contradict him. He has never felt the chill at the nape of the neck that makes you look over your shoulder when, passing from the Tiber's golden light, you move into some great bloc of shadow. By some fallen column, by some chaste ruin, the thieves of integrity wait, some bishop's whore, some nephew-of-a-nephew, some monied seducer with furred breath; he feels, sometimes, fortunate to have escaped that city with his soul intact.

"Put simply," he says, "the Pope's spies will guess what Stephen's about while he is still packing his vestments, and the cardinals and the secretaries will have time to fix their prices. If you must send him, give him a great deal of ready money. Those cardinals don't take promises; what they really like is a bag of gold to placate their bankers, because they're mostly run out of credit." He shrugs. "I know this."

"I should send you," the cardinal says, jolly. "You could offer Pope Clement a loan."

Why not? He knows the money markets; it could probably be arranged. If he were Clement, he would borrow heavily this year to hire in troops to ring his territories. It's probably too late; for the summer season's fighting, you need to be recruiting by Candlemas. He says, "Will you not start the king's suit within your own jurisdiction? Make him take the first steps, then he will see if he really wants what he says he wants."

"That is my intention. What I mean to do is to convene a small court here in London. We will approach him in a shocked fashion: King Harry, you appear to have lived all these years in an unlawful manner, with a woman not your wife. He hates—saving His Majesty—to appear in the wrong: which is where we must put him, very firmly. Possibly he will forget that the original scruples were his. Possibly he will shout at us, and hasten in a fit of indignation back to the queen. If not, then I must have the dispensation revoked, here or in Rome, and if I succeed in parting him from Katherine I shall marry him, smartly, to a French princess."

No need to ask if the cardinal has any particular princess in mind. He has not one but two or three. He never lives in a single reality, but in a shifting shadow-mesh of diplomatic possibilities. While he is doing his best to keep the king married to Queen Katherine and her

Spanish-Imperial family, by begging Henry to forget his scruples, he will also plan for an alternative world, in which the king's scruples must be heeded, and the marriage to Katherine is void. Once that nullity is recognized—and the last eighteen years of sin and suffering wiped from the page—he will readjust the balance of Europe, allying England with France, forming a power bloc to oppose the young Emperor Charles, Katherine's nephew. And all outcomes are likely, all outcomes can be managed, even massaged into desirability: prayer and pressure, pressure and prayer, everything that comes to pass will pass by God's design, a design reenvisaged and redrawn, with helpful emendations, by the cardinal. He used to say, "The king will do such and such." Then he began to say, "We will do such and such." Now he says, "This is what I will do."

"But what will happen to the queen?" he asks. "If he casts her off, where will she go?"

"Convents can be comfortable."

"Perhaps she will go home to Spain."

"No, I think not. It is another country now. It is—what?—twenty-seven years since she landed in England." The cardinal sighs. "I remember her, at her coming-in. Her ships, as you know, had been delayed by the weather, and she had been day upon day tossed in the Channel. The old king rode down the country, determined to meet her. She was then at Dogmersfield, at the Bishop of Bath's palace, and making slow progress toward London; it was November and, yes, it was raining. At his arriving, her household stood upon their Spanish manners: the princess must remain veiled, until her husband sees her on her wedding day. But you know the old king!"

He did not, of course; he was born on or about the date the old king, a renegade and a refugee all his life, fought his way to an unlikely throne. Wolsey talks as if he himself had witnessed everything, eyewitnessed it, and in a sense he has, for the recent past arranges itself only in the patterns acknowledged by his superior mind, and agreeable to his eye. He smiles. "The old king, in his later years, the least thing could arouse his suspicion. He made some show of reining back to confer with his escort, and then he leapt—he was still a lean man—from the saddle, and told the Spanish, to their faces, he would see her or else. My land and my laws, he said; we'll have no veils here. Why may I not see her, have I been cheated, is she deformed, is it that you are proposing to marry my son Arthur to a monster?"

Thomas thinks, he was being unnecessarily Welsh.

"Meanwhile her women had put the little creature into bed; or said they had, for they thought that in bed she would be safe against him. Not a bit. King Henry strode through the rooms, looking as if he had in mind to tear back the bedclothes. The women bundled her into some decency. He burst into the chamber. At the sight of her, he forgot his Latin. He stammered and backed out like a tongue-tied boy." The cardinal chuckled. "And then when she first danced at court—our poor prince Arthur sat smiling on the dais, but the little girl could hardly sit still in her chair—no one knew the Spanish dances, so she took to the floor with one of her ladies. I will never forget that turn of her head, that moment when her beautiful red hair slid over one shoulder . . . There was no man who saw it who didn't imagine—though the dance was in fact very sedate . . . Ah dear. She was sixteen."

The cardinal looks into space and Thomas says, "God forgive you?"

"God forgive us all. The old king was constantly taking his lust to confession. Prince Arthur died, then soon after the queen died, and when the old king found himself a widower he thought he might marry Katherine himself. But then . . ." He lifts his princely shoulders. "They couldn't agree over the dowry, you know. The old fox, Ferdinand, her father. He would fox you out of any payment due. But our present Majesty was a boy of ten when he danced at his brother's wedding, and, in my belief, it was there and then that he set his heart on the bride."

They sit and think for a bit. It's sad, they both know it's sad. The old king freezing her out, keeping her in the kingdom and keeping her poor, unwilling to miss the part of the dowry he said was still owing, and equally unwilling to pay her widow's portion and let her go. But then it's interesting too, the extensive diplomatic contacts the little girl picked up during those years, the expertise in playing off one interest against another. When Henry married her he was eighteen, guileless. His father was no sooner dead than he claimed Katherine for his own. She was older than he was, and years of anxiety had sobered her and taken something from her looks. But the real woman was less vivid than the vision in his mind; he was greedy for what his older brother had owned. He felt again the little tremor of her hand, as she had rested it on his arm when he was a boy of ten. It was as if she had trusted him, as if—he told his intimates—she had recognized that she was never meant to be Arthur's wife, except in name; her body was reserved for him, the second son, upon whom she turned her beautiful blue-gray eyes, her compliant smile. She always loved me, the king would say. Seven years or so of diplomacy, if you can call it that, kept me from her side. But now I need fear no one. Rome has dispensed. The papers are in order. The alliances are set in place. I have married a virgin, since my poor brother did not touch her; I have married an alliance, her Spanish relatives; but, above all, I have married for love.

And now? Gone. Or as good as gone: half a lifetime waiting to be expunged, eased from the record.

"Ah, well," the cardinal says. "What will be the outcome? The king expects his own way, but she, she will be hard to move."

There is another story about Katherine, a different story. Henry went to France to have a little war; he left Katherine as regent. Down came the Scots; they were well beaten, and at Flodden the head of their king cut off. It was Katherine, that pink-and-white angel, who proposed to send the head in a bag by the first crossing, to cheer up her husband in his camp. They dissuaded her; told her it was, as a gesture, un-English. She sent, instead, a letter. And with it, the surcoat in which the Scottish king had died, which was stiffened, black and crackling with his pumped-out blood.

The fire dies, an ashy log subsiding; the cardinal, wrapped in his dreams, rises from his chair and personally kicks it. He stands looking down, twisting the rings on his fingers, lost in thought. He shakes himself and says, "Long day. Go home. Don't dream of Yorkshiremen."

Thomas Cromwell is now a little over forty years old. He is a man of strong build, not tall. Various expressions are available to his face, and one is readable: an expression of stifled amusement. His hair is dark, heavy and waving, and his small eyes, which are of very strong sight, light up in conversation: so the Spanish ambassador will tell us, quite soon. It is said he knows by heart the entire New Testament in Latin, and so as a servant of the cardinal is apt—ready with a text if abbots flounder. His speech is low and rapid, his manner assured; he is at home in courtroom or waterfront, bishop's palace or inn yard. He can draft a contract, train a falcon, draw a map, stop a street fight, furnish a house and fix a jury. He will quote you a nice point in the old authors, from Plato to Plautus and back again. He knows new poetry, and can say it in Italian. He works all hours, first up and last to bed. He makes money and he spends it. He will take a bet on anything.

He rises to leave, says, "If you did have a word with God and the sun came out, then the king could ride out with his gentlemen, and if he were not so fretted and confined then his spirits would rise, and he might not be thinking about Leviticus, and your life would be easier."

"You only partly understand him. He enjoys theology, almost as much as he enjoys riding out."

He is at the door. Wolsey says, "By the way, the talk at court . . . His Grace the Duke of Norfolk is complaining that I have raised an evil spirit, and directed it to follow him about. If anyone mentions it to you . . . just deny it."

He stands in the doorway, smiling slowly. The cardinal smiles too, as if to say, I have saved the good wine till last. Don't I know how to make you happy? Then the cardinal drops his head over his papers. He is a man who, in England's service, scarcely needs to sleep; four hours will refresh him, and he will be up when Westminster's bells have rung in another wet, smoky, lightless April day. "Good night," he says. "God bless you, Tom."

Outside his people are waiting with lights to take him home. He has a house in Stepney but tonight he is going to his town house. A hand on his arm: Rafe Sadler, a slight young man with pale eyes. "How was Yorkshire?"

Rafe's smile flickers; the wind pulls the torch flame into a rainy blur. "I haven't to speak of it; the cardinal fears it will give us bad dreams."

Rafe frowns. In all his twenty-one years he has never had bad dreams; sleeping securely under the Cromwell roof since he was seven, first at Fenchurch Street and now at the Austin Friars, he has grown up with a tidy mind, and his nighttime worries are all rational ones: thieves, loose dogs, sudden holes in the road.

"The Duke of Norfolk . . ." he says, then, "no, never mind. Who's been asking for me while I've been away?"

The damp streets are deserted; the mist is creeping from the river. The stars are stifled in damp and cloud. Over the city lies the sweet, rotting odor of yesterday's unrecollected sins. Norfolk kneels, teeth chattering, beside his bed; the cardinal's late-night pen scratches, scratches, like a rat beneath his mattress. While Rafe, by his side, gives him a digest of the office news, he formulates his denial, for whom it may concern: "His Grace the cardinal wholly rejects any imputation that he has sent an evil spirit to wait upon the Duke of Norfolk. He deprecates the suggestion in the strongest possible terms. No headless calf, no fallen angel in the shape of loll-tongued dog, no crawling pre-used winding-sheet, no Lazarus or animated cadaver has been sent by His Grace to pursue His Grace: nor is any such pursuit pending."

Someone is screaming, down by the quays. The boatmen are singing. There is a faint, faraway splashing; perhaps they are drowning someone. "My lord cardinal makes this statement without prejudice to his right to harass and distress my lord of Norfolk by means of any fantasma which he may in his wisdom elect: at any future date, and without notice given: subject only to the lord cardinal's views in the matter."

This weather makes old scars ache. But he walks into his house as if it were midday: smiling, and imagining the trembling duke. It is one o'clock. Norfolk, in his mind, is still kneeling. A black-faced imp with a trident is pricking his calloused heels.

III

At Austin Friars

1527

izzie is still up. When she hears the servants let him in, she comes out with his little dog under her arm, fighting and squealing. "Forget where you lived?"

He sighs.

"How was Yorkshire?"

He shrugs.

"The cardinal?"

He nods.

"Eaten?"

"Yes."

"Tired?"

"Not really."

"Drink?"

"Yes."

"Rhenish?"

"Why not."

The paneling has been painted. He walks into the subdued green and golden glow. "Gregory—"

"Letter?"

"Of sorts."

She gives him the letter and the dog, while she fetches the wine. She sits down, taking a cup herself.

"He greets us. As if there were only one of us. Bad Latin."

"Ah, well," she says.

"So, listen. He hopes you are well. Hopes I am well. Hopes his lovely sisters Anne and little Grace are well. He himself is well. And now no more for lack of time, your dutiful son, Gregory Cromwell."

"Dutiful?" she says. "Just that?"

"It's what they teach them."

The dog Bella nibbles his fingertips, her round innocent eyes shining at him like alien moons. Liz looks well, if worn by her long day; wax tapers stand tall and straight behind her. She is wearing the string of pearls and garnets that he gave her at New Year's.

"You're sweeter to look at than the cardinal," he says.

"That's the smallest compliment a woman ever received."

"And I've been working on it all the way from Yorkshire." He shakes his head. "Ah well!" He holds Bella up in the air; she kicks her legs in glee. "How's business?"

Liz does a bit of silk-work. Tags for the seals on documents; fine net cauls for ladies at court. She has two girl apprentices in the house, and an eye on fashion; but she complains, as always, about the middlemen, and the price of thread. "We should go to Genoa," he says. "I'll teach you to look the suppliers in the eye."

"I'd like that. But you'll never get away from the cardinal."

"He tried to persuade me tonight that I should get to know people in the queen's household. The Spanish-speakers."

"Oh?"

"I told him my Spanish wasn't so good."

"Not good?" She laughs. "You weasel."

"He doesn't have to know everything I know."

"I've been visiting in Cheapside," she says. She names one of her old friends, a master jeweler's wife. "Would you like the news? A big emerald was ordered and a setting commissioned, for a ring, a woman's ring." She shows him the emerald, big as her thumbnail. "Which arrived, after a few anxious weeks, and they were cutting it in Antwerp." Her fingers flick outward. "Shattered!"

"So who bears the loss?"

"The cutter says he was swindled and it was a hidden flaw in the base. The importer says, if it was so hidden, how could I be expected to know? The cutter says, so collect damages from your supplier . . ."

"They'll be at law for years. Can they get another?"

"They're trying. It must be the king, so we think. Nobody else in London would be in the market for a stone of that size. So who's it for? It isn't for the queen."

The tiny Bella now lies back along his arm, her eyes blinking, her tail gently stirring. He thinks, I shall be curious to see if and when an emerald ring appears. The cardinal will tell me. The cardinal says, it's all very well, this business of holding the king off and angling after presents, but he will have her in his bed this summer, for sure, and by the autumn he'll be tired of her, and pension her off; if he doesn't, I will. If Wolsey's going to import a fertile French princess, he doesn't want her first weeks spoiled by scenes of spite with superseded concubines. The king, Wolsey thinks, ought to be more ruthless about his women.

Liz waits for a moment, till she knows she isn't going to get a hint. "Now, about Gregory," she says. "Summer coming. Here, or away?"

Gregory is coming up thirteen. He's at Cambridge, with his tutor. He's sent his nephews, his sister Bet's sons, to school with him; it's something he is glad to do for the family. The summer is for their recreation; what would they do in the city? Gregory has little interest in his books so far, though he likes to be told stories, dragon stories, stories of green people who live in the woods; you can drag him squealing through a passage of Latin if you persuade him that over the page there's a sea serpent or a ghost. He likes to be in the woods and fields and he likes to hunt. He has plenty of growing to do, and we hope he will grow tall. The king's maternal grandfather, as all old men will tell you, stood six foot four. (His father, however, was more the size of Morgan Williams.) The king stands six foot two, and the cardinal can look him in the eye. Henry likes to have about him men like his brother-in-law Charles Brandon, of a similar impressive height and breadth of padded shoulder. Height is not the fashion in the back alleys; and, obviously, not in Yorkshire.

He smiles. What he says about Gregory is, at least he isn't like I was, when I was his age; and when people say, what were you like? he says, oh, I used to stick knives in people. Gregory would never do that;

so he doesn't mind—or minds less than people think—if he doesn't really get to grips with declensions and conjugations. When people tell him what Gregory has failed to do, he says, "He's busy growing." He understands his need to sleep; he never got much sleep himself, with Walter stamping around, and after he ran away he was always on the ship or on the road, and then he found himself in an army. The thing people don't understand about an army is its great, unpunctuated wastes of inaction: you have to scavenge for food, you are camped out somewhere with a rising water level because your mad capitaine says so, you are shifted abruptly in the middle of the night into some indefensible position, so you never really sleep, your equipment is defective, the gunners keep causing small unwanted explosions, the crossbowmen are either drunk or praying, the arrows are ordered up but not here yet, and your whole mind is occupied by a seething anxiety that things are going to go badly because *il principe,* or whatever little worshipfulness is in charge today, is not very good at the basic business of thinking. It didn't take him many winters to get out of fighting and into supply. In Italy, you could always fight in the summer, if you felt like it. If you wanted to go out.

"Asleep?" Liz says.

"No. But dreaming."

"The Castile soap came. And your book from Germany. It was packaged as something else. I almost sent the boy away."

In Yorkshire, which smelled of unwashed men, wearing sheepskins and sweating with anger, he had dreams about the Castile soap.

❖

Later she says, "So who is the lady?"

His hand, resting on her familiar but lovely left breast, removes itself in bewilderment. "What?" Does she think he has taken up with some woman in Yorkshire? He falls onto his back and wonders how to persuade her this is not so; if necessary he'll take her there, and then she'll see.

"The emerald lady?" she says. "I only ask because people say the king is wanting to do something very strange, and I can't really believe it. But that is the word in the city."

Really? Rumor has advanced, in the fortnight while he has been north among the slope-heads.

"If he tries this," she says, "then half the people in the world will be against it."

He had only thought, and Wolsey had only thought, that the Emperor and Spain would be against it. *Only* the Emperor. He smiles in the dark, hands behind his head. He doesn't say, which people, but waits for Liz to tell him. "All women," she says. "All women everywhere in England. All women who have a daughter but no son. All women who have lost a child. All women who have lost any hope of having a child. All women who are forty."

She puts her head on his shoulder. Too tired to speak, they lie side by side, in sheets of fine linen, under a quilt of yellow turkey satin. Their bodies breathe out the faint borrowed scent of sun and herbs. In Castilian, he remembers, he can insult people.

"Are you asleep now?"

"No. Thinking."

"Thomas," she says, sounding shocked, "it's three o'clock."

And then it is six. He dreams that all the women of England are in bed, jostling and pushing him out of it. So he gets up, to read his German book, before Liz can do anything about it.

It's not that she says anything; or only, when provoked, she says, "My prayer book is good reading for me." And indeed she does read her prayer book, taking it in her hand absently in the middle of the day—but only half stopping what she's doing—interspersing her murmured litany with household instructions; it was a wedding present, a book of hours, from her first husband, and he wrote her new married name in it, Elizabeth Williams. Sometimes, feeling jealous, he would like to write other things, contrarian sentiments: he knew Liz's first husband, but that doesn't mean he liked him. He has said, Liz, there's Tyndale's book, his New Testament, in the locked chest there, read it, here's the key; she says, you read it to me if you're so keen, and he says, it's in English, read it for yourself: that's the point, Lizzie. You read it, you'll be surprised what's not in it.

He'd thought this hint would draw her: seemingly not. He can't imagine himself reading to his household; he's not, like Thomas More, some sort of failed priest, a frustrated preacher. He never sees More—a star in another firmament, who acknowledges him with a grim nod—without wanting to ask him, what's wrong with you? Or what's wrong with me? Why does everything you know, and everything you've learned, confirm you in what you believed before? Whereas in my case, what I grew up with, and what I thought I believed, is chipped away a little and a little, a fragment then a piece and then a piece more. With every month that passes, the corners are knocked off the certainties of this world: and the next world too. Show me where it says, in the Bible, "Purgatory." Show me where it says "relics, monks, nuns." Show me where it says "Pope."

He turns back to his German book. The king, with help from Thomas More, has written a book against Luther, for which the Pope has granted him the title of Defender of the Faith. It's not that he loves Brother Martin himself; he and the cardinal agree it would be better if Luther had never been born, or better if he had been born more subtle. Still, he keeps up with what's written, with what's smuggled through the Channel ports, and the little East Anglian inlets, the tidal creeks where a small boat with dubious cargo can be beached and pushed out again, by moonlight, to sea. He keeps the cardinal informed, so that when More and his clerical friends storm in, breathing hellfire about the newest heresy, the cardinal can make calming gestures, and say, "Gentlemen, I am already informed." Wolsey will burn books, but not men. He did so, only last October, at St. Paul's Cross: a holocaust of the English language, and so much rag-rich paper consumed, and so much black printers' ink.

The Testament he keeps in the chest is the pirated edition from Antwerp, which is easier to get hold of than the proper German printing. He knows William Tyndale; before London got too hot for him, he lodged six months with Humphrey Monmouth, the master draper, in the city. He is a principled man, a hard man, and Thomas More calls him the Beast; he looks as if he has never laughed in his life, but then, what's there to laugh about, when you're driven from your native shore? His Testament is in octavo, nasty cheap paper: on the title page, where the printer's colophon and address should be, the words PRINTED IN UTOPIA. He hopes Thomas More has seen one of these. He is tempted to show him, just to see his face.

He closes the new book. It's time to get on with the day. He knows he has not time to put the text into Latin himself, so it can be discreetly circulated; he should ask somebody to do it for him, for love or money. It is surprising how much love there is, these days, between those who read German.

By seven, he is shaved, breakfasted and wrapped beautifully in fresh unborrowed linen and dark fine wool. Sometimes, at this hour, he misses Liz's father; that good old man, who would always be up early, ready to drop a flat hand on his head and say, enjoy your day, Thomas, on my behalf.

He had liked old Wykys. He first came to him on a legal matter. In those days he was—what, twenty-six, twenty-seven?—not long back from abroad, prone to start a sentence in one language and finish it in another. Wykys had been shrewd and had made a tidy fortune in the wool trade. He was a Putney man originally, but that wasn't why he employed him; it was because he came recommended and came cheap. At their first conference, as Wykys laid out the papers, he had said, "You're Walter's lad, aren't you? So what happened? Because, by God, there was no one rougher than you were when you were a boy."

He would have explained, if he'd known what sort of explanation Wykys would understand. I gave up fighting because, when I lived in Florence, I looked at frescoes every day? He said, "I found an easier way to be."

Latterly, Wykys had grown tired, let the business slide. He was still sending broadcloth to the north German market, when—in his opinion, with wool so long in the fleece these days, and good broadcloth hard to weave—he ought to be getting into kerseys, lighter cloth like that, exporting through Antwerp to Italy. But he listened—he was a good listener—to the old man's gripes, and said, "Things are changing. Let me take you to the cloth fairs this year."

Wykys knew he should show his face in Antwerp and Bergen op Zoom, but he didn't like the crossing. "He'll be all right with me," he told Mistress Wykys. "I know a good family where we can stay."

"Right, Thomas Cromwell," she said. "Make a note of this. No strange Dutch drinks. No women. No banned preachers in cellars. I know what you do."

"I don't know if I can stay out of cellars."

"Here's a bargain. You can take him to a sermon if you don't take him to a brothel."

Mercy, he suspects, comes from a family where John Wycliffe's writings are preserved and quoted, where the scriptures in English have always been known; scraps of writing hoarded, forbidden verses locked in the head. These things come down the generations, as eyes and noses come down, as meekness or the capacity for passion, as muscle power or the need to take a risk. If you must take risks these days, better the preacher than the whore; eschew Monsieur Breakbone, known in Florence as the Neapolitan Fever, and in Naples, no doubt, as Florence Rot. Good sense enforces abstinence—in any part of Europe, these islands included. Our lives are limited in this way, as the lives of our forefathers were not.

On the boat, he listened to the usual grievances from fellow passengers: these bastard pilots, lanes not marked, English monopolies. The merchants of the Hanse would rather their own men brought the ships up to Gravesend: Germans are a pack of thieves, but they know how to bring a boat upstream. Old Wykys was queasy when they put out to sea. He stayed on deck, making himself useful; you must have been a ship's boy, master, one of the crew said. Once in Antwerp, they made their way to the sign of the Holy Ghost. The servant opening the door shouted, "It's Thomas come back to us," as if he'd risen from the dead. When the three old men came out, the three brothers from the boat, they clucked, "Thomas, our poor foundling, our runaway, our little beaten-up friend. Welcome, come in and get warm!"

Nowhere else but here is he still a runaway, still a little, beaten boy.

Their wives, their daughters, their dogs covered him in kisses. He left old Wykys by the fireside—it is surprising how international is the language of old men, swapping tips on salves for aches, commiserating with petty wretchednesses and discussing the whims and demands of their wives. The youngest brother would translate, as usual: straight-faced, even when the terms became anatomical.

He had gone out drinking with the three brothers' three sons. *"Wat will je?"* they teased him. "The old man's business? His wife when he dies?"

"No," he said, surprising himself. "I think I want his daughter."

"Young?"

"A widow. Young enough."

When he got back to London he knew he could turn the business around. Still, he needed to think of the day-to-day. "I've seen your stock," he said to Wykys. "I've seen your accounts. Now show me your clerks."

That was the key, of course, the key that would unlock profit. People are always the key, and if you can look them in the face you can be pretty sure if they're honest and up to the job. He tossed out the dubious chief clerk—saying, you go, or we go to law—and replaced him with a stammering junior, a boy he'd been told was stupid. Timid, was all he was; he looked over his work each night, mildly and wordlessly indicating each error and omission, and in four weeks the boy was both competent and keen, and had taken to following him about like a puppy. Four weeks invested, and a few days down at the docks, checking who was on the take: by the year end, Wykys was back in profit.

Wykys stumped away after he showed him the figures. "Lizzie?" he yelled. "Lizzie? Come downstairs."

She came down.

"You want a new husband. Will he do?"

She stood and looked him up and down. "Well, Father. You didn't pick him for his looks." To him, her eyebrows raised, she said, "Do you *want* a wife?"

"Should I leave you to talk it over?" old Wykys said. He seemed baffled: seemed to think they should sit down and write a contract there and then.

Almost, they did. Lizzie wanted children; he wanted a wife with city contacts and some money behind her. They were married in weeks. Gregory arrived within the year. Bawling, strong, one hour old, plucked from the cradle: he kissed the infant's fluffy skull and said, I shall be as tender to you as my father was not to me. For what's the point of breeding children, if each generation does not improve on what went before?

❖

So this morning—waking early, brooding on what Liz said last night—he wonders, why should my wife worry about women who have no sons? Possibly it's something women do: spend time imagining what it's like to be each other.

One can learn from that, he thinks.

It's eight o'clock. Lizzie is down. Her hair is pushed under a linen cap and her sleeves turned back. "Oh, Liz," he says, laughing at her. "You look like a baker's wife."

"You mind your manners," she says. "Pot-boy."

Rafe comes in: "First back to my lord cardinal?" Where else, he says. He gathers his papers for the day. Pats his wife, kisses his dog. Goes out. The morning is drizzly but brightening, and before they reach York Place it is clear the cardinal has been as good as his word. A wash of sunlight lies over the river, pale as the flesh of a lemon.

PART TWO

I

Visitation

1529

hey are taking apart the cardinal's house. Room by room, the king's men are stripping York Place of its owner. They are bundling up parchments and scrolls, missals and memoranda and the volumes of his personal accounts; they are taking even the ink and the quills. They are prizing from the walls the boards on which the cardinal's coat of arms is painted.

They arrived on a Sunday, two vengeful grandees: the Duke of Norfolk a bright-eyed hawk, the Duke of Suffolk just as keen. They told the cardinal he was dismissed as Lord Chancellor, and demanded he hand over the Great Seal of England. He, Cromwell, touched the cardinal's arm. A hurried conference. The cardinal turned back to them, gracious: it appears a written request from the king is necessary; have you one? Oh: careless of you. It requires a lot of face to keep so calm; but then the cardinal has face.

"You want us to ride back to Windsor?" Charles Brandon is incredulous. "For a piece of paper? When the situation's plain?"

That's like Suffolk; to think the letter of the law is some kind of luxury. He whispers to the cardinal again, and the cardinal says, "No, I think we'd better tell them, Thomas . . . not prolong the matter beyond its natural life . . . My lords, my lawyer here says I can't give you the Seal, written request or not. He says that properly speaking I should only hand it to the Master of the Rolls. So you'd better bring him with you."

He says, lightly, "Be glad we told you, my lords. Otherwise it would have been three trips, wouldn't it?"

Norfolk grins. He likes a scrap. "Am obliged, master," he says.

When they go Wolsey turns and hugs him, his face gleeful. Though it is the last of their victories and they know it, it is important to show ingenuity; twenty-four hours is worth buying, when the king is so changeable. Besides, they enjoyed it. "Master of the Rolls," Wolsey says. "Did you know that, or did you make it up?"

❖

Monday morning the dukes are back. Their instructions are to turn out the occupants this very day, because the king wants to send in his own builders and furnishers and get the palace ready to hand over to the Lady Anne, who needs a London house of her own.

He's prepared to stand and argue the point: have I missed something? This palace belongs to the archdiocese of York. When was Lady Anne made an archbishop?

But the tide of men flooding in by the water stairs is sweeping them away. The two dukes have made themselves scarce, and there's nobody to argue with. What a terrible sight, someone says: Master Cromwell balked of a fight. And now the cardinal's ready to go, but where? Over his customary scarlet, he is wearing a traveling cloak that belongs to someone else; they are confiscating his wardrobe piece by piece, so he has to grab what he can. It is autumn, and though he is a big man he feels the cold.

They are overturning chests and tipping out their contents. They scatter across the floor, letters from Popes, letters from the scholars of Europe: from Utrecht, from Paris, from San Diego de Compostela; from Erfurt, from Strassburg, from Rome. They are packing his gospels and taking them for the king's libraries. The texts are heavy to hold in the arms, and awkward as if they breathed; their pages are made of slunk vellum from stillborn calves, reveined by the illuminator in tints of lapis and leaf-green.

They take down the tapestries and leave the bare blank walls. They are rolled up, the woolen monarchs, Solomon and Sheba; as they are brought into coiled proximity, their eyes are filled by each other, and their tiny lungs breathe in the fiber of bellies and thighs. Down come the cardinal's hunting scenes, the scenes of secular pleasure: the sportive peasants splashing in ponds, the stags at bay, the hounds in cry, the spaniels held on leashes of silk and the mastiffs with their collars of spikes: the huntsmen with their studded belts and knives, the ladies on horseback with jaunty caps, the rush-fringed pond, the mild sheep at pasture, and the bluish feathered treetops, running away into a long plumed distance, to a scene of chalky bluffs and a white sailing sky.

The cardinal looks at the scavengers as they go about their work. "Have we refreshments for our visitors?"

In the two great rooms that adjoin the gallery they have set up trestle tables. Each trestle is twenty feet long and they are bringing up more. In the Gilt Chamber they have laid out the cardinal's gold plate, his jewels and precious stones, and they are deciphering his inventories and calling out the weight of the plate. In the Council Chamber they are stacking his silver and parcel-gilt. Because everything is listed, down to the last dented pan from the kitchens, they have put baskets under the tables so they can throw in any item unlikely to catch the eye of the king. Sir William Gascoigne, the cardinal's treasurer, is moving constantly between the rooms, preoccupied, talking, directing the attention of the commissioners to any corner, any press and chest that he thinks they may have overlooked.

Behind him trots George Cavendish, the cardinal's gentleman usher; his face is raw and open with dismay. They bring out the cardinal's vestments, his copes. Stiff with embroidery, strewn with pearls, encrusted with gemstones, they seem to stand by themselves. The raiders knock down each one as if they are knocking down Thomas Becket. They itemize it, and having reduced it to its knees and broken its spine, they toss it into their traveling crates. Cavendish flinches: "For God's sake, gentlemen, line those chests with a double thickness of cambric. Would you shred the fine work that has taken nuns a lifetime?" He turns: "Master Cromwell, do you think we can get these people out before dark?"

"Only if we help them. If it's got to be done, we can make sure they do it properly."

This is an indecent spectacle: the man who has ruled England, reduced. They have brought out bolts of fine holland, velvets and grosgrain, sarcenet and taffeta, scarlet by the yard: the scarlet silk in which he braves the summer heat of London, the crimson brocades that keep his blood warm when snow falls on Westminster and whisks in sleety eddies over the Thames. In public the cardinal wears red, just red, but in various weights, various weaves, various degrees of pigment and dye, but all of them the best of their kind, the best reds to be got for money. There have been days when, swaggering out, he would say, "Right, Master Cromwell, price me by the yard!"

And he would say, "Let me see," and walk slowly around the cardinal; and saying, "May I?," he would pinch a sleeve between an expert forefinger and thumb; and standing back, he would view him, to estimate his girth—year on year, the cardinal expands—and so come up with a figure. The cardinal would clap his hands, delighted. "Let the begrudgers behold us! On, on, on." His procession would form up, his silver crosses, his sergeants at arms with their axes of gilt: for the cardinal went nowhere, in public, without a procession.

So day by day, at his request and to amuse him, he would put a value on his master. Now the king has sent an army of clerks to do it. But he would like to take away their pens by force and write across their inventories: Thomas Wolsey is a man beyond price.

"Now, Thomas," the cardinal says, patting him. "Everything I have, I have from the king. The king gave it to me, and if it pleases him to take York Place fully furnished, I am sure we own other houses, we have other roofs to shelter under. This is not Putney, you know." The cardinal holds on to him. "So I forbid you to hit anyone." He affects to be pressing his arms by his sides, in smiling restraint. The cardinal's fingers tremble.

The treasurer Gascoigne comes in and says, "I hear Your Grace is to go straight to the Tower."

"Do you?" he says. "Where did you hear that?"

"Sir William Gascoigne," the cardinal says, measuring out his name, "what do you suppose I have done that would make the king want to send me to the Tower?"

"It's like you," he says to Gascoigne, "to spread every story you're told. Is that all the comfort you've got to offer—walk in here with evil rumors? Nobody's going to the Tower. We're going"—and the household waits, breath held, as he improvises—"to Esher. And your job," he can't help giving Gascoigne a little shove in the chest, "is to keep an eye on all these strangers and see that everything that's taken out of here gets where it's meant to go, and that nothing goes missing by the way, because if it does you'll be beating on the gates of the Tower and begging them to take you in, to get away from me."

Various noises: mainly, from the back of the room, a sort of stifled cheer. It's hard to escape the feeling that this is a play, and the cardinal is in it: the Cardinal and his Attendants. And that it is a tragedy.

Cavendish tugs at him, anxious, sweating. "But Master Cromwell, the house at Esher is an empty house, we haven't a pot, we haven't a knife or a spit, where will my lord cardinal sleep, I doubt we have a bed aired, we have neither linen nor firewood nor . . . and how are we going to get there?"

"Sir William," the cardinal says to Gascoigne, "take no offense from Master Cromwell, who is, upon the occasion, blunt to a fault; but take what is said to heart. Since everything I have proceeds from the king, everything must be delivered back in good order." He turns away, his lips twitching. Except when he teased the dukes yesterday, he hasn't smiled in a month. "Tom," he says, "I've spent years teaching you not to talk like that."

Cavendish says to him, "They haven't seized my lord cardinal's barge yet. Nor his horses."

"No?" He lays a hand on Cavendish's shoulder: "We go upriver, as many as the barge will take. Horses can meet us at—at Putney, in fact—and then we will . . . borrow things. Come on, George Cavendish, exercise some ingenuity, we've done more difficult things in these last years than get the household to Esher."

Is this true? He's never taken much notice of Cavendish, a sensitive sort of man who talks a lot about table napkins. But he's trying to think of a way to put some military backbone into him, and the best way lies in suggesting that they are brothers from some old campaign.

"Yes, yes," Cavendish says, "we'll order up the barge."

Good, he says, and the cardinal says, Putney? and he tries to laugh. He says, well, Thomas, you told Gascoigne, you did; there's something about that man I never have liked, and he says, why did you keep him then? and the cardinal says, oh, well, one does, and again the cardinal says, Putney, eh?

He says, "Whatever we face at journey's end, we shall not forget how nine years ago, for the meeting of two kings, Your Grace created a golden city in some sad damp fields in Picardy. Since then, Your Grace has only increased in wisdom and the king's esteem."

He is speaking for everyone to hear; and he thinks, that occasion was about peace, notionally, whereas this occasion, we don't know what this is, it is the first day of a long or a short campaign; we had better dig in and hope our supply lines hold. "I think we will manage to find some fire irons and soup kettles and whatever else George Cavendish thinks we can't do without. When I remember that Your Grace provisioned the king's great armies, that went to fight in France."

"Yes," the cardinal says, "and we all know what you thought about our campaigns, Thomas."

Cavendish says, "What?" and the cardinal says, "George, don't you call to mind what my man Cromwell said in the House of Commons, was it five years past, when we wanted a subsidy for the new war?"

"But he spoke against Your Grace!"

Gascoigne—who hangs doggedly to this conversation—says, "You didn't advance yourself there, master, speaking against the king and my lord cardinal, because I do remember your speech, and I assure you so will others, and you bought yourself no favors there, Cromwell."

He shrugs. "I didn't mean to buy favor. We're not all like you, Gascoigne. I wanted the Commons to take some lessons from the last time. To cast their minds back."

"You said we'd lose."

"I said we'd be bankrupted. But I tell you, all our wars would have ended much worse without my lord cardinal to supply them."

"In the year 1523—" Gascoigne says.

"Must we refight this now?" says the cardinal.

"—the Duke of Suffolk was only fifty miles from Paris."

"Yes," he says, "and do you know what fifty miles is, to a half-starved infantryman in winter, when he sleeps on wet ground and wakes up cold? Do you know what fifty miles is to a baggage train, with carts up to the axles in mud? And as for the glories of 1513—God defend us."

"Tournai! Thérouanne!" Gascoigne shouts. "Are you blind to what occurred? Two French towns taken! The king so valiant in the field!"

If we were in the field now, he thinks, I'd spit at your feet. "If you like the king so much, go and work for him. Or do you already?"

The cardinal clears his throat softly. "We all do," Cavendish says, and the cardinal says, "Thomas, we are the works of his hand."

❖

When they get out to the cardinal's barge his flags are flying: the Tudor rose, the Cornish choughs. Cavendish says, wide-eyed, "Look at all these little boats, waffeting up and down." For a moment, the cardinal thinks the Londoners have turned out to wish him well. But as he enters the barge, there are sounds of hooting and booing from the boats; spectators crowd the bank, and though the cardinal's men keep them back, their intent is clear enough. When the oars begin to row upstream, and not downstream to the Tower, there are groans and shouted threats.

It is then that the cardinal collapses, falling into his seat, beginning to talk, and talks, talks, talks, all the way to Putney. "Do they hate me so much? What have I done but promote their trades and show them my goodwill? Have I sown hatred? No. Persecuted none. Sought remedies every year when wheat was scarce. When the apprentices rioted, begged the king on my knees with tears in my eyes to spare the offenders, while they stood garlanded with the nooses that were to hang them."

"The multitude," Cavendish says, "is always desirous of a change. They never see a great man set up but they must pull him down—for the novelty of the thing."

"Fifteen years Chancellor. Twenty in his service. His father's before that. Never spared myself . . . rising early, watching late . . ."

"There, you see," Cavendish says, "what it is to serve a prince! We should be wary of their vacillations of temper."

"Princes are not obliged to consistency," he says. He thinks, I may forget myself, lean across and push you overboard.

The cardinal has not forgotten himself, far from it; he is looking back, back twenty years to the young king's accession. "Put him to work, said some. But I said, no, he is a young man. Let him hunt, joust, and fly his hawks and falcons . . ."

"Play instruments," Cavendish says. "Always plucking at something or other. And singing."

"You make him sound like Nero."

"Nero?" Cavendish jumps. "I never said so."

"The gentlest, wisest prince in Christendom," says the cardinal. "I will not hear a word against him from any man."

"Nor shall you," he says.

"But what I would do for him! Cross the Channel as lightly as a man might step across a stream of piss in the street." The cardinal shakes his head. "Waking and sleeping, on horseback or at my beads . . . twenty years . . ."

"Is it something to do with the English?" Cavendish asks earnestly. He's still thinking of the uproar back there when they embarked; and even now, people are running along the banks, making obscene signs and whistling. "Tell us, Master Cromwell, you've been abroad. Are they particularly an ungrateful nation? It seems to me that they like change for the sake of it."

"I don't think it's the English. I think it's just people. They always hope there may be something better."

"But what do they get by the change?" Cavendish persists. "One dog sated with meat is replaced by a hungrier dog who bites nearer the bone. Out goes the man grown fat with honor, and in comes a hungry and a lean man."

He closes his eyes. The river shifts beneath them, dim figures in an allegory of Fortune. Decayed Magnificence sits in the center. Cavendish, leaning at his right like a Virtuous Councillor, mutters words of superfluous and belated advice, to which the sorry magnate inclines his head; he, like a Tempter, is seated on the left, and the cardinal's great hand, with its knuckles of garnet and tourmaline, grips his own hand painfully. George would certainly go in the river, except that what he's saying, despite the platitudes, makes a bleak sense. And why? Stephen Gardiner, he thinks. It may not be proper to call the cardinal a dog grown fat, but Stephen is definitely hungry and lean, and has been promoted by the king to a place as his own private secretary. It is not unusual for the cardinal's staff to transfer in this way, after careful nurture in the Wolsey school of craft and diligence; but still, this places Stephen as the man who—if he manages his duties properly— may be closer than anyone to the king, except perhaps for the gentle- man who attends him at his close-stool and hands him a diaper cloth. I wouldn't so much mind, he thinks, if Stephen got that job.

The cardinal closes his eyes. Tears are seeping from beneath his lids. "For it is a truth," says Cavendish, "that fortune is inconstant, fickle and mutable . . ."

All he has to do is to make a strangling motion, quickly, while the cardinal has his eyes shut. Cavendish, putting a hand to his throat, takes the point. And then they look at each other, sheepish. One of them has said too much; one of them has felt too much. It is not easy to know where the balance rests. His eyes scan the banks of the Thames. Still, the cardinal weeps and grips his hand.

As they move upriver, the littoral ceases to alarm. It is not because, in Putney, Englishmen are less fickle. It's just that they haven't heard yet.

❖

The horses are waiting. The cardinal, in his capacity as a churchman, has always ridden a large strong mule; though, since he has hunted with kings for twenty years, his stable is the envy of every nobleman. Here the beast stands, twitching long ears, in its usual scarlet trap- pings, and by him Master Sexton, the cardinal's fool.

"What in God's name is he doing here?" he asks Cavendish.

Sexton comes forward and says something in the cardinal's ear;

the cardinal laughs. "Very good, Patch. Now, help me mount, there's a good fellow."

But Patch—Master Sexton—is not up to the job. The cardinal seems weakened; he seems to feel the weight of his flesh hanging on his bones. He, Cromwell, slides from his saddle, nods to three of the stouter servants. "Master Patch, hold Christopher's head." When Patch pretends not to know that Christopher is the mule, and puts a headlock on the man next to him, he says, oh, for Jesus' sake, Sexton, get out of the way, or I'll stuff you in a sack and drown you.

The man who's nearly had his head pulled off stands up, rubs his neck; says, thanks, Master Cromwell, and hobbles forward to hold the bridle. He, Cromwell, with two others, hauls the cardinal into the saddle. The cardinal looks shamefaced. "Thank you, Tom." He laughs shakily. "That's you told, Patch."

They are ready to ride. Cavendish looks up. "Saints protect us!" A single horseman is heading downhill at a gallop. "An arrest!"

"By one man?"

"An outrider," says Cavendish, and he says, Putney's rough but you don't have to send out scouts. Then someone shouts, "It's Harry Norris." Harry throws himself from his mount. Whatever he's come to do, he's in a lather about it. Harry Norris is one of the king's closest friends; he is, to be exact, the Groom of the Stool, the man who hands the diaper cloth.

Wolsey sees, immediately, that the king wouldn't send Norris to take him into custody. "Now, Sir Henry, get your breath back. What can be so urgent?"

Norris says, beg pardon, my lord, my lord cardinal, sweeps off his feathered cap, wipes his face with his arm, smiles in his most engaging fashion. He speaks to the cardinal gracefully: the king has commanded him to ride after His Grace and overtake him, and speak words of comfort to him and give him this ring, which he knows well—a ring which he holds out, in the palm of his glove.

The cardinal scrambles from his mule and falls to the ground. He takes the ring and presses it to his lips. He's praying. Praying, thanking Norris, calling for blessings on his sovereign. "I have nothing to send him. Nothing of value to send to the king." He looks around him, as if his eye might light on something he can send; a tree? Norris tries to get him on his feet, ends up kneeling beside him, kneeling—this neat and charming man—in the Putney mud. The message he's giving the cardinal, it seems, is that the king only appears displeased, but is not really displeased; that he knows the cardinal has enemies; that he himself, Henricus Rex, is not one of them; that this show of force is only to satisfy those enemies; that he is able to recompense the cardinal with twice as much as has been taken from him.

The cardinal begins to cry. It's starting to rain, and the wind blows the rain across their faces. The cardinal speaks to Norris fast, in a low voice, and then he takes a chain from around his neck and tries to hang it around Norris's neck, and it gets tangled up in the fastenings of his riding cape and several people rush forward to help and fail, and Norris gets up and begins to brush himself down with one glove while clutching the chain in the other. "Wear it," the cardinal begs him, "and when you look at it think of me, and commend me to the king."

Cavendish jolts up, riding knee-to-knee. "His reliquary!" George is upset, astonished. "To part with it like this! It is a piece of the true Cross!"

"We'll get him another. I know a man in Pisa makes them ten for five florins and a round dozen for cash up front. And you get a certificate with St. Peter's thumbprint, to say they're genuine."

"For shame!" Cavendish says, and twitches his horse away.

Now Norris is backing away too, his message delivered, and they are trying to get the cardinal back on his mule. This time, four big men step forward, as if it were routine. The play has turned into some kind of low comic interlude; that, he thinks, is why Patch is here. He rides over and says, looking down from the saddle, "Norris, can we have all this in writing?"

Norris smiles, says, "Hardly, Master Cromwell; it's a confidential message to my lord cardinal. My master's words were meant only for him."

"So what about this recompense you mention?"

Norris laughs—as he always does, to disarm hostility—and whispers, "I think it might be figurative."

"I think it might be, too." Double the cardinal's worth? Not on Henry's income. "Give us back what's been taken. We don't ask double."

Norris's hand goes to the chain, now slung about his neck. "But it all proceeds from the king. You can't call it theft."

"I didn't call it theft."

Norris nods, thoughtful. "No more did you."

"They shouldn't have taken the vestments. They belong to my lord as churchman. What will they have next? His benefices?"

"Esher—which is where you are going, are you not?—is of course one of the houses which my lord cardinal holds as Bishop of Winchester."

"And?"

"He remains for the while in that estate and title, but . . . shall we say . . . it must come under the king's consideration? You know my lord cardinal is indicted under the statutes of praemunire, for asserting a foreign jurisdiction in the land."

"Don't teach me the law."

Norris inclines his head.

He thinks, since last spring, when things began to go wrong, I should have persuaded my lord cardinal to let me manage his revenues, and put some money away abroad where they can't get it; but then he would never admit that anything was wrong. Why did I let him rest so cheerful?

Norris's hand is on his horse's bridle. "I was ever a person who admired your master," he says, "and I hope that in his adversity he will remember that."

"I thought he wasn't in adversity? According to you."

How simple it would be, if he were allowed to reach down and shake some straight answers out of Norris. But it's not simple; this is what the world and the cardinal conspire to teach him. Christ, he thinks, by my age I ought to know. You don't get on by being original. You don't get on by being bright. You don't get on by being strong. You get on by being a subtle crook; somehow he thinks that's what Norris is, and he feels an irrational dislike taking root, and he tries to dismiss it, because he prefers his dislikes rational, but after all, these circumstances are extreme, the cardinal in the mud, the humiliating tussle to get him back in the saddle, the talking, talking on the barge, and worse, the talking, talking on his knees, as if Wolsey's unraveling, in a great unweaving of scarlet thread that might lead you back into a scarlet labyrinth, with a dying monster at its heart.

"Master Cromwell?" Norris says.

He can hardly say what he's thinking; so he looks down at Norris, his expression softened, and says, "Thanks for this much comfort."

"Well, take my lord cardinal out of the rain. I'll tell the king how I found him."

"Tell him how you knelt in the mud together. He might be amused."

"Yes." Norris looks sad. "You never know what will do it."

It is at this point that Patch starts screaming. The cardinal, it seems—casting around for a gift—has given him to the king. Patch, he has often said, is worth a thousand pounds. He is to go with Norris, no time like the present; and it takes four more of the cardinal's men to subdue him to the purpose. He fights. He bites. He lashes out with fists and feet. Till he is thrown onto a baggage mule, stripped of its baggage; till he begins to cry, hiccupping, his ribs heaving, his stupid feet dangling, his coat torn and the feather in his hat broken off to a stub.

"But Patch," the cardinal says, "my dear fellow. You shall see me often, once the king and I understand each other again. My dear Patch, I will write you a letter, a letter of your own. I shall write it tonight," he promises, "and put my big seal on it. The king will cherish you; he is the kindest soul in Christendom."

Patch wails on a single thin note, like someone taken by the Turks and impaled.

There, he says to Cavendish, he's more than one kind of fool. He shouldn't have drawn attention to himself, should he.

❖

Esher: the cardinal dismounts under the shadow of old Bishop Wayneflete's keep, surmounted by octagonal towers. The gateway is set into a defensive wall topped with a walkway; stern enough at first sight, but the whole thing is built of brick, ornamented and prettily inlaid. "You couldn't fortify it," he says. Cavendish is silent. "George, you're supposed to say, 'But the need could never arise.'"

The cardinal's not used the place since he built Hampton Court. They've sent messages ahead, but has anything been done? Make my lord comfortable, he says, and goes straight down to the kitchens. At Hampton Court, the kitchens have running water; here, nothing's running but the cooks' noses. Cavendish is right. In fact it is worse than he thinks. The larders are impoverished and such supplies as they have show signs of ill-keeping and plunder. There are weevils in the flour. There are mouse droppings where the pastry should be rolled. It is nearly Martinmas, and they have not even thought of salting their beef. The *batterie de cuisine* is an insult, and the stockpot is mildewed. There are a number of small boys sitting by the hearth, and, for cash down, they can be induced into scouring and scrubbing; children take readily to novelty, and the idea of cleaning, it seems, is novel to them.

My lord, he says, needs to eat and drink now; and he needs to eat and drink for . . . how long we don't know. This kitchen must be put in order for the winter ahead. He finds someone who can write, and dictates his orders. His eyes are fixed on the kitchen clerk. On his left hand he counts off the items: you do this, then this, then thirdly this. With his right hand, he breaks eggs into a basin, each one with a hard professional tap, and between his fingers the white drips, sticky and slow, from the yolk. "How old is this egg? Change your supplier. I want a nutmeg. Nutmeg? Saffron?" They look at him as if he's speaking Greek. Patch's thin scream is still hurting his ears. Dusty angels look down on him as he pounds back to the hall.

It is late before they get the cardinal into any sort of bed worthy of the name. Where is his household steward? Where is his comptroller? By this time, he feels it is true that he and Cavendish are old survivors of a campaign. He stays up with Cavendish—not that there are beds, if they wanted them—working out what they need to keep the cardinal in reasonable comfort; they need plates, unless my lord's going to dine off dented pewter, they need bedsheets, table linen, firewood. "I will send some people," he says, "to sort out the kitchens. They will be Italian. It will be violent at first, but then after three weeks it will work."

Three weeks? He wants to set those children cleaning the copper. "Can we get lemons?" he asks, just as Cavendish says, "So who will be Chancellor now?"

I wonder, he thinks, are there rats down there? Cavendish says, "Recall His Grace of Canterbury?"

Recall him—fifteen years after the cardinal chivvied him out of that office? "No, Warham's too old." And too stubborn, too unaccommodating to the king's wishes. "And not the Duke of Suffolk"—because in his view Charles Brandon is no brighter than Christopher the mule, though better at fighting and fashion and generally showing off—"not Suffolk, because the Duke of Norfolk won't have him."

"And vice versa." Cavendish nods. "Bishop Tunstall?"

"No. Thomas More."

"But, a layman and a commoner? And when he's so opposed in the matter of the king's marriage suit?"

He nods, yes, yes, it will be More. The king is known for putting out his conscience to high bidders. Perhaps he hopes to be saved from himself.

"If the king offers it—and I see that, as a gesture, he might—surely Thomas More won't accept?"

"He will."

"Bet?" says Cavendish.

They agree to the terms and shake hands on it. It takes their mind off the urgent problem, which is the rats, and the cold; which is the question of how they can pack a household staff of several hundred, retained at Westminster, into the much smaller space at Esher. The cardinal's staff, if you include his principal houses, and count them up from priests, law clerks, down to floor-sweepers and laundresses, is about six hundred souls. They expect three hundred following them immediately. "As things stand, we'll have to break up the household," Cavendish says. "But we've no ready money for wages."

"I'm damned if they're going unpaid," he says, and Cavendish says, "I think you are anyway. After what you said about the relic."

He catches George's eye. They start to laugh. At least they've got something worthwhile to drink; the cellars are full, which is lucky, Cavendish says, because we'll need a drink over the next weeks. "What do you think Norris meant?" George says. "How can the king be in two minds? How can my lord cardinal be dismissed if he doesn't want to dismiss him? How can the king give way to my lord's enemies? Isn't the king master over all the enemies?"

"You would think so."

"Or is it *her*? It must be. He's frightened of her, you know. She's a witch."

He says, don't be childish. George says, she is so a witch: the Duke of Norfolk says she is, and he's her uncle, he should know.

It's two o'clock, then it's three; sometimes it's freeing, to think you don't have to go to bed because there isn't a bed. He doesn't need to think of going home; there's no home to go to, he's got no family left. He'd rather be here drinking with Cavendish, huddled in a corner of the great chamber at Esher, cold and tired and frightened of the future, than think about his family and what he's lost. "Tomorrow," he says, "I'll get my clerks down from London and we'll try and make sense of what my lord still has by way of assets, which won't be easy as they've taken all the paperwork. His creditors won't be inclined to pay up when they know what's happened. But the French king pays him a pension, and if I remember it's always in arrears . . . Maybe he'd like to send a bag of gold, pending my lord's return to favor. And you— you can go looting."

❖

Cavendish is hollow-faced and hollow-eyed when he throws him onto a fresh horse at first light. "Call in some favors. There's hardly a gentleman in the realm that doesn't owe my lord cardinal something."

It's late October, the sun a coin barely flipped above the horizon. "Keep him cheerful," Cavendish says. "Keep him talking. Keep him talking about what Harry Norris said . . ."

"Off you go. If you should see the coals on which St. Lawrence was roasted, we could make good use of them here."

"Oh, don't," Cavendish begs. He has come far since yesterday, and is able to make jokes about holy martyrs; but he drank too much last night, and it hurts him to laugh. But not to laugh is painful too. George's head droops, the horse stirs beneath him, his eyes are full of bafflement. "How did it come to this?" he asks. "My lord cardinal kneeling in the dirt. How could it happen? How in the world could it?"

He says, "Saffron. Raisins. Apples. And cats, get cats, huge starving ones. I don't know, George, where do cats come from? Oh, wait! Do you think we can get partridges?"

If we can get partridges we can slice the breasts, and braise them at the table. Whatever we can do that way, we will; and so, if we can help it, my lord won't be poisoned.

II

An Occult History of Britain

1521–1529

O nce, in the days of time immemorial, there was a king of Greece who had thirty-three daughters. Each of these daughters rose up in revolt and murdered her husband. Perplexed as to how he had bred such rebels, but not wanting to kill his own flesh and blood, their princely father exiled them and set them adrift in a rudderless ship.

Their ship was provisioned for six months. By the end of this period, the winds and tides had carried them to the edge of the known earth. They landed on an island shrouded in mist. As it had no name, the eldest of the killers gave it hers: Albina.

When they hit shore, they were hungry and avid for male flesh. But there were no men to be found. The island was home only to demons.

The thirty-three princesses mated with the demons and gave birth to a race of giants, who in turn mated with their mothers and produced more of their own kind. These giants spread over the whole landmass of Britain. There were no priests, no churches and no laws. There was also no way of telling the time.

After eight centuries of rule, they were overthrown by Trojan Brutus.

The great-grandson of Aeneas, Brutus was born in Italy; his mother died in giving birth to him, and his father, by accident, he killed with an arrow. He fled his birthplace and became leader of a band of men who had been slaves in Troy. Together they embarked on a voyage north, and the vagaries of wind and tide drove them to Albina's coast, as the sisters had been driven before. When they landed they were forced to do battle with the giants, led by Gogmagog. The giants were defeated and their leader thrown into the sea.

Whichever way you look at it, it all begins in slaughter. Trojan Brutus and his descendants ruled till the coming of the Romans. Before London was called Lud's Town, it was called New Troy. And we were Trojans.

Some say the Tudors transcend this history, bloody and demonic as it is: that they descend from Brutus through the line of Constantine, son of St. Helena, who was a Briton. Arthur, High King of Britain, was Constantine's grandson. He married up to three women, all called Guinevere, and his tomb is at Glastonbury, but you must understand that he is not really dead, only waiting his time to come again.

His blessed descendant Prince Arthur of England was born in the year 1486, eldest son of Henry, the first Tudor king. This Arthur married Katherine the princess of Aragon, died at fifteen and was buried in Worcester Cathedral. If he were alive now, he would be King of England. His younger brother Henry would likely be Archbishop of Canterbury, and would not (at least, we devoutly hope not) be in pursuit of a woman of whom the cardinal hears nothing good: a woman to whom, several years before the dukes walk in to despoil him, he will need to turn his attention; whose history, before ruin seizes him, he will need to comprehend.

Beneath every history, another history.

❖

The lady appeared at court at the Christmas of 1521, dancing in a yellow dress. She was—what?—about twenty years old. Daughter of the diplomat Thomas Boleyn, she has been brought up since childhood in the Burgundian court at Mechelen and Brussels, and more recently in Paris, moving in Queen Claude's train between the pretty chateaux of the Loire. Now she speaks her native tongue with a slight, unplaceable accent, strewing her sentences with French words when she pretends she can't think of the English. At Shrovetide, she dances in a court masque. The ladies are costumed as Virtues, and she takes the part of

Perseverance. She dances gracefully but briskly, with an amused expression on her face, a hard, impersonal touch-me-not smile. Soon she has a little trail of petty gentlemen following her; and one not so petty gentleman. The rumor spreads that she is going to marry Harry Percy, the Earl of Northumberland's heir.

The cardinal hauls in her father. "Sir Thomas Boleyn," he says, "speak to your daughter, or I will. We brought her back from France to marry her into Ireland, to the Butlers' heir. Why does she tarry?"

"The Butlers . . ." Sir Thomas begins, and the cardinal says, "Oh yes? The Butlers what? Any problem you have there, I'll fix the Butlers. What I want to know is, did you put her up to it? Conniving in corners with that foolish boy? Because, Sir Thomas, let me make myself plain: I won't have it. The king won't have it. It must be stopped."

"I have scarcely been in England these last months. Your Grace cannot think that I am party to the scheme."

"No? You would be surprised what I can think. Is this your best excuse? That you can't govern your own children?"

Sir Thomas is looking wry and holding out his hands. He's on the verge of saying, young people today . . . But the cardinal stops him. The cardinal suspects—and has confided his suspicion—that the young woman is not enticed by the prospect of Kilkenny Castle and its frugal amenities, nor by the kind of social life that will be available to her when, on special occasions, she hacks on the poor dirt roads to Dublin.

"Who's that?" Boleyn says. "In the corner there?"

The cardinal waves a hand. "Just one of my legal people."

"Send him out."

The cardinal sighs.

"Is he taking notes of this conversation?"

"Are you, Thomas?" the cardinal calls. "If so, stop it at once."

Half the world is called Thomas. Afterward, Boleyn will never be sure if it was him.

"Look now, my lord," he says, his voice playing up and down the diplomat's scales: he is frank, a man of the world, and his smile says, now Wolsey, now Wolsey, you're a man of the world too. "They're young." He makes a gesture, designed to impersonate frankness. "She caught the boy's eye. It's natural. I've had to break it to her. She knows it can't proceed. She knows her place."

"Good," the cardinal says, "because it's below a Percy. I mean," he adds, "below, in the dynastic sense. I am not speaking of what one might do in a haystack on a warm night."

"He doesn't accept it, the young man. They tell him to marry Mary Talbot, but . . ." and Boleyn gives a little careless laugh, "he doesn't care to marry Mary Talbot. He believes he is free to choose his wife."

"Choose his—!" the cardinal breaks off. "I never heard the like. He's not some plowboy. He's the man who will have to hold the north for us, one of these days, and if he doesn't understand his position in the world then he must learn it or forfeit it. The match already made with Shrewsbury's daughter is a fit match for him, and a match made by me, and agreed by the king. And the Earl of Shrewsbury, I can tell you, doesn't take kindly to this sort of moonstruck clowning by a boy who's promised to his daughter."

"The difficulty is . . ." Boleyn allows a discreet diplomatic pause. "I think that, Harry Percy and my daughter, they may have gone a little far in the matter."

"What? You mean we are speaking of a haystack and a warm night?"

From the shadows he watches; he thinks Boleyn is the coldest, smoothest man he has ever seen.

"From what they tell me, they have pledged themselves before witnesses. How can it be undone, then?"

The cardinal smashes his fist on the table. "I'll tell you how. I shall get his father down from the borders, and if the prodigal defies him, he will be tossed out of his heirdom on his prodigal snout. The earl has other sons, and better. And if you don't want the Butler marriage called off, and your lady daughter shriveling unmarriageable down in Sussex and costing you bed and board for the rest of her life, you will forget any talk of pledges, and witnesses—who are they, these witnesses? I know those kinds of witnesses who never show their faces when I send for them. So never let me hear it. Pledges. Witnesses. Contracts. God in Heaven!"

Boleyn is still smiling. He is a poised, slender man; it takes the effort of every finely tuned muscle in his body to keep the smile on his face.

"I do not ask you," says Wolsey, relentless, "whether in this matter you have sought the advice of your relatives in the Howard family. I should be reluctant to think that it was with their agreement that you launched yourself on this scheme. I should be sorry to hear the Duke of Norfolk was apprised of this: oh, very sorry indeed. So let me not hear it, eh? Go and ask your relatives for some *good* advice. Marry the girl into Ireland before the Butlers hear any rumor that she's spoiled goods. Not that I'd mention it. But the court does talk."

Sir Thomas has two spots of angry red on his cheekbones. He says, "Finished, my lord cardinal?"

"Yes. Go."

Boleyn turns, in a sweep of dark silks. Are those tears of temper in his eyes? The light is dim, but he, Cromwell, is of very strong sight. "Oh, a moment, Sir Thomas . . ." the cardinal says. His voice loops across the room and pulls his victim back. "Now, Sir Thomas, remember your ancestry. The Percy family comprise, I do think, the noblest in the land. Whereas, notwithstanding your remarkable good fortune in marrying a Howard, the Boleyns were in trade once, were they not? A person of your name was Lord Mayor of London, not so? Or have I mixed up your line with some Boleyns more distinguished?"

Sir Thomas's face has drained; the scarlet spots have vanished from his cheeks, and he is almost fainting with rage. As he quits the room, he whispers, "Butcher's boy." And as he passes the clerk—whose beefy hand lies idly on his desk—he sneers, "Butcher's dog."

❖

The door bangs. The cardinal says, "Come out, dog." He sits laughing, with his elbows on his desk and his head in his hands. "Mark and learn," he says. "You can never advance your own pedigree—and God knows, Tom, you were born in a more dishonorable estate than me—so the trick is always to keep them scraped up to their own standards. They made the rules; they cannot complain if I am the strictest enforcer. Percys above Boleyns. Who does he think he is?"

"Is it good policy to make people angry?"

"Oh, no. But it amuses me. My life is hard and I find I want amusement." The cardinal casts on him a kindly eye; he suspects he may be this evening's further diversion, now that Boleyn has been torn into strips and dropped on the ground like orange peel. "Who need one look up to? The Percys, the Staffords, the Howards, the Talbots: yes. Use a long stick to stir them, if you must. As for Boleyn—well, the king likes him, and he is an able man. Which is why I open all his letters, and have done for years."

"So has your lordship heard—no, forgive me, it is not fit for your ears."

"What?" says the cardinal.

"It is only rumor. I should not like to mislead Your Grace."

"You cannot speak and not speak. You must tell me now."

"It's only what the women are saying. The silk women. And the cloth merchants' wives." He waits, smiling. "Which is of no interest to you, I'm sure."

Laughing, the cardinal pushes back his chair, and his shadow rises with him. Firelit, it leaps. His arm darts out, his reach is long, his hand is like the hand of God.

But when God closes his hand, his subject is across the room, back to the wall.

The cardinal gives ground. His shadow wavers. It wavers and comes to rest. He is still. The wall records the movement of his breath. His head inclines. In a halo of light he seems to pause, to examine his handful of nothing. He splays his fingers, his giant firelit hand. He places it flat on his desk. It vanishes, melted into the cloth of damask. He sits down again. His head is bowed; his face, half-dark.

He Thomas, also Tomos, Tommaso and Thomaes Cromwell, withdraws his past selves into his present body and edges back to where he was before. His single shadow slides against the wall, a visitor not sure of his welcome. Which of these Thomases saw the blow coming? There are moments when a memory moves right through you. You shy, you duck, you run; or else the past takes your fist and actuates it, without the intervention of will. Suppose you have a knife in your fist? That's how murder happens.

He says something, the cardinal says something. They break off. Two sentences go nowhere. The cardinal resumes his chair. He hesitates before him; he sits down. The cardinal says, "I really would like the London gossip. But I wasn't planning to beat it out of you."

The cardinal bows his head, frowns at a paper on his desk; he is allowing time for the difficult moment to pass, and when he speaks again his tone is measured and easy, like a man telling anecdotes after supper. "When I was a child, my father had a friend—a customer, really—who was of a florid complexion." He touches his sleeve, in illustration. "Like this . . . scarlet. Revell was his name, Miles Revell." His hand drifts to rest again, palm downward on the blackish damask. "For some reason I used to believe . . . though I dare say he was an honest citizen, and liked a glass of Rhenish . . . I used to believe he was a drinker of blood. I don't know . . . some story I suppose that I had heard from my nurse, or from some other silly child . . . and then when my father's apprentices knew about it—only because I was foolish enough to whine and cry—they would shout out, 'Here comes Revell for his cup of blood, run, Thomas Wolsey . . .' I used to flee as if the devil were after me. Put the marketplace between us. I marvel that I didn't fall under a wagon. I used to run, and never look. Even today," he says—he picks up a wax seal from the desk, turns it over, turns it over, puts it down—"even today, when I see a fair, florid man—let us say, the Duke of Suffolk—I feel inclined to burst into tears." He pauses. His gaze comes to rest. "So, Thomas . . . can't a cleric stand up, unless you think he's after your blood?" He picks up the seal again; he turns it over in his fingers; he averts his eyes; he begins to play with words. "Would a bishop abash you? A parish clerk panic you? A deacon disconcert?"

He says, "What is the word? I don't know in English . . . an *estoc* . . ."

Perhaps there is no English word for it: the short-bladed knife that, at close quarters, you push up under the ribs. The cardinal says, "And this was . . . ?"

This was some twenty years ago. The lesson is learned and learned well. Night, ice, the still heart of Europe; a forest, lakes silver beneath a pattern of winter stars; a room, firelight, a shape slipping against the wall. He didn't see his assassin, but he saw his shadow move.

"All the same . . ." says the cardinal. "It's forty years since I saw Master Revell. He will be long dead, I suppose. And your man?" He hesitates. "Long dead too?"

It is the most delicate way that can be contrived, to ask a man if he has killed someone.

"And in Hell, I should think. If your lordship pleases."

That makes Wolsey smile; not the mention of Hell, but the bow to the breadth of his jurisdiction. "So if you attacked the young Cromwell, you went straight to the fiery pit?"

"If you had seen him, my lord. He was too dirty for Purgatory. The Blood of the Lamb can do much, we are told, but I doubt if it could have wiped this fellow clean."

"I am all for a spotless world," Wolsey says. He looks sad. "Have you made a good confession?"

"It was a long time ago."

"Have you made a good confession?"

"My lord cardinal, I was a soldier."

"Soldiers have hope of Heaven."

He looks up into Wolsey's face. There's no knowing what he believes. He says, "We all have that." Soldiers, beggars, sailors, kings.

"So you were a ruffian in your youth," the cardinal says. "*Ça ne fait rien.*" He broods. "This dirty fellow who attacked you . . . he was not, in fact, in holy orders?"

He smiles. "I didn't ask."

"These tricks of memory . . ." the cardinal says. "Thomas, I shall try not to move without giving you warning. And in that way we shall do very well together."

But the cardinal looks him over; he is still puzzling. It is early in their association and his character, as invented by the cardinal, is at this stage a work in progress; in fact, perhaps it is this evening that sets it going? In the years to come, the cardinal will say, "I often wonder, about the monastic ideal—especially as applied to the young. My servant Cromwell, for instance—his youth was secluded, spent almost entirely in fasting, prayer and study of the Church Fathers. That's why he's so wild nowadays."

And when people say, is he?—recalling, as best they can, a man who seems peculiarly discreet; when they say, really? Your man Cromwell? the cardinal will shake his head and say, but I try to mend matters, of course. When he breaks the windows we just call in the glaziers and part with the cash. As for the procession of aggrieved young women . . . Poor creatures, I pay them off . . .

But tonight he is back to business; hands clasped on his desk, as if holding together the evening passed. "Come now, Thomas, you were telling me of a rumor."

"The women judge from orders to the silk merchants that the king has a new—" He breaks off and says, "My lord, what do you call a whore when she is a knight's daughter?"

"Ah," the cardinal says, entering into the problem. "To her face, 'my lady.' Behind her back—well, what is her name? Which knight?"

He nods to where, ten minutes ago, Boleyn stood.

The cardinal looks alarmed. "Why did you not speak up?"

"How could I have introduced the topic?"

The cardinal bows to the difficulty.

"But it is not the Boleyn lady new at court. Not Harry Percy's lady. It is her sister."

"I see." The cardinal drops back in his chair. "Of course."

Mary Boleyn is a kind little blonde, who is said to have been passed all around the French court before coming home to this one, scattering goodwill, her frowning little sister trotting always at her heels.

"Of course, I have followed the direction of His Majesty's eye," the cardinal says. He nods to himself. "Are they now close? Does the queen know? Or can't you say?"

He nods. The cardinal sighs. "Katherine is a saint. Still, if I were a saint, and a queen, perhaps I would feel I could take no harm from Mary Boleyn. Presents, eh? What sort? Not lavish, you say? I am sorry for her then; she should seize her advantage while it lasts. It's not that our king has so many adventures, though they do say . . . they say that when His Majesty was young, not yet king, it was Boleyn's wife who relieved him of his virgin state."

"Elizabeth Boleyn?" He is not often surprised. "This one's *mother*?"

"The same. Perhaps the king lacks imagination in that way. Not that I ever believed it . . . If we were at the other side, you know," he gestures in the direction of Dover, "we wouldn't even try to keep track of the women. My friend King François—they do say he once oozed up to the lady he'd been with the night before, gave her a formal kiss of the hand, asked her name, and wished they might be better friends." He bobs his head, liking the success of his story. "But Mary won't cause difficulties. She's an easy armful. The king could do worse."

"But her family will want to get something out of it. What did they get before?"

"The chance to make themselves useful." Wolsey breaks off and makes a note. He can imagine its content: what Boleyn can have, if he asks nicely. The cardinal looks up. "So should I have been, in my interview with Sir Thomas—how shall I put it—more douce?"

"I don't think my lord could have been sweeter. Witness his face when he left us. The picture of soothed gratification."

"Thomas, from now on, any London gossip," he touches the damask cloth, "bring it right here to me. Don't trouble about the source. Let the trouble be mine. And I promise never to assault you. Truly."

"It is forgotten."

"I doubt that. Not if you've carried the lesson all these years." The cardinal sits back; he considers. "At least she is married." Mary Boleyn, he means. "So if she whelps, he can acknowledge it or not, as he pleases. He has a boy from John Blount's daughter and he won't want too many."

Too large a royal nursery can be encumbering to a king. The example of history and of other nations shows that the mothers fight for status, and try to get their brats induced somehow into the line of succession. The son Henry acknowledges is known as Henry Fitzroy; he is a handsome blond child made in the king's own image. His father has created him Duke of Somerset and Duke of Richmond; he is not yet ten years old, and the senior nobleman in England.

Queen Katherine, whose boys have all died, takes it patiently: that is to say, she suffers.

❖

When he leaves the cardinal, he is miserably angry. When he thinks back to his earlier life—that boy half-dead on the cobbles in Putney—he feels no tenderness for him, just a faint impatience: why doesn't he get up? For his later self—still prone to getting into fights, or at least being in the place where a fight might occur—he feels something like contempt, washed with a queasy anxiety. That was the way of the world: a knife in the dark, a movement on the edge of vision, a series of warnings which have worked themselves into flesh. He has given the cardinal a shock, which is not his job; his job, as he has defined it at this time, is to feed the cardinal information and soothe his temper and understand him and embellish his jokes. What went wrong was an accident of timing only. If the cardinal had not moved so fast; if he had not been so edgy, not knowing how he could signal to him to be less despotic to Boleyn. The trouble with England, he thinks, is that it's so poor in gesture. We shall have to develop a hand signal for "Back off, our prince is fucking this man's daughter." He is surprised that the Italians have not done it. Though perhaps they have, and he just never caught on.

❖

In the year 1529, my lord cardinal newly disgraced, he will think back to that evening.

He is at Esher; it is the lightless, fireless night, when the great man has gone to his (possibly damp) bed, and there is only George Cavendish to keep his spirits alive. What happened next, he asked George, with Harry Percy and Anne Boleyn?

He knew the story only in the cardinal's chilly and dismissive rendition. But George said, "I shall tell you how it was. Now. Stand up, Master Cromwell." He does it. "A little to the left. Now, which would you like to be? My lord cardinal, or the young heir?"

"Oh, I see, is it a play? You be the cardinal. I don't feel equal to it."

Cavendish adjusts his position, turning him imperceptibly from the window, where night and bare trees are their audience. His gaze rests on the air, as if he were seeing the past: shadowy bodies, moving in this lightless room. "Can you look troubled?" George asks. "As if you were brooding upon mutinous speech, and yet dare not speak? No, no, not like that. You are youthful, gangling, your head drooping, you are blushing." Cavendish sighs. "I believe you never blushed in your life, Master Cromwell. Look." Cavendish sets his hands, gently, on his upper arms. "Let us change roles. Sit here. You be the cardinal."

At once he sees Cavendish transformed. George twitches, he fumbles, he all but weeps; he becomes the quaking Harry Percy, a young man in love. "Why should I not match with her?" he cries. "Though she be but a simple maid—"

"Simple?" he says. "Maid?"

George glares at him. "The cardinal never said that!"

"Not at the time, I agree."

"Now I am Harry Percy again. 'Though she be but a simple maid, her father a mere knight, yet her lineage is good—'"

"She's some sort of cousin of the king's, isn't she?"

"Some sort of cousin?" Cavendish again breaks up his role, indignant. "My lord cardinal would have their descent unfolded before him, all drawn up by the heralds."

"So what shall I do?"

"Just pretend! Now: her forebears are not without merit, young Percy argues. But the stronger the boy argues, the more my lord cardinal waxes into a temper. The boy says, we have made a contract of matrimony, which is as good as a true marriage . . ."

"Does he? I mean, did he?"

"Yes, that was the sense of it. Good as a true marriage."

"And what did my lord cardinal do there?"

"He said, good God, boy, what are you telling me? If you have involved yourself in any such false proceeding, the king must hear of it. I shall send for your father, and between us we will contrive to annul this folly of yours."

"And Harry Percy said?"

"Not much. He hung his head."

"I wonder the girl had any respect for him."

"She didn't. She liked his title."

"I see."

"So then his father came down from the north—will you be the earl, or will you be the boy?"

"The boy. I know how to do it now."

He jumps to his feet and imitates penitence. It seems they had a long talk in a long gallery, the earl and the cardinal; then they had a glass of wine. Something strong, it must have been. The earl stamped the length of the gallery, then sat down, Cavendish said, on a bench where the waiting-boys used to rest between orders. He called his heir to stand before him, and took him apart in front of the servants.

" 'Sir,' " says Cavendish, " 'thou hast always been a proud, presumptuous, disdainful and very unthrift waster.' So that was a good start, wasn't it?"

"I like," he says, "the way you remember the exact words. Did you write them down at the time? Or do you use some license?"

Cavendish looks sly. "No one exceeds your own powers of memory," he says. "My lord cardinal asks for an accounting of something or other, and you have all the figures at your fingertips."

"Perhaps I invent them."

"Oh, I don't think so." Cavendish is shocked. "You couldn't do that for long."

"It is a method of remembering. I learned it in Italy."

"There are people, in this household and elsewhere, who would give much to know the whole of what you learned in Italy."

He nods. Of course they would. "But now, where were we? Harry Percy, who is as good as married, you say, to Lady Anne Boleyn, is standing before his father, and the father says . . . ?"

"That if he comes into the title, he would be the death of his noble house—he would be the last earl of Northumberland there ever was. And 'Praise be to God,' he says, 'I have more choice of boys . . .' And he stamped off. And the boy was left crying. He had his heart set on Lady Anne. But the cardinal married him to Mary Talbot, and now they're as miserable as dawn on Ash Wednesday. And the Lady Anne said—well, we all laughed at the time—she said that if she could work my lord cardinal any displeasure, she would do it. Can you think how we laughed? Some sallow chit, forgive me, a knight's daughter, to menace my lord cardinal! Her nose out of joint because she could not have an earl! But we could not know how she would rise and rise."

He smiles.

"So tell me," Cavendish says, "what did we do wrong? I'll tell you. All along, we were misled, the cardinal, young Harry Percy, his father, you, me—because when the king said, Mistress Anne is not to marry into Northumberland, I think, I think, the king had his eye cast on her, all that long time ago."

"While he was close with Mary, he was thinking about sister Anne?"

"Yes, yes!"

"I wonder," he says, "how it can be that, though all these people think they know the king's pleasure, the king finds himself at every turn impeded." At every turn, thwarted: maddened and baffled. The Lady Anne, whom he has chosen to amuse him, while the old wife is cast off and the new wife brought in, refuses to accommodate him at all. How can she refuse? Nobody knows.

Cavendish looks downcast because they have not continued the play. "You must be tired," he says.

"No, I'm just thinking. How has my lord cardinal . . ." Missed a trick, he wants to say. But that is not a respectful way to speak of a cardinal. He looks up. "Go on. What happened next?"

❖

In May 1527, feeling embattled and bad-tempered, the cardinal opens a court of inquiry at York Place, to look into the validity of the king's marriage. It's a secret court; the queen is not required to appear, or even be represented; she's not even supposed to know, but all Europe knows. It is Henry who is ordered to appear, and produce the dispensation that allowed him to marry his brother's widow. He does so, and he is confident that the court will find the document defective in some way. Wolsey is prepared to say that the marriage is open to doubt. But he does not know, he tells Henry, what the legatine court can do for him, beyond this preparatory step; since Katherine, surely, is bound to appeal to Rome.

Six times (to the world's knowledge) Katherine and the king have lived in hope of an heir. "I remember the winter child," Wolsey says. "I suppose, Thomas, you would not be back in England then. The queen was taken unexpectedly with pains and the prince was born early, just at the turn of the year. When he was less than an hour old I held him in my arms, the sleet falling outside the windows, the chamber alive with firelight, the dark coming down by three o'clock, and the tracks of birds and beasts covered that night by the snow, every mark of the old world wiped out, and all our pain abolished. We called him the New Year's prince. We said he would be the richest, the most beautiful, the most devoted. The whole of London was lit up in celebration . . . He breathed fifty-two days, and I counted every one of them. I think that if he had lived, our king might have been—I do not say a better king, for that could hardly be—but a more contented Christian."

The next child was a boy who died within an hour. In the year 1516 a daughter was born, the Princess Mary, small but vigorous. The year following, the queen miscarried a male child. Another small princess lived only a few days; her name would have been Elizabeth, after the king's own mother.

Sometimes, says the cardinal, the king speaks of his mother, Elizabeth Plantagenet, and tears stand in his eyes. She was, you know, a lady of great beauty and calm, so meek under the misfortunes God sent her. She and the old king were blessed with many children, and some of them died. But, says the king, my brother Arthur was born to my mother and father within a year of their marriage, and followed, in not too long a time, by another goodly son, which was me. So why have I been left, after twenty years, with one frail daughter whom any vagrant wind may destroy?

By now they are, this long-married couple, dragged down by the bewildered consciousness of sin. Perhaps, some people say, it would be a kindness to set them free? "I doubt Katherine will think so," the cardinal says. "If the queen has a sin laid on her conscience, believe me, she will shrive it. If it takes the next twenty years."

What have I done? Henry demands of the cardinal. What have I done, what has she done, what have we done together? There is no answer the cardinal can make, even though his heart bleeds for his most benevolent prince; there is no answer he can make, and he detects something not entirely sincere in the question; he thinks, though he will not say so, except in a small room alone with his man of business, that no rational man could worship a God so simply vengeful, and he believes the king is a rational man. "Look at the examples before us," he says. "Dean Colet, that great scholar. Now he was one of twenty-two children, and the only one to live past infancy. Some would suggest that to invite such attrition from above, Sir Henry Colet and his wife must have been monsters of iniquity, infamous through Christendom. But in fact, Sir Henry was Lord Mayor of London—"

"Twice."

"—and made a very large fortune, so in no way was he slighted by the Almighty, I would say; but rather received every mark of divine favor."

It's not the hand of God kills our children. It's disease and hunger and war, rat bites and bad air and the miasma from plague pits; it's bad harvests like the harvest this year and last year; it's careless nurses. He says to Wolsey, "What age is the queen now?"

"She will be forty-two, I suppose."

"And the king says she can have no more children? My mother was fifty-two when I was born."

The cardinal stares at him. "Are you sure?" he says: and then he laughs, a merry, easy laugh that makes you think, it's good to be a prince of the church.

"Well, about that, anyway. Over fifty." They were hazy about these things in the Cromwell family.

"And did she survive the ordeal? She did? I congratulate both of you. But don't tell people, will you?"

The living result of the queen's labors is the diminutive Mary—not really a whole princess, perhaps two-thirds of one. He has seen her when he has been at court with the cardinal, and thought she was about the size of his daughter Anne, who is two or three years younger.

Anne Cromwell is a tough little girl. She could eat a princess for breakfast. Like St. Paul's God, she is no respecter of persons, and her eyes, small and steady as her father's, fall coldly on those who cross her; the family joke is, what London will be like when our Anne becomes Lord Mayor. Mary Tudor is a pale, clever doll with fox-colored hair, who speaks with more gravity than the average bishop. She was barely ten years old when her father sent her to Ludlow to hold court as Princess of Wales. It was where Katherine had been taken as a bride; where her husband, Arthur, died; where she herself almost died in that year's epidemic, and lay bereft, weakened and forgotten, till the old king's wife paid out of her private purse to have her brought back to London, day by painful day, in a litter. Katherine had hidden—she hides so much—any grief at the parting with her daughter. She herself is daughter of a reigning queen. Why should Mary not rule England? She had taken it as a sign that the king was content.

But now she knows different.

❖

As soon as the secret hearing is convened, Katherine's stored-up grievances come pouring out. According to her, the whole business is the fault of the cardinal. "I told you," Wolsey said. "I told you it would be. Look for the hand of the king in it? Look for the will of the king? No, she cannot do that. For the king, in her eyes, is immaculate."

Ever since Wolsey rose in the king's service, the queen claims, he has been working to push her out of her rightful place as Henry's confidante and adviser. He has used every means he can, she says, to drive me from the king's side, so that I know nothing of his projects, and so that he, the cardinal, should have the direction of all. He has prevented my meetings with the ambassador of Spain. He has put spies in my household—my women are all spies for him.

The cardinal says, wearily, I have never favored the French, nor the Emperor neither: I have favored peace. I have not stopped her seeing the Spanish ambassador, only made the quite reasonable request that she should not see him alone, so that I might have some check on what insinuations and lies he presents to her. The ladies of her household are English gentlewomen who have a right to wait upon their queen; after almost thirty years in England, would she have nothing but Spaniards? As for driving her from the king's side, how could I do that? For years his conversation was "The queen must see this" and "Katherine will like to hear of this, we must go to her straightaway." There never was a lady who knew better her husband's needs.

She knows them; for the first time, she doesn't want to comply with them.

Is a woman bound to wifely obedience, when the result will be to turn her out of the estate of wife? He, Cromwell, admires Katherine: he likes to see her moving about the royal palaces, as wide as she is high, stitched into gowns so bristling with gemstones that they look as if they are designed less for beauty than to withstand blows from a sword. Her auburn hair is faded and streaked with gray, tucked back under her gable hood like the modest wings of a city sparrow. Under her gowns she wears the habit of a Franciscan nun. Try always, Wolsey says, to find out what people wear under their clothes. At an earlier stage in life this would have surprised him; he had thought that under their clothes people wore their skin.

❖

There are many precedents, the cardinal says, that can help the king in his current concerns. King Louis XII was allowed to set aside his first wife. Nearer home, his own sister Margaret, who had first married the King of Scotland, divorced her second husband and remarried. And the king's great friend Charles Brandon, who is now married

to his youngest sister, Mary, had an earlier alliance put aside in circumstances that hardly bear inquiry.

But set against that the fact that the church is not in the business of
breaking up established marriages or bastardizing children. If the
dispensation was technically defective, or in any other way defective,
why can it not be mended with a new one? So Pope Clement may
think, Wolsey says.

When he says this, the king shouts. He can shrug that off, the
shouting; one grows accustomed, and he watches how the cardinal
behaves, as the storm breaks over his head; half-smiling, civil, regret-
ful, he waits for the calm that succeeds it. But Wolsey is becoming
uneasy, waiting for Boleyn's daughter—not the easy armful, but the
younger girl, the flat-chested one—to drop her coy negotiations and
please the king. If she would do this, the king would take an easier
view of life and talk less about his conscience; after all, how could he,
in the middle of an amour? But some people suggest that she is bargaining with the king; some say that she wants to be the new wife;
which is laughable, Wolsey says, but then the king is infatuated, so
perhaps he doesn't demur, not to her face. He has drawn the cardinal's
attention to the emerald ring Lady Anne now wears, and has told him
the provenance and the price. The cardinal looked shocked.

After the Harry Percy debacle, the cardinal had got Anne sent
down to her family house at Hever, but she had insinuated herself
back to court somehow, among the queen's ladies, and now he never
knows where she'll be, and whether Henry will disappear from his
grasp because he's chasing her across country. He thinks of calling in
her father, Sir Thomas, and telling him off again, but—even without
mentioning the old rumor about Henry and Lady Boleyn—how can
you explain to a man that as his first daughter was a whore, so his
second one should be too: insinuating that it's some sort of family
business he puts them into?

"Boleyn is not rich," he says. "I'd get him in. Cost it out for him.
The credit side. The debit side."

"Ah yes," the cardinal says, "but you are the master of practical
solutions, whereas I, as a churchman, have to be careful not actively to

recommend that my monarch embark on a studied course of adultery." He moves the quills around on his desk, shuffles some papers. "Thomas, if you are ever . . . How shall I put it?"

He cannot imagine what the cardinal might say next.

"If you are ever close to the king, if you should find, perhaps after I am gone . . ." It's not easy to speak of nonexistence, even if you've already commissioned your tomb. Wolsey cannot imagine a world without Wolsey. "Ah well. You know I would prefer you to his service, and never hold you back, but the difficulty is . . ."

Putney, he means. It is the stark fact. And since he's not a churchman, there are no ecclesiastical titles to soften it, as they have softened the stark fact of Ipswich.

"I wonder," Wolsey says, "would you have patience with our sovereign lord? When it is midnight and he is up drinking and giggling with Brandon, or singing, and the day's papers not yet signed, and when you press him he says, I'm for my bed now, we're hunting tomorrow . . . If your chance comes to serve, you will have to take him as he is, a pleasure-loving prince. And he will have to take you as you are, which is rather like one of those square-shaped fighting dogs that low men tow about on ropes. Not that you are without a fitful charm, Tom."

The idea that he or anyone else might come to have Wolsey's hold over the king is about as likely as Anne Cromwell becoming Lord Mayor. But he doesn't altogether discount it. One has heard of Jeanne d'Arc; and it doesn't have to end in flames.

He goes home and tells Liz about the fighting dogs. She also thinks it strikingly apt. He doesn't tell her about the fitful charm, in case it's something only the cardinal can see.

❖

The court of inquiry is just about to break up, leaving the matter for further advisement, when the news comes from Rome that the Emperor's Spanish and German troops, who have not been paid for months, have run wild through the Holy City paying themselves, plundering the treasuries and stoning the artworks. Dressed satirically in stolen vestments, they have raped the wives and virgins of

Rome. They have tumbled to the ground statues and nuns, and smashed their heads on the pavements. A common soldier has stolen the head of the lance that opened the side of Christ, and has attached it to the shaft of his own murderous weapon. His comrades have torn up antique tombs and tipped out the human dust, to blow away in the wind. The Tiber brims with fresh bodies, the stabbed and the strangled bobbing against the shore. The most grievous news is that the Pope is taken prisoner. As the young Emperor, Charles, is nominally in charge of these troops, and presumably will assert his authority and take advantage of the situation, King Henry's matrimonial cause is set back. Charles is the nephew of Queen Katherine, and while he is in the Emperor's hands, Pope Clement is not likely to look favorably on any appeals passed up from the legate in England.

Thomas More says that the imperial troops, for their enjoyment, are roasting live babies on spits. Oh, he would! says Thomas Cromwell. Listen, soldiers don't do that. They're too busy carrying away everything they can turn into ready money.

Under his clothes, it is well known, More wears a jerkin of horsehair. He beats himself with a small scourge, of the type used by some religious orders. What lodges in his mind, Thomas Cromwell's, is that somebody makes these instruments of daily torture. Someone combs the horsehair into coarse tufts, knots them and chops the blunt ends, knowing that their purpose is to snap off under the skin and irritate it into weeping sores. Is it monks who make them, knotting and snipping in a fury of righteousness, chuckling at the thought of the pain they will cause to persons unknown? Are simple villagers paid— how, by the dozen?—for making flails with waxed knots? Does it keep farmworkers busy during the slow winter months? When the money for their honest labor is put into their hands, do the makers think of the hands that will pick up the product?

We don't have to invite pain in, he thinks. It's waiting for us: sooner rather than later. Ask the virgins of Rome.

He thinks, also, that people ought to be found better jobs.

❖

Let us, says the cardinal at this point, take a step back from the situation. He suffers some genuine alarm; it has always been clear to him that one of the secrets of stability in Europe is to have the papacy independent, and in the clutches of neither France nor the Emperor. But his nimble mind is already skipping toward some advantage for Henry.

Suppose, he says—for in this emergency, it will be to me that Pope Clement looks to hold Christendom together—suppose I were to cross the Channel, stop off in Calais to reassure our people there and suppress any unhelpful rumors, then travel into France and conduct face-to-face talks with their king, then progress to Avignon, where they know how to host a papal court, and where the butchers and the bakers, the candlestick-makers and the keepers of lodgings and indeed the whores have lived in hope these many years. I would invite the cardinals to meet me, and set up a council, so that the business of church government could be carried on while His Holiness is suffering the Emperor's hospitality. If the business brought before this council were to include the king's private matter, would we be justified in keeping so Christian a monarch waiting on the resolution of military events in Italy? Might we not rule? It ought not to be beyond the wit of men or angels to send a message to Pope Clement, even in captivity, and the same men or angels will bring a message back—surely endorsing our ruling, for we will have heard the full facts. And when, of course, in due time—and how we all look for that day—Pope Clement is restored to perfect liberty, he will be so grateful for the good order kept in his absence that any little matter of signatures or seals will be a formality. Voilà—the King of England will be a bachelor.

❖

Before this can happen the king has to talk to Katherine; he can't always be hunting somewhere else, while she waits for him, patient, implacable, his place set for supper in her private apartments. It is June 1527; well barbered and curled, tall and still trim from certain angles, and wearing white silk, the king makes his way to his wife's apartments. He moves in a perfumed cloud made of the essence of roses: as if he owns all the roses, owns all the summer nights.

His voice is low, gentle, persuasive, and full of regret. If he were free, he says, if there were no impediment, it is she, above all women, that he would choose for his wife. The lack of sons wouldn't matter; God's will be done. He would like nothing better than to marry her all over again: lawfully, this time. But there it is: it can't be managed. She was his brother's wife. Their union has offended divine law.

You can hear what Katherine says. That wreck of a body, held together by lacing and stays, encloses a voice that you can hear as far as Calais; it resounds from here to Paris, from here to Madrid, to Rome. She is standing on her status, she is standing on her rights; the windows are rattled, from here to Constantinople.

What a woman she is, Thomas Cromwell remarks in Spanish: to no one in particular.

❖

By mid-July the cardinal is making his preparations for the voyage across the Narrow Sea. The warm weather has brought sweating sickness to London, and the city is emptying. A few have gone down already and many more are imagining they have it, complaining of headaches and pains in their limbs. The gossip in the shops is all about pills and infusions, and friars in the streets are doing a lucrative trade in holy medals. This plague came to us in the year 1485, with the armies that brought us the first Henry Tudor. Now every few years it fills the graveyards. It kills in a day. Merry at breakfast, they say: dead by noon.

So the cardinal is relieved to be quitting the city, though he cannot embark without the entourage appropriate for a prince of the church. He must persuade King François of the efforts he should make, in Italy, to free Pope Clement by military action; he must assure François of the King of England's amity and assistance, but without committing any troops or funds. If God gives him a following wind, he will bring back not only an annulment, but a treaty of mutual aid between England and France, one which will make the young Emperor's large jaw quiver, and draw a tear from his narrow Habsburg eye.

So why is he not more cheerful, as he strides about his private chamber at York Place? "What will I get, Cromwell, if I gain everything I ask? The queen, who does not like me, will be cast off and, if the king persists in his folly, the Boleyns brought in, who do not like me either; the girl has a spite against me, her father I've made a fool of for years, and her uncle, Norfolk, would see me dead in a ditch. Do you think this plague will be over by the time I return? They say these visitations are all from God, but I can't pretend to know his purposes. While I'm away you should get out of the city yourself."

He sighs; is the cardinal his only work? No; he is just the patron who demands the most constant attendance. Business always increases. When he works for the cardinal, in London or elsewhere, he pays his own expenses and those of the staff he sends out on Wolsey business. The cardinal says, reimburse yourself, and trusts him to take a fair percentage on top; he doesn't quibble, because what is good for Thomas Cromwell is good for Thomas Wolsey—and vice versa. His legal practice is thriving, and he is able to lend money at interest, and arrange bigger loans, on the international market, taking a broker's fee. The market is volatile—the news from Italy is never good two days together—but as some men have an eye for horseflesh or cattle to be fattened, he has an eye for risk. A number of noblemen are indebted to him, not just for arranging loans, but for making their estates pay better. It is not a matter of exactions from tenants, but, in the first place, giving the landowner an accurate survey of land values, crop yield, water supply, built assets, and then assessing the potential of all these; next, putting in bright people as estate managers, and with them setting up an accounting system that makes yearly sense and can be audited. Among the city merchants, he is in demand for his advice on trading partners overseas. He has a sideline in arbitration, commercial disputes mostly, as his ability to assess the facts of a case and give a swift impartial decision is trusted here, in Calais and in Antwerp. If you and your opponent can at least concur on the need to save the costs and delays of a court hearing, then Cromwell is, for a fee, your man; and he has the pleasant privilege, often enough, of sending away both sides happy.

These are good days for him: every day a fight he can win. "Still serving your Hebrew God, I see," remarks Sir Thomas More. "I mean, your idol Usury." But when More, a scholar revered through Europe, wakes up in Chelsea to the prospect of morning prayers in Latin, he wakes up to a creator who speaks the swift patois of the markets; when More is settling in for a session of self-scourging, he and Rafe are sprinting to Lombard Street to get the day's exchange rates. Not that he sprints, quite; an old injury drags sometimes, and when he's tired a foot turns inward, as if he's walking back toward himself. People suggest it is the legacy of a summer with Cesare Borgia. He likes the stories they tell about him. But where's Cesare now? He's dead.

"Thomas Cromwell?" people say. "That is an ingenious man. Do you know he has the whole of the New Testament by heart?" He is the very man if an argument about God breaks out; he is the very man for telling your tenants twelve good reasons why their rents are fair. He is the man to cut through some legal entanglement that's ensnared you for three generations, or talk your sniffling little daughter into the marriage she swears she will never make. With animals, women and timid litigants, his manner is gentle and easy; but he makes your creditors weep. He can converse with you about the Caesars or get you Venetian glassware at a very reasonable rate. Nobody can outtalk him, if he wants to talk. Nobody can better keep their head, when markets are falling and weeping men are standing on the street tearing up letters of credit. "Liz," he says one night, "I believe that in a year or two we'll be rich."

She is embroidering shirts for Gregory with a black-work design; it's the same one the queen uses, for she makes the king's shirts herself.

"If I were Katherine I'd leave the needle in them," he says.

She grins. "I know you would."

Lizzie had grown silent and stern when he told her how the king had spoken, at the meeting with Katherine. He had told her they should separate, pending a judgment on their marriage; perhaps she would retire from court? Katherine had said no; she said that would not be possible; she said she would seek advice from canon lawyers, and that he, himself, should equip himself with better lawyers, and better priests; and then, after the shouting was done, the people with their ears pressed to the walls had heard Katherine crying. "He doesn't like her crying."

"Men say," Liz reaches for her scissors, "'I can't endure it when women cry'—just as people say, 'I can't endure this wet weather.' As if it were nothing to do with the men at all, the crying. Just one of those things that happen."

"I've never made you cry, have I?"

"Only with laughter," she says.

Conversation fades into an easy silence; she is embroidering her own thoughts, he is plotting what to do with his money. He is supporting two young scholars, not belonging to the family, through Cambridge University; the gift blesses the giver. I could increase those endowments, he thinks, and—"I suppose I should make a will," he says.

She reaches out for his hand. "Tom, don't die."

"Good God, no, I'm not proposing it."

He thinks, I may not be rich yet but I am lucky. Look how I got out from under Walter's boots, from Cesare's summer, and a score of bad nights in back alleys. Men, it is supposed, want to pass their wisdom to their sons; he would give a great deal to protect his own son from a quarter of what he knows. Where does Gregory's sweet nature come from? It must be the result of his mother's prayers. Richard Williams, Kat's boy, is sharp, keen and forward. Christopher, his sister Bet's boy, is clever and willing too. And then he has Rafe Sadler, whom he trusts as he would trust his son; it's not a dynasty, he thinks, but it's a start. And quiet moments like this are rare, because his house is full of people every day, people who want to be taken to the cardinal. There are artists looking for a subject. There are solemn Dutch scholars with books under their arms, and Lübeck merchants unwinding at length solemn Germanic jokes; there are musicians in transit tuning up strange instruments, and noisy conclaves of agents for the Italian banks; there are alchemists offering recipes and astrologers offering favorable fates, and lonely Polish fur traders who've wandered by to see if someone speaks their language; there are printers, engravers, translators and cipherers; and poets, garden designers, cabalists and geometricians. Where are they tonight?

"Hush," Liz says. "Listen to the house."

At first, there is no sound. Then the timbers creak, breathe. In the chimneys, nesting birds shuffle. A breeze blows from the river, faintly shivering the tops of trees. They hear the sleeping breath of children, imagined from other rooms. "Come to bed," he says.

The king can't say that to his wife. Or, with any good effect, to the woman they say he loves.

❖

Now the cardinal's many bags are packed for France; his entourage yields little in splendor to the one with which he crossed seven years ago to the Field of the Cloth of Gold. His itinerary is leisurely, before he embarks: Dartford, Rochester, Faversham, Canterbury for three or four days, prayers at the shrine of Becket.

So, Thomas, he says, if you know the king's had Anne, get a letter to me the very day. I'll only trust it if I hear it from you. How will you know it's happened? I should think you'll know by his face. And if you have not the honor of seeing it? Good point. I wish I had presented you; I should have taken the chance while I had it.

"If the king doesn't tire of Anne quickly," he tells the cardinal, "I don't see what you are to do. We know princes please themselves, and usually it's possible to put some gloss on their actions. But what case can you make for Boleyn's daughter? What does she bring him? No treaty. No land. No money. How are you to present it as a creditable match at all?"

Wolsey sits with his elbows on his desk, his fingers dabbing his closed lids. He takes a great breath, and begins to talk: he begins to talk about England.

You can't know Albion, he says, unless you can go back before Albion was thought of. You must go back before Caesar's legions, to the days when the bones of giant animals and men lay on the ground where one day London would be built. You must go back to the New

Troy, the New Jerusalem, and the sins and crimes of the kings who rode under the tattered banners of Arthur and who married women who came out of the sea or hatched out of eggs, women with scales and fins and feathers; beside which, he says, the match with Anne looks less unusual. These are old stories, he says, but some people, let us remember, do believe them.

He speaks of the deaths of kings: of how the second Richard vanished into Pontefract Castle and was murdered there or starved; how the fourth Henry, the usurper, died of a leprosy which so scarred and contracted his body that it was the size of a manikin or child. He talks of the fifth Henry's victories in France, and the price, not in money, to be paid for Agincourt. He talks of the French princess whom that great prince married; she was a sweet lady, but her father was insane and believed that he was made of glass. From this marriage—Fifth Henry and the Glass Princess—sprung another Henry who ruled an England dark as winter, cold, barren, calamitous. Edward Plantagenet, son of the Duke of York, came as the first sign of spring: he was a native of Aries, the sign under which the whole world was made.

When Edward was eighteen years old, he seized the kingdom, and he did it because of a sign he received. His troops were baffled and battle-weary, it was the darkest time of one of God's darkest years, and he had just heard the news that should have broken him: his father and his youngest brother had been captured, mocked and slaughtered by the Lancastrian forces. It was Candlemas; huddled in his tent with his generals, he prayed for the slaughtered souls. St. Blaise's Day came: February 3, black and icy. At ten in the morning, three suns rose in the sky: three blurred discs of silver, sparkling and hazy through particles of frost. Their garland of light spread over the sorry fields, over the sodden forests of the Welsh borderlands, over his demoralized and unpaid troops. His men knelt in prayer on the frozen ground. His knights genuflected to the sky. His whole life took wing and soared. In that wash of brilliant light he saw his future. When no one else could see, he could see: and that is what it means to be a king. At the Battle of Mortimer's Cross he took prisoner one Owen Tudor. He beheaded him in Hereford marketplace and set his head to rot on the market cross. An unknown woman brought a basin of water and washed the severed head; she combed its bloody hair.

From then on—St. Blaise's Day, the three suns shining—every time he touched his sword he touched it to win. Three months later he was in London and he was king. But he never saw the future again, not clearly as he had that year. Dazzled, he stumbled through his kingship as through a mist. He was entirely the creature of astrologers, of holy men and fantasists. He didn't marry as he should, for foreign advantage, but became enmeshed in a series of half-made, half-broken promises to an unknown number of women. One of them was a Talbot girl, Eleanor by name, and what was special about her? It was said she was descended—in the female line—from a woman who was a swan. And why did he fasten his affection, finally, on the widow of a Lancastrian knight? Was it because, as some people thought, her cold blond beauty raised his pulse? It was not exactly that; it was that she claimed descent from the serpent woman, Melusine, whom you may see in old parchments, winding her coils about the Tree of Knowledge and presiding over the union of the moon and the sun. Melusine faked her life as an ordinary princess, a mortal, but one day her husband saw her naked and glimpsed her serpent's tail. As she slid from his grip she predicted that her children would found a dynasty that would reign forever: power with no limit, guaranteed by the devil. She slid away, says the cardinal, and no one ever saw her again.

Some of the candles have gone out; Wolsey does not call for more lights. "So you see," he says, "King Edward's advisers were planning to marry him to a French princess. As I . . . as I have intended. And look what happened instead. Look how he chose."

"How long is that? Since Melusine?"

It is late; the whole great palace of York Place is quiet, the city sleeping; the river creeping in its channels, silting its banks. In these matters, the cardinal says, there is no measure of time; these spirits slip from our hands and through the ages, serpentine, mutable, sly.

"But the woman King Edward married—she brought, did she not, a claim to the throne of Castile? Very ancient, very obscure?"

The cardinal nods. "That was the meaning of the three suns. The throne of England, the throne of France, the throne of Castile. So when our present king married Katherine, he was moving closer to his ancient rights. Not that anyone, I imagine, dared put it in those terms to Queen Isabella and King Ferdinand. But it is as well to remember, and mention from time to time, that our king is the ruler of three kingdoms. If each had their own."

"By your account, my lord, our king's Plantagenet grandfather beheaded his Tudor great-grandfather."

"A thing to know. But not to mention."

"And the Boleyns? I thought they were merchants, but should I have known they had serpent fangs, or wings?"

"You are laughing at me, Master Cromwell."

"Indeed not. But I want the best information, if you are leaving me to watch this situation for you."

The cardinal talks then about killing. He talks about sin: about what's to be expiated. He talks about the sixth King Henry, murdered in the Tower; of King Richard, born under Scorpio, the sign of secret dealings, tribulation and vice. At Bosworth, where the Scorpian died, bad choices were made; the Duke of Norfolk fought on the losing side, and his heirs were turned out of their dukedom. They had to work hard, long and hard, to get it back. So do you wonder, he says, why the Norfolk that is now shakes sometimes, if the king is in a temper? It's because he thinks he will lose all he has, at an angry man's whim.

The cardinal sees his man make a mental note; and he speaks of the loose rattling bones under the paving of the Tower, those bones bricked into staircases and mulched into the Thames mud. He talks about King Edward's two vanished sons, the younger of them prone to stubborn resurrections that almost threw Henry Tudor out of his kingdom. He speaks of the coins the Pretender struck, stamped with their message to the Tudor king: "Your days are numbered. You are weighed in the balance: and found wanting."

He speaks of the fear that was then, of the return of civil war. Katherine was contracted to be married into England, had been called "Princess of Wales" since she was three years old; but before her family would let her embark from Corunna, they exacted a price in blood and bone. They asked Henry to turn his attention to the chief Plantagenet claimant, the nephew of King Edward and wicked King Richard, whom he had held in the Tower since he was a child of ten. To gentle pressure, King Henry capitulated; the White Rose, aged twenty-four, was taken out into God's light and air, in order to have his head cut off. But there is always another White Rose; the Plantagenets breed, though not unsupervised. There will always be the need for more killing; one must, says the cardinal, have the stomach for it, I suppose, though I don't know I ever have; I am always ill when there is an execution. I pray for them, these old dead people. I even pray for wicked King Richard sometimes, though Thomas More tells me he is burning in Hell.

Wolsey looks down at his own hands, twists the rings on his fingers. "I wonder," he murmurs. "Wonder which it is." Those who envy the cardinal say he has a ring which enables its owner to fly, and allows him to encompass the death of his enemies. It detects poisons, renders ferocious beasts harmless, ensures the favor of princes, and protects against drowning.

"I suppose other people know, my lord. Because they have employed conjurers, to try to get it copied."

"If I knew, I'd get it copied myself. I'd give one to you."

"I picked up a snake once. In Italy."

"Why did you do that?"

"For a bet."

"Was it poisonous?"

"We didn't know. That was the point of the bet."

"Did it bite you?"

"Of course."

"Why of course?"

"It wouldn't be much of a story, would it? If I'd put it down unharmed, and away it slid?"

Unwillingly, the cardinal laughs. "What will I do without you," he says, "among the double-tongued French?"

❖

In the house at Austin Friars, Liz is in bed but she stirs in her sleep. She half wakes, says his name and inches into his arms. He kisses her hair and says, "Our king's grandfather married a serpent."

Liz murmurs, "Am I awake or asleep?" A heartbeat, and she slides away from him, and turns over, throwing out an arm; he wonders what she will dream. He lies awake, thinking. All that Edward did, his battles, his conquests, he did with Medici money behind him; their letters of credit were more important than signs and wonders. If King Edward was, as many people say, not the son of his father at all, not the son of the Duke of York; if King Edward's mother, as some people do believe, had bred him from an honest English soldier, an archer called Blaybourne; then if Edward married a serpent woman, his offspring would be . . . Unreliable, is the word that comes to mind. If all the old stories are to be believed, and some people, let us remember, do believe them, then our king is one part bastard archer, one part hidden serpent, one part Welsh, and all of him in debt to the Italian banks . . . He too slides, drifts toward sleep. His accounting fails; the spectral world moves in, where pages of figures used to be. Try always, the cardinal says, to learn what people wear under their clothes, for it's not just their skin. Turn the king inside out, and you will find his scaly ancestors: his warm, solid, serpentine flesh.

When in Italy he had picked up a snake for a bet, he had to hold it till they counted ten. They counted, rather slowly, in the slower languages: *eins, zwei, drei* . . . At four, the startled snake flicked its head and bit him. Between four and five he tightened his grip. Now some cried, "Blood of Christ, drop it!" Some prayed and some swore, some just kept on counting. The snake looked sick; when they had all reached ten, and not before, he eased its coiled body gently to the ground, and let it slip away into its future.

There was no pain, but one could see clearly the puncture wound.

On instinct, he tasted it, almost bit his own wrist. He noticed, surprised by it, the private, white, English flesh of his inner arm; he saw the narrow blue-green veins into which the snake had slipped the poison.

He collected his winnings. He waited to die, but he never did die. If anything, he got stronger, quick to hide and quick to strike. There was no Milanese quartermaster could outbawl him, no bought-in Bernese capitaine who would not fall back before his grim reputation for blood first and bargaining later. Tonight is hot, it is July; he is asleep; he dreams. Somewhere in Italy, a snake has children. He calls his children Thomas; they carry in their heads pictures of the Thames, of muddy shallow banks beyond the reach of the tide, beyond the wash of the water.

Next morning when he wakes, Liz is still sleeping. The sheets are damp. She is warm and flushed, her face smooth like a young girl's. He kisses her hairline. She tastes of salt. She murmurs, "Tell me when you are coming home."

"Liz, I'm not going," he says. "I'm not going with Wolsey." He leaves her. His barber comes to shave him. He sees his own eyes in a polished mirror. They look alive; serpent eyes. What a strange dream, he says to himself.

As he goes downstairs he thinks he sees Liz following him. He thinks he sees the flash of her white cap. He turns, and says, "Liz, go back to bed . . ." But she's not there. He is mistaken. He picks up his papers and goes to Gray's Inn.

❖

It is recess. The business is not legal; the discussion is of texts, and the whereabouts of Tyndale (somewhere in Germany), and the immediate problem is a fellow lawyer (so who shall say he should not be there, visiting Gray's Inn?) called Thomas Bilney, who is a priest also, and a fellow of Trinity Hall. "Little Bilney" he's called, on account of his short stature and wormlike attributes; he sits twisting on a bench, and talking about his mission to lepers.

"The scriptures, to me, are as honey," says Little Bilney, swiveling his meager bottom, and kicking his shrunken legs. "I am drunk on the word of God."

"For Christ's sake, man," he says. "Don't think you can crawl out of your hole because the cardinal is away. Because now the Bishop of London has his hands free, not to mention our friend in Chelsea."

"Masses, fasting, vigils, pardons out of Purgatory . . . all useless," Bilney says. "This is revealed to me. All that remains, in effect, is to go to Rome and discuss it with His Holiness. I am sure he will come over to my way of thinking."

"You think your viewpoint is original, do you?" he says gloomily. "Still, at that, it may be, Father Bilney. If you think the Pope would welcome your advice in these matters."

He goes out, saying, there's one who will jump into the fire, given an invitation. Masters, be careful there.

❖

He doesn't take Rafe to these meetings. He will not draw any member of his household into dangerous company. The Cromwell household is as orthodox as any in London, and as pious. They must be, he says, irreproachable.

The rest of the day is nothing to remember. He would have been home early, if he had not arranged to meet up in the German enclave, the Steelyard, with a man from Rostock, who brought along a friend from Stettin, who offered to teach him some Polish.

It's worse than Welsh, he says at the end of the evening. I'll need a lot of practice. Come to my house, he says. Give us notice and we'll pickle some herring; otherwise, it's potluck.

❖

There's something wrong when you arrive home at dusk but torches are burning. The air is sweet and you feel so well as you walk in, you feel young, unscarred. Then you see the dismayed faces; they turn away at the sight of you.

Mercy comes and stands before him, but here is no mercy. "Say it," he begs her.

She looks away when she says, I am so sorry.

He thinks it's Gregory; he thinks his son is dead. Then he half knows, because where is Liz? He begs her, "Say it."

"We looked for you. We said, Rafe, go and see if he's at Gray's Inn, bring him back, but the gatekeepers denied they'd seen you the whole day. Rafe said, trust me, I'll find him, if I go over the whole city: but not a sign of you."

He remembers the morning: the damp sheets, her damp forehead. Liz, he thinks, didn't you fight? If I had seen your death coming, I would have taken him and beaten in his death's head; I would have crucified him against the wall.

The little girls are still up, though someone has put them into their nightdresses, as if it were any ordinary night. Their legs and feet are bare and their nightcaps, round lace bonnets made by their mother, are knotted under their chins with a resolute hand. Anne's face is like a stone. She has Grace's hand tucked in her fist. Grace looks up at him, dubious. She almost never sees him; why is he here? But she trusts him and lets him lift her, without protest, into his arms. Against his shoulder she tumbles at once into sleep, her arms flung around his neck, the crown of her head tucked beneath his chin. "Now, Anne," he says, "we must take Grace to bed, because she is little. I know you are not ready to sleep yet, but you must go in beside her, because she may wake and feel cold."

"I may feel cold," Anne says.

Mercy walks before him to the children's room. Grace is put down without waking. Anne cries, but she cries in silence. I'll sit with them, Mercy says: but he says, "I will." He waits until Anne's tears stop flowing, and her hand slackens in his.

These things happen; but not to us.

"Now let me see Liz," he says.

The room—which this morning was only their bedroom—is lively with the scent of the herbs they are burning against contagion. They have lit candles at her head and feet. They have bound up her jaw with linen, so already she does not look like herself. She looks like the dead; she looks fearless, and as if she could judge you; she looks flat-

ter and deader than people he has seen on battlefields, with their guts
spilled.

❖

He goes down, to get an account of her deathbed; to deal with the
household. At ten this morning, Mercy said, she sat down: Jesu, I am
so weary. In the middle of the day's business. Not like me, is it? she'd
said. I said, it's not like you, Liz. I put my hand to her forehead, and
I said, Liz, my darling . . . I told her, lie down, get to bed with you, you
have to sweat this out. She said, no, give me a few minutes, I'm dizzy,
perhaps I need to eat a little something, but we sat down at the table
and she pushed her food away . . .

He would like her to shorten her account, but he understands her
need to tell it over, moment by moment, to say it out loud. It is like a
package of words she is making, to hand to him: this is yours now.

At midday Elizabeth lay down. She was shivering, though her skin
burned. She said, is Rafe in the house? Tell him to go and find Thomas.
And Rafe did go, and any number of people went, and they didn't
find you.

At half past twelve, she said, tell Thomas to look after the children.
And then what? She complained her head ached. But nothing to me,
no message? No; she said she was thirsty. Nothing more. But then Liz,
she never did say much.

At one o'clock, she called for a priest. At two, she made her confession. She said she had once picked up a snake, in Italy. The priest said
it was the fever speaking. He gave her absolution. And he could not
wait, Mercy said, he could not wait to get out of the house, he was so
afraid he might take the contagion and die.

At three in the afternoon, she declined. At four, she put off the
burden of this life.

I suppose, he says, she will want to be buried with her first husband.

Why should you think that?

Because I came more lately. He walks away. There is no point in
writing the usual directions about mourning clothes, beadsmen, candles. Like all the others touched by this sickness, Liz must be buried

quickly. He will not be able to send for Gregory or call the family together. The rule is for the household to hang a bunch of straw outside
the door as sign of infection, and then restrict entry for forty days,
and go abroad as little as possible.

Mercy comes in and says, a fever, it could be any fever, we don't
have to admit to the sweat . . . If we all stayed at home, London would
come to a standstill.

"No," he says. "We must do it. My lord cardinal made these rules
and it would not be proper for me to scant them."

Mercy says, where were you anyway? He looks into her face; he
says, you know Little Bilney? I was with him; I warned him, I said
he will jump into the fire.

And later? Later I was learning Polish.

Of course. You would be, she says.

She doesn't expect to make sense of it. He never expects to make
any better sense of it than it makes now. He knows the whole of the
New Testament by heart, but find a text: find a text for this.

Later, when he thinks back to that morning, he will want to catch
again that flash of her white cap: though when he turned, no one was
there. He would like to picture her with the bustle and warmth of the
household behind her, standing in the doorway, saying, "Tell me when
you are coming home." But he can only picture her alone, at the door;
and behind her is a wasteland, and a blue-tinged light.

He thinks of their wedding night; her trailing taffeta gown, her
little wary gesture of hugging her elbows. Next day she said, "That's all
right then."

And smiled. That's all she left him. Liz who never did say much.

❖

For a month he is at home: he reads. He reads his Testament, but he
knows what it says. He reads Petrarch, whom he loves, reads how he
defied the doctors: when they had given him up to fever he lived still,
and when they came back in the morning, he was sitting up writing.
The poet never trusted any doctor after that; but Liz left him too fast
for physician's advice, good or bad, or for the apothecary with his

cassia, his galingale, his wormwood, and his printed cards with prayers on.

He has got Niccolò Machiavelli's book *Principalities;* it is a Latin edition, shoddily printed in Naples, which seems to have passed through many hands. He thinks of Niccolò on the battlefield; of Niccolò in the torture chamber. He feels he is in the torture chamber but he knows that one day he will find the door out, because it is he who has the key. Someone says to him, what is in your little book? and he says, a few aphorisms, a few truisms, nothing we didn't know before.

Whenever he looks up from his book, Rafe Sadler is there. Rafe is a slight boy, and the game with Richard and the others is to pretend not to see him, and say, "I wonder where Rafe is?" They are as pleased with this joke as a bunch of three-year-olds might be. Rafe's eyes are blue, his hair is sandy-brown, and you couldn't take him for a Cromwell. But still he is a tribute to the man who brought him up: dogged, sardonic, quick on the uptake.

He and Rafe read a book about chess. It is a book printed before he was born, but it has pictures. They frown over them, perfecting their game. For what seems like hours, neither of them makes a move. "I was a fool," Rafe says, a forefinger resting on the head of a pawn. "I should have found you. When they said you weren't at Gray's Inn, I should have known you were."

"How could you have known? I'm not reliably where I shouldn't be. Are you moving that pawn, or just patting it?"

"J'adoube." Rafe snatches his hand away.

For a long time they sit gazing at their pieces, at the configuration which locks them in place. They see it coming: stalemate. "We're too good for each other."

"Perhaps we ought to play against other people."

"Later. When we can wipe out all-comers."

Rafe says, "Ah, wait!" He seizes his knight and makes it leap. Then he looks at the result, aghast.

"Rafe, you are *foutu.*"

"Not necessarily." Rafe rubs his forehead. "You might yet do something stupid."

"Right. You live in hope."

Voices murmur. Sunlight outside. He feels he could almost sleep, but when he sleeps Liz Wykys comes back, cheerful and brisk, and when he wakes he has to learn the lack of her all over again.

From a distant room a child is crying. Footsteps overhead. The crying stops. He picks up his king and looks at the base of it, as if to see how it is made. He murmurs, *"J'adoube."* He puts it back where it was.

❖

Anne Cromwell sits with him, as the rain falls, and writes her beginner's Latin in her copy book. By St. John's Day she knows all common verbs. She is quicker than her brother and he tells her so. "Let me see," he says, holding out his hand for her book. He finds that she has written her name over and over, "Anne Cromwell, Anne Cromwell . . ."

News comes from France of the cardinal's triumphs, parades, public Masses and extempore Latin orations. It seems that, once disembarked, he has stood on every high altar in Picardy and granted the worshippers remission of their sins. That's a few thousand Frenchmen free to start all over again.

The king is chiefly at Beaulieu, a house in Essex he has recently bought from Sir Thomas Boleyn, whom he has made Viscount Rochford. All day he hunts, undeterred by the wet weather. In the evening he entertains. The Duke of Suffolk and the Duke of Norfolk join him at private suppers, which they share with the new viscount. The Duke of Suffolk is his old friend and if the king said, knit me some wings so I may fly, he would say, what color? The Duke of Norfolk is, of course, chief of the Howard family and Boleyn's brother-in-law: a sinewy little twitcher, always twitching after his own advantage.

He does not write to the cardinal to tell him that everybody in England is saying that the king means to marry Anne Boleyn. He doesn't have the news the cardinal wants, so he doesn't write at all. He gets his clerks to do it, to keep the cardinal updated on his legal affairs, his finances. Tell him we are all well here, he says. Tender him my respects and my duty. Tell him how much we would like to see his face.

No one else in their household falls sick. This year London has escaped lightly—or at least, everyone says so. Prayers of thanksgiving are offered in the city churches; or prayers of appeasement, perhaps one should call them? In the little conclaves that meet at night, God's purpose is interrogated. London knows that it sins. As the Bible tells us, "A merchant shall hardly keep himself from doing wrong." And elsewhere it is stated, "He that maketh haste to be rich shall not be innocent." It is a sure sign of troubled minds, the habit of quotation. "Whom the Lord loveth he correcteth."

By early September, the plague has run its course and the family is able to gather to pray for Liz. Now she can have the ceremonies that were denied her when she left them so suddenly. Black coats are given to twelve poor men of the parish, the same mourners who would have followed her coffin; and each man in the family has pledged seven years of Masses for her soul. On the day appointed, the weather clears briefly, and there is a chill in the air. "The harvest is passed, the summer is ended, and we are not saved."

The small child Grace wakes in the night and says that she sees her mother in her shroud. She does not cry like a child, noisy and hiccupping, but like a grown woman, weeping tears of dread.

"All the rivers run into the sea, but the seas are not yet full."

❖

Morgan Williams shrinks year by year. Today especially he looks small and gray and harassed, as he grips his arm and says, "Why are the best taken? Ah, why are they?" Then, "I know you were happy with her, Thomas."

They are back at Austin Friars, a swarm of women and children and robust men whom mourning hardly takes out of their customary black, the garb of lawyers and merchants, of accountants and brokers. There is his sister, Bet Wellyfed; her two boys, her little daughter Alice. There is Kat; his sisters have their heads together, deciding who shall move in to help out Mercy with the girls, "until you marry again, Tom."

His nieces, two good little girls, still clutch their rosary beads. They stare around them, unsure what they must do next. Ignored, as the people talk over their heads, they lean against the wall, and flick their eyes at each other. Slowly, they slide down the wall, straight-backed, till they are the height of two-year-olds, and balancing on their heels. "Alice! Johane!" someone snaps; slowly they rise, solemn-faced, to their proper heights. Grace approaches them; silently they trap her, take off her cap, shake out her blond hair and begin to plait it. While the brothers-in-law talk about what the cardinal is doing in France, his attention strays toward her. Grace's eyes grow wide as her cousins draw her hair back tight. Her mouth opens in a silent gape, like a fish's mouth. When one squeak escapes her, it is Liz's sister, the elder Johane, who crosses the room and scoops her up. Watching Johane, he thinks, as he often has, how alike the sisters are: were.

His daughter Anne turns her back on the women, slides her arm into her uncle's. "We're talking about the Low Countries trade," Morgan tells her.

"One thing's for sure, Uncle, they won't be pleased in Antwerp if Wolsey signs a treaty with the French."

"That's what we're saying to your father. But, oh, he will stick by his cardinal. Come, Thomas! You don't like the French any more than we do."

He knows, as they do not, how much the cardinal needs the friendship of King François; without one of the major powers of Europe to speak for him, how will the king get his divorce?

"Treaty of Perpetual Peace? Let's think, when was the last Perpetual Peace? I give it three months." It is his brother-in-law Wellyfed who speaks, laughing; and John Williamson, who is Johane's husband, asks will they take bets on it: three months, six? Then he remembers they're at a solemn occasion. "Sorry, Tom," he says, and breaks into a spasm of coughing.

Johane's voice cuts across it: "If the old gamester keeps coughing like this, the winter will finish him off, and then I'll marry you, Tom."

"Will you?"

"Oh, for sure. As long as I get the right piece of paper from Rome."

The party smile and hide their smiles. They give each other knowing looks. Gregory says, why is that funny? You can't marry your wife's sister, can you? He and his boy cousins go off into a corner to talk about private subjects—Bet's boys Christopher and Will, Kat's boys Richard and Walter—why did they call that child Walter? Did they need a reminder of their father, lurking around after his death, to remind them not to get too happy? The family never meet but he thanks God that Walter's not with them anymore. He tells himself he should have more kindness toward his father, but his kindness extends only to paying for Masses for his soul.

In the year before he came back to England for good, he had crossed and recrossed the sea, undecided; he had so many friends in Antwerp, besides good business contacts, and as the city expanded, which it did every year, it seemed more and more the right place to be. If he was homesick, it was for Italy: the light, the language, Tommaso as he'd been there. Venice had cured him of any nostalgia for the banks of the Thames. Florence and Milan had given him ideas more flexible than those of people who'd stayed at home. But something pulled at him—curiosity about who was dead and who'd been born, a desire to see his sisters again, and laugh—one can always laugh somehow—about their upbringing. He had written to Morgan Williams to say, I'm thinking of London next. But don't tell my father. Don't tell him I'm coming home.

During the early months they tried to coax him. Look, Walter's settled down, you wouldn't know him. He's eased back on the drink. Well, he knew it was killing him. He keeps out of the law courts these days. He's even served his turn as churchwarden.

What? he said. And he didn't get drunk on the altar wine? He didn't make off with the candle funds?

Nothing they said could persuade him down to Putney. He waited more than a year, till he was married and a father. Then he felt safe to go.

It was more than twelve years he'd been out of England. He'd been taken aback by the change in people. He left them young and they had softened or sharpened into middle age. The lissom were lean now and dried out. The plump were plumper. Fine features had blurred and softened. Bright eyes were duller. There were some people he didn't recognize at all, not at first glance.

But he would have known Walter anywhere. As his father walked toward him he thought, I'm seeing myself, in twenty, thirty years, if I'm spared. They said that drink had nearly done for him, but he didn't look half-dead. He looked as he had always looked: as if he could knock you down, and might decide to do it. His short strong body had broadened and coarsened. His hair, thick and curling, had hardly a thread of gray. His glance was skewering; small eyes, bright and golden-brown. You need good eyes in a smithy, he used to say. You need good eyes wherever you are, or they'll rob you blind.

"Where've you been?" Walter said. Where once he would have sounded angry, he now sounded merely irritated. It was as if his son had been on a message to Mortlake, and had taken his time over it.

"Oh . . . here and there," he said.

"You look like a foreigner."

"I am a foreigner."

"So what have you been doing?"

He could imagine himself saying, "This and that." He did say it.

"And what sort of this and that are you doing now?"

"I'm learning the law."

"Law!" Walter said. "If it weren't for the so-called law, we would be lords. Of the manor. And a whole lot of other manors round here."

That is, he thinks, an interesting point to make. If you get to be a lord by fighting, shouting, being bigger, better, bolder and more shameless than the next man, Walter should be a lord. But it's worse than that; Walter thinks he's entitled. He'd heard it all his childhood: the Cromwells were a rich family once, we had estates. "When, where?" he used to say. Walter would say, "Somewhere in the north, up there!" and yell at him for quibbling. His father didn't like to be disbelieved even when he was telling you an outright lie. "So how did we come to such a low place?" he would ask, and Walter would say it was because of lawyers and cheats and lawyers who are all cheats, and who thieve land away from its owners. Understand it if you can, Walter would say, for I can't—and I'm not stupid, boy. How dare they drag me into court and fine me for running beasts on the so-called common? If all had their own, that would be my common.

Now, if the family's land was in the north, how could that be? No point saying this—in fact, it's the quickest way to get a lesson from Walter's fist. "But was there no money?" he'd persist. "What happened to it?"

Just once, when he was sober, Walter had said something that sounded true, and was, by his lights, eloquent: I suppose, he said, I suppose we pissed it away. I suppose once it's gone it's gone. I suppose fortune, when it's lost, it will never visit again.

He thought about it, over the years. On that day when he went back to Putney, he'd asked him, "If ever the Cromwells were rich, and I were to go after what's left, would that content you?"

His tone was meant to be soothing but Walter was hard to soothe. "Oh yes, and share it out, I suppose? You and bloody Morgan that you're so thick with. That's my money, if all have their own."

"It would be family money." What are we doing, he thought, quarreling right off, rowing within five minutes over this nonexistent wealth? "You have a grandson now." He added, not aloud, "And you aren't coming anywhere near him."

"Oh, I have those already," Walter said. "Grandsons. What is she, some Dutch girl?"

He told him about Liz Wykys. Admitting, therefore, that he had been in England long enough to marry and have a child. "Caught yourself a rich widow," Walter said, sniggering. "I suppose that was more important than coming to see me. It would be. I suppose you thought I'd be dead. Lawyer, is it? You were always a talker. A slap in the mouth couldn't cure it."

"But God knows you tried."

"I suppose you don't admit to the smithy work now. Or helping your uncle John and sleeping among the turnip shavings."

"Good God, father," he'd said, "they didn't eat turnips at Lambeth Palace. Cardinal Morton eat turnips! What are you thinking?"

When he was a little boy and his uncle John was a cook for the great man, he used to run away to Lambeth to the palace, because the chances of getting fed were better. He used to hang around by the entrance nearest the river—Morton hadn't built his big gateway then—and watch the people come and go, asking who was who and recognizing them next time by the colors of their clothes and the animals and objects painted on their shields. "Don't stand about," people bellowed at him, "make yourself useful."

Other children than he made themselves useful in the kitchen by fetching and carrying, their small fingers employed in plucking songbirds and hulling strawberries. Each dinnertime the household officers formed up in procession in the passages off the kitchens, and they carried in the tablecloths and the Principal Salt. His uncle John measured the loaves and if they were not just right they were tossed into a basket for the lower household. Those that passed his test he counted as they went in; standing by him, pretending to be his deputy, he learned to count. Into the great hall would go the meats and the cheeses, the sugared fruits and the spiced wafers, to the archbishop's table—he was not a cardinal then. When the scrapings and remnants came back they were divided up. First choice to the kitchen staff. Then to the almshouse and the hospital, the beggars at the gate. What wasn't fit for them would go down the line to the children and the pigs.

Each morning and evening the boys earned their keep by running up the back staircases with beer and bread to put in the cupboards for the young gentlemen who were the cardinal's pages. The pages were of good family. They would wait at table and so become intimate with great men. They would hear their talk and learn from it. When they were not at the table they were learning out of great volumes from their music masters and other masters, who passed up and down the house holding nosegays and pomanders, who spoke in Greek. One of the pages was pointed out to him: Master Thomas More, whom the archbishop himself says will be a great man, so deep his learning already and so pleasant his wit.

One day he brought a wheaten loaf and put it in the cupboard and lingered, and Master Thomas said, "Why do you linger?" But he did not throw anything at him. "What is in that great book?" he asked, and Master Thomas replied, smiling, "Words, words, just words."

Master More is fourteen this year, someone says, and is to go to Oxford. He doesn't know where Oxford is, or whether he wants to go there or has just been sent. A boy can be sent; and Master Thomas is not yet a man.

Fourteen is twice seven. Am I seven? he asks. Don't just say yes. Tell me am I? His father says, for God's sake, Kat, make him up a birthday. Tell him anything, but keep him quiet.

When his father says, I'm sick of the sight of you, he leaves Putney and sets off to Lambeth. When Uncle John says, we have plenty of boys this week, and the devil finds work for idle hands, he sets off back to Putney. Sometimes he gets a present to take home. Sometimes it is a brace of pigeons with their feet tied together, and gaping bloody beaks. He walks along the riverbank whirling them about his head, and they look as if they are flying, till somebody shouts at him, stop that! He can't do anything without someone shouting. Is it any wonder, John says, when you are into any mischief going, prone to giving back answers and always reliably to be found where you shouldn't be?

In a small cold room off the kitchen passages there is a woman called Isabella, who makes marzipan figures, for the archbishop and his friends to make plays with after supper. Some of the figures are heroes, such as Prince Alexander, Prince Caesar. Some are saints; today I am making St. Thomas, she says. One day she makes marzipan beasts and gives him a lion. You can eat it, she says; he would rather keep it, but Isabella says it will soon fall to pieces. She says, "Haven't you got a mother?"

He learns to read from the scribbled orders for wheat flour or dried beans, for barley and for ducks' eggs, that come out of the stewards' pantries. For Walter, the point of being able to read is to take advantage of people who can't; for the same purpose one must learn to write. So his father sends him to the priest. But again he is always in the wrong, for priests have such strange rules; he should come to the lesson specially, not on his way from whatever else he is doing, not carrying a toad in a bag, or knives that want sharpening, and not cut and bruised either, from one of those doors (doors called Walter) that he is always walking into. The priest shouts, and forgets to feed him, so he takes off to Lambeth again.

On the days when he turns up in Putney, his father says, where by the sweet saints have you been: unless he's busy inside, on top of a stepmother. Some of the stepmothers last such a short time that his father's done with them and kicked them out by the time he gets home, but Kat and Bet tell him about them, screeching with laughter. Once when he comes in, dirty and wet, that day's stepmother says, "Who does this boy belong to?" and tries to kick him out into the yard.

One day when he is nearly home he finds the first Bella lying in the street, and he sees that nobody wants her. She is no longer than a small-sized rat and so shocked and cold that she doesn't even cry. He carries her home in one hand, and in the other a small cheese wrapped in sage leaves.

The dog dies. His sister Bet says, you can get another. He looks in the street but never finds one. There are dogs, but they belong to somebody.

It can take a long time to get to Putney from Lambeth and some-times he eats the present, if it's not raw. But if he only gets a cabbage, he kicks it and rolls it and thrashes it till it is utterly, utterly destroyed.

At Lambeth he follows the stewards around and when they say a number he remembers it; so people say, if you haven't time to write it down, just tell John's nephew. He will cast an eye on a sack of what-ever's been ordered in, then warn his uncle to check if it's short weight.

At night at Lambeth, when it's still light and all the pots have been scoured, the boys go outside onto the cobbles and play at football. Their shouts rise into the air. They curse and barge into each other, and till somebody yells to stop, they fight with their fists and sometimes bite each other. From the open window above, the young gentlemen sing a part-song in the high careful voices they learn.

Sometimes the face of Master Thomas More appears. He waves to him, but Master Thomas looks down without recognition at the chil-dren below. He smiles impartially; his white scholar's hand draws close the shutter. The moon rises. The pages go to their truckle-beds. The kitchen children wrap themselves in sacking and sleep by the hearth.

He remembers one night in summer when the footballers had stood silent, looking up. It was dusk. The note from a single recorder wavered in the air, thin and piercing. A blackbird picked up the note, and sang from a bush by the water gate. A boatman whistled back from the river.

❖

1527: when the cardinal comes back from France, he immediately begins ordering up banquets. French ambassadors are expected, to set the seal on his concordat. Nothing, he says, nothing, will be too good for these gentlemen.

The court leaves Beaulieu on August 27. Soon afterward, Henry meets the returned cardinal, face-to-face for the first time since early June. "You will hear that the king's reception of me was cold," Wolsey says, "but I can tell you it was not. She—Lady Anne—was present . . . this is true."

On the face of it, a large part of his mission has been a failure. The cardinals would not meet him at Avignon: made the excuse that they didn't want to go south in the heat. "But now," he says, "I have a better plan. I will ask the Pope to send me a co-legate, and I will try the king's matter in England."

While you were in France, he says, my wife, Elizabeth, died.

The cardinal looks up. His hands fly to his heart. His right hand creeps down to the crucifix he wears. He asks how it occurred. He listens. His thumb runs over the tortured body of God: over and over, as if it were any lump of metal. He bows his head. He murmurs, "Whom the Lord loveth . . ." They sit in silence. To break the silence, he begins to ask the cardinal unnecessary questions.

He scarcely needs an account of the tactics of the summer just past. The cardinal has promised to help finance a French army which will go into Italy and try to expel the Emperor. While this is happening, the Pope, who has lost not just the Vatican but the papal states, and seen Florence throw out his Medici relatives, will be grateful and obliged to King Henry. But as for any long-term rapprochement with the French—he, Cromwell, shares the skepticism of his friends in the city. If you have been in the street in Paris or Rouen, and seen a mother pull her child by the hand, and say, "Stop that squalling, or I'll fetch an Englishman," you are inclined to believe that any accord between the countries is formal and transient. The English will never be forgiven for the talent for destruction they have always displayed when they get off their own island. English armies laid waste to the land they moved through. As if systematically, they performed every action proscribed by the codes of chivalry, and broke every one of the laws of war. The battles were nothing; it was what they did between the battles that left its mark. They robbed and raped for forty miles around the line of their march. They burned the crops in the fields, and the houses with the people inside them. They took bribes in coin and in kind and when they were encamped in a district they made the people pay for every day on which they were left unmolested. They killed priests and hung them up naked in the marketplaces. As if they were infidels, they ransacked the churches, packed the chalices in their baggage, fueled their cooking fires with precious books; they scattered relics and stripped altars. They found out the families of the dead and demanded that the living ransom them; if the living could not pay, they torched the corpses before their eyes, without ceremony, without a single prayer, disposing of the dead as one might the carcasses of diseased cattle.

This being so, the kings may forgive each other; the people scarcely can. He does not say this to Wolsey, who has enough bad news waiting for him. During his absence, the king had sent his own envoy to Rome for secret negotiations. The cardinal had found it out; and it had come to nothing, of course. "But if the king is less than frank with me, it does nothing to aid our cause."

He has never before met with such double-dealing. The fact is, the king knows his case is weak in law. He knows this, but does not want to know it. In his own mind, he has convinced himself he was never married and so is now free to marry. Let us say, his will is convinced, but not his conscience. He knows canon law, and where he does not know it already he has made himself expert. Henry, as the younger brother, was brought up and trained for the church, and for the highest offices within it. "If His Majesty's brother Arthur had lived," Wolsey says, "then His Majesty would have been the cardinal, and not me. Now there's a thought. Do you know, Thomas, I haven't had a day off since . . . since I was on the boat, I suppose. Since the day I was seasick, starting at Dover."

They had once crossed the Narrow Sea together. The cardinal had lain below, calling on God, but he, being used to the voyage, spent the time on deck, making drawings of the sails and rigging, and of notional ships with notional rigging, and trying to persuade the captain— "yourself not offended," he said—that there was a way of going faster. The captain thought it over and said, "When you fit out a merchant ship of your own, you can do it that way. Of course, any Christian vessel will think you're pirates, so don't look for help if you get in difficulties. Sailors," he explained, "don't like anything new."

"Nor does anyone else," he'd said. "Not as far as I can see."

There cannot be new things in England. There can be old things freshly presented, or new things that pretend to be old. To be trusted, new men must forge themselves an ancient pedigree, like Walter's, or enter into the service of ancient families. Don't try to go it alone, or they'll think you're pirates.

This summer, with the cardinal back on dry land, he remembers that voyage. He waits for the enemy to come alongside, and for the hand-to-hand fighting to begin.

But for now he goes down to the kitchens, to see how they are getting on with their masterpieces to impress the French envoys. They have got the steeple on their sugar-paste model of St. Paul's, but they are having trouble with the cross and ball on top. He says, "Make marzipan lions—the cardinal wants them."

They roll their eyes and say, will it never end?

Since he returned from France their master has been uncharacteristically sour. It is not just the overt failures that make him grumble, but the dirty work behind the scenes. Squibs and slanders were printed against him and as fast as he could buy them up there was a new batch on the street. Every thief in France seemed to converge on his baggage train; at Compiègne, though he mounted a day-and-night guard on his gold plate, a little boy was found to be going up and down the back stairs, passing out the dishes to some great robber who had trained him up.

"What happened? Did you catch him?"

"The great robber was put in the pillory. The boy ran away. Then one night, some villain sneaked into my chamber, and carved a device by the window . . ." And next morning, a shaft of early sun, creeping through mist and rain, had picked out a gallows, from which dangled a cardinal's hat.

❖

Once again the summer has been wet. He could swear it has never been light. The harvest will be ruined. The king and the cardinal exchange recipes for pills. The king lays down cares of state should he happen to sneeze, and prescribes for himself an easy day of music-making or strolling—if the rain abates—in his gardens. In the afternoon, he and Anne sometimes retire and are private. The gossip is that she allows him to undress her. In the evenings, good wine keeps the chills out, and Anne, who reads the Bible, points out strong scriptural commendations to him. After supper he grows thoughtful, says he supposes the King of France is laughing at him; he supposes the Emperor is laughing too. After dark the king is sick with love. He is melancholy, sometimes unreachable. He drinks and sleeps heavily, sleeps alone; he wakes, and because he is a strong man and a young man still he is optimistic, clearheaded, ready for the new day. In daylight, his cause is hopeful.

The cardinal doesn't stop work if he's ill. He just goes on at his desk, sneezing, aching, and complaining.

In retrospect, it is easy to see where the cardinal's decline began, but at the time it was not easy. Look back, and you remember being at sea. The horizon dipped giddily, and the shoreline was lost in mist.

October comes, and his sisters and Mercy and Johane take his dead wife's clothes and cut them up carefully into new patterns. Nothing is wasted. Every good bit of cloth is made into something else.

At Christmas the court sings:

As the holly groweth green
And never changes hue
So I am, and ever hath been,
Unto my lady true.

Green groweth the holly, so doth the ivy.
Though winter blasts blow ever so high.

As the holly groweth green,
With ivy all alone,
When flowers cannot be seen
And green-wood leaves be gone,
Green groweth the holly.

❖

Spring 1528: Thomas More, ambling along, genial, shabby. "Just the man," he says. "Thomas, Thomas Cromwell. Just the man I want to see."

He is genial, always genial; his shirt collar is grubby. "Are you bound for Frankfurt this year, Master Cromwell? No? I thought the cardinal might send you to the fair, to get among the heretic booksellers. He is spending a deal of money buying up their writings, but the tide of filth never abates."

More, in his pamphlets against Luther, calls the German shit. He says that his mouth is like the world's anus. You would not think that such words would proceed from Thomas More, but they do. No one has rendered the Latin tongue more obscene.

"Not really my business," Cromwell says, "heretics' books. Heretics abroad are dealt with abroad. The church being universal."

"Oh, but once these Bible men get over to Antwerp, you know . . . What a town it is! No bishop, no university, no proper seat of learning, no proper authorities to stop the proliferation of so-called translations, translations of scripture which in my opinion are malicious and willfully misleading . . . But you know that, of course, you spent some years there. And now Tyndale's been sighted in Hamburg, they say. You'd know him, wouldn't you, if you saw him?"

"So would the Bishop of London. You yourself, perhaps."

"True. True." More considers it. He chews his lip. "And you'll say to me, well, it's not work for a lawyer, running after false translations. But I hope to get the means to proceed against the brothers for sedition, do you see?" The brothers, he says; his little joke; he drips with disdain. "If there is a crime against the state, our treaties come into play, and I can have them extradited. To answer for themselves in a straiter jurisdiction."

"Have you found sedition in Tyndale's writing?"

"Ah, Master Cromwell!" More rubs his hands together. "I relish you, I do indeed. Now I feel as a nutmeg must do when it's grated. A lesser man—a lesser lawyer—would say, 'I have read Tyndale's work, and I find no fault there.' But Cromwell won't be tripped—he casts it back, he asks me, rather, have you read Tyndale? And I admit it. I have studied the man. I have picked apart his so-called translations, and I have done it letter by letter. I read him, of course, I do. By license. From my bishop."

"It says in Ecclesiasticus, 'he that toucheth pitch shall be defiled.' Unless his name's Thomas More."

"Well now, I knew you were a Bible reader! Most apt. But if a priest hears a confession, and the matter be wanton, does that make the priest a wanton fellow himself?" By way of diversion, More takes his hat off, and absently folds it up in his hands; he creases it in two; his bright, tired eyes glance around, as if he might be confuted from all sides. "And I believe the Cardinal of York has himself licensed his young divines at Cardinal College to read the sectaries' pamphlets. Perhaps he includes you in his dispensations. Does he?"

It would be strange for him to include his lawyer; but then it's strange work for lawyers altogether. "We have come around in a circle," he says.

More beams at him. "Well, after all, it's spring. We shall soon be dancing around the maypole. Good weather for a sea voyage. You could take the chance to do some wool-trade business, unless it's just men you're fleecing these days? And if the cardinal asked you to go to Frankfurt, I suppose you'd go? Now if he wants some little monastery knocked down, when he thinks it has good endowments, when he thinks the monks are old, Lord bless them, and a little wandering in their wits; when he thinks the barns are full and the ponds well stocked with fish, the cattle fat and the abbot old and lean . . . off you go, Thomas Cromwell. North, south, east or west. You and your little apprentices."

If another man were saying this, he'd be trying to start a fight. When Thomas More says it, it leads to an invitation to dinner. "Come out to Chelsea," he says. "The talk is excellent, and we shall like you to add to it. Our food is simple, but good."

Tyndale says a boy washing dishes in the kitchen is as pleasing to the eye of God as a preacher in the pulpit or the apostle on the Galilee shore. Perhaps, he thinks, I won't mention Tyndale's opinion.

More pats his arm. "Have you no plans to marry again, Thomas? No? Perhaps wise. My father always says, choosing a wife is like putting your hand into a bag full of writhing creatures, with one eel to six snakes. What are the chances you will pull out the eel?"

"Your father has married, what, three times?"

"Four." He smiles. The smile is real. It crinkles the corner of his eyes. "Your beadsman, Thomas," he says, as he ambles away.

When More's first wife died, her successor was in the house before the corpse was cold. More would have been a priest, but human flesh called to him with its inconvenient demands. He did not want to be a bad priest, so he became a husband. He had fallen in love with a girl of sixteen, but her sister, at seventeen, was not yet married; he took the elder, so that her pride should not be hurt. He did not love her; she could not read or write; he hoped that might be amended, but seemingly not. He tried to get her to learn sermons by heart, but she grumbled and was stubborn in her ignorance; he took her home to her father, who suggested beating her, which made her so frightened that she swore she would complain no more. "And she never did," More will say. "Though she didn't learn any sermons either." It seems he thought the negotiations had been satisfactory: honor preserved all round. The stubborn woman gave him children, and when she died at twenty-four, he married a city widow, getting on in years and advanced in stubbornness: another one who couldn't read. There it is: if you are so lenient with yourself as to insist on living with a woman, then for the sake of your soul you should make it a woman you really don't like.

Cardinal Campeggio, whom the Pope is sending to England at Wolsey's request, was a married man before he was a priest. It makes him especially suitable to help Wolsey—who of course has no experience of marital problems—on the next stage of the journey to thwart the king in his heart's desire. Though the imperial army has withdrawn from Rome, a spring of negotiations has failed to yield any definite result. Stephen Gardiner has been in Rome, with a letter from the cardinal, praising the Lady Anne, trying to disabuse the Pope of any notion he may entertain that the king is being willful and whimsical in his choice of bride. The cardinal had sat long over the letter listing her virtues, writing it in his own hand. "Womanly modesty . . . chastity . . . can I say chastity?"

"You'd better."

The cardinal looked up. "Know something?" He hesitated, and returned to his letter. "Apt to bear children? Well, her family is fertile. Loving and faithful daughter of the church . . . Perhaps stretching a point . . . They say she has the scriptures in French set up in her chamber, and lets her women read them, but I would have no positive knowledge of that . . ."

"King François allows the Bible in French. She learned her scriptures there, I suppose."

"Ah, but women, you see. Women reading the Bible, there's another point of contention. Does she know what Brother Martin thinks is a woman's place? We shouldn't mourn, he says, if our wife or daughter dies in childbirth—she's only doing what God made her for. Very harsh, Brother Martin, very intractable. And perhaps she is not a Bible woman. Perhaps it is a slur on her. Perhaps it is just that she is out of patience with churchmen. I wish she did not blame me for her difficulties. Not blame me so very much."

Lady Anne sends friendly messages to the cardinal, but he thinks she does not mean them. "If," Wolsey had said, "I saw the prospect of an annulment for the king, I would go to the Vatican in person, have my veins opened and allow the documents to be written in my own blood. Do you think, if Anne knew that, it would content her? No, I didn't think so, but if you see any of the Boleyns, make them the offer. By the way, I suppose you know a person called Humphrey Monmouth? He is the man who had Tyndale in his house for six months, before he ran off to wherever. They say he sends him money still, but that can't possibly be true, as how would he know where to send? Monmouth ... I am merely mentioning his name. Because ... now why am I?" The cardinal had closed his eyes. "Because I am merely mentioning it."

The Bishop of London has already filled his own prisons. He is locking up Lutherans and sectaries in Newgate and the Fleet, with common criminals. There they remain until they recant and do public penance. If they relapse they will be burned; there are no second chances.

When Monmouth's house is raided, it is clear of all suspect writings. It's almost as if he was forewarned. There are neither books nor letters that link him to Tyndale and his friends. All the same, he is taken to the Tower. His family is terrified. Monmouth is a gentle and fatherly man, a master draper, well liked in his guild and the city at large. He loves the poor and buys cloth even when trade is bad, so the weavers may keep in work. No doubt the imprisonment is designed to break him; his business is tottering by the time he is released. They have to let him go, for lack of evidence, because you can't make anything of a heap of ashes in the hearth.

Monmouth himself would be a heap of ashes, if Thomas More had his way. "Not come to see us yet, Master Cromwell?" he says. "Still breaking dry bread in cellars? Come now, my tongue is sharper than you deserve. We must be friends, you know."

It sounds like a threat. More moves away, shaking his head: "We must be friends."

Ashes, dry bread. England was always, the cardinal says, a miserable country, home to an outcast and abandoned people, who are working slowly toward their deliverance, and who are visited by God with special tribulations. If England lies under God's curse, or some evil spell, it has seemed for a time that the spell has been broken, by the golden king and his golden cardinal. But those golden years are over, and this winter the sea will freeze; the people who see it will remember it all their lives.

❖

Johane has moved into the house at Austin Friars with her husband, John Williamson, and her daughter little Johane—Jo, the children call her, seeing she is too small for a full name. John Williamson is needed in the Cromwell business. "Thomas," says Johane, "what exactly is your business these days?"

In this way she detains him in talk. "Our business," he says, "is making people rich. There are many ways to do this and John is going to help me out with them."

"But John won't have to deal with my lord cardinal, will he?"

The gossip is that people—people of influence—have complained to the king, and the king has complained to Wolsey, about the monastic houses he has closed down. They don't think of the good use to which the cardinal has put the assets; they don't think of his colleges, the scholars he maintains, the libraries he is founding. They're only interested in getting their own fingers in the spoils. And because they've been cut out of the business, they pretend to believe the monks have been left naked and lamenting in the road. They haven't. They've been transferred elsewhere, to bigger houses better run. Some of the younger ones have been let go, boys who have no calling to the life. Questioning them, he usually finds they know nothing, which makes nonsense of the abbeys' claims to be the light of learning. They can stumble through a Latin prayer, but when you say, "Go on then, tell me what it means," they say, "Means, master?" as if they thought that words and their meanings were so loosely attached that the tether would snap at the first tug.

"Don't worry about what people say," he tells Johane. "I take responsibility for it, I do, alone."

The cardinal has received the complaints with a supreme hauteur.

He has grimly noted in his file the names of the complainers. Then he has taken out of his file the list, and handed it over to his man, with a tight smile. All he cares for are his new buildings, his banners flying, his coat of arms embossed on the brickwork, his Oxford scholars; he's plundering Cambridge to get the brightest young doctors over to Cardinal College. There was trouble before Easter, when the dean found six of the new men in possession of a number of forbidden books. Lock them up, by all means, Wolsey said, lock them up and reason with them. If the weather is not too hot, or not too wet, I might come up and reason with them myself.

No use trying to explain this to Johane. She only wants to know her husband's not within arrow-shot of the slanders that are flying. "You know what you're doing, I suppose." Her eyes dart upward. "At least, Tom, you always look as if you do."

Her voice, her footstep, her raised eyebrow, her pointed smile, everything reminds him of Liz. Sometimes he turns, thinking that Liz has come into the room.

❖

The new arrangements confuse Grace. She knows her mother's first husband was called Tom Williams; they name him in their household prayers. Is Uncle Williamson therefore his son? she asks.

Johane tries to explain it. "Save your breath," Anne says. She taps her head. Her bright little fingers bounce from the seed pearls of her cap. "Slow," she says.

Later, he says to her, "Grace isn't slow, just young."

"I never remember I was as foolish as that."

"They're all slow, except us? Is that right?"

Anne's face says, more or less, that is right. "Why do people marry?"

"So there can be children."

"Horses don't marry. But there are foals."

"Most people," he says, "feel it increases their happiness."

"Oh, yes, that," Anne says. "May I choose my husband?"

"Of course," he says; meaning, up to a point.

"Then I choose Rafe."

For a minute, for two minutes together, he feels his life might mend. Then he thinks, how could I ask Rafe to wait? He needs to set up his own household. Even five years from now, Anne would be a very young bride.

"I know," she says. "And time goes by so slowly."

It's true; one always seems to be waiting for something. "You seem to have thought it through," he says. You don't have to spell out to her, keep this to yourself, because she knows to do that; you don't have to lead this female child through a conversation with the little shifts and demurs that most women demand. She's not like a flower, a nightin-gale: she's like . . . like a merchant adventurer, he thinks. A look in the eye to skewer your intentions, and a deal done with a slap of the palm.

She pulls off her cap; she twists the seed pearls in her fingers, and tugs at a strand of her dark hair, stretching it and pulling out its wave. She scoops up the rest of her hair, twists it and wraps it around her neck. "I could do that twice," she says, "if my neck were smaller." She sounds fretful. "Grace thinks I cannot marry Rafe because we are re-lated. She thinks everybody who lives in a house must be cousins."

"You are not Rafe's cousin."

"Are you sure?"

"I am sure. Anne . . . put your cap back on. What will your aunt say?"

She makes a face. It is a face imitative of her aunt Johane. "Oh, Thomas," she murmurs, "you are always so sure!"

He raises a hand to cover his smile. For a moment Johane seems less worrying. "Put your cap on," he says mildly.

She squashes it back onto her head. She is so little, he thinks; but still, she'd be better suited by a helmet. "How did Rafe come here?" she says.

❖

He came here from Essex, because that's where his father happened to be at the time. His father, Henry, was a steward to Sir Edward Belknap, who was a cousin of the Grey family, and so related to the Marquis of Dorset, and the marquis was Wolsey's patron, when the cardinal was a scholar at Oxford. So yes, cousins come into it; and the fact that, when he had only been back in England for a year or two, he was already somehow in the cardinal's affinity, though he had never set eyes on the great man himself; already he, Cromwell, was a man useful to employ. He worked for the Dorset family on various of their tangled lawsuits. The old marchioness had him tracking down bed hangings and carpets for her. Send that. Be here. To her, all the world was a menial. If she wanted a lobster or a sturgeon, she ordered it up, and if she wanted good taste she ordered it in the same way. The marchioness would run her hand over Florentine silks, making little squeaks of pleasure. "You bought it, Master Cromwell," she would say. "And very beautiful it is. Your next task is to work out how we pay for it."

Somewhere in this maze of obligations and duties, he met Henry Sadler, and agreed to take his son into his household. "Teach him all you know," Henry proposed, a little fearfully. He arranged to collect Rafe on his way back from business in his part of the country, but he picked a bad day for it: mud and drenching rain, clouds chasing in from the coast. It was not much after two when he splashed up to the door, but the light was already failing; Henry Sadler said, can't you stay, you won't make it to London before they close the gates. I ought to try to get home tonight, he said. I have to be in court, and then there'll be my Lady Dorset's debt collectors to see off, and you know how that is . . . Mistress Sadler glanced fearfully outside, and down at her child: from whom she must now part, trusting him, at the age of seven, to the weather and the roads.

This is not harsh, this is usual. But Rafe was so small that he almost thought it harsh. His baby curls had been cropped and his ginger hair stood up at the crown. His mother and father knelt down and patted him. Then they swaddled and pulled and knotted him into multiple layers of overwrapped padding, so that his slight frame swelled into the likeness of a small barrel. He looked down at the child and out at the rain and thought, sometimes I should be warm and dry like other men; how do they contrive it while I never can? Mistress Sadler knelt and took her son's face in her hands. "Remember everything we have told you," she whispered. "Say your prayers. Master Cromwell, please see he says his prayers."

When she looked up he saw that her eyes were blurred with tears and he saw that the child could not bear it, and was shaking inside his vast wrappings and about to howl. He threw his cloak around himself. A scatter of raindrops flew from it, baptized the scene. "Well, Rafe, what do you think? If you're man enough . . ." He held out his gauntleted hand. The child's hand slotted into it. "Shall we see how far we get?"

We'll do this fast so you don't look back, he thought. The wind and rain drove the parents back from the open door. He threw Rafe into the saddle. The rain came at them horizontally. On the outskirts of London the wind dropped. He lived at Fenchurch Street then. At the door a servant held out his arms in an offer to take Rafe, but he said, "We drowned men will stick together."

The child had become a dead weight in his arms, shrinking flesh inside seven sodden layers of interwrapped wool. He stood Rafe before the fire; vapors rose from him. Roused by the warmth, he put up small frozen fingers and tentatively began to unpick, to unravel himself. What place is this, he said, in a distinct, polite tone.

"London," he said. "Fenchurch Street. Home."

He took a linen towel and gently blotted from his face the journey just passed. He rubbed his head. Rafe's hair stood up in spikes. Liz came in. "Heaven direct me: boy or hedgehog?" Rafe turned his face to her. He smiled. He slept on his feet.

❖

When the sweat comes back this summer, 1528, people say, as they did last year, that you won't get it if you don't think about it. But how can you not? He sends the girls out of London; first to the Stepney house, and then beyond. This time the court is infected. Henry tries to outride the plague, moving from one hunting lodge to the next. Anne is sent to Hever. The fever breaks out there among the Boleyn family and the lady's father goes down first. He lives; her sister Mary's husband dies. Anne falls ill but within twenty-four hours she is reported back on her feet. Still, it can wreck a woman's looks. You don't know what outcome to pray for, he says to the cardinal.

The cardinal says, "I am praying for Queen Katherine . . . and also for the dear Lady Anne. I am praying for King François's armies in Italy, that they may meet with success, and yet not so much success that they forget how they need their friend and ally King Henry. I am praying for the king's Majesty and all his councillors, and for the beasts in the field, and for the Holy Father and the Curia, may their decisions be guided from above. I am praying for Martin Luther, and for all those infected with his heresy, and for all who combat him, most especially the Chancellor of the Duchy of Lancaster, our dear friend Thomas More. Against all common sense and observation, I am praying for a good harvest, and for the rain to stop. I am praying for everybody. I am praying for everything. That is what it is, to be a cardinal. Only when I say to the Lord, 'Now, about Thomas Cromwell—' does God say to me, 'Wolsey, what have I told you? Don't you know when to give up?'"

When the infection reaches Hampton Court, the cardinal seals himself off from the world. Only four servants are allowed to approach him. When he reemerges, he does look as if he has been praying.

At the end of the summer, when the girls come back to London, they have grown and Grace's hair has been bleached by the sun. She is shy of him and he wonders if now she can only associate him with that night when he carried her to bed, after she had been told her mother was dead. Anne says, next summer, whatever happens, I prefer to stay with you. The sickness has left the city, but the cardinal's prayers have met with variable success. The harvest is poor; the French are losing badly in Italy and their commander has died of plague.

Autumn comes. Gregory goes back to his tutor; his reluctance is clear enough, though little about Gregory is clear to him. "What is it," he asks him, "what's wrong?" The boy won't say. With other people, he is sunny and lively, but with his father guarded and polite, as if to keep a formal distance between them. He says to Johane, "Is Gregory frightened of me?"

Quick as a needle into canvas, she darts at him. "He's not a monk, has he cause?" Then she softens. "Thomas, why should he be? You're a kind father; in fact, I think too much so."

"If he doesn't want to go back to his tutor, I could send him to Antwerp to my friend Stephen Vaughan."

"Gregory will never make a man of business."

"No." You can't see him beating out a deal on interest rates with one of the Fuggers' agents or some sniggering de' Medici clerk. "So what will I do with him?"

"I'll tell you what to do—when he is ready, marry him well. Gregory is a gentleman. Anyone can see that."

Anne is eager to make a start with Greek. He is thinking who best to teach her, asking around. He wants someone congenial, whom he can talk to over supper, a young scholar who will live in the house. He regrets the choice of tutor he's made for his son and nephews, but he won't take them away at this point. The man is quarrelsome, and to be sure there was a sad episode when one of the boys set fire to his room, because he'd been reading in bed with a candle. "It wouldn't be Gregory, would it?" he'd said, always hopeful; the master seemed to think he was treating it as a joke. And he's always sending him bills that he believes he's paid; I need a household accountant, he thinks.

He sits at his desk, piled high with drawings and plans from Ipswich and Cardinal College, with craftsmen's estimates and bills for Wolsey's planting schemes. He examines a scar in the palm of his hand; it is an old burn mark, and it looks like a twist of rope. He thinks about Putney. He thinks about Walter. He thinks about the jittery sidestep of a skittish horse, the smell of the brewery. He thinks about the kitchen at Lambeth, and about the towheaded boy who used to bring the eels. He remembers taking the eel-boy by the hair and dipping his head in a tub of water, and holding it under. He thinks, did I really do that? I wonder why. The cardinal's probably right, I am beyond redemption. The scar sometimes itches; it is as hard as a spur of bone. He thinks, I need an accountant. I need a Greek tutor. I need Johane, but who says I can have what I need?

He opens a letter. It is from a priest called Thomas Byrd. He is in want of money, and it seems the cardinal owes him some. He makes a note, to have it checked out and paid, then picks up the letter again. It mentions two men, two scholars, Clerke and Sumner. He knows the names. They are two of the six college men, the Oxford men who had the Lutheran books. Lock them up and reason with them, the cardinal had said. He holds the letter and glances away from it. He knows something bad is coming; its shadow moves on the wall.

He reads. Clerke and Sumner are dead. The cardinal should be told, the writer says. Having no other secure place, the Dean saw fit to shut them in the college cellars, the deep cold cellars intended for storing fish. Even in that silent place, secret, icy, the summer plague sought them out. They died in the dark and without a priest.

All summer we have prayed and not prayed hard enough. Had the cardinal simply forgotten his heretics? I must go and tell him, he thinks.

It is the first week in September. His suppressed grief becomes anger. But what can he do with anger? It also must be suppressed.

But when at last the year turns, and the cardinal says, Thomas, what shall I give you for a New Year gift?, he says, "Give me Little Bilney." And without waiting for the cardinal to answer he says, "My lord, he has been in the Tower for a year. The Tower would frighten anyone, but Bilney is a timid man and not strong and I am afraid he is straitly kept, and my lord, you remember Sumner and Clerke and how they died. My lord, use your power, write letters, petition the king if you must. Let him go."

The cardinal leans back. He puts his fingertips together. "Thomas," he says. "My dear Thomas Cromwell. Very well. But Father Bilney must go back to Cambridge. He must give up his project of going to Rome and addressing the Pope to bring him to a right way of thinking. There are very deep vaults under the Vatican, and my arm will not be able to reach him there."

It is at the tip of his tongue to say, "You could not reach into the cellars of your own college." But he stops himself. Heresy—his brush with it—is a little indulgence that the cardinal allows him. He is always glad to have the latest bad books filleted, and any gossip from the Steelyard, where the German merchants live. He is happy to turn over a text or two, and enjoy an after-supper debate. But for the cardinal, any contentious point must be wrapped around and around again with a fine filament of words, fine as split hairs. Any dangerous opinion must be so plumped out with laughing apologies that it is as fat and harmless as the cushions you lean on. It is true that when he was told of the deaths underground, my lord was moved to tears. "How could I not have known?" he said. "Those fine young men!"

He cries easily in recent months, though that does not mean his tears are less genuine; and indeed now he wipes away a tear, because he knows the story: Little Bilney at Gray's Inn, the man who spoke Polish, the futile messengers, the dazed children, Elizabeth Cromwell's face set in the fixed severity of death. He leans across his desk and says, "Thomas, please don't despair. You still have your children. And in time you may wish to marry again."

I am a child, he thinks, who cannot be consoled. The cardinal places his hand over his. The strange stones flicker in the light, showing their depths: a garnet like a blood bubble; a turquoise with a silver sheen; a diamond with a yellow-gray blink, like the eye of a cat.

He will never tell the cardinal about Mary Boleyn, though the impulse will arise. Wolsey might laugh, he might be scandalized. He has to smuggle him the content, without the context.

❖

Autumn 1528: he is at court on the cardinal's business. Mary is running toward him, her skirts lifted, showing a fine pair of green silk stockings. Is her sister Anne chasing her? He waits to see.

She stops abruptly. "Ah, it's you!"

He wouldn't have thought Mary knew him. She puts one hand against the paneling, catching her breath, and the other against his shoulder, as if he were just part of the wall. Mary is still dazzlingly pretty; fair, soft-featured. "My uncle, this morning," she says. "My uncle Norfolk. He was roaring against you. I said to my sister, who is this terrible man, and she said—"

"He's the one who looks like a wall?"

Mary takes her hand away. She laughs, blushes, and with a little heave of her bosom tries to get her breath back.

"What was my lord of Norfolk's complaint?"

"Oh . . ." she flaps a hand to fan herself, "he said, cardinals, legates, it was never merry in England when we had cardinals among us. He says the Cardinal of York is despoiling the noble houses, he says he will have all to rule himself, and the lords to be like schoolboys creeping in for a whipping. Not that you should take any notice of what I say . . ."

She looks fragile, breathless still: but his eyes tell her to talk. She gives a little laugh and says, "My brother George roared too. He said that the Cardinal of York was born in a hospital for paupers and he employs a man who was born in the gutter. My lord father said, come now, my dear boy, you lose nothing if you are exact: not quite a gutter, but a brewer's yard, I believe, for he's certainly no gentleman." Mary takes a step back. "You look a gentleman. I like your gray velvet, where did you find that?"

"Italy."

He has been promoted, from being the wall. Mary's hand creeps back; absorbed, she strokes him. "Could you get me some? Though a bit sober for a woman, perhaps?"

Not for a widow, he thinks. The thought must show on his face because Mary says, "That's it, you see. William Carey's dead."

He bows his head and is very correct; Mary alarms him. "The court misses him sadly. As you must yourself."

A sigh. "He was kind. Given the circumstances."

"It must have been difficult for you."

"When the king turned his mind to Anne, he thought that, knowing how things are done in France, she might accept a . . . a certain position, in the court. And in his heart, as he put it. He said he would give up all other mistresses. The letters he has written, in his own hand . . ."

"Really?"

The cardinal always says that you can never get the king to write a letter himself. Even to another king. Even to the Pope. Even when it might make a difference.

"Yes, since last summer. He writes and then sometimes, where he would sign Henricus Rex . . ." She takes his hand, turns up his palm, and with her forefinger traces a shape. "Where he should sign his name, instead he draws a heart—and he puts their initials in it. Oh, you mustn't laugh . . ." She can't keep the smile off her face. "He says he is suffering."

He wants to say, Mary, these letters, can you steal them for me?

"My sister says, this is not France, and I am not a fool like you, Mary. She knows I was Henry's mistress and she sees how I'm left. And she takes a lesson from it."

He is almost holding his breath: but she's reckless now, she will have her say.

"I tell you, they will ride over Hell to marry. They have vowed it. Anne says she will have him and she cares not if Katherine and every Spaniard is in the sea and drowned. What Henry wants he will have, and what Anne wants she will have, and I can say that, because I know them both, who better?" Her eyes are soft and welling with tears. "So that is why," she says, "why I miss William Carey, because now she is everything, and I am to be swept out after supper like the old rushes. Now I'm no one's wife, they can say anything they like to me. My father says I'm a mouth to feed and my uncle Norfolk says I'm a whore."

As if he didn't make you one. "Are you short of money?"

"Oh, yes!" she says. "Yes, yes, yes, and no one has even thought about that! No one has even asked me that before. I have children. You know that. I need . . ." She presses her fingers against her mouth, to stop it trembling. "If you saw my son . . . well, why do you think I called him Henry? The king would have owned him as his son, just as he has owned Richmond, but my sister forbade it. He does what she says. She means to give him a prince herself, so she doesn't want mine in his nursery."

Reports have been sent to the cardinal: Mary Boleyn's child is a healthy boy with red-gold hair and lively appetites. She has a daughter, older, but in the context that's not so interesting, a daughter. He says, "What age is your son now, Lady Carey?"

"Three in March. My girl Catherine is five." Again she touches her lips, in consternation. "I'd forgotten . . . your wife died. How could I forget?" How would you even know, he wonders, but she answers him at once. "Anne knows everything about people who work for the cardinal. She asks questions and writes the answers in a book." She looks up at him. "And you have children?"

"Yes . . . do you know, no one ever asks me that either?" He leans one shoulder against the paneling, and she moves an inch closer, and their faces soften, perhaps, from their habitual brave distress, and into the conspiracy of the bereft. "I have a big boy," he says, "he's at Cambridge with a tutor. I have a little girl called Grace; she's pretty and she has fair hair, though I don't . . . My wife was not a beauty, and I am as you see. And I have Anne, Anne wants to learn Greek."

"Goodness," she says. "For a woman, you know . . ."

"Yes, but she says, 'Why should Thomas More's daughter have the preeminence?' She has such good words. And she uses them all."

"You like her best."

"Her grandmother lives with us, and my wife's sister, but it's not . . . for Anne it's not the best arrangement. I could send her into some other household, but then . . . well, her Greek . . . and I hardly see her as it is." It feels like the longest speech, unless to Wolsey, that he's made for some time. He says, "Your father should be providing properly for you. I'll ask the cardinal to speak to him." The cardinal will enjoy that, he thinks.

"But I need a new husband. To stop them calling me names. Can the cardinal get husbands?"

"The cardinal can do anything. What kind of husband would you like?"

She considers. "One who will take care of my children. One who can stand up to my family. One who doesn't die." She touches her fingertips together.

"You should ask for someone young and handsome too. Don't ask, don't get."

"Really? I was brought up in the other tradition."

Then you had a different upbringing from your sister, he thinks. "In the masque, at York Place, do you remember . . . were you Beauty, or Kindness?"

"Oh . . ." she smiles, "that must be, what, seven years ago? I don't remember. I've dressed up so many times."

"Of course, you are still both."

"That's all I used to care about. Dressing up. I remember Anne, though. She was Perseverance."

He says, "Her particular virtue may be tested."

Cardinal Campeggio came here with a brief from Rome to obstruct. Obstruct and delay. Do anything, but avoid giving judgment.

"Anne is always writing letters, or writing in her little book. She walks up and down, up and down. When she sees my lord father she holds up a palm to him, don't dare speak . . . and when she sees me, she gives me a little pinch. Like . . ." Mary demonstrates an airy pinch, with the fingers of her left hand. "Like that." She strokes the fingers of her right hand along her throat, till she reaches the little pulsing dip above her collarbone. "There," she says. "Sometimes I am bruised. She thinks to disfigure me."

"I'll talk to the cardinal," he says.

"Do." She waits.

He needs to go. He has things to do.

"I no longer want to be a Boleyn," she says. "Or a Howard. If the king would recognize my boy it would be different, but as it is I don't want any more of these masques and parties and dressing up as Virtues. They have no virtues. It's all show. If they don't want to know me, I don't want to know them. I'd rather be a beggar."

"Really . . . it doesn't have to come to that, Lady Carey."

"Do you know what I want? I want a husband who upsets them. I want to marry a man who frightens them."

There is a sudden light in her blue eyes. An idea has dawned. She rests one delicate finger on the gray velvet she so admires, and says softly, "Don't ask, don't get."

Thomas Howard for an uncle? Thomas Boleyn for a father? The king, in time, for a brother?

"They'd kill you," he says.

He thinks he shouldn't enlarge on the statement: just let it stand as fact.

She laughs, bites her lip. "Of course. Of course they would. What am I thinking? Anyway, I'm grateful for what you have done already. For an interval of peace this morning—because when they're shouting about you, they're not shouting about me. One day," she says, "Anne will want to talk to you. She'll send for you and you'll be flattered. She'll have a little job for you, or she'll want some advice. So before that happens, you can have my advice. Turn around and walk the other way."

She kisses the tip of her forefinger and touches it to his lips.

The cardinal does not need him that night, so he goes home to Austin Friars. His feeling is to put distance between himself and any Boleyns at all. There are some men, possibly, who would be fascinated by a woman who had been a mistress to two kings, but he is not one of them. He thinks about sister Anne, why she should take any interest in him; possibly she has information through what Thomas More calls "your evangelical fraternity," and yet this is puzzling: the Boleyns don't seem like a family who think much about their souls. Uncle Norfolk has priests to do that for him. He hates ideas and never reads a book. Brother George is interested in women, hunting, clothes, jewelry and tennis. Sir Thomas Boleyn, the charming diplomat, is interested only in himself.

He would like to tell somebody what occurred. There is no one he can tell, so he tells Rafe. "I think you imagined it," Rafe says severely. His pale eyes open wide at the story of the initials inside the heart, but he doesn't even smile. He confines his incredulity to the marriage proposal. "She must have meant something else."

He shrugs; it's hard to see what. "The Duke of Norfolk would fall on us like a pack of wolves," Rafe says. "He would come round and set fire to our house." He shakes his head.

"But the pinching. What remedy?"

"Armor. Evidently," says Rafe.

"It might raise questions."

"Nobody's looking at Mary these days." He adds accusingly, "Except you."

With the arrival of the papal legate in London, the quasi-regal household of Anne Boleyn is broken up. The king does not want the issue confused; Cardinal Campeggio is here to deal with his qualms about his marriage to Katherine, which are quite separate, he will insist, from any feelings he may entertain about Lady Anne. She is packed off to Hever, and her sister goes with her. A rumor floats back to London, that Mary is pregnant. Rafe says, "Saving your presence, master, are you sure you only leaned against the wall?" The dead husband's family says it can't be his child, and the king is denying it too. It's sad to see the alacrity with which people assume the king is lying. How does Anne like it? She'll have time to get over her sulks, while she's rusticated. "Mary will be pinched black and blue," Rafe says.

People all over town tell him the gossip, without knowing quite how interested he is. It makes him sad, it makes him dubious, it makes him wonder about the Boleyns. Everything that passed between himself and Mary he now sees, hears, differently. It makes his skin creep, to think that if he had been flattered, susceptible, if he had said yes to her, he might soon have become father to a baby that looked nothing like a Cromwell and very like a Tudor. As a trick, you must admire it. Mary may look like a doll but she's not stupid. When she ran down the gallery showing her green stockings, she had a sharp eye out for prey. To the Boleyns, other people are for using and discarding. The feelings of others mean nothing, or their reputations, their family name.

He smiles, at the thought of the Cromwells having a family name. Or any reputation to defend.

Whatever has happened, nothing comes of it. Perhaps Mary was mistaken, or the talk was simply malice; God knows, the family invite it. Perhaps there was a child, and she lost it. The story peters out, with no definite conclusion. There is no baby. It is like one of the cardinal's strange fairy tales, where nature itself is perverted and women are serpents and appear and disappear at will.

Queen Katherine had a child that disappeared. In the first year of her marriage to Henry, she miscarried, but the doctors said that she was carrying twins, and the cardinal himself remembers her at court with her bodices loosened and a secret smile on her face. She took to her rooms for her confinement; after a time, she emerged tight-laced, with a flat belly, and no baby.

It must be a Tudor speciality.

A little later, he hears that Anne has taken the wardship of her sister's son, Henry Carey. He wonders if she intends to poison him. Or eat him.

❖

New Year's 1529: Stephen Gardiner is in Rome, issuing certain threats to Pope Clement, on the king's behalf; the content of the threats has not been divulged to the cardinal. Clement is easily panicked at the best of times, and it is not surprising that, with Master Stephen breathing sulfur in his ear, he falls ill. They are saying that he is likely to die, and the cardinal's agents are around and about in Europe, taking soundings and counting heads, chinking their purses cheerfully. There would be a swift solution to the king's problem, if Wolsey were Pope. He grumbles a little about his possible eminence; the cardinal loves his country, its May garlands, its tender birdsong. In his nightmares he sees squat spitting Italians, a forest of nooses, a corpse-strewn plain. "I shall want you to come with me, Thomas. You can stand by my side and move quick if any of those cardinals tries to stab me."

He pictures his master stuck full of knives, as St. Sebastian is stuck full of arrows. "Why does the Pope have to be in Rome? Where is it written?"

A slow smile spreads over the cardinal's face. "Bring the Holy See home. Why not?" He loves a bold plan. "I couldn't bring it to London, I suppose? If only I were Archbishop of Canterbury, I could hold my papal court at Lambeth Palace . . . but old Warham does hang on and on, he always balks me . . ."

"Your Grace could move to your own see."

"York is so remote. I couldn't have the papacy in Winchester, you don't think? Our ancient English capital? And nearer the king?"

What an unusual regime this will turn out to be. The king at supper, with the Pope, who is also his Lord Chancellor . . . Will the king have to hand him his napkin, and serve him first?

When news comes of Clement's recovery, the cardinal doesn't say, a glorious chance lost. He says, Thomas, what shall we do next? We must open the legatine court, it can be no longer delayed. He says, "Go and find me a man called Anthony Poynes."

He stands, arms folded, waiting for further and better particulars.

"Try the Isle of Wight. And fetch me Sir William Thomas, whom I believe you will find in Carmarthen—he's elderly, so tell your men to go slowly."

"I don't employ anyone slow." He nods. "Still, I take the point. Don't kill the witnesses."

The trial of the king's great matter is approaching. The king intends to show that when Queen Katherine came to him she was not a virgin, having consummated her marriage with his brother Arthur. To that end he is assembling the gentlemen who attended the royal couple after their wedding at Baynard's Castle, then later at Windsor, where the court moved in November that year, and later at Ludlow, where they were sent to play at Prince and Princess of Wales. "Arthur," Wolsey says, "would have been about your age, Thomas, if he had lived." The attendants, the witnesses, are at least a generation older. And so many years have gone by—twenty-eight, to be precise. How good can their memories be?

It should never have come to this—to this public and unseemly exposure. Cardinal Campeggio has implored Katherine to bow to the king's will, accept that her marriage is invalid and retire to a convent. Certainly, she says sweetly, she will become a nun: if the king will become a monk.

Meanwhile she presents reasons why the legatine court should not try the issue. It is still *sub judice* at Rome, for one thing. For another, she is a stranger, she says, in a strange country; she ignores the decades in which she's been intimate with every twist and turn of English policy. The judges, she claims, are biased against her; certainly, she has reason to believe it. Campeggio lays hand on heart, and assures her he would give an honest judgment, even if he were in fear of his life. Katherine finds him too intimate with his co-legate; anyone who has spent much time with Wolsey, she thinks, no longer knows what honesty is.

Who is advising Katherine? John Fisher, Bishop of Rochester. "Do you know what I can't endure about that man?" the cardinal says. "He's all skin and bone. I abhor your skeletal prelate. It makes the rest of us look bad. One looks . . . corporeal."

He is in his corporeal pomp, his finest scarlet, when the king and queen are summoned before the two cardinals at Blackfriars. Everyone had supposed that Katherine would send a proxy, but instead she appears in person. The whole bench of bishops is assembled. The king answers to his name, in a full, echoing voice, speaking out of his big bejeweled chest. He, Cromwell, would have advised a motion of the hand, a murmur, a dip of the head to the court's authority. Most humility, in his view, is pretense; but the pretense can be winning.

The hall is packed. He and Rafe are far-off spectators. Afterward, when the queen has made her statement—a few men have been seen to cry—they come out into the sunshine. Rafe says, "If we had been nearer, we could have seen whether the king could meet her eye."

"Yes. That is really all anyone needs to know."

"I'm sorry to say it, but I believe Katherine."

"Hush. Believe nobody."

Something blots out the light. It is Stephen Gardiner, black and scowling, his aspect in no way improved by his trip to Rome.

"Master Stephen!" he says. "How was your journey home? Never pleasant, is it, to come back empty-handed? I've been feeling sorry for you. I suppose you did your best, such as it is."

Gardiner's scowl deepens. "If this court can't give the king what he wants, your master will be finished. And then it is I who will feel sorry for you."

"Except you won't."

"Except I won't," Gardiner concedes; and moves on.

The queen does not return for the sordid parts of the proceedings. Her counsel speaks for her; she has told her confessor how her nights with Arthur left her untouched, and she has given him permission to break the seal of the confessional and make her assertion public. She has spoken before the highest court there is, God's court; would she lie, to the damnation of her soul?

Besides, there is another point, which everyone has in mind. After Arthur died, she was presented to prospective bridegrooms—to the old king, as it may be, or to the young Prince Henry—as fresh meat. They could have brought a doctor, who would have looked at her. She would have been frightened, she would have cried; but she would have complied. Perhaps now she wishes it had been so; that they had brought in a strange man with cold hands. But they never asked her to prove what she claimed; perhaps people were not so shameless in those days. The dispensations for her marriage to Henry were meant to cover either case: she was/was not a virgin. The Spanish documents are different from the English documents, and that is where we should be now, among the subclauses, studying paper and ink, not squabbling in a court of law over a shred of skin and a splash of blood on a linen sheet.

If he had been her adviser, he would have kept the queen in court, however much she squealed. Because, would the witnesses have spoken, to her face, as they spoke behind her back? She would be ashamed to face them, gnarled and grizzled and each equipped with perfect recollection; but he would have had her greet them cordially, and declare she would never have recognized them, after so much time gone by; and ask if they have grandchildren, and whether the summer heat eases their elderly aches and pains? The greater shame would be theirs: would they not hesitate, would they not falter, under the steady gaze of the queen's honest eyes?

Without Katherine present, the trial becomes a bawdy entertainment. The Earl of Shrewsbury is before the court, a man who fought with the old king at Bosworth. He recalls his own long-ago wedding night, when he was, like Prince Arthur, a boy of fifteen; never had a woman before, he says, but did his duty to his bride. On Arthur's wedding night, he and the Earl of Oxford had taken the prince to Katherine's chamber. Yes, says the Marquis of Dorset, and I was there too; Katherine lay under the coverlet, the prince got into bed beside her. "No one is willing to swear to having climbed in with them," Rafe whispers. "But I wonder they haven't found someone."

The court must make do with evidence of what was said next morning. The prince, coming out of the bridal chamber, said he was thirsty and asked Sir Anthony Willoughby for a cup of ale. "Last night I was in Spain," he said. A little boy's crude joke, dragged back into the light; the boy has been, these thirty years, a corpse. How lonely it is to die young, to go down into the dark without any company! Maurice St. John is not there with him, in his vault at Worcester Cathedral: nor Mr. Cromer nor William Woodall, nor any of the men who heard him say, "Masters, it is good pastime to have a wife."

When they have listened to all this, and they come out into the air, he feels strangely cold. He puts a hand to his face, touches his cheekbone. Rafe says, "It would be a poor sort of bridegroom who would come out in the morning and say, 'Good day, masters. Nothing done!' He was boasting, wasn't he? That was all. They've forgotten what it's like to be fifteen."

Even as the court is sitting, King François in Italy is losing a battle. Pope Clement is preparing to sign a new treaty with the Emperor, Queen Katherine's nephew. He doesn't know this when he says, "This is a bad day's work. If we want Europe to laugh at us, they've every reason now."

He looks sideways at Rafe, whose particular problem, clearly, is that he cannot imagine anyone, even a hasty fifteen-year-old, wanting to penetrate Katherine. It would be like copulation with a statue. Rafe, of course, has not heard the cardinal on the subject of the queen's former attractions. "Well, I reserve judgment. Which is what the court will do. It's all they can do." He says, "Rafe, you are so much closer in these matters. I can't remember being fifteen."

"Surely? Were you not fifteen or so when you fetched up in France?"

"Yes, I must have been." Wolsey: "Arthur would have been about your age, Thomas, if he had lived." He remembers a woman in Dover, up against a wall; her small crushable bones, her young, bleak, pallid face. He feels a small sensation of panic, loss; what if the cardinal's joke isn't a joke, and the earth is strewn with his children, and he has never done right by them? It is the only honest thing to be done: look after your children. "Rafe," he says, "do you know I haven't made my will? I said I would but I never did. I think I should go home and draft it."

"Why?" Rafe looks amazed. "Why now? The cardinal will want you."

"Come home." He takes Rafe's arm. On his left side, a hand touches his: fingers without flesh. A ghost walks: Arthur, studious and pale. King Henry, he thinks, you raised him; now you put him down.

❖

July 1529: Thomas Cromwell of London, gentleman. Being whole in body and memory. To his son Gregory six hundred and sixty-six pounds thirteen shillings and four pence. And featherbeds, bolsters and the quilt of yellow turkey satin, the joined bed of Flanders work and the carved press and the cupboards, the silver and the silver gilt and twelve silver spoons. And leases of farms to be held for him by the executors till he comes to full age, and another two hundred pounds for him in gold at that date. Money to the executors for the upbringing and marriage portions of his daughter Anne, and his little daughter Grace. A marriage portion for his niece Alice Wellyfed; gowns, jackets and doublets to his nephews; to Mercy all sorts of household stuff and some silver and anything else the executors think she should have. Bequests to his dead wife's sister Johane, and her husband, John Williamson, and a marriage portion to her daughter, also Johane. Money to his servants. Forty pounds to be divided between forty poor maidens on their marriage. Twenty pounds for mending the roads. Ten pounds toward feeding poor prisoners in the London jails.

His body to be buried in the parish where he dies: or at the direction of his executors.

The residue of his estate to be spent on Masses for his parents.

To God his soul. To Rafe Sadler his books.

❖

When the summer plague comes back, he says to Mercy and Johane, shall we send the children out?

In which direction, Johane says: not challenging him, just wanting to know.

Mercy says, can anyone outrun it? They take comfort from a belief that since the infection killed so many last year, it won't be so violent this year; which he does not think is necessarily true, and he thinks they seem to be endowing this plague with a human or at least bestial intelligence: the wolf comes down on the sheepfold, but not on the nights when the men with dogs are waiting for him. Unless they think the plague is more than bestial or human—that it is God behind it—God, up to his old tricks. When he hears the bad news from Italy, about Clement's new treaty with the Emperor, Wolsey bows his head and says, "My Master is capricious." He doesn't mean the king.

On the last day of July, Cardinal Campeggio adjourns the legatine court. It is, he says, the Roman holidays. News comes that the Duke of Suffolk, the king's great friend, has hammered the table before Wolsey, and threatened him to his face. They all know the court will never sit again. They all know the cardinal has failed.

That evening with Wolsey he believes, for the first time, that the cardinal will come down. If he falls, he thinks, I come down with him. His reputation is black. It is as if the cardinal's joke has been incarnated: as if he wades through streams of blood, leaving in his wake a trail of smashed glass and fires, of widows and orphans. Cromwell, people say: that's a bad man. The cardinal will not talk about what is happening in Italy, or what has happened in the legate's court. He says, "They tell me the sweating sickness is back. What shall I do? Shall I die? I have fought four bouts with it. In the year . . . what year? . . . I think it was 1518 . . . now you will laugh, but it was so—when the sweat had finished with me, I looked like Bishop Fisher. My flesh was wasted. God picked me up and rattled my teeth."

"Your Grace was wasted?" he says, trying to raise a smile. "I wish you'd had your portrait made then."

Bishop Fisher has said in court—just before the Roman holidays set in—that no power, human or divine, could dissolve the marriage of the king and queen. If there's one thing he'd like to teach Fisher, it's not to make grand overstatements. He has an idea of what the law can do, and it's different from what Bishop Fisher thinks.

Until now, every day till today, every evening till this, if you told Wolsey a thing was impossible, he'd just laugh. Tonight he says— when he can be brought to the point—my friend King François is beaten and I am beaten too. I don't know what to do. Plague or no plague, I think I may die.

"I must go home," he says. "But will you bless me?"

He kneels before him. Wolsey raises his hand, and then, as if he has forgotten what he's doing, lets it hover in midair. He says, "Thomas, I am not ready to meet God."

He looks up, smiling. "Perhaps God is not ready to meet you."

"I hope that you will be with me when I die."

"But that will be at some distant date."

He shakes his head. "If you had seen how Suffolk set on me today. He, Norfolk, Thomas Boleyn, Thomas Lord Darcy, they have been waiting only for this, for my failure with this court, and now I hear they are devising a book of articles, they are drawing up a list of accusations, how I have reduced the nobility, and so forth—they are making a book called—what will they call it?—'Twenty Years of Insults'? They are brewing some stewpot into which they are pouring the dregs of every slight, as they conceive it, by which they mean every piece of truth I have told them . . ." He takes a great rattling breath, and looks at the ceiling, which is embossed with the Tudor rose.

"There will be no such stewpots in Your Grace's kitchen," he says. He gets up. He looks at the cardinal, and all he can see is more work to be done.

❖

"Liz Wykys," Mercy says, "wouldn't have wanted her girls dragged about the countryside. Especially as Anne, to my knowledge, cries if she does not see you."

"Anne?" He is amazed. "Anne cries?"

"What did you think?" Mercy asks, with some asperity. "Do you think your children don't love you?"

He lets her make the decision. The girls stay at home. It's the wrong decision. Mercy hangs outside their door the signs of the sweating sickness. She says, how has this happened? We scour, we scrub the floors, I do not think you will find in the whole of London a cleaner house than ours. We say our prayers. I have never seen a child pray as Anne does. She prays as if she's going into battle.

Anne falls ill first. Mercy and Johane shout at her and shake her to keep her awake, since they say if you sleep you will die. But the pull of the sickness is stronger than they are, and she falls exhausted against the bolster, struggling for breath, and falls further, into black stillness, only her hand moving, the fingers clenching and unclenching. He takes it in his own and tries to still it, but it is like the hand of a soldier itching for a fight.

Later she rouses herself, asks for her mother. She asks for the copybook in which she has written her name. At dawn the fever breaks. Johane bursts into tears of relief, and Mercy sends her away to sleep. Anne struggles to sit up, she sees him clearly, she smiles, she says his name. They bring a basin of water strewn with rose petals, and wash her face; her finger reaches out, tentative, to push the petals below the water, so each of them becomes a vessel shipping water, a cup, a perfumed grail.

But when the sun comes up her fever rises again. He will not let them begin it again, the pinching and pummeling, the shaking; he gives her into God's hands, and asks God to be good to her. He talks to her but she makes no sign that she hears. He is not, himself, afraid of contagion. If the cardinal can survive this plague four times, I am sure I am in no danger, and if I die, I have made my will. He sits with her, watching her chest heaving, watching her fight and lose. He is not there when she dies—Grace has already taken sick, and he is seeing her put to bed. So he is out of the room, just, and when they usher him in, her stern little face has relaxed into sweetness. She looks passive, placid; her hand is already heavy, and heavy beyond his bearing.

He comes out of the room; he says, "She was already learning Greek." Of course, Mercy says: she was a wonderful child, and your true daughter. She leans against his shoulder and cries. She says, "She was clever and good, and in her way, you know, she was beautiful."

His thought had been: she was learning Greek: perhaps she knows it now.

Grace dies in his arms; she dies easily, as naturally as she was born. He eases her back against the damp sheet: a child of impossible perfection, her fingers uncurling like thin white leaves. I never knew her, he thinks; I never knew I had her. It has always seemed impossible to him that some act of his gave her life, some unthinking thing that he and Liz did, on some unmemorable night. They had intended the name to be Henry for a boy, Katherine for a girl, and, Liz had said, that will do honor to your Kat as well. But when he had seen her, swaddled, beautiful, finished and perfect, he had said quite another thing, and Liz had agreed. We cannot earn grace. We do not merit it.

He asks the priest if his elder daughter can be buried with her copybook, in which she has written her name: Anne Cromwell. The priest says he has never heard of such a thing. He is too tired and angry to fight.

His daughters are now in Purgatory, a country of slow fires and ridged ice. Where in the Gospels does it say "Purgatory"?

Tyndale says, now abideth faith, hope and love, even these three; but the greatest of these is love.

Thomas More thinks it is a wicked mistranslation. He insists on "charity." He would chain you up, for a mistranslation. He would, for a difference in your Greek, kill you.

He wonders again if the dead need translators; perhaps in a moment, in a simple twist of unbecoming, they know everything they need to know.

Tyndale says, "Love never falleth away."

❖

October comes in. Wolsey presides, as usual, over the meetings of the king's council. But in the law courts, as Michaelmas term opens, writs are moved against the cardinal. He is charged with success. He is charged with the exercise of power. Specifically, he is charged with asserting a foreign jurisdiction in the king's realm—that is to say, with exercising his role as papal legate. What they mean to say is this: he is *alter rex.* He is, he has always been, more imperious than the king. For that, if it is a crime, he is guilty.

So now they swagger into York Place, the Duke of Suffolk, the Duke of Norfolk: the two great peers of the realm. Suffolk, his blond beard bristling, looks like a pig among truffles; a florid man, he remembers, turns my lord cardinal sick. Norfolk looks apprehensive, and as he turns over the cardinal's possessions, it is clear that he expects to find wax figures, perhaps of himself, perhaps with long pins stuck through them. The cardinal has done his feats by a compact with the devil; that is his fixed opinion.

He, Cromwell, sends them away. They come back. They come back with further and higher commissions and better signatures, and they bring with them the Master of the Rolls. They take the Great Seal from my lord cardinal.

Norfolk glances sideways at him, and gives him a fleeting, ferrety grin. He doesn't know why.

"Come and see me," the duke says.

"Why, my lord?"

Norfolk turns down his mouth. He never explains.

"When?"

"No hurry," Norfolk says. "Come when you've mended your manners."

It is October 19, 1529.

III

Make or Mar

ALL HALLOWS 1529

alloween: the world's edge seeps and bleeds. This is the time when the tally-keepers of Purgatory, its clerks and jailers, listen in to the living, who are praying for the dead. At this time of year, with their parish, he and Liz would keep vigil. They would pray for Henry Wykys, her father; for Liz's dead husband, Thomas Williams; for Walter Cromwell, and for distant cousins; for half-forgotten names, long-dead half sisters and lost stepchildren.

Last night he kept the vigil alone. He lay awake, wishing Liz back; waiting for her to come and lie beside him. It's true he is at Esher with the cardinal, not at home at the Austin Friars. But, he thought, she'll know how to find me. She'll look for the cardinal, drawn through the space between worlds by incense and candlelight. Wherever the cardinal is, I will be.

At some point he must have slept. When daylight came, the room felt so empty it was empty even of him.

❖

All Hallows Day: grief comes in waves. Now it threatens to capsize him. He doesn't believe that the dead come back; but that doesn't stop him from feeling the brush of their fingertips, wing tips, against his shoulder. Since last night they have been less individual forms and faces than a solid aggregated mass, their flesh slapping and jostling together, their texture dense like sea creatures, their faces sick with an undersea sheen.

Now he stands in a window embrasure, Liz's prayer book in hand. His daughter Grace liked to look at it, and today he can feel the imprint of her small fingers under his own. These are Our Lady's prayers for the canonical hours, the pages illuminated by a dove, a vase of lilies. The office is Matins, and Mary kneels on a floor of checkered tiles. The angel greets her, and the words of his greeting are written on a scroll, which unfurls from his clasped hands as if his palms are speaking. His wings are colored: heaven-blue.

He turns the page. The office is Lauds. Here is a picture of the Visitation. Mary, with her neat little belly, is greeted by her pregnant cousin, St. Elizabeth. Their foreheads are high, their brows plucked, and they look surprised, as indeed they must be; one of them is a virgin, the other advanced in years. Spring flowers grow at their feet, and each of them wears an airy crown, made of gilt wires as fine as blond hairs.

He turns a page. Grace, silent and small, turns the page with him. The office is Prime. The picture is the Nativity: a tiny white Jesus lies in the folds of his mother's cloak. The office is Sext: the Magi proffer jeweled cups; behind them is a city on a hill, a city in Italy, with its bell tower, its view of rising ground and its misty line of trees. The office is None: Joseph carries a basket of doves to the temple. The office is Vespers: a dagger sent by Herod makes a neat hole in a shocked infant. A woman throws up her hands in protest, or prayer: her eloquent, helpless palms. The infant corpse scatters three drops of blood, each one shaped like a tear. Each bloody tear is a precise vermilion.

He looks up. Like an afterimage, the form of the tears swims in his eyes; the picture blurs. He blinks. Someone is walking toward him. It is George Cavendish. His hands wash together, his face is a mask of concern.

Let him not speak to me, he prays. Let George pass on.

"Master Cromwell," he says, "I believe you are crying. What is this? Is there bad news about our master?"

He tries to close Liz's book, but Cavendish reaches out for it. "Ah, you are praying." He looks amazed.

Cavendish cannot see his daughter's fingers touching the page, or his wife's hands holding the book. George simply looks at the pictures, upside down. He takes a deep breath and says, "Thomas . . . ?"

"I am crying for myself," he says. "I am going to lose everything, everything I have worked for, all my life, because I will go down with the cardinal—no, George, don't interrupt me—because I have done what he asked me to do, and been his friend, and the man at his right hand. If I had stuck to my work in the city, instead of hurtling about the countryside making enemies, I'd be a rich man—and you, George, I'd be inviting you out to my new country house, and asking your advice on furniture and flower beds. But look at me! I'm finished."

George tries to speak: he utters a consolatory bleat.

"Unless," he says. "Unless, George. What do you think? I've sent my boy Rafe to Westminster."

"What will he do there?"

But he is crying again. The ghosts are gathering, he feels cold, his position is irretrievable. In Italy he learned a memory system, so he can remember everything: every stage of how he got here. "I think," he says, "I should go after him."

"Please," says Cavendish, "not before dinner."

"No?"

"Because we need to think how to pay off my lord's servants."

A moment passes. He enfolds the prayer book to himself; he holds it in his arms. Cavendish has given him what he needs: an accountancy problem. "George," he says, "you know my lord's chaplains have flocked here after him, all of them earning—what?—a hundred, two hundred pounds a year, out of his liberality? So, I think . . . we will make the chaplains and the priests pay off the household servants, because what I think is, what I notice is, that his servants love my lord more than his priests do. So, now, let's go to dinner, and after dinner I will make the priests ashamed, and I will make them open their veins and bleed money. We need to give the household a quarter's wages at least, and a retainer. Against the day of my lord's restoration."

"Well," says George, "if anyone can do it, you can."

He finds himself smiling. Perhaps it's a grim smile, but he never thought he would smile today. He says, "When that's done, I shall leave you. I shall be back as soon as I have made sure of a place in the Parliament."

"But it meets in two days . . . How will you manage it now?"

"I don't know, but someone must speak for my lord. Or they will kill him."

He sees the hurt and shock; he wants to take the words back; but it is true. He says, "I can only try. I'll make or mar, before I see you again."

George almost bows. "Make or mar," he murmurs. "It was ever your common saying."

Cavendish walks about the household, saying, Thomas Cromwell was reading a prayer book. Thomas Cromwell was crying. Only now does George realize how bad things are.

❖

Once, in Thessaly, there was a poet called Simonides. He was commissioned to appear at a banquet, given by a man called Scopas, and recite a lyric in praise of his host. Poets have strange vagaries, and in his lyric Simonides incorporated verses in praise of Castor and Pollux, the Heavenly Twins. Scopas was sulky, and said he would pay only half the fee: "As for the rest, get it from the Twins."

A little later, a servant came into the hall. He whispered to Simonides; there were two young men outside, asking for him by name.

He rose and left the banqueting hall. He looked around for the two young men, but he could see no one.

As he turned back, to go and finish his dinner, he heard a terrible noise, of stone splitting and crumbling. He heard the cries of the dying, as the roof of the hall collapsed. Of all the diners, he was the only one left alive.

The bodies were so broken and disfigured that the relatives of the dead could not identify them. But Simonides was a remarkable man. Whatever he saw was imprinted on his mind. He led each of the relatives through the ruins; and pointing to the crushed remains, he said, there is your man. In linking the dead to their names, he worked from the seating plan in his head.

It is Cicero who tells us this story. He tells us how, on that day, Simonides invented the art of memory. He remembered the names, the faces, some sour and bloated, some blithe, some bored. He remembered exactly where everyone was sitting, at the moment the roof fell in.

PART THREE

I

Three-Card Trick

WINTER 1529–SPRING 1530

ohane: "You say, 'Rafe, go and find me a seat in the new Parliament.' And off he goes, like a girl who's been told to bring the washing in."

"It was harder than that," Rafe says.

Johane says, "How would you know?"

Seats in the Commons are, largely, in the gift of lords; of lords, bishops, the king himself. A scanty handful of electors, if pressured from above, usually do as they're told.

Rafe has got him Taunton. It's Wolsey terrain; they wouldn't have let him in if the king had not said yes, if Thomas Howard had not said yes. He had sent Rafe to London to scout the uncertain territory of the duke's intentions: to find out what lies behind that ferrety grin. "Am obliged, master."

Now he knows. "The Duke of Norfolk," Rafe says, "believes my lord cardinal has buried treasure, and he thinks you know where it is."

❖

They talk alone. Rafe: "He'll ask you to go and work for him."

"Yes. Perhaps not in so many words."

He watches Rafe's face as he weighs up the situation. Norfolk is already—unless you count the king's bastard son—the realm's premier nobleman. "I assured him," Rafe says, "of your respect, your . . . your reverence, your desire to be at his—erm—"

"Commandment?"

"More or less."

"And what did he say?"

"He said, 'Hmm.'"

He laughs. "And was that his tone?"

"It was his tone."

"And his grim nod?"

"Yes."

Very well. I dry my tears, those tears from All Hallows Day. I sit with the cardinal, by the fire at Esher in a room with a smoking chimney. I say, my lord, do you think I would forsake you? I locate the man in charge of chimneys and hearths. I give him orders. I ride to London, to Blackfriars. The day is foggy, St. Hubert's Day. Norfolk is waiting, to tell me he will be a good lord to me.

❖

The duke is now approaching sixty years old, but concedes nothing to the calendar. Flint-faced and keen-eyed, he is lean as a gnawed bone and as cold as an ax head; his joints seem knitted together of supple chain links, and indeed he rattles a little as he moves, for his clothes conceal relics: in tiny jeweled cases he has shavings of skin and snippets of hair, and set into medallions he wears splinters of martyrs' bones. "Marry!" he says, for an oath, and "By the Mass!," and sometimes takes out one of his medals or charms from wherever it is hung about his person, and kisses it in a fervor, calling on some saint or martyr to stop his current rage getting the better of him. "St. Jude give me patience!" he will shout; probably he has mixed him up with Job, whom he heard about in a story when he was a little boy at the knee of his first priest. It is hard to imagine the duke as a little boy, or in any way younger or different from the self he presents now. He thinks the Bible a book unnecessary for laypeople, though he understands priests make some use of it. He thinks book-reading an affectation altogether, and wishes there were less of it at court. His niece is always reading, Anne Boleyn, which is perhaps why she is unmarried at the age of twenty-eight. He does not see why it's a gentleman's business to write letters; there are clerks for that.

Now he fixes an eye, red and fiery. "Cromwell, I am content you are a burgess in the Parliament."

He bows his head. "My lord."

"I spoke to the king for you and he is also content. You will take his instructions in the Commons. And mine."

"Will they be the same, my lord?"

The duke scowls. He paces; he rattles a little; at last he bursts out, "Damn it all, Cromwell, why are you such a . . . person? It isn't as if you could afford to be."

He waits, smiling. He knows what the duke means. He is a person, he is a presence. He knows how to edge blackly into a room so that you don't see him; but perhaps those days are over.

"Smile away," says the duke. "Wolsey's household is a nest of vipers. Not that . . ." he touches a medal, flinching, "God forbid I should . . ."

Compare a prince of the church to a serpent. The duke wants the cardinal's money, and he wants the cardinal's place at the king's side: but then again, he doesn't want to burn in Hell. He walks across the room; he slaps his hands together; he rubs them; he turns. "The king is preparing to quarrel with you, master. Oh yes. He will favor you with an interview because he wishes to understand the cardinal's affairs, but he has, you will learn, a very long and exact memory, and what he remembers, master, is when you were a burgess of the Parliament before this, and how you spoke against his war."

"I hope he doesn't think still of invading France."

"God damn you! What Englishman does not! We own France. We have to take back our own." A muscle in his cheek jumps; he paces, agitated; he turns, he rubs his cheek; the twitch stops, and he says, in a voice perfectly matter-of-fact, "Mind you, you're right."

He waits. "We can't win," the duke says, "but we have to fight as if we can. Hang the expense. Hang the waste—money, men, horses, ships. That's what's wrong with Wolsey, you see. Always at the treaty table. How can a butcher's son understand—"

"*La gloire?*"

"Are you a butcher's son?"

"A blacksmith's."

"Are you really? Shoe a horse?"

He shrugs. "If I were put to it, my lord. But I can't imagine—"

"You can't? What can you imagine? A battlefield, a camp, the night before a battle—can you imagine that?"

"I was a soldier myself."

"Were you so? Not in any English army, I'll be bound. There, you see." The duke grins, quite without animosity. "I knew there was something about you. I knew I didn't like you, but I couldn't put my finger on it. Where were you?"

"Garigliano."

"With?"

"The French."

The duke whistles. "Wrong side, lad."

"So I noticed."

"With the French," he chuckles. "With the French. And how did you scramble out of that disaster?"

"I went north. Got into . . ." He's going to say money, but the duke wouldn't understand trading in money. "Cloth," he says. "Silk, mostly. You know what the market is, with the soldier over there."

"By the Mass, yes! Johnnie Freelance—he puts his money on his back. Those Switzers! Like a troupe of play-actors. Lace, stripes, fancy hats. Easy target, that's all. Longbowman?"

"Now and then." He smiles. "On the short side for that."

"Me too. Now, Henry draws a bow. Very nice. Got the height for it. Got the arm. Still. We won't win many battles like that anymore."

"Then how about not fighting any? Negotiate, my lord. It's cheaper."

"I tell you, Cromwell, you've got face, coming here."

"My lord—you sent for me."

"Did I?" Norfolk looks alarmed. "It's come to that?"

❖

The king's advisers are preparing no fewer than forty-four charges against the cardinal. They range from the violation of the statutes of praemunire—that is to say, the upholding of a foreign jurisdiction within the king's realm—to buying beef for his household at the same price as the king; from financial malfeasance to failing to halt the spread of Lutheran heresies.

The law of praemunire dates from another century. No one who is alive now quite knows what it means. From day to day it seems to mean what the king says it means. The matter is argued in every talking shop in Europe. Meanwhile, my lord cardinal sits, and sometimes mutters to himself, and sometimes speaks aloud, saying, "Thomas, my colleges! Whatever happens to my person, my colleges must be saved. Go to the king. Whatever vengeance, for whatever imagined injury, he would like to wreak on me, he surely cannot mean to put out the light of learning?"

In exile at Esher, the cardinal paces and frets. The great mind which once revolved the affairs of Europe now cogitates ceaselessly on its own losses. He lapses into silent inactivity, brooding as the light fails; for God's sake, Thomas, Cavendish begs him, don't tell him you're coming if you're not.

I won't, he says, and I am coming, but sometimes I am held up. The House sits late and before I leave Westminster I have to gather up the letters and petitions to my lord cardinal, and talk with all the people who want to send messages but don't want them put into writing.

I understand, Cavendish says; but Thomas, he wails, you can't imagine what it's like here at Esher. What time is it? my lord cardinal says. What time will Cromwell be here? And in an hour, again: Cavendish, what time is it? He has us out with lights, and reporting on the weather; as if you, Cromwell, were a person to be impeded by hailstorms or ice. Then next he will ask, what if he has met with some accident on the road? The road from London is full of robbers; wasteland and heathland, as the light fails, are creeping with the agents of malefice. From that he will pass on to say, this world is full of snares and delusions, and into many of them I have fallen, miserable sinner that I am.

When he, Cromwell, finally throws off his riding cloak and collapses into a chair by the fire—God's blood, that smoking chimney—the cardinal is at him before he can draw breath. What said my lord of Suffolk? How looked my lord of Norfolk? The king, have you seen him, did he speak to you? And Lady Anne, is she in health and good looks? Have you worked any device to please her—because we must please her, you know?

He says, "There is one short way to please that lady, and that is to crown her queen." He closes his lips on the topic of Anne and has no more to say. Mary Boleyn says she has noticed him, but till recently Anne gave no sign of it. Her eyes passed over him on their way to someone who interested her more. They are black eyes, slightly protuberant, shiny like the beads of an abacus; they are shiny and always in motion, as she makes calculations of her own advantage. But Uncle Norfolk must have said to her, "There goes the man who knows the cardinal's secrets," because now when he comes into her sight her long neck darts; those shining black beads go click, click, as she looks him up and down and decides what use can be got out of him. He supposes she is in health, as the year creeps toward its end; not coughing like a sick horse, for instance, or gone lame. He supposes she is in good looks, if that's what you like.

One night, just before Christmas, he arrives late at Esher and the cardinal is sitting alone, listening to a boy play the lute. He says, "Mark, thank you, go now." The boy bows to the cardinal; he favors him, barely, with the nod suitable for a burgess in the Parliament. As he withdraws from the room the cardinal says, "Mark is very adept, and a pleasant boy—at York Place, he was one of my choristers. I think I shouldn't keep him here, but send him to the king. Or to Lady Anne, perhaps, as he is such a pretty young thing. Would she like him?"

The boy has lingered at the door to drink in his praises. A hard Cromwellian stare—the equivalent of a kick—sends him out. He wishes people would not ask him what the Lady Anne would and would not like.

The cardinal says, "Does Lord Chancellor More send me any message?"

He drops a sheaf of papers on the table. "You look ill, my lord."

"Yes, I am ill. Thomas, what shall we do?"

"We shall bribe people," he says. "We shall be liberal and open-handed with the assets Your Grace has left—for you still have benefices to dispose of, you still have land. Listen, my lord—even if the king takes all you have, people will be asking, can the king truly bestow what belongs to the cardinal? No one to whom he makes a grant will be sure in their title, unless you confirm it. So you still have, my lord, you still have cards in your hand."

"And after all, if he meant to bring a treason . . ." his voice falters, "if . . ."

"If he meant to charge you with treason you would be in the Tower by now."

"Indeed—and what use would I be to him, head in one place, body in another? This is how it is: the king thinks, by degrading me, to give a sharp lesson to the Pope. He thinks to indicate, I as King of England am master in my own house. Oh, but is he? Or is Lady Anne master, or Thomas Boleyn? A question not to be asked, not outside this room."

The battle is, now, to get the king alone; to find out his intentions, if he knows them himself, and broker a deal. The cardinal urgently needs ready cash, that's the first skirmish. Day after day, he waits for an interview. The king extends a hand, takes from him what letters he proffers, glancing at the cardinal's seal. He does not look at him, saying merely an absent "Thanks." One day he does look at him, and says, "Master Cromwell, yes . . . I cannot talk about the cardinal." And as he opens his mouth to speak, the king says, "Don't you understand? I cannot talk about him." His tone is gentle, puzzled. "Another day," he says. "I will send for you. I promise."

When the cardinal asks him, "How did the king look today?" he says, he looks as if he does not sleep.

The cardinal laughs. "If he does not sleep it is because he does not hunt. This icy ground is too hard for the hounds' pads, they cannot go out. It is lack of fresh air, Thomas. It is not his conscience."

Later, he will remember that night toward the end of December when he found the cardinal listening to music. He will run it through his mind, twice and over again.

Because as he is leaving the cardinal, and contemplating again the road, the night, he hears a boy's voice, speaking behind a half-open door: it is Mark, the lute-player. ". . . so for my skill he says he will prefer me to Lady Anne. And I shall be glad, because what is the use of being here when any day the king may behead the old fellow? I think he ought, for the cardinal is so proud. Today is the first day he ever gave me a good word."

A pause. Someone speaks, muffled; he cannot tell who. Then the boy: "Yes, for sure the lawyer will come down with him. I say 'lawyer,' but who is he? Nobody knows. They say he has killed men with his own hands and never told it in confession. But those hard kinds of men, they always weep when they see the hangman."

He is in no doubt that it is his own execution Mark looks forward to. Beyond the wall, the boy runs on: "So when I am with Lady Anne she is sure to notice me, and give me presents." A giggle. "And look on me with favor. Don't you think? Who knows where she may turn while she is still refusing the king?"

A pause. Then Mark: "She is no maid. Not she."

What an enchanting conversation: servants' talk. Again comes a muffled answer, and then Mark: "Could she be at the French court, do you think, and come home a maid? Any more than her sister could? And Mary was every man's hackney."

But this is nothing. He is disappointed. I had hopes of particulars; this is just the *on dit*. But still he hesitates, and doesn't move away.

"Besides, Tom Wyatt has had her, and everybody knows it, down in Kent. I have been down to Penshurst with the cardinal, and you know that palace is near to Hever, where the lady's family is, and the Wyatts' house an easy ride away."

Witnesses? Dates?

But then, from the unseen person, "Shh!" Again, a soft giggle.

One can do nothing with this. Except bear it in mind. The conversation is in Flemish: language of Mark's birthplace.

❖

Christmas comes, and the king, with Queen Katherine, keeps it at Greenwich. Anne is at York Place; the king can come upriver to see her. Her company, the women say, is exacting; the king's visits are short, few and discreet.

At Esher the cardinal takes to his bed. Once he would never have done that, though he looks ill enough to justify it. He says, "Nothing will happen while the king and Lady Anne are exchanging their New Year kisses. We are safe from incursions till Twelfth Night." He turns his head, against his pillows. Says, vehement, "Body of Christ, Cromwell. Go home."

The house at the Austin Friars is decorated with wreaths of holly and ivy, of laurel and ribboned yew. The kitchen is busy, feeding the living, but they omit this year their usual songs and Christmas plays. No year has brought such devastation. His sister Kat, her husband, Morgan Williams, have been plucked from this life as fast as his daughters were taken, one day walking and talking and next day cold as stones, tumbled into their Thames-side graves and dug in beyond reach of the tide, beyond sight and smell of the river; deaf now to the sound of Putney's cracked church bell, to the smell of wet ink, of hops, of malted barley, and the scent, still animal, of woolen bales; dead to the autumn aroma of pine resin and apple candles, of soul cakes baking. As the year ends two orphans are added to his house, Richard and the child Walter. Morgan Williams, he was a big talker, but he was shrewd in his own way, and he worked hard for his family. And Kat—well, latterly she understood her brother about as well as she understood the motions of the stars: "I can never add you up, Thomas," she'd say, which was his failure entirely, because who had taught her, except him, to count on her fingers, and puzzle out a tradesman's bill?

If he were to give himself a piece of advice for Christmas, he'd say, leave the cardinal now or you'll be out on the streets again with the three-card trick. But he only gives advice to those who are likely to take it.

They have a big gilded star at the Austin Friars, which they hang in their great hall on New Year's Eve. For a week it shines out, to welcome their guests at Epiphany. From summer onward, he and Liz would be thinking of costumes for the Three Kings, coveting and hoarding scraps of any strange cloth they saw, any new trimmings; then from October, Liz would be sewing in secrecy, improving on last year's robes by patching them over with new shining panels, quilting a shoulder and weighting a hem, and building each year some fantastical new crowns. His part was to think what the gifts would be, that the kings had in their boxes. Once a king had dropped his casket in shock when the gift began to sing.

This year no one has the heart to hang up the star; but he visits it, in its lightless storeroom. He slides off the canvas sleeves that protect its rays, and checks that they are unchipped and unfaded. There will be better years, when they will hang it up again; though he cannot imagine them. He eases back the sleeves, pleased at how ingeniously they have been made and how exactly they fit. The Three Kings' robes are packed into a chest, as also the sheepskins for the children who will be sheep. The shepherds' crooks lean in a corner; from a peg hang angel's wings. He touches them. His finger comes away dusty. He shifts his candle out of danger, then lifts them from the peg and gently shakes them. They make a soft sound of hissing, and a faint amber perfume washes into the air. He hangs them back on the peg; passes over them the palm of his hand, to soothe them and still their shiver. He picks up his candle. He backs out and closes the door. He pinches out the light, turns the lock and gives the key to Johane.

He says to her, "I wish we had a baby. It seems such a long time since there was a baby in the house."

"Don't look at me," Johane says.

He does, of course. He says, "Does John Williamson not do his duty by you these days?"

She says, "His duty is not my pleasure."

As he walks away he thinks, that's a conversation I shouldn't have had.

On New Year's Day, when night falls, he is sitting at his writing table; he is writing letters for the cardinal, and sometimes he crosses the room to his counting board and pushes the counters about. It seems that in return for a formal guilty plea to the praemunire charges, the king will allow the cardinal his life, and a measure of liberty; but whatever money is left him, to maintain his state, will be a fraction of his former income. York Place has been taken already, Hampton Court is long gone, and the king is thinking of how to tax and rob the rich bishopric of Winchester.

Gregory comes in. "I brought you lights. My aunt Johane said, go in to your father."

Gregory sits. He waits. He fidgets. He sighs. He gets up. He crosses to his father's writing table and hovers in front of him. Then, as if someone had said, "Make yourself useful," he reaches out timidly and begins to tidy the papers.

He glances up at his son, while keeping his head down over his task. For the first time, perhaps, since Gregory was a baby, he notices his hands, and he is struck by what they have become: not childish paws, but the large, white untroubled hands of a gentleman's son. What is Gregory doing? He is putting the documents into a stack. On what principle is he doing it? He can't read them, they're the wrong way up. He's not filing them by subject. Is he filing them by date? For God's sake, what is he doing?

He needs to finish this sentence, with its many vital subclauses. He glances up again, and recognizes Gregory's design. It is a system of holy simplicity: big papers on the bottom, small ones on top.

"Father . . ." Gregory says. He sighs. He crosses to the counting board. With a forefinger he inches the counters about. Then he scoops them together, picks them up and clicks them into a tidy pile.

He looks up at last. "That was a calculation. It wasn't just where I dropped them."

"Oh, sorry," Gregory says politely. He sits down by the fire and tries not to disturb the air as he breathes.

The mildest eyes can be commanding; under his son's gaze, he asks, "What is it?"

"Do you think you can stop writing?"

"A minute," he says, holding up a delaying hand; he signs the letter, his usual form: "Your assured friend, Thomas Cromwell." If Gregory is going to tell him that someone else in the house is mortally ill, or that he, Gregory, has offered himself in marriage to the laundry girl, or that London Bridge has fallen down, he must be ready to take it like a man; but he must sand and seal this. He looks up. "Yes?"

Gregory turns his face away. Is he crying? It would not be surprising, would it, as he has cried himself, and in public? He crosses the room. He sits down opposite his son, by the hearth. He takes off his cap of velvet and runs his hands back through his hair.

For a long time no one speaks. He looks down at his own thick-fingered hands, scars and burn marks hidden in the palms. He thinks, gentleman? So you call yourself, but who do you hope to mislead? Only the people who have never seen you, or the people you keep distanced with courtesy, legal clients and your fellows in the Commons, colleagues at Gray's Inn, the household servants of courtiers, the courtiers themselves . . . His mind strays to the next letter he must write. Then Gregory says, his voice small as if he had receded into the past, "Do you remember that Christmas, when there was the giant in the pageant?"

"Here in the parish? I remember."

"He said, 'I am a giant, my name is Marlinspike.' They said he was as tall as the Cornhill maypole. What's the Cornhill maypole?"

"They took it down. The year of the riots. Evil May Day, they called it. You were only a baby then."

"Where's the maypole now?"

"The city has it in store."

"Shall we have our star again next year?"

"If our fortunes look up."

"Shall we be poor now the cardinal is down?"

"No."

The little flames leap and flare, and Gregory looks into them. "You remember the year I had my face dyed black, and I was wrapped in a black calfskin? When I was a devil in the Christmas play?"

"I do." His face softens. "I remember."

Anne had wanted to be dyed, but her mother had said it was not suitable for a little girl. He wishes he had said that Anne must have her turn as a parish angel—even if, being dark, she had to wear one of the parish's yellow knitted wigs, which slipped sideways, or fell over the children's eyes.

The year that Grace was an angel, she had wings made of peacock feathers. He himself had contrived it. The other little girls were dowdy goose creatures, and their wings fell off if they caught them on the corners of the stable. But Grace stood glittering, her hair entwined with silver threads; her shoulders were trussed with a spreading, shivering glory, and the rustling air was perfumed as she breathed. Lizzie said, Thomas, there's no end to you, is there? She has the best wings the city has ever seen.

Gregory stands up; he comes to kiss him good night. For a moment his son leans against him, as if he were a child; or as if the past, the pictures in the fire, were an intoxication.

Once the boy has gone to bed he sweeps his papers out of the tidy stack he has made. He refolds them. He sorts them with the endorsement out, ready for filing. He thinks of Evil May Day. Gregory did not ask, why were there riots? The riots were against foreigners. He himself had not long been home.

❖

As 1530 begins, he does not hold an Epiphany feast, because so many people, sensible of the cardinal's disgrace, would be obliged to refuse his invitation. Instead, he takes the young men to Gray's Inn, for the Twelfth Night revels. He regrets it almost at once; this year they are noisier, and more bawdy, than any he remembers.

The law students make a play about the cardinal. They make him flee from his palace at York Place, to his barge on the Thames. Some fellows flap dyed sheets, to impersonate the river, and then others run up and throw water on them from leather buckets. As the cardinal scrambles into his barge, there are hunting cries, and one benighted fool runs into the hall with a brace of otter hounds on a leash. Others come with nets and fishing rods, to haul the cardinal back to the bank.

The next scene shows the cardinal floundering in the mud at Putney, as he runs to his bolt-hole at Esher. The students halloo and cry as the cardinal weeps and holds up his hands in prayer. Of all the people who witnessed this, who, he wonders, has offered it up as a comedy? If he knew, or if he guessed, the worse for them.

The cardinal lies on his back, a crimson mountain; he flails his hands; he offers his bishopric of Winchester to anyone who can get him back on his mule. Some students, under a frame draped with donkey skins, enact the mule, which turns about and jokes in Latin, and farts in the cardinal's face. There is much wordplay about bishoprics and bishops' pricks, which might pass as witty if they were streetsweepers, but he thinks law students should do better. He rises from his place, displeased, and his household has no choice but to stand up with him and walk out.

He stops to have a word with some of the benchers: how was this allowed to go forward? The Cardinal of York is a sick man, he may die, how will you and your students stand then before your God? What sort of young men are you breeding here, who are so brave as to assail a great man who has fallen on evil times—whose favor, a few short weeks ago, they would have begged for?

The benchers follow him, apologizing; but their voices are lost in the roars of laughter that billow out from the hall. His young household are lingering, casting glances back. The cardinal is offering his harem of forty virgins to anyone who will help him mount; he sits on the ground and laments, while a flaccid and serpentine member, knitted of red wool, flops out from under his robes.

Outside, lights burn thin in the icy air. "Home," he says. He hears Gregory whisper, "We can only laugh if he permits us."

"Well, after all," he hears Rafe say, "he is the man in charge."

He falls back a step, to speak with them. "Anyway, it was the wicked Borgia Pope, Alexander, who kept forty women. And none of them were virgins, I can tell you."

Rafe touches his shoulder. Richard walks on his left, sticking close. "You don't have to hold me up," he says mildly. "I'm not like the cardinal." He stops. He laughs. He says, "I suppose it was . . ."

"Yes, it was quite entertaining," Richard says. "His Grace must have been five feet around his waist."

The night is loud with the noise of bone rattles, and alive with the flames of torches. A troop of hobby horses clatters past them, singing, and a party of men wearing antlers, with bells at their heels. As they near home a boy dressed as an orange rolls past, with his friend, a lemon. "Gregory Cromwell!" they call out, and to him as their senior they courteously raise, in lieu of hats, an upper slice of rind. "God send you a good new year."

"The same to you," he calls. And, to the lemon: "Tell your father to come and see me about that Cheapside lease."

They get home. "Go to bed," he says. "It's late." He feels it best to add, "God see you safe till morning."

They leave him. He sits at his worktable. He remembers Grace, at the end of her evening as an angel: standing in the firelight, her face white with fatigue, her eyes glittering, and the eyes of her peacock's wings shining in the firelight, each like a topaz, golden, smoky. Liz said, "Stand away from the fire, sweetheart, or your wings will catch alight." His little girl backed off, into shadow; the feathers were the colors of ash and cinders as she moved toward the stairs, and he said, "Grace, are you going to bed in your wings?"

"Till I say my prayers," she said, darting a look over her shoulder. He followed her, afraid for her, afraid of fire and some other danger, but he did not know what. She walked up the staircase, her plumes rustling, her feathers fading to black.

Ah, Christ, he thinks, at least I'll never have to give her to anyone else. She's dead and I'll not have to sign her away to some purse-mouthed petty gent who wants her dowry. Grace would have wanted a title. She would have thought because she was lovely he should buy her one: Lady Grace. I wish my daughter Anne were here, he thinks, I wish Anne were here and promised to Rafe Sadler. If Anne were older. If Rafe were younger. If Anne were still alive.

Once more he bends his head over the cardinal's letters. Wolsey is writing to the rulers of Europe, to ask them to support him, vindicate him, fight his cause. He, Thomas Cromwell, wishes the cardinal would not, or if he must, could the encryption be more tricky? Is it not treasonable for Wolsey to urge them to obstruct the king's purpose? Henry would deem it is. The cardinal is not asking them to make war on Henry, on his behalf: he's merely asking them to withdraw their approval of a king who very much likes to be liked.

He sits back in his chair, hands over his mouth, as if to disguise his opinion from himself. He thinks, I am glad I love my lord cardinal, because if I did not, and I were his enemy—let us say I am Suffolk, let us say I am Norfolk, let us say I am the king—I would be putting him on trial next week.

The door opens. "Richard? You can't sleep? Well, I knew it. The play was too exciting for you."

It is easy to smile now, but Richard does not smile; his face is in shadow. He says, "Master, I have a question to put to you. Our father is dead and you are our father now."

Richard Williams, and Walter-named-after-Walter Williams: these are his sons. "Sit down," he says.

"So shall we change our name to yours?"

"You surprise me. The way things are with me, the people called Cromwell will be wanting to change their names to Williams."

"If I had your name, I should never disown it."

"Would your father like it? You know he believed he had his descent from Welsh princes."

"Ah, he did. When he'd had a drink, he would say, who will give me a shilling for my principality?"

"Even so, you have the Tudor name in your descent. By some accounts."

"Don't," Richard pleads. "It makes beads of blood stand out on my forehead."

"It's not that hard." He laughs. "Listen. The old king had an uncle, Jasper Tudor. Jasper had two bastard daughters, Joan and Helen. Helen was Gardiner's mother. Joan married William ap Evan—she was your grandmother."

"Is that all? Why did my father make it sound so deep? But if I am the king's cousin," Richard pauses, "and Stephen Gardiner's cousin . . . what good can it do me? We're not at court and not likely to be, now the cardinal . . . well . . ." He looks away. "Sir . . . when you were on your travels, did you ever think you would die?"

"Yes. Oh, yes."

Richard looks at him: how did that feel?

"I felt," he said, "irritated. It seemed a waste, I suppose. To come so far. To cross the sea. To die for . . ." He shrugs. "God knows why."

Richard says, "Every day I light a candle for my father."

"Does that help you?"

"No. I just do it."

"Does he know you do it?"

"I can't imagine what he knows. I know the living must comfort each other."

"This comforts me, Richard Cromwell."

Richard gets up, kisses his cheek. "Good night. *Cysga'n dawel.*"

Sleep well; it is the familiar form for those who are close to home. It is the usage for fathers, for brothers. It matters what name we choose, what name we make. The people lose their name who lie dead on the field of battle, the ordinary corpses of no lineage, with no herald to search for them and no chantry, no perpetual prayers. Morgan's bloodline won't be lost, he is sure of it, though he died in a busy year for death, when London was never out of black. He touches his throat, where the medal would have been, the holy medal that Kat gave him; his fingers are surprised not to find it there. For the first time he understands why he took it off and slid it into the sea. It was so that no living hand could take it. The waves took it, and the waves have it still.

❖

The chimney at Esher continues to smoke. He goes to the Duke of Norfolk—who is always ready to see him—and asks him what is to be done about the cardinal's household.

In this matter, both dukes are helpful. "Nothing is more malcontent," says Norfolk, "than a masterless man. Nothing more dangerous. Whatever one thinks of the Cardinal of York, he was always well served. Prefer them to me, send them in my direction. They will be my men."

He directs a searching look at Cromwell. Who turns away. Knows himself coveted. Wears an expression like an heiress: sly, coy, cold.

He is arranging a loan for the duke. His foreign contacts are less than excited. The cardinal down, he says, the duke has risen, like the morning sun, and sitteth at Henry's right hand. Tommaso, they say, seriously, you are offering what as guarantee? Some old duke who may be dead tomorrow—they say he is choleric? You are offering a duke-dom as security, in that barbaric island of yours, which is always breaking out into civil war? And another war coming, if your willful king will set aside the Emperor's aunt, and install his whore as queen?

Still: he'll get terms. Somewhere.

Charles Brandon says, "You here again, Master Cromwell, with your lists of names? Is there anyone you specially recommend to me?"

"Yes, but I am afraid he is a man of a lowly stamp, and more fit that I should confer with your kitchen steward—"

"No, tell me," says the duke. He can't bear suspense.

"It's only the hearths and chimneys man, hardly a matter for Your Grace . . ."

"I'll have him, I'll have him," Charles Brandon says. "I like a good fire."

Thomas More, the Lord Chancellor, has put his signature first on all the articles against Wolsey. They say one strange allegation has been added at his behest. The cardinal is accused of whispering in the king's ear and breathing into his face; since the cardinal has the French pox, he intended to infect our monarch.

When he hears this he thinks, imagine living inside the Lord Chan-cellor's head. Imagine writing down such a charge and taking it to the printer, and circulating it through the court and through the realm, putting it out there to where people will believe anything; putting it out there, to the shepherds on the hills, to Tyndale's plowboy, to the beggar on the roads and the patient beast in its byre or stall; out there to the bitter winter winds, and to the weak early sun, and the snowdrops in the London gardens.

❖

It is a wan morning, low unbroken cloud; the light, filtering sparely through glass, is the color of tarnished pewter. How brightly colored the king is, like the king in a new pack of cards: how small his flat blue eye.

There is a crowd of gentlemen around Henry Tudor; they ignore his approach. Only Harry Norris smiles, gives him a polite good morning. At a signal from the king, the gentlemen retire to a distance; bright in their riding cloaks—it is a hunting morning—they flutter, eddy, cluster; they whisper, one to another, and conduct a discourse in nods and shrugs.

The king glances out of the window. "So," he says, "how is . . . ?" He seems reluctant to name the cardinal.

"He cannot be well till he has Your Majesty's favor."

"Forty-four charges," the king says. "Forty-four, master."

"Saving Your Majesty, there is an answer to each one, and given a hearing we would make them."

"Could you make them here and now?"

"If Your Majesty would care to sit."

"I heard you were a ready man."

"Would I come here unprepared?"

He has spoken almost without thinking. The king smiles. That fine curl of the red lip. He has a pretty mouth, almost like a woman's; it is too small for his face. "Another day I would put you to the test," he says. "But my lord Suffolk is waiting for me. Will the cloud lift, do you think? I wish I'd gone out before Mass."

"I think it will clear," he says. "A good day to be chasing something."

"Master Cromwell?" The king turns, he looks at him, astonished. "You are not of Thomas More's opinion, are you?"

He waits. He cannot imagine what the king is going to say.

"*La chasse.* He thinks it barbaric."

"Oh, I see. No, Your Majesty, I favor any sport that's cheaper than battle. It's rather that . . ." How can he put it? "In some countries, they hunt the bear, and the wolf and the wild boar. We once had these animals in England, when we had our great forests."

"My cousin France has boar to hunt. From time to time he says he will ship me some. But I feel . . ."

You feel he is taunting you.

"We usually say," Henry looks straight at him, "we usually say, we gentlemen, that the chase prepares us for war. Which brings us to a sticky point, Master Cromwell."

"It does indeed," he says, cheerful.

"You said, in the Parliament, some six years ago, that I could not afford a war."

It was seven years: 1523. And how long has this audience lasted? Seven minutes? Seven minutes and he is sure already. There's no point backing off; do that and Henry will chase you down. Advance, and he may just falter. He says, "No ruler in the history of the world has ever been able to afford a war. They're not affordable things. No prince ever says, 'This is my budget, so this is the kind of war I can have.' You enter into one and it uses up all the money you've got, and then it breaks you and bankrupts you."

"When I went into France in the year 1513 I captured the town of Thérouanne, which in your speech you called—"

"A doghole, Majesty."

"A doghole," the king repeats. "How could you say so?"

He shrugs. "I've been there."

A flash of anger. "And so have I, at the head of my army. Listen to me, master—you said I should not fight because the taxes would break the country. What is the country for, but to support its prince in his enterprise?"

"I believe I said—saving Your Majesty—we didn't have the gold to see you through a year's campaign. All the bullion in the country would be swallowed by the war. I have read there was a time when people exchanged leather tokens, for want of metal coins. I said we would be back to those days."

"You said I was not to lead my troops. You said if I was taken, the country couldn't put up the ransom. So what do you want? You want a king who doesn't fight? You want me to huddle indoors like a sick girl?"

"That would be ideal, for fiscal purposes."

The king takes a deep ragged breath. He's been shouting. Now— and it's a narrow thing—he decides to laugh. "You advocate prudence. Prudence is a virtue. But there are other virtues that belong to princes."

"Fortitude."

"Yes. Cost that out."

"It doesn't mean courage in battle."

"Do you read me a lesson?"

"It means fixity of purpose. It means endurance. It means having the strength to live with what constrains you."

Henry crosses the room. Stamp, stamp, stamp in his riding boots; he is ready for *la chasse*. He turns, rather slowly, to show his majesty to better effect: wide and square and bright. "We will pursue this. What constrains me?"

"The distance," he says. "The harbors. The terrain, the people. The winter rains and the mud. When Your Majesty's ancestors fought in France, whole provinces were held by England. From there we could supply, we could provision. Now that we have only Calais, how can we support an army in the interior?"

The king stares out into the silver morning. He bites his lip. Is he in a slow fury, simmering, bubbling to boiling point? He turns, and his smile is sunny. "I know," he says. "So when we next go into France, we will need a seacoast."

Of course. We need to take Normandy. Or Brittany. That's all.

"Well reasoned," the king says. "I bear you no ill will. Only I suppose you have no experience in policy, or the direction of a campaign."

He shakes his head. "None."

"You said—before, I mean, in this speech of yours to the Parliament—that there was one million pounds in gold in the realm."

"I gave a round figure."

"But how would you find that figure?"

"I trained in the Florentine banks. And in Venice."

The king stares at him. "Howard said you were a common soldier."

"That too."

"Anything else?"

"What would Your Majesty like me to be?"

The king looks him full in the face: a rare thing with him. He looks back; it is his habit. "Master Cromwell, your reputation is bad."

He inclines his head.

"You don't defend yourself?"

"Your Majesty is able to form his own opinion."

"I can. I will."

At the door, the guards part their spears; the gentlemen step aside and bow; Suffolk pounds in. Charles Brandon: he looks too hot in his clothes. "You ready?" he says to the king. "Oh, Cromwell." He grins. "How's your fat priest?"

The king flushes with displeasure. Brandon doesn't notice. "You know," he chuckles, "they say the cardinal once rode out with his servant, and checked his horse at the head of a valley, where looking down he saw a very fair church and its lands about. He says to his servant, Robin, who owns that? I would that were my benefice! Robin says, It is, my lord, it is."

His story meets with poor success, but he laughs at it himself.

He says, "My lord, they tell that story all over Italy. Of this cardinal, or that."

Brandon's face falls. "What, the same story?"

"*Mutatis mutandis.* The servant isn't called Robin."

The king meets his eye. He smiles.

Leaving, he pushes past the gentlemen, and who should he meet but the king's Secretary! "Good morning, good morning!" he says. He doesn't often repeat things, but the moment seems to call for it.

Gardiner is rubbing his great blue hands together. "Cold, no?" he says. "And how was that, Cromwell? Unpleasant, I think?"

"On the contrary," he says. "Oh, and he's going out with Suffolk; you'll have to wait." He walks on, but then turns. There is a pain like a dull bruise inside his chest. "Gardiner, can't we drop this?"

"No," Gardiner says. His drooping eyelids flicker. "No, I don't see that we can."

"Fine," he says. He walks on. He thinks, you wait. You may have to wait a year or two, but you just wait.

❖

Esher, two days later: he is hardly through the gateway when Cavendish comes hurtling across the courtyard. "Master Cromwell! Yesterday the king—"

"Calmly, George," he advises.

"—yesterday he sent us four cartloads of furnishings—come and see! Tapestry, plate, bed hangings—was it by your suit?"

Who knows? He hadn't asked for anything directly. If he had, he'd have been more specific. Not that hanging, but this hanging, which my lord likes; he likes goddesses, rather than virgin martyrs, so away with St. Agnes, and let's have Venus in a grove. My lord likes Venetian glassware; take away these battered silver goblets.

He looks contemptuous as he inspects the new stuff. "Only the best for you boys from Putney," Wolsey says. "It is possible," he adds, almost apologizing, "that what the king appointed for me was not in fact what was sent. That inferior substitutions were made, by inferior persons."

"That is entirely possible," he says.

"Still. Even so. We are more comfortable for it."

"The difficulty is," Cavendish says, "we need to move. This whole house needs to be scrubbed out and aired."

"True," the cardinal says. "St. Agnes, bless her, would be knocked over by the smell of the privies."

"So will you make suit to the king's council?"

He sighs. "George, what is the point? Listen. I'm not talking to Thomas Howard. I'm not talking to Brandon. I'm talking to him."

The cardinal smiles. A fat paternal beam.

❖

He is surprised—as they thrash out a financial settlement for the cardinal—at Henry's grasp of detail. Wolsey has always said that the king has a fine mind, as quick as his father's, but more comprehensive. The old king grew narrow as he aged; he kept a hard hand on England; there was no nobleman he did not hold by a debt or bond, and he said frankly that if he could not be loved he would be feared. Henry has a different nature, but what is it? Wolsey laughs and says, I should write you a handbook. But as he walks in the gardens of the little lodge at Richmond, where the king has allowed him to remove, the cardinal's mind becomes clouded, he talks about prophecies, and about the downfall of the priests of England, which he says is foretold, and will now happen.

Even if you don't believe in omens—and he doesn't, personally—he can see the problem. For if the cardinal is guilty of a crime in asserting his jurisdiction as legate, are not all those clerics, from bishops downward, who assented to his legacy, also guilty? He can't be the only person who's thinking about this; but mostly, his enemies can't see past the cardinal himself, his vast scarlet presence on the horizon; they fear it will loom up again, ready for revenge. "These are bad times for proud prelates," says Brandon, when next they meet. He sounds jaunty, a man whistling to keep his courage up. "We need no cardinals in this realm."

"And he," the cardinal says, furious, "he, Brandon, when he married the king's sister out of hand—when he married her in the first days of her widowhood, knowing the king intended her for another monarch—his head would have been parted from his body, if I, a simple cardinal, had not pleaded for him to the king."

I, a simple cardinal.

"And what excuse did Brandon make?" the cardinal says. "'Oh, Your Majesty, your sister Mary cried. How she did cry and beg me to marry her myself! I never saw a woman cry so!' So he dried her tears and got himself up to a dukedom! And now he talks as if he's held his title since the Garden of Eden. Listen, Thomas, if men of sound learning and good disposition come to me—as Bishop Tunstall comes, as Thomas More comes—and plead that the church must be reformed, why then I listen. But Brandon! To talk about proud prelates! What was he? The king's horsekeeper! And I've known horses with more wit."

"My lord," Cavendish pleads, "be more temperate. And Charles Brandon, you know, was of an ancient family, a gentleman born."

"Gentleman, he? A swaggering braggart. That's Brandon." The cardinal sits down, exhausted. "My head aches," he says. "Cromwell, go to court and bring me better news."

Day by day he takes his instructions from Wolsey at Richmond, and rides to wherever the king is. He thinks of the king as a terrain into which he must advance, with no seacoast to supply him.

He understands what Henry has learned from his cardinal: his floating diplomacy, his science of ambiguity. He sees how the king has applied this science to the slow, trackless, dubious ruin of his minister. Every kindness, Henry matches with a cruelty, some further charge or forfeiture. Till the cardinal moans, "I want to go away."

"Winchester," he suggests, to the dukes. "My lord cardinal is willing to proceed to his palace there."

"What, so near the king?" Brandon says. "We are not fools to ourselves, Master Cromwell."

Since he, the cardinal's man, is with Henry so often, rumors have run all over Europe that Wolsey is about to be recalled. The king is cutting a deal, people say, to have the church's wealth in exchange for Wolsey's return to favor. Rumors leak from the council chamber, from the privy chamber: the king does not like his new setup. Norfolk is found ignorant; Suffolk is accused of having an annoying laugh.

He says, "My lord won't go north. He is not ready for it."

"But I want him north," Howard says. "Tell him to go. Tell him Norfolk says he must be on the road and out of here. Or—and tell him this—I will come where he is, and I will tear him with my teeth."

"My lord." He bows. "May I substitute the word 'bite'?"

Norfolk approaches him. He stands far too close. His eyes are bloodshot. Every sinew is jumping. He says, "Substitute nothing, you misbegotten—" The duke stabs a forefinger into his shoulder. "You . . . person," he says; and again, "you nobody from Hell, you whore-spawn, you cluster of evil, you lawyer."

He stands there, pushing away, like a baker pressing the dimples into a batch of manchet loaves. Cromwell flesh is firm, dense and impermeable. The ducal finger just bounces off.

Before they left Esher, one of the cats that had been brought in to kill the vermin gave birth to a litter in the cardinal's own rooms. What presumption, in an animal! But wait—new life, in the cardinal's suite? Could that be an *omen*? One day, he fears, there will be an omen of another sort: a dead bird will fall down that smoking chimney, and then—oh, woe is us!—he'll never hear the last of it.

But for the while the cardinal is amused, and puts the kittens on a cushion in an open chest, and watches as they grow. One of them is black and hungry, with a coat like wool and yellow eyes. When it is weaned he brings it home. He takes it from under his coat, where it has been sleeping curled against his shoulder. "Gregory, look." He holds it out to his son. "I am a giant, my name is Marlinspike."

Gregory looks at him, wary, puzzled. His glance flinches; his hand pulls away. "The dogs will kill it," he says.

Marlinspike goes down to the kitchen, to grow stout and live out his beastly nature. There is a summer ahead, though he cannot imagine its pleasures; sometimes when he's walking in the garden he sees him, a half-grown cat, lolling watchful in an apple tree, or snoring on a wall in the sun.

❖

Spring 1530: Antonio Bonvisi, the merchant, invites him to supper at his fine tall house on Bishopsgate. "I won't be late," he tells Richard, expecting that it will be the usual tense gathering, everyone cross and hungry: for even a rich Italian with an ingenious kitchen cannot find a hundred ways with smoked eel or salt cod. The merchants in Lent miss their mutton and malmsey, their nightly grunt in a featherbed with wife or mistress; from now to Good Friday their knives will be out for some cutthroat intelligence, some mean commercial advantage.

But it is a grander occasion than he thought; the Lord Chancellor is there, among a company of lawyers and aldermen. Humphrey Monmouth, whom More once locked up, is seated well away from the great man; More looks at his ease, holding the company captive with one of his stories about that great scholar Erasmus, his dear friend. But when he looks up and sees him, Cromwell, he falls silent halfway through a sentence; he casts his eyes down, and an opaque and stony look grows on his face.

"Did you want to talk about me?" he asks. "You can do it while I'm here, Lord Chancellor. I have a thick skin." He knocks back a glass of wine and laughs. "Do you know what Brandon is saying? He can't fit my life together. My travels. The other day he called me a Jewish peddler."

"And was that to your face?" his host asks politely.

"No. The king told me. But then my lord cardinal calls Brandon a horsekeeper."

Humphrey Monmouth says, "You have the entrée these days, Thomas. And what do you think, now you are a courtier?"

There are smiles around the table. Because, of course, the idea is so ridiculous, the situation so temporary. More's people are city people, no grander; but he is *sui generis,* a scholar and a wit. And More says, "Perhaps we should not press the point. There are delicate issues here. There is a time to be silent."

An elder of the drapers' guild leans across the table and warns, his voice low: "Thomas More said, when he took his seat, that he won't discuss the cardinal, or the Lady either."

He, Cromwell, looks around at the company. "The king surprises me, though. What he will tolerate."

"From you?" More says.

"I mean Brandon. They're going to hunt: he walks in and shouts, are you ready?"

"Your master the cardinal found it a constant battle," Bonvisi says, "in the early years of the reign. To stop the king's companions becoming too familiar with him."

"He wanted only himself to be familiar," More suggests.

"Though, of course, the king may raise up whom he will."

"Up to a point, Thomas," Bonvisi says; there is some laughter.

"And the king enjoys his friendships. That is good, surely?"

"A soft word, from you, Master Cromwell."

"Not at all," Monmouth says. "Master Cromwell is known as one who does everything for his friends."

"I think . . ." More stops; he looks down at the table. "In all truth, I am not sure if one can regard a prince as a friend."

"But surely," Bonvisi says, "you've known Henry since he was a child."

"Yes, but friendship should be less exhausting . . . it should be restorative. Not like . . ." More turns to him, for the first time, as if inviting comment. "I sometimes feel it is like . . . like Jacob wrestling with the angel."

"And who knows," he says, "what that fight was about?"

"Yes, the text is silent. As with Cain and Abel. Who knows?"

He senses a little disquiet around the table, among the more pious, the less sportive; or just those keen for the next course. What will it be? Fish!

"When you speak to Henry," More says, "I beg you, speak to the good heart. Not the strong will."

He would pursue it, but the aged draper waves for more wine, and asks him, "How's your friend Stephen Vaughan? What's new in Antwerp?" The conversation is about trade then; it is about shipping, interest rates; it is no more than a background hum to unruly speculation. If you come into a room and say, this is what we're not talking about, it follows that you're talking about nothing else. If the Lord Chancellor weren't here it would be just import duties and bonded warehouses; we would not be thinking of the brooding scarlet cardinal, and our starved Lenten minds would not be occupied by the image of the king's fingers creeping over a resistant, quick-breathing and virginal bosom. He leans back and fixes his gaze on Thomas More. In time there is a natural pause in conversation, a lull; and after a quarter hour in which he has not spoken, the Lord Chancellor breaks into it, his voice low and angry, his eyes on the remnants of what he has eaten. "The Cardinal of York," he says, "has a greed that will never be appeased, for ruling over other men."

"Lord Chancellor," Bonvisi says, "you are looking at your herring as if you hate it."

Says the gracious guest, "There's nothing wrong with the herring."

He leans forward, ready for this fight; he means not to let it pass. "The cardinal is a public man. So are you. Should he shrink from a public role?"

"Yes." More looks up. "Yes, I think, a little, he should. A little less evident appetite, perhaps."

"It's late," Monmouth says, "to read the cardinal a lesson in humility."

"His real friends have read it long ago, and been ignored."

"And you count yourself his friend?" He sits back, arms folded. "I'll tell him, Lord Chancellor, and by the blood of Christ he will find it a consolation, as he sits in exile and wonders why you have slandered him to the king."

"Gentlemen . . ." Bonvisi rises in his chair, edgy.

"No," he says, "sit down. Let's have this straight. Thomas More here will tell you, I would have been a simple monk, but my father put me to the law. I would spend my life in church, if I had the choice. I am, as you know, indifferent to wealth. I am devoted to things of the spirit. The world's esteem is nothing to me." He looks around the table. "So how did he become Lord Chancellor? Was it an accident?"

The doors open; Bonvisi jumps to his feet; relief floods his face. "Welcome, welcome," he says. "Gentlemen: the Emperor's ambassador."

It is Eustache Chapuys, come in with the desserts; the new ambassador, as one calls him, though he has been in the post since fall. He stands poised on the threshold, so they may know him and admire: a little crooked man, in a doublet slashed and puffed, blue satin billowing through black; beneath it, his little black spindly legs. "I regret to be so late," he says. He simpers. *"Les dépêches, toujours les dépêches."*

"That's the ambassador's life." He looks up and smiles. "Thomas Cromwell."

"Ah, c'est le juif errant!"

At once the ambassador apologizes: while smiling around, as if bemused, at the success of his joke.

Sit down, sit down, says Bonvisi, and the servants bustle, the cloths are swept away, the company rearranges itself more informally, except for the Lord Chancellor, who goes on sitting where he's sitting. Preserved autumn fruits come in, and spiced wine, and Chapuys takes a place of honor beside More.

"We will speak French, gentlemen," says Bonvisi.

French, as it happens, is the first language of the ambassador of the Empire and Spain; and like any other diplomat, he will never take the trouble to learn English, for how will that help him in his next posting? So kind, so kind, he says, as he eases himself back in the carved chair their host has vacated; his feet do not quite touch the floor. More rouses himself then; he and the ambassador put their heads together. He watches them; they glance back at him resentfully; but looking is free.

In a tiny moment when they pause, he cuts in. "Monsieur Chapuys? You know, I was talking with the king recently about those events, so regrettable, when your master's troops plundered the Holy City. Perhaps you can advise us? We don't understand them even now."

Chapuys shakes his head. "Most regrettable events."

"Thomas More thinks it was the secret Mohammedans in your army who ran wild—oh, and my own people, of course, the wandering Jews. But before this, he has said it was the Germans, the Lutherans, who raped the poor virgins and desecrated the shrines. In all cases, as the Lord Chancellor says, the Emperor must blame himself; but to whom should we attach blame? Are you able to help us out?"

"My dear Sir Chancellor!" The ambassador is shocked. His eyes turn toward Thomas More. "Did you speak so, of my imperial master?" A glance flicked over his shoulder, and he drops into Latin.

The company, linguistically agile, sit and smile at him. He advises, pleasantly, "If you wish to be half secret, try Greek. *Allez*, Monsieur Chapuys, rattle away! The Lord Chancellor will understand you."

The party breaks up soon after, the Lord Chancellor rising to go; but before he does, he makes a pronouncement to the company, in English. "Master Cromwell's position," he says, "is indefensible, it seems to me. He is no friend to the church, as we all know, but he is friend to one priest. And that priest the most corrupt in Christendom."

With the curtest of nods he takes his leave. Even Chapuys does not warrant more. The ambassador looks after him, dubious, biting his lip: as if to say, I looked for more help and friendship there. Everything Chapuys does, he notices, is like something an actor does. When he thinks, he casts his eyes down, places two fingers to his forehead. When he sorrows, he sighs. When he is perplexed, he wags his chin, he half-smiles. He is like a man who has wandered inadvertently into a play, who has found it to be a comedy, and decided to stay and see it through.

❖

The supper is over; the company dwindles away, into the early dusk. "Perhaps sooner than you would have liked?" he says, to Bonvisi.

"Thomas More is my old friend. You should not come here and bait him."

"Oh, have I spoiled your party? You invited Monmouth; was that not to bait him?"

"No, Humphrey Monmouth is my friend too."

"And I?"

"Of course."

They have slid back naturally into Italian. "Tell me something that intrigues me," he says. "I want to know about Thomas Wyatt." Wyatt went to Italy, having attached himself to a diplomatic mission, rather suddenly: three years ago now. He had a disastrous time there, but that's for another evening; the question is, why did he run away from the English court in such haste?

"Ah. Wyatt and Lady Anne," Bonvisi says. "An old story, I'd have thought?"

Well, perhaps, he says, but he tells him about the boy Mark, the musician, who seems sure Wyatt's had her; if the story's bouncing around Europe, among servants and menials, what are the odds the king hasn't heard?

"A part of the art of ruling, I suppose, is to know when to shut your ears. And Wyatt is handsome," Bonvisi says, "in the English style, of course. He is tall, he is blond, my countrymen marvel at him; where do you breed such people? And so assured, of course. And a poet!"

He laughs at his friend because, like all the Italians, he can't say "Wyatt": it comes out "Guiett," or something like that. There was a man called Hawkwood, a knight of Essex, used to rape and burn and murder in Italy, in the days of chivalry; the Italians called him *Acuto*, the Needle.

"Yes, but Anne . . ." He senses, from his glimpses of her, that she is unlikely to be moved by anything so impermanent as beauty. "These few years she has needed a husband, more than anything: a name, an establishment, a place from which she can stand and negotiate with the king. Now, Wyatt's married. What could he offer her?"

"Verses?" says the merchant. "It wasn't diplomacy took him out of England. It was that she was torturing him. He no longer dared be in the same room with her. The same castle. The same country." He shakes his head. "Aren't the English odd?"

"Christ, aren't they?" he says.

"You must take care. The Lady's family, they are pushing a little against the limit of what can be done. They are saying, why wait for the Pope? Can we not make a marriage contract without him?"

"It would seem to be the way forward."

"Try one of these sugared almonds."

He smiles. Bonvisi says, "Tommaso, I may give you some advice? The cardinal is finished."

"Don't be so sure."

"Yes, and if you did not love him, you would know it was true."

"The cardinal has been nothing but good to me."

"But he must go north."

"The world will chase him. You ask the ambassadors. Ask Chapuys. Ask them who they report to. We have them at Esher, at Richmond. *Toujours les dépêches.* That's us."

"But that is what he is accused of! Running a country within the country!"

He sighs. "I know."

"And what will you do about it?"

"Ask him to be more humble?"

Bonvisi laughs. "Ah, Thomas. Please, you know when he goes north you will be a man without a master. That is the point. You are seeing the king, but it is only for now, while he works out how to give the cardinal a payoff that will keep him quiet. But then?"

He hesitates. "The king likes me."

"The king is an inconstant lover."

"Not to Anne."

"That is where I must warn you. Oh, not because of Guiett . . . not because of any gossip, any light thing said . . . but because it must all end soon . . . she will give way, she is just a woman . . . think how foolish a man would have been if he had linked his fortunes to those of the Lady's sister, who came before her."

"Yes, just think."

He looks around the room. That's where the Lord Chancellor sat. On his left, the hungry merchants. On his right, the new ambassador. There, Humphrey Monmouth the heretic. There, Antonio Bonvisi. Here, Thomas Cromwell. And there are ghostly places set, for the Duke of Suffolk large and bland, for Norfolk jangling his holy medals and shouting "By the Mass!" There is a place set for the king, and for the doughty little queen, famished in this penitential season, her belly quaking inside the stout armor of her robes. There is a place set for Lady Anne, glancing around with her restless black eyes, eating nothing, missing nothing, tugging at the pearls around her little neck. There is a place for William Tyndale, and one for the Pope; Clement looks at the candied quinces, too coarsely cut, and his Medici lip curls. And there sits Brother Martin Luther, greasy and fat: glowering at them all, and spitting out his fish bones.

A servant comes in. "Two young gentlemen are outside, master, asking for you by name."

He looks up. "Yes?"

"Master Richard Cromwell and Master Rafe. With servants from your household, waiting to take you home."

He understands that the whole purpose of the evening has been to warn him: to warn him off. He will remember it, the fatal *placement*: if it proves fatal. That soft hiss and whisper, of stone destroying itself; that distant sound of walls sliding, of plaster crumbling, of rubble crashing onto fragile human skulls? That is the sound of the roof of Christendom, falling on the people below.

Bonvisi says, "You have a private army, Tommaso. I suppose you have to watch your back."

"You know I do." His glance sweeps the room: one last look. "Good night. It was a good supper. I liked the eels. Will you send your cook to see mine? I have a new sauce to brighten the season. One needs mace and ginger, some dried mint leaves chopped—"

His friend says, "I beg of you. I implore you to be careful."

"—a little, but a very little garlic—"

"Wherever you dine next, pray do not—"

"—and of breadcrumbs, a scant handful . . ."

"—sit down with the Boleyns."

II

Entirely Beloved Cromwell

SPRING–DECEMBER 1530

e arrives early at York Place. The baited gulls, penned in their keeping yards, are crying out to their free brothers on the river, who wheel screaming and diving over the palace walls. The car-men are pushing up from the river goods incoming, and the courts smell of baking bread. Some children are bringing fresh rushes, tied in bundles, and they greet him by name. For their civility, he gives each of them a coin, and they stop to talk. "So, you are going to the evil lady. She has bewitched the king, you know? Do you have a medal or a relic, master, to protect you?"

"I had a medal. But I lost it."

"You should ask our cardinal," one child says. "He will give you another."

The scent of the rushes is sharp and green; the morning is fine. The rooms of York Place are familiar to him, and as he passes through them toward the inner chambers he sees a half-familiar face and says, "Mark?"

The boy detaches himself from the wall where he is leaning. "You're about early. How are you?"

A sulky shrug.

"It must feel strange to be back here at York Place, now the world is so altered."

"No."

"You don't miss my lord cardinal?"

"No."

"You are happy?"

"Yes."

"My lord will be pleased to know." To himself he says, as he moves away, you may never think of us, Mark, but we think of you. Or at least I do, I think of you calling me a felon and predicting my death. It is true that the cardinal always says, there are no safe places, there are no sealed rooms, you may as well stand on Cheapside shouting out your sins as confess to a priest anywhere in England. But when I spoke to the cardinal of killing, when I saw a shadow on the wall, there was no one to hear; so if Mark reckons I'm a murderer, that's only because he thinks I look like one.

❖

Eight anterooms: in the last, where the cardinal should be, he finds Anne Boleyn. Look, there are Solomon and Sheba, unrolled again, back on the wall. There is a draft; Sheba eddies toward him, rosy, round, and he acknowledges her: Anselma, lady made of wool, I thought I'd never see you again.

He had sent word back to Antwerp, applied discreetly for news; Anselma was married, Stephen Vaughan said, and to a younger man, a banker. So if he drowns or anything, he said, let me know. Vaughan writes back: Thomas, come now, isn't England full of widows? And fresh young girls?

Sheba makes Anne look bad: sallow and sharp. She stands by the window, her fingers tugging and ripping at a sprig of rosemary. When she sees him, she drops it, and her hands dip back into her trailing sleeves.

In December, the king gave a banquet, to celebrate her father's elevation to be Earl of Wiltshire. The queen was elsewhere, and Anne sat where Katherine should sit. There was frost on the ground, frost in the atmosphere. They only heard of it, in the Wolsey household. The Duchess of Norfolk (who is always furious about something) was furious that her niece should have precedence. The Duchess of Suffolk, Henry's sister, refused to eat. Neither of these great ladies spoke to Boleyn's daughter. Nevertheless, Anne had taken her place as the first lady of the kingdom.

But now it's the end of Lent, and Henry has gone back to his wife; he hasn't the face to be with his concubine as we move toward the week of Christ's Passion. Her father is abroad, on diplomatic business; so is her brother George, now Lord Rochford; so is Thomas Wyatt, the poet whom she tortures. She's alone and bored at York Place; and she's reduced to sending for Thomas Cromwell, to see if he offers any amusement.

A flurry of little dogs—three of them—run away from her skirts, yapping, darting toward him. "Don't let them out," Anne says, and with practiced and gentle hands he scoops them up—they are the kind of dogs, Bellas, with ragged ears and tiny wafting tails, that any merchant's wife would keep, across the Narrow Sea. By the time he has given them back to her, they have nibbled his fingers and his coat, licked his face and yearned toward him with goggling eyes: as if he were someone they had so much longed to meet.

Two of them he sets gently on the floor; the smallest he hands back to Anne. "*Vous êtes gentil,*" she says, "and how my babies like you! I could not love, you know, those apes that Katherine keeps. *Les singes enchaînés.* Their little hands, their little necks fettered. My babies love me for myself."

She's so small. Her bones are so delicate, her waist so narrow; if two law students make one cardinal, two Annes make one Katherine. Various women are sitting on low stools, sewing or rather pretending to sew. One of them is Mary Boleyn. She keeps her head down, as well she might. One of them is Mary Shelton, a bold pink-and-white Boleyn cousin, who looks him over, and—quite obviously—says to herself, Mother of God, is that the best Lady Carey thought she could get? Back in the shadows there is another girl, who has her face turned away, trying to hide. He does not know who she is, but he understands why she's looking fixedly at the floor. Anne seems to inspire it; now that he's put the dogs down, he's doing the same thing.

"*Alors,*" Anne says softly, "suddenly, everything is about you. The king does not cease to quote Master Cromwell." She pronounces it as if she can't manage the English: Cremuel. "He is so right, he is at all points correct . . . Also, let us not forget, Maître Cremuel makes us laugh."

"I see the king does sometimes laugh. But you, madam? In your situation? As you find yourself?"

A black glance, over her shoulder. "I suppose I seldom. Laugh. If I think. But I had not thought."

"This is what your life has come to."

Dusty fragments, dried leaves and stems, have fallen down her skirts. She stares out at the morning.

"Let me put it this way," he says. "Since my lord cardinal was reduced, how much progress have you seen in your cause?"

"None."

"No one knows the workings of Christian countries like my lord cardinal. No one is more intimate with kings. Think how bound to you he would be, Lady Anne, if you were the means of erasing these misunderstandings and restoring him to the king's grace."

She doesn't answer.

"Think," he says. "He is the only man in England who can obtain for you what you need."

"Very well. Make his case. You have five minutes."

"Otherwise, I can see you're really busy."

Anne looks at him with dislike, and speaks in French. "What do you know of how I occupy my hours?"

"My lady, are we having this conversation in English or French? Your choice entirely. But let's make it one or the other, yes?"

He sees a movement from the corner of his eye; the half-hidden girl has raised her face. She is plain and pale; she looks shocked.

"You are indifferent?" Anne says.

"Yes."

"Very well. In French."

He tells her again: the cardinal is the only man who can deliver a good verdict from the Pope. He is the only man who can deliver the king's conscience, and deliver it clean.

She listens. He will say that for her. He has always wondered how well women can hear, beneath the muffling folds of their veils and hoods, but Anne does give the impression that she is hearing what he has said. She waits him out, at least; she doesn't interrupt, until at last she does: so, she says, if the king wants it, and the cardinal wants it, he who was formerly the chief subject in the kingdom, then I must say, Master Cremuel, it is all taking a marvelous long while to come to pass!

From her corner her sister adds, barely audible, "And she's not getting any younger."

Not a stitch have the women added to their sewing since he has been in the room.

"One may resume?" he asks, persuading her. "There is a moment left?"

"Oh yes," Anne says. "But a moment only: in Lent I ration my patience."

He tells her to dismiss the slanderers who claim that the cardinal obstructed her cause. He tells her how it distresses the cardinal that the king should not have his heart's desire, which was ever the cardinal's desire too. He tells her how all the king's subjects repose their hopes in her, for an heir to the throne; and how he is sure they are right to do so. He reminds her of the many gracious letters she has written to the cardinal in times past: all of which he has on file.

"Very nice," she says, when he stops. "Very nice, Master Cremuel, but try again. One thing. One simple thing we asked of the cardinal, and he would not. One simple thing."

"You know it was not simple."

"Perhaps I am a simple person," Anne says. "Do you feel I am?"

"You may be. I hardly know you."

The reply incenses her. He sees her sister smirk. You may go, Anne says: and Mary jumps up, and follows him out.

❖

Once again Mary's cheeks are flushed, her lips are parted. She's brought her sewing with her, which he thinks is strange; but perhaps, if she leaves it behind, Anne pulls the stitches out. "Out of breath again, Lady Carey?"

"We thought she might run up and slap you. Will you come again? Shelton and I can't wait."

"She can stand it," he says, and Mary says, indeed, she likes a skirmish with someone on her own level. What are you working there? he asks, and she shows him. It is Anne's new coat of arms. On everything, I suppose, he says, and she smiles broadly, oh yes, her petticoats, her handkerchiefs, her coifs and her veils; she has garments that no one ever wore before, just so she can have her arms sewn on, not to mention the wall hangings, the table napkins . . .

"And how are you?"

She looks down, glance swiveling away from him. "Worn down. Frayed a little, you might say. Christmas was . . ."

"They quarreled. So one hears."

"First he quarreled with Katherine. Then he came here for sympathy. Anne said, what! I told you not to argue with Katherine, you know you always lose. If he were not a king," she says with relish, "one could pity him. For the dog's life they lead him."

"There have been rumors that Anne—"

"Yes, but she's not. I would be the first to know. If she thickened by an inch, it would be me who let out her clothes. Besides, she can't, because they don't. They haven't."

"She'd tell you?"

"Of course—out of spite!" Still Mary will not meet his eyes. But she seems to feel she owes him information. "When they are alone, she lets him unlace her bodice."

"At least he doesn't call you to do it."

"He pulls down her shift and kisses her breasts."

"Good man if he can find them."

Mary laughs; a boisterous, unsisterly laugh. It must be audible within, because almost at once the door opens and the small hiding girl maneuvers herself around it. Her face is grave, her reserve complete; her skin is so fine that it is almost translucent. "Lady Carey," she says, "Lady Anne wants you."

She speaks their names as if she is making introductions between two cockroaches.

Mary snaps, oh, by the saints! and turns on her heel, whipping her train behind her with the ease of long practice.

❦

To his surprise, the small pale girl catches his glance; behind the retreating back of Mary Boleyn, she raises her own eyes to Heaven.

❖

Walking away—eight antechambers back to the rest of his day—he knows that Anne has stepped forward to a place where he can see her, the morning light lying along the curve of her throat. He sees the thin arch of her eyebrow, her smile, the turn of her head on her long slender neck. He sees her speed, intelligence and rigor. He didn't think she would help the cardinal, but what do you lose by asking? He thinks, it is the first proposition I have put to her; probably not the last.

There was a moment when Anne gave him all her attention: her skewering dark glance. The king, too, knows how to look; blue eyes, their mildness deceptive. Is this how they look at each other? Or in some other way? For a second he understands it; then he doesn't. He stands by a window. A flock of starlings settles among the tight black buds of a bare tree. Then, like black buds unfolding, they open their wings; they flutter and sing, stirring everything into motion, air, wings, black notes in music. He becomes aware that he is watching them with pleasure: that something almost extinct, some small gesture toward the future, is ready to welcome the spring; in some spare, desperate way, he is looking forward to Easter, the end of Lenten fasting, the end of penitence. There is a world beyond this black world. There is a world of the possible. A world where Anne can be queen is a world where Cromwell can be Cromwell. He sees it; then he doesn't. The moment is fleeting. But insight cannot be taken back. You cannot return to the moment you were in before.

❖

In Lent, there are butchers who will sell you red meat, if you know where to go. At Austin Friars he goes down to talk to his kitchen staff, and says to his chief man, "The cardinal is sick, he is dispensed from Lent."

His cook takes off his hat. "By the Pope?"

"By me." He runs his eye along the row of knives in their racks, the cleavers for splitting bones. He picks one up, looks at its edge, decides it needs sharpening and says, "Do you think I look like a murderer? In your good opinion?"

A silence. After a while, Thurston proffers, "At this moment, master, I would have to say . . ."

"No, but suppose I were making my way to Gray's Inn . . . Can you picture to yourself? Carrying a folio of papers and an inkhorn?"

"I do suppose a clerk would be carrying those."

"So you can't picture it?"

Thurston takes off his hat again, and turns it inside out. He looks at it as if his brains might be inside it, or at least some prompt as to what to say next. "I see how you would look like a lawyer. Not like a murderer, no. But if you will forgive me, master, you always look like a man who knows how to cut up a carcass."

He has the kitchen make beef olives for the cardinal, stuffed with sage and marjoram, neatly trussed and placed side by side in trays, so that the cooks at Richmond need do nothing but bake them. Show me where it says in the Bible, a man shall not eat beef olives in March.

He thinks of Lady Anne, her unslaked appetite for a fight; the sad ladies about her. He sends those ladies some flat baskets of small tarts, made of preserved oranges and honey. To Anne herself he sends a dish of almond cream. It is flavored with rose water and decorated with the preserved petals of roses, and with candied violets. He is above riding across the country, carrying food himself; but not that much above it. It's not so many years since the Frescobaldi kitchen in Florence; or perhaps it is, but his memory is clear, exact. He was clarifying calf's-foot jelly, chatting away in his mixture of French, Tuscan and Putney, when somebody shouted, "Tommaso, they want you upstairs." His movements were unhurried as he nodded to a kitchen child, who brought him a basin of water. He washed his hands, dried them on a linen cloth. He took off his apron and hung it on a peg. For all he knows, it is there still.

He saw a young boy—younger than him—on hands and knees, scrubbing the steps. He sang as he worked:

"Scaramella va alla guerra
Colla lancia et la rotella
La zombero boro borombetta,
La boro borombo . . ."

"If you please, Giacomo," he said. To let him pass, the boy moved aside, into the curve of the wall. A shift of the light wiped the curiosity from his face, blanking it, fading his past into the past, washing the future clean. Scaramella is off to war . . . But I've been to war, he thought.

He had gone upstairs. In his ears the roll and stutter of the song's military drum. He had gone upstairs and never come down again. In a corner of the Frescobaldi countinghouse, a table was waiting for him. *Scaramella fa la gala,* he hummed. He had taken his place. Sharpened a quill. His thoughts bubbled and swirled, Tuscan, Putney, Castilian oaths. But when he committed his thoughts to paper they came out in Latin and perfectly smooth.

❖

Even before he walks in from the kitchens at Austin Friars, the women of the house know that he has been to see Anne.

"So," Johane demands. "Tall or short?"

"Neither."

"I'd heard she was very tall. Sallow, is she not?"

"Yes, sallow."

"They say she is graceful. Dances well."

"We did not dance."

Mercy says, "But what do you think? A friend to the gospel?"

He shrugs. "We did not pray."

Alice, his little niece: "What was she wearing?"

Ah, I can tell you that; he prices and sources her, hood to hem, foot to fingertip. For her headdress Anne affects the French style, the round hood flattering the fine bones of her face. He explains this, and though his tone is cool, mercantile, the women somehow do not appreciate it.

"You don't like her, do you?" Alice says, and he says it's not for him to have an opinion; or you either, Alice, he says, hugging her and making her giggle. The child Jo says, our master is in a good mood. This squirrel trim, Mercy says, and he says, Calabrian. Alice says, oh, Calabrian, and wrinkles her nose; Johane remarks, I must say, Thomas, it seems you got close.

"Are her teeth good?" Mercy says.

"For God's sake, woman: when she sinks them into me, I'll let you know."

❖

When the cardinal had heard that the Duke of Norfolk was coming out to Richmond to tear him with his teeth, he had laughed and said, "Marry, Thomas, time to be going."

But to go north, the cardinal needs funding. The problem is put to the king's council, who fall out, and continue the quarrel in his hearing. "After all," Charles Brandon says, "one can't let an archbishop creep away to his enthronement like a servant who's stolen the spoons."

"He's done more than steal the spoons," Norfolk says. "He's eaten the dinner that would have fed all England. He's filched the tablecloth, by God, and drunk the cellar dry."

The king can be elusive. One day when he thinks he has an appointment to meet Henry, he gets Master Secretary instead. "Sit down," Gardiner says. "Sit down and listen to me. Contain yourself in patience, while I put you straight on a few matters."

He watches him ranging to and fro, Stephen the noonday devil. Gardiner is a man with bones loose-jointed, his lines flowing with menace; he has great hairy hands, and knuckles which crack when he folds his right fist into his left palm.

He takes away the menace conveyed, and the message. Pausing in the doorway, he says mildly, "Your cousin sends greetings."

Gardiner stares at him. His eyebrows bristle, like a dog's hackles. He thinks that Cromwell presumes—

"Not the king," he says soothingly. "Not His Majesty. I mean your cousin Richard Williams."

Aghast, Gardiner says, "That old tale!"

"Oh, come," he says. "It's no disgrace to be a royal bastard. Or so we think, in my family."

"In your family? What grasp have they on propriety? I have no interest in this young person, recognize no kinship with him, and I will do nothing for him."

"Truly, you don't need to. He calls himself Richard Cromwell now." As he is going—really going, this time—he adds, "Don't let it keep you awake, Stephen. I have been into the matter. You may be related to Richard, but you are not related to me."

He smiles. Inside, he is beside himself with rage, running with it, as if his blood were thin and full of dilute venom like the uncolored blood of a snake. As soon as he gets home to Austin Friars, he hugs Rafe Sadler and makes his hair stand up in spikes. "Heaven direct me: boy or hedgehog? Rafe, Richard, I am feeling penitent."

"It is the season," Rafe says.

"I want," he says, "to become perfectly calm. I want to be able to get into the coop without ruffling the chickens' feathers. I want to be less like Uncle Norfolk, and more like Marlinspike."

He has a long soothing talk in Welsh with Richard, who laughs at him because old words are fading from his memory, and he is forever sliding through bits of English, with a sly borderlands intonation. He gives his little nieces the pearl and coral bracelets he bought them weeks ago, but forgot to give. He goes down to the kitchen and makes suggestions, all of them cheerful.

He calls his household staff together, his clerks. "We need to plan it," he says, "how the cardinal will be made comfortable on the road north. He wants to go slowly so the people can admire him. He needs to arrive in Peterborough for Holy Week, and from there shift by stages to Southwell, where he will plan his further progress to York. The archbishop's palace at Southwell has good rooms, but still we may need to get builders in . . ."

George Cavendish has told him that the cardinal has taken to spending time in prayer. There are some monks at Richmond whose company he has sought; they spell out to him the value of thorns in the flesh and salt in the wound, the merits of bread and water and the somber delights of self-flagellation. "Oh, that settles it," he says, annoyed. "We have to get him on the road. He'd be better off in Yorkshire."

He says to Norfolk, "Well, my lord, how shall we do this? Do you want him gone or not? Yes? Then come to the king with me."

Norfolk grunts. Messages are sent. A day or so later, they find themselves together in an antechamber. They wait. Norfolk paces. "Oh, by St. Jude!" the duke says. "Shall we get some fresh air? Or don't you lawyers need it?"

They stroll in the gardens; or, he strolls, the duke stamps. "When do the flowers come out?" the duke says. "When I was a boy, we never had flowers. It was Buckingham, you know, who brought in this knot garden sort of stuff. Oh dear, it was fancy!"

The Duke of Buckingham, keen gardener, had his head cut off for treason. That was 1521: less than ten years ago. It seems sad to mention it now, in the presence of the spring: singing from every bush, every bough.

A summons is received. As they proceed to their interview, the duke balks and jibs; his eye rolls and his nostrils distend, his breath comes short. When the duke lays a hand on his shoulder, he is forced to slow his pace, and they scuffle along—he resisting his impulse to pull away—like two war veterans in a beggars' procession. *Scaramella va alla guerra* . . . Norfolk's hand is trembling.

But it is only when they get into the presence that he fully understands how it rattles the old duke to be in a room with Henry Tudor. The gilded ebullience makes him shrink inside his clothes. Henry greets them cordially. He says it is a wonderful day and pretty much a wonderful world. He spins around the room, arms wide, reciting some verses of his own composition. He will talk about anything except the cardinal. Frustrated, Norfolk turns a dusky red, and begins to mutter. Dismissed, they are backing out. Henry calls, "Oh, Cromwell . . ."

He and the duke exchange glances. "By the Mass . . ." mutters the duke.

Hand behind his back, he indicates, be gone, my lord Norfolk, I'll catch up with you later.

Henry stands with arms folded, eyes on the ground. He says nothing till he, Cromwell, has come close. "A thousand pounds?" Henry whispers.

It is on the tip of his tongue to say, that will be a start on the ten thousand which, to the best of my knowledge and belief, you have owed the Cardinal of York for a decade now.

He doesn't say it, of course. At such moments, Henry expects you to fall to your knees—duke, earl, commoner, light and heavy, old and young. He does it; scar tissue pulls; few of us, by our forties, are not carrying injuries.

The king signals, you can get up. He adds, his tone curious, "The Duke of Norfolk shows you many marks of friendship and favor."

The hand on the shoulder, he means: the minute and unexpected vibration of ducal palm against plebeian muscle and bone. "The duke is careful to preserve all distinctions of rank." Henry seems relieved.

An unwelcome thought creeps into his head: what if you, Henry Tudor, were to be taken ill and fall at my feet? Am I allowed to pick you up, or must I send for an earl to do it? Or a bishop?

Henry walks away. He turns and says, in a small voice, "Every day I miss the Cardinal of York." There is a pause. He whispers, take the money with our blessing. Don't tell the duke. Don't tell anyone. Ask your master to pray for me. Tell him it is the best I can do.

The thanks he makes, still from his kneeling situation, is eloquent and extensive. Henry looks at him bleakly and says, dear God, Master Cromwell, you can talk, can't you?

He goes out, face composed, fighting the impulse to smile broadly. *Scaramella fa la gala* . . . "Every day I miss the Cardinal of York."

Norfolk says, what, what, what did he say? Oh, nothing, he says. Just some special hard words he wants me to convey to the cardinal.

❖

The itinerary is drawn up. The cardinal's effects are put on coastal barges, to be taken to Hull and go overland from there. He himself has beaten the bargees down to a reasonable rate.

He tells Richard, you know, a thousand pounds isn't much when you have a cardinal to move. Richard asks, "How much of your own money is sunk in this enterprise?"

Some debts should never be tallied, he says. "I myself, I know what is owed me, but by God I know what I owe."

To Cavendish he says, "How many servants is he taking?"

"Only a hundred and sixty."

"Only." He nods. "Right."

Hendon. Royston. Huntingdon. Peterborough. He has men riding ahead, with precise instructions.

❖

That last night, Wolsey gives him a package. Inside it is a small and hard object, a seal or ring. "Open it when I'm gone."

People keep walking in and out of the cardinal's private chamber, carrying chests and bundles of papers. Cavendish wanders through, holding a silver monstrance.

"You will come north?" the cardinal says.

"I'll come to fetch you, the minute the king summons you back." He believes and does not believe that this will happen.

The cardinal gets to his feet. There is a constraint in the air. He, Cromwell, kneels for a blessing. The cardinal holds out a hand to be kissed. His turquoise ring is missing. The fact does not evade him. For a moment, the cardinal's hand rests on his shoulder, fingers spread, thumb in the hollow of his collarbone.

It is time he was gone. So much has been said between them that it is needless to add a marginal note. It is not for him now to gloss the text of their dealings, nor append a moral. This is not the occasion to embrace. If the cardinal has no more eloquence to offer, he surely has none. Before he has reached the door of the room the cardinal has turned back to the fireplace. He pulls his chair to the blaze, and raises a hand to shield his face; but his hand is not between himself and the fire, it is between himself and the closing door.

He makes for the courtyard. He falters; in a smoky recess where the light has extinguished itself, he leans against the wall. He is crying. He says to himself, let George Cavendish not come by and see me, and write it down and make it into a play.

He swears softly, in many languages: at life, at himself for giving way to its demands. Servants walk past, saying, "Master Cromwell's horse is here for him! Master Cromwell's escort at the gate!" He waits till he is in command of himself, and exits, disbursing coins.

When he gets home, the servants ask him, are we to paint out the cardinal's coat of arms? No, by God, he says. On the contrary, repaint it. He stands back for a look. "The choughs could look more lively. And we need a better scarlet for the hat."

He hardly sleeps. He dreams of Liz. He wonders if she would know him, the man he vows that soon he will be: adamant, mild, a keeper of the king's peace.

❖

Toward dawn, he dozes; he wakes up thinking, the cardinal just now will be mounting his horse; why am I not with him? It is April 5. Johane meets him on the stairs; chastely, she kisses his cheek.

"Why does God test us?" she whispers.

He murmurs, "I do not feel we will pass."

He says, perhaps I should go up to Southwell myself? I'll go for you, Rafe says. He gives him a list. Have the whole of the archbishop's palace scrubbed out. My lord will be bringing his own bed. Draft in kitchen staff from the King's Arms. Check the stabling. Get in musicians. Last time I passed through I noticed some pigsties up against the palace wall. Find out the owner, pay him off and knock them down. Don't drink in the Crown; the ale is worse than my father's.

Richard says, "Sir . . . it is time to let the cardinal go."

"This is a tactical retreat, not a rout."

They think he's gone but he's only gone into a back room. He skulks among the files. He hears Richard say, "His heart is leading him."

"It is an experienced heart."

"But can a general organize a retreat when he doesn't know where the enemy is? The king is so double in this matter."

"One could retreat straight into his arms."

"Jesus. You think our master is double too?"

"Triple at least," Rafe says. "Look, there was no profit for him, ever, in deserting the old man—what would he get but the name of deserter? Perhaps something is to be got by sticking fast. For all of us."

"Off you go then, swine-boy. Who else would think about the pigsties? Thomas More, for instance, would never think about them."

"Or he would be exhorting the pig-keeper, my good man, Easter approacheth—"

"—hast thou prepared to receive Holy Communion?" Rafe laughs. "By the way, Richard, hast thou?"

Richard says, "I can get a piece of bread any day in the week."

❖

During Holy Week, reports come in from Peterborough: more people have crowded in to look at Wolsey than have been in that town in living memory. As the cardinal moves north he follows him on the map of these islands he keeps in his head. Stamford, Grantham, Newark; the traveling court arrives in Southwell on April 28. He, Cromwell, writes to soothe him, he writes to warn him. He is afraid that the Boleyns, or Norfolk, or both, have found some way of implanting a spy in the cardinal's retinue.

The ambassador Chapuys, hurrying away from an audience with the king, has touched his sleeve, drawn him aside. "Monsieur Cremuel, I thought to call at your house. We are neighbors, you know."

"I should like to welcome you."

"But people inform me you are often with the king now, which is pleasant, is it not? Your old master, I hear from him every week. He has become solicitous about the queen's health. He asks if she is in good spirits, and begs her to consider that soon she will be restored to the king's bosom. And bed." Chapuys smiles. He is enjoying himself. "The concubine will not help him. We know you have tried with her and failed. So now he turns back to the queen."

He is forced to ask, "And the queen says?"

"She says, I hope God in his mercy finds it possible to forgive the cardinal, for I never can." Chapuys waits. He does not speak. The ambassador resumes: "I think you are sensible of the tangle of wreckage that will be left if this divorce is granted, or, shall we say, somehow extorted from His Holiness? The Emperor, in defense of his aunt, may make war on England. Your merchant friends will lose their livelihoods, and many will lose their lives. Your Tudor king may go down, and the old nobility come into their own."

"Why are you telling me this?"

"I am telling all Englishmen."

"Door-to-door?"

He is meant to pass to the cardinal this message: that he has come to the end of his credit with the Emperor. What will that do but drive him into an appeal to the French king? Either way, treason lies.

He imagines the cardinal among the canons at Southwell, in his chair in the chapter house, presiding beneath the high vaulting like a prince at his ease in some forest glade, wreathed by carvings of leaves and flowers. They are so supple that it is as if the columns, the ribs have quickened, as if stone has burst into florid life; the capitals are decked with berries, finials are twisted stems, roses entangle the shafts, flowers and seeds flourish on one stalk; from the foliage, faces peers, the faces of dogs, of hares, of goats. There are human faces, too, so lifelike that perhaps they can change their expression; perhaps they stare down, astonished, at the portly scarlet form of his patron; and perhaps in the silence of the night, when the canons are sleeping, the stone men whistle and sing.

In Italy he learned a memory system and furnished it with pictures. Some are drawn from wood and field, from hedgerow and copse: shy hiding animals, eyes bright in the undergrowth. Some are foxes and deer, some are griffins, dragons. Some are men and women: nuns, warriors, doctors of the church. In their hands he puts unlikely objects, St. Ursula a crossbow, St. Jerome a scythe, while Plato bears a soup ladle and Achilles a dozen damsons in a wooden bowl. It is no use hoping to remember with the help of common objects, familiar faces. One needs startling juxtapositions, images that are more or less peculiar, ridiculous, even indecent. When you have made the images, you place them about the world in locations you choose, each one with its parcel of words, of figures, which they will yield you on demand. At Greenwich, a shaven cat may peep at you from behind a cupboard; at the palace of Westminster, a snake may leer down from a beam and hiss your name.

Some of these images are flat, and you can walk on them. Some are clothed in skin and walk around in a room, but perhaps they are men with their heads on backward, or with tufted tails like the leopards in coats of arms. Some scowl at you like Norfolk, or gape at you, like my lord Suffolk, with bewilderment. Some speak, some quack. He keeps them, in strict order, in the gallery of his mind's eye.

Perhaps it is because he is used to making these images that his head is peopled with the cast of a thousand plays, ten thousand interludes. It is because of this practice that he tends to glimpse his dead wife lurking in a stairwell, her white face upturned, or whisking around a corner of the Austin Friars, or the house at Stepney. Now the image is beginning to merge with that of her sister Johane, and everything that belonged to Liz is beginning to belong to her: her half-smile, her questioning glance, her way of being naked. Till he says, enough, and scrubs her out of his mind.

Rafe rides up the country with messages to Wolsey too secret to put into letters. He would go himself, but though Parliament is prorogued he cannot get away, because he is afraid of what might be said about Wolsey if he is not there to defend him; and at short notice the king might want him, or Lady Anne. "And although I am not with you in person," he writes, "yet be assured I am, and during my life shall be, with Your Grace in heart, spirit, prayer and service . . ."

The cardinal replies: he is "mine own good, trusty and most assured refuge in this my calamity." He is "mine own entirely beloved Cromwell."

He writes to ask for quails. He writes to ask for flower seeds. "Seeds?" Johane says. "He is planning to take root?"

❖

Twilight finds the king melancholy. Another day of regress, in his campaign to be a married man again; he denies, of course, that he is married to the queen. "Cromwell," he says, "I need to find my way to ownership of those . . ." He looks sidelong, not wishing to say what he means. "I understand there are legal difficulties. I do not pretend to understand them. And before you begin, I do not want them explained."

The cardinal has endowed his Oxford college, as also the school at Ipswich, with land that will produce an income in perpetuity. Henry wants their silver and gold plate, their libraries, their yearly revenues and the land that produces the revenues; and he does not see why he should not have what he wants. The wealth of twenty-nine monasteries has gone into those foundations—suppressed by permission of the Pope, on condition that the proceeds were used for the colleges. But do you know, Henry says, I am beginning to care very little about the Pope and his permissions?

It is early summer. The evenings are long and the grass, the air, scented. You would think that a man like Henry, on a night like this, could go to whichever bed he pleases. The court is full of eager women. But after this interview he will walk in the garden with Lady Anne, her hand resting on his arm, deep in conversation; then he will go to his empty bed, and she, one presumes, to hers.

When the king asks him what he hears from the cardinal, he says that he misses the light of His Majesty's countenance; that preparations for his enthronement at York are in hand. "Then why doesn't he get to York? It seems to me he delays and delays." Henry glares at him. "I will say this for you. You stick by your man."

"I have never had anything from the cardinal other than kindness. Why would I not?"

"And you have no other master," the king says. "My lord Suffolk asks me, where does the fellow spring from? I tell him there are Cromwells in Leicestershire, Northamptonshire—landed people, or once they were. I suppose you are from some unfortunate branch of that family?"

"No."

"You may not know your own forebears. I shall ask the heralds to look into it."

"Your Majesty is kind. But they will have scant success."

The king is exasperated. He is failing to take advantage of what is on offer: a pedigree, however meager. "My lord cardinal told me you were an orphan. He told me you were brought up in a monastery."

"Ah. That was one of his little stories."

"He told me little stories?" Several expressions chase each other across the king's face: annoyance, amusement, a wish to call back times past. "I suppose he did. He told me that you had a loathing of those in the religious life. That was why he found you diligent in his work."

"That was not the reason." He looks up. "May I speak?"

"Oh, for God's sake," Henry cries. "I wish someone would."

He is startled. Then he understands. Henry wants a conversation, on any topic. One that's nothing to do with love, or hunting, or war. Now that Wolsey's gone, there's not much scope for it; unless you want to talk to a priest of some stripe. And if you send for a priest, what does it come back to? To love; to Anne; to what you want and can't have.

"If you ask me about the monks, I speak from experience, not prejudice, and though I have no doubt that some foundations are well governed, my experience has been of waste and corruption. May I suggest to Your Majesty that, if you wish to see a parade of the seven deadly sins, you do not organize a masque at court but call without notice at a monastery? I have seen monks who live like great lords, on the offerings of poor people who would rather buy a blessing than buy bread, and that is not Christian conduct. Nor do I take the monasteries to be the repositories of learning some believe they are. Was Grocyn a monk, or Colet, or Linacre, or any of our great scholars? They were university men. The monks take in children and use them as servants, they don't even teach them dog Latin. I don't grudge them some bodily comforts. It cannot always be Lent. What I cannot stomach is hypocrisy, fraud, idleness—their worn-out relics, their thread-bare worship, and their lack of invention. When did anything good last come from a monastery? They do not invent, they only repeat, and what they repeat is corrupt. For hundreds of years the monks have held the pen, and what they have written is what we take to be our history, but I do not believe it really is. I believe they have suppressed the history they don't like, and written one that is favorable to Rome."

Henry appears to look straight through him, to the wall behind. He waits. Henry says, "Dogholes, then?"

He smiles.

Henry says, "Our history . . . As you know, I am gathering evidence. Manuscripts. Opinions. Comparisons, with how matters are ordered in other countries. Perhaps you would consult with those learned gentlemen. Put a little direction into their efforts. Talk to Dr. Cranmer—he will tell you what is needed. I could make good use of the money that flows yearly to Rome. King François is richer by far than I am. I do not have a tenth of his subjects. He taxes them as he pleases. For my part, I must call Parliament. If I do not, there are riots." He adds, bitterly, "And riots if I do."

"Take no lessons from King François," he says. "He likes war too much, and trade too little."

Henry smiles faintly. "You do not think so, but to me that is the remit of a king."

"There is more tax to be raised when trade is good. And if taxes are resisted, there may be other ways."

Henry nods. "Very well. Begin with the colleges. Sit down with my lawyers."

Harry Norris is there to show him out of the king's private rooms. Not smiling for once, rather stern, he says, "I wouldn't be his tax collector."

He thinks, are the most remarkable moments of my life to be spent under the scrutiny of Henry Norris?

"He killed his father's best men. Empson, Dudley. Didn't the cardinal get one of their houses?"

A spider scuttles from under a stool and presents him with a fact. "Empson's house on Fleet Street. Granted the ninth of October, the first year of this reign."

"This glorious reign," Norris says: as if he were issuing a correction.

❖

Gregory is fifteen as summer begins. He sits a horse beautifully, and there are good reports of his swordsmanship. His Greek . . . well, his Greek is where it was.

But he has a problem. "People in Cambridge are laughing at my greyhounds."

"Why?" The black dogs are a matched pair. They have curving muscled necks and dainty feet; they keep their eyes lowered, mild and demure, till they sight prey.

"They say, why would you have dogs that people can't see at night? Only felons have dogs like that. They say I hunt in the forests, against the law. They say I hunt badgers, like a churl."

"What do you want?" he asks. "White ones, or some spots of color?"

"Either would be correct."

"I'll take your black dogs." Not that he has time to go out, but Richard or Rafe will use them.

"But what if people laugh?"

"Really, Gregory," Johane says. "This is your father. I assure you, no one will dare laugh."

When the weather is too wet to hunt, Gregory sits poring over *The Golden Legend;* he likes the lives of the saints. "Some of these things are true," he says, "some not." He reads *Le Morte d'Arthur,* and because it is the new edition they crowd around him, looking over his shoulder at the title page. "Here beginneth the first book of the most noble and worthy prince King Arthur sometime King of Great Britain . . ." In the forefront of the picture, two couples embrace. On a high-stepping horse is a man with a mad hat, made of coiled tubes like fat serpents. Alice says, sir, did you wear a hat like that when you were young, and he says, I had a different color for each day in the week, but mine were bigger.

Behind this man, a woman rides pillion. "Do you think this represents Lady Anne?" Gregory asks. "They say the king does not like to be parted from her, so he perches her up behind him like a farmer's wife." The woman has big eyes, and looks sick from jolting; it might just be Anne. There is a small castle, not much taller than a man, with a plank for a drawbridge. The birds, circling above, look like flying daggers. Gregory says, "Our king takes his descent from this Arthur. He was never really dead but waited in the forest biding his time, or possibly in a lake. He is several centuries old. Merlin is a wizard. He comes later. You will see. There are twenty-one chapters. If it keeps on raining I mean to read them all. Some of these things are true and some of them lies. But they are all good stories."

❖

When the king next calls him to court, he wants a message sent to Wolsey. A Breton merchant whose ship was seized by the English eight years ago is complaining he has not had the compensation promised. No one can find the paperwork. It was the cardinal who handled the case—will he remember it? "I'm sure he will," he says. "That will be the ship with powdered pearls for ballast, the hold packed with unicorns' horns?"

God forbid! says Charles Brandon; but the king laughs and says, "That will be the one."

"If the sums are in doubt, or indeed the whole case, may I look after it?"

The king hesitates. "I'm not sure you have a *locus standi* in the matter."

It is at this moment that Brandon, quite unexpectedly, gives him a testimonial. "Harry, let him. When this fellow has finished, the Breton will be paying you."

Dukes revolve in their spheres. When they confer, it is not for pleasure in each other's society; they like to be surrounded by their own courts, by men who reflect them and are subservient to them. For pleasure, they are as likely to be found with a kennelman as another duke; so it is that he spends an amiable hour with Brandon, looking over the king's hounds. It is not yet the season for hunting the hart, so the running dogs are well fed in their kennels; their musical barking rises into the evening air, and the tracking dogs, silent as they are trained to be, rise on their hind legs and watch, dripping saliva, the progress of their suppers. The kennel children are carrying baskets of bread and bones, buckets of offal and basins of pigs'-blood pottage. Charles Brandon inhales, appreciative: like a dowager in a rose garden.

A huntsman calls forward a favorite bitch, white patched with chestnut, Barbada, four years old. He straddles her and pulls back her head to show her eyes, clouded with a fine film. He will hate to kill her, but he doubts she will be much use this season. He, Cromwell, cups the bitch's jaw in his hand. "You can draw off the membrane with a curved needle. I've seen it done. You need a steady hand and to be quick. She doesn't like it, but then she won't like to be blind." He runs his hand over her ribs, feels the panicked throb of her little animal heart. "The needle must be very fine. And just this length." He shows them, between finger and thumb. "Let me talk to your smith."

Suffolk looks sideways at him. "You're a useful sort of man."

They walk away. The duke says, "Look here. The problem is my wife." He waits. "I have always wanted Henry to have what he wants, I have always been loyal to him. Even when he was talking about cutting my head off because I'd married his sister. But now, what am I to do? Katherine is the queen. Surely? My wife was always a friend of hers. She's beginning to talk of, I don't know, I'd give my life for the queen, that sort of thing. And for Norfolk's niece to have precedence over my wife, who was Queen of France—we can't live with it. You see?"

He nods. I see. "Besides," the duke says, "I hear Wyatt is due back from Calais." Yes, and? "I wonder if I ought to tell him. Tell Henry, I mean. Poor devil."

"My lord, leave it alone," he says. The duke lapses into what, in another man, you would call silent thought.

❖

Summer: the king is hunting. If he wants him, he has to chase him, and if he is sent for, he goes. Henry visits, on his summer progress, his friends in Wiltshire, in Sussex, in Kent, or stays at his own houses, or the ones he has taken from the cardinal. Sometimes, even now, the queen in her stout little person rides out with a bow, when the king hunts within one of his great parks, or in some lord's park, where the deer are driven to the archers. Lady Anne rides too—on separate occasions—and enjoys the pursuit. But there is a season to leave the ladies at home, and ride into the forest with the trackers and the running hounds; to rise before dawn when the light is clouded like a pearl; to consult with the huntsman, and then unharbor the chosen stag. You do not know where the chase will end, or when.

Harry Norris says to him, laughing, your turn soon, Master Cromwell, if he continues to favor you as he does. A word of advice: as the day begins, and you ride out, pick a ditch. Picture it in your mind. When he has worn out three good horses, when the horn is blowing for another chase, you will be dreaming of that ditch, you will imagine lying down in it: dead leaves and cool ditch-water will be all you desire.

He looks at Norris: his charming self-deprecation. He thinks, you were with my cardinal at Putney, when he fell on his knees in the dirt; did you offer the pictures in your head to the court, to the world, to the students of Gray's Inn? For if not you, then who?

In the forest you may find yourself lost, without companions. You may come to a river which is not on a map. You may lose sight of your quarry, and forget why you are there. You may meet a dwarf, or the living Christ, or an old enemy of yours; or a new enemy, one you do not know until you see his face appear between the rustling leaves, and see the glint of his dagger. You may find a woman asleep in a bower of leaves. For a moment, before you don't recognize her, you will think she is someone you know.

❖

At Austin Friars, there is little chance to be alone, or alone with just one person. Every letter of the alphabet watches you. In the counting-house there is young Thomas Avery, whom you are training up to take a grip on your private finances. Midway through the letters comes Marlinspike, strolling in the garden with his observant golden eyes. Toward the end of the alphabet comes Thomas Wriothesley pronounced Risley. He is a bright young man, twenty-five or so and well connected, son of York Herald, nephew to Garter King-at-Arms. In Wolsey's household he worked under your direction, then was carried away by Gardiner, as Master Secretary, to work for him. Now he is sometimes at court, sometimes at Austin Friars. He's Stephen's spy, the children say—Richard and Rafe.

Master Wriothesley is tall, with red-blond hair, but without the propensity of others of that complexion—the king, let's say—to grow pink when gratified, or mottled when crossed; he is always pale and cool, always his handsome self, always composed. At Trinity Hall he was a great actor in the students' plays, and he has certain affectations, a consciousness of himself, of how he appears; they mimic him behind his back, Richard and Rafe, and say, "My name is Wri-oth-es-ley, but as I wish to spare you effort, you can call me Risley." They say, he only complicates his name like that so he can come here and sign things, and use up our ink. They say, you know Gardiner, he is too angry to use long names, Gardiner just calls him "you." They are pleased with this joke and for a while, every time Mr. W. appears, they shout, "It's you!"

Have mercy, he says, on Master Wriothesley. Cambridge men should have our respect.

He would like to ask them, Richard, Rafe, Master Wriothesley call me Risley: do I look like a murderer? There is a boy who says I do.

This year, there has been no summer plague. Londoners give thanks on their knees. On St. John's Eve, the bonfires burn all night. At dawn, white lilies are carried in from the fields. The city daughters with shivering fingers weave them into drooping garlands, to pin on the city's gates, and on city doors.

He thinks about that little girl like a white flower; the girl with Lady Anne, who maneuvered herself around the door. It would have been easy to find out her name, except he didn't, because he was busy finding out secrets from Mary. Next time he sees her . . . but what's the use of thinking of it? She will come of some noble house. He had meant to write to Gregory and say, I have seen such a sweet girl, I will find out who she is and, if I steer our family adroitly in the next few years, perhaps you can marry her.

He has not written this. In his present precarious situation, it would be about as useful as the letters Gregory used to write to him:

Dear father, I hope you are well. I hope your dog is well. And now no more for lack of time.

❖

Lord Chancellor More says, "Come and see me, and we'll talk about Wolsey's colleges. I feel sure the king will do something for the poor scholars. Do come. Come and see my roses before the heat spoils them. Come and see my new carpet."

It is a muted, gray day; when he arrives at Chelsea, Master Secretary's barge is tied up, the Tudor flag limp in the sultry air. Beyond the gatehouse, the redbrick house, new-built, offers its bright facade to the river. He strolls toward it, through the mulberry trees. Standing in the porch, under the honeysuckle, Stephen Gardiner. The grounds at Chelsea are full of small pet animals, and as he approaches, and his host greets him, he sees that the Chancellor of England is holding a lop-eared rabbit with snowy fur; it hangs peacefully in his hands, like ermine mittens.

"Is your son-in-law Roper with us today?" Gardiner asks. "A pity. I hoped to see him change his religion again. I wanted to witness it."

"A garden tour?" More offers.

"I thought that we might see him sit down a friend of Luther, as formerly he was, yet come back to the church by the time they bring in the currants and gooseberries."

"Will Roper is now settled," More says, "in the faith of England and of Rome."

He says, "It's not really a good year for soft fruit."

More looks at him out of the tail of his eye; he smiles. He chats genially as he leads them into the house. Lolloping after them comes Henry Pattinson, a servant of More's he sometimes calls his fool, and to whom he allows license. The man is a great brawler; normally you take in a fool to protect him, but in Pattinson's case it's the rest of the world needs protection. Is he really simple? There's something sly in More, he enjoys embarrassing people; it would be like him to have a fool that wasn't. Pattinson's supposed to have fallen from a church steeple and hit his head. At his waist, he wears a knotted string which he sometimes says is his rosary; sometimes he says it is his scourge. Sometimes he says it is the rope that should have saved him from his fall.

Entering the house, you meet the family hanging up. You see them painted life-size before you meet them in the flesh; and More, conscious of the double effect it makes, pauses, to let you survey them, to take them in. The favorite, Meg, sits at her father's feet with a book on her knee. Gathered loosely about the Lord Chancellor are his son John; his ward Anne Cresacre, who is John's wife; Margaret Giggs, who is also his ward; his aged father, Sir John More; his daughters Cicely and Elizabeth; Pattinson, with goggle eyes; and his wife, Alice, with lowered head and wearing a cross, at the edge of the picture. Master Holbein has grouped them under his gaze, and fixed them forever: as long as no moth consumes, no flame or mold or blight.

In real life there is something fraying about their host, a suspicion of unraveling weave; being at his leisure, he wears a simple wool gown. The new carpet, for their inspection, is stretched out on two trestle tables. The ground is not crimson but a blush color: not rose madder, he thinks, but a red dye mixed with whey. "My lord cardinal liked turkey carpets," he murmurs. "The Doge once sent him sixty." The wool is soft wool from mountain sheep, but none of them were black sheep; where the pattern is darkest the surface has already a brittle feel, from patchy dyeing, and with time and use it may flake away. He turns up the corner, runs his fingertips over the knots, counting them by the inch, in an easy accustomed action. "This is the Ghiordes knot," he says, "but the pattern is from Pergamon—you see there within the octagons, the eight-pointed star?" He smooths down the corner, and walks away from it, turns back, says "there"—he walks forward, puts a tender hand on the flaw, the interruption in the weave, the lozenge slightly distorted, warped out of true. At worst, the carpet is two carpets, pieced together. At best, it has been woven by the village's Pattinson, or patched together last year by Venetian slaves in a backstreet workshop. To be sure, he needs to turn the whole thing over. His host says, "Not a good buy?"

It's beautiful, he says, not wanting to spoil his pleasure. But next time, he thinks, take me with you. His hand skims the surface, rich and soft. The flaw in the weave hardly matters. A turkey carpet is not on oath. There are some people in this world who like everything squared up and precise, and there are those who will allow some drift at the margins. He is both these kinds of person. He would not allow, for example, a careless ambiguity in a lease, but instinct tells him that sometimes a contract need not be drawn too tight. Leases, writs, statutes, all are written to be read, and each person reads them by the light of self-interest. More says, "What do you think, gentlemen? Walk on it, or hang it on the wall?"

"Walk on it."

"Thomas, your luxurious tastes!" And they laugh. You would think they were friends.

They go out to the aviary; they stand deep in talk, while finches flit and sing. A small grandchild toddles in; a woman in an apron shadows him, or her. The child points to the finches, makes sounds expressive of pleasure, flaps its arms. It eyes Stephen Gardiner; its small mouth turns down. The nurse swoops in, before tears ensue; how must it be, he asks Stephen, to have such effortless power over the young? Stephen scowls.

More takes him by the arm. "Now, about the colleges," he says. "I have spoken to the king, and Master Secretary here has done his best—truly, he has. The king may refound Cardinal College in his name, but for Ipswich I see no hope, after all it is only . . . I am sorry to say this, Thomas, but it is only the birthplace of a man now disgraced, and so has no special claim on us."

"It is a shame for the scholars."

"It is, of course. Shall we go in to supper?"

❖

In More's great hall, the conversation is exclusively in Latin, though More's wife, Alice, is their hostess and does not have a word of it. It is their custom to read a passage of scripture, by way of a grace. "It is Meg's turn tonight," More says.

He is keen to show off his darling. She takes the book, kissing it;

over the interruptions of the fool, she reads in Greek. Gardiner sits with his eyes shut tight; he looks, not holy, but exasperated. He watches Margaret. She is perhaps twenty-five. She has a sleek, darting head, like the head of the little fox which More says he has tamed; all the same, he keeps it in a cage for safety.

The servants come in. It is Alice's eye they catch as they place the dishes; here, madam, and here? The family in the picture don't need servants, of course; they exist just by themselves, floating against the wall. "Eat, eat," says More. "All except Alice, who will burst out of her corset."

At her name she turns her head. "That expression of painful surprise is not native to her," More says. "It is produced by scraping back her hair and driving in great ivory pins, to the peril of her skull. She believes her forehead is too low. It is, of course. Alice, Alice," he says, "remind me why I married you."

"To keep house, Father," Meg says in a low voice.

"Yes, yes," More says. "A glance at Alice frees me from stain of concupiscence."

He is conscious of an oddity, as if time has performed some loop or snared itself in a noose; he has seen them on the wall as Hans froze them, and here they enact themselves, wearing their various expressions of aloofness or amusement, benignity and grace: a happy family. He prefers their host as Hans painted him; the Thomas More on the wall, you can see that he's thinking, but not what he's thinking, and that's the way it should be. The painter has grouped them so skillfully that there's no space between the figures for anyone new. The outsider can only soak himself into the scene, as an unintended blot or stain; certainly, he thinks, Gardiner is a blot or stain. The Secretary waves his black sleeves; he argues vigorously with their host. What does St. Paul mean when he says Jesus was made a little lower than the angels? Do Hollanders ever make jokes? What is the proper coat of arms of the Duke of Norfolk's heir? Is that thunder in the distance, or will this heat keep up? Just as in the painting, Alice has a little monkey on a gilt chain. In the painting it plays about her skirts. In life, it sits in her lap and clings to her like a child. Sometimes she lowers her head and talks to it, so that no one else can hear.

More takes no wine, though he serves it to his guests. There are several dishes, which all taste the same—flesh of some sort, with a gritty sauce like Thames mud—and then junkets, and a cheese which he says one of his daughters has made—one of his daughters, wards, stepdaughters, one of the women of whom the house is full. "Because one must keep them employed," he says. "They cannot always be at their books, and young women are prone to mischief and idleness."

"For sure," he mutters. "They'll be fighting in the streets next." His eyes are drawn unwillingly to the cheese; it is pitted and wobbling, like the face of a stable boy after a night out.

"Henry Pattinson is excitable tonight," More says. "Perhaps he should be bled. I hope his diet has not been too rich."

"Oh," says Gardiner, "I have no anxieties on that score."

Old John More—who must be eighty now—has come in for supper, and so they yield the conversation to him; he is fond of telling stories. "Did you ever hear of Humphrey Duke of Gloucester and the beggar who claimed to be blind? Did you ever hear of the man who didn't know the Virgin Mary was a Jew?" Of such a sharp old lawyer one hopes for more, even in his dotage. Then he begins on anecdotes of foolish women, of which he has a vast collection, and even when he falls asleep, their host has more. Lady Alice sits scowling. Gardiner, who has heard all these stories before, is grinding his teeth.

"Look there at my daughter-in-law Anne," More says. The girl lowers her eyes; her shoulders tense, as she waits for what is coming. "Anne craved—shall I tell them, my dear?—she craved a pearl necklace. She did not cease to talk about it, you know how young girls are. So when I gave her a box that rattled, imagine her face. Imagine her face again when she opened it. What was inside? Dried peas!"

The girl takes a deep breath. She raises her face. He sees the effort it costs her. "Father," she says, "don't forget to tell the story of the woman who didn't believe the world was round."

"No, that's a good one," More says.

When he looks at Alice, staring at her husband with painful concentration, he thinks, she still doesn't believe it.

After supper they talk about wicked King Richard. Many years ago Thomas More began to write a book about him. He could not decide whether to compose in English or Latin, so he has done both, though he has never finished it, or sent any part of it to the printer. Richard was born to be evil, More says; it was written on him from his birth. He shakes his head. "Deeds of blood. Kings' games."

"Dark days," says the fool.

"Let them never come again."

"Amen." The fool points to the guests. "Let these not come again either."

There are people in London who say that John Howard, grandfather of the Norfolk that is now, was more than a little concerned in the disappearance of the children who went into the Tower and never came out again. The Londoners say—and he reckons the Londoners know— that it was on Howard's watch that the princes were last seen; though Thomas More thinks it was Constable Brakenbury who handed the keys to the killers. Brakenbury died at Bosworth; he can't come out of his grave and complain.

The fact is, Thomas More is thick with the Norfolk that is now, and keen to deny that his ancestor helped disappear anyone, let alone two children of royal blood. In his mind's eye he frames the present duke: in one dripping, sinewy hand he holds a small golden-haired corpse, and in the other hand the kind of little knife a man brings to table to cut his meat.

He comes back to himself: Gardiner, jabbing the air, is pressing the Lord Chancellor on his evidence. Presently the fool's grumbling and groaning become unbearable. "Father," Margaret says, "please send Henry out." More rises to scold him, take him by the arm. All eyes follow him. But Gardiner takes advantage of the lull. He leans in, speaks English in an undertone. "About Master Wriothesley. Remind me. Is he working for me, or for you?"

"For you, I would have thought, now he is made a Clerk of the Signet. They assist Master Secretary, do they not?"

"Why is he always at your house?"

"He's not a bound apprentice. He may come and go."

"I suppose he's tired of churchmen. He wants to know what he can learn from . . . whatever it is you call yourself, these days."

"A person," he says placidly. "The Duke of Norfolk says I'm a person."

"Master Wriothesley has his eye on his advantage."

"I hope we all have that. Or why did God give us eyes?"

"He thinks of making his fortune. We all know that money sticks to your hands."

Like the aphids to More's roses. "No," he sighs. "It passes through them, alas. You know, Stephen, how I love luxury. Show me a carpet, and I'll walk on it."

The fool scolded and ejected, More rejoins them. "Alice, I have told you about drinking wine. Your nose is glowing." Alice's face grows stiff, with dislike and a kind of fear. The younger women, who understand all that is said, bow their heads and examine their hands, fiddling with their rings and turning them to catch the light. Then something lands on the table with a thud, and Anne Cresacre, provoked into her native tongue, cries, "Henry, stop that!" There is a gallery above with oriel windows; the fool, leaning through one of them, is peppering them with broken crusts. "Don't flinch, masters," he shouts. "I am pelting you with God."

He scores a hit on the old man, who wakes with a start. Sir John looks about him; with his napkin, he wipes dribble from his chin. "Now, Henry," More calls up. "You have wakened my father. And you are blaspheming. And wasting bread."

"Dear Lord, he should be whipped," Alice snaps.

He looks around him; he feels something which he identifies as pity, a heavy stirring beneath the breastbone. He believes Alice has a good heart; continues to believe it even when, taking his leave, permitted to thank her in English, she raps out, "Thomas Cromwell, why don't you marry again?"

"No one will have me, Lady Alice."

"Nonsense. Your master may be down but you're not poor, are

you? Got your money abroad, that's what I'm told. Got a good house, haven't you? Got the king's ear, my husband says. And from what my sisters in the city say, got everything in good working order."

"Alice!" More says. Smiling, he takes her wrist, shakes her a little. Gardiner laughs: his deep bass chuckle, like laughter through a crack in the earth.

When they go out to Master Secretary's barge, the scent of the gardens is heavy in the air. "More goes to bed at nine o'clock," Stephen says.

"With Alice?"

"People say not."

"You have spies in the house?"

Stephen doesn't answer.

It is dusk; lights bob in the river. "Dear God, I am hungry," Master Secretary complains. "I wish I had kept back one of the fool's crusts. I wish I had laid hands on the white rabbit; I'd eat it raw."

He says, "You know, he daren't make himself plain."

"Indeed he dare not," Gardiner says. Beneath the canopy, he sits hunched into himself, as if he were cold. "But we all know his opinions, which I think are fixed and impervious to argument. When he took office, he said he would not meddle with the divorce, and the king accepted that, but I wonder how long he will accept it."

"I didn't mean, make himself plain to the king. I meant, to Alice."

Gardiner laughs. "True, if she understood what he said about her she'd send him down to the kitchens and have him plucked and roasted."

"Suppose she died? He'd be sorry then."

"He'd have another wife in the house before she was cold. Someone even uglier."

He broods: foresees, vaguely, an opportunity for placing bets. "That young woman," he says. "Anne Cresacre. She is an heiress, you know? An orphan?"

"There was some scandal, was there not?"

"After her father died her neighbors stole her, for their son to marry. The boy raped her. She was thirteen. This was in Yorkshire . . . that's how they go on there. My lord cardinal was furious when he heard of it. It was he who got her away. He put her under More's roof because he thought she'd be safe."

"So she is."

Not from humiliation. "Since More's son married her, he lives off her lands. She has a hundred a year. You'd think she could have a string of pearls."

"Do you think More is disappointed in his boy? He shows no talent for affairs. Still, I hear you have a boy like that. You'll be looking for an heiress for him soon." He doesn't reply. It's true; John More, Gregory Cromwell, what have we done to our sons? Made them into idle young gentlemen—but who can blame us for wanting for them the ease we didn't have? One thing about More, he's never idled for an hour, he's passed his life reading, writing, talking toward what he believes is the good of the Christian commonwealth. Stephen says, "Of course you may have other sons. Aren't you looking forward to the wife Alice will find you? She is warm in your praises."

He feels afraid. It is like Mark, the lute player: people imagining what they cannot know. He is sure he and Johane have been secret. He says, "Don't you ever think of marrying?"

A chill spreads over the waters. "I am in holy orders."

"Oh, come on, Stephen. You must have women. Don't you?"

The pause is so long, so silent, that he can hear the oars as they dip into the Thames, the little splash as they rise; he can hear the ripples in their wake. He can hear a dog barking, from the southern shore. The Secretary asks, "What kind of Putney inquiry is that?"

The silence lasts till Westminster. But on the whole, not too bad a trip. As he mentions, disembarking, neither of them has thrown the other in the river. "I'm waiting till the water's colder," Gardiner says. "And till I can tie weights to you. You have a trick of resurfacing, don't you? By the way, why am I bringing you to Westminster?"

"I am going to see Lady Anne."

Gardiner is affronted. "You didn't say so."

"Should I report all my plans to you?"

He knows that is what Gardiner would prefer. The word is that the king is losing patience with his council. He shouts at them, "The cardinal was a better man than any of you, for managing matters." He thinks, if my lord cardinal comes back—which by a caprice of the king's he may, any time now—then you're all dead, Norfolk, Gardiner, More. Wolsey is a merciful man, but surely: only up to a point.

❖

Mary Shelton is in attendance; she looks up, simpers. Anne is sumptuous in her nightgown of dark silk. Her hair is down, her delicate feet bare inside kidskin slippers. She is slumped in a chair, as if the day has beaten the spirit out of her. But still, as she looks up, her eyes are sparkling, hostile. "Where've you been?"

"Utopia."

"Oh." She is interested. "What passed?"

"Dame Alice has a little monkey that sits on her knee at table."

"I hate them."

"I know you do."

He walks about. Anne lets him treat her fairly normally, except when she has a sudden, savage seizure of I-who-will-be-Queen, and slaps him down. She examines the toe of her slipper. "They say that Thomas More is in love with his own daughter."

"I think they may be right."

Anne's sniggering laugh. "Is she a pretty girl?"

"No. Learned though."

"Did they talk about me?"

"They never mention you in that house." He thinks, I should like to hear Alice's verdict.

"Then what was the talk?"

"The vices and follies of women."

"I suppose you joined it? It's true, anyway. Most women are foolish. And vicious. I have seen it. I have lived among the women too long."

He says, "Norfolk and my lord your father are very busy seeing ambassadors. France, Venice, the Emperor's man—just in these last two days."

He thinks, they are working to entrap my cardinal. I know it.

"I did not think you could afford such good information. Though they say you have spent a thousand pounds on the cardinal."

"I expect to get it back. From here and there."

"I suppose people are grateful to you. If they have received grants out of the cardinal's lands."

He thinks, your brother George, Lord Rochford, your father, Thomas, Earl of Wiltshire, haven't they got rich from the cardinal's fall? Look at what George is wearing these days, look at the money he spends on horses and girls; but I don't see much sign of gratitude from the Boleyns. He says, "I just take my conveyancer's fee."

She laughs. "You look well on it."

"Do you know, there are ways and ways . . . Sometimes people just tell me things."

It is an invitation. Anne drops her head. She is on the verge of becoming one of those people. But perhaps not tonight. "My father says, one can never be sure of that person, one can never tell who he's working for. I should have thought—but then I am only a woman—that it is perfectly obvious that you're working for yourself."

That makes us alike, he thinks: but does not quite say.

Anne yawns, a little catlike yawn. "You're tired," he says. "I shall go. By the way, why did you send for me?"

"We like to know where you are."

"So why does your lord father not send for me, or your brother?"

She looks up. It may be late, but not too late for Anne's knowing smile. "They do not think you would come."

❖

August: the cardinal writes to the king, a letter full of complaint, saying that he is being hounded by his creditors, "wrapped in misery and dread"—but the stories that come back are different. He is holding dinners, and inviting all the local gentry. He is dispensing charity on his old princely scale, settling lawsuits, and sweet-talking estranged husbands and wives into sharing a roof again.

Call-Me-Risley was up in Southwell in June, with William Brereton of the king's privy chamber: getting the cardinal's signature on a petition Henry is circulating, which he means to send to the Pope. It's Norfolk's idea, to get the peers and bishops to sign up to this letter asking Clement to let the king have his freedom. It contains certain murky, unspecific threats, but Clement's used to being threatened—no one's better at spinning a question out, setting one party against the other, playing ends against the middle.

The cardinal looks well, according to Wriothesley. And his building work, it seems, has gone beyond repairs and a few renovations. He has been scouring the country for glaziers, joiners, and for plumbers; it is ominous when my lord decides to improve the sanitation. He never had a parish church but he built the tower higher; never lodged anywhere where he did not draw up drainage plans. Soon there will be earthworks, culverts and pipes laid. Next he will be installing fountains. Wherever he goes he is cheered by the people.

"The people?" Norfolk says. "They'd cheer a Barbary ape. Who cares what they cheer? Hang 'em all."

"But then who will you tax?" he says, and Norfolk looks at him fearfully, unsure if he's made a joke.

Rumors of the cardinal's popularity don't make him glad, they make him afraid. The king has given Wolsey a pardon, but if he was offended once, he can be offended again. If they could think up forty-four charges, then—if fantasy is unconstrained by truth—they can think up forty-four more.

He sees Norfolk and Gardiner with their heads together. They look up at him; they glare and don't speak.

Wriothesley stays with him, in his shadow and footsteps, writes his most confidential letters, those to the cardinal and the king. He never says, I am too tired. He never says, it is late. He remembers all that he is required to remember. Even Rafe is not more perfect.

It is time to bring the girls into the family business. Johane complains of her daughter's poor sewing, and it seems that, transferring the needle surreptitiously into her wrong hand, the child has devised an awkward little backstitch which you would be hard-pushed to imitate. She gets the job of sewing up his dispatches for the north.

❖

September 1530: the cardinal leaves Southwell, traveling by easy stages to York. The next part of his progress becomes a triumphal procession. People from all over the countryside flock to him, ambushing him at wayside crosses so that he can lay his magical hands on their children; they call it "confirmation," but it seems to be some older sacrament. They pour in by the thousand, to gape at him; and he prays for them all.

"The council has the cardinal under observation," Gardiner says, swishing past him. "They have had the ports closed."

Norfolk says, "Tell him if I ever see him again, I will chew him up, bones, flesh and gristle." He writes it down just so and sends it up-country: "bones, flesh and gristle." He can hear the crunch and snap of the duke's teeth.

On October 2 the cardinal reaches his palace at Cawood, ten miles from York. His enthronement is planned for November 7. News comes that he has called a convocation of the northern church; it is to meet at York the day after his enthronement. It is a signal of his independence; some may think it is a signal of revolt. He has not informed the king, he has not informed old Warham, Archbishop of Canterbury; he can hear the cardinal's voice, soft and amused, saying, now, Thomas, why do they need to know?

Norfolk calls him in. His face is crimson and he froths a little at the mouth as he starts to shout. He has been seeing his armorer for a fitting, and is still wearing sundry parts—his cuirass, his garde-reins—so that he looks like an iron pot wobbling to the boil. "Does he think he can dig in up there and carve himself a kingdom? Cardinal's hat not enough for him, only a crown will do for Thomas bloody Wolsey the bleeding butcher's boy, and I tell you, I tell you . . ."

He drops his gaze in case the duke should stop to read his thoughts. He thinks, my lord would have made such an excellent king; so benign, so sure and suave in his dealings, so equitable, so swift and so discerning. His rule would have been the best rule, his servants the best servants; and how he would have enjoyed his state.

His glance follows the duke as he bobs and froths; but to his surprise, when the duke turns, he smites his own metaled thigh, and a tear—at the pain, or something else—bubbles into his eye. "Ah, you think me a hard man, Cromwell. I am not such a hard man that I don't see how you are left. Do you know what I say? I say I don't know one man in England who would have done what you have done, for a man disgraced and fallen. The king says so. Even him, Chapuys, the Emperor's man, he says, you cannot fault what's-he-called. I say, it's a pity you ever saw Wolsey. It's a pity you don't work for me."

"Well," he says, "we all want the same thing. For your niece to be queen. Can we not work together?"

Norfolk grunts. There is something amiss, in his view, with that word "together," but he cannot articulate what it is. "Do not forget your place."

He bows. "I am mindful of your lordship's continuing favor."

"Look here, Cromwell, I wish you would come down and see me at home at Kenninghall, and talk to my lady wife. She's a woman of monstrous demands. She thinks I shouldn't keep a woman in the house, for my pleasant usage, you know? I say, where else should she be? Do you want me to disturb myself on a winter's night and venture out on the icy roads? I don't seem to be able to express myself correctly to her; do you think you could come down and put my case?" He says, hastily, "Not now, of course. No. More urgent . . . see my niece . . ."

"How is she?"

"In my view," Norfolk says, "Anne's out for bloody murder. She wants the cardinal's guts in a dish to feed her spaniels, and his limbs nailed over the city gates of York."

❖

It is a dark morning and your eyes naturally turn toward Anne, but something shadowy is bobbing about, on the fringes of the circle of light. Anne says, "Dr. Cranmer is just back from Rome. He brings us no good news, of course."

They know each other; Cranmer has worked from time to time for the cardinal, as indeed who has not? Now he is active in the king's case. They embrace cautiously: Cambridge scholar, person from Putney.

He says, "Master, why would you not come to our college? To Cardinal College, I mean? His Grace was very sorry you would not. We would have made you comfortable."

"I think he wanted more permanence," Anne says, sneering.

"But with respect, Lady Anne, the king has almost said to me that he will take over the Oxford foundation himself." He smiles. "Perhaps it can be called after you?"

This morning Anne wears a crucifix on a gold chain. Sometimes her fingers pull at it impatiently, and then she tucks her hands back in her sleeves. It is so much a habit with her that people say she has something to hide, a deformity; but he thinks she is a woman who doesn't like to show her hand. "My uncle Norfolk says Wolsey goes about with eight hundred armed men at his back. They say he has letters from Katherine—is that true? They say Rome will issue a decree telling the king to separate from me."

"That would be a clear mistake on Rome's part," Cranmer says.

"Yes it would. Because he won't be told. Is he some parish clerk, the King of England? Or some child? This would not happen in France; their king keeps his churchmen under his hand. Master Tyndale says, 'One king, one law, is God's ordinance in every realm.' I have read his book, *The Obedience of a Christian Man*. I myself have shown it to the king and marked the passages that touch on his authority. The subject must obey his king as he would his God; do I have the sense of it? The Pope will learn his place."

Cranmer looks at her with a half-smile; she's like a child who you're teaching to read, who dazzles you by sudden aptitude.

"Wait," she says, "I have something to show you." She darts a look. "Lady Carey . . ."

"Oh, please," Mary says. "Do not give it currency."

Anne snaps her fingers. Mary Boleyn moves forward into the light, a flash of blond hair. "Give it," Anne says. It is a paper, which she unfolds. "I found this in my bed, would you believe? As it happened, it was a night when that sickly milk-faced creeper had turned down the sheet, and of course I could not get any sense out of her, she cries if you look at her sideways. So I cannot know who put it there."

She unfolds a drawing. There are three figures. The central figure is the king. He is large and handsome, and to make sure you don't miss him he is wearing a crown. On either side of him is a woman; the one on the left has no head. "That's the queen," she says, "Katherine. And that's me." She laughs. "Anne *sans tête*."

Dr. Cranmer holds out his hand for the paper. "Give it to me, I'll destroy it."

She crumples it in her fist. "I can destroy it myself. There is a prophecy that a queen of England will be burned. But a prophecy does not frighten me, and even if it is true, I will run the risk."

Mary stands, like a statue, in the position where Anne left her; her hands are joined, as if the paper were still between them. Oh, Christ, he thinks, to see her out of here; to take her to somewhere she could forget she is a Boleyn. She asked me once. I failed her. If she asked me again, I would fail her again.

Anne turns against the light. Her cheeks are hollow—how thin she is now—her eyes are alight. *"Ainsi sera,"* she says. "Never mind who grudges it, it will happen. I mean to have him."

On their way out, he and Dr. Cranmer do not speak, till they see the little pale girl coming toward them, the sickly milk-faced creeper, carrying folded linen.

"I think this is the one who cries," he says. "So do not look at her sideways."

"Master Cromwell," she says, "this may be a long winter. Send us some more of your orange tarts."

"I haven't seen you for so long . . . What have you been doing, where have you been?"

"Sewing mostly." She considers each question separately. "Where I'm sent."

"And spying, I think."

She nods. "I'm not very good at it."

"I don't know. You're very small and unnoticeable."

He means it as a compliment; she blinks, in acknowledgment. "I don't speak French. So don't you, if you please. It gives me nothing to report."

"Who are you spying for?"

"My brothers."

"Do you know Dr. Cranmer?"

"No," she says; she thinks it's a real question.

"Now," he instructs her, "you must say who you are."

"Oh. I see. I'm John Seymour's daughter. From Wolf Hall."

He is surprised. "I thought his daughters were with Queen Katherine."

"Yes. Sometimes. Not now. I told you. I go where I'm sent."

"But not where you are appreciated."

"I am, in the one way. You see, Lady Anne will not refuse any of the queen's ladies who want to spend time with her." She raises her eyes, a pale momentary brightness. "Very few do."

Every rising family needs information. With the king considering himself a bachelor, any little girl can hold the key to the future, and not all his money is on Anne. "Well, good luck," he says. "I'll try to keep it in English."

"I would be obliged." She bows. "Dr. Cranmer."

He turns to watch her as she patters off in the direction of Anne Boleyn. A small suspicion enters his mind, about the paper in the bed. But no, he thinks. That is not possible.

Dr. Cranmer says, smiling, "You have a wide acquaintance among the court ladies."

"Not very wide. I still don't know which daughter that was, there are three at least. And I suppose Seymour's sons are ambitious."

"I hardly know them."

"The cardinal brought Edward up. He's sharp. And Tom Seymour is not such a fool as he pretends."

"The father?"

"Stays in Wiltshire. We never see him."

"One could envy him," Dr. Cranmer murmurs.

Country life. Rural felicity. A temptation he has never known. "How long were you at Cambridge, before the king called you up?"

Cranmer smiles. "Twenty-six years."

They are both dressed for riding. "You are going back to Cambridge today?"

"Not to stay. The family"—the Boleyns, he means—"want to have me at hand. And you, Master Cromwell?"

"A private client. I can't make a living from Lady Anne's black looks."

Boys wait with their horses. From various folds of his garments Dr. Cranmer produces objects wrapped in cloth. One of them is a carrot cut carefully lengthways, and another a wizened apple, quartered. As if he were a child, fair-minded with a treat, he gives him two slices of carrot and half the apple, to feed to his own horse; as he does so, he says, "You owe much to Anne Boleyn. More than perhaps you think. She has formed a good opinion of you. I'm not sure she cares to be your sister-in-law, mind . . ."

The beasts bend their necks, nibbling, their ears flicking in appreciation. It is a moment of peace, like a benediction. He says, "There are no secrets, are there?"

"No. No. Absolutely none." The priest shakes his head. "You asked why I would not come to your college."

"I was making conversation."

"Still . . . as we heard it in Cambridge, you performed such labors for the foundation . . . the students and Fellows all commend you . . . no detail escapes Master Cromwell. Though to be sure, this comfort on which you pride yourselves . . ." His tone, smooth and unemphatic, doesn't change. "In the fish cellar? Where the students died?"

"My lord cardinal did not take that lightly."

Cranmer says, lightly, "Nor did I."

"My lord was never a man to ride down another for his opinions. You would have been safe."

"I assure you he would have found no heresy in me. Even the Sorbonne could not fault me. I have nothing to be afraid of." A wan smile.

"But perhaps . . . ah well . . . perhaps I'm just a Cambridge man at heart."

❖

He says to Wriothesley, "Is he? At all points orthodox?"

"It's hard to say. He doesn't like monks. You should get on."

"Was he liked at Jesus College?"

"They say he was a severe examiner."

"I suppose he doesn't miss much. Although. He thinks Anne is a virtuous lady." He sighs. "And what do we think?"

Call-Me-Risley snorts. He has just married—a connection of Gardiner's—but his relations with women are not, on the whole, gentle.

"He seems a melancholy sort of man," he says. "The kind who wants to live retired from the world."

Wriothesley's fair eyebrows rise, almost imperceptibly. "Did he tell you about the barmaid?"

❖

When Cranmer comes to the house, he feeds him the delicate meat of the roe deer; they take supper privately, and he gets his story from him, slowly, slowly and easily. He asks the doctor where he comes from, and when he says, nowhere you know, he says, try me, I've been to most places.

"If you had been to Aslockton, you wouldn't know you were there. If a man goes fifteen miles to Nottingham, let him only spend the night away, and it vanishes clear from his mind." His village has not even a church; only some poor cottages and his father's house, where his family has lived for three generations.

"Your father is a gentleman?"

"He is indeed." Cranmer sounds faintly shocked: what else could he be? "The Tamworths of Lincolnshire are among my connections. The Cliftons of Clifton. The Molyneux family, of whom you will have heard. Or have you?"

"And you have much land?"

"If I had thought, I would have brought the ledgers."

"Forgive me. We men of business . . ."

Eyes rest on him, assessing. Cranmer nods. "A small acreage. And I am not the eldest. But he brought me up well. Taught me horsemanship. He gave me my first bow. He gave me my first hawk to train."

Dead, he thinks, the father long dead: still looking for his hand in the dark.

"When I was twelve he sent me to school. I suffered there. The master was harsh."

"To you? Or others as well?"

"If I am honest, I only thought of myself. I was weak, no doubt. I suppose he sought out weakness. Schoolmasters do."

"Could you not complain to your father?"

"I wonder now why I did not. But then he died. I was thirteen. Another year and my mother sent me to Cambridge. I was glad of the escape. To be from under his rod. Not that the flame of learning burned bright. The east wind put it out. Oxford—Magdalen especially, where your cardinal was—it was everything in those days."

He thinks, if you were born in Putney, you saw the river every day, and imagined it widening out to the sea. Even if you had never seen the ocean you had a picture of it in your head from what you had been told by foreign people who sometimes came upriver. You knew that one day you would go out into a world of marble pavements and peacocks, of hillsides buzzing with heat, the fragrance of crushed herbs rising around you as you walked. You planned for what your journeys would bring you: the touch of warm terra-cotta, the night sky of another climate, alien flowers, the stone-eyed gaze of other people's saints. But if you were born in Aslockton, in flat fields under a wide sky, you might just be able to imagine Cambridge: no farther.

"A man from my college," Dr. Cranmer says tentatively, "was told by the cardinal that as an infant you were stolen by pirates."

He stares at him for a moment, then smiles in slow delight. "How I miss my master. Now he has gone north, there is no one to invent me."

Dr. Cranmer, cautious: "So it is not true? Because I wondered if there was doubt over whether you were baptized. I fear it could be a question, in such an event."

"But the event never took place. Really. Pirates would have given me back."

Dr. Cranmer frowns. "You were an unruly child?"

"If I'd known you then, I could have knocked down your schoolmaster for you."

Cranmer has stopped eating; not that he has tasted much. He thinks, at some level of his being this man will always believe I am a heathen; I will never disabuse him now. He says, "Do you miss your studies? Your life has been disrupted since the king made you an ambassador and had you tossed on the high seas."

"In the Bay of Biscay, when I was coming from Spain, we had to bail out the ship. I heard the sailors' confessions."

"They must have been something to hear." He laughs. "Shouted over the noise of the storm."

After that strenuous journey—though the king was pleased with his embassy—Cranmer might have dropped back into his old life, except that he had mentioned, meeting Gardiner in passing, that the European universities might be polled on the king's case. You've tried the canon lawyers; now try the theologians. Why not? the king said; bring me Dr. Cranmer and put him in charge of it. The Vatican said it had nothing against the idea, except that the divines should not be offered money: a merry caveat, coming from a Pope with the surname of de' Medici. To him, this initiative seems nearly futile—but he thinks of Anne Boleyn, he thinks of what her sister had said: she's not getting any younger. "Look, you've found a hundred scholars, at a score of universities, and some say the king is right—"

"Most—"

"And if you find two hundred more, what will it matter? Clement isn't open to persuasion now. Only to pressure. And I don't mean moral pressure."

"But it's not Clement we have to persuade of the king's case. It's all of Europe. All Christian men."

"I'm afraid the Christian women may be harder still."

Cranmer drops his eyes. "I could never persuade my wife of anything. I would never have thought to try." He pauses. "We are two widowers, I think, Master Cromwell, and if we are to become colleagues, I must not leave you wondering, or at the mercy of stories that people will bring to you."

The light is fading around them while he talks, and his voice, each murmur, each hesitation, trails away into the dusk. Outside the room where they sit, where the house is going on its nightly course, there is a banging and scraping, as if trestles were being moved, and a faint sound of cheering and whooping. But he ignores it, settles his attention on the priest. Joan, an orphan, he says, servant in a gentleman's house where he used to visit; no people of her own, no marriage portion; he pitied her. A whisper in a paneled room raises spirits from the fens, fetches the dead: Cambridge twilights, damp seeping from the marshes and rush lights burning in a bare swept room where an act of love takes place. I could not help but marry her, Dr. Cranmer says, and indeed, how can a man help marrying? His college took away his fellowship, of course, you cannot have married fellows. And naturally she had to leave her place, and not knowing what else to do with her, he lodged her at the Dolphin, which is kept by some connections of his, some—he confesses, not without a downward glance—some relations of his, yes it is true that some of his people keep the Dolphin.

"It's nothing to be ashamed of. The Dolphin is a good house."

Ah, you know it: and he bites his lip.

He studies Dr. Cranmer: his way of blinking, the cautious finger he lays to his chin, his eloquent eyes and his pale praying hands. So Joan was not, he says, she was not, you see, a barmaid, whatever people say, and I know what they do say. She was a wife with a child in her belly, and he a poor scholar, preparing to live with her in honest poverty, but that didn't happen, in the event. He thought he might find a position as secretary to some gentleman, or as a tutor, or that he might earn a living by his pen, but all that scheming was to no avail. He thought they might move from Cambridge, even from England, but they didn't have to, in the end. He hoped some connection of his would do something for him, before the child was born: but when Joan died in labor, no one could do anything for him, not anymore. "If the child had lived I would have salvaged something. As it was, no one knew what to say to me. They did not know whether to condole with me on losing my wife, or congratulate me because Jesus College had taken me back. I took holy orders; why not? All that, my marriage, the child I thought I would have, my colleagues seemed to regard it as some sort of miscalculation. Like losing your way in the woods. You get home and never think of it again."

"There are some strange cold people in this world. It is priests, I think. Saving your presence. Training themselves out of natural feeling. They mean it for the best, of course."

"It was not a mistake. We did have a year. I think of her every day."

The door opens; it is Alice bringing in lights. "This is your daughter?"

Rather than explain his family, he says, "This is my lovely Alice. This is not your job, Alice?"

She bobs, a small genuflection to a churchman. "No, but Rafe and the others want to know what you are talking about so long. They are waiting to know if there will be a dispatch to the cardinal tonight. Jo is standing by with her needle and thread."

"Tell them I will write in my own hand, and we will send it tomorrow. Jo may go to bed."

"Oh, we are not going to bed. We are running Gregory's greyhounds up and down the hall and making a noise fit to wake the dead."

"I can see why you don't want to break off."

"Yes, it is excellent," Alice says. "We have the manners of scullery maids and no one will ever want to marry us. If our aunt Mercy had behaved like us when she was a girl, she would have been knocked round the head till she bled from the ears."

"Then we live in happy times," he says.

When she has gone, and the door is closed behind her, Cranmer says, "The children are not whipped?"

"We try to teach them by example, as Erasmus suggests, though we all like to race the dogs up and down and make a noise, so we are not doing very well in that regard." He does not know if he should smile; he has Gregory; he has Alice, and Johane and the child Jo, and in the corner of his eye, at the periphery of his vision, the little pale girl who spies on the Boleyns. He has hawks in his mews who move toward the sound of his voice. What has this man?

"I think of the king's advisers," Dr. Cranmer says. "The sort of men who are about him now."

And he has the cardinal, if the cardinal still thinks well of him after all that has passed. If he dies, he has his son's sable hounds to lie at his feet.

"They are able men," Cranmer says, "who will do anything he wants, but it seems to me—I do not know how it seems to you—that they are utterly lacking in any understanding of his situation . . . any compunction or kindness. Any charity. Or love."

"It is what makes me think he will bring the cardinal back."

Cranmer studies his face. "I am afraid that cannot happen now."

He has a wish to speak, to express the bottled rage and pain he feels. He says, "People have worked to make misunderstandings between us. To persuade the cardinal that I am not working for his interests, only for my own, that I have been bought out, that I see Anne every day—"

"Of course, you do see her . . ."

"How else can I know how to move next? My lord cannot know, he cannot understand, what it's like here now."

Cranmer says gently, "Should you not go to him? Your presence would dispel any doubt."

"There is no time. The snare is set for him and I dare not move."

❖

There is a chill in the air; the summer birds have flown, and black-winged lawyers are gathering for the new term in the fields of Lincoln's Inn and Gray's. The hunting season—or at least, the season when the king hunts every day—will soon be over. Whatever is happening elsewhere, whatever deceits and frustrations, you can forget them in the field. The hunter is among the most innocent of men; living in the moment makes him feel pure. When he returns in the evening, his body aches, his mind is full of pictures of leaves and sky; he does not want to read documents. His miseries, his perplexities have receded, and they will stay away, provided—after food and wine, laughter and exchange of stories—he gets up at dawn to do it all over again.

But the winter king, less occupied, will begin to think about his conscience. He will begin to think about his pride. He will begin to prepare the prizes for those who can deliver him results.

It is an autumn day, whitish sun flitting behind the loosening, flickering leaves. They go into the butts. The king likes to do more than one thing at once: talk, direct arrows at a target. "Here we will be alone," he says, "and I will be free to open my mind to you."

In fact, the population of a small village—as it might be, Aslockton—is circulating around them. The king does not know what "alone" means. Is he ever by himself, even in his dreams? "Alone" means without Norfolk clattering after him. "Alone" means without Charles Brandon, who in a summer fit of fury the king advised to make himself scarce and not come within fifty miles of the court. "Alone" means just with my yeoman of the bow and his menials, alone with my gentlemen of the privy chamber, who are my select and private friends. Two of these gentlemen, unless he is with the queen, sleep at the foot of his bed; so they have been on duty for some years now.

When he sees Henry draw his bow, he thinks, I see now he is royal. At home or abroad, in wartime or peacetime, happy or aggrieved, the king likes to practice several times in the week, as an Englishman should; using his height, the beautiful trained muscles of his arms, shoulders and chest, he sends his arrows snapping straight to the eye of the target. Then he holds out his arm, for someone to unstrap and restrap the royal armguard; for someone to change his bow, and bring him a choice. A cringing slave hands a napkin, to mop his forehead, and picks it up from where the king has dropped it; and then, exasperated, one shot or two falling wide, the King of England snaps his fingers, for God to change the wind.

The king shouts, "From various quarters I receive the advice that I should consider my marriage dissolved in the eyes of Christian Europe, and may remarry as I please. And soon."

He doesn't shout back.

"But others say . . ." The breeze blows, his words are carried off, toward Europe.

"I am one of the others."

"Dear Jesus," Henry says. "I will be unmanned by it. How long do you suppose my patience lasts?"

He hesitates to say, you are still living with your wife. You share a roof, a court, wherever you move together, she on the queen's side, you on the king's; you told the cardinal she was your sister not your wife, but if today you do not shoot well, if the breeze is not in your favor or you find your eyes blurred by sudden tears, it is only sister Katherine whom you can tell; you can admit no weakness or failure to Anne Boleyn.

He has studied Henry through his practice round. He has taken up a bow at his invitation, which causes some consternation in the ranks of the gentlemen who stud the grass and lean against trees, wearing their fallen-fruit silks of mulberry, gold and plum. Though Henry shoots well, he has not the action of a born archer; the born archer lays his whole body into the bow. Compare him with Richard Williams, Richard Cromwell as he is now. His grandfather ap Evan was an artist with the bow. He never saw him, but you can bet he had muscles like cords and every one in use from the heels up. Studying the king, he is satisfied that his great-grandfather was not the archer Blaybourne, as the story says, but Richard, Duke of York. His grandfather was royal; his mother was royal; he shoots like a gentleman amateur, and he is king through and through.

The king says, you have a good arm, a good eye. He says disparagingly, oh, at this distance. We have a match every Sunday, he says, my household. We go to Paul's for the sermon and then out to Moorfields, we meet up with our fellow guildsmen and destroy the butchers and the grocers, and then we have a dinner together. We have grudge matches with the vintners . . .

Henry turns to him, impulsive: what if I came with you one week? If I came in disguise? The Commons would like it, would they not? I could shoot for you. A king should show himself, sometimes, don't you feel? It would be amusing, yes?

Not very, he thinks. He cannot swear to it, but he thinks there are tears in Henry's eyes. "For sure we would win," he says. It is what you would say to a child. "The vintners would be roaring like bears."

It begins to drizzle, and as they walk toward a sheltering clump of trees, a pattern of leaves shadows the king's face. He says, Nan threatens to leave me. She says that there are other men and she is wasting her youth.

❖

Norfolk, panicking, that last week of October 1530: "Listen. This fellow here," he jerks his thumb, rudely, at Brandon—who is back at court, of course he is back—"this fellow here, a few years ago, he charged at the king in the lists, and nearly killed him. Henry had not put his visor down, God alone knows why—but these things happen. My lord here ran his lance—bam!—into the king's headpiece, and the lance shattered—an inch, one inch, from his eye."

Norfolk has hurt his right hand, by the force of his demonstration. Wincing, but furious, earnest, he presses on. "One year later, Henry is following his hawk—it's that cut-up sort of country, flat, deceptive, you know it—he comes to a ditch, he drives in a pole to help him cross, the infernal instrument breaks, God rot it, and there's His Majesty facedown and stunned in a foot of water and mud, and if some servant hadn't clawed him out, well, gentlemen, I shudder to think."

He thinks, that's one question answered. In case of peril, you may pick him up. Fish him out. Whatever.

"Suppose he dies?" Norfolk demands. "Supposing a fever carries him away or he comes off his horse and breaks his neck? Then what? His bastard, Richmond? I've nothing against him, he's a fine boy, and Anne says I should get him married to my daughter Mary, Anne's no fool, let's put a Howard everywhere, she says, everywhere the king looks. Now I have no quarrel with Richmond, except he was born out of wedlock. Can he reign? Ask yourselves this. How did the Tudors get the crown? By title? No. By force? Exactly. By God's grace they won the battle. The old king, he had such a fist as you will go many a mile to meet, he had great books into which he entered his grudges and he forgave, when? Never! That's how one rules, masters." He turns to his audience, to the councillors waiting and watching and to the gentlemen of the court and the bedchamber; to Henry Norris, to his friend William Brereton, to Master Secretary Gardiner; to, incidentally, as it happens, Thomas Cromwell, who is increasingly where he shouldn't be. He says, "The old king bred, and by the help of Heaven he bred sons. But when Arthur died, there were swords sharpened in Europe, and they were sharpened to carve up this kingdom. Henry that is now, he was a child, nine years old. If the old king had not staggered on a few more years, the wars would have been to fight all over again. A child cannot hold England. And a bastard child? God give me strength! And it's November again!"

It's hard to fault what the duke says. He understands it all; even that last cry, wrung from the duke's heart. It's November, and a year has passed since Howard and Brandon walked into York Place and demanded the cardinal's chain of office, and turned him out of his house.

There is a silence. Then someone coughs, someone sighs. Someone— probably Henry Norris—laughs. It is he who speaks. "The king has one child born in wedlock."

Norfolk turns. He flushes, a deep mottled purple. "Mary?" he says. "That talking shrimp?"

"She will grow up."

"We are all waiting," Suffolk says. "She has now reached fourteen, has she not?"

"But her face," Norfolk says, "is the size of my thumbnail." The duke shows off his digit to the company. "A woman on the English throne, it flies in the face of nature."

"Her grandmother was Queen of Castile."

"She cannot lead an army."

"Isabella did."

Says the duke, "Cromwell, why are you here? Listening to the talk of gentlemen?"

"My lord, when you shout, the beggars on the street can hear you. In Calais."

Gardiner has turned to him; he is interested. "So you think Mary can rule?"

He shrugs. "It depends who advises her. It depends who she marries."

Norfolk says, "We have to act soon. Katherine has half the lawyers of Europe pushing paper for her. This dispensation. That dispensation. The other dispensation with the different bloody wording that they say they've got in Spain. It doesn't matter. This has gone beyond paper."

"Why?" Suffolk says. "Is your niece in foal?"

"No! More's the pity. Because if she were, he'd have to do something."

"What?" Suffolk says.

"I don't know. Grant his own divorce?"

There is a shuffle, a grunt, a sigh. Some look at the duke; some look at their shoes. There's no man in the room who doesn't want Henry to have what he wants. Their lives and fortunes depend on it. He sees the path ahead: a tortuous path through a flat terrain, the horizon deceptively clear, the country intersected by ditches, and the present Tudor, a certain amount of mud bespattering his person and his face, fished gasping into clear air. He says, "That good man who pulled the king out of the ditch, what was his name?"

Norfolk says, drily, "Master Cromwell likes to hear of the deeds of those of low birth."

He doesn't suppose any of them will know. But Norris says, "I know. His name was Edmund Mody."

Muddy, more like, Suffolk says. He yells with laughter. They stare at him.

✣

It is All Souls' Day: as Norfolk puts it, November again. Alice and Jo have come to speak to him. They are leading Bella—the Bella that is now—on a ribbon of pink silk. He looks up: may I be of service to you two ladies?

Alice says, "Master, it is more than two years since my aunt Elizabeth died, your lady wife. Will you write to the cardinal, and ask him to ask the Pope to let her out of Purgatory?"

He says, "What about your aunt Kat? And your little cousins, my daughters?"

The children exchange glances. "We don't think they have been there so long. Anne Cromwell was proud of her working of numbers and boasted that she was learning Greek. Grace was vain of her hair and used to state that she had wings, this was a lie. We think perhaps they must suffer more. But the cardinal could try."

Don't ask, don't get, he thinks.

Alice says, encouragingly, "You have been so active in the cardinal's business that he would not refuse. And although the king does not favor the cardinal anymore, surely the Pope favors him?"

"And I expect," says Jo, "that the cardinal writes to the Pope every day. Though I do not know who sews his letters. And I suppose the cardinal might send him a present for his trouble. Some money, I mean. Our aunt Mercy says that the Pope does nothing except on cash terms."

"Come with me," he says. They exchange glances. He sweeps them along before him. Bella's small legs race. Jo drops her lead, but still Bella runs behind.

Mercy and the elder Johane are sitting together. The silence is not companionable. Mercy is reading, murmuring the words to herself. Johane is staring at the wall, sewing in her lap. Mercy marks her place. "What's this, an embassy?"

"Tell her," he says. "Jo, tell your mother what you have been asking me."

Jo starts to cry. It is Alice who speaks up and puts their case. "We want our aunt Liz to come out of Purgatory."

"What have you been teaching them?" he asks.

Johane shrugs. "Many grown persons believe what they believe."

"Dear God, what is going on under this roof? These children believe the Pope can go down to the underworld with a bunch of keys. Whereas Richard denies the sacrament—"

"What?" Johane's mouth falls open. "He does what?"

Mercy says, "Richard is right. When the good Lord said, this is my body, he meant, this signifies my body. He did not license priests to be conjurers."

"But he said, it is. He did not say, this is like my body, he said, it is. Can God lie? No. He is incapable of it."

"God can do anything," Alice says.

Johane stares at her. "You little minx."

"If my mother were here, she would slap you for that."

"No fighting," he says. "Please?" The Austin Friars is like the world in little. These few years it's been more like a battlefield than a household; or like one of the tented encampments in which the survivors look in despair at their shattered limbs and spoiled expectations. But they are his to direct, these last hardened troops; if they are not to be flattened in the next charge it is he who must teach them the defensive art of facing both ways, faith and works, Pope and new brethren, Katherine and Anne. He looks at Mercy, who is smirking. He looks at Johane, a high color in her cheeks. He turns away from Johane and his thoughts, which are not precisely theological. He says to the children, "You have done nothing wrong." But their faces are stricken, and he coaxes them: "I shall give you a present, Jo, for sewing the cardinal's letters; and I shall give you a present, Alice, I am sure that we do not need a reason. I shall give you marmosets."

They look at each other. Jo is tempted. "Do you know where to get them?"

"I think so. I have been to the Lord Chancellor's house, and his wife has such a creature, and it sits on her knee and attends to everything she says."

Alice says, "They are not the fashion now."

"Though we thank you," says Mercy.

"Though we thank you," Alice repeats. "But marmosets are not seen at court since Lady Anne came up. To be fashionable, we should like Bella's puppies."

"In time," he says. "Perhaps." The room is full of undercurrents, some of which he does not understand. He picks up his dog, tucks her under his arm and goes off to see how to provide some more money for brother George Rochford. He sits Bella on his desk, to take a nap among his papers. She has been sucking the end of her ribbon, and attempting subtly to undo the knot at her throat.

❖

On November 1, 1530, a commission for the cardinal's arrest is given to Harry Percy, the young Earl of Northumberland. The earl arrives at Cawood to arrest him, forty-eight hours before his planned arrival in York for his investiture. He is taken to Pontefract Castle under guard, from there to Doncaster, and from there to Sheffield Park, the home of the Earl of Shrewsbury. Here at Talbot's house he falls ill. On November 26 the Constable of the Tower arrives, with twenty-four men at arms, to escort him south. From there he travels to Leicester Abbey. Three days later he dies.

What was England, before Wolsey? A little offshore island, poor and cold.

❖

George Cavendish comes to Austin Friars. He cries as he talks. Sometimes he dries his tears and moralizes. But mostly he cries. "We had not even finished our dinner," he says. "My lord was taking his dessert when young Harry Percy walked in. He was spattered with mud from the road, and he had the keys in his hands, he had taken them from the porter already, and set sentries on the stairs. My lord rose to his feet, he said, Harry, if I'd known, I'd have waited dinner for you. I fear we've almost finished the fish. Shall I pray for a miracle?

"I whispered to him, my lord, do not blaspheme. Then Harry Percy came forward: my lord, I arrest you for high treason."

Cavendish waits. He waits for him to erupt in fury? But he puts his fingers together, joined as if he were praying. He thinks, Anne arranged this, and it must have given her an intense and secret pleasure; vengeance deferred, for herself, for her old lover, once berated by the cardinal and sent packing from the court. He says, "How did he look? Harry Percy?"

"He was shaking from head to foot."

"And my lord?"

"Demanded his warrant, his commission. Percy said, there are items in my instructions you may not see. So, said my lord, if you will not show it, I shall not surrender to you, so here's a pretty state of affairs, Harry. Come, George, my lord said to me, we will go into my rooms, and have some conference. They followed him on his heels, the earl's party, so I stood in the door and I barred the way. My lord cardinal walked into his chamber, mastering himself, and when he turned he said, Cavendish, look at my face: I am not afraid of any man alive."

He, Cromwell, walks away so that he does not have to see the man's distress. He looks at the wall, at the paneling, at his new linenfold paneling, and runs his index finger across its grooves. "When they took him from the house, the townspeople were assembled outside. They knelt in the road and wept. They asked God to send vengeance on Harry Percy."

God need not trouble, he thinks: I shall take it in hand.

"We were riding south. The weather was closing in. At Doncaster it was late when we arrived. In the street the townsfolk were packed shoulder to shoulder, and each person holding up a candle against the dark. We thought they would disperse, but they stood all night in the road. And their candles burned down. And it was daylight, of a sort."

"It must have put heart into him. Seeing the crowds."

"Yes, but by then—I did not say, I should have told you—he had gone a week without eating."

"Why? Why did he do that?"

"Some say he meant to destroy himself. I cannot believe it, a Christian soul . . . I ordered him a dish of warden pears, roasted with spices—did I do right?"

"And he ate?"

"A little. But then he put his hand to his chest. He said, there is something cold inside me, cold and hard like a whetstone. And that was where it began." Cavendish gets up. Now he too walks about the room. "I called for an apothecary. He made a powder and I had him pour it into three cups. I drank off one. He, the apothecary, he drank another. Master Cromwell, I trusted nobody. My lord took his powder and presently the pain eased, and he said, there, it was wind, and we laughed, and I thought, tomorrow he will be better."

"Then Kingston came."

"Yes. How could we tell my lord, the Constable of the Tower is here to fetch you? My lord sat down on a packing case. He said, William Kingston? William Kingston? He kept on saying his name."

And all that time a weight in his chest, a whetstone, a steel, a sharpening knife in his gut.

"I said to him, now take it cheerfully, my lord. You will come before the king and clear your name. And Kingston said the same, but my lord said, you are leading me into a fool's paradise. I know what is provided for me, and what death is prepared. That night we did not sleep. My lord voided black blood from his bowels. The next morning he was too weak to stand, and so we could not ride. But then we did ride. And so we came to Leicester.

"The days were very short, the light poor. On Monday morning at eight he woke. I was just then bringing in the small wax lights, and setting them along the cupboard. He said, whose is that shadow that leaps along the wall? And he cried your name. God forgive me, I said you were on the road. He said, the ways are treacherous. I said, you know Cromwell, the devil does not delay him—if he says he is on the road he will be here."

"George, make this story short, I cannot bear it."

But George must have his say: next morning at four, a bowl of chicken broth, but he would not eat it. Is this not a meatless day? He asked for the broth to be taken away. By now he had been ill for eight days, continually voiding his bowels, bleeding and in pain, and he said, believe me, death is the end of this.

Put my lord in a difficulty, and he will find a way; with his craft and cunning, he will find a way, an exit. Poison? If so, then by his own hand.

It was eight next morning when he drew his last breath. Around his bed, the click of rosary beads; outside the restive stamp of horses in their stalls, the thin winter moon shining down on the London road.

"He died in his sleep?" He would have wished him less pain.

George says, no, he was speaking to the last. "Did he speak of me again?"

Anything? A word?

I washed him, George says, laid him out for burial. "I found, under his fine holland shirt, a belt of hair . . . I am sorry to tell you, I know you are not a lover of these practices, but so it was. I think he never did this till he was at Richmond among the monks."

"What became of it? This belt of hair?"

"The monks of Leicester kept it."

"God Almighty! They'll make it pay."

"Do you know, they could provide nothing better than a coffin of plain boards?" Only when he says this does George Cavendish give way; only at this point does he swear and say, by the passion of Christ, I heard them knocking it together. When I think of the Florentine sculptor and his tomb, the black marble, the bronze, the angels at his head and foot . . . But I saw him dressed in his archbishop's robes, and I opened his fingers to put into his hand his crozier, just as I thought I would see him hold it when he was enthroned at York. It was only two days away. Our bags were packed and we were ready for the road; till Harry Percy walked in.

"You know, George," he says, "I begged him, be content with what you have clawed back from ruin, go to York, be glad to be alive . . . In the course of things, he would have lived another ten years, I know he would."

"We sent for the mayor and all the city officials, so that they could see him in his coffin, so there could be no false rumors that he was living and escaped to France. Some made remarks about his low birth, by God I wish you had been there—"

"I too."

"For to your face, Master Cromwell, they had not done it, nor would they dare. When the light failed we kept vigil, with the tapers burning around his coffin, till four in the morning, which you know is the canonical hour. Then we heard Mass. At six we laid him in the crypt. There left him."

Six in the morning, a Wednesday, the feast of St. Andrew the

Apostle. I, a simple cardinal. There left him and rode south, to find the king at Hampton Court. Who says to George, "I would not for twenty thousand pounds that the cardinal had died."

"Look, Cavendish," he says, "when you are asked what the cardinal said in his last days, tell them nothing."

George raises his eyebrows. "I already have. Told them nothing. The king questioned me. My lord Norfolk."

"If you tell Norfolk anything, he will twist it into treason."

"Still, as he is Lord Treasurer, he has paid me my back wages. I was three-quarters of the year in arrears."

"What were you paid, George?"

"Ten pounds a year."

"You should have come to me."

These are the facts. These are the figures. If the Lord of the Under-world rose up tomorrow in the privy chamber, and offered a dead man back, fresh from the grave, fresh from the crypt, the miracle of Lazarus for £20,000—Henry Tudor would be pushed to scrape it together. Norfolk as Lord Treasurer? Fine; it doesn't matter who holds the title, who holds the clanking keys to the empty chests.

"Do you know," he says, "if the cardinal could say, as he used to say to me, Thomas, what would you like for a New Year's gift, I would say, I would like sight of the nation's accounts."

Cavendish hesitates; he begins to speak; he stops; he starts again. "The king said certain things to me. At Hampton Court. 'Three may keep counsel, if two are away.'"

"It is a proverb, I think."

"He said, 'If I thought my cap knew my counsel, I would cast it into the fire.'"

"I think that also is a proverb."

"He means to say that he will not choose any adviser now: not my lord of Norfolk, nor Stephen Gardiner, or anyone, any person to be close to him, to be so close as the cardinal was."

He nods. That seems a reasonable interpretation.

Cavendish looks ill. It is the strain of the long sleepless nights, of the vigil around the coffin. He is worried about various sums of money the cardinal had on the journey, which he did not have when he died. He is worried about how to get his own effects from Yorkshire to his home; apparently Norfolk has promised him a cart and a transport allowance. He, Cromwell, talks about this while he thinks about the king, and out of sight of George folds his fingers, one by one, tight into the palm of his hand. Mary Boleyn traced, in his palm, a certain shape; he thinks, Henry, I have your heart in my hand.

When Cavendish has gone, he goes to his secret drawer and takes out the package that the cardinal gave him on the day he began his journey north. He unwinds the thread that binds it. It snags, knots, he works at it patiently; before he had expected it, the turquoise ring rolls into his palm, cold as if it came from the tomb. He pictures the cardinal's hands, long-fingered, white and unscarred, steady for so many years on the wheel of the ship of state; but the ring fits as if it had been made for him.

The cardinal's scarlet clothes now lie folded and empty. They cannot be wasted. They will be cut up and become other garments. Who knows where they will get to over the years? Your eye will be taken by a crimson cushion or a patch of red on a banner or ensign. You will see a glimpse of them in a man's inner sleeve or in the flash of a whore's petticoat.

Another man would go to Leicester to see where he died and talk to the abbot. Another man would have trouble imagining it, but he has no trouble. The red of a carpet's ground, the flush of the robin's breast or the chaffinch, the red of a wax seal or the heart of the rose: implanted in his landscape, cered in his inner eye, and caught in the glint of a ruby, in the color of blood, the cardinal is alive and speaking. Look at my face: I am not afraid of any man alive.

❖

At Hampton Court in the great hall they perform an interlude; its name is "The Cardinal's Descent into Hell." It takes him back to last year, to Gray's Inn. Under the eye of the officials of the king's household, the carpenters have been working furiously and for bonus rates, erecting frames upon which to drape canvas cloths painted with scenes of torture. At the back of the hall, the screens are entirely hung with flames.

The entertainment is this: a vast scarlet figure, supine, is dragged across the floor, howling, by actors dressed as devils. There are four devils, one for each limb of the dead man. The devils wear masks. They have tridents with which they prick the cardinal, making him twitch and writhe and beg. He had hoped the cardinal died without pain but Cavendish had said no. He died conscious, talking of the king. He had started out of sleep and said, whose is that shadow on the wall?

The Duke of Norfolk walks around the hall chortling, "Isn't it good, eh? It's good enough to be printed! By the Mass, that's what I shall do! I shall have it printed, so I can take it home with me, and at Christmas we can play it all over again."

Anne sits laughing, pointing, applauding. He has never seen her like this before: lit up, glowing. Henry sits frozen by her side. Sometimes he laughs, but he thinks if you could get close you would see that his eyes are afraid. The cardinal rolls across the floor, kicking out at the demons, but they harry him, in their wooly suits of black, and cry, "Come, Wolsey, we must fetch you to Hell, for our master Beelzebub is expecting you to supper."

When the scarlet mountain pops up his head and asks, "What wines does he serve?" he almost forgets himself and laughs. "I'll have no English wine," the dead man declares. "None of that cats' piss my lord of Norfolk lays on."

Anne crows; she points; she points to her uncle; the noise rises high to the roof beams with the smoke from the hearth, the laughing and chanting from the tables, the howling of the fat prelate. No, they assure him, the devil is a Frenchman, and there are catcalls and whistles, and songs break out. The devils now catch the cardinal's head in a noose. They haul him to his feet, but he fights them. The flailing punches are not all fake, and he hears their grunts, as the breath is knocked out of them. But there are four hangmen, and one great scarlet bag of nothingness, who chokes, who claws; the court cries, "Let him down! Let him down alive!"

The actors throw up their hands; they prance back and let him fall.

When he rolls on the ground, gasping, they thrust their forks into him and wind out lengths of scarlet woolen bowel.

The cardinal utters blasphemies. He utters farts, and fireworks blast out from corners of the hall. From the corner of his eye, he sees a woman run away, a hand over her mouth; but Uncle Norfolk marches about, pointing: "Look, there his guts are wound out, as the hangman would draw them! Why, I'd pay to see this!"

Someone calls, "Shame on you, Thomas Howard, you'd have sold your own soul to see Wolsey down." Heads turn, and his head turns, and nobody knows who has spoken; but he thinks it might be, could it be, Thomas Wyatt? The gentlemen devils have dusted themselves down and got their breath back. Shouting "Now!" they pounce; the cardinal is dragged off to Hell, which is located, it seems, behind the screens at the back of the hall.

He follows them behind the screens. Pages run out with linen towels for the actors, but the satanic influx knocks them aside. At least one of the children gets an elbow in the eye, and drops his bowl of steaming water on his feet. He sees the devils wrench off their masks, and toss them, swearing, into a corner; he watches as they try to claw off their knitted devil-coats. They turn to each other, laughing, and begin to pull them over each other's heads. "It's like the shirt of Nessus," George Boleyn says, as Norris wrenches him free.

George tosses his head to settle his hair back into place; his white skin has flared from contact with the rough wool. George and Henry Norris are the hand-devils, who seized the cardinal by his forepaws. The two foot-devils are still wrestling each other from their trappings. They are a boy called Francis Weston, and William Brereton, who—like Norris—is old enough to know better. They are so absorbed in themselves—cursing, laughing, calling for clean linen—that they do not notice who is watching them and anyway they do not care. They splash themselves and each other, they towel away their sweat, they rip the shirts from the pages' hands, they drop them over their heads. Still wearing their cloven hooves, they swagger out to take their bow.

In the center of the space they have vacated, the cardinal lies inert, shielded from the hall by the screens; perhaps he is sleeping.

He walks up to the scarlet mound. He stops. He looks down. He waits. The actor opens one eye. "This must be Hell," he says. "This must be Hell, if the Italian is here."

The dead man pulls off his mask. It is Sexton, the fool: Master Patch. Master Patch, who screamed so hard, a year ago, when they wanted to part him from his master.

Patch holds out a hand, to be helped to his feet, but he does not take it. The man scrambles up by himself, cursing. He begins to pull off his scarlet, dragging and tearing at the cloth. He, Cromwell, stands with his arms folded, his writing hand tucked into a hidden fist. The fool casts away his padding, fat pillows of wool. His body is scrawny, wasted, his chest furred with wiry hairs. He speaks: "Why you come to my country, Italian? Why you no stay in your own country, ah?"

Sexton is a fool, but he's not soft in the head. He knows well he's not an Italian.

"You should have stayed over there," Patch says, in his own London voice. "Have your own walled town by now. Have a cathedral. Have your own marzipan cardinal to eat after dinner. Have it all for a year or two, eh, till a bigger brute comes along and knocks you off the trough?"

He picks up the costume Patch has cast off. Its red is the fiery, cheap, quick-fading scarlet of Brazil-wood dye, and it smells of alien sweat. "How can you act this part?"

"I act what part I'm paid to act. And you?" He laughs: his shrill bark, which passes as mad. "No wonder your humor's so bitter these days. Nobody's paying you, eh? Monsieur Cremuel, the retired mercenary."

"Not so retired. I can fix you."

"With that dagger you keep where once was your waist." Patch springs away, he capers. He, Cromwell, leans against the wall; he watches him. He can hear a child sobbing, somewhere out of sight; perhaps it is the little boy who has been hit in the eye, now slapped again for dropping the bowl, or perhaps just for crying. Childhood was like that; you are punished, then punished again for protesting. So, one learns not to complain; it is a hard lesson, but one never lost.

Patch is trying out various postures, obscene gestures; as if preparing for some future performance. He says, "I know what ditch you were spawned in, Tom, and it was a ditch not far from mine." He turns to the hall, where, unseen and beyond the dividing screen, the king, presumably, continues his pleasant day. Patch plants his legs apart, he sticks out his tongue. "The fool has said in his heart, there is no Pope." He turns his head; he grins. "Come back in ten years, Master Cromwell, and tell me who's the fool then."

"You're wasting your jokes on me, Patch. Wearing out your stock-in-trade."

"Fools can say anything."

"Not where my writ runs."

"And where is that? Not even in the backyard where you were christened in a puddle. Come and meet me here, ten years today, if you're still alive."

"You would have a fright if I was dead."

"Because I'll stand still, and let you knock me down."

"I could crack your skull against the wall now. They'd not miss you."

"True," Master Sexton says. "They would roll me out in the morning and lay me on a dunghill. What's one fool? England is full of them."

❖

He is surprised there is any daylight left; he had thought it was deepest night. In these courts, Wolsey lingers; he built them. Turn any corner, and you will think you will see my lord, with a scroll of draftsman's plans in his hands, his glee at his sixty turkey carpets, his hope to lodge and entertain the finest mirror-makers of Venice—"Now, Thomas, you will add to your letter some Venetian endearments, some covert phrases that will suggest, in the local dialect and the most delicate way possible, that I pay top rates."

And he will add that the people of England are welcoming to foreigners and that the climate of England is benign. That golden birds sing on golden branches, and a golden king sits on a hill of coins, singing a song of his own composition.

When he gets home to Austin Friars he walks into a space that feels strange and empty. It has taken hours to get back from Hampton Court and it is late. He looks at the place on the wall where the cardinal's arms blaze out: the scarlet hat, at his request, recently retouched. "You can paint them out now," he says.

"And what shall we paint else, sir?"

"Leave a blank."

"We could have a pretty allegory?"

"I'm sure." He turns and walks away. "Leave a space."

III

The Dead Complain of Their Burial

CHRISTMASTIDE 1530

he knocking at the gate comes after midnight. His watchman rouses the household, and when he goes downstairs—wearing a savage expression and in all other respects fully dressed—he finds Johane in her nightgown, her hair down, asking, "What is this about?" Richard, Rafe, the men of the household steer her aside; standing in the hall at Austin Friars is William Brereton of the privy chamber, with an armed escort. They have come to arrest me, he thinks. He walks up to Brereton. "Good Christmas, William? Are you up early, or down late?"

Alice and Jo appear. He thinks of that night when Liz died, when his daughters stood forlorn and bewildered in their night-shifts, waiting for him to come home. Jo begins to cry. Mercy appears and sweeps the girls away. Gregory comes down, dressed to go out. "Here if you want me," he says diffidently.

"The king is at Greenwich," Brereton says. "He wants you now." He has ordinary ways of showing his impatience: slapping his glove against his palm and tapping his foot.

"Go back to bed," he tells his household. "The king wouldn't order me to Greenwich to arrest me; it doesn't happen that way." Though he hardly knows how it happens; he turns to Brereton. "What does he want me for?"

Brereton's eyes are roaming around, to see how these people live.

"I really can't enlighten you."

He looks at Richard, and sees how badly he wants to give this lordling a smack in the mouth. That would have been me, once, he thinks. But now I am as sweet as a May morning. They go out, Richard, Rafe, himself, his son, into the dark and the raw cold.

A party of link-men are waiting with lights. A barge is waiting at the nearest landing stairs. It is so far to the Palace of Placentia, the Thames so black, that they could be rowing along the river Styx. The boys sit opposite him, huddled, not talking, looking like one composite relative; though Rafe of course is not his relative. I'm getting like Dr. Cranmer, he thinks: the Tamworths of Lincolnshire are among my connections, the Cliftons of Clifton, the Molyneux family, of whom you will have heard, or have you? He looks up at the stars but they seem dim and far away; which, he thinks, they probably are.

So what should he do? Should he try for some conversation with Brereton? The family's lands are in Staffordshire, Cheshire, on the Welsh borders. Sir Randal has died this year and his son has come into a fat inheritance, a thousand a year at least in Crown grants, another three hundred or so from local monasteries . . . He is adding up in his head. It is none too soon to inherit; the man must be his own age, or nearly that. His father, Walter, would have got on with the Breretons, a quarrelsome crew, great disturbers of the peace. He recalls a proceeding against them in Star Chamber, would be fifteen years back . . . It doesn't seem likely to furnish a topic. Nor does Brereton seem to want one.

Every journey ends; terminates, at some pier, some mist-shrouded wharf, where torches are waiting. They are to go at once to the king, deep into the palace, to his private rooms. Harry Norris is waiting for them; who else? "How is he now?" Brereton says. Norris rolls his eyes.

"Well, Master Cromwell," he says, "we do meet under the strangest circumstances. Are these your sons?" He smiles, glancing around their faces. "No, clearly not. Unless they have divers mothers."

He names them: Master Rafe Sadler, Master Richard Cromwell, Master Gregory Cromwell. He sees a flicker of dismay on his son's face, and clarifies: "This is my nephew. This, my son."

"You only to go in," Norris says. "Come now, he is waiting." Over his shoulder, he says, "The king is afraid he may take cold. Will you look out the russet nightgown, the one with the sables?"

Brereton grunts some reply. Poor work, shaking out the furs, when you could be up in Chester, waking the populace, beating a drum around the city walls.

❖

It is a spacious chamber with a high carved bed; his eye flickers over it. In the candlelight, the bed hangings are ink-black. The bed is empty. Henry sits on a velvet stool. He seems to be alone, but there is a dry scent in the room, a cinnamon warmth, that makes him think that the cardinal must be in the shadows, holding the pithed orange, packed with spices, that he always carried when he was among a press of people. The dead, for sure, would want to ward off the scent of the living; but what he can see, across the room, is not the cardinal's shadowy bulk, but a pale drifting oval that is the face of Thomas Cranmer.

The king turns his head toward him as he enters. "Cromwell, my dead brother came to me in a dream."

He does not answer. What is a sensible answer to this? He watches the king. He feels no temptation to laugh. The king says, "During the twelve days, between Christmas Day and Epiphany, God permits the dead to walk. This is well known."

He says gently, "How did he look, your brother?"

"He looked as I remember him . . . but he was pale, very thin. There was a white fire around him, a light. But you know, Arthur would have been in his forty-fifth year now. Is that your age, Master Cromwell?"

"About," he says.

"I am good at telling people's ages. I wonder who Arthur would have looked like, if he had lived. My father, probably. Now, I am like my grandfather."

He thinks the king will say, who are you like? But no: he has established that he has no ancestors.

"He died at Ludlow. In winter. The roads impenetrable. They had to take his coffin in an oxcart. A prince of England, to go in a cart. I cannot think that was well done."

Now Brereton comes in, with the russet velvet, sable-lined. Henry stands up and sheds one layer of velvet, gains another, plusher and denser. The sable lining creeps down over his hands, as if he were a monster-king, growing his own fur. "They buried him at Worcester," he says. "But it troubles me. I never saw him dead."

Dr. Cranmer says, from the shadows, "The dead do not come back to complain of their burial. It is the living who are exercised about these matters."

The king hugs his robe about him. "I never saw his face till now in my dream. And his body, shining white."

"But it is not his body," Cranmer says. "It is an image formed in Your Majesty's mind. Such images are *quasi corpora*, like bodies. Read Augustine."

The king does not look as if he wants to send out for a book. "In my dream he stood and looked at me. He looked sad, so sad. He seemed to say I stood in his place. He seemed to say, you have taken my kingdom, and you have used my wife. He has come back to make me ashamed."

Cranmer says, faintly impatient, "If Your Majesty's brother died before he could reign, that was God's will. As for your supposed marriage, we all know and believe that it was clean contrary to scripture. We know the man in Rome has no power to dispense from the law of God. That there was a sin, we acknowledge; but with God there is mercy enough."

"Not for me," Henry says. "When I come to judgment my brother will plead against me. He has come back to make me ashamed and I must bear it." The thought enrages him. "I, I alone."

Cranmer is about to speak; he catches his eye, imperceptibly shakes his head. "Did your brother Arthur speak to you, in your dream?"

"No."

"Did he make any sign?"

"No."

"Then why believe he means Your Majesty anything but good? It seems to me you have read into his face what was not really there, which is a mistake we make with the dead. Listen to me." He puts his hand upon the royal person, on his sleeve of russet velvet, on his arm, and he grasps it hard enough to make himself felt. "You know the lawyers' saying '*Le mort saisit le vif*'? The dead grip the living. The prince dies but his power passes at the moment of his death, there is no lapse, no interregnum. If your brother visited you, it is not to make you ashamed, but to remind you that you are vested with the power of both the living and the dead. This is a sign to you to examine your kingship. And exert it."

Henry looks up at him. He is thinking. He is stroking his sable cuff and his expression is lost. "Is this possible?"

Again Cranmer begins to speak. Again he cuts him off. "You know what is written on the tomb of Arthur?"

"*Rex quondam rexque futurus.* The former king is the future king."

"Your father made it sure. A prince coming out of Wales, he made good the word given to his ancestors. Out of his lifetime's exile he came back and claimed his ancient right. But it is not enough to claim a country; it must be held. It must be held and made secure, in every generation. If your brother seems to say that you have taken his place, then he means you to become the king that he would have been. He himself cannot fulfill the prophecy, but he wills it to you. For him, the promise, and for you, the performance of it."

The king's eyes move to Dr. Cranmer, who says, stiffly, "I cannot see anything against it. I still counsel against heeding dreams."

"Oh, but," he says, "the dreams of kings are not like the dreams of other men."

"You may be right."

"But why now?" Henry says, reasonably enough. "Why does he come back now? I have been king for twenty years."

He bites back the temptation to say, because you are forty and he is telling you to grow up. How many times have you enacted the stories of Arthur—how many masques, how many pageants, how many companies of players with paper shields and wooden swords? "Because this is the vital time," he says. "Because now is the time to become the ruler you should be, and to be sole and supreme head of your kingdom. Ask Lady Anne. She will tell you. She will say the same."

"She does," the king admits. "She says we should no longer bow to Rome."

"And should your father appear to you in a dream, take it just as you take this one. That he has come to strengthen your hand. No father wishes to see his son less powerful than himself."

Henry slowly smiles. From the dream, from the night, from the night of shrouded terrors, from maggots and worms, he seems to uncurl, and stretch himself. He stands up. His face shines. The fire stripes his robe with light, and in its deep folds flicker ocher and fawn, colors of earth, of clay. "Very well," he says. "I see. I understand it all now. I knew who to send for. I always know." He turns and speaks into the darkness. "Harry Norris? What time is it? Is it four o'clock? Have my chaplain robe for Mass."

"Perhaps I could say Mass for you," Dr. Cranmer suggests, but Henry says, "No, you are tired. I've kept you from your beds, gentlemen."

It is as easy as that, as peremptory. They find themselves turned out. They pass the guards. They walk in silence, back to their people, the man Brereton shadowing them. At last, Dr. Cranmer says, "Neat work."

He turns. Now he wants to laugh but he dare not laugh.

"A deft touch, 'and should your father appear to you . . .' I take it you don't like to be roused too often in the small hours."

"My household was alarmed."

The doctor looks sorry then, as if he might have been frivolous. "Of course," he murmurs. "Because I am not a married man, I do not think of these things."

"I am not a married man, either."

"No. I forgot."

"You object to what I said?"

"It was perfect in every way. As if you had thought of it in advance."

"How could I?"

"Indeed. You are a man of vigorous invention. Still . . . for the gospel, you know . . ."

"For the gospel, I count it a good night's work."

"But I wonder," Cranmer says, almost to himself. "I wonder what you think the gospel is. Do you think it is a book of blank sheets on which Thomas Cromwell imprints his desires?"

He stops. He puts a hand on his arm and says, "Dr. Cranmer, look at me. Believe me. I am sincere. I cannot help it if God has given me a sinner's aspect. He must mean something by it."

"I dare say." Cranmer smiles. "He has arranged your face on purpose to disconcert our enemies. And that hand of yours, to take a grip on circumstance—when you took the king's arm in your grasp, I winced myself. And Henry, he felt it." He nods. "You are a person of great force of will."

Clerics can do this: speak about your character. Give verdicts: this one seems favorable, though the doctor, like a fortune-teller, has told him no more than he already knew. "Come," Cranmer says, "your boys will be fretting to see you safe."

Rafe, Gregory, Richard, cluster round him: what's happened? "The king had a dream."

"A dream?" Rafe is shocked. "He got us out of bed for a dream?"

"Believe me," Brereton says, "he gets one out of bed for less than that."

"Dr. Cranmer and I agree that a king's dreams are not as other men's dreams."

Gregory asks, "Was it a bad dream?"

"Initially. He thought it was. It isn't now."

They look at him, not understanding, but Gregory understands. "When I was small I dreamed of demons. I thought they were under my bed, but you said, it can't be so, you don't get demons our side of the river, the guards won't let them over London Bridge."

"So are you terrified," Richard says, "if you cross the river to Southwark?"

Gregory says, "Southwark? What is Southwark?"

"Do you know," Rafe says, in a schoolmaster's tone, "there are times when I see a spark of something in Gregory. Not a blaze, to be sure. Just a spark."

"That you should mock! With a beard like that."

"Is that a beard?" Richard says. "Those scant red bristles? I thought there was some negligence by the barber."

They are hugging each other, wild with relief. Gregory says, "We thought the king had committed him to some dungeon."

Cranmer nods, tolerant, amused. "Your children love you."

Richard says, "We cannot do without the man in charge."

It will be many hours till dawn. It is like the lightless morning on which the cardinal died. There is a smell of snow in the air.

"I suspect he will want us again," Cranmer says. "When he has thought about what you have said to him and, shall we say, followed where his thoughts lead him?"

"Still, I shall go back to the city and show my face." Change my clothes, he thinks, and wait for the next thing. To Brereton he says, "You know where to find me. William."

A nod, and he walks away. "Dr. Cranmer, tell the Lady we did a good night's work for her." He throws his arm around his son's shoulder, whispers, "Gregory, those Merlin stories you read—we are going to write some more."

Gregory says, "Oh, I didn't finish them. The sun came out."

❖

Later that day he walks back into a paneled chamber at Greenwich. It is the last day of 1530. He eases off his gloves, kidskin scented with amber. The fingers of his right hand touch the turquoise ring, settling it in place.

"The council is waiting," the king says. He is laughing, as if at some personal triumph. "Go and join them. They will give you your oath."

Dr. Cranmer is with the king; very pale, very silent. The doctor nods, to acknowledge him; and then, surprisingly, a smile floods his face, lighting up the whole afternoon.

An air of improvisation hangs over the next hour. The king does not want to wait and it is a matter of which councillors can be found at short notice. The dukes are in their own countries, holding their Christmas courts. Old Warham is with us, Archbishop of Canterbury.

It is fifteen years since Wolsey kicked him out of his post as Lord Chancellor; or, as the cardinal always put it, relieved him of worldly office, so allowing him the opportunity, in his last years, to embrace a life of prayer. "Well, Cromwell," he says. "You a councillor! What the world comes to!" His face is seamed, his eyes are dead-fish eyes. His hands shake a little as he proffers the holy book.

Thomas Boleyn is with us, Earl of Wiltshire, Lord Privy Seal. The Lord Chancellor is here; he thinks in irritation, why can More never get a proper shave? Can't he make time, shorten his whipping schedule? As More moves into the light, he sees that he is more disheveled than usual, his face gaunt, plum-colored stains under his eyes. "What's happened to you?"

"You didn't hear. My father died."

"That good old man," he says. "We will miss his wise counsel in the law."

And his tedious stories. I don't think.

"He died in my arms." More begins to cry; or rather, he seems to diminish, and his whole body to leak tears. He says, he was the light of my life, my father. We are not those great men, we are a shadow of what they were. Ask your people at Austin Friars to pray for him. "It's strange, Thomas, but since he went, I feel my age. As if I were just a boy, till a few days ago. But God has snapped his fingers, and I see my best years are behind me."

"You know, after Elizabeth died, my wife . . ." And then, he wants to say, my daughters, my sister, my household decimated, my people never out of black, and now my cardinal lost . . . But he will not admit, for even a moment, that sorrow has sapped his will. You cannot get another father, but he would hardly want to; as for wives, they are two-a-penny with Thomas More. "You do not believe it now, but feeling will come back. For the world and all you must do in it."

"You have had your losses, I know. Well, well." The Lord Chancellor sniffs, he sighs, shakes his head. "Let us do this necessary thing."

It is More who begins to read him the oath. He swears to give faithful counsel, in his speech to be plain, impartial, in his manner secret, in his allegiance true. He is getting on to wise counsel and discreet, when the door flies open and Gardiner swoops in, like a crow that's spied a dead sheep. "I don't think you can do this without Master Secretary," he says, and Warham says mildly, by the Blessed Rood, must we start swearing him all over again?

Thomas Boleyn is stroking his beard. His eye has fallen on the cardinal's ring, and his expression has moved from the shocked to the merely sardonic. "If we do not know the procedure," he says, "I feel sure Thomas Cromwell has a note of it. Give him a year or two, and we may all find ourselves superfluous."

"I am sure I shall not live to see it," Warham says. "Lord Chancellor, shall we get on? Oh, you poor man! Weeping again. I am very sorry for you. But death comes to us all."

Dear God, he thinks, if that's the best you get from the Archbishop of Canterbury, I could do the job.

He swears to uphold the king's authorities. His preeminences, his jurisdictions. He swears to uphold his heirs and lawful successors, and he thinks of the bastard child Richmond, and Mary the talking shrimp, and the Duke of Norfolk showing off his thumbnail to the company. "Well, that's done," says the archbishop. "And amen to it, for what choice have we? Shall we have a glass of wine warmed? This cold gets into the bones."

Thomas More says, "Now you are a member of the council, I hope you will tell the king what he ought to do, not merely what he can do. If the lion knew his own strength, it would be hard to rule him."

Outside it is sleeting. Dark flakes fall into the waters of the Thames. England stretches away from him, low red sun on fields of snow.

He thinks back to the day York Place was wrecked. He and George Cavendish stood by as the chests were opened and the cardinal's vestments taken out. The copes were sewn in gold and silver thread, with patterns of golden stars, with birds, fishes, harts, lions, angels, flowers and Catherine wheels. When they were repacked and nailed into their traveling chests, the king's men delved into the boxes that held the albs and cottas, each folded, by an expert touch, into fine pleats. Passed hand to hand, weightless as resting angels, they glowed softly in the light; loose one, a man said, let us see the quality of it. Fingers tugged at the linen bands; here, let me, George Cavendish said. Freed, the cloth drifted against the air, dazzling white, fine as a moth's wing. When the lids of the vestments chests were raised there was the smell of cedar and spices, somber, distant, desert-dry. But the floating angels had been packed away in lavender; London rain washed against the glass, and the scent of summer flooded the dim afternoon.

PART FOUR

I

Arrange Your Face

1531

hether it is through pain or fear, or some defect of nature; whether because of the summer heat, or the sound of hunting horns winding into the distance, or the spinning of sparkling dust in empty rooms; or whether it is that the child has lost sleep, while from dawn onward her father's decamping household was packed up around her; for whatever reason, she is shrunken into herself, and her eyes are the color of ditch-water. Once, as he is going through the preliminary Latin politenesses, he sees her grip tighten on the back of her mother's chair. "Madam, your daughter should sit." In case a contest of wills should ensue, he picks up a stool and places it, with a decisive thud, by Katherine's skirts.

The queen leans back, rigid inside her boned bodice, to whisper to her daughter. The ladies of Italy, seemingly carefree, wore constructions of iron beneath their silks. It took infinite patience, not just in negotiation, to get them out of their clothes.

Mary drops her head to whisper back; she hints, in Castilian, that it is her woman's disorder. Two pairs of eyes rise to meet his. The girl's glance is almost unfocused; she sees him, he supposes, as a bulky mass of shadow, in a space welling with distress. Stand up straight, Katherine murmurs: like a princess of England. Braced against the chair back, Mary takes a deep breath. She turns to him her plain pinched face: hard as Norfolk's thumbnail.

It is early afternoon, very hot. The sun casts against the wall shifting squares of lilac and gold. The shriveled fields of Windsor are laid out below them. The Thames shrinks from its banks.

The queen speaks in English. "Do you know who this is? This is Master Cromwell. Who now writes all the laws."

Caught awkwardly between languages, he says, "Madam, shall we go on in English, or Latin?"

"Your cardinal would ask the same question. As if I were a stranger here. I will say to you, as I said to him, that I was first addressed as Princess of Wales when I was three years old. I was sixteen when I came here to marry my lord Arthur. I was a virgin and seventeen when he died. I was twenty-four years old when I became Queen of England, and I will say for the avoidance of doubt that I am at present aged forty-six, and still queen, and by now, I believe, a sort of Englishwoman. But I shall not repeat to you everything that I told the cardinal. I imagine he left you notes of these things."

He feels he should bow. The queen says, "Since the year began they have brought certain bills into Parliament. Until now Master Cromwell's talent was for money lending, but now he finds he has a talent for legislation too—if you want a new law, just ask him. I hear that at night you take the drafts to your house in—where is your house?" She makes it sound like "your dog-hole."

Mary says, "These laws are written against the church. I wonder that our lords allow it."

"You know," the queen says, "that the Cardinal of York was accused under the praemunire laws of usurping your lord father's jurisdiction as ruler of England. Now Master Cromwell and his friends find all the clergy complicit in that crime, and ask them to pay a fine of more than one hundred thousand pounds."

"Not a fine. We call it a benevolence."

"I call it extortion." She turns to her daughter. "If you ask why the church is not defended, I can only tell you that there are noblemen in this land"—Suffolk, she means, Norfolk—"who have been heard to say they will pull the power of the church down, that never again will they suffer—they use the word—a churchman to grow so great as our late legate. That we need no new Wolsey, I concur. With the attacks on the bishops, I do not concur. Wolsey was to me an enemy. That does not alter my feelings toward our Holy Mother the church."

He thinks, Wolsey was to me a father and a friend. That does not alter my feelings toward our Holy Mother the church.

"You and Speaker Audley, you put your heads together by candlelight." The queen mentions the Speaker's name as if she were saying "your kitchen boy." "And when the morning comes you induce the king to describe himself as head of the church in England."

"Whereas," the child says, "the Pope is head of the church everywhere, and from the throne of St. Peter flows the lawfulness of all government. From no other source."

"Lady Mary," he says, "will you not sit?" He catches her just as she folds at the knees, and eases her down onto the stool. "It is just the heat," he says, so she will not be ashamed. She turns up her eyes, shallow and gray, with a look of simple gratitude; and as soon as she is seated the look is replaced by an expression as stony as the wall of a town under siege.

"You say 'induce,'" he tells Katherine. "But Your Highness, above anyone, knows that the king cannot be led."

"But he may be enticed." She turns to Mary, whose arms have crept over her belly. "So your father the king is named head of the church, and to soothe the conscience of the bishops, they have caused this formula to be inserted: 'as far as the law of Christ allows.'"

"What does that mean?" Mary says. "It means nothing."

"Your Highness, it means everything."

"Yes. It is very clever."

"I beg you," he says, "to consider it in this way, that the king has merely defined a position previously held, one that ancient precedents—"

"—invented these last months—"

"—show as his right."

Under her clumsy gable hood, Mary's forehead is slick with sweat. She says, "What is defined can be redefined, yes?"

"Indeed," her mother says. "And redefined in favor of the church—if only I fall in with their wishes, and put myself out of the estate of queen and wife."

The princess is right, he thinks. There is room for negotiation. "Nothing here is irrevocable."

"No, you wait to see what I will bring to your treaty table." Katherine holds out her hands—little, stubby, puffy hands—to show that they are empty. "Only Bishop Fisher defends me. Only he has been constant. Only he is able to tell the truth, which is that the House of Commons is full of heathens." She sighs, her hands fall at her sides. "And now under what persuasion has my husband ridden off without a farewell? He has not done so before. Never."

"He means to hunt out of Chertsey for a few days."

"With the woman," Mary says. "The person."

"Then he will ride by way of Guildford to visit Lord Sandys—he wants to see his handsome new gallery at the Vyne." His tone is easy, soothing, like the cardinal's; perhaps too much so? "From there, depending on the weather, and the game, he will go to William Paulet at Basing."

"I am to follow, when?"

"He will return in a fortnight, God willing."

"A fortnight," Mary says. "Alone with the person."

"Before then, madam, you are to go to another palace—he has chosen the More, in Hertfordshire, which you know is very comfortable."

"Being the cardinal's house," Mary says, "it would be lavish."

My own daughters, he thinks, would never have spoken so. "Princess," he says, "will you, of your charity, cease to speak ill of a man who never did you harm?"

Mary blushes from neckline to hairline. "I did not mean to fail in charity."

"The late cardinal is your godfather. You owe him your prayers."

Her eyes flicker toward him; she looks cowed. "I pray to shorten his term in Purgatory . . ."

Katherine interrupts her. "Send a box to Hertfordshire. Send a package. Do not seek to send me."

"You shall have your whole court. The household is ready for two hundred."

"I shall write to the king. You may carry the letter. My place is with him."

"My advice," he says, "take this gently. Or he may . . ." He indicates the princess. His hands join and drift apart. Separate you.

The child is fighting down pain. Her mother is fighting down grief and anger, and disgust and fear. "I expected this," she says, "but I did not expect he would send a man like you to tell me." He frowns: does she think it would come better from Norfolk? "They say you had a trade as a blacksmith; is that correct?"

Now she will say, shoe a horse?

"It was my father's trade."

"I begin to understand you." She nods. "The blacksmith makes his own tools."

❖

Half a mile of chalk walls, a mirror for the glare, bounce at him a white heat. In the shadow of a gateway, Gregory and Rafe are jostling and pushing, insulting each other with culinary insults he has taught them: Sir, you are a fat Fleming, and spread butter on your bread. Sir, you are a Roman pauper, may your offspring eat snails. Master Wriothesley is leaning in the sun and watching them, with a lazy smile; butterflies garland his head.

"Oh, it's you," he says. Wriothesley looks gratified. "You look fit to be painted, Master Wriothesley. A doublet of azure, and a shaft of light precisely placed."

"Sir? Katherine says?"

"She says our precedents are fake."

Rafe: "Does she understand that you and Dr. Cranmer sat up all night over them?"

"Oh, wild times!" Gregory says. "Seeing the dawn in, with Dr. Cranmer!"

He throws an arm around Rafe's bony little shoulders and squeezes him; it is a liberation to be away from Katherine, from the girl flinching like a whipped bitch. "Once I myself, with Giovannino—well, with some boys I knew—" He stops: what is this? I don't tell stories about myself.

"Please . . ." Wriothesley says.

"Well, we had a statue made, a smirking little god with wings, and then we beat it with hammers and chains to make it antique, and we hired a muleteer and drove it to Rome and sold it to a cardinal." Such a hot day, when they were ushered into his presence: hazy, thunder in the distance, and white dust from building sites hanging in the air. "I remember he had tears in his eyes when he paid us. 'To think that on these charming little feet and these sweet pinions, the gaze of the Emperor Augustus may have rested.' When the Portinari boys set off for Florence they were staggering under the weight of their purses."

"And you?"

"I took my cut and stayed on to sell the mules."

They head downhill through the inner courts. Emerging into the sun, he shades his eyes as if to see through the tangle of treetops that runs into the distance. "I told the queen, let Henry go in peace. Or he might not let the princess move with her up-country."

Wriothesley says, surprised, "But it is decided. They are to be separated. Mary is to go to Richmond."

He did not know. He hopes his hesitation is not perceptible. "Of course. But the queen had not been told, and it was worth a try, yes?"

See how useful Master Wriothesley is. See how he brings us intelligence from Secretary Gardiner. Rafe says, "It is harsh. To use the little girl against her mother."

"Harsh, yes . . . but the question is, have you picked your prince? Because that is what you do, you choose him, and you know what he is. And then, when you have chosen, you say yes to him—yes, that is possible, yes, that can be done. If you don't like Henry, you can go abroad and find another prince, but I tell you—if this were Italy, Katherine would be cold in her tomb."

"But you swore," Gregory says, "that you respected the queen."

"So I do. And I would respect her corpse."

"You would not work her death, would you?"

He halts. He takes his son's arm, turns him to look into his face. "Retrace our steps through this conversation." Gregory pulls away. "No, listen, Gregory. I said, you give way to the king's requests. You open the way to his desires. That is what a courtier does. Now, understand this: it is impossible that Henry should require me or any other person to harm the queen. What is he, a monster? Even now he has affection for her; how could he not? And he has a soul he hopes may be saved. He confesses every day to one or another of his chaplains. Do you think the Emperor does so much, or King Francis? Henry's heart, I assure you, is a heart full of feeling; and Henry's soul, I swear, is the most scrutinized soul in Christendom."

Wriothesley says, "Master Cromwell, he is your son, not an ambassador."

He lets Gregory go. "Shall we get on the river? There might be a breeze."

In the Lower Ward, six couples of hunting dogs stir and yelp in the cages on wheels which are going to carry them across country. Tails waving, they are clambering over each other, twisting ears and nipping, their yaps and howls adding to the sense of near-panic that has taken over the castle. It's more like the evacuation of a fort than the start of a summer progress. Sweating porters are heaving the king's furnishings onto carts. Two men with a studded chest have got wedged in a doorway. He thinks of himself on the road, a bruised child, loading wagons to get a lift. He wanders over. "How did this happen, boys?"

He steadies one corner of the chest and backs them off into the shadows; adjusts the degree of rotation with a flip of his hand; a moment's fumbling and slipping, and they burst into the light, shouting, "Here she goes!" as if they had thought of it themselves. Be packing for the queen next, he says, for the cardinal's palace at the More, and they say, surprised, is that so, master, and what if the queen won't go? He says, then we will roll her up in a carpet and put her on your cart. He hands out coins: ease up, it's too hot to work so hard. He saunters back to the boys. A man leads up horses ready for harnessing to the hounds' wagons, and as soon as they catch their scent the dogs set up an excited barking, which can still be heard as they get on the water.

The river is brown, torpid; on the Eton bank, a group of listless swans glides in and out of the weeds. Their boat bobs beneath them; he says, "Is that not Sion Madoc?"

"Never forget a face, eh?"

"Not when it's ugly."

"Have you seen yourself, *bach*?" The boatman has been eating an apple, core and all; fastidious, he flicks the pips over the side.

"How's your dad?"

"Dead." Sion spits the stalk out. "Any of these yours?"

"Me," Gregory says.

"That's mine." Sion nods to the opposite oar, a lump of a lad who reddens and looks away. "Your dad used to shut up shop in this weather. Put the fire out and go fishing."

"Lashing the water with his rod," he says, "and punching the lights out of the fish. Jump in and drag them gasping out of the green deep. Fingers through the gills: 'What are you looking at, you scaly whoreson? Are you looking at me?'"

"He not being one to sit and enjoy the sunshine," Madoc explains. "I could tell you stories, about Walter Cromwell."

Master Wriothesley's face is a study. He does not understand how much you can learn from boatmen, their argot blasphemous and rapid. At twelve he spoke it fluently, his mother tongue, and now it flows back into his mouth, something natural, something dirty. There are tags of Greek he has mastered, which he exchanges with Thomas Cranmer, with Call-Me-Risley: early language, unblighted, like tender fruit. But never does a Greek scholar pin back your ears as Sion does now, with Putney's opinion of the fucking Bullens. Henry goes to it with the mother, good luck to him. He goes to it with the sister, what's a king for? But it's got to stop somewhere. We're not beasts of the field. Sion calls Anne an eel, he calls her a slippery dipper from the slime, and he remembers what the cardinal had called her: my serpentine enemy. Sion says, she goes to it with her brother; he says, what, her brother George?

"Any brother she's got. Those kind keep it in the family. They do filthy French tricks, like—"

"Can you keep your voice down?" He looks around, as if spies might be swimming by the boat.

"—and that's how she trusts herself she don't give in to Henry, because if she lets him do it and she gets a boy he's, thanks very much, now clear off, girl—so she's, oh, Your Highness, I never could allow—because she knows that very night her brother's inside her, licking her up to the lungs, and then he's, excuse me, sister, what shall I do with this big package—she says, oh, don't distress yourself, my lord brother, shove it up the back entry, it'll come to no harm there."

Thanks, he says, I had no idea how they were managing.

The boys have got about one word in three. Sion gets a tip. It's worth anything, to be reacquainted with the Putney imagination. He will cherish Sion's simper: very unlike the real Anne.

Later, at home, Gregory says, "Ought people to speak like that? And be paid for it?"

"He was speaking his mind." He shrugs. "So, if you want to know people's minds . . ."

"Call-Me-Risley is frightened of you. He says that when you were coming from Chelsea with Master Secretary, you threatened to throw him out of his own barge and drown him."

That is not precisely his memory of the conversation.

"And does Call-Me think I would do it?"

"Yes. He thinks you would do anything."

❖

At New Year's he had given Anne a present of silver forks with handles of rock crystal. He hopes she will use them to eat with, not to stick in people.

"From Venice!" She is pleased. She holds them up, so the handles catch and splinter the light.

He has brought another present, for her to pass on. It is wrapped in a piece of sky-blue silk. "It is for the little girl who always cries."

Anne's mouth opens a little. "Don't you know?" Her eyes brim with black glee. "Come, so I can tell you in your ear." Her cheek brushes his. Her skin is faintly perfumed: amber, rose. "Sir John Seymour?

Dear Sir John? Old Sir John, as people call him?" Sir John is not, perhaps, more than a dozen years older than himself, but amiability can
be aging; with his sons Edward and Tom now the young men about
court, he does give the impression of having eased into retirement.
"Now we understand why we never see him," Anne murmurs. "Now
we know what he does down in the country."

"Hunting, I thought."

"Yes, and he has netted Catherine Fillol, Edward's wife. They were
taken in the act, but I cannot find out where, whether in her bed, or his,
or in a meadow, a hayloft—yes, cold, to be sure, but they were keeping
each other warm. And now Sir John has confessed it all, man to man,
telling his son to his face that he's had her every week since the wedding, so that's about two years and, say, six months, so . . ."

"You could round it off to a hundred and twenty times, assuming
they abstain at the major feasts . . ."

"Adulterers don't stop for Lent."

"Oh, and I thought they did."

"She's had two babies, so allow respite for her lying-in . . . And they
are boys, you know. So Edward is . . ." He imagines how Edward is. That
pure hawk's profile. "He is cutting them out of the family. They are to be
bastards. She, Catherine Fillol, she's to be put in a convent. I think he
should put her in a cage! He is asking for an annulment. As for dear Sir
John, I think we will not see him at court soon."

"Why are we whispering? I must be the last person in London to
hear."

"The king hasn't heard. And you know how proper he is. So if
someone is to come to him joking about it, let it not be me or you."

"And the daughter? Jane, is it?"

Anne sniggers. "Pasty-face? Gone down to Wiltshire. Her best move
would be to follow the sister-in-law into a nunnery. Her sister Lizzie
married well, but no one wants Milksop, and now no one will." Her eyes
fall on his present; she says, suddenly anxious, jealous, "What is it?"

"Only a book of needlework patterns."

"As long as it is nothing to tax her wits. Why would you send her a
present?"

"I feel sorry for her." More now, of course.

"Oh. You don't like her, do you?" The correct answer is, no, my lady Anne, I only like you. "Because, is it proper for you to send her a present?"

"It is not as if it is tales out of Boccaccio."

She laughs. "They could tell Boccaccio a tale, those sinners at Wolf Hall."

❖

Thomas Hitton, a priest, was burned just as February went out; taken up by Fisher, Bishop of Rochester, as a smuggler of Tyndale's scriptures. Soon afterward, rising from the bishop's frugal table, a dozen guests had collapsed, vomiting, rigid with pain, and been taken, pale and almost pulseless, to their beds and the ministrations of the doctors. Dr. Butts said the broth had done it; from testimony of the waiting-boys, it was the only dish they had tasted in common.

There are poisons nature herself brews, and he, before putting the bishop's cook to the torture, would have visited the kitchens and passed a skimmer over the stockpot. But no one else doubts there has been a crime.

Presently the cook admits to adding to the broth a white powder, which someone gave him. Who? Just a man. A stranger who had said it would be a good joke, to give Fisher and his guests a purge.

The king is beside himself: rage and fear. He blames heretics. Dr. Butts, shaking his head, pulling his lower lip, says that poison is what Henry fears worse than Hell itself.

Would you put poison in a bishop's dinner because a stranger told you it would be a laugh? The cook won't say more, or perhaps he has reached a stage beyond saying. The interrogation has been mismanaged then, he says to Butts; I wonder why. The doctor, a man who loves the gospel, laughs sourly and says, "If they wanted the man to talk, they should have called in Thomas More."

The word is that the Lord Chancellor has become a master in the twin arts of stretching and compressing the servants of God. When heretics are taken, he stands by at the Tower while the torture is applied.

It is reported that in his gatehouse at Chelsea he keeps suspects in the stocks, while he preaches at them and harries them: the name of your printer, the name of the master of the ship that brought these books into England. They say he uses the whip, the manacles and the torment-frame they call Skeffington's Daughter. It is a portable device, into which a man is folded, knees to chest, with a hoop of iron across his back; by means of a screw, the hoop is tightened until his ribs crack. It takes art to make sure the man does not suffocate: for if he does, everything he knows is lost.

❖

Over the next week, two dinner guests die; Fisher himself rallies. It is possible, he thinks, that the cook did speak, but that what he said was not for the ears of the ordinary subject.

He goes to see Anne. A thorn between two roses, she is sitting with her cousin Mary Shelton, and her brother's wife, Jane, Lady Rochford. "My lady, do you know the king has devised a new form of death for Fisher's cook? He is to be boiled alive."

Mary Shelton gives a little gasp, and flushes as if some gallant had pinched her. Jane Rochford drawls, "*Vere dignum et justum est, aequum et salutare.*" She translates for Mary: "Apt."

Anne's face wears no expression at all. Even a man as literate as he can find nothing there to read. "How will they do it?"

"I did not ask about the mechanics. Would you like me to inquire? I think it will involve hoisting him up in chains, so that the crowd can see his skin peeling off and hear him screaming."

To be fair to Anne, if you walked up to her and said, you are to be boiled, she would probably shrug: *c'est la vie.*

Fisher is in bed for a month. When he is up and about he looks like a walking corpse. The intercession of angels and saints has not sufficed to heal his sore gut and put the flesh back on his bones.

These are days of brutal truth from Tyndale. Saints are not your friends and they will not protect you. They cannot help you to salvation. You cannot engage them to your service with prayers and candles, as you might hire a man for the harvest. Christ's sacrifice was done on

Calvary; it is not done in the Mass. Priests cannot help you to Heaven; you need no priest to stand between you and your God. No merits of yours can save you: only the merits of the living Christ.

March: Lucy Petyt, whose husband is a master grocer and a member of the Commons, comes to see him at Austin Friars. She is wearing black lambskin—imported, at a guess—and a modest gray worsted gown; Alice receives her gloves and surreptitiously slides in a finger to appraise the silk lining. He rises from his desk and takes her hands, drawing her to the fire and pressing upon her a cup of warm spiced wine. Her hands shake as she cradles the cup and she says, "I wish John had this. This wine. This fire."

It was snowing at dawn on the day of the raid on Lion's Quay, but soon a wintery sun was up, scouring windowpanes and casting the paneled rooms of city houses into sharp relief, ravines of shadows and cold floods of light. "That is what I cannot get out of my mind," Lucy says, "the cold." And More himself, his face muffled in furs, standing at the door with his officers, ready to search the warehouse and their own rooms. "I was the first there," she says, "and I kept him hovering with pleasantries—I called up, my dear, here is the Lord Chancellor come on parliamentary business." The wine floods into her face, loosens her tongue. "I kept saying, have you breakfasted, sir, are you sure, and the servants were weaving under his feet, impeding him"—she gives a little, mirthless, whooping laugh—"and all the time John was stowing his papers behind a panel—"

"You did well, Lucy."

"When they walked upstairs John was ready for him—oh, Lord Chancellor, welcome to my poor house—but the poor hapless man, he had cast his Testament under his desk, my eye went straight to it, I wonder their eyes didn't follow mine."

An hour's search realized nothing; so are you sure, John, the Chancellor said, that you have none of these new books, because I was informed you had? (And Tyndale lying there, like a poison stain on the tiles.) I don't know who could have told you that, said John Petyt. I was proud of him, Lucy says, holding out her cup for more wine, I was proud that he spoke up. More said, it is true I have found nothing today, but you must go with these men. Mr. Lieutenant, will you take him?

John Petyt is not a young man. At More's direction he sleeps on a pad of straw laid on the flagstones; visitors have been admitted only so that they can take back to his neighbors the news of how ill he looks. "We have sent food and warm clothes," Lucy says, "and been turned away on the Lord Chancellor's orders."

"There's a tariff for bribes. You pay the jailers. You need ready money?"

"If I do I shall come to you." She puts the cup down on his desk. "He cannot lock us all up."

"He has prisons enough."

"For bodies, yes. But what are bodies? He can take our goods, but God will prosper us. He can close the booksellers, but still there will be books. They have their old bones, their glass saints in windows, their candles and shrines, but God has given us the printing press." Her cheeks glow. She glances down to the drawings on his desk. "What are these, Master Cromwell?"

"The plans for my garden. I am hoping to buy some of the houses at the back of here, I want the land."

She smiles. "A garden . . . It is the first pleasant thing I have heard of in a while."

"I hope you and John will come and enjoy it."

"And this . . . You are going to build a tennis court?"

"If I get the ground. And here, you see, I mean to plant an orchard." Tears well into her eyes. "Speak to the king. We count on you."

He hears a footstep: Johane's. Lucy's hand flies to her mouth. "God forgive me . . . For a moment I took you for your sister."

"The mistake is made," Johane says. "And sometimes persists. Mistress Petyt, I am very sorry to hear your husband is in the Tower. But you have brought this on yourselves. You people were the first to throw calumnies at the late cardinal. But now I suppose you wish you had him back."

Lucy goes out without a further word, only one long look over her shoulder. Outside he hears Mercy greet her; she will get a more sisterly word there. Johane walks to the fire and warms her hands. "What does she think you can do for her?"

"Go to the king. Or to Lady Anne."

"And will you? Do not," she says, "do not do it." She scrubs away a tear with her knuckle; Lucy has upset her. "More will not rack him. Word will get out, and the city would not have it. But he may die anyway." She glances up at him. "She is quite old, you know, Lucy Petyt. She ought not to wear gray. Do you see how her cheeks have fallen in? She won't have any more children."

"I get the point," he says.

Her hand clenches on her skirt. "But what if he does? What if he does rack him? And he gives names?"

"What's that to me?" He turns away. "He already knows my name."

❖

He speaks to Lady Anne. What can I do? she asks, and he says, you know how to please the king, I suppose; she laughs and says, what, my maidenhead for a grocer?

He speaks to the king when he is able, but the king gives him a blank stare and says the Lord Chancellor knows his business. Anne says, I have tried, I myself as you know have put Tyndale's books into his hand, his royal hand; could Tyndale, do you think, come back into this kingdom? In winter they negotiated, letters crossing the Channel. In spring, Stephen Vaughan, his man in Antwerp, set up a meeting: evening, the concealing dusk, a field outside the city walls. Cromwell's letter put into his hand, Tyndale wept: I want to come home, he said, I am sick of this, hunted city to city and house to house. I want to come home and if the king would just say yes, if he would say yes to the scriptures in our mother tongue, he can choose his translator, I will never write more. He can do with me what he pleases, torture me or kill me, but only let the people of England hear the gospel.

Henry has not said no. He had not said, never. Though Tyndale's translation and any other translation is banned, he may, one day, permit a translation to be made by a scholar he approves. How can he say less? He wants to please Anne.

But summer comes, and he, Cromwell, knows he has gone to the brink and must feel his way back. Henry is too timid, Tyndale too intransigent. His letters to Stephen sound a note of panic: abandon ship. He does not mean to sacrifice himself to Tyndale's truculence; dear God, he says, More, Tyndale, they deserve each other, these mules that pass for men. Tyndale will not come out in favor of Henry's divorce; nor, for that matter, will the monk Luther. You'd think they'd sacrifice a fine point of principle, to make a friend of the King of England: but no.

And when Henry demands, "Who is Tyndale to judge me?" Tyndale snaps a message back, quick as word can fly: one Christian man may judge another.

"A cat may look at a king," he says. He is cradling Marlinspike in his arms, and talking to Thomas Avery, the boy he's teaching his trade. Avery has been with Stephen Vaughan, so he can learn the practice among the merchants over there, but any boat may bring him to Austin Friars with his little bag, inside it a woolen jerkin, a few shirts. When he comes clattering in he shouts out for Mercy, for Johane, for the little girls, for whom he brings comfits and novelties from street traders. On Richard, on Rafe, on Gregory if he's about, he lands a few punches by way of saying I'm back, but always he keeps his bag tucked under his arm.

The boy follows him into his office. "Did you never feel homesick, master, when you were on your travels?"

He shrugs: I suppose if I'd had a home. He puts the cat down, opens the bag. He fishes up on his finger a string of rosary beads; for show, says Avery, and he says, good boy. Marlinspike leaps onto his desk; he peers into the bag, dabbing with a paw. "The only mice in there are sugar ones." The boy pulls the cat's ears, tussles with him. "We don't have any little pets in Master Vaughan's house."

"He's all business, Stephen. And very stern, these days."

"He says, Thomas Avery, what time did you get in last night? Have you written to your master? Been to Mass? As if he cares for the Mass! It's all but, how's your bowels?"

"Next spring you can come home."

As they speak he is unrolling the jerkin. With a shake he turns it inside out, and with a small pair of scissors begins to slit open a seam. "Neat stitching . . . Who did this?"

The boy hesitates; he colors. "Jenneke."

He draws out from the lining the thin, folded paper. Unwraps it: "She must have good eyes."

"She does."

"And lovely eyes too?" He glances up, smiling. The boy looks him in the face. For a moment he seems startled, and as if he will speak; then he drops his gaze and turns away.

"Just tormenting you, Tom, don't take it to heart." He is reading Tyndale's letter. "If she is a good girl, and in Stephen's household, what harm?"

"What does Tyndale say?"

"You carried it without reading it?"

"I would rather not know. In case."

In case you found yourself Thomas More's guest. He holds the letter in his left hand; his right hand curls loosely into a fist. "Let him come near my people. I'll drag him out of his court at Westminster and beat his head on the cobbles till I knock into him some sense of the love of God and what it means."

The boy grins and flops down on a stool. He, Cromwell, glances again at the letter. "Tyndale says, he thinks he can never come back, even if my lady Anne were queen . . . a project he does nothing to aid, I must say. He says he would not trust a safe conduct, even if the king himself were to sign it, while Thomas More is alive and in office, because More says you need not keep a promise you have made to a heretic. Here. You may as well read. Our Lord Chancellor respects neither ignorance nor innocence."

The boy flinches, but he takes the paper. What a world is this, where promises are not kept. He says gently, "Tell me who is Jenneke. Do you want me to write to her father for you?"

"No." Avery looks up, startled; he is frowning. "No, she's an orphan. Master Vaughan keeps her at his own charge. We are all teaching her English."

"No money to bring you, then?"

The boy looks confused. "I suppose Stephen will give her a dowry." The day is too mild for a fire. The hour is too early for a candle. In lieu of burning, he tears up Tyndale's message. Marlinspike, his ears pricked, chews a fragment of it. "Brother cat," he says. "He ever loved the scriptures."

Scriptura sola. Only the gospel will guide and console you. No use praying to a carved post or lighting a candle to a painted face. Tyndale says "gospel" means good news, it means singing, it means dancing: within limits, of course. Thomas Avery says, "Can I truly come home next spring?"

John Petyt at the Tower is to be allowed to sleep in a bed: no chance, though, that he will go home to Lion's Quay.

Cranmer said to him, when they were talking late one night, St. Augustine says we need not ask where our home is, because in the end we all come home to God.

❖

Lent saps the spirits, as of course it is designed to do. Going in again to Anne, he finds the boy Mark, crouched over his lute and picking at something doleful; he flicks a finger against his head as he breezes past, and says, "Cheer it up, can't you?"

Mark almost falls off his stool. It seems to him they are in a daze, these people, vulnerable to being startled, to being ambushed. Anne, waking out of her dream, says, "What did you just do?"

"Hit Mark. Only," he demonstrates, "with one finger."

Anne says, "Mark? Who? Oh. Is that his name?"

This spring, 1531, he makes it his business to be cheerful. The cardinal was a great grumbler, but he always grumbled in some entertaining way. The more he complained, the more cheerful his man Cromwell became; that was the arrangement.

The king is a complainer too. He has a headache. The Duke of Suffolk is stupid. The weather is too warm for the time of year. The country is going to the dogs. He's anxious too; afraid of spells, and of people thinking bad thoughts about him in any specific or unspecific way. The more anxious the king becomes, the more tranquil becomes his new servant, the more hopeful, the more staunch. And the more the king snips and carps, the more do his petitioners seek out the company of Cromwell, so unfailing in his amiable courtesy.

At home, Jo comes to him looking perplexed. She is a young lady now, with a womanly frown, a soft crinkle of flesh on her forehead, which Johane, her mother, has too. "Sir, how shall we paint our eggs at Easter?"

"How did you paint them last year?"

"Every year before this we gave them hats like the cardinal's." She watches his face, to read back the effect of her words; it is his own habit exactly, and he thinks, not only your children are your children. "Was it wrong?"

"Not at all. I wish I'd known. I would have taken him one. He would have liked it."

Jo puts her soft little hand into his. It is still a child's hand, the skin scuffed over the knuckles, the nails bitten. "I am of the king's council now," he says. "You can paint crowns if you like."

This piece of folly with her mother, this ongoing folly, it has to stop. Johane knows it too. She used to make excuses, to be where he was. But now, if he's at Austin Friars, she's at the house in Stepney.

"Mercy knows," she murmurs in passing.

The surprise is it took her so long, but there is a lesson here; you think people are always watching you, but that is guilt, making you jump at shadows. But finally, Mercy finds she has eyes in her head, and a tongue to speak, and picks a time when they can be alone. "They tell me that the king has found a way around at least one of his stumbling blocks. I mean, the difficulty of how he can marry Lady Anne, when her sister Mary has been in his bed."

"We have had all the best advice," he says easily. "Dr. Cranmer at my recommendation sent to Venice, to a learned body of rabbis, to take opinions on the meaning of the ancient texts."

"So it is not incest? Unless you have actually been married to one sister?"

"The divines say not."

"How much did that cost?"

"Dr. Cranmer wouldn't know. The priests and the scholars go to the negotiating table, then some less godly sort of man comes after them, with a bag of money. They don't have to meet each other, coming in or going out."

"It hardly helps your case," she says bluntly.

"There is no help in my case."

"She wants to talk to you. Johane."

"What's there to say? We all know—" We all know it can go nowhere. Even though her husband, John Williamson, is still coughing: one is always half listening for it, here and at Stepney, the annunciatory wheezing on a stairway or in the next room; one thing about John Williamson, he'll never take you by surprise. Dr. Butts has recommended him country air, and keeping away from fumes and smoke. "It was a moment of weakness," he says. Then . . . what? Another moment. "God sees all. So they tell me."

"You must listen to her." Mercy's face, when she turns back, is incandescent. "You owe her that."

❖

"The way it seems to me, it seems like part of the past." Johane's voice is unsteady; with a little twitch of her fingers she settles her half-moon hood and drifts her veil, a cloud of silk, over one shoulder. "For a long time, I didn't think Liz was really gone. I expected to see her walk in one day."

It has been a constant temptation to him, to have Johane beautifully dressed, and he has dealt with it by, as Mercy says, throwing money at the London goldsmiths and mercers, so the women of Austin Friars are bywords among the city wives, who say behind their hands (but with a worshipful murmur, almost a genuflection), dear God, Thomas Cromwell, the money must be flowing in like the grace of God.

"So now I think," she says, "that what we did because she was dead, when we were shocked, when we were sorry, we have to leave off that now. I mean, we are still sorry. We will always be sorry."

He understands her. Liz died in another age, when the cardinal was still in his pomp, and he was the cardinal's man. "If," she says, "you would like to marry, Mercy has her list. But then, you probably have your own list. With nobody on it we know.

"If, of course," she says, "if John Williamson had—God forgive me but every winter I think it is his last—then of course I, without question, I mean, at once, Thomas, as soon as decent, not clasping hands over his coffin . . . but then the church wouldn't allow it. The law wouldn't."

"You never know," he says.

She throws out her hands, words flood out of her. "They say you intend to, what you intend, to break the bishops and make the king head of the church and take away his revenues from the Holy Father and give them to Henry, then Henry can declare the law if he likes and put off his wife as he likes and marry Lady Anne and he will say what is a sin and what not and who can be married. And the Princess Mary, God defend her, will be a bastard and after Henry the next king will be whatever child that lady gives him."

"Johane . . . when Parliament meets again, would you like to come down and tell them what you've just said? Because it would save a lot of time."

"You can't," she says, aghast. "The Commons will not vote it. The Lords will not. Bishop Fisher will not allow it. Archbishop Warham. The Duke of Norfolk. Thomas More."

"Fisher is ill. Warham is old. Norfolk, he said to me only the other day, 'I am tired'—if you will permit his expression—'of fighting under the banner of Katherine's stained bedsheet, and if Arthur could enjoy her, or if he couldn't, who gives a—who cares anymore?'" He is rapidly altering the duke's words, which were coarse in the extreme. "'Let my niece Anne come in,' he said, 'and do her worst.'"

"What is her worst?" Johane's mouth is ajar; the duke's words will be rolling down Gracechurch Street, rolling to the river and across the bridge, till the painted ladies in Southwark are passing them mouth to mouth like ulcers; but that's the Howards for you, that's the Boleyns; with or without him, news of Anne's character will reach London and the world.

"She provokes the king's temper," he says. "He complains Katherine never in her life spoke to him as Anne does. Norfolk says she uses language to him you wouldn't use to a dog."

"Jesu! I wonder he doesn't whip her."

"Perhaps he will, when they're married. Look, if Katherine were to withdraw her suit from Rome, if she were to submit to judgment of her case in England, or if the Pope were to concede to the king's wishes, then all this—everything you've said, it won't happen, it will be just—" His hand makes a smooth, withdrawing motion, like the rolling up of a parchment. "If Clement were to come to his desk one morning, not quite awake, and sign with his left hand some piece of paper he's not read, well, who could blame him? And then I leave him, we leave him, undisturbed, in possession of his revenues, in possession of his authority, because now Henry only wants one thing, and that is Anne in his bed; but time marches on and he is beginning to think, believe me, of other things he might want."

"Yes. Like his own way."

"He's a king. He's used to it."

"And if the Pope is still stubborn?"

"He'll go begging for his revenue."

"Will the king take the money of Christian people? The king is rich."

"There you are wrong. The king is poor."

"Oh. Does he know it?"

"I'm not sure he knows where his money comes from, or where it goes. While my lord cardinal was alive, he never wanted for a jewel in his hat or a horse or a handsome house. Henry Norris keeps his privy purse, but besides that he has too much of a hand in the revenue for my liking. Henry Norris," he tells her before she can ask, "is the bane of my life." He is always, he does not add, with Anne when I need to see her alone.

"I suppose if Henry wants his supper, he can come here. Not this Henry Norris. I mean, Henry our pauper king." She stands up; she sees herself in the glass; she ducks, as if shy of her own reflection, and arranges her face into an expression lighter, more curious and detached, less personal; he sees her do it, lift her eyebrows a fraction, curve up her lips at the corner. I could paint her, he thinks; if I had the skill. I have looked at her so long; but looking doesn't bring back the dead, the harder you look the faster and the farther they go. He had never supposed Liz Wykys was smiling down from Heaven on what he was doing with her sister. No, he thinks, what I've done is push Liz into the dark; and something comes back to him, that Walter once said, that his mother used to say her prayers to a little carved saint she'd had in her bundle when she came down as a young woman from the north, and she used to turn it away before she got into bed with him. Walter had said, dear God, Thomas, it was St. fucking Felicity if I'm not mistaken, and her face was to the wall for sure the night I got you.

Johane walks about the room. It is a large room and filled with light. "All these things," she says, "these things we have now. The clock. That new chest you had Stephen send you from Flanders, the one with the carving of the birds and flowers, I heard with my own ears you say to Thomas Avery, oh, tell Stephen I want it, I don't care what it costs. All these painted pictures of people we don't know, all these, I don't know what, lutes and books of music, we never used to have them, when I was a girl I never used to look at myself in a mirror, but now I look at myself every day. And a comb, you gave me an ivory comb. I never had one of my own. Liz used to plait my hair and push it under my hood, and then I did hers, and if we didn't look how we ought to look, somebody soon told us."

Why are we so attached to the severities of the past? Why are we so proud of ourselves for having endured our fathers and our mothers, the fireless days and the meatless days, the cold winters and the sharp tongues? It's not as if we had a choice. Even Liz, once when they were young, when she'd seen him early in the morning putting Gregory's shirt to warm before the fire, even Liz had said sharply, don't do that, he'll expect it every day.

He says, "Liz—I mean, Johane . . ."

You've done that once too often, her face says.

"I want to be good to you. Tell me what I can give you."

He waits for her to shout, as women do, do you think you can buy me, but she doesn't, she listens, and he thinks she is entranced, her face intent, her eyes on his, as she learns his theory about what money can buy. "There was a man in Florence, a friar, Fra Savonarola, he induced all the people to think beauty was a sin. Some people think he was a magician and they fell under his spell for a season, they made fires in the streets and they threw in everything they liked, everything they had made or worked to buy, bolts of silk, and linen their mothers had embroidered for their marriage beds, books of poems written in the poet's hand, bonds and wills, rent-rolls, title deeds, dogs and cats, the shirts from their backs, the rings from their fingers, women their veils, and do you know what was worst, Johane—they threw in their mirrors. So then they couldn't see their faces and know how they were different from the beasts in the field and the creatures screaming on the pyre. And when they had melted their mirrors they went home to their empty houses, and lay on the floor because they had burned their beds, and when they got up next day they were aching from the hard floor and there was no table for their breakfast because they'd used the table to feed the bonfire, and no stool to sit on because they'd chopped it into splinters, and there was no bread to eat because the bakers had thrown into the flames the basins and the yeast and the flour and the scales. And you know the worst of it? They were sober. Last night they took their wineskins . . ." He turns his arm, in a mime of a man lobbing something into a fire. "So they were sober and their heads were clear, but they looked around and they had nothing to eat, nothing to drink and nothing to sit on."

"But that wasn't the worst. You said the mirrors were the worst. Not to be able to look at yourself."

"Yes. Well, so I think. I hope I can always look myself in the face. And you, Johane, you should always have a fine glass to see yourself. As you're a woman worth looking at."

You could write a sonnet, Thomas Wyatt could write her a sonnet, and not make this effect . . . She turns her head away, but through the thin film of her veil he can see her skin glow. Because women will coax: tell me, just tell me something, tell me your thoughts; and this he has done.

They part friends. They even manage without one last time for old time's sake. Not that they are parted, really, but now they are on different terms. Mercy says, "Thomas, when you're cold and under a stone, you'll talk yourself out of your grave."

The household is quiet, calm. The turmoil of the city is locked outside the gate; he is having the locks renewed, the chains reinforced. Jo brings him an Easter egg. "Look, we have saved this one for you." It is a white egg with no speckles. It is featureless, but a single curl, the color of onionskin, peeps out from under a lopsided crown. You pick your prince and you know what he is: or do you?

The child says, "My mother sends a message: tell your uncle, for a present, I'd like a drinking cup made of the shell of a griffin's egg. It's a lion with the head and wings of a bird; it's died out now, so you can't get them anymore."

He says, "Ask her what color she wants."

Jo plants a kiss on his cheek.

He looks into the glass and the whole bright room comes bouncing back to him: lutes, portraits, silk hangings. In Rome there was a banker called Agostino Chigi. In Siena, where he came from, they maintained he was the richest man in the world. When Agostino had the Pope around for dinner he fed him on gold plates. Then he looked at the aftermath—the sprawled, sated cardinals, the mess they left behind, the half-picked bones and fish skeletons, the oyster shells and the orange rinds—and he said, stuff it, let's save the washing-up.

The guests tossed their plates out of the open windows and straight into the Tiber. The soiled table linen flew after them, white napkins unfurling like greedy gulls diving for scraps. Peals of Roman laughter unfurled into the Roman night.

Chigi had netted the banks, and he had divers standing by for whatever escaped. Some sharp-eyed servant of his upper household stood by the bank when dawn came, and checked off the list, pricking with a pin each item retrieved as it came up from the deep.

❖

1531: it is the summer of the comet. In the long dusk, beneath the curve of the rising moon and the light of the strange new star, black-robed gentlemen stroll arm in arm in the garden, speaking of salvation. They are Thomas Cranmer, Hugh Latimer, the priests and clerks of Anne's household detached and floated to Austin Friars on a breeze of theological chitchat: where did the church go wrong? How can we drift her into the right channel again? "It would be a mistake," he says, watching them from the window, "to think any of those gentlemen agree one with the other on any point of the interpretation of scripture. Give them a season's respite from Thomas More, and they will fall to persecuting each other."

Gregory is sitting on a cushion and playing with his dog. He is whisking her nose with a feather and she is sneezing to amuse him. "Sir," he says, "why are your dogs always called Bella and always so small?"

Behind him at an oak table, Nikolaus Kratzer, the king's astronomer, sits with his astrolabe before him, his paper and ink. He puts down his pen and looks up. "Master Cromwell," he says lightly, "either my calculations are wrong, or the universe is not as we think it."

He says, "Why are comets bad signs? Why not good signs? Why do they prefigure the fall of nations? Why not their rise?"

Kratzer is from Munich, a dark man of his own age with a long humorous mouth. He comes here for the company, for the good and learned conversation, some of it in his own language. The cardinal had been his patron, and he had made him a beautiful gold sundial. When he saw it the great man had flushed with pleasure. "Nine faces, Nikolaus! Seven more than the Duke of Norfolk."

In the year 1456 there was a comet like this one. Scholars recorded it, Pope Calixtus excommunicated it, and it may be that there are one or two old men alive who saw it. Its tail was noted down as saber-shaped, and in that year the Turks laid siege to Belgrade. It is as well to take note of any portents the heavens may offer; the king seeks the best advice. The alignment of the planets in Pisces, in the autumn of 1524, was followed by great wars in Germany, the rise of Luther's sect, uprisings among common men and the deaths of 100,000 of the Emperor's subjects; also, three years of rain. The sack of Rome was foretold, a full ten years before the event, by noises of battle in the air and under the ground: the clash of invisible armies, steel clattering against steel, and the spectral cries of dying men. He himself was not in Rome to hear it, but he has met many men who say they have a friend who knows a man who was.

He says, "Well, if you can answer for reading the angles, I can check your workings."

Gregory says, "Dr. Kratzer, where does the comet go, when we are not looking at it?"

The sun has declined; birdsong is hushed; the scent of the herb beds rises through the open window. Kratzer is still, a man transfixed by prayer or Gregory's question, gazing down at his papers with his long knuckly fingers joined. Down below in the garden, Dr. Latimer glances up and waves to him. "Hugh is hungry. Gregory, fetch our guests in."

"I will run over the figures first." Kratzer shakes his head. "Luther says, God is above mathematics."

Candles are brought in for Kratzer. The wood of the table is black in the dusk, and the light settles against it in trembling spheres. The scholar's lips move, like the lips of a monk at vespers; liquid figures spill from his pen. He, Cromwell, turns in the doorway and sees them. They flitter from the table, skim and melt into the corners of the room.

❖

Thurston comes stumping up from the kitchens. "I sometimes wonder what people think goes on here! Give some dinners, or we shall be undone. All these hunting gentlemen, and ladies too, they have sent us enough meat to feed an army."

"Send it to the neighbors."

"Suffolk is sending us a buck every day."

"Monsieur Chapuys is our neighbor, he doesn't get many presents."

"And Norfolk—"

"Give it out at the back gate. Ask the parish who's hungry."

"But it is the butchering! The skinning, the quartering!"

"I'll come and give you a hand, shall I?"

"You can't do that!" Thurston wrings his apron.

"It will be a pleasure." He eases off the cardinal's ring.

"Sit still! Sit still, and be a gentleman, sir. Indict something, can you not? Write a law! Sir, you must forget you ever knew these businesses."

He sits back down again, with a heavy sigh. "Are our benefactors getting letters of thanks? I had better sign them myself."

"They are thanking and thanking," Thurston says. "A dozen of clerks scribbling away."

"You must take on more kitchen boys."

"And you more scribblers."

If the king asks for him, he goes out of London to where the king is. August finds him in a group of courtiers watching Anne, standing in a pool of sunlight, dressed as Maid Marian and shooting at a target. "William Brereton, good day," he says. "You are not in Cheshire?"

"Yes. Despite appearances, I am."

I asked for that. "Only I thought you would be hunting in your own country."

Brereton scowls. "Must I account to you for my movements?"

In her green glade, in her green silks, Anne is fretting and fuming. Her bow is not to her liking. In a temper, she casts it on the grass.

"She was the same in the nursery." He turns to find Mary Boleyn at his side: an inch closer than anyone else would be.

"Where's Robin Hood?" His eyes are on Anne. "I have dispatches."

"He won't look at them till sundown."

"He will not be occupied then?"

"She is selling herself by the inch. The gentlemen all say you are advising her. She wants a present in cash for every advance above her knee."

"Not like you, Mary. One push backward and, good girl, here's fourpence."

"Well. You know. If kings are doing the pushing." She laughs. "Anne has very long legs. By the time he comes to her secret part he will be bankrupt. The French wars will be cheap, in comparison."

Anne has knocked away Mistress Shelton's offer of another bow. She stalks toward them across the grass. The golden caul that holds her hair glitters with diamond points. "What's this, Mary? Another assault on Master Cromwell's reputation?" There is some giggling from the group. "Have you any good news for me?" she asks him. Her voice softens, and her look. She puts a hand on his arm. The giggling stops.

In a north-facing closet, out of the glare, she tells him, "I have news for you, in fact. Gardiner is to get Winchester."

Winchester was Wolsey's richest bishopric; he carries all the figures in his head. "The preference may render him amenable."

She smiles: a twist of her mouth. "Not to me. He has worked to get rid of Katherine, but he would rather I did not replace her. Even to Henry he makes no secret of that. I wish he were not Secretary. You—"

"Too soon."

She nods. "Yes. Perhaps. You know they have burned Little Bilney? While we have been in the woods playing thieves."

Bilney was taken before the Bishop of Norwich, caught preaching in the open fields and handing out to his audience pages of Tyndale's gospels. The day he was burned it was windy, and the wind kept blowing the flames away from him, so it was a long time before he died. "Thomas More says he recanted when he was in the fire."

"That is not what I hear from people who saw it."

"He was a fool," Anne says. She blushes, deep angry red. "People must say whatever will keep them alive, till better times come. That is no sin. Would not you?" He is not often hesitant. "Oh, come, you have thought about it."

"Bilney put himself into the fire. I always said he would. He recanted before and was let go, so he could be granted no more mercy."

Anne drops her eyes. "How fortunate we are, that we never come to the end of God's." She seems to shake herself. She stretches her arms. She smells of green leaves and lavender. In the dusk her diamonds are as cool as raindrops. "The King of Outlaws will be home. We had better go and meet him." She straightens her spine.

The harvest is getting in. The nights are violet and the comet shines over the stubble fields. The huntsmen call in the dogs. After Holy Cross Day the deer will be safe. When he was a child this was the time for the boys who had been living wild on the heath all summer to come home and make their peace with their fathers, stealing in on a harvest supper night when the parish was in drink. Since before Whitsun they had lived by scavenging and beggars' tricks, snaring birds and rabbits and cooking them in their iron pot, chasing any girls they saw back screaming to their houses, and on wet and cold nights sneaking into outhouses and barns, to keep warm by singing and telling riddles and jokes. When the season was over it was time for him to sell the cauldron, taking it door-to-door and talking up its merits. "This pot is never empty," he would claim. "If you've only some fish-heads, throw them in and a halibut will swim up."

"Is it holed?"

"This pot is sound, and if you don't believe me, madam, you can piss in it. Come, tell me what you will give me. There is no pot to equal this since Merlin was a boy. Toss in a mouse from your trap and the next thing you know it's a spiced boar's head with the apple ready in its mouth."

"How old are you?" a woman asks him.

"That I couldn't say."

"Come back next year, and we can lie in my feather bed."

He hesitates. "Next year I'm run away."

"You're going on the road as a traveling show? With your pot?"

"No, I thought I'd be a robber on the heath. Or a bear-keeper's a steady job."

The woman says, "I hope it keeps fine for you."

❖

That night, after his bath, his supper, his singing, his dancing, the king wants a walk. He has country tastes, likes what you call hedge wine, nothing strong, but these days he knocks back his first drink quickly and nods to signal for more; so he needs Francis Weston's arm to steady him as he leaves the table. A heavy dew has fallen, and gentlemen with torches squelch over the grass. The king takes a few breaths of damp air. "Gardiner," he says. "You don't get on."

"I have no quarrel with him," he says blandly.

"Then he has a quarrel with you." The king vanishes into blackness; next he speaks from behind a torch flame, like God out of the burning bush. "I can manage Stephen. I have his measure. He is the kind of robust servant I need, these days. I don't want men who are afraid of controversy."

"Your Majesty should come inside. These night vapors are not healthy."

"Spoken like the cardinal." The king laughs.

He approaches on the king's left hand. Weston, who is young and lightly built, is showing signs of buckling at the knees. "Lean on me, sir," he advises. The king locks an arm around his neck, in a sort of wrestling hold. Bear-keeper's a steady job. For a moment he thinks the king is crying.

He didn't run away the next year, for bear-keeping or any other trade. It was next year that the Cornishmen came roaring up the country, rebels bent on burning London and taking the English king and bending him to their Cornish will. Fear went before their army, for they were known for burning ricks and ham-stringing cattle, for firing houses with the people inside, for slaughtering priests and eating babies and trampling altar bread.

The king lets him go abruptly. "Away to our cold beds. Or is that only mine? Tomorrow you will hunt. If you are not well mounted we will provide. I will see if I can tire you out, though Wolsey said it was a thing impossible. You and Gardiner, you must learn to pull together. This winter you must be yoked to the plow."

It is not oxen he wants, but brutes who will go head-to-head, injure and maim themselves in the battle for his favor. It's clear his chances with the king are better if he doesn't get on with Gardiner than if he does. Divide and rule. But then, he rules anyway.

❖

Though Parliament has not been recalled, Michaelmas term is the busiest he has ever known. Fat files of the king's business arrive almost hourly, and the Austin Friars fills up with city merchants, monks and priests of various sorts, petitioners for five minutes of his time. As if they sense something, a shift of power, a coming spectacle, small groups of Londoners begin to gather outside his gate, pointing out the liveries of the men who come and go: the Duke of Norfolk's man, the Earl of Wiltshire's servant. He looks down on them from a window and feels he recognizes them; they are sons of the men who every autumn stood around gossiping and warming themselves by the door of his father's forge. They are boys like the boy he used to be: restless, waiting for something to happen.

He looks down at them and arranges his face. Erasmus says that you must do this each morning before you leave your house: "put on a mask, as it were." He applies that to each place, each castle or inn or nobleman's seat, where he finds himself waking up. He sends some money to Erasmus, as the cardinal used to do. "To buy him his gruel," he used to say, "and keep the poor soul in quills and ink." Erasmus is surprised; he has heard only bad things of Thomas Cromwell.

From the day he was sworn into the king's council, he has had his face arranged. He has spent the early months of the year watching the faces of other people, to see when they register doubt, reservation, rebellion—to catch that fractional moment before they settle into the suave lineaments of the courtier, the facilitator, the yes-man. Rafe says to him, we cannot trust Wriothesley, and he laughs: I know where I am with Call-Me. He is well connected at court, but got his start in the cardinal's household: as who did not? But Gardiner was his master at Trinity Hall, and he has watched us both rise in the world. He has seen us put on muscle, two fighting dogs, and he cannot decide where to put his money. He says to Rafe, I might in his place feel the same; it was easy in my day, you just put your shirt on Wolsey. He has no fear of Wriothesley, or anyone like him. You can calculate the actions of unprincipled men. As long as you feed them they'll run at your heels. Less calculable, more dangerous, are men like Stephen Vaughan, men who write to you, as Vaughan does: Thomas Cromwell, I would do anything for you. Men who say they understand you, whose embrace is so tight and ungiving they will carry you over the abyss.

At Austin Friars he has beer and bread sent out to the men who stand at the gate: broth, as the mornings get sharper. Thurston says, well, if you aim to be feeding the whole district. It's only last month, he says, that you were complaining the larders were overflowing and the cellars were full. St. Paul tells us we must know how to flourish in times of abasement and times of abundance, with a full stomach and an empty. He goes down to the kitchens to talk to the boys Thurston has taken on. They shout up with their names and what they can do, and gravely he notes their abilities in a book: Simon, can dress a salad and play a drum, Matthew, he can say his Pater Noster. All these *garzoni* must be trainable. One day they must be able to walk upstairs, as he did, and take a seat in the countinghouse. All must have warm and decent clothes, and be encouraged to wear them, not sell them, for he remembers from his days at Lambeth the profound cold of storerooms; in Wolsey's kitchens at Hampton Court, where the chimneys draw well and confine the heat, he has seen stray snowflakes drifting in the rafters and settling on sills.

When in the crisp mornings at dawn he comes out of his house with his entourage of clerks, the Londoners are already assembling. They drop back and watch him, neither friendly nor hostile. He calls out good morning to them and may God bless you, and some of them shout good morning back. They pull off their caps and, because he is a king's councillor, they stand bareheaded till he has gone by.

❖

October: Monsieur Chapuys, the Emperor's ambassador, comes to Austin Friars to dine, and Stephen Gardiner is on the menu. "No sooner appointed to Winchester, than sent abroad," Chapuys says. "And how do you think King Francis will like him? What can he do as a diplomat that Sir Thomas Boleyn cannot? Though I suppose he is *parti pris*. Being the lady's father. Gardiner more . . . ambivalent, you would say? More disinterested, that is the word. I cannot see what King Francis will get out of supporting the match, unless your king were to offer him—what? Money? Warships? Calais?"

At table with the household, Monsieur Chapuys has talked pleasantly of verse, portraiture, and his university years in Turin; turning to Rafe, whose French is excellent, he has spoken of falconry, as a thing likely to interest young men. "You must go out with our master," Rafe tells him. "It is almost his only recreation these days."

Monsieur Chapuys turns his bright little eyes upon him. "He plays kings' games now."

Rising from table, Chapuys praises the food, the music, the furnishings. One can see his brain turning, hear the little clicks, like the gins of an elaborate lock, as he encodes his opinions for his dispatches to his master the Emperor.

Afterward, in his cabinet, the ambassador unleashes his questions; rattling on, not pausing for a reply. "If the Bishop of Winchester is in France, how will Henry do without his Secretary? Master Stephen's embassy cannot be short. Perhaps this is your chance to creep closer, do you think? Tell me, is it true Gardiner is Henry's bastard cousin? And your boy Richard, also? Such things perplex the Emperor. To have a king who is so very little royal. It is perhaps no wonder he seeks to wed a poor gentlewoman."

"I would not call Lady Anne poor."

"True, the king has enriched her family." Chapuys smirks. "Is it usual in this country, to pay the girl for her services in advance?"

"Indeed it is—you should remember it—I should be sorry to see you chased down the street."

"You advise her, Lady Anne?"

"I look over accounts. It is not much to do, for a dear friend."

Chapuys laughs merrily. "A friend! She is a witch, you know? She has put the king under an enchantment, so he risks everything—to be cast out of Christendom, to be damned. And I think he half knows it. I have seen him under her eye, his wits scattered and fleeing, his soul turning and twisting like a hare under the eye of a hawk. Perhaps she has enchanted you too." Monsieur Chapuys leans forward and rests, on his own hand, his little monkey's paw. "Break the enchantment, *mon cher ami*. You will not regret it. I serve a most liberal prince."

❖

November: Sir Henry Wyatt stands in the hall at Austin Friars; he looks at the blank space on the wall, where the cardinal's arms have been painted out. "He has only been gone a year, Thomas. To me it seems more. They say that when you are an old man one year is the same as the next. I can tell you that is not true."

Oh, come sir, the little girls shout, you are not so old you cannot tell a story. They tow him toward one of the new velvet armchairs and enthrone him. Sir Henry would be everyone's father, if they had their choice, everyone's grandfather. He has served in the treasury of this Henry, and the Henry before him; if the Tudors are poor, it's not his fault.

Alice and Jo have been out in the garden, trying to catch the cat. Sir Henry likes to see a cat honored in a household; at the children's request, he will explain why.

"Once," he begins, "in this land of England, there arose a cruel tyrant by the name of Richard Plantagenet—"

"Oh, they were wicked folk of that name," Alice bursts out. "And do you know, there are still some of them left?"

There is laughter. "Well, it is true," Alice shouts, her cheeks burning.

"—and I, your servant Wyatt who relates this tale, was cast by this tyrant into a dungeon, to sleep upon the straw, a dungeon with but one small window, and that window barred . . ."

Winter came on, Sir Henry says, and I had no fire; I had no food or water, for the guards forgot me. Richard Cromwell sits listening, chin on hand; he exchanges a look with Rafe; both of them glance at him, and he makes a little gesture, damping down the horror of the past. Sir Henry, they know, was not forgotten at the Tower. His guards laid white-hot knives against his flesh. They pulled out his teeth.

"So what must I do?" says Sir Henry. "Lucky for me, my dungeon was damp. I drank the water that ran down the wall."

"And for food?" Jo says. Her voice is low and thrilled.

"Ah, now we come to the best part of the tale." One day, Sir Henry says, when I thought if I did not eat I was likely to die, I perceived that the light of my little window was blocked; looking up, what should I see, but the form of a cat, a black-and-white London cat. "Now, Pusskins," I said to her; and she mewed, and in doing so, she let fall her burden. And what had she brought me?

"A pigeon!" shouts Jo.

"Mistress, either you have been a prisoner yourself, or heard this tale before."

The girls have forgotten that he does not have a cook, a spit, a fire; the young men drop their eyes, flinching from the mental picture of a prisoner tearing apart, with fettered hands, a mass of feathers swarming with bird lice.

"Now, the next news I heard, lying on the straw, was the ringing of bells, and a cry in the streets, A Tudor! A Tudor! Without the cat's gift, I would not have lived to hear it, or hear the key turn in the lock, and King Henry himself cry, Wyatt, is that you? Come forth to your reward!"

Some forgivable exaggeration here. King Henry had not been in that cell, but King Richard had; it was he who oversaw the heating of the knife, and listened, his head tilted slightly, as Henry Wyatt screamed; who sidled away, fastidious, from the odor of burning flesh, and ordered the knife to be reheated, and applied again.

They say that Little Bilney, the night before he was burned, held his fingers in a candle flame, and called on Jesus to teach him how to endure the pain. That was not wise, to maim yourself before the event; wise or not, he thinks of it. "Now, Sir Henry," Mercy says, "you must tell us the lion tale, because we won't sleep if we don't hear it."

"Well, really that is my son's tale, he should be here."

"If he were," Richard says, "the ladies would all be making goggle eyes at him, and sighing—yes you would, Alice—and they would not care about any lion tale."

When Sir Henry was mended after his imprisonment he became a powerful man at court, and an admirer sent him a present of a lion cub. At Allington Castle I brought her up like my child, he says, till, as a girl will, she developed a mind of her own. One careless day, and mine the fault, she came out of her cage. Leontina, I called to her, stand till I lead you back; but then she crouched, quite silent, and sighted me, and her eyes were like fire. It was then I realized, he says, that I was not her father, for all that I had cherished her: I was her dinner.

Alice says, a hand to her mouth, "Sir Henry, you thought your last hour had come."

"Indeed I did, and so it had, if it had not been that my son Thomas chanced to step into the courtyard. In a second he saw my peril, and called out to her, Leontina, here to me; and she turned her head. In that moment, her glare distracted, I stepped back a pace, and another. Look at me, Thomas called. Now that day he was dressed very brightly, with long fluttering sleeves, and a loose gown the wind got inside, and his hair being fair, you know, which he wore long, he must have looked like a flame, I think, tall and flickering in the sun, and for a moment she stood, puzzling, and I stepped away, back and back . . ."

Leontina turns; she crouches; leaving the father, she begins to stalk the son. You can see her padding feet and feel the stink of blood on her breath. (Meanwhile he, Henry Wyatt, in a cold lather of fear, backs off, backs away, in the direction of help.) In his soft enchanting voice, in loving murmurs, in the accents of prayer, Tom Wyatt speaks to the lion, asking St. Francis to open her brutish heart to grace. Leontina watches. She listens. She opens her mouth. She roars: "What does she say?"

"Fee, fi, fo and fum, I smell the blood of an Englishman."

Tom Wyatt stands still as a statue. Grooms with nets creep across the court. Leontina is within feet of him, but once again she checks, listening. She stands, uncertain, ears twitching. He can see the pink drool from her jaw and smell her musty fur. She crouches back on her haunches. He scents her breath. She is ready to spring. He sees her muscles quiver, her jaw stretch; she leaps—but she spins in the air, an arrow stinging her ribs. She whirls, smashes at the barb, cries out, moans; another arrow thuds into her dense flank, and as she circles again, whining, the nets drop over her. Sir Henry, striding calmly toward her, places his third arrow in her throat.

Even as she dies she roars. She coughs blood and strikes out. One of the grooms bears her claw mark to this day. Her pelt can be seen on the wall at Allington. "And you will come and visit me, young ladies," Sir Henry says. "And you can see what a brute she was."

"Tom's prayers were not answered," Richard says, smiling. "St. Francis did nothing about it, so far as I can see."

"Sir Henry," Jo pulls at his sleeve, "you have not said the best part."

"No. I forgot. So then my son Tom walks away, the hero of the hour, and is sick into a bush."

The children release their breath. They all applaud. In its time the story had reached court, and the king—he was younger then, sweet in disposition—was a little awed by it. When he sees Tom even now, he will nod, and murmur to himself, "Tom Wyatt. He can tame lions."

❖

When Sir Henry, who is fond of soft fruit, has eaten some fat brambles with yellow cream, he says, "A word with you alone," and they withdraw. If I were in your place, Sir Henry says, I'd ask him to make you Keeper of the Jewel House. "From that post, when I had it, I found I had an overview of the revenue."

"Ask him how?"

"Get Lady Anne to ask him."

"Perhaps your son could help by asking Anne."

Sir Henry laughs; or rather, he indicates with a little ahem that he knows a joke has been made. By the account of drinkers in Kent alehouses, and the backstairs servants at court (the musician Mark for one), Anne has done Thomas Wyatt all the favors a man might reasonably ask, even in a brothel.

"I mean to retire from court this year," Sir Henry says. "It's time I wrote my will. May I name you as executor?"

"You do me honor."

"There is no one I'd rather trust with my affairs. You've the steadiest hand I know."

He smiles, puzzled; nothing in his world seems steady to him.

"I understand you," Wyatt says. "I know our old fellow in scarlet nearly brought you down. But look at you, eating almonds, with all your teeth in your head, and your household around you, and your affairs prospering, and men like Norfolk speaking to you civil." Whereas, he doesn't need to add, a year ago they were wiping their feet on you. Sir Henry breaks up, in his fingers, a cinnamon wafer, and dabs it onto his tongue, a careful, secular Eucharist. It is forty years, more, since the Tower, but his smashed-up jaw still stiffens and plagues him with pain. "Thomas, I have something to ask you . . . Will you keep an eye on my son? Be a father to him?"

"Tom is, what, twenty-eight? He may not like another father."

"You cannot do worse than I did. I have much to regret, his marriage chiefly . . . He was seventeen, he did not want it, it was I who wanted it, because her father was Baron Cobham, and I wanted to keep my place up among my neighbors in Kent. Tom was always good to look at, a kind boy and courteous as well, you'd have thought he would have done for the girl, but I don't know if she was faithful to him a month. So then, of course, he paid her in kind . . . the place is full of his doxies, open a closet at Allington and some wench falls out of it. He roams off abroad and what comes of that? He ends up a prisoner in Italy, I shall never understand that affair. Since Italy he's had even less sense. Write you a piece of terza rima, of course, but sit down and work out where his money's gone . . ." He rubs his chin. "But there you have it. When all's said, there is no braver boy than my boy."

"Will you come back now, and join the company? You know we take a holiday when you visit us."

Sir Henry levers himself upright. He is a portly man, though he lives on pottage and mashes. "Thomas, how did I get old?"

When they return to the hall it is to find a play in progress. Rafe is acting the part of Leontina and the household is roaring him on. It is not that the boys don't believe the lion tale; it is just that they like to put their own words to it. He extends a peremptory hand to Richard, who has been standing on a joint-stool, squealing. "You are jealous of Tom Wyatt," he says.

"Ah, don't be out of temper with us, master." Rafe resumes human form and throws himself onto a bench. "Tell us about Florence. Tell us what else you did, you and Giovannino."

"I don't know if I should. You will make a play of it."

Ah, do, they persuade him, and he looks around: Rafe encourages him with a purr. "Are we sure Call-Me-Risley is not here? Well . . . when we had a day off, we used to take down buildings."

"Take them down?" Henry Wyatt says. "Did you so?"

"What I mean is, blow them up. But not without the owner's permission. Unless we thought they were crumbling and a danger to passersby. We only charged for explosive materials. Not for our expertise."

"Which was considerable, I suppose?"

"It's a lot of digging for a few seconds of excitement. But I knew some boys who went into it as a profession. In Florence," he says, "it was just what you might do for your recreation. Like fishing. It kept us out of trouble." He hesitates. "Well, no, it didn't. Not really."

Richard says, "Did Call-Me tell Gardiner? About your Cupid?"

"What do you think?"

The king had said to him, I hear you antiqued a statue. The king was laughing, but perhaps also making a note; laughing because the joke's against clerics, against cardinals, and he's in the mood for such a joke.

Secretary Gardiner: "Statue, statute, not much difference."

"One letter is everything, in legislating. But my precedents are not faked."

"Stretched?" Gardiner says.

"Majesty, the Council of Constance granted your ancestor, Henry V, such control over the church in England as no other Christian king exercised in his realm."

"The concessions were not applied. Not with consistency. Why is that?"

"I don't know. Incompetence?"

"But we have better councillors now?"

"Better kings, Your Majesty."

Behind Henry's back, Gardiner makes a gargoyle face at him. He almost laughs.

❖

The legal term closes. Anne says, come and eat a poor Advent supper with me. We'll use forks.

He goes, but he doesn't like the company. She has made pets of the king's friends, the gentlemen of his privy chamber: Henry Norris, William Brereton, those people, and her brother, of course, Lord Rochford. Anne is brittle in their company, and as ruthless with their compliments as a housewife snapping the necks of larks for the table. If her precise smile fades for a moment, they all lean forward, anxious to know how to please her. A bigger set of fools you would go far to seek.

For himself, he can go anywhere, he has been anywhere. Brought up on the table talk of the Frescobaldi family, the Portinari family, and latterly at the cardinal's table among the savants and wits, he is unlikely to find himself at a loss among the pretty people Anne gathers around her. God knows, they do their best, the gentlemen, to make him uncomfortable; he imports his own comfort, his calm, his exact and pointed conversation. Norris, who is a witty man, and not young, stultifies himself by keeping such company: and why? Proximity to Anne makes him tremble. It is almost a joke, but a joke that nobody tells.

After that first occasion, Norris follows him out, touches his sleeve, and brings him to a standstill, face-to-face. "You don't see it, do you? Anne?"

He shakes his head.

"So what would be your idea? Some fat frau from your travels?"

"A woman I could love, would be a woman in whom the king has no interest at all."

"If that is a piece of advice, tell it to your friend Wyatt's son."

"Oh, I think young Wyatt has worked it out. He is a married man. He says to himself, from your deprivations make a verse. Don't we all grow wiser, from pinpricks to the *amour propre*?"

"Can you look at me," Norris says, "and think I grow wiser?"

He hands Norris his handkerchief. Norris mops his face and gives the handkerchief back. He thinks of St. Veronica, swabbing with her veil the features of the suffering Christ; he wonders if, when he gets home, Henry's gentlemanly features will be imprinted on the cloth, and if so, will he hang the result on the wall? Norris turns away, with a little laugh: "Weston—young Weston, you know—he is jealous of a boy she brings in to sing for us some nights. He is jealous of the man who comes in to mend the fire, or the maid who pulls her stockings off. Every time she looks at you, he keeps count, he says, there, there, do you see, she is looking at that fat butcher, she looked at him fifteen times in two hours."

"It was the cardinal who was the fat butcher."

"To Francis, one tradesman's the same as the next."

"I quite see that. Give you good night."

Night, Tom, Norris says, batting him on the shoulder, absent, distracted, almost as if they were equals, as if they were friends; his eyes are turned back to Anne, his steps are turned back to his rivals.

One tradesman the same as the next? Not in the real world. Any man with a steady hand and a cleaver can call himself a butcher: but without the smith, where does he get that cleaver? Without the man who works in metal, where are your hammers, your scythes, your sickles, scissors and planes? Your arms and armor, your arrowheads, your pikes and your guns? Where are your ships at sea and their anchors? Where are your grappling hooks, your nails, latches, hinges, pokers and tongs? Where are your spits, kettles, trivets, your harness rings, buckles and bits? Where are your knives?

He remembers the day they heard the Cornish army was coming. He was—what—twelve? He was in the forge. He had cleaned the big bellows and he was oiling the leather. Walter came over and looked at it. "Wants caulking."

"Right," he said. (This was the kind of conversation he had with Walter.)

"It won't do itself."

"I said, right, right, I'm doing it!"

He looked up. Their neighbor Owen Madoc stood in the doorway. "They're on the march. Word's all down the river. Henry Tudor ready to fight. The queen and the little ones in the Tower."

Walter wipes his mouth. "How long?"

Madoc says, "God knows. Those fuckers can fly."

He straightens up. Into his hand has floated a four-pound hammer with an ash shaft.

❖

The next few days they worked till they were ready to drop. Walter undertook body armor for his friends, and he to put an edge on anything that can cut, tear, lacerate rebel flesh. The men of Putney have no sympathy with these heathens. They pay their taxes: why not the Cornish? The women are afraid that the Cornishmen will outrage their honor. "Our priest says they only do it to their sisters," he says, "so you'll be all right, our Bet. But then again, the priest says they have cold scaly members like the devil, so you might want the novelty."

Bet throws something at him. He dodges. It's always the excuse for breakages, in that house: I threw it at Thomas. "Well, I don't know what you like," he says.

That week, rumors proliferate. The Cornishmen work under the ground, so their faces are black. They are half-blind and so you can catch them in a net. The king will give you a shilling for each you catch, two shillings if it's a big one. Just how big are they? Because they shoot arrows a yard long.

Now all household objects are seen in a new light. Skewers, spits, larding needles: anything for defense at close quarters. The neighbors are paying out to Walter's other business, the brewery, as if they think the Cornishmen mean to drink England dry. Owen Madoc comes in and commissions a hunting knife, hand-guard, blood gutter and twelve-inch blade. "Twelve-inch?" he says. "You'll be flailing around and cut your ear off."

"You'll not be so pert when the Cornish seize you. They spit children like you and roast them on bonfires."

"Can't you just slap them with an oar?"

"I'll slap your jaw shut," Owen Madoc bellows. "You little fucker, you had a bad name before you were born."

He shows Owen Madoc the knife he has made for himself, slung on a cord under his shirt: its stub of blade, like a single, evil tooth. "What do you think?"

"Christ," Madoc says. "Be careful who you leave it in."

❖

He says to his sister Kat—just resting his four-pound hammer on her windowsill at the Pegasus—why did I have a bad name before I was born?

Ask Morgan Williams, she says. He'll tell you. Oh, Tom, Tom, she says. She grabs his head and kisses it. You don't put yourself out there. Let him fight.

She hopes the Cornish will kill Walter. She doesn't say so, but he knows it.

When I am the man of this family, he says, things will be different, I can tell you.

Morgan tells him—blushing, for he is a very proper man—that boys used to follow his mother in the street, shouting "Look at the old mare in foal!"

His sister Bet says, "Another thing those Cornish have got, they have got a giant called Bolster, who's in love with St. Agnes and he follows her around and the Cornish bear her image on their flags and so he's coming to London after them."

"Bolster?" he sneers. "I expect he's that big."

"Oh, you will see," Bet says. "Then you won't be so quick with your answers."

The women of the district, Morgan says, clucked around his mother pretending concern: what will it be when it's born, she's like the side of a house!

Then when he came into this world, bawling, with clenched fists and wet black curls, Walter and his friends reeled through Putney, singing. They shouted, "Come and get it, girls!" and "Barren wives served here!"

They never noted the date. He said to Morgan, I don't mind. I don't have a natal chart. So I don't have a fate.

As fate had it, there was no battle in Putney. For the outriders and escapees, the women were ready with bread knives and razors, the men to bludgeon them with shovels and mattocks, to hollow them with adzes and to spike them on butchers' steels. The big fight was at

Blackheath instead: Cornishmen cut up into little pieces, minced by the Tudor in his military mincing machine. All of them safe: except from Walter.

His sister Bet says, "You know that giant, Bolster? He hears that St. Agnes is dead. He's cut his arm and in sorrow his blood has flowed into the sea. It's filled up a cave that can never be filled, which goes into a hole, which goes down beneath the bed of the sea and into the center of the earth and into Hell. So he's dead."

"Oh, good. Because I was really worried about Bolster."

"Dead till next time," his sister says.

So on a date unknown, he was born. At three years old, he was collecting kindling for the forge. "See my little lad?" Walter would say, batting him fondly around the head. His fingers smelled of burning, and his palm was solid and black.

In recent years, of course, scholars have tried to give him a fate; men learned in reading the heavens have tried to work him back from what he is and how he is, to when he was born. Jupiter favorably aspected, indicating prosperity. Mercury rising, offering the faculty of quick and persuasive speech. Kratzer says, if Mars is not in Scorpio, I don't know my trade. His mother was fifty-two and they thought she could neither conceive nor deliver a child. She hid her powers and disguised him under draperies, deep inside her, for as long as she could contrive. He came out and they said, what is it?

❖

In mid-December, James Bainham, a barrister of the Middle Temple, abjures his heresies before the Bishop of London. He has been tortured, the city says, More himself questioning him while the handle of the rack is turned and asking him to name other infected members of the Inns of Court. A few days later, a former monk and a leather-seller are burned together. The monk had run in consignments of books through the Norfolk ports and then, stupidly enough, through St. Katharine's Dock, where the Lord Chancellor was waiting to seize them. The leather-seller had possession of Luther's *Liberty of a Christian Man*, the text copied out in his own hand. These are men he knows, the disgraced and broken Bainham, the monk Bayfield, John Tewkesbury, who God knows was no doctor of theology. That's how the year goes out, in a puff of smoke, a pall of human ash hanging over Smithfield.

❖

On New Year's Day, he wakes before dawn to see Gregory at the foot of his bed. "You'd better come. Tom Wyatt's been taken up."

He is out of bed instantly; his first thought is that More has struck into the heart of Anne's circle. "Where is he? They've not taken him to Chelsea?"

Gregory sounds mystified. "Why would they take him to Chelsea?"

"The king cannot allow—it comes too near him—Anne has books, she has shown them to him—he himself has read Tyndale—what next, is More going to arrest the king?" He reaches for a shirt.

"It's nothing to do with More. It's some fools taken up for making a riot in Westminster, they were in the street leaping over bonfires and took to smashing windows, you know how it goes . . ." Gregory's voice is weary. "Then they go fighting the watch and they get locked up, and a message comes, will Master Cromwell go down and give the turnkey a New Year's present?"

"Christ," he says. He sits down on the bed, suddenly conscious of his nakedness, of feet, shins, thighs, cock, his pelt of body hair, bristling chin: and the sweat that has broken out across his shoulders. He pulls on his shirt. "They'll have to take me as they find me," he says. "And I'll have my breakfast first."

Gregory says, with light malice, "You agreed to be a father to him. This is what being a father means."

He stands up. "Get Richard."

"I'll come."

"Come if you must, but I want Richard in case there's trouble."

There is no trouble, only a bit of haggling. Dawn is breaking when the young gentlemen reel out into the air, haggard, battered, their clothes torn and dirty. "Francis Weston," he says, "good morning, sir."

He thinks, if I'd known you were here, I'd have left you. "Why are you not at court?"

"I am," the boy says, on an outgust of sour breath. "I am at Greenwich. I am not here. Do you understand?"

"Bilocation," he says. "Right."

"Oh, Jesus. Oh, Jesus my Redeemer." Thomas Wyatt stands in the bright snowy light, rubbing his head. "Never again."

"Till next year," Richard says.

He turns, to see a last shambling figure fall out into the street. "Francis Bryan," he says. "I should have known this enterprise would not be complete without you. Sir."

Exposed to the first chill of the new year, Lady Anne's cousin shakes himself like a wet dog. "By the tits of Holy Agnes, it's freezing." His doublet is ripped and his shirt collar torn off, and he has only one shoe. He clutches at his hose to keep them up. Five years ago, he lost an eye in the joust; now he has lost his eyepatch, and the livid socket is on view. He looks around, with what ocular equipment remains. "Cromwell? I don't remember you were with us last night."

"I was in my bed and would be glad if I were there still."

"Why not go back?" Risking dangerous slippage, he throws his hands out. "Which of the city wives is waiting for you? Do you have one for each of the twelve days of Christmas?" He almost laughs, till Bryan adds, "Don't you sectaries hold your women in common?"

"Wyatt," he turns away, "get him to cover himself, or his parts will be frostbitten. Bad enough to be without an eye."

"Say thank you." Thomas Wyatt bellows, and thumps his companions. "Say thank you to Master Cromwell and pay him back what you owe him. Who else would be up so early on a holiday, and with his purse open? We could have been there till tomorrow."

They do not look like men who have a shilling between them. "Never mind," he says. "I'll put it on the account."

II

"Alas, What Shall I Do for Love?"

SPRING 1532

ime now to consider the compacts that hold the world together: the compact between ruler and ruled, and that between husband and wife. Both these arrangements rest on a sedulous devotion, the one to the interests of the other. The master and husband protect and provide; the wife and servant obey. Above masters, above husbands, God rules all. He counts up our petty rebellions, our human follies. He reaches out his long arm, hand bunched into a fist.

Imagine debating these matters with George, Lord Rochford. He is as witty a young man as any in England, polished and well read; but today what fascinates him is the flame-colored satin that is pulled through his slashed velvet oversleeve. He keeps coaxing the little puffs of fabric with a fingertip, pleating and nudging them and encouraging them to grow bigger, so that he looks like one of those jugglers who run balls down their arms.

It is time to say what England is, her scope and boundaries: not to count and measure her harbor defenses and border walls, but to estimate her capacity for self-rule. It is time to say what a king is, and what trust and guardianship he owes his people: what protection from foreign incursions moral or physical, what freedom from the pretensions of those who would like to tell an Englishman how to speak to his God.

Parliament meets mid-January. The business of the early spring is breaking the resistance of the bishops to Henry's new order, putting in place legislation that—though for now it is held in suspension—will cut revenues to Rome, make his supremacy in the church no mere form of words. The Commons drafts a petition against the church courts, so arbitrary in their proceedings, so presumptuous in their claimed jurisdiction; it questions their jurisdiction, their very existence. The papers pass through many hands, but finally he himself works through the night with Rafe and Call-Me-Risley, scribbling amendments between the lines. He is flushing out the opposition: Gardiner, although he is the king's Secretary, feels obliged to lead his fellow prelates into the charge.

The king sends for Master Stephen. When he goes in, the hair on his neck is bristling and he is shrinking inside his skin like a mastiff being led toward a bear. The king has a high voice, for a big man, and it rises when he is angry to an ear-throbbing shriek. Are the clergy his subjects, or only half his subjects? Perhaps they are not his subjects at all, for how can they be, if they take an oath to obey and support the Pope? Should they not, he yells, be taking an oath to me?

When Stephen comes out he leans against the painted paneling. At his back a troupe of painted nymphs are frisking in a glade. He takes out a handkerchief but seems to have forgotten why; he twists it in his great paw, wrapping it around his knuckles like a bandage. Sweat trickles down his face.

He, Cromwell, calls for assistance. "My lord the bishop is ill." They bring a stool and Stephen glares at it, glares at him, then sits down with caution, as if he is not able to trust the joinery. "I take it you heard him?"

Every word. "If he does lock you up, I'll make sure you have some small comforts."

Gardiner says, "God damn you, Cromwell. Who are you? What office do you hold? You're nothing. Nothing."

We have to win the debate, not just knock our enemies down. He has been to see Christopher St. German, the aged jurist, whose word is respected all over Europe. The old man entertains him civilly at his house. There is no man in England, he says, who does not believe our church is in need of reform which grows more urgent by the year, and if the church cannot do it, then the king in Parliament must, and can.

This is the conclusion I have come to, after some decades of studying the subject.

Of course, the old man says, Thomas More does not agree with me. Perhaps his time has passed. Utopia, after all, is not a place one can live.

When he meets the king, Henry rages about Gardiner: disloyalty, he shouts, ingratitude. Can he remain my Secretary, when he has set himself up in direct opposition to me? (This is the man whom Henry himself praised as a stout controversialist.) He sits quietly, watching Henry, trying by stillness to defuse the situation; to wrap the king in a blanketing silence, so that he, Henry, can listen to himself. It is a great thing, to be able to divert the wrath of the Lion of England. "I think . . ." he says softly, "with Your Majesty's permission, what I think . . . The Bishop of Winchester, as we know, likes arguing. But not with his king. He would not dare to do that for sport." He pauses. "So his views, though mistaken, are honestly held."

"Indeed, but—" The king breaks off. Henry has heard his own voice, the voice he used to the cardinal when he brought him down. Gardiner is not Wolsey—if only in the sense that, if he is sacrificed, few will remember him with regret. And yet it suits him, for the moment, to have the snarling bishop still in his post; he has a care for Henry's reputation in Europe, and he says, "Majesty, Stephen has served you as an ambassador to the limit of his powers, and it would be better to reconcile him, by honest persuasion, than to force his hand by the weight of your displeasure. It is the more pleasant course, and there is more honor in it."

He watches Henry's face. He is alive to anything that concerns honor.

"Is that the advice you would always give?"

He smiles. "No."

"You are not wholly determined I should govern in a spirit of Christian meekness?"

"No."

"I know you dislike Gardiner."

"That is why Your Majesty should consider my advice."

He thinks, you owe me, Stephen. The bill will come in by and by.

At his own house he meets with parliamentarians and gentlemen from the Inns of Court and the city livery companies; with Thomas Audley, who is Mr. Speaker, and his protégé Richard Riche, a golden-haired young man, pretty as a painted angel, who has an active, quick and secular mind; with Rowland Lee, a robust outspoken cleric, the least priestly man you would find in a long day's march. In these months, the ranks of his city friends are thinned by sickness and unnatural death. Thomas Somer, whom he has known for years, has died just after release from the Tower, where he was shut up for distributing the gospel in English; fond of fine clothes and fast horses, Somer was a man of irrepressible spirits, till at last he had his reckoning with the Lord Chancellor. John Petyt has been released but he is too sick to take any more part in the Commons. He visits him; he is confined to his chamber now. It is painful to hear him fighting for breath. The spring of 1532, the year's first warm weather, does nothing to ease him. I feel, he says, as if there is an iron hoop around my chest, and they are drawing it tighter. He says, Thomas, will you look after Luce when I die?

Sometimes, if he walks in the gardens with the burgesses or with Anne's chaplains, he feels the absence of Dr. Cranmer at his right-hand side. He has been away since January, as the king's ambassador to the Emperor; on his travels, he will visit scholars in Germany to canvass support for the king's divorce. He had said to him, "What shall I do if, while you are away, the king has a dream?"

Cranmer had smiled. "You worked it by yourself, last time. I was only there to nod it through."

He sees the animal Marlinspike, his paws hanging as he drapes himself from a black bough. He points him out. "Gentlemen, that was the cardinal's cat." At the sight of the visitors Marlinspike darts along the boundary wall, and with a whisk of his tail disappears, into the unknown territory beyond.

Down in the kitchens at Austin Friars, the *garzoni* are learning to make spiced wafers. The process involves a good eye, exact timing and a steady hand. There are so many points at which it can go wrong. The mixture must have the right dropping consistency, the plates of the long-handled irons must be well greased and hot. When you press the plates together there is an animal shriek as they meet, and steam hisses into the air. If you panic and release the pressure you will have a claggy mess to scrape away. You must wait till the steam dies down, and then you start counting. If you miss a beat the smell of scorching permeates the air. A second divides the successes from the failures.

When he brings into the Commons a bill to suspend the payment of annates to Rome, he suggests a division of the House. This is far from usual, but amid shock and grumbling the members comply: for the bill to this side, against the bill to the other side. The king is present; he watches, he learns who is for him and who against, and at the end of the process he gives his councillor a grim nod of approval. In the Lords this tactic will not serve. The king has to go in person, three times, and argue his own case. The old aristocracy—proud families like the Exeter clan, with their own claim to the throne—are for Pope and Katherine and are not afraid to say so: or not yet. But he is identifying his enemies and, where he can, splitting them.

Once the kitchen boys have made a single commendable wafer, Thurston has them turn out a hundred more. It becomes second nature, the flick of the wrist with which one rolls the half-set wafer onto the handle of a wooden spoon and then flips it onto the drying rack to crisp. The successes—with time, they should all be successes—are stamped with the badges of the Tudors, and stacked by the dozen in the pretty inlaid boxes in which they will come to the table, each frail golden disk perfumed with rose water. He sends a batch to Thomas Boleyn.

As father of the queen-to-be, Wiltshire thinks he deserves some special title, and has let it be known it would not be disagreeable to him to be known as Monseigneur. He confers with him, his son and their friends, then walks to see Anne, through the chambers at Whitehall. Month by month her state is greater, but he goes through with a bow from her people. At court and in the offices of Westminster he dresses not a whit above his gentleman's station, in loose jackets of Lemster wool so fine they flow like water, in purples and indigos so near black that it looks as if the night has bled into them; his cap of black velvet sits on his black hair, so that the only points of light are his darting eyes and the gestures of his solid, fleshy hands; those, and flashes of fire from Wolsey's turquoise ring.

At Whitehall—York Place, as it was—the builders are still in. For Christmas, the king had given Anne a bedroom. He led her to it himself, to see her gasp at the wall hangings, which were of cloth of silver and cloth of gold, the carved bed hung with crimson satin embroidered with images of flowers and children. Henry Norris had reported to him that Anne had failed to gasp; she had just looked around the room slowly, smiled, blinked. Then she had remembered what she ought to do; she pretended to feel faint at the honor, and it was only when she swayed and the king locked his arms around her that the gasp came. I do devoutly hope, Norris had said, that we shall all at least once in our lives cause a woman to utter that sound.

When Anne had expressed her thanks, kneeling, Henry had to leave, of course; to leave the shimmering room, trailing her by the hand, and go back to the New Year's feast, to the public scrutiny of his expression: in the certainty that news of it would be conveyed all over Europe, by land and sea, in and out of cipher.

When at the end of his walk through the cardinal's old rooms he finds Anne sitting with her ladies, she already knows, or seems to know, what her father and brother have said. They think they are fixing her tactics, but she is her own best tactician, and able to think back and judge what has gone wrong; he admires anyone who can learn from mistakes. One day, the windows open to the wingbeats of nest-building birds, she says, "You once told me that only the cardinal could set the king free. Do you know what I think now? I think Wolsey was the last person to do it. Because he was so proud, because he wanted to be Pope. If he had been more humble, Clement would have obliged him."

"There may be something in that."

"I suppose we should take a lesson," Norris says.

They turn together. Anne says, "Really, should we?" and he says, "What lesson would that be?"

Norris is at a loss.

"None of us are likely to be cardinals," Anne says. "Even Thomas, who aspires to most things, would not aspire to that."

"Oh? I wouldn't put money on it." Norris slouches off, as only a silken gentleman can slouch, and leaves him behind with the women.

"So, Lady Anne," he says, "when you are reflecting on the late cardinal, do you take time to pray for his soul?"

"I think God has judged him, and my prayers, if I make them or if I do not, are of no effect."

Mary Boleyn says, gently, "He is teasing you, Anne."

"If it were not for the cardinal, you would be married to Harry Percy."

"At least," she snaps, "I would occupy the estate of wife, which is an honorable estate, but now—"

"Oh, but cousin," Mary Shelton says, "Harry Percy has gone mad. Everybody knows it. He is spending all his money."

Mary Boleyn laughs. "So he is, and my sister supposes it is his disappointment over her that is to blame."

"My lady," he turns to Anne, "you would not like to be in Harry Percy's country. For you know he would do as those northern lords do, and keep you in a freezing turret up a winding stair, and only let you come down for your dinner. And just as you are seated, and they are bringing in a pudding made of oatmeal mixed with the blood of cattle they have got in a raid, my lord comes thundering in, swinging a sack—oh, sweetheart, you say, a present for me? and he says, aye, madam, if it please you, and opens the sack and into your lap rolls the severed head of a Scot."

"Oh, that is horrible," Mary Shelton whispers. "Is that what they do?" Anne puts her hand to her mouth, laughing.

"And you know," he says, "that for your dinner you would prefer a lightly poached breast of chicken, sliced into a cream sauce with tarragon. And also a fine aged cheese imported by the ambassador of Spain, which he intended no doubt for the queen, but which somehow found its way to my house."

"How could I be better served?" Anne asks. "A band of men on the highway, waylaying Katherine's cheese."

"Well, having staged such a coup, I must go . . ." he gestures to the lute-player in the corner, "and leave you with your goggle-eyed lover."

Anne darts a look at the boy Mark. "He does goggle. True."

"Shall I send him off? The place is full of musicians."

"Leave him," Mary says. "He's a sweet boy."

Mary Boleyn stands up. "I'll just . . ."

"Now Lady Carey is going to have one of her conferences with Master Cromwell," Mary Shelton says, in a tone of giving agreeable information.

Jane Rochford: "She is going to offer him her virtue again."

"Lady Carey, what can you not say before us all?" But Anne nods. He may go. Mary may go. Presumably Mary is to carry messages that she, Anne, is too delicate to convey direct.

Outside: "Sometimes I need to breathe." He waits. "Jane and our brother George, you know they hate each other? He won't go to bed with her. If he is not with some other woman he sits up at night with Anne in her rooms. They play cards. They play Pope Julius till the dawn comes. Did you know the king pays her gambling debts? She needs more income, and a house of her own, a retreat, not too far from London, somewhere on the river—"

"Whose house has she in mind?"

"I don't think she means to turn anyone out."

"Houses tend to belong to somebody." Then a thought strikes him. He smiles.

She says, "I told you to stay away from her, once. But now we cannot do without you. Even my father and my uncle say so. Nothing is done, nothing, without the king's favor, without his constant company, and nowadays when you are not with Henry he wants to know where you are." She steps back, appraises him for a moment as if he were a stranger. "My sister, too."

"I want a job, Lady Carey. It isn't enough to be a councillor. I need an official place in the household."

"I'll tell her."

"I want a post in the Jewel House. Or the Exchequer."

She nods. "She made Tom Wyatt a poet. She made Harry Percy a madman. I'm sure she has some ideas about what to make you."

❖

A few days before Parliament met, Thomas Wyatt had come to apologize for getting him out of bed before dawn on New Year's Day. "You have every right to be angry with me, but I've come to ask you not to be. You know how it is at New Year's. Toasts are drunk, and the bowl goes round, and you must drain the bowl."

He watches Wyatt as he walks about the room, too curious and restless and half-shy to sit down and make his amends face-to-face. He turns the painted globe of the world, and rests his forefinger on England. He stops to look at pictures, at a little altarpiece, and he turns, questioning; it was my wife's, he says, I keep it for her sake. Master Wyatt wears a jacket of a stiffened cream brocade trimmed with sables, which he probably cannot afford; he wears a doublet of tawny silk. He has tender blue eyes and a mane of golden hair, thinning now. Sometimes he puts his fingertips to his head, tentative, as if he still has his New Year's headache; really, he is checking his hairline, to see if it has receded in the last five minutes. He stops and looks at himself in the mirror; he does this very often. Dear God, he says. Rolling about the streets with that crowd. I'm too old for such behavior. But too young to lose my hair. Do you think women care about it? Much? Do you think if I grew a beard it would distract . . . No, probably not. But perhaps I will anyway. The king's beard looks well, does it not?

He says, "Didn't your father give you any advice?"

"Oh yes. Drink off a bowl of milk before you go out. Stewed quinces in honey—do you think that works?"

He is trying not to laugh. He wants to take it seriously, his new post as Wyatt's father. He says, "I mean, did he never advise you to stay away from women in whom the king is interested?"

"I did stay away. You remember I went to Italy? After that I was in Calais for a year. How much staying away can a man do?"

A question from his own life; he recognizes it. Wyatt sits down on a small stool. He props his elbows on his knees. He holds his head, fingertips on his temples. He is listening to his own heartbeat; he is thinking; perhaps he is composing a verse? He looks up. "My father says that now Wolsey is dead you're the cleverest man in England. So can you understand this, if I say it just once? If Anne is not a virgin, that's none of my doing."

He pours him a glass of wine. "Strong," Wyatt says, after he has downed it. He looks into the depth of the glass, at his own fingers holding it. "I must say more, I think."

"If you must, say it here, and just once."

"Is anyone hiding behind the arras? Somebody told me there are servants at Chelsea who report to you. No one's servants are safe, these days, there are spies everywhere."

"Tell me in what day there were not spies," he says. "There was a child in More's house, Dick Purser, More took him in out of guilt after he was orphaned—I cannot say More killed the father outright, but he had him in the pillory and in the Tower, and it broke his health. Dick told the other boys he did not believe God was in the Communion host, so More had him whipped before the whole household. Now I have brought him here. What else could I do? I will take in any others he ill-treats."

Smiling, Wyatt passes his hand over the Queen of Sheba: that is to say, over Anselma. The king has given him Wolsey's fine tapestry. Early in the year, when he went in to speak to him at Greenwich, the king had seen him raise his eyes to her in greeting, and had said, with a sideways smile, do you know this woman? I used to, he said, explaining himself, excusing himself; the king said, no matter, we all have our follies in youth, and you can't marry everyone, can you . . . He had said in a low voice, I have in mind that this belonged to the Cardinal of York, and then, more briskly, when you go home make a place for her; I think she should come to live with you.

He gives himself a glass of wine, and another to Wyatt; says, "Gardiner has people outside the gate, watching who comes and goes. This is a city house, it is not a fortress—but if anybody's here who shouldn't be, my household does enjoy kicking them out. We quite like fighting. I'd prefer to put my past behind me, but I'm not allowed to. Uncle Norfolk keeps reminding me I was a common soldier, and not even in his army."

"You call him that?" Wyatt laughs. "Uncle Norfolk?"

"Between ourselves. But I don't need to remind you of what the Howards think is due to them. And you've grown up Thomas Boleyn's neighbor, so you know not to cross him, whatever you feel about his daughter. I hope you don't feel anything—do you?"

"For two years," Wyatt says, "I was sick to my soul to think of any other man touching her. But what could I offer? I am a married man, and not the duke or prince she was fishing for, either. She liked me, I think, or she liked to have me in thrall to her, it amused her. We would be alone, she would let me kiss her, and I always thought . . . but that is Anne's tactic, you see, she says yes, yes, yes, then she says no."

"And of course, you are such a gentleman."

"What, I should have raped her? If she says stop she means it— Henry knows that. But then another day would come and again she would let me kiss her. Yes, yes, yes, no. The worst of it is her hinting, her boasting almost, that she says no to me but yes to others—"

"Who are?"

"Oh, names, names would spoil her pastime. It must be so arranged that every man you see, at court or down in Kent, you think, is he the one? Is it him, or him? So you are continually asking yourself why you've fallen short, why you can never please her, why you never get the chance."

"I should think you write the best poems. You can comfort yourself there. His Majesty's verses can be a little repetitive, not to say self-centered."

"That song of his, 'Pastime with Good Company.' When I hear it there is something inside me, like a little dog, that wants to howl."

"True, the king is past forty. It is melancholy to hear him sing of the days when he was young and stupid." He watches Wyatt. The young man looks dazed, as if he has a persistent pain between his eyes. He is claiming that Anne no longer torments him, but that's not how it looks. He says, brutal as a butcher, "So how many lovers do you think she has had?"

Wyatt looks down at his feet. He looks at the ceiling. He says, "A dozen? Or none? Or a hundred? Brandon tried to tell Henry she was soiled goods. But he sent Brandon away from court. Imagine if I tried. I doubt I'd get out of the room alive. Brandon forced himself to speak, because he thinks, come the day she gives in to Henry, what then? Will he not know?"

"Give her credit. She must have thought of that. Besides, the king is no judge of maidenheads. He admits as much. With Katherine, it took him twenty years to puzzle out his brother had been there before him."

Wyatt laughs. "When the day comes, or the night, Anne can hardly say that to him."

"Listen. This is my view of the case. Anne does not concern herself with her wedding night because there is no cause for concern." He wants to say, because Anne is not a carnal being, she is a calculating being, with a cold slick brain at work behind her hungry black eyes. "I believe any woman who can say no to the King of England and keep on saying it, has the wit to say no to any number of men, including you, including Harry Percy, including anyone else she may choose to torment for her own sport while she is arranging her career in the way it suits her. So I think, yes, you've been made into a fool, but not quite in the way you thought."

"That is meant as consolation?"

"It should console you. If you'd really been her lover I would fear for you. Henry believes in her virginity. What else can he believe? But he will prove jealous, once they're married."

"As they will be? Married?"

"I am working hard with Parliament, believe me, and I think I can break the bishops. And after that, God knows . . . Thomas More says that in the reign of King John when England was placed under an interdict by the Pope, the cattle didn't breed, the corn ceased to ripen, the grass stopped growing and birds fell out of the air. But if that starts to happen," he smiles, "I'm sure we can reverse our policy."

"Anne has asked me: Cromwell, what does he really believe?"

"So you have conversations? And about me? Not just yes, yes, yes, no? I'm flattered."

Wyatt looks unhappy. "You couldn't be wrong? About Anne?"

"It's possible. For the moment I take her at her own valuation. It suits me. It suits us both."

As Wyatt is leaving: "You must come back soon. My girls have heard how handsome you are. You can keep your hat on, if you think they might be disillusioned."

Wyatt is the king's regular tennis partner. Therefore he knows about humbled pride. He fetches up a smile.

"Your father told us all about the lion. The boys have made a play out of it. Perhaps you would like to come one day and take your own role?"

"Oh, the lion. Nowadays, I think back on it, and it doesn't seem to me like a thing I would do. Stand still, in the open, and draw it on." He pauses. "More like something you would do, Master Cromwell."

❖

Thomas More comes to Austin Friars. He refuses food, he refuses drink, though he looks in need of both.

The cardinal would not have taken no for an answer. He would have made him sit down and eat syllabub. Or, if it were the season, given him a large plate of strawberries and a very small spoon.

More says, "In these last ten years the Turks have taken Belgrade. They have lit their campfires in the great library at Buda. It is only two years since they were at the gates of Vienna. Why would you want to make another breach in the walls of Christendom?"

"The King of England is not an infidel. Nor am I."

"Are you not? I hardly know whether you pray to the god of Luther and the Germans, or some heathen god you met with on your travels, or some English deity of your own invention. Perhaps your faith is for purchase. You would serve the Sultan if the price was right."

Erasmus says, did nature ever create anything kinder, sweeter or more harmonious than the character of Thomas More?

He is silent. He sits at his desk—More has caught him at work—with his chin propped on his fists. It is a pose that shows him, probably, to some combative advantage.

The Lord Chancellor looks as if he might rend his garments: which could only improve them. One could pity him, but he decides not to. "Master Cromwell, you think because you are a councillor you can negotiate with heretics, behind the king's back. You are wrong. I know about your letters that come and go to Stephen Vaughan, I know he has met with Tyndale."

"Are you threatening me? I'm just interested."

"Yes," More says sadly. "Yes, that is precisely what I am doing."

He sees that the balance of power has shifted between them: not as officers of state, but as men.

When More leaves, Richard says to him, "He ought not. Threaten you, I mean. Today, because of his office, he walks away, but tomorrow, who knows?"

He thinks, I was a child, nine or so, I ran off into London and saw an old woman suffer for her faith. The memory floods into his body and he walks away as if he sails on its tide, saying over his shoulder, "Richard, see if the Lord Chancellor has his proper escort. If not, give him one, and try to put him on a boat back to Chelsea. We cannot have him wandering about London, haranguing anyone at whose gate he may arrive."

He says the last bit in French, he does not know why. He thinks of Anne, her hand outstretched, drawing him toward her: *Maître Cremuel, à moi.*

He cannot remember the year but he remembers the late April weather, fat raindrops dappling the pale new leaves. He cannot remember the reason for Walter's temper, but he can remember the fear he felt in the pith of his being, and his heart banging against his ribs. In those days if he couldn't hide out with his uncle John at Lambeth he would get himself into the town and see who he could pick up with—see if he could earn a penny by running errands up and down to the quays, by carrying baskets or loading barrows. If you whistled for him, he came; lucky, he knows now, not to have got in with lowlifes who would lead him to be branded or whipped, or to be one of the small corpses fished out of the river. At that age you have no judgment. If somebody said, good sport over there, he followed the pointing finger. He had nothing against the old woman, but he had never seen a burning.

What's her crime? he said, and they said, she is a Loller. That's one who says the God on the altar is a piece of bread. What, he said, bread like the baker bakes? Let this child forward, they said. Let him be instructed, it will do him good to see up close, so he always goes to Mass after this and obeys his priest. They pushed him to the front of the crowd. Come here, sweetheart, stand with me, a woman said. She had a broad smile and wore a clean white cap. You get a pardon for your sins just for watching it, she said. Any that bring faggots to the burning, they get forty days' release from Purgatory.

When the Loller was led out between the officers the people jeered and shouted. He saw that she was a grandmother, perhaps the oldest person he had ever seen. The officers were nearly carrying her. She had no cap or veil. Her hair seemed to be torn out of her head in patches. People behind him said, no doubt she did that herself, in desperation at her sin. Behind the Loller came two monks, parading like fat gray rats, crosses in their pink paws. The woman in the clean cap squeezed his shoulder: like a mother might do, if you had one. Look at her, she said, eighty years old, and steeped in wickedness. A man said, not much fat on her bones, it won't take long unless the wind changes.

But what's her sin? he said.

I told you. She says the saints are but wooden posts.

Like that post they're chaining her to?

Aye, just like that.

The post will burn too.

They can get another next time, the woman said. She took her hand from his shoulder. She balled her two hands into fists and punched them in the air, and from the depth of her belly she let loose a scream, a halloo, in a shrill voice like a demon. The press of people took up the cry. They seethed and pushed forward for a view, they catcalled and whistled and stamped their feet. At the thought of the horrible thing he would see he felt hot and cold. He twisted to look up into the face of the woman who was his mother in this crowd. You watch, she said. With the gentlest brush of her fingers she turned his face to the spectacle. Pay attention now. The officers took chains and bound the old person to the stake.

The stake was on top of a pile of stones, and some gentlemen came, and priests, bishops perhaps, he did not know. They called out to the Loller to put off her heresies. He was close enough to see her lips moving but he could not hear what she said. What if she changes her mind now, will they let her go? Not they, the woman chuckled. Look, she is calling on Satan to help her. The gentlemen withdrew. The officers banked up wood and bales of straw around the Loller. The woman tapped him on the shoulder; let's hope it's damp, eh? This is a good view, last time I was at the back. The rain had stopped, the sun broken through. When the executioner came with a torch, it was pale in the sunshine, barely more than a slick movement, like the movement of eels in a bag. The monks were chanting and holding up a cross to the Loller, and it was only when they skipped backward, at the first billow of smoke, that the crowd knew the fire was set.

They surged forward, roaring. Officers made a barrier with staves and shouted in great deep voices, back, back, back, and the crowd shrieked and fell back, and then came on again, roaring and chanting, as if it were a game. Eddies of smoke spoiled their view, and the crowd beat it aside, coughing. Smell her! they cried. Smell the old sow! He had held his breath, not to breathe her in. In the smoke the Loller was screaming. Now she calls on the saints! they said. The woman bent down and said in his ear, do you know that in the fire they bleed? Some people think they just shrivel up, but I've seen it before and I know.

By the time the smoke cleared and they could see again, the old woman was well ablaze. The crowd began cheering. They had said it would not take long but it did take long, or so it seemed to him, before the screaming stopped. Does nobody pray for her, he said, and the woman said, what's the point? Even after there was nothing left to scream, the fire was stoked. The officers trod around the margins, stamping out any wisps of straw that flew off, kicking back anything bigger.

When the crowd drifted home, chattering, you could tell the ones who'd been on the wrong side of the fire, because their faces were gray with wood-ash. He wanted to go home but again he thought of Walter, who had said that morning he was going to kill him by inches. He watched the officers strike with their iron bars at the human debris that was left. The chains retained the remnants of flesh, sucking and clinging. Approaching the men, he asked, how hot must the fire be, to burn bone? He expected them to have knowledge in the matter. But they didn't understand his question. People who are not smiths think all fires are the same. His father had taught him the colors of red: sunset red, cherry red, the bright yellow-red with no name unless its name is scarlet.

The Loller's skull was left on the ground, the long bones of her arms and legs. Her broken rib cage was not much bigger than a dog's. A man took an iron bar and thrust it through the hole where the woman's left eye had been. He scooped up the skull and positioned it on the stones, so it was looking at him. Then he hefted his bar and brought it down on the crown. Even before the blow landed he knew it was false, skewed. Shattered bone, like a star, flew away into the dirt, but the most part of the skull was intact. Jesus, the man said. Here, lad, do you want a go? One good swipe will stove her in.

Usually he said yes to any invitation. But now he backed away, his hands behind his back. God's blood, the man said, I wish I could afford to be choosy. Soon after that it came on to rain. The men wiped their hands, blew their noses and walked off the job. They threw down their iron bars amid what was left of the Loller. It was just splinters of bone now, and thick sludgy ash. He picked up one of the iron bars, in case he needed a weapon. He fingered its tapered end, which was cut like a chisel. He did not know how far he was from home, and whether Walter might come for him. He wondered how you kill a person by inches, whether by burning them or cutting them up. He should have asked the officers while they were here, for being servants of the city they would know.

The stink of the woman was still in the air. He wondered if she was in Hell now, or still about the streets, but he was not afraid of ghosts. They had put up a stand for the gentlemen, and though the canopy was taken down, it was high enough off the ground to crouch underneath for shelter. He prayed for the woman, thinking it could do no harm. He moved his lips as he prayed. Rainwater gathered above him and fell in great drops through the planking. He counted the time between drops and caught them in his cupped hand. He did this just for a pastime. Dusk fell. If it were an ordinary day he would have been hungry by now and gone looking for food.

In the twilight certain men came, and women too; he knew, because there were women, that they were not officers or people who would hurt him. They drew together, making a loose circle around the stake on its pile of stones. He ducked out from under the stand and approached them. You will be wondering what has happened here, he said. But they did not look up or speak to him. They fell to their knees and he thought they were praying. I have prayed for her too, he said.

Have you? Good lad, one of the men said. He didn't even glance up. If he looks at me, he thought, he will see that I am not good, but a worthless boy who goes off with his dog and forgets to make the brine bath for the forge, so when Walter shouts Where's the fucking slake-tub, it's not there. With a sick lurch of his stomach he remembered what he'd not done and why he was to be killed. He almost cried out. As if he were in pain.

He saw now that the men and women were not praying. They were on their hands and knees. They were friends of the Loller, and they were scraping her up. One of the women knelt, her skirts spread, and held out an earthenware pot. His eyes were sharp even in the gloom, and out of the sludge and muck he picked a fragment of bone. Here's some, he said. The woman held out the bowl. Here's another.

One of the men stood apart, some way off. Why does he not help us? he said.

He is the watchman. He will whistle if the officers come.

Will they take us up?

Hurry, hurry, another man said.

When they had got a bowlful, the woman who was holding it said, "Give me your hand."

Trusting, he held it out to her. She dipped her fingers into the bowl. She placed on the back of his hand a smear of mud and grit, fat and ash. "Joan Boughton," she said.

Now, when he thinks back on this, he wonders at his own faulty memory. He has never forgotten the woman, whose last remnants he carried away as a greasy smudge on his own skin, but why is it that his life as a child doesn't seem to fit, one bit with the next? He can't remember how he got back home, and what Walter did instead of killing him by inches, or why he'd run off in the first place without making the brine. Perhaps, he thinks, I spilled the salt and I was too frightened to tell him. That seems likely. One fear creates a dereliction, the offense brings on a greater fear, and there comes a point where the fear is too great and the human spirit just gives up and a child wanders off numb and directionless and ends up following a crowd and watching a killing.

He has never told anyone this story. He doesn't mind talking to Richard, to Rafe about his past—within reason—but he doesn't mean to give away pieces of himself. Chapuys comes to dinner very often and sits beside him, teasing out bits of his life story as he teases tender flesh from the bone.

Some tell me your father was Irish, Eustache says. He waits, poised.

It is the first I have heard of it, he says, but I grant you, he was a mystery even to himself. Chapuys sniffs; the Irish are a very violent people, he says. "Tell me, is it true you fled from England at fifteen, having escaped from prison?"

"For sure," he says. "An angel struck off my chains."

That will give him something to write home. "I put the allegation to Cremuel, who answered me with a blasphemy, unfit for your Imperial ear." Chapuys is never stuck for something to put in dispatches. If news is scant he sends the gossip. There is the gossip he picks up, from dubious sources, and the gossip he feeds him on purpose. As Chapuys doesn't speak English, he gets his news in French from Thomas More, in Italian from the merchant Antonio Bonvisi, and in God knows what—Latin?—from Stokesley, the Bishop of London, whose table he also honors. Chapuys is peddling the idea to his master the Emperor that the people of England are so disaffected by their king that, given encouragement by a few Spanish troops, they will rise in revolt. Chapuys is, of course, deeply misled. The English may favor Queen Katherine—broadly, it seems they do. They may mislike or fail to understand recent measures in the Parliament. But instinct tells him this; they will knit together against foreign interference. They like Katherine because they have forgotten she is Spanish, because she has been here for a long time. They are the same people who rioted against foreigners, on Evil May Day; the same people, narrow-hearted, stubborn, attached to their patch of ground. Only overwhelming force—a coalition, say, of Francis and the Emperor—will budge them. We cannot, of course, rule out the possibility that such a coalition may occur.

When dinner is over, he walks Chapuys back to his people, to his big solid boys, bodyguards, who lounge about, chatting in Flemish, often about him. Chapuys knows he has been in the Low Countries; does he think he doesn't understand the language? Or is this some elaborate double-bluff?

There were days, not too long past, days since Lizzie died, when he'd woken in the morning and had to decide, before he could speak to anybody, who he was and why. There were days when he'd woken from dreams of the dead and searching for them. When his waking self trembled, at the threshold of deliverance from his dreams.

But those days are not these days.

Sometimes, when Chapuys has finished digging up Walter's bones and making his own life unfamiliar to him, he feels almost impelled to speak in defense of his father, his childhood. But it is no use to justify yourself. It is no good to explain. It is weak to be anecdotal. It is wise to conceal the past even if there is nothing to conceal. A man's power is in the half-light, in the half-seen movements of his hand and the unguessed-at expression of his face. It is the absence of facts that frightens people: the gap you open, into which they pour their fears, fantasies, desires.

❖

On April 14, 1532, the king appoints him Keeper of the Jewel House. From here, Henry Wyatt had said, you are able to take an overview of the king's income and outgoings.

The king shouts, as if to any courtier passing, "Why should I not, tell me why should I not, employ the son of an honest blacksmith?"

He hides his smile, at this description of Walter; so much more flattering than any the Spanish ambassador has arrived at. The king says, "What you are, I make you. I alone. Everything you are, everything you have, will come from me."

The thought gives him a pleasure you can hardly grudge. Henry is so well disposed these days, so openhanded and amenable, that you must forgive him the occasional statement of his position, whether it is necessary or not. The cardinal used to say, the English will forgive a king anything, until he tries to tax them. He also used to say, it doesn't really matter what the title of the office is. Let any colleague on the council turn his back, he would turn again to find that I was doing his job.

He is in a Westminster office one day in April when Hugh Latimer walks in, just released from custody at Lambeth Palace. "Well?" Hugh says. "You might leave off your scribble, and give me your hand."

He rises from his desk and embraces him, dusty black coat, sinew, bone. "So you made Warham a pretty speech?"

"I made it extempore, in my fashion. It came fresh from my mouth as from the mouth of a babe. Perhaps the old fellow is losing his appetite for burnings now his own end is so near. He is shriveling like a seedpod in the sun, when he moves you can hear his bones rattle. Anyway, I cannot account for it, but here you see me."

"How did he keep you?"

"Bare walls my library. Fortunately, my brain is furnished with texts. He sent me off with a warning. Told me if I did not smell of the fire then I smelled of the frying pan. It has been said to me before. It must be ten years now, since I came up for heresy before the Scarlet Beast." He laughs. "But Wolsey, he gave me my preacher's license back.

And the kiss of peace. And my dinner. So? Are we any nearer a queen who loves the gospel?"

A shrug. "We—they—are talking to the French. There is a treaty in the air. Francis has a gaggle of cardinals who might lend us their voices in Rome."

Hugh snorts. "Still waiting on Rome."

"That is how it must be."

"We will turn Henry. We will turn him to the gospel."

"Perhaps. Not suddenly. A little and a little."

"I am going to ask Bishop Stokesley to allow me to visit our brother Bainham. Will you come?"

Bainham is the barrister who was taken up by More last year and tortured. Just before Christmas he came before the Bishop of London. He abjured, and was free by February. He is a natural man; he wanted to live, how not? But once he was free his conscience would not let him sleep. One Sunday he walked into a crowded church and stood up before all the people, Tyndale's Bible in his hand, and spoke a profession of his faith. Now he is in the Tower waiting to know the date of his execution.

"So?" Latimer says. "You will or you won't?"

"I should not give ammunition to the Lord Chancellor."

I might sap Bainham's resolve, he thinks. Say to him, believe anything, brother, swear to it and cross your fingers behind your back. But then, it hardly matters what Bainham says now. Mercy will not operate for him, he must burn.

Hugh Latimer lopes away. The mercy of God operates for Hugh. The Lord walks with him, and steps with him into a wherry, to disembark under the shadow of the Tower; this being so, there is no need for Thomas Cromwell.

More says it does not matter if you lie to heretics, or trick them into a confession. They have no right to silence, even if they know speech will incriminate them; if they will not speak, then break their fingers, burn them with irons, hang them up by their wrists. It is legitimate, and indeed More goes further; it is blessed.

There is a group from the House of Commons who dine with

priests at the Queen's Head tavern. The word comes from them, and spreads among the people of London, that anyone who supports the king's divorce will be damned. So devoted is God to the cause of these gentlemen, they say, that an angel attends the sittings of Parliament with a scroll, noting down who votes and how, and smudging a sooty mark against the names of those who fear Henry more than the Almighty.

At Greenwich, a friar called William Peto, the head in England of his branch of the Franciscan order, preaches a sermon before the king, in which he takes as his text and example the unfortunate Ahab, seventh king of Israel, who lived in a palace of ivory. Under the influence of the wicked Jezebel he built a pagan temple and gave the priests of Baal places in his retinue. The prophet Elijah told Ahab that the dogs would lick his blood, and so it came to pass, as you would imagine, since only the successful prophets are remembered. The dogs of Samaria licked Ahab's blood. All his male heirs perished. They lay unburied in the streets. Jezebel was thrown out of a window of her palace. Wild dogs tore her body into shreds.

Anne says, "I am Jezebel. You, Thomas Cromwell, are the priests of Baal." Her eyes are alight. "As I am a woman, I am the means by which sin enters this world. I am the devil's gateway, the cursed ingress. I am the means by which Satan attacks the man, whom he was not bold enough to attack, except through me. Well, that is their view of the situation. My view is that there are too many priests with scant learning and smaller occupation. And I wish the Pope and the Emperor and all Spaniards were in the sea and drowned. And if anyone is to be thrown out of a palace window . . . *alors,* Thomas, I know who I would like to throw. Except the child Mary, the wild dogs would not find a scrap of flesh to gnaw, and Katherine, she is so fat she would bounce."

❖

When Thomas Avery comes home, he lowers to the flagstones the traveling chest in which he carries everything he owns, and rises with open arms to hug his master like a child. News of his government promotion has reached Antwerp. It seems Stephen Vaughan turned brick-red with pleasure and drank off a whole cup of wine without cutting it with water.

Come in, he says, there are fifty people here to see me but they can wait, come and tell me how is everyone across the sea. Thomas Avery starts talking at once. But inside the doorway of his room, he stops. He is looking at the tapestry given by the king. His eyes search it, then turn to his master's face, and then back to the tapestry. "Who is that lady?"

"You can't guess?" He laughs. "It is Sheba visiting Solomon. The king gave it to me. It was my lord cardinal's. He saw I liked it. And he likes to give presents."

"It must be worth a fair sum." Avery looks at it with respect, like the keen young accountant he is.

"Look," he says to him, "I have another present, what do you think of this? It is perhaps the only good thing ever to come out of a monastery. Brother Luca Pacioli. It took him thirty years to write."

The book is bound in deepest green with a tooled border of gold, and its pages are edged in gilt, so that it blazes in the light. Its clasps are studded with blackish garnets, smooth, translucent. "I hardly dare open it," the boy says.

"Please. You will like it."

It is *Summa de Arithmetica*. He unclasps it to find a woodcut of the author with a book before him, and a pair of compasses. "This is a new printing?"

"Not quite, but my friends in Venice have just now remembered me. I was a child, of course, when Luca wrote it, and you were not even thought of." His fingertips barely touch the page. "Look, here he treats of geometry, do you see the figures? Here is where he says you don't go to bed until the books balance."

"Master Vaughan quotes that maxim. It has caused me to sit up till dawn."

"And I." Many nights in many cities. "Luca, you know, he was a poor man. He came out of Sansepulcro. He was a friend of artists and he became a perfect mathematician in Urbino, which is a little town up in the mountains, where Count Federigo the great condottiere had his library of over a thousand books. He was magister at the university in Perugia, later in Milan. I wonder why such a man would remain a monk, but of course there have been practitioners of algebra and geometry who have been thrown into dungeons as magicians, so perhaps he thought the church would protect him . . . I heard him lecture in Venice, it will be more than twenty years ago now, I was your age, I suppose. He spoke about proportion. Proportion in building, in music, in paintings, in justice, in the commonwealth, the state; about how rights should be balanced, the power of a prince and his subjects, how the wealthy citizen should keep his books straight and say his prayers and serve the poor. He spoke about how a printed page should look. How a law should read. Or a face, what makes it beautiful."

"Will he tell me in this book?" Thomas Avery glances up again at the Queen of Sheba. "I suppose they knew, who made the tapestry."

"How is Jenneke?"

The boy turns the leaves with reverent fingers. "It is a beautiful book. Your friends in Venice must admire you very much."

So Jenneke is no more, he thinks. She is dead or she is in love with someone else. "Sometimes," he says, "my friends in Italy send me new poems, but I think all the poems are in here . . . Not that a page of figures is a verse, but anything that is precise is beautiful, anything that balances in all its parts, anything that is proportionate . . . do you think so?"

He wonders at the power Sheba has to draw the boy's eyes. It is impossible he should have seen Anselma, ever met her, heard of her. I told Henry about her, he thinks. One of those afternoons when I told my king a little, and he told me a lot: how he shakes with desire when he thinks of Anne, how he has tried other women, tried them as an expedient to take the edge off lust, so that he can think and talk and act as a reasoning man, but how he has failed with them . . . A strange admission, but he thinks it justifies him, he thinks it verifies the rightness of his pursuit, for I chase but one hind, he says, one strange deer timid and wild, and she leads me off the paths that other men have trod, and by myself into the depths of the wood.

"Now," he says, "we will put this book on your desk. So that you can be consoled by it when nothing seems to add up at all."

He has great hopes of Thomas Avery. It's easy to employ some child who will total the columns and push them under your nose, get them initialed and then lock them in a chest. But what's the point of that? The page of an accounts book is there for your use, like a love poem. It's not there for you to nod and then dismiss it; it's there to open your heart to possibility. It's like the scriptures: it's there for you to think about, and initiate action. Love your neighbor. Study the market. Increase the spread of benevolence. Bring in better figures next year.

❖

The date of James Bainham's execution is fixed for April 30. He cannot go to the king, not with any hope of a pardon. Long ago Henry was given the title of Defender of the Faith; he is keen to show he deserves it still.

At Smithfield in the stand put up for the dignitaries he meets the Venetian ambassador, Carlo Capello. They exchange a bow. "In what capacity are you here, Cromwell? As friend of this heretic, or by virtue of your position? In fact, what is your position? The devil alone knows."

"And I am sure he will tell Your Excellency, when you next have a private talk."

Wrapped in his sheet of flames, the dying man calls out, "The Lord forgive Sir Thomas More."

❖

On May 15, the bishops sign a document of submission to the king. They will not make new church legislation without the king's license, and will submit all existing laws to a review by a commission which will include laymen—members of Parliament and the king's appointees. They will not meet in Convocation without the king's permission.

Next day, he stands in a gallery at Whitehall, which looks down on an inner court, a garden, where the king waits, and the Duke of Norfolk busies to and fro. Anne is in the gallery beside him. She is wearing a dark red gown of figured damask, so heavy that her tiny white shoulders seem to droop inside it. Sometimes—in a kind of fellowship of the imagination—he imagines resting his hand upon her shoulder and following with his thumb the scooped hollow between her collarbone and her throat; imagines with his forefinger tracking the line of her breast as it swells above her bodice, as a child follows a line of print.

She turns her head and half-smiles. "Here he comes. He is not wearing the Lord Chancellor's chain. What can he have done with it?"

Thomas More looks round-shouldered and despondent. Norfolk looks tense. "My uncle has been trying to arrange this for months," Anne says. "But the king will not be brought to it. He doesn't want to lose More. He wants to please everybody. You know how it is."

"He knew Thomas More when he was young."

"When I was young I knew sin."

They turn, and smile at each other. "Look now," Anne says. "Do you suppose that is the Seal of England, that he has got in that leather bag?"

When Wolsey gave up the Great Seal, he dragged out the process for two days. But now the king, in the private paradise below, is waiting with open hand.

"So who now?" Anne says. "Last night he said, my Lord Chancellors are nothing but grief to me. Perhaps I shall do without one."

"The lawyers will not like that. Somebody must rule the courts."

"Then who do you say?"

"Put it in his mind to appoint Mr. Speaker. Audley will do an honest job. Let the king try him in the role *pro tem,* if he will, and then if he does not like him he need not confirm it. But I think he will like him. Audley is a good lawyer and he is his own man, but he understands how to be useful. And he understands me, I think."

"To think that someone does! Shall we go down?"

"You cannot resist it?"

"No more can you."

They go down the inner staircase. Anne places her fingertips lightly on his arm. In the garden below, nightingales are hung in cages. Struck mute, they huddle against the sunlight. A fountain pit-patters into a basin. A scent of thyme rises from the herb beds. From inside the palace, an unseen someone laughs. The sound is cut off as if a door had closed. He stoops and picks a sprig of the herb, bruises its scent into his palm. It takes him to another place, far from here. More makes his bow to Anne. She barely nods. She curtsies deeply to Henry, and arranges herself by his side, her eyes on the ground. Henry clutches her wrist; he wants to tell her something, or just be alone with her.

"Sir Thomas?" He offers his hand. More turns away. Then he thinks better of it; he turns back and takes it. His fingertips are ashy cold.

"What will you do now?"

"Write. Pray."

"My recommendation would be write only a little, and pray a lot."

"Now, is that a threat?" More is smiling.

"It may be. My turn, don't you think?"

When the king saw Anne, his face had lit up. His heart is ardent; in his councillor's hand, it burns to the touch.

❖

He catches Gardiner at Westminster, in one of those smoky back courts where the sunlight never reaches. "My lord bishop?"

Gardiner draws together his beetle brows.

"Lady Anne has asked me to think about a country house for her."

"What is that to me?"

"Let me unfold to you," he says, "the way my thoughts proceed. It should be somewhere near the river, convenient for Hampton Court, and for her barge to Whitehall and Greenwich. Somewhere in good repair, as she has no patience, she will not wait. Somewhere with pretty gardens, well established . . . Then I think, what about Stephen's manor at Hanworth, that the king leased him when he became Master Secretary?"

Even in the dim light he can see the thoughts chasing each other through Stephen's brain. Oh my moat and my little bridges, my rose gardens and strawberry beds, my herb garden, my beehives, my ponds and orchard, oh my Italianate terra-cotta medallions, my intarsia, my gilding, my galleries, my seashell fountain, my deer park.

"It would be graceful in you to offer her the lease, before it becomes a royal command. A good deed to set against the bishops' stubbornness? Oh, come on, Stephen. You have other houses. It isn't as if you'll be sleeping under a haystack."

"If I were," the bishop says, "I should expect one of your boys along with a ratting dog, to dig me out of my dreams."

Gardiner's rodent pulses jump; his wet black eyes gleam. He is squeaking inside with indignation and stifled fury. But part of him may be relieved, when he thinks about it, that the bill has come in so early, and that he can meet its terms.

Gardiner is still Master Secretary, but he, Cromwell, now sees the king almost every day. If Henry wants advice, he can give it, or if the subject is outside his remit, he will find someone else who can. If the king has a complaint, he will say, leave it with me: if, by your royal favor, I may proceed? If the king is in a good humor he is ready to laugh, and if the king is miserable he is gentle and careful with him. The king has begun a course of dissimulation, which the Spanish ambassador, sharp-eyed as ever, has not failed to notice. "He sees you in private, not in his presence chamber," he says. "He prefers if his nobles do not know how often he consults with you. If you were a smaller man, you could be brought in and out in a laundry basket. As it is, I think those so-spiteful privy chamber gentlemen cannot fail to tell their friends, who will mutter at your success, and circulate slanders against you, and plot to bring you down." The ambassador smiles and says, "If I may proffer an image which will appeal to you—do I hit the nail on the head?"

In a letter from Chapuys to the Emperor, one which happens to go by way of Mr. Wriothesley, he learns of his own character. Call-Me reads it out to him: "He says your antecedents are obscure, your youth reckless and wild, that you are a heretic of long standing, a disgrace to the office of councillor; but personally, he finds you a man of good cheer, liberal, openhanded, gracious . . ."

"I knew he liked me. I should ask him for a job."

"He says that the way you got into the king's confidence, you promised you would make him the richest king England has ever had."

He smiles.

Late in May, two fish of prodigal size are caught in the Thames, or rather they are washed up, dying, on the muddy shore. "Am I expected to do something about it?" he says, when Johane brings the news in.

"No," she says. "At least, I don't think so. It's a portent, isn't it? It's an omen, that's all."

❖

In late July, he has a letter from Cranmer in Nuremberg. Before this he has written from the Low Countries, asking for advice on his commercial negotiations with the Emperor, matters in which he feels out of his depth; from towns along the Rhine, he has written hopefully that the Emperor must come to an accommodation with the Lutheran princes, as he needs their help against the Turks on the frontier. He writes of how he struggles to become an adept in England's usual diplomatic game: proffering the King of England's friendship, dangling promises of English gold, while actually failing to provide any.

But this letter is different. It is dictated, written in a clerk's hand. It talks of the workings of the holy spirit in the heart. Rafe reads it out to him, and points out, down at the bottom and running up the left margin, a few words in Cranmer's own script: "Something has occurred. Not to be trusted to a letter. It may make a stir. Some would say I have been rash. I shall need your advice. Keep this secret."

"Well," Rafe says, "let us run up and down Cheap: 'Thomas Cranmer has a secret, we don't know what it is!'"

❖

A week later Hans turns up at Austin Friars. He has rented a house in Maiden Lane and is staying at the Steelyard while it is fixed up for him. "Let me see your new picture, Thomas," he says, walking in. He stands before it. Folds his arms. Steps back a pace. "You know these people? The likeness is good?"

Two Italian bankers, confederates, looking toward the viewer but longing to exchange glances; one in silks, one in fur; a vase of carnations, an astrolabe, a goldfinch, a glass through which the sand has half run; through an arched window, a ship rigged with silk, its sails translucent, drifting in a mirror sea. Hans turns away, pleased. "How does he get that expression in the eye, so hard yet so sly?"

"How is Elsbeth?"

"Fat. Sad."

"Is it surprising? You go home, give her a child, come away again."

"I don't reckon to be a good husband. I just send the money home."

"How long will you stay with us?"

Hans grunts, downs his cup of wine and talks about what he's left behind: talk about Basle, about the Swiss cantons and cities. Riots and pitched battles. Images, not images. Statues, not statues. It is the body of God, it is not the body of God, it is sort of the body of God. It is his blood, it is not his blood. Priests may marry, they may not. There are seven sacraments, there are three. The crucifix we creep to on our knees and reverence with our lips, or the crucifix we chop it up and burn it in the public square. "I am no Pope-lover but I get tired of it. Erasmus has run off to Freiburg to the papists and now I have run off to you and Junker Heinrich. That's what Luther calls your king. 'His Disgrace, the King of England.'" He wipes his mouth. "All I ask is to do some good work and be paid for it. And I prefer not to have my efforts wiped out by some sectary with a pail of whitewash."

"You came here looking for peace and ease?" He shakes his head. "Too late."

"I was just going over London Bridge and I saw someone had attacked the Madonna's statue. Knocked off the baby's head."

"That was done a while back. It would be that devil Cranmer. You know what he is when he's taken a drink."

Hans grins. "You miss him. Who would have thought you would be friends?"

"Old Warham is not well. If he dies this summer, Lady Anne will ask for Canterbury for my friend."

Hans is surprised. "Not Gardiner?"

"He's spoiled his chance with the king."

"He is his own worst enemy."

"I wouldn't say that."

Hans laughs. "It would be a great promotion for Dr. Cranmer. He will not want it. Not he. So much pomp. He likes his books."

"He will take it. It will be his duty. The best of us are forced against the grain."

"What, you?"

"It is against the grain to have your old patron come and threaten me in my own house, and take it quietly. As I do. Have you been to Chelsea?"

"Yes. They are a sad household."

"It was given out that he was resigning on grounds of ill health. So as not to embarrass anybody."

"He says he has a pain here," Hans rubs his chest, "and it comes on him when he starts to write. But the others look well enough. The family on the wall."

"You need not go to Chelsea for commissions now. The king has me at work at the Tower, we are restoring the fortifications. He has builders and painters and gilders in, we are stripping out the old royal apartments and making something finer, and I am going to build a new lodging for the queen. In this country, you see, the kings and queens lie at the Tower the night before they are crowned. When Anne's day comes there will be plenty of work for you. There will be pageants to design, banquets, and the city will be ordering gold and silver plate to present to the king. Talk to the Hanse merchants, they will want to make a show. Get them planning. Secure yourself the work before half the craftsmen in Europe are here."

"Is she to have new jewels?"

"She is to have Katherine's. He has not lost all sense."

"I would like to paint her. Anna Bolena."

"I don't know. She may not want to be studied."

"They say she is not beautiful."

"No, perhaps she is not. You would not choose her as a model for a Primavera. Or a statue of the Virgin. Or a figure of Peace."

"What then, Eve? Medusa?" Hans laughs. "Don't answer."

"She has great presence, esprit . . . You may not be able to put it in a painting."

"I see you think I am limited."

"Some subjects resist you, I feel sure."

Richard comes in. "Francis Bryan is here."

"Lady Anne's cousin." He stands up.

"You must go to Whitehall. Lady Anne is breaking up the furniture and smashing the mirrors."

He swears under his breath. "Take Master Holbein in to dinner."

❖

Francis Bryan is laughing so hard that his horse twitches under him, uneasy, and skitters sideways, to the danger of passersby. By the time they get to Whitehall he has pieced this story together: Anne has just heard that Harry Percy's wife, Mary Talbot, is preparing to petition Parliament for a divorce. For two years, she says, her husband has not shared her bed, and when finally she asked him why, he said he could not carry on a pretense any longer; they were not really married, and never had been, since he was married to Anne Boleyn.

"My lady is enraged," Bryan says. His eyepatch, sewn with jewels, winks as he giggles. "She says Harry Percy will spoil everything for her. She cannot decide between striking him dead with one blow of a sword or teasing him apart over forty days of public torture, like they do in Italy."

"Those stories are much exaggerated."

He has never witnessed, or quite believed in, Lady Anne's uncontrolled outbursts of temper. When he is admitted she is pacing, her hands clasped, and she looks small and tense, as if someone has knitted her and drawn the stitches too tight. Three ladies—Jane Rochford, Mary Shelton, Mary Boleyn—are following her with their eyes. A small carpet, which perhaps ought to be on the wall, is crumpled on the floor. Jane Rochford says, "We have swept up the broken glass." Sir Thomas Boleyn, Monseigneur, sits at a table, a heap of papers before him. George sits by him on a stool. George has his head in his hands. His sleeves are only medium-puffed. The Duke of Norfolk is staring into the hearth, where a fire is laid but not lit, perhaps attempting through the power of his gaze to make the kindling spark.

"Shut the door, Francis," George says, "and don't let anybody else in." He is the only person in the room who is not a Howard.

"I suggest we pack Anne's bags and send her down to Kent," Jane Rochford says. "The king's anger, once roused—"

George: "Say no more, or I may strike you."

"It is my honest advice." Jane Rochford, God protect her, is one of those women who doesn't know when to stop. "Master Cromwell, the king has indicated there must be an inquiry. It must come before the council. It cannot be fudged this time. Harry Percy will give testimony unimpeded. The king cannot do all he has done, and all he means to do, for a woman who is concealing a secret marriage."

"I wish I could divorce you," George says. "I wish you had a pre-contract, but Jesus, no chance of that, the fields were black with men running in the other direction."

Monseigneur holds up a hand. "Please."

Mary Boleyn says, "What is the use of calling in Master Cromwell, and not telling him what has already occurred? The king has already spoken to my lady sister."

"I deny everything," Anne says. It is as if the king is standing before her.

"Good," he says. "Good."

"That the earl spoke to me of love, I allow. He wrote me verse, and I being then a young girl, and thinking no harm of it—"

He almost laughs. "Verse? Harry Percy? Do you still have it?"

"No. Of course not. Nothing written."

"That makes it easier," he says gently. "And of course there was no promise, or contract, or even talk of them."

"And," Mary says, "no consummation of any kind. There could not be. My sister is a notorious virgin."

"And how was the king, was he—"

"He walked out of the room," Mary says, "and left her standing."

Monseigneur looks up. He clears his throat. "In this exigency, there are a variety, and number of approaches, it seems to me, that one might—"

Norfolk explodes. He pounds up and down on the floor, like Satan in a Corpus Christi play. "Oh, by the thrice-beshitten shroud of Lazarus! While you are selecting an approach, my lord, while you are taking a view, your lady daughter is slandered up and down the country, the king's mind is poisoned, and this family's fortune is unmaking before your eyes."

"Harry Percy," George says; he holds up his hands. "Listen, will you let me speak? As I understand it, Harry Percy was persuaded once to forget his claims, so if he was fixed once—"

"Yes," Anne says, "but the cardinal fixed him, and most unfortunately the cardinal is dead."

There is a silence: a silence sweet as music. He looks, smiling, at Anne, at Monseigneur, at Norfolk. If life is a chain of gold, sometimes God hangs a charm on it. To prolong the moment, he crosses the room and picks up the fallen hanging. Narrow loom. Indigo ground. Asymmetrical knot. Isfahan? Small animals march stiffly across it, weaving through knots of flowers. "Look," he says. "Do you know what these are? Peacocks."

Mary Shelton comes to peer over his shoulder. "What are those snake things with legs?"

"Scorpions."

"Mother Mary, do they not bite?"

"Sting." He says, "Lady Anne, if the Pope cannot stop you becoming queen, and I do not think he can, Harry Percy should not be in your way."

"So shift him out of it," Norfolk says.

"I can see why it would not be a good idea for you, as a family—"

"Do it," Norfolk says. "Beat his skull in."

"Figuratively," he says. "My lord."

Anne sits down. Her face is turned away from the women. Her little hands are drawn into fists. Monseigneur shuffles his papers. George, lost in thought, takes off his cap and plays with its jeweled pin, testing the point against the pad of his forefinger.

He has rolled the hanging up, and he presents it gently to Mary Shelton. "Thank you," she whispers, blushing as if he had proposed something intimate. George squeaks; he has succeeded in pricking himself. Uncle Norfolk says bitterly, "You fool of a boy."

Francis Bryan follows him out.

"Please feel you can leave me now, Sir Francis."

"I thought I would go with you. I want to learn what you do."

He checks his stride, slaps his hand flat into Bryan's chest, spins him sideways and hears the thud of his skull against the wall. "In a hurry," he says.

Someone calls his name. Master Wriothesley rounds a corner. "Sign of Mark and the Lion. Five minutes' walk."

Call-Me has had men following Harry Percy since he came to London. His concern has been that Anne's ill-wishers at court—the Duke of Suffolk and his wife, and those dreamers who believe Katherine will come back—have been meeting with the earl and encouraging him in a view of the past that would be useful, from their point of view. But seemingly no meetings have occurred: unless they are held in bathhouses on the Surrey bank.

Call-Me turns sharply down an alley, and they emerge into a dirty inn yard. He looks around; two hours with a broom and a willing heart, and you could make it respectable. Mr. Wriothesley's handsome red-gold head shines like a beacon. St. Mark, creaking above his head, is tonsured like a monk. The lion is small and blue and has a smiling face. Call-Me touches his arm: "In there." They are about to duck into a side door, when from above there is a shrill whistle. Two women lean out of a window, and with a whoop and a giggle flop their bare breasts over the sill. "Jesu," he says. "More Howard ladies."

Inside Mark and the Lion, various men in Percy livery are slumped over tables and lying under them. The Earl of Northumberland is drinking in a private room. It would be private, except there is a serving hatch through which faces keep leering. The earl sees him. "Oh. I was half expecting you." Tense, he runs his hands through his cropped hair, and it stands up in bristles all over his head.

He, Cromwell, goes to the hatch, holds up one finger to the spectators, and slams it in their face. But he is soft-voiced as ever when he sits down with the boy and says, "Now, my lord, what is to be done here? How can I help you? You say you can't live with your wife. But she is as lovely a lady as any in this kingdom, if she has faults I never heard of them, so why can you not agree?"

But Harry Percy is not here to be handled like a timid falcon. He is here to shout and weep. "If I could not agree with her on our wedding day, how can I agree now? She hates me because she knows we are not properly married. Why has only the king a conscience in the matter, why not I, if he doubts his marriage he shouts about it to the whole of Christendom, but when I doubt mine he sends the lowest man in his employ to sweet-talk me and tell me to go back home and make the best of it. Mary Talbot knows I was pledged to Anne, she knows where my heart lies and always will. I told the truth before, I said we had made a compact before witnesses and therefore neither of us was free. I swore it and the cardinal bullied me out of it; my father said he would strike me out of his line, but my father is dead and I am not afraid to speak the truth anymore. Henry may be king but he is stealing another man's wife; Anne Boleyn is rightfully my wife, and how will he stand on the day of judgment, when he comes before God naked and stripped of his retinue?"

He hears him out. The slide and tumble into incoherence . . . true love . . . pledges . . . swore she would give her body to me, allowed me such freedom as only a betrothed woman would allow . . .

"My lord," he says. "You have said what you have to say. Now listen to me. You are a man whose money is almost spent. I am a man who knows how you have spent it. You are a man who has borrowed all over Europe. I am a man who knows your creditors. One word from me, and your debts will be called in."

"Oh, and what can they do?" Percy says. "Bankers have no armies."

"Neither have you armies, my lord, if your coffers are empty. Look at me now. Understand this. You hold your earldom from the king.

Your task is to secure the north. Percys and Howards between them defend us against Scotland. Now suppose Percy cannot do it. Your men will not fight for a kind word—"

"They are my tenants, it is their duty to fight."

"But my lord, they need supply, they need provision, they need arms, they need walls and forts in good repair. If you cannot ensure these things you are worse than useless. The king will take your title away, and your land, and your castles, and give them to someone who will do the job you cannot."

"He will not. He respects all ancient titles. All ancient rights."

"Then let's say I will." Let's say I will rip your life apart. Me and my banker friends.

How can he explain to him? The world is not run from where he thinks. Not from his border fortresses, not even from Whitehall. The world is run from Antwerp, from Florence, from places he has never imagined; from Lisbon, from where the ships with sails of silk drift west and are burned up in the sun. Not from castle walls, but from countinghouses, not by the call of the bugle but by the click of the abacus, not by the grate and click of the mechanism of the gun but by the scrape of the pen on the page of the promissory note that pays for the gun and the gunsmith and the powder and shot.

"I picture you without money and title," he says. "I picture you in a hovel, wearing homespun, and bringing home a rabbit for the pot. I picture your lawful wife, Anne Boleyn, skinning and jointing this rabbit. I wish you every happiness."

Harry Percy slumps over the table. Angry tears spring out of his eyes.

"You were never pre-contracted," he says. "Any silly promises you made had no effect in law. Whatever understanding you think you had, you didn't have it. And there is another matter, my lord. If ever you say one more word about Lady Anne's freedom"—he packs into one word a volume of disgust—"then you will answer to me and the Howards and the Boleyns, and George Rochford will have no tender care of your person, and my lord Wiltshire will humble your pride, and as for the Duke of Norfolk, if he hears the slightest imputation against his niece's honor he will drag you out of whatever hole you are cowering in and bite your bollocks off. Now," he says, resuming his former amiability, "is that clear, my lord?" He crosses the room and opens the serving hatch again. "You can peer in again now." Faces appear; or, to be truthful, just bobbing foreheads, and eyes. In the doorway he pauses and turns back to the earl. "And I will tell you this, for the avoidance of doubt. If you think Lady Anne loves you, you could not be more mistaken. She hates you. The only service you can do her now, short of dying, is to unsay what you said to your poor wife, and take any oath that is required of you, to clear her path to become Queen of England."

On the way out he says to Wriothesley, "I feel sorry for him really." Call-Me laughs so hard he has to lean against the wall.

❖

Next day he is early for the meeting of the king's council. The Duke of Norfolk takes his place at the head of the table, then shifts out of it when word comes that the king himself will preside. "And Warham is here," someone says: the door opens, nothing happens, then slowly very slowly the ancient prelate shuffles in. He takes his seat. His hands tremble as they rest on the cloth before him. His head trembles on his neck. His skin is parchment-colored, like the drawing that Hans made of him. He looks around the table with a slow lizard blink.

He crosses the room and stands across the table from Warham, inquiring after his health, by way of a formality; it is clear he is dying. He says, "This prophetess you harbor in your diocese. Eliza Barton. How is she getting on?"

Warham barely looks up. "What is it you want, Cromwell? My commission found nothing against the girl. You know that."

"I hear she is telling her followers that if the king marries Lady Anne he has only a year to reign."

"I could not swear to that. I have not heard it with my own ears."

"I understand Bishop Fisher has been to see her."

"Well . . . or she to see him. One or the other. Why should he not? She is a blessed young woman."

"Who is controlling her?"

Warham's head looks as if it will wobble off his shoulders. "She may be unwise. She may be misled. After all, she is a simple country girl. But she has a gift, I am sure of it. When people come into her company, she can tell them at once what is troubling them. What sins are weighing on their conscience."

"Indeed? I must go and see her. I wonder if she would know what's troubling me?"

"Peace," Thomas Boleyn says. "Harry Percy is here."

The earl comes in between two of his minders. His eyes are red, and a whiff of stale vomit suggests he has resisted the efforts of his people to scrub him down. The king comes in. It is a warm day and he wears pale silks. Rubies cluster on his knuckles like bubbles of blood. He takes his seat. He rests his flat blue eye on Harry Percy.

Thomas Audley—standing in as Lord Chancellor—leads the earl through his denials. Pre-contracted? No. Promises of any kind? No carnal—I so regret to mention—knowledge? Upon my honor, no, no and no.

"Sad to say, we shall need more than your word of honor," the king says. "Matters have gone so far, my lord."

Harry Percy looks panic-stricken. "Then what more must I do?"

He says softly, "Approach His Grace of Canterbury, my lord. He is holding out the Book."

This, anyway, is what the old man is trying to do. Monseigneur tries to assist him, and Warham bats his hands away. Gripping the table, making the cloth slide, he hauls himself to his feet. "Harry Percy, you have chopped and changed in this matter, you have asserted it, denied it, asserted it, now you are brought here to deny it again, but this time not only in the sight of men. Now . . . will you put your hand on this Bible, and swear before me and in the presence of the king and his council that you are free from unlawful knowledge of Lady Anne, and free from any marriage contract with her?"

Harry Percy rubs his eyes. He extends his hand. His voice shakes. "I swear."

"All done," the Duke of Norfolk says. "You'd wonder how the

whole thing got about in the first place, wouldn't you?" He walks up to Harry Percy and grips him by the elbow. "We shall hear no more of this, boy?"

The king says, "Howard, you have heard him take his oath, cease to trouble him now. Some of you assist the archbishop, you see he is not well." His mood softened, he smiles around at his councillors. "Gentlemen, we will go to my private chapel, and see Harry Percy take Holy Communion to seal his oath. Then Lady Anne and I will spend the afternoon in reflection and prayer. I shall not want to be disturbed."

Warham shuffles up to the king. "Winchester is robing to say Mass for you. I am going home to my diocese." With a murmur, Henry leans to kiss his ring. "Henry," the archbishop says, "I have seen you promote within your own court and council persons whose principles and morals will hardly bear scrutiny. I have seen you deify your own will and appetite, to the sorrow and scandal of Christian people. I have been loyal to you, to the point of violation of my own conscience. I have done much for you, but now I have done the last thing I will ever do."

❖

At Austin Friars, Rafe is waiting for him. "Yes?"

"Yes."

"So now?"

"Now Harry Percy can borrow more money, and edge himself nearer his ruin. A progress which I shall be pleased to facilitate." He sits down. "I think one day I will have that earldom off him."

"How would you do that, sir?" He shrugs: don't know. "You would not want the Howards to have more sway in the borders than they do already."

"No. No, possibly not." He broods. "Can you look out the papers about Warham's prophetess?"

While he waits, he opens the window and looks down into the garden. The pink of the roses in his arbors has been bleached out by the sun. I am sorry for Mary Talbot, he thinks; her life will not be easier after this. For a few days, a few days only, she instead of Anne was the talk of the king's court. He thinks of Harry Percy, walking in to arrest the cardinal, keys in his hand: the guard he set, around the dying man's bed.

He leans out of the window. I wonder if peach trees would be possible? Rafe brings in the bundle.

He cuts the tape and straightens out the letters and memoranda. This unsavory business all started six years ago, at a broken-down chapel on the edge of Kentish marshland, when a statue of the Virgin began to attract pilgrims, and a young woman, by name Elizabeth Barton, started to put on shows for them. What did the statue do in the first place, to get attention? Move, probably: or weep blood. The girl is an orphan, brought up in the household of one of Warham's land agents. She has a sister, no other family. He says to Rafe, "Nobody took any notice of her till she was twenty or so, and then she had some kind of illness, and when she got better she started to have visions, and speak in alien voices. She says she's seen St. Peter at the gates of Heaven with his keys. She's seen St. Michael weighing souls. If you ask her where your dead relatives are, she can tell you. If it's Heaven, she speaks in a high voice. If it's Hell, in a deep voice."

"The effect could be comic," Rafe says.

"Do you think so? What irreverent children I have brought up." He reads, then looks up. "She sometimes goes without food for nine days. Sometimes she falls suddenly to the ground. Not surprising, is it? She suffers spasms, torsions and trances. It sounds most displeasant. She was interviewed by my lord cardinal, but . . ." his hand sifts the papers, "nothing here, no record of the meeting. I wonder what happened. Probably he tried to get her to eat her dinner, she wouldn't have liked that. By this . . ." he reads, ". . . she is in a convent in Canterbury. The broken-down chapel has got a new roof and money is rolling in to the local clergy. There are cures. The lame walk, the blind see. Candles light by themselves. The pilgrims are thick upon the roads. Why do I feel I have heard this story before? She has a flock of monks and priests about her, who direct the people's eyes heavenward while picking their pockets. And we can presume it is these same monks and priests who have instructed her to hawk around her opinion on the subject of the king's marriage."

"Thomas More has met her. As well as Fisher."

"Yes, I keep that in mind. Oh, and . . . look here . . . Mary Magdalene has sent her a letter, illuminated in gold."

"Can she read it?"

"Yes, it seems she can." He looks up. "What do you think? The king will endure being called names, if it is by a holy virgin. I suppose he is used to it. Anne berates him often enough."

"Possibly he is afraid."

Rafe has been to court with him; evidently, he understands Henry better than some people who have known him all his life. "Indeed he is. He believes in simple maids who can talk to saints. He is disposed to believe in prophecies, whereas I . . . I think we let it run for a time. See who visits her. Who makes offerings. Certain noble ladies have been in touch with her, wanting their fortunes told and their mothers prayed out of Purgatory."

"My lady Exeter," Rafe says.

Henry Courtenay, Marquis of Exeter, is the king's nearest male relative, being a grandson of old King Edward; hence, useful to the Emperor, when he comes with his troops to boot out Henry and put a new king on the throne. "If I were Exeter, I wouldn't let my wife dance attendance on some addle-witted girl who is feeding her fantasies that one day she will be queen." He begins to refold the papers. "This girl, you know, she claims she can raise the dead."

❖

At John Petyt's funeral, while the women are upstairs sitting with Lucy, he convenes an impromptu meeting downstairs at Lion's Quay, to talk to his fellow merchants about disorder in the city. Antonio Bonvisi, More's friend, excuses himself and says he will go home; "The Trinity bless and prosper you," he says, withdrawing and taking with him the mobile island of chill which has followed him since his unexpected arrival. "You know," he says, turning at the door, "if there is a question of help for Mistress Petyt, I shall be glad—"

"No need. She is left wealthy."

"But will the city let her take the business on?"

He cuts him off: "I have that in hand."

Bonvisi nods and goes out. "Surprising he should show his face." John Parnell, of the Drapers' Company, has a history of clashes with More. "Master Cromwell, if you are taking charge of this, does it mean—do you have it in mind to speak to Lucy?"

"Me? No."

Humphrey Monmouth says, "Shall we have our meeting first, and broker marriages later? We are concerned, Master Cromwell, as you must be, as the king must be . . . we are all, I think," he looks around, "we are all, now Bonvisi has left us, friendly to the cause for which our late brother Petyt was, in effect, a martyr, but it is for us to keep the peace, to disassociate ourselves from outbreaks of blasphemy . . ."

In one city parish last Sunday, at the sacred moment of the elevation of the host, and just as the priest pronounced, *"hoc est enim corpus meum,"* there was an outbreak of chanting, *"hoc est corpus, hocus pocus."* And in an adjacent parish, at the commemoration of the saints, where the priest requires us to remember our fellowship with the holy martyrs, *"cum Joanne, Stephano, Mathia, Barnaba, Ignatio, Alexandro, Marcellino, Petro . . ."* some person had shouted out, "and don't forget me and my cousin Kate, and Dick with his cockle-barrel on Leadenhall, and his sister Susan and her little dog Posset."

He puts his hand over his mouth. "If Posset needs a lawyer, you know where I am."

"Master Cromwell," says a crabbed elder from the Skinners' Company, "you convened this gathering. Set us an example in gravity."

"There are ballads made," Monmouth says, "about Lady Anne— the words are not repeatable in this company. Thomas Boleyn's servants complain they are called names on the street. Ordure thrown on their livery. Masters must keep a hand on their apprentices. Disloyal talk should be reported."

"To whom?"

He says, "Try me."

He finds Johane at Austin Friars. She has made some excuse to stay at home: a summer cold. "Ask me what secret I know," he says.

For appearances' sake, she polishes the tip of her nose. "Let me see. You know to a shilling what the king has in his treasury?"

"I know to the farthing. Not that. Ask me. Sweet sister."

When she has guessed enough, he tells her, "John Parnell is going to marry Luce."

"What? And John Petyt not cold?" She turns away, to get over whatever she is feeling. "Your brethren stick together. Parnell's household is not clean from sectaries. He has a servant in Bishop Stokesley's prison, so I hear."

Richard Cromwell puts his head around the door. "Master. The Tower. Bricks. Five shilling the thousand."

"No."

"Right."

"You'd think she'd marry a safer sort of man."

He goes to the door. "Richard, come back." Turns to Johane. "I don't think she knows any."

"Sir?"

"Get it down by sixpence, and check every batch. What you should do is choose a few in every load, and take a close interest in them."

Johane in the room behind him: "Anyway, you did the wise thing."

"For instance, measure them . . . Johane, did you think I'd get married out of some sort of inadvertence? By accident?"

"I'm sorry?" Richard says.

"Because if you keep measuring them, it throws brickmakers into a panic, and you'll see by their faces if they're trying any tricks."

"I expect you have some lady in view. At court. The king has given you a new office—"

"Clerk of the Hanaper. Yes. A post in the chancery finances . . . It hardly signs the flowery trail to a love affair." Richard has gone, clattering downstairs. "Do you know what I think?"

"You think you should wait. Till she, that woman, is queen."

"I think it's the transport that pushes the cost up. Even by barge. I should have cleared some ground and built my own kilns."

❖

Sunday, September 1, at Windsor: Anne kneels before the king to receive the title of Marquess of Pembroke. The Garter knights in their stalls watch her, the noble ladies of England flank her, and (the duchess having refused, and spat out an oath at the suggestion) Norfolk's daughter Mary bears her coronet on a cushion; the Howards and the Boleyns are *en fête*. Monseigneur caresses his beard, nods and smiles as he receives murmured congratulations from the French ambassador. Bishop Gardiner reads out Anne's new title. She is vivid in red velvet and ermine, and her black hair falls, virgin-style, in snaky locks to her waist. He, Cromwell, has organized the income from fifteen manors to support her dignity.

A *Te Deum* is sung. A sermon is preached. When the ceremony is over, and the women stoop to pick up her train, he sees a flash of blue, like a kingfisher, and glances up to see John Seymour's little daughter among the Howard ladies. A warhorse raises his head at the sound of trumpets, and great ladies look up and smile; but as the musicians play a flourish, and the procession leaves St. George's Chapel, she keeps her pale face downturned, her eyes on her toes as if she fears tripping.

At the feast Anne sits beside Henry on the dais, and when she turns to speak to him her black lashes brush her cheeks. She is almost there now, almost there, her body taut like a bowstring, her skin dusted with gold, with tints of apricot and honey; when she smiles, which she does often, she shows small teeth, white and sharp. She is planning to commandeer Katherine's royal barge, she tells him, and have the device "H&K" burned away, all Katherine's badges obliterated. The king has sent for Katherine's jewels, so she can wear them on the projected trip to France. He has spent an afternoon with her, two afternoons, three, in the fine September weather, with the king's goldsmith beside her making drawings, and he as master of the jewels adding suggestions; Anne wants new settings made. At first Katherine had refused to give up the jewels. She had said she could not part with the property of the Queen of England and put it into the hands of the disgrace of Christendom. It had taken a royal command to make her hand over the loot.

Anne refers everything to him; she says, laughing, "Cromwell, you are my man." The wind is set fair and the tide is running for him. He can feel the tug of it under his feet. His friend Audley must surely be confirmed as Chancellor; the king is getting used to him. Old courtiers have resigned, rather than serve Anne; the new comptroller of the household is Sir William Paulet, a friend of his from Wolsey days. So many of the new courtiers are his friends from Wolsey days. And the cardinal didn't employ fools.

After the Mass and Anne's installation, he attends the Bishop of Winchester as he disrobes, gets out of his canonicals into gear more suitable for secular celebrations. "Are you going to dance?" he asks him. He sits on a stone window ledge, half attentive to what is going on in the courts below, the musicians carrying in pipes and lutes, harps and rebecs, hautboys, viols and drums. "You could cut a good figure. Or don't you dance now you're a bishop?"

Stephen's conversation is on a track of its own. "You'd think it would be enough for any woman, wouldn't you, to be made a marquess in her own right? She'll give way to him now. Heir in the belly, please God, before Christmas."

"Oh, you wish her success?"

"I wish his temper soothed. And some result out of this. Not to do it all for nothing."

"Do you know what Chapuys is saying about you? That you keep two women in your household, dressed up as boys."

"Do I?" He frowns. "Better, I suppose, than two boys dressed up as women. Now that would be opprobrious." Stephen gives a bark of laughter. They stroll together toward the feast. Trolly-lolly, the musicians sing. "Pastime with good company, I love and shall until I die." The soul is musical by nature, the philosophers say. The king calls up

Thomas Wyatt to sing with him, and the musician Mark. "Alas, what shall I do for love? For love, alas, what shall I do?"

"Anything he can think of," Gardiner says. "There is no limit, that I can see."

He says, "The king is good to those who think him good." He floats it to the bishop, below the music.

"Well," Gardiner says, "if your mind is infinitely flexible. As yours, I see, would have to be."

He speaks to Mistress Seymour. "Look," she says. She holds up her sleeves. The bright blue with which she has edged them, that king-fisher flash, is cut from the silk in which he wrapped her present of needlework patterns. How do matters stand now at Wolf Hall, he asks, as tactfully as he can: how do you ask after a family, in the wake of incest? She says in her clear little voice, "Sir John is very well. But then Sir John is always very well."

"And the rest of you?"

"Edward angry, Tom restless, my lady mother grinding her teeth and banging the doors. The harvest coming in, the apples on the bough, the maids in the dairy, our chaplain at his prayers, the hens laying, the lutes in tune, and Sir John . . . Sir John as always is very well. Why don't you make some business in Wiltshire and ride down to inspect us? Oh, and if the king gets a new wife, she will need matrons to attend her, and my sister Liz is coming to court. Her husband is the Governor of Jersey, you know him, Anthony Oughtred? I would rather go up-country to the queen, myself. But they say she is moving again, and her household is being reduced."

"If I were your father . . . no . . ." he rephrases it, "if I were to advise you, it would be to serve Lady Anne."

"The marquess," she says. "Of course, it is good to be humble. She makes sure we are."

"Just now it is difficult for her. I think she will soften, when she has her heart's desire." Even as he says it, he knows it is not true.

Jane lowers her head, looks up at him from under her eyelids. "That is my humble face. Do you think it will serve?"

He laughs. "It would take you anywhere."

When the dancers are resting, fanning themselves, from the galliards, pavanes and almanes, he and Wyatt sing the little soldiers' air: Scaramella to the war has gone, with his shield, his lance. It is melancholy, as songs are, whatever the words, when the light is failing and the human voice, unaccompanied, fades in the shadows of the room. Charles Brandon asks him, "What is it about, that song, is it about a lady?"

"No, it is just about a boy who goes off to war."

"What are his fortunes?"

Scaramella fa la gala. "It's all one big holiday to him."

"Those were better days," the duke says. "Soldiering."

The king sings to the lute, his voice strong, true, plangent: "As I Walked the Woods So Wild." Some women weep, a little the worse for strong Italian wines.

At Canterbury, Archbishop Warham lies cold on a slab; coins of the realm are laid on his eyelids, as if to seal into his brain for eternity the image of his king. He is waiting to go down under the pavement of the cathedral, in the dank charnel vacancy by Becket's bones. Anne sits still as a statue, her eyes on her lover. Only her restless fingers move; she clutches on her lap one of her little dogs, and her hands run over and over its fur, twisting its curls. As the last note dies, candles are brought in.

❖

October, and we are going to Calais—a train two thousand strong, stretched from Windsor to Greenwich, from Greenwich across the green fields of Kent to Canterbury: to a duke an entourage of forty, to a marquess thirty-five, to an earl twenty-four, while a viscount must scrape by with twenty, and he with Rafe and any clerks he can pack into the ships' rat-holes. The king is to meet his brother France, who intends to oblige him by speaking to the Pope in favor of his new marriage. François has offered to marry one of his three sons—his three sons, how God must love him—to the Pope's niece, Catherine de' Medici; he says he will make it a precondition of the match that Queen Katherine is refused leave to appeal her case to Rome, and that his

brother England is allowed to settle his marital affairs in his own jurisdiction, using his own bishops.

These two potent monarchs will see each other for the first time
since the meeting called the Field of the Cloth of Gold, which the cardinal arranged. The king says the trip must cost less than that occasion, but when he is questioned on specifics he wants more of that and
two of those—everything bigger, plusher, more lavish, and with more
gilding. He is taking his own cooks and his own bed, his ministers
and musicians, his horses, dogs and falcons, and his new marquess,
whom Europe calls his concubine. He is taking the possible claimants
to the throne, including the Yorkist Lord Montague, and the Lancastrian Nevilles, to show how tame they are and how secure are the
Tudors. He is taking his gold plate, his linen, his pastry chefs and
poultry-pickers and poison-taster, and he is even taking his own wine:
which you might think is superfluous, but what do you know?

Rafe, helping him pack his papers: "I understand that King Francis
will speak to Rome for the king's cause. But I am not sure what he gets
out of this treaty."

"Wolsey always said that the making of a treaty is the treaty. It
doesn't matter what the terms are, just that there are terms. It's the
goodwill that matters. When that runs out, the treaty is broken, whatever the terms say."

It is the processions that matter, the exchange of gifts, the royal
games of bowls, the tilts, jousts and masques: these are not prelimi-
naries to the process, they are the process itself. Anne, accustomed to
the French court and French etiquette, sets out the difficulties in store.
"If the Pope were to visit him, then France could advance toward him,
perhaps meeting him in a courtyard. But two monarchs meeting,
once they are in sight, should take the same number of steps toward
each other. And this works, unless one monarch—*hélas*—were to take
very small steps, forcing the other to cover the ground."

"By God," Charles Brandon bursts out, "such a man would be a
knave. Would Francis do that?"

Anne looks at him, lids half-lowered. "My lord Suffolk, is your lady
wife ready for the journey?"

Suffolk reddens. "My wife is a former Queen of France."

"I am aware of it. François will be pleased to see her again. He thought her very beautiful. Though of course, she was young then."

"My sister is beautiful still," Henry says, pacific. But a tempest is boiling up inside Charles Brandon, and it breaks with a yell like a crack of thunder: "You expect her to wait on you? On Boleyn's daughter? Pass you your gloves, madam, and serve you first at dinner? Make your mind up to it—that day will never come."

Anne turns to Henry, her hand fastening on his arm. "Before your face he humiliates me."

"Charles," Henry says, "leave us now and come back when you are master of yourself. Not a moment before." He sighs, makes a sign: Cromwell, go after him.

The Duke of Suffolk is seething and steaming. "Fresh air, my lord," he suggests.

Autumn has come already; there is a raw wind from the river. It lifts a flurry of sodden leaves, which flap in their path like the flags of some miniature army. "I always think Windsor is a cold place. Don't you, my lord? I mean the situation, not just the castle?" His voice runs on, soothing, low. "If I were the king, I would spend more time at the palace in Woking. You know it never snows there? At least, not once in twenty years."

"If you were king?" Brandon stumps downhill. "If Anne Boleyn can be queen, why not?"

"I take that back. I should have used a more humble expression."

Brandon grunts. "She will never appear, my wife, in the train of that harlot."

"My lord, you had better think her chaste. We all do."

"Her lady mother trained her up, and she was a great whore, let me tell you. Liz Boleyn, Liz Howard as was—she was the first to take Henry to bed. I know these things, I am his oldest friend. Seventeen, and he didn't know where to put it. His father kept him like a nun."

"But none of us believe that story now. About Monseigneur's wife."

"*Monseigneur!* Christ in Heaven."

"He likes to be called that. It is no harm."

"Her sister Mary trained her up, and Mary was trained in a brothel. Do you know what they do, in France? My lady wife told me. Well, not told me, but she wrote it down for me, in Latin. The man has a cock-stand, and she takes it in her mouth! Can you imagine such a thing? A woman who can do such a filthy proceeding, can you call that a virgin?"

"My lord . . . if your wife will not go to France, if you cannot persuade her . . . shall we say that she is ill? It would be something you could do for the king, whom you know is your friend. It would save him from—" He almost says, from the lady's harsh tongue. But he backs out of that sentence, and says something else. "It would save face."

Brandon nods. They are still heading toward the river, and he tries to check their pace because soon Anne will expect him back with news of an apology. When the duke turns to him, his face is a picture of misery. "It's true, anyway. She is ill. Her beautiful little"—he makes a gesture, his hands cupping the air—"all fallen away. I love her anyway. She's as thin as a wafer. I say to her, Mary, I will wake up one day, and I won't be able to find you, I'll take you for a thread in the bed linen."

"I am so sorry," he says.

He rubs his face. "Ah, God. Go back to Harry, will you? Tell him we can't do this."

"He will expect you to come to Calais, if your lady wife cannot."

"I don't like to leave her, you see?"

"Anne is unforgiving," he says. "Hard to please, easy to offend. My lord, be guided by me."

Brandon grunts. "We all are. We must be. You do everything, Cromwell. You are everything now. We say, how did it happen? We ask ourselves." The duke sniffs. "We ask ourselves, but by the steaming blood of Christ we have no bloody answer."

The steaming blood of Christ. It's an oath worthy of Thomas Howard, the senior duke. When did he become the interpreter of dukes, their explainer? He asks himself but he has no bloody answer. When he returns to the king and the queen-to-be, they are looking lovingly into each other's faces. "The Duke of Suffolk begs pardon," he says. Yes, yes, the king says. I'll see you tomorrow, but not too early. You would think they were already man and wife, a languorous night before them, filled with marital delights. You would think so, except he has Mary Boleyn's word for it that the marquisate has bought Henry only the right to caress her sister's inner thigh. Mary tells him this, and doesn't even put it in Latin. Whenever she spends time alone with the king, Anne reports back to her relations, no detail spared. You have to admire her; her measured exactness, her restraint. She uses her body like a soldier, conserving its resources; like one of the masters in the anatomy school at Padua, she divides it up and names every part, this my thigh, this my breast, this my tongue.

"Perhaps in Calais," he says. "Perhaps he will get what he wants then."

"She will have to be sure." Mary walks away. She stops and turns back, her face troubled. "Anne says, Cromwell is my man. I don't like her to say that."

In ensuing days, other questions emerge to torment the English party. Which royal lady will be hostess to Anne when they meet the French? Queen Eleanor will not—you cannot expect it, as she is the Emperor's sister, and family feeling is touched by His Disgrace's abandonment of Katherine. Francis's sister, the Queen of Navarre, pleads illness rather than receive the King of England's mistress. "Is it the same illness that afflicts the poor Duchess of Suffolk?" Anne asks. Perhaps, Francis suggests, it would be appropriate if the new marquess were to be met by the Duchess of Vendôme, his own *maîtresse en titre*?

Henry is so angry that it gives him a toothache. Dr. Butts comes with his chest of specifics. A narcotic seems kindest, but when the king wakes he is still so mortified that for a few hours there seems no solution but to call the expedition off. Can they not comprehend, can they not grasp, that Anne is no man's mistress, but a king's bride-to-be? But to comprehend that is not in Francis's nature. He would never wait more than a week for a woman he wanted. Pattern of chivalry, he? Most Christian king? All he understands, Henry bellows, is rutting like a stag. But I tell you, when his rut is done, the other harts will put him down. Ask any hunter!

It is suggested, finally, that the solution will be to leave the future queen behind in Calais, on English soil where she can suffer no insult, while the king meets Francis in Boulogne. Calais, a small city, should be more easily contained than London, even if people line up at the harborside to shout *"Putain!"* and "Great Whore of England." If they sing obscene songs, we will simply refuse to understand them.

At Canterbury, with the royal party in addition to the pilgrims from all nations, every house is packed from cellars to eaves. He and Rafe are lodged in some comfort and near the king, but there are lords in flea-bitten inns and knights in the back rooms of brothels, pilgrims forced into stables and outhouses and sleeping out under the stars. Luckily, the weather is mild for October. Any year before this, the king would have gone to pray at Becket's shrine and leave a rich offering. But Becket was a rebel against the Crown, not the sort of archbishop we like to encourage at the moment. In the cathedral the incense is still hanging in the air from Warham's interment, and prayers for his soul are a constant drone like the buzz of a thousand hives. Letters have gone to Cranmer, lying somewhere in Germany at the Emperor's traveling court. Anne has begun to refer to him as the Archbishop-Elect. No one knows how long he'll take getting home. With his secret, Rafe says.

Of course, he says, his secret, written down the side of the page.

Rafe visits the shrine. It is his first time. He comes back wide-eyed, saying it is covered in jewels the size of goose eggs.

"I know. Are they real, do you think?"

"They show you a skull, they say it's Becket's, it's smashed up by the knights but it's held together with a silver plate. For ready money, you can kiss it. They have a tray of his finger bones. They have his snotty handkerchief. And a bit of his boot. And a vial they shake up for you, they say it's his blood."

"At Walsingham, they have a vial of the Virgin's milk."

"Christ, I wonder what that is?" Rafe looks sick. "The blood, you can tell it's water with some red soil in it. It floats about in clumps."

"Well, pick up that goose quill, plucked from the pinions of the angel Gabriel, and we will write to Stephen Vaughan. We may have to set him on the road, to bring Thomas Cranmer home."

"It can't be soon enough," Rafe says. "Just wait, master, till I wash Becket off my hands."

Though he will not go to the shrine, the king wants to show himself to the people, Anne by his side. Leaving Mass, against all advice he walks out among the crowds, his guards standing back, his councillors around him. Anne's head darts, on the slender stem of her neck, turning to catch the comments that come her way. People stretch out their hands to touch the king.

Norfolk, at his elbow, stiff with apprehension, eyes everywhere: "I don't care for this proceeding, Master Cromwell." He himself, having once been quick with a knife, is alert for movements below the eyeline. But the nearest thing to a weapon is an outsize cross, wielded by a bunch of Franciscan monks. The crowd gives way to them, to a huddle of lay priests in their vestments, a contingent of Benedictines from the abbey, and in the midst of them a young woman in the habit of a Benedictine nun.

"Majesty?"

Henry turns. "By God, this is the Holy Maid," he says. The guards move in, but Henry holds up a hand. "Let me see her." She is a big girl, and not so young, perhaps twenty-eight; plain face, dusky, excited, with an urgent flush. She pushes toward the king, and for a second he sees him through her eyes: a blur of red-gold and flushed skin, a ready, priapic body, a hand like a ham that stretches out to take her by her nunly elbow. "Madam, you have something to say to me?"

She tries to curtsy, but his grip won't let her. "I am advised by Heaven," she says, "by the saints with whom I converse, that the heretics around you must be put into a great fire, and if you do not light that fire, then you yourself will burn."

"Which heretics? Where are they? I do not keep heretics about my person."

"Here is one."

Anne shrinks against the king; against the scarlet and gold of his jacket she melts like wax.

"And if you enter into a form of marriage with this unworthy woman, you will not reign seven months."

"Come, madam, seven months? Round it off, can you not? What sort of a prophet says 'seven months'?"

"That is what Heaven tells me."

"And when the seven months are up, who will replace me? Speak up, say who you would like to be king instead of me."

The monks and priests are trying to draw her away; this was not part of their plan. "Lord Montague, he is of the blood. The Marquis of Exeter, he is blood royal." She in turn tries to pull away from the king. "I see your lady mother," she says, "surrounded by pale fires."

Henry drops her as if her flesh were hot. "My mother? Where?"

"I have been looking for the Cardinal of York. I have searched Heaven, Hell and Purgatory, but the cardinal is not there."

"Surely she is mad?" Anne says. "She is mad and must be whipped. If she is not, she must be hanged."

One of the priests says, "Madam, she is a very holy person. Her speech is inspired."

"Get her out of my way," Anne says.

"Lightning will strike you," the nun tells Henry. He laughs uncertainly.

Norfolk erupts into the group, teeth clenched, fist raised. "Drag her back to her whorehouse, before she feels this, by God!" In the mêlée, one monk hits another with the cross; the Maid is drawn backward, still prophesying; the noise from the crowd rises, and Henry grasps Anne by the arm and pulls her back the way they came. He himself follows the Maid, sticking close to the back of the group, till the crowd thins and he can tap one of the monks on the arm and ask to speak to her. "I was a servant of Wolsey," he says. "I want to hear her message."

Some consultation, and they let him through. "Sir?" she says.

"Could you try again to find the cardinal? If I were to make an offering?"

She shrugs. One of the Franciscans says, "It would have to be a substantial offering."

"Your name is?"

"I am Father Risby."

"I can no doubt meet your expectations. I am a wealthy man."

"Would you want simply to locate the soul, to help your own prayers, or were you thinking in terms of a chantry, perhaps, an endowment?"

"Whatever you recommend. But of course I'd need to know he wasn't in Hell. There would be no point throwing away good Masses on a hopeless case."

"I'll have to talk to Father Bocking," the girl says.

"Father Bocking is this lady's spiritual director."

He inclines his head. "Come again and ask me," the girl says. She turns and is lost in the crowd. He parts with some money there and then, to the entourage. For Father Bocking, whoever he may be. As it seems Father Bocking does the price list and keeps the accounts.

❖

The nun has plunged the king into gloom. How would you feel if you were told you'd be struck by lightning? By evening he complains of a headache, a pain in his face and jaw. "Go away," he tells his doctors. "You can never cure it, so why should you now? And you, madam," he says to Anne, "have your ladies put you to bed, I do not want chatter, I cannot stand piercing voices."

Norfolk grumbles under his breath: the Tudor, always something the matter with him.

At Austin Friars, if anyone gets a sniffle or a sprain, the boys perform an interlude called "If Norfolk were Dr. Butts." Got a toothache? Pull them out! Trapped your finger? Hack your hand off! Pain in the head? Slice it off, you've got another.

Now Norfolk pauses, in backing out of the presence. "Majesty, she didn't say the lightning would in fact kill you."

"No more did she," Brandon says cheerily.

"Not dead but dethroned, not dead but stricken and scorched, that's something to look forward to, is it?" Pitifully indicating his circumstances, the king barks for a servant to bring logs and a page to warm some wine. "Am I to sit here, the King of England, with a miserable fire and nothing to drink?" He does look cold. He says, "She saw my lady mother."

"Your Majesty," he says, cautious, "you know that in the cathedral one of the windows has an image of your lady mother in glass? And would not the sun shine through, so it would seem as if she was in a dazzle of light? I think that is what the nun has seen."

"You don't believe these visions?"

"I think perhaps she can't tell what she sees in the outside world from what is inside her head. Some people are like that. She is to be pitied, perhaps. Though not too much."

The king frowns. "But I loved my mother," he says. Then: "Buckingham set much store by visions. He had a friar who prophesied for him. Told him he would be king." He does not need to add, Buckingham was a traitor and is more than ten years dead.

❖

When the court sails for France he is in the king's party, on the *Swallow*. He stands on deck watching England recede, with the Duke of Richmond, Henry's bastard, excited to be on his first sea voyage, and to be in his father's company too. Fitzroy is a handsome boy of thirteen, fair-haired, tall for his age but slender: Henry as he must have been as a young prince, and endowed with a proper sense of himself and his own dignity. "Master Cromwell," he says, "I have not seen you since the cardinal came down." A moment's awkwardness. "I am glad you prosper. Because it is said in the book called *The Courtier* that in men of base degree we often see high gifts of nature."

"You read Italian, sir?"

"No, but parts of that book have been put into English for me. It is a very good book for me to read." A pause. "I wish"—he turns his head, lowering his voice—"I wish the cardinal were not dead. Because now the Duke of Norfolk is my guardian."

"And I hear Your Grace is to marry his daughter Mary."

"Yes. I do not want to."

"Why not?"

"I have seen her. She has no breasts."

"But she has a good wit, my lord. And time may remedy the other matter, before you live together. If your people will translate for you that part of Castiglione's book that relates to gentlewomen and their qualities, I'm sure you will find that Mary Howard has all of them."

Let's hope, he thinks, it won't turn out like Harry Percy's match, or George Boleyn's. For the girl's sake too; Castiglione says that everything that can be understood by men can be understood by women, that their apprehension is the same, their faculties, no doubt their loves and hates. Castiglione was in love with his wife, Ippolita, but she died when he had only had her four years. He wrote a poem for her, an elegy, but he wrote it as if Ippolita was writing: the dead woman speaking to him.

In the ship's wake the gulls cry like lost souls. The king comes on deck and says his headache has cleared. He says, "Majesty, we were talking of Castiglione's book. You have found time to read it?"

"Indeed. He extols *sprezzatura*. The art of doing everything gracefully and well, without the appearance of effort. A quality princes should cultivate, too." He adds, rather dubious, "King Francis has it."

"Yes. But besides *sprezzatura* one must exhibit at all times a dignified public restraint. I was thinking I might commission a translation as a gift for my lord Norfolk."

It must be in his mind, the picture of Thomas Howard in Canterbury, threatening to punch the holy nun. Henry grins. "You should do it."

"Well, if he would not take it as a reproach. Castiglione recommends that a man should not curl his hair nor pluck his eyebrows. And you know my lord does both."

The princeling frowns at him. "My lord of Norfolk?" Henry unleashes an unregal yell of laughter, neither dignified nor restrained. It is welcome to his ears. The ship's timbers creak. The king steadies himself with a hand on his shoulder. The wind stiffens the sails. The sun dances over the water. "An hour and we will be in port."

❖

Calais, this outpost of England, her last hold on France, is a town where he has many friends, many customers, many clients. He knows it, Watergate and Lantern Gate, St. Nicholas Church and Church of Our Lady, he knows its towers and bulwarks, its markets, courts and quays, Staple Inn where the Governor lodges, and the houses of the Whethill and Wingfield families, houses with shady gardens where gentlemen live in pleasant retreat from an England they claim they no longer understand. He knows the fortifications—crumbling—and beyond the city walls the lands of the Pale, its woods, villages and marshes, its sluices, dikes and canals. He knows the road to Boulogne, and the road to Gravelines, which is the Emperor's territory, and he knows that either monarch, Francis or Charles, could take this town with one determined push. The English have been here for two hundred years, but in the streets now you hear more French and Flemish spoken.

The Governor greets His Majesty; Lord Berners, old soldier and scholar, is the pattern of old-fashioned virtue, and if it were not for his limp, and his evident anxiety about the vast expenses he is about to incur, he would be straight out of the book called *The Courtier.* He has even arranged to lodge the king and the marquess in rooms with an interconnecting door. "I think that will be very suitable, my lord," he says. "As long as there is a sturdy bolt on both sides."

Because Mary told him, before they left dry land, "Till now she wouldn't, but now she would, but he won't. He tells her he must be sure that if she gets a child it's born in wedlock."

The monarchs are to meet for five days in Boulogne, then five days in Calais. Anne is aggrieved at the thought of being left behind. He can see by her restlessness that she knows this is a debatable land, where things might happen you cannot foretell. Meanwhile he has private business to transact. He leaves even Rafe behind, and slips away to an inn in a back court off Calkwell Street.

❖

It is a low sort of place, and smells of wood smoke, fish and mold. On a side wall is a watery mirror through which he glimpses his own face, pale, only his eyes alive. For a moment it shocks him; you do not expect to see your own image in a hovel like this.

He sits at a table and waits. After five minutes there is a disturbance of the air at the back of the room. But nothing happens. He has anticipated they will keep him waiting; to pass the time, he runs over in his head the figures for last year's receipts to the king from the Duchy of Cornwall. He is about to move on to the figures submitted by the Chamberlain of Chester, when a dark shape materializes, and resolves itself into the person of an old man in a long gown. He totters forward, and in time two others follow him. You could change any one for another: hollow coughs, long beards. According to some precedence which they negotiate by grunting, they take their seats on a bench opposite. He hates alchemists, and these look like alchemists to him: nameless splashes on their garments, watering eyes, vapor-induced sniffles. He greets them in French. They shudder, and one of them asks in Latin if they are not going to have anything to drink. He calls for the boy, and asks him without much hope what he suggests. "Drink somewhere else?" the boy offers.

A jug of something vinegary comes. He lets the old men drink deeply before he asks, "Which of you is Maître Camillo?"

They exchange glances. It takes them as long as it takes the Graiae to pass their single shared eye.

"Maître Camillo has gone to Venice."

"Why?"

Some coughing. "For consultations."

"But he does mean to return to France?"

"Quite likely."

"The thing you have, I want it for my master."

A silence. How would it be, he thought, if I take the wine away till they say something useful? But one preempts him, snatching up the jug; his hand shakes, and the wine washes over the table. The others bleat with irritation.

"I thought you might bring drawings," he says.

They look at each other. "Oh, no."

"But there are drawings?"

"Not as such."

The spilled wine begins to soak into the splintered wood. They sit in miserable silence and watch this happen. One of them occupies himself in working his finger through a moth hole in his sleeve.

He shouts to the boy for a second jug. "We do not wish to disoblige you," the spokesman says. "You must understand that Maître Camillo is, for now, under the protection of King Francis."

"He intends to make a model for him?"

"That is possible."

"A working model?"

"Any model would be, by its nature, a working model."

"Should he find the terms of his employment in the least unsatisfactory, my master Henry would be happy to welcome him in England."

There is another pause, till the jug is fetched and the boy has gone. This time, he does the pouring himself. The old men exchange glances again, and one says, "The magister believes he would dislike the English climate. The fogs. And also, the whole island is covered with witches."

The interview has been unsatisfactory. But one must begin somewhere. As he leaves he says to the boy, "You might go and swab the table."

"I may as well wait till they've upset the second jug, monsieur."

"True. Take them in some food. What do you have?"

"Pottage. I wouldn't recommend it. It looks like what's left when a whore's washed her shift."

"I never knew the Calais girls to wash anything. Can you read?"

"A little."

"Write?"

"No, monsieur."

"You should learn. Meanwhile use your eyes. If anyone else comes to talk to them, if they bring out any drawings, parchments, scrolls, anything of that kind, I want to know."

The boy says, "What is it, monsieur? What are they selling?"

He almost tells him. What harm could it do? But then in the end he can't think of the right words.

❖

Partway through the talks in Boulogne, he has a message that Francis would like to see him. Henry deliberates before giving him permission; face-to-face, monarchs should deal only with fellow monarchs, and lords and churchmen of high rank. Since they landed, Brandon and Howard, who were friendly enough on board ship, have been distant with him, as if to make it quite clear to the French that they accord him no status; he is some whim of Henry's, they pretend, a novelty councillor who will soon vanish in favor of a viscount, baron or bishop.

The French messenger tells him, "This is not an audience."

"No," he says, "I understand. Nothing of that sort."

Francis sits waiting, attended only by a handful of courtiers, for what is not an audience. He is a beanpole of a man, his elbows and knees jutting at the air, his big bony feet restless inside vast padded slippers. "Cremuel," he says. "Now, let me understand you. You are a Welshman."

"No, Your Highness."

Sorrowful dog eyes; they look him over, they look him over again. "Not a Welshman."

He sees the French king's difficulty. How has he got his passport to the court, if he is not from some family of humble Tudor retainers? "It was the late cardinal who induced me into the king's business."

"Yes, I know that," Francis says, "but I think to myself there is something else going on here."

"That may be, Highness," he says crisply, "but it's certainly not being Welsh."

Francis touches the tip of his pendulous nose, bending it farther toward his chin. Choose your prince: you wouldn't like to look at this one every day. Henry is so wholesome, in his fleshy, scrubbed pink-

and-whiteness. Francis says, his glance drifting away, "They say you once fought for the honor of France."

Garigliano: for a moment he lowers his eyes, as if he's remembering a very bad accident in the street: some mashing and irretrievable mangling of limbs. "On a most unfortunate day."

"Still . . . these things pass. Who now remembers Agincourt?"

He almost laughs. "It is true," he says. "A generation or two, or three . . . four . . . and these things are nothing."

Francis says, "They say you are in very good standing with That Lady." He sucks his lip. "Tell me, I am curious, what does my brother king think? Does he think she is a maid? Myself, I never tried her. When she was here at court she was young, and as flat as a board. Her sister, however—"

He would like to stop him but you can't stop a king. His voice runs over naked Mary, chin to toes, and then flips her over like a griddle cake and does the other side, nape to heels. An attendant hands him a square of fine linen, and as he finishes he dabs the corner of his mouth: and hands the kerchief back.

"Well, enough," Francis says. "I see you will not admit to being Welsh, so that is the end of my theories." The corners of his mouth turn up; his elbows work a little; his knees twitch; the not-audience is over. "Monsieur Cremuel," he says, "we may not meet again. Your sudden fortunes may not last. So, come, give me your hand, like a soldier of France. And put me in your prayers."

He bows. "Your beadsman, sir."

As he leaves, one of the courtiers steps forward, and murmuring, "A gift from His Highness," hands him a pair of embroidered gloves.

❖

Another man, he supposes, would be pleased, and try them on. For his part, he pinches the fingers, and finds what he is looking for. Gently, he shakes the glove, his hand cupped.

He goes straight to Henry. He finds him in the sunshine, playing a game of bowls with some French lords. Henry can make a game of bowls as noisy as a tournament: whooping, groaning, shouting of odds, wails, oaths. The king looks up at him, his eyes saying, "Well?" His eyes say, "Alone," the king's say, "Later," and not a word is spoken, but all the time the king keeps up his joking and backslapping, and he straightens up, watching his wood glide over the shorn grass, and points in his direction. "You see this councillor of mine? I warn you, never play any game with him. For he will not respect your ancestry. He has no coat of arms and no name, but he believes he is bred to win."

One of the French lords says, "To lose gracefully is an art that every gentleman cultivates."

"I hope to cultivate it too," he says. "If you see an example I might follow, please point it out."

For they are all, he notices, intent on winning this game, on taking a piece of gold from the King of England. Gambling is not a vice, if you can afford to do it. Perhaps I could issue him with gaming tokens, he thinks, redeemable only if presented in person at some office in Westminster: with tortuous paperwork attached, and fees to clerks, and a special seal to be affixed. That would save us some money.

But the king's wood moves smoothly toward the marker ball. Henry is winning the game anyway. From the French, a spatter of polite applause.

❖

When he and the king are alone, he says, "Here's something you will like."

Henry likes surprises. With a thick forefinger, his pink clean English nail, he nudges the ruby about on the back of his hand. "It is a good stone," he says. "I am a judge of these things." A pause. "Who is the principal goldsmith here? Ask him to wait on me. It is a dark stone, Francis will know it again; I will wear it on my own finger before our meetings are done. France shall see how I am served." He is in high good humor. "However, I shall give you the value." He nods, to dismiss him. "Of course, you will compound with the goldsmith to put a higher valuation on it, and arrange to split the profit with him . . . but I shall be liberal in the matter."

Arrange your face.

The king laughs. "Why would I trust a man with my business, if he could not manage his own? One day Francis will offer you a pension. You must take it. By the way, what did he ask you?"

"He asked if I were Welsh. It seemed a great question with him, I was sorry to be so disappointing."

"Oh, you are not disappointing," Henry says. "But the moment you are, I will let you know."

Two hours. Two kings. What do you know, Walter? He stands in the salty air, talking to his dead father.

❖

When Francis comes back with his brother king to Calais, it is Anne who leads him out to dance after the evening's great feast. There is color in her cheeks, and her eyes sparkle behind her gilded mask. When she lowers the mask and looks at the King of France, she wears a strange half-smile, not quite human, as if behind the mask were another mask. You can see his jaw drop; you can see him begin to drool. She entwines her fingers with his, and leads him to a window seat. They speak in French for an hour, whispering, his sleek dark head leaning toward her; sometimes they laugh, looking into each other's eyes. No doubt they are discussing the new alliance; he seems to think she has another treaty tucked down her bodice. Once Francis lifts her hand. She pulls back, half-resisting, and for one moment it seems he intends to lay her little fingers upon his unspeakable codpiece. Everyone knows that Francis has recently taken the mercury cure. But no one knows if it has worked.

Henry is dancing with the wives of Calais notables: gigue, saltarello. Charles Brandon, his sick wife forgotten, is making his partners scream by throwing them in the air so that their skirts fly up. But Henry's glance keeps straying down the hall to Anne, to Francis. His spine is stiff with his personal terror. His face expresses smiling agony.

Finally, he thinks, I must end this: can it be true, he wonders, that as a subject should, I really love my king?

He ferrets Norfolk out of the dark corner where he is hiding, for fear that he should be commanded to partner the Governor's wife. "My lord, fetch your niece away. She has done enough diplomacy. Our king is jealous."

"What? What the devil is his complaint now?" Yet Norfolk sees at a glance what is happening. He swears, and crosses the room— through the dancers, not round them. He takes Anne by her wrist, bending it back as if to snap it. "By your leave, Highness. My lady, we shall dance." He jerks her to her feet. Dance they do, though it bears no relation to any dance seen in any hall before this. On the duke's part, a thundering with demon hooves; on her part, a blanched caper, one arm held like a broken wing.

He looks across at Henry. The king's face expresses a sober, righteous satisfaction. Anne should be punished, and by whom except her kin? The French lords huddle together, sniggering. Francis looks on with narrowed eyes.

❖

That night the king withdraws from company early, dismissing even the gentlemen of his privy chamber; only Henry Norris is in and out, trailed by an underling carrying wine, fruit, a large quilt, then a pan of coals; it has turned chilly. The women, in their turn, have become brisk and snappish. Anne's raised voice has been heard. Doors slam. As he is talking to Thomas Wyatt, Mistress Shelton comes careering toward him. "My lady wants a Bible!"

"Master Cromwell can recite the whole New Testament," Wyatt says helpfully.

The girl looks agonized. "I think she wants it to swear on."

"In that case I'm no use to her."

Wyatt catches her hands. "Who's going to keep you warm tonight, young Shelton?" She pulls away from him, shoots off in pursuit of the scriptures. "I'll tell you who. Henry Norris."

He looks after the girl. "She draws lots?"

"I have been lucky."

"The king?"

"Perhaps."

"Recently?"

"Anne would pull out their hearts and roast them."

He feels he should not go far, in case Henry calls for him. He finds a corner for a game of chess with Edward Seymour. Between moves, "Your sister Jane . . ." he says.

"Odd little creature, isn't she?"

"What age would she be?"

"I don't know . . . twenty or so? She walked around at Wolf Hall saying, 'These are Thomas Cromwell's sleeves,' and nobody knew what she was talking about." He laughs. "Very pleased with herself."

"Has your father made a match for her?"

"There was some talk of—" He looks up. "Why do you ask?"

"Just distracting you."

Tom Seymour bursts through the door. "Good e'en, grandfer," he shouts at his brother. He knocks his cap off and ruffles his hair. "There are women waiting for us."

"My friend here advises not." Edward dusts his cap. "He says they're just the same as Englishwomen but dirtier."

"Voice of experience?" Tom says.

Edward resettles his cap primly. "How old would our sister Jane be?"

"Twenty-one, twenty-two. Why?"

Edward looks down at the board, reaches for his queen. He sees how he's trapped. He glances up in appreciation. "How did you manage that?"

❖

Later, he sits with a blank piece of paper before him. He means to write a letter to Cranmer and cast it to the four winds, send it searching through Europe. He picks up his pen but does not write. He revisits in his mind his conversation with Henry, about the ruby. His king imagines he would take part in a backstairs deceit, the kind that might have entertained him in the days when he antiqued cupids and sold them to cardinals. But to defend yourself against such accusations makes you seem guilty. If Henry does not fully trust him, is it surprising? A prince is alone: in his council chamber, in his bedchamber, and finally in Hell's antechamber, stripped—as Harry Percy said—for Judgment.

This visit has compacted the court's quarrels and intrigues, trapped them in the small space within the town's walls. The travelers have become as intimate with each other as cards in a pack: contiguous, but their paper eyes blind. He wonders where Tom Wyatt is, and in what sort of trouble. He doesn't think he can sleep: though not because he's worried about Wyatt. He goes to the window. The moon, as if disgraced, trails rags of black cloud.

In the gardens, torches burn in wall brackets, but he walks away from the light. The faint push and pull of the ocean is steady and insistent as his own heartbeat. He knows he shares this darkness, and within a moment there is a footstep, a rustle of skirts, a faint breathy gulp, a hand sliding on his arm. "You," Mary says.

"Me."

"Do you know they unbolted the door between them?" She laughs, a merciless giggle. "She is in his arms, naked as she was born. She can't change her mind now."

"Tonight I thought they would quarrel."

"They did. They like quarreling. She claims Norfolk has broken her arm. Henry called her a Magdalene and some other names I forget, I think they were Roman ladies. Not Lucrece."

"No. At least, I hope not. What did she want the Bible for?"

"To swear him. Before witnesses. Me. Norris. He made a binding promise. They are married in God's sight. And he swears he will marry her again in England and crown her queen when spring comes."

He thinks of the nun, at Canterbury: if you enter into a form of marriage with this unworthy woman, you will not reign seven months.

"So now," Mary says, "it is just a question of whether he will find he is able to do the deed."

"Mary." He takes her hand. "Don't frighten me."

"Henry is timid. He thinks you expect a kingly performance. But if he is shy, Anne will know how to help." She adds, carefully, "I mean to say, I have advised her." She slides her hand onto his shoulder. "So now, what about us? It has been a weary struggle to bring them here. I think we have earned our recreation."

No answer. "You're not still frightened of my uncle Norfolk?"

"Mary, I am terrified of your uncle Norfolk."

Still, that's not the reason, not the reason why he hesitates, not quite pulling away. Her lips brush his. She asks, "What are you thinking?"

"I was thinking that if I were not the king's most dutiful servant, it would be possible to be on the next boat out."

"Where would we go?"

He doesn't remember inviting a friend. "East. Though I grant this would not be a good starting point." East of the Boleyns, he thinks. East of everybody. He is thinking of the Middle Sea, not these northern waters; and one night especially, a warm midnight in a house in Larnaca: Venetian lights spilling out onto the dangerous waterfront, the slap of slave feet on tiles, a perfume of incense and coriander. He puts an arm around Mary, encountering something soft, totally unexpected: fox fur. "Clever of you," he says.

"Oh, we brought everything. Every stitch. In case we are here till winter."

A glow of light on flesh. Her throat very white, very soft. All things seem possible, if the duke stays indoors. His fingertip teases out the fur till fur meets flesh. Her shoulder is warm, scented and a little damp. He can feel the bounce of her pulse.

A sound behind him. He turns, dagger in hand. Mary screams, pulls at his arm. The point of the weapon comes to rest against a man's doublet, under the breastbone. "All right, all right," says a sober, irritated English voice. "Put that away."

"Heavens," Mary says. "You almost murdered William Stafford."

He backs the stranger into the light. When he sees his face, not till then, he draws back the blade. He doesn't know who Stafford is: somebody's horse-keeper? "William, I thought you weren't coming," Mary says.

"If I didn't, it seems you had a reserve."

"You don't know what a woman's life is! You think you've fixed something with a man, and you haven't. He says he'll meet you, and he doesn't turn up."

It is a cry from the heart. "Give you good night," he says. Mary turns as if to say, oh, don't go. "Time I said my prayers."

A wind has blown up from the Narrow Sea, snapping at the rigging in the harbor, rattling the windows inland. Tomorrow, he thinks, it may rain. He lights a candle and goes back to his letter. But his letter has no attraction for him. Leaves flurry from the gardens, from the orchards. Images move in the air beyond the glass, gulls blown like ghosts: a flash of his wife Elizabeth's white cap, as she follows him to the door on her last morning. Except that she didn't: she was sleeping, wrapped in damp linen, under the yellow turkey quilt. If he thinks of the fortune that brought him here he thinks equally of the fortune that brought him to that morning five years ago, going out of Austin Friars a married man, files of Wolsey's business under his arm: was he happy then? He doesn't know.

That night in Cyprus, long ago now, he had been on the verge of handing his resignation to his bank, or at least of asking them for letters of introduction to take him east. He was curious to see the Holy Land, its plant life and people, to kiss the stones where the disciples had walked, to bargain in the hidden quarters of strange cities and in black tents where veiled women scuttle like cockroaches into corners. That night his fortunes had been in equipoise. In the room behind him, as he looked out over the harbor lights, he heard a woman's throaty laughter, her soft *"al-hamdu lillah"* as she shook the ivory dice in her hand. He heard her spill them, heard them rattle and come to rest: "What is it?"

East is high. West is low. Gambling is not a vice, if you can afford to do it.

"It is three and three."

Is that low? You must say it is. Fate has not given him a shove, more of a gentle tap. "I shall go home."

"Not tonight, though. It is too late for the tide."

Next day he felt the gods at his back, like a breeze. He turned back toward Europe. Home then was a narrow shuttered house on a quiet canal, Anselma kneeling, creamily naked under her trailing night-gown of green damask, its sheen blackish in candlelight; kneeling before the small silver altarpiece she kept in her room, which was precious to her, she had told him, the most precious thing I own. Excuse me just a moment, she had said to him; she prayed in her own language, now coaxing, now almost threatening, and she must have teased from her silver saints some flicker of grace, or perceived some deflection in their glinting rectitude, because she stood up and turned to him, saying, "I'm ready now," tugging apart the silk ties of her gown so that he could take her breasts in his hands.

III

Early Mass

NOVEMBER 1532

afe is standing over him, saying it is seven o'clock already. The king has gone to Mass. He has slept in a bed of phantoms. "We did not want to wake you. You never sleep late."

The wind is a muted sigh in the chimneys. A handful of rain like gravel rattles against the window, swirls away, and is thrown back again. "We may be in Calais for some time," he says.

When Wolsey had gone to France, five years ago, he had asked him to watch the situation at court and to pass on a report of when the king and Anne went to bed. He had said, how will I know when it happens? The cardinal had said, "I should think you'll know by his face."

The wind has dropped and the rain respited by the time he reaches the church, but the streets have turned to mud, and the people waiting to see the lords come out still have their coats pulled over their heads, like a new race of walking decapitees. He pushes through the crowd, then threads and whispers his way through the gathered gentlemen: *s'il vous plaît, c'est urgent,* make way for a big sinner. They laugh and let him through.

Anne comes out on the Governor's arm. He looks tense—it seems his gout is troubling him—but he is attentive to her, murmuring pleasantries to which he gets no response; her expression is adjusted to a careful blankness. The king has a Wingfield lady on his arm, face uptilted, chattering. He is taking no notice of her at all. He looks large, broad, benign. His regal glance scans the crowd. It alights on him. The king smiles.

As he leaves the church, Henry puts on his hat. It is a big hat, a new hat. And in that hat there is a feather.

PART FIVE

I

Anna Regina

1533

he two children sit on a bench in the hall of Austin Friars. They are so small that their legs stick straight out in front of them, and as they are still in smocks one cannot tell their sex. Under their caps, their dimpled faces beam. That they look so fat and contented is a credit to the young woman, Helen Barre, who now unwinds the thread of her tale: daughter of a bankrupt small merchant out of Essex, wife of one Matthew Barre, who beat her and deserted her, "leaving me," she says, indicating, "with that one in my belly."

The neighbors are always coming at him with parish problems. Unsafe cellar doors. A noisome goose house. A husband and wife who shout and bang pans all night, so the next house can't get to sleep. He tries not to fret if these things cut into his time, and he minds Helen less than a goose house. Mentally, he takes her out of cheap shrunken wool and re-dresses her in some figured velvet he saw yesterday, six shillings the yard. Her hands, he sees, are skinned and swollen from rough work; he supplies kid gloves.

"Though when I say he deserted me, it may be that he is dead. He was a great drinker and a brawler. A man who knew him told me he came off worst in a fight, and I should seek him at the bottom of the river. But someone else saw him on the quays at Tilbury, with a traveling bag. So which am I—wife or widow?"

"I will look into it. Though I think you would rather I didn't find him. How have you lived?"

"When he went first I was stitching for a sailmaker. Since I came up to London to search, I've been hiring out by the day. I have been in the laundry at a convent near Paul's, helping at the yearly wash of their bed linen. They find me a good worker, they say they will give me a pallet in the attics, but they won't take the children."

Another instance of the church's charity. He runs up against them all the time. "We cannot have you a slave to a set of hypocrite women. You must come here. I am sure you will be useful. The house is filling up all the time, and I am building, as you see." She must be a good girl, he thinks, to turn her back on making a living in the obvious way; if she walked along the street, she wouldn't be short of offers. "They tell me you would like to learn to read, so you can read the gospel."

"Some women I met took me to what they call a night school. It was in a cellar at Broadgate. Before that, I knew Noah, the Three Kings, and father Abraham, but St. Paul I had never heard of. At home on our farm we had pucks who used to turn the milk and blow up thunderstorms, but I am told they are not Christians. I wish we had stayed farming, for all that. My father was no hand at town life." Her eyes, anxious, follow the children. They have launched themselves off the bench and toddled across the flagstones to see the picture that is growing on the wall, and their every step causes her to hold her breath. The workman is a German, a young boy Hans recommended for a simple job, and he turns around—he speaks no English—to explain to the children what he is doing. A rose. Three lions, see them jump. Two black birds.

"Red," the elder child cries.

"She knows colors," Helen says, pink with pride. "She is also beginning on one-two-three."

The space where the arms of Wolsey used to be is being repainted with his own newly granted arms: *azure, on a fess between three lions rampant or, a rose gules, barbed vert, between two Cornish choughs proper.* "You see, Helen," he says, "those black birds were Wolsey's emblem." He laughs. "There are people who hoped they would never see them again."

"There are other people, of our sort, who do not understand it."

"You mean night school people?"

"They say, how can a man who loves the gospel, have loved such a man as that?"

"I never liked his haughty manners, you know, and his processions every day, the state he kept. And yet there was never a man more active in the service of England since England began. And also," he says sadly, "when you came into his confidence, he was a man of such grace and ease . . . Helen, can you come here today?" He is thinking of those nuns and the yearly wash of their bed linen. He is imagining the cardinal's appalled face. Laundry women followed his train as whores follow an army, hot from their hour-by-hour exertions. At York Place he had a bath made, deep enough for a man to stand up in it, the room heated by a stove such as you find in the Low Countries, and many a time he had negotiated business with the cardinal's bobbing, boiled-looking head. Henry has taken it over now, and splashes about in it with favored gentlemen, who submit to being ducked under the water and half-drowned by their lord, if his mood takes him that way.

The painter offers the brush to the elder child. Helen glows. "Careful, darling," she says. A blob of blue is applied. You are a little adept, the painter says. *"Gefällt es Ihnen, Herr Cromwell, sind Sie stolz darauf?"*

He says to Helen, he asks if I am pleased and proud. She says, if you are not, your friends will be proud for you.

I am always translating, he thinks: if not language to language, then person to person. Anne to Henry. Henry to Anne. Those days when he wants soothing, and she is as prickly as a holly bush. Those times—they do occur—when his gaze strays after another woman, and she follows it, and storms off to her own apartments. He, Cromwell, goes about like some public poet, carrying assurances of desire, each to each.

It is hardly three o'clock, and already the room is half dark. He picks up the younger child, who flops against his shoulder and falls asleep with the speed at which someone pushed falls off a wall. "Helen," he says, "this household is full of pert young men, and they will all put themselves forward in teaching you to read, bringing you presents and trying to sweeten your days. Do learn, and take the presents, and be happy here with us, but if anyone is too forward, you must tell me, or tell Rafe Sadler. He is the boy with the little red beard. Though I should not say boy." It will be twenty years, soon, since he brought Rafe in from his father's house, a lowering, dark day like this, rain bucketing from the heavens, the child slumped against his shoulder as he carried him into his hall at Fenchurch Street.

❖

The storms had kept them in Calais for ten days. Ships out of Boulogne were wrecked, Antwerp flooded, much of the countryside put under water. He would like to get messages to his friends, inquiring after their lives and property, but the roads are impassable, Calais itself a floating island upon which a happy monarch reigns. He goes to the king's lodgings to ask for an audience—business doesn't stop in bad weather—but he is told, "The king cannot see you this morning. He and Lady Anne are composing some music for the harp."

Rafe catches his eye and they walk away. "Let us hope in time they have a little song to show for it."

Thomas Wyatt and Henry Norris get drunk together in a low tavern. They swear eternal friendship. But their followers have a fight in the inn yard and roll each other in mud.

He never sets eyes on Mary Boleyn. Presumably she and Stafford have found some bolt-hole where they can compose together.

By candlelight, at noon, Lord Berners shows him his library, limping energetically from desk to desk, handling with care the old folios from which he has made his scholarly translations. Here is a romance of King Arthur: "When I started reading it I almost gave up the project. It was clear to me it was too fantastical to be true. But little by little, as I read, you know, it appeared to me that there was a moral in this tale." He does not say what it is. "And here is Froissart done into English, which His Majesty himself bade me undertake. I could not do other, for he had just lent me five hundred pounds. Would you like to see my translations from the Italian? They are private ones, I have not sent them to the printer."

He spends an afternoon with the manuscripts, and they discuss them at supper. Lord Berners holds a position, chancellor of the exchequer, which Henry has given him for life, but because he is not in London and attending to it, it does not bring him in much money, or the influence it should. "I know you are a good man for business. Might you in confidence look over my accounts? They're not what you'd call in order."

Lord Berners leaves him alone with the dog's breakfast that he calls his ledgers. An hour passes: the wind whistles across the rooftops, the candle flames tremble, hail batters the glass. He hears the scrape of his host's bad foot: an anxious face peers around the door. "What joy?"

All he can find is money owing. This is what you get for devoting yourself to scholarship and serving the king across the sea, when you could be at court with sharp teeth and eyes and elbows, ready to seize your advantage. "I wish you'd called on me earlier. There are always things that can be done."

"Ah, but who knew you, Master Cromwell?" the old man says. "One exchanged letters, yes. Wolsey's business, king's business. But I never knew you. It did not seem at all likely I should know you, until now."

On the day they are finally ready to embark, the boy from the alchemists' inn turns up. "You at last! What have you got for me?"

The boy displays his empty hands, and launches into English, of a sort. "*On dit* those magi have retoured to Paris."

"Then I am disappointed."

"You are hard to find, monsieur. I go to the place where le roi Henri and the Grande Putain are lodged, '*je cherche milord Cremuel,*' and the persons there laughed at me and beat me."

"That is because I am not a milord."

"In that case, I do not know what a milord in your country looks like." He offers the boy a coin for his efforts, and another for the beating, but he shakes his head. "I thought to take service with you, monsieur. I have made up my mind to go traveling."

"Your name is?"

"Christophe."

"You have a family name?"

"*Ça ne fait rien.*"

"You have parents?"

A shrug.

"Your age?"

"What age would you say?"

"I know you can read. Can you fight?"

"There is much fighting *chez vous*?"

Christophe has his own squat build; he needs feeding up, but a year or two from now he will be hard to knock over. He puts him at fifteen, no more. "You are in trouble with the law?"

"In France," he says, disparagingly: as one might say, in far Cathay. "You are a thief?"

The boy makes a jabbing motion, invisible knife in his fist.

"You left someone dead?"

"He didn't look well."

He grins. "You're sure you want Christophe for your name? You can change it now, but not later."

"You understand me, monsieur."

Christ, of course I do. You could be my son. Then he looks at him closely, to make sure that he isn't; that he isn't one of these brawling children the cardinal spoke of, whom he has left by the Thames, and not impossibly by other rivers, in other climes. But Christophe's eyes are a wide, untroubled blue. "You are not afraid of the sea voyage?" he asks. "In my house in London there are many French speakers. You'll soon be one of us."

Now at Austin Friars, Christophe pursues him with questions. Those magi, what is it they have? Is it a *carte* of buried treasure? Is it—he flaps his arms—the instructions for one to make a flying machine? Is it a machine to *faire* great explosions, or a military dragon, breathes out fire?

He says, "Have you ever heard of Cicero?"

"No. But I am prepared to hear of him. Till today I have never heard of Bishop Gardineur. *On dit* you have stole his strawberry beds and give them to the king's mistress, and now he intends . . ." the boy breaks off, and again gives his impression of a military dragon, "to ruin you utterly and pursue you unto death."

"And well beyond, if I know my man."

There have been worse accounts of his situation. He wants to say, she is not a mistress, not anymore, but the secret—though it must soon be an open secret—is not his to tell.

❖

January 25, 1533, dawn, a chapel at Whitehall, his friend Rowland Lee as priest, Anne and Henry take their vows, confirm the contract they made in Calais: almost in secret, with no celebration, just a huddle of witnesses, the married pair both speechless except for the small admissions of intent forced out of them by the ceremony. Henry Norris is pale and sober: was it kind to make him witness it twice over, Anne being given to another man?

William Brereton is a witness, as he is in attendance in the king's privy chamber. "Are you truly here?" he asks him. "Or are you somewhere else? You gentlemen tell me you can bilocate, like great saints."

Brereton glares. "You've been writing letters up to Chester."

"The king's business. How not?"

They must do this in a mutter, as Rowland joins the hands of bride and groom. "I'll tell you just once. Keep away from my family's affairs. Or you'll come off worse, Master Cromwell, than you can imagine."

Anne is attended by only one lady, her sister. As they leave—the king towing his wife, hand on her upper arm, toward a little harp music—Mary turns and gives him a sumptuous smile. She holds up her hand, thumb and finger an inch apart.

She had always said, I will be the first to know. It will be me who lets out her bodices.

He calls William Brereton back, politely; he says, you have made a mistake in threatening me.

He goes back to his office in Westminster. He wonders, does the king know yet? Probably not.

He sits down to his drafting. They bring in candles. He sees the shadow of his own hand moving across the paper, his own unconcealable fist unmasked by velvet glove. He wants nothing between himself and the weave of the paper, the black running line of ink, so he takes off his rings, Wolsey's turquoise and Francis's ruby—at New Year's, the king slid it from his own finger and gave it back to him, in the setting the Calais goldsmith had made, and said, as rulers do, in a rush of confidence, now that will be a sign between us, Cromwell, send a paper with this and I shall know it comes from your hand even if you lack your seal.

A confidant of Henry's who was standing by—it was Nicholas Carew—had remarked, His Majesty's ring fits you without adjustment. He said, so it does.

He hesitates, his quill hovering. He writes, "This realm of England is an Empire." *This realm of England is an Empire, and so has been accepted in the world, governed by one Supreme Head and King . . .*

At eleven o'clock, when the day has brightened as much as it will, he eats dinner with Cranmer in his lodging at Cannon Row, where he is living till his new dignity is conferred and he can move into Lambeth Palace. He has been practicing his new signature, Thomas Elect of Canterbury. Soon he will dine in state, but today, like a threadbare scholar, he shoves his papers aside while some table linen is laid and they bring in the salt fish, over which he signs a grace.

"That won't improve it," he says. "Who's cooking for you? I'll send someone over."

"So, is the marriage made?" It is like Cranmer to wait to be told: to work six hours in silent patience, head down over his books.

"Yes, Rowland was up to his office. He didn't wed her to Norris, or the king to her sister." He shakes out his napkin. "I know a thing. But you must coax it from me."

He is hoping that Cranmer, by way of coaxing, will impart the secret he promised in his letter, the secret written down the side of the page. But it must have been some minor indiscretion, now forgotten. And because Canterbury Elect is occupied in poking uncertainly at scales and skin, he says, "She, Anne, she is already having a child."

Cranmer glances up. "If you tell it in that tone, people will think you take the credit yourself."

"Are you not astonished? Are you not pleased?"

"I wonder what fish this purports to be?" Cranmer says with mild interest. "Naturally I am delighted. But I knew it, you see, because this marriage is clean—why would not God bless it with offspring? And with an heir?"

"Of course, with an heir. Look." He takes out the papers he has been working on. Cranmer washes his fishy fingers and hunches toward the candle flame. "So after Easter," he says, reading, "it will be against the law and the king's prerogative to make an appeal in any matter to the Pope. So there is Katherine's suit dead and buried. And I, Canterbury, can decide the king's cause in our own courts. Well, this has been long enough coming."

He laughs. "You were long enough coming." Cranmer was in Mantua when he heard of the honor the king intended for him. He began his journey circuitously: Stephen Vaughan met him at Lyons, and hustled him over the winter roads and through the snowdrifts of Picardy to the boat. "Why did you delay? Doesn't every boy want to be an archbishop? Though not me, if I think back. What I wanted was my own bear."

Cranmer looks at him, his expression speculative. "I'm sure that could be arranged for you."

Gregory has asked him, how will we know when Dr. Cranmer is making a joke? He has told him, you won't, they are as rare as apple blossom in January. And now, for some weeks, he will be half fearful that a bear will turn up at his door. As they part that day, Cranmer glances up from the table and says, "Of course, I don't officially know."

"About the child?"

"About the marriage. As I am to be judge in the matter of the king's old marriage, it would not be proper for me to hear that his new one has already taken place."

"Right," he says. "What Rowland gets up to in the early hours of the morning is a matter for himself alone." He leaves Cranmer with head bowed over the remains of their meal, as if studying to reassemble the fish.

As our severance from the Vatican is not yet complete, we cannot have a new archbishop unless the Pope appoints him. Delegates in Rome are empowered to say anything, promise anything, *pro tem*, to get Clement to agree. The king says, aghast, "Do you know how much the papal bulls cost, for Canterbury? And that I shall have to pay for them? And you know how much it costs to install him?" He adds, "It must be done properly, of course, nothing omitted, nothing scanted."

"It will be the last money Your Majesty sends to Rome, if it rests with me."

"And do you know," the king says, as if he has discovered something astonishing, "that Cranmer has not a penny of his own? He can contribute nothing."

He borrows the money, on the Crown's behalf, from a rich Genovese he knows called Salvago. To persuade him into the loan, he sends around to his house an engraving which he knows Sebastian covets. It shows a young man standing in a garden, his eyes turned upward to an empty window, at which it is to be hoped very soon a lady will appear; her scent hangs already in the air, and birds on the boughs look inquiringly into the vacancy, ready to sing. In his two hands the young man holds a book; it is a book shaped like a heart.

Cranmer sits on committees every day, in back rooms at Westminster. He is writing a paper for the king, to show that even if his brother's marriage to Katherine was not consummated, it does not affect the case for the annulment, for certainly they intended to be married, and that intention creates affinity; also, in the nights they spent together, it must have been their intention to make children, even if they did not go about it the right way. In order not to make a liar out of Henry or Katherine, one or the other, the committee men think up circumstances in which the match may have been partly consummated, or somewhat consummated, and to do this they have to imagine every disaster and shame that can occur between a man and a woman alone in a room in the dark. Do you like the work, he inquires; looking at their hunched and dusty persons, he judges them to have the experience they need. Cranmer in his writing keeps calling the queen "the most serene Katherine," as if to separate her untroubled face, framed by a linen pillow, from the indignities being forced on her lower body: the boy's fumbling and scrabbling, the pawing at her thighs.

Meanwhile Anne, the hidden Queen of England, breaks free from her gentleman companions as she walks through a gallery at White-hall; she laughs as she breaks into a trot, almost a skip, and they reach out to contain her, as if she is dangerous, but she flings their hands away from her, laughing. "Do you know, I have a great longing to eat apples? The king says it means I am having a baby, but I tell him no, no, it can't be that . . ." She whirls around, around again. She flushes, tears bounce out of her eyes and seem to fly away from her like the waters of an unregulated fountain.

Thomas Wyatt pushes through the crowd. "Anne . . ." He snatches at her hands, he pulls her toward him. "Anne, hush, sweetheart . . . hush . . ." She collapses into hiccupping sobs, folding herself against his shoulder. Wyatt holds her fast; his eyes travel around, as if he had found himself naked in the road, and is looking for some traveler to come along with a garment to cover his shame. Among the bystanders is Chapuys; the ambassador makes a rapid, purposeful exit, his little legs working, a sneer stamped on his face.

So that's the news sped to the Emperor. It would have been good if the old marriage were out, the new marriage in, confirmed to Europe before Anne's happy state were announced. But then, life is never perfect for the servant of a prince; as Thomas More used to say, we should not look to go to Heaven on feather beds.

Two days later he is alone with Anne; she is tucked into a window embrasure, eyes closed, basking like a cat in a scarce shaft of winter sun. She stretches out her hand to him, hardly knowing who he is; any man will do? He takes her fingertips. Her black eyes snap open. It's like a shop when the shutters are taken down: good morning, Master Cromwell, what can we sell each other today?

"I am tired of Mary," she says. "And I would like to be rid of her."

Does she mean Katherine's daughter, the princess? "She should be married," she says, "and out of my way. I never want to have to see her.

I don't want to have to think about her. I have long imagined her married to some obscure person."

He waits, still wondering.

"I don't suppose she would be a bad wife, for somebody who was prepared to keep her chained to the wall."

"Ah. Mary your sister."

"What did you think? Oh," she laughs, "you thought I meant Mary the king's bastard. Well, now you put it in my mind, she should be married too. What age is she?"

"Seventeen this year."

"And still a dwarf?" Anne doesn't wait for an answer. "I shall find some old gentleman for her, some very honorable feeble old gentleman, who will get no children on her and whom I will pay to stay away from court. But as for Lady Carey, what is to be done? She cannot marry you. We tease her that you are her choice. Some ladies have a secret preference for common men. We say, Mary, oh, how you long to repose in the arms of the blacksmith . . . even at the thought, you are growing hot."

"Are you happy?" he asks her.

"Yes." She drops her eyes, and her small hands rest on her rib cage. "Yes, because of this. You see," she says slowly, "I was always desired. But now I am valued. And that is a different thing, I find."

He pauses, to let her think her own thoughts: which he sees are precious to her. "So," she says, "you have a nephew Richard, a Tudor of sorts, though I am sure I cannot understand how that came about."

"I can draw out for you the tree of descent."

She shakes her head, smiling. "I wouldn't give you the trouble. Since this," her fingers slip downward, "I wake up in the morning and I scarcely remember my name. I always wondered why women were foolish, and now I know."

"You mentioned my nephew."

"I have seen him with you. He looks a determined boy. He might do for her. What she wants are furs and jewels. You can give her those, can't you? And a child in the cradle every other year. As for who fathers it, you can make your own household arrangements about that."

"I thought," he says, "that your sister had an attachment?"

He doesn't want revenge: just clarification.

"Does she? Oh well, Mary's attachments . . . usually passing and sometimes very odd—as you know, don't you." It's not a question. "Bring them to court, your children. Let's see them."

He leaves her, eyes closing again, edging into marginal warmth, the small sort of sunbeam that is all February offers.

The king has given him lodgings within the old palace at Westminster, for when he works too late to get home. This being so, he has to walk mentally through his rooms at Austin Friars, picking up his memory images from where he has left them on windowsills and under stools and in the woolen petals of the flowers strewn in the tapestry at Anselma's feet. At the end of a long day he takes supper with Cranmer and with Rowland Lee, who stamps between the various working parties, urging them along. Sometimes Audley joins them, the Lord Chancellor, but they keep no state, just sit down like a bunch of inky students, and talk till it's Cranmer's bedtime. He wants to work them out, these people, test how far he can rely on them, and find out their weaknesses. Audley is a prudent lawyer who can sift a sentence like a cook sifting a sack of rice for grit. An eloquent speaker, he is tenacious of a point, and devoted to his career; now that he's Chancellor he aims to make an income to go with the office. As for what he believes, it's up for negotiation; he believes in Parliament, in the king's power exercised in Parliament, and in matters of faith . . . let's say his convictions are flexible. As for Lee, he wonders if he believes in God at all—though it doesn't stop him having a bishopric in his sights. He says, "Rowland, will you take Gregory into your household? I think Cambridge has done all that it can for him. And I admit that Gregory has done nothing for Cambridge."

"I'll take him up the country with me," Rowland says, "when I go to have a row with the northern bishops. He is a good boy, Gregory. Not the most forward, but I can understand that. We'll make him useful yet."

"You don't intend him for the church?" Cranmer asks.

"I said," growls Rowland, "we'll make him useful."

At Westminster his clerks are in and out, with news and gossip and paperwork, and he keeps Christophe with him, supposedly to look after his clothes, but really to make him laugh. He misses the music they have nightly at Austin Friars, and the women's voices, heard from other rooms.

He is at the Tower most days of the week, persuading the foremen to keep their men working through frost and rain; checking the pay-master's accounts, and making a new inventory of the king's jewels and plate. He calls on the Wardens of the Mint, and suggests a spot check on the weight of the king's coinage. "What I should like to do," he says, "is make our English coins so sound that the merchants over the sea won't even bother weighing them."

"Do you have authority for this?"

"Why, what are you hiding?"

He has written a memorandum for the king, setting out the sources of his yearly revenues, and detailing through which government of-fices they pass. It is remarkably concise. The king reads it and reads it again. He turns the paper over to see if anything convoluted and inex-plicable is written on the back. But there is nothing more than meets his eye.

"It's not news," he says, half apologetic. "The late cardinal carried it in his head. I shall keep calling at the Mint. If Your Majesty pleases."

At the Tower he calls on a prisoner, John Frith. At his request, which does not count for nothing, the prisoner is cleanly kept above-ground, with warm bedding, sufficient food, a supply of wine, paper, ink; though he has advised him to put away his writings if he hears the key in his lock. He stands by while the turnkey admits him, his eyes on the ground, not liking what he is going to see; but John Frith rises from his table, a gentle, slender young boy, a scholar in Greek, and says, Master Cromwell, I knew you would come.

When he takes Frith's hands he finds them all bones, cold and dry and with telltale traces of ink. He thinks, he cannot be so delicate, if he has lived so long. He was one of the scholars shut in the cellar at Wolsey's college, where the Bible men were held because there was no other secure place. When the summer plague struck underground,

Frith lay in the dark with the corpses, till someone remembered to let him out.

"Master Frith," he says, "if I had been in London when you were taken—"

"But while you were in Calais, Thomas More was at work."

"What made you come back into England? No, don't tell me. If you were going about Tyndale's work, I had better not know it. They say you have taken a wife, is that correct? In Antwerp? The one thing the king cannot abide—no, many things he cannot abide—but he hates married priests. And he hates Luther, and you have translated Luther into English."

"You put the case so well, for my prosecution."

"You must help me to help you. If I could get you an audience with the king . . . you would have to be prepared, he is a most astute theologian . . . do you think you could soften your answers, to accommodate him?"

The fire is built up but the room is still cold. You cannot get away from the mists and exhalations of the Thames. Frith says, his voice barely audible, "Thomas More still has some credit with the king. And he has written him a letter, saying," he manages to smile, "that I am Wycliffe, Luther and Zwingli rolled together and tied up in string— one reformer stuffed inside another, as for a feast you might parcel a pheasant inside a chicken inside a goose. More means to dine on me, so do not injure your credit by asking for mercy. As for softening my answers . . . I believe, and I will say before any tribunal—"

"Do not, John."

"I will say before any tribunal what I will say before my last judge— the Eucharist is but bread, of penance we have no need, Purgatory is an invention ungrounded in scripture—"

"If some men come to you and say, come with us, Frith, you go with them. They will be my men."

"You think you can take me out of the Tower?"

Tyndale's Bible says, with God shall nothing be unpossible. "If not out of the Tower, then when you are taken to be questioned, that will be your chance. Be ready to take it."

"But to what purpose?" Frith speaks kindly, as if speaking to a young pupil. "You think you can keep me at your house and wait for the king to change his mind? I should have to break out of there, and walk to Paul's Cross, and say before the Londoners what I have already said."

"Your witness cannot wait?"

"Not on Henry. I might wait till I was old."

"They will burn you."

"And you think I cannot bear the pain. You are right, I cannot. But they will give me no choice. As More says, it hardly makes a man a hero, to agree to stand and burn once he is chained to a stake. I have written books and I cannot unwrite them. I cannot unbelieve what I believe. I cannot unlive my life."

He leaves him. Four o'clock: the river traffic sparse, a fine and penetrative vapor creeping between air and water.

Next day, a day of crisp blue cold, the king comes down in the royal barge to see the progress of the work, with the new French envoy; they are confidential, the king walking with a hand on de Dinteville's shoulder, or rather on his padding; the Frenchman is wearing so many layers that he seems broader than the doorways, but he is still shivering. "Our friend here must get some sport to warm his blood," the king says, "and he is a bungler with the bow—when we went into the butts last, he shook so much I thought he would shoot himself in the foot. He complains we are not serious falconers, so I have said he should go out with you, Cromwell."

Is this a promise of time off? The king strolls away and leaves them. "Not if it's cold like this," the envoy says. "I'm not standing in a field with the wind whistling, it will be the death of me. When shall we see the sun again?"

"Oh, about June. But the falcons will be molting by then. I aim to have mine flying again in August, so *nil desperandum*, monsieur, we shall have some sport."

"You wouldn't postpone this coronation, would you?" It's always so; after a little chaff and chat, out of his mouth pops an ambassador's purpose. "Because when my master made the treaty, he didn't expect

Henry to be flaunting his supposed wife and her big belly. If he were to keep her quietly, it would be a different matter."

He shakes his head. There will be no postponement. Henry claims he has the support of the bishops, the nobles, judges, Parliament and the people; Anne's coronation is his chance to prove it. "Never mind," he says. "Tomorrow we entertain the papal nuncio. You will see how my master will manage him."

Henry calls down to them, from the walls, "Come up here, sir, see the prospect of my river."

"Do you wonder I shake?" the Frenchman says with passion. "Do you wonder I tremble before him? My river. My city. My salvation, cut out and embroidered just for me. My personally tailored English god." He swears under his breath, and begins to climb.

When the papal nuncio comes to Greenwich, Henry takes him by the hand and tells him frankly how his ungodly councillors torment him, and how he longs for a return of perfect amity with Pope Clement.

You could watch Henry every day for a decade and not see the same thing. Choose your prince: he admires Henry more and more. Sometimes he seems hapless, sometimes feckless, sometimes a child, sometimes master of his trade. Sometimes he seems an artist, in the way his eye ranges over his work; sometimes his hand moves and he doesn't seem to see it move. If he had been called to a lower station in life, he could have been a traveling player, and leader of his troupe.

At Anne's command, he brings his nephew to court, Gregory too; Rafe the king already knows, for he is always at his elbow. The king stands gazing for a long time at Richard. "I see it. Indeed I do."

There is nothing in Richard's face, as far as he can see, to show that he has Tudor blood, but the king is looking at him with the eye of a man who wants relatives. "Your grandfather ap Evan the archer was a great servant to the king my father. You have a fine build. I should like to see you in the tilt yard. I should like to see you carry your colors in the joust."

Richard bows. And then the king, because he is the essence of courtesy, turns to Gregory, and says, "And you, Master Gregory, you are a very fine young man too."

As the king walks away, Gregory's face opens in simple pleasure. He puts his hand on his arm, the place the king has touched, as if transferring regal grace to his fingertips. "He is very splendid. He is so splendid. Beyond anything I ever thought. And to speak to me!" He turns to his father. "How do you manage to speak to him every day?"

Richard gives him a sideways look. Gregory thumps him on the arm. "Never mind your grandfather the archer, what would he say if he knew your father was *that* big?" He shows between finger and thumb the stature of Morgan Williams. "I have been riding at the ring these many years. I have been riding at the Saracen's image and putting my lance just so, thud, right over his black Saracen's heart."

"Yes," Richard says patiently, "but, squib, you will find a living knight a tougher proposition than a wooden infidel. You never think of the cost—armor of show quality, a stable of trained horses—"

"We can afford it," he says. "It seems our days as foot soldiers are behind us."

That night at Austin Friars he asks Richard to come to speak with him alone after supper. Possibly he is at fault, in putting it as a business proposition, spelling out to him what Anne has suggested about his marriage. "Build nothing on it. We have yet to get the king's approval."

Richard says, "But she doesn't know me."

He waits, for objections; not knowing someone, is that an objection? "I won't force you."

Richard looks up. "Are you sure?"

When have I, when have I ever forced anyone to do anything, he starts to say: but Richard cuts in, "No, you don't, I agree, it's just that you are practiced at persuading, and sometimes it's quite difficult, sir, to distinguish being persuaded by you from being knocked down in the street and stamped on."

"I know Lady Carey is older than you, but she is very beautiful, I think the most beautiful woman at court, and she is not as witless as everyone thinks, and she has not got any of her sister's malice in her." In a strange way, he thinks, she has been a good friend to me. "And instead of being the king's unrecognized cousin, you would be his brother-in-law. We would all profit."

"A title, perhaps. For me, and for you. Brilliant matches for Alice and Jo. What about Gregory? A countess at least for him." Richard's voice is flat. Is he talking himself into it? It's hard to tell. With many people, most people perhaps, the book of their heart lies open to him, but there are times when it's easier to read outsiders than your own family. "And Thomas Boleyn would be my father-in-law. And Uncle Norfolk would really be our uncle."

"Imagine his face."

"Oh, his face. Yes, one would go barefoot over hot coals to see his expression."

"Think about it. Don't tell anybody."

Richard goes out with a bob of the head but without another word. It seems he interprets "don't tell anybody" as "don't tell anybody but Rafe," because ten minutes later Rafe comes in, and stands looking at him, with his eyebrows raised. Redheaded people can look quite strained when they are raising eyebrows that aren't really there. He says, "You need not tell Richard that Mary Boleyn once proposed herself to me. There's nothing between us. It won't be like Wolf Hall, if that's what you're thinking."

"And what if the bride thinks different? I wonder you don't marry her to Gregory."

"Gregory is too young. Richard is twenty-three, it is a good age to marry if you can afford it. And you have passed it—it's time you married too."

"I'm going, before you find a Boleyn for me." Rafe turns back and says softly, "Only this, sir, and I think it is what gives Richard pause . . . all our lives and fortunes depend now on that lady, and as well as being mutable she is mortal, and the whole history of the king's marriage tells us a child in the womb is not an heir in the cradle."

❖

In March, news comes from Calais that Lord Berners has died. The afternoon in his library, the storm blowing outside: it seems when he looks back a haven of peace, the last hour he had to himself. He wants to make an offer for his books—a generous one, to help Lady Berners—but the folios seem to have jumped off their desks and walked, some in the direction of Francis Bryan, the old man's nephew, and some to another connection of his, Nicholas Carew. "Would you forgive his debts," he asks Henry, "at least for his wife's lifetime? You know he leaves—"

"No sons." Henry's mind has moved ahead: once I was in that unhappy state, no sons, but soon I shall have my heir.

He brings Anne some majolica bowls. The word MASCHIO is painted on the outside, and inside are pictures of plump blond-haired babies, each with a coy little phallus. She laughs. The Italians say for a boy you have to keep warm, he tells her. Heat up your wine to heat up your blood. No cold fruit, no fish.

Jane Seymour says, "Do you think it's already decided, what it will be, or does God decide later? Do you think it knows itself, what it is? Do you think if we could see inside you, we would be able to tell?"

"Jane, I wish you were still down in Wiltshire," Mary Shelton says.

Anne says, "You needn't cut me up, Mistress Seymour. It is a boy, and no one is to say or think otherwise." She frowns, and you can see her bending, concentrating, the great force of her will.

"I'd like a baby," Jane says.

"Watch yourself," Lady Rochford tells her. "If your belly shows, mistress, we'll have you bricked up alive."

"In her family," Anne says, "they'd give her a bouquet. They don't know what continence means, down at Wolf Hall."

Jane is flushed and trembling. "I meant no harm."

"Leave her," Anne says. "It's like baiting a field mouse." She turns to him. "Your bill is not passed yet. Tell me what is the delay."

The bill, she means, to forbid appeals to Rome. He begins to explain to her the strength of the opposition, but she raises her eyebrows and says, "My father is speaking for you in the Lords, and Norfolk. So who dare oppose us?"

"I shall have it through by Easter, depend upon it."

"The woman we saw in Canterbury, they say her people are printing a book of her prophecies."

"That may be, but I shall make sure no one reads it."

"They say on St. Catherine's Day last, while we were at Calais, she saw a vision of the so-called princess Mary crowned queen." Her voice runs on, fluid, rapid, these are my enemies, this prophetess and those about her, Katherine who is plotting with the Emperor, her daughter Mary the supposed heir, Mary's old governess Margaret Pole, Lady Salisbury, she and all her family are my enemies, her son Lord Montague, her son Reginald Pole, who is abroad, people talk of his claim to the throne so why can he not be brought back, his loyalty examined? Henry Courtenay, the Marquis of Exeter, he believes he has a claim, but when my son is born that will put him out of his conceit. Lady Exeter, Gertrude, she is forever complaining that noblemen are being put down from their places by men of low birth, and you know who she means by that.

My lady, her sister says softly, do not distress yourself.

I am not distressed, Anne says. Her hand over the growing child, she says calmly, "These people want me dead."

The days are still short, the king's temper shorter. Chapuys bows and writhes before him, twisting and grimacing, as if he had in mind to ask Henry to dance. "I have read with some perplexity certain conclusions reached by Dr. Cranmer—"

"My archbishop," the king says coldly; at great expense, the anointing has taken place.

"—conclusions regarding Queen Katherine—"

"Who? You mean my late brother's wife, the Princess of Wales?"

"—for Your Majesty knows that dispensations were issued in such form as to allow your own marriage to be valid, whether or not that former marriage was consummated."

"I do not want to hear the word *dispensation*," Henry says. "I do not want to hear you mention what you call my marriage. The Pope has no power to make incest licit. I am no more Katherine's husband than you are."

Chapuys bows.

"If the contract had not been void," Henry says, patient for the last time, "God would not have punished me with the loss of my children."

"We do not know the blessed Katherine is beyond childbearing." He looks up with a sly, delicate glance.

"Tell me, why do you think I do this?" The king sounds curious. "Out of lust? Is that what you think?"

Kill a cardinal? Divide your country? Split the church? "It seems extravagant," Chapuys murmurs.

"But that is what you think. That is what you tell the Emperor. You are wrong. I am the steward of my country, sir, and if I now take a wife in a union blessed by God, it is to have a son by her."

"But there is no guarantee that Your Majesty will have a son. Or any living children at all."

"Why would I not?" Henry reddens. He is on his feet, shouting, angry tears spilling down his face. "Am I not a man like other men? Am I not? Am I not?"

He is a game little terrier, the Emperor's man; but even he knows that when you've made a king cry it's time to back off. On the way out he says—dusting himself down, with his accustomed, self-deprecatory flutter—"There is a distinction to be drawn between the welfare of the country and the welfare of the Tudor line. Or do you not think so?"

"So who is your preferred candidate for the throne? You favor Courtenay, or Pole?"

"You should not sneer at persons of royal blood." Chapuys shakes out his sleeves. "At least now I am officially informed of the lady's state, whereas before I could only deduce it from certain spectacles of folly I had witnessed . . . Do you know how much you are staking, Cremuel, on the body of one woman? Let us hope no evil comes near her, eh?"

He takes the ambassador by the arm, wheels him around. "What evil? Say what you mean."

"If you would let go your grip on my jacket. Thank you. Very soon you resort to manhandling people, which shows, as they say, your breeding." His words are full of bravado, but he is trembling. "Look around you and see how by her pride and her presumption she offends your own nobility. Her own uncle has no stomach for her tricks. The king's oldest friends make excuses to stay away from court."

"Wait till she's crowned," he says. "Watch them come running."

On April 12, Easter Sunday, Anne appears with the king at High

Mass, and is prayed for as Queen of England. His bill went through Parliament just yesterday; he expects a modest reward, and before the royal party go in to break their fast, the king waves him over and gives him Lord Berners's old post, chancellor of the exchequer. "Berners suggested you for it." Henry smiles. He likes giving; like a child, he enjoys anticipating how pleased you will be.

During Mass, his mind had wandered through the city. What noisome goose houses have they waiting for him at home? What rows in the street, what babies left on church steps, what unruly apprentices with whom he will please have a word? Have Alice and Jo painted Easter eggs? They are too grown up now, but they are content to be the children of the house until the next generation comes along. It's time he put his mind to husbands for them. Anne, if she had lived, could be married by now, and to Rafe, as he is still not spoken for. He thinks of Helen Barre; how fast she gets on with her reading, how they cannot do without her at Austin Friars. He believes now that her husband is dead, and he thinks, I must talk to her, I must tell her she is free. She is too proper to show any pleasure, but who would not like to know that she is no longer subject to a man like that?

Through Mass, Henry keeps up a constant buzz of talk. He sorts papers and passes them up and down to his councillors; only at the consecration does he throw himself to his knees in a fever of reverence, as the miracle takes place and a wafer becomes God. As soon as the priest says, "*Ite, missa est,*" he whispers, come to me in my closet, alone.

First the assembled courtiers must make their bows to Anne. Her ladies sweep back and leave her alone in a little sunlit space. He watches them, watches the gentlemen and councillors, among whom, on this feast day, are many of the king's boyhood friends. He watches Sir Nicholas Carew in particular; nothing is wanting in his reverence to his new queen, but he cannot help a downturn of his mouth. Arrange your face, Nicholas Carew, your ancient family face. He hears Anne saying, these are my enemies: he adds Carew to the list.

Behind the chambers of state are the king's own rooms, which only his intimates see, where he is served by his gentlemen, and where he can be free of ambassadors and spies. This is Henry Norris's ground, and Norris gently congratulates him on his new appointment, and moves away, soft-footed.

"You know Cranmer is to convene a court to make a formal dissolution of the . . ." Henry has said he does not want to hear any more about his marriage, so he will not even say the word. "I have asked him to convene at the priory at Dunstable, because it is, what, ten, twelve miles to Ampthill, where she is lodged—so she can send her lawyers, if she likes. Or come to the court herself. I want you to go to see her, go secretly, just talk to her—"

Make sure she springs no surprises.

"Leave Rafe with me while you are gone." At being so easily understood, the king relaxes into good humor. "I can rely on him to say what Cromwell would say. You have a good boy there. And he is better than you are at keeping his face straight. I see you, when we sit in council, with your hand before your mouth. Sometimes, you know, I want to laugh myself." He drops into a chair, covers his face as if to shade his eyes. He sees that, once again, the king is about to cry. "Brandon says my sister is dying. There is no more the doctors can do for her. You know that fair hair she had once, hair like silver—my daughter had that. When she was seven she was the image of my sister, like a saint painted on a wall. Tell me, what am I to do with my daughter?"

He waits, till he knows it is a real question. "Be good to her, sir. Conciliate her. She should not suffer."

"But I must make her a bastard. I need to settle England on my lawful children."

"Parliament will do it."

"Yes." He sniffs. Scrubs his tears away. "After Anne is crowned. Cromwell, one thing, and then we will have our breakfast, because I am really very hungry. This project of a match for my cousin Richard . . ."

He thinks his way, rapidly, around the nobility of England. But no, he sees it's his Richard, Richard Cromwell. "Lady Carey . . ." The king's voice softens. "Well, I have thought it over, and I think, no. Or at least, not at this time."

He nods. He understands his reason. When Anne understands it, she will spit nails.

"Sometimes it is a solace to me," Henry says, "not to have to talk and talk. You were born to understand me, perhaps."

That is one view of their situations. He was six years or so in this world before Henry came into it, years of which he made good use. Henry takes off his embroidered cap, throws it down, runs his hands through his hair. Like Wyatt's golden mane, his hair is thinning, and it exposes the shape of his massive skull. For a moment he seems like a carved statue, like a simpler form of himself, or one of his own ancestors: one of the race of giants that roamed Britain, and left no trace of themselves except in the dreams of their petty descendants.

He goes back to Austin Friars as soon as he can get away. Surely he can have one day off? The crowds outside his gate have dispersed, as Thurston has fed them an Easter dinner. He goes out to the kitchen first, to give his man a slap on the head and a gold piece. "A hundred open maws, I swear," Thurston says. "And by supper time they'll be round again."

"It is a shame there should be beggars."

"Beggars my arse. What comes out of this kitchen is so good, there are aldermen out there, with their hoods up so we don't know them. And I have a houseful here, whether you are with us or not—I have Frenchmen, Germans, I have Florentiners, they all claim to know you and they all want their dinner to their own liking, I have their servants down here, pinch of that, soupçon of the other. We must feed fewer, or build another kitchen."

"I'll get it in hand."

"Master Rafe says for the Tower you have bought out the whole of a quarry in Normandy. He says the Frenchmen are all undermined, and dropping into holes in the ground."

Such beautiful stone. The color of butter. Four hundred men on the payroll, and anyone standing about instantly redeployed to the building work at Austin Friars. "Thurston, don't let anybody put pinches or soupçons in our dinner." He thinks, that's how Bishop Fisher nearly died; unless it was an unboiled stockpot after all. You could never fault

Thurston's stockpot. He goes and views it, bubbling away. "Where is Richard, do you know?"

"Chopping onions on the back step. Oh, you mean Master Richard? Upstairs. Eating. Where's anybody?"

He goes up. The Easter eggs, he sees, bear his own unmistakable features. Jo has painted his hat and his hair on one, so he seems to be wearing a cap with earflaps. She has given him at least two chins. "Well, sir," Gregory says, "it is true you are getting stout. When Stephen Vaughan was here he could not believe you."

"My master the cardinal waxed like the moon," he says. "It is a mystery, because he hardly sat down to dine but he would be leaping up to deal with some exigency, and even when he was at the table he could hardly eat for talking. I feel sorry for myself. I have not broken bread since last night." He breaks it, and says, "Hans wants to paint me."

"I hope he can run fast," Richard says.

"Richard—"

"Have your dinner."

"My breakfast. No, never mind it. Come."

"The happy bridegroom," Gregory says, taunting.

"You," his father threatens him, "are going north with Rowland Lee. If you think I'm a hard man, wait till you meet Rowland."

In his office, he says, "How is your practice in the lists?"

"Good. Cromwells will knock down all comers."

He is afraid for his son; that he will fall, be maimed, be killed. Afraid for Richard too; these boys are the hope of his house. Richard says, "So am I? The happy bridegroom?"

"The king says no. It is not because of my family, or your family—he calls you his cousin. He is, at this moment, his disposition to us, I would say it is excellent. But he needs Mary for himself. The child is due in late summer and he is afraid to touch Anne. And he does not wish to resume his celibate life."

Richard looks up. "He said this?"

"He left me to understand it. And as I understand it, I convey it to you, and we are both amazed, but we get over it."

"I suppose if the sisters were more alike, one could begin to understand it."

"I suppose," he says, "one could."

"And he is the head of our church. No wonder foreigners laugh."

"If he were a model of conduct in his private life, one would be . . . surprised . . . but for me, you see, I can only concern myself with his kingship. If he were oppressive, if he were to override Parliament, if he were to pay no heed to the Commons and govern only for himself . . . But he does not . . . so I cannot concern myself with how he behaves to his women."

"But if he were not king . . ."

"Oh, I agree. You'd have him locked up. But again, Richard, leave aside Mary and he has behaved well enough. He hasn't filled a nursery with his bastards, as the Scottish kings do. There have been women, but who can name them? Only Richmond's mother, and the Boleyns. He has been discreet."

"I dare say Katherine knew their names."

"Who can say he will be a faithful husband? Will you?"

"I may not get the chance."

"On the contrary, I have a wife for you. Thomas Murfyn's girl? A Lord Mayor's daughter is not a bad prospect. And your fortune will more than match hers, I will make sure of that. And Frances likes you. I know because I have asked her."

"You have asked my wife to marry me?"

"Since I was dining there yesterday—no point in delay, was there?"

"Not really." Richard laughs. He stretches back in his chair. His body—his capable, admirable body, which has impressed the king so much—is rinsed with relief. "Frances. Good. I like Frances."

Mercy approves. He cannot think how she would have taken to Lady Carey; he had not broached the topic with the women. She says, "Don't leave it too long to make a match for Gregory. He is very young, I know. But some men never grow up until they have a son of their own."

He hasn't thought about it, but it might be true. In that case, there's hope for the kingdom of England.

Two days later he is back at the Tower. The time goes quickly between Easter and Whit, when Anne will be crowned. He inspects her new apartments and orders in braziers to help dry out the plaster. He wants to get on with the frescoes—he wishes Hans would come down, but he is painting de Dinteville and says he needs to push on with it, as the ambassador is petitioning Francis for his recall, a whining letter on every boat. For the new queen we are not going to have those hunting scenes you see painted everywhere, or grim virgin saints with the instruments of their torture, but goddesses, doves, white falcons, canopies of green leaves. In the distance, cities seated on the hills: in the foreground, temples, groves, fallen columns and hot blue skies delineated, as within a frame, by borders of Vitruvian colors, quicksilver and cinnabar, burnt ocher, malachite, indigo and purple. He unrolls the sketches the craftsmen have made. Minerva's owl spreads her wings across a panel. A barefoot Diana fits an arrow to her bow. A white doe watches her from the trees. He scribbles a direction to the overseer: arrow to be picked out in gold. All goddesses have dark eyes. Like a wing tip from the dark, dread brushes him: what if Anne dies? Henry will want another woman. He will bring her to these rooms. Her eyes may be blue. We will have to scour away the faces and paint them again, against the same cities, the same violet hills.

Outside he stops to watch a fight. A stonemason and the bricklayer's gaffer are swiping at each other with battens. He stands in the ring with the trowel men. "What's it about?"

"Nuffing. Stone men have to fight brick men."

"Like Lancaster and York?"

"Like that."

"Have you ever heard of the field called Towton? The king tells me more than twenty thousand Englishmen died."

The man gapes at him. "Who were they fighting?"

"Each other."

It was Palm Sunday, the year 1461. The armies of two kings met in the driving snow. King Edward, the king's grandfather, was the winner, if you can say there was a winner at all. Corpses made a bobbing bridge across the river. Uncounted numbers crawled away, rolled and tumbled in their own blood: some blinded, some disfigured, some maimed for life.

The child in Anne's womb is the guarantee of no more civil war. He is the beginning, the start of something, the promise of another country.

He walks into the fight. He bellows at them to stop. He gives them both a push and they bowl over backward: two crumbly Englishmen, snappable bones, chalky teeth. Victors of Agincourt. He's glad Chapuys isn't there to see.

❖

The trees are in full leaf when he rides into Bedfordshire, with a small train on unofficial business. Christophe rides beside him and pesters him: you have said you will tell me who is Cicero, and who is Reginald Pole.

"Cicero was a Roman."

"A general?"

"No, he left that to others. As I, for example, might leave it to Norfolk."

"Oh, Norferk." Christophe subjects the duke to his peculiar pronunciation. "He is one who pisses on your shadow."

"Dear God, Christophe! I've heard of spitting on someone's shadow."

"Yes, but we speak of Norferk. And Cicero?"

"We lawyers try to memorize all his speeches. If any man were walking around today with all of Cicero's wisdom in his head he would be . . ." He would be what? "Cicero would be on the king's side," he says.

Christophe is not much impressed. "Pole, he is a general?"

"A priest. That is not quite true . . . He has offices in the church, but he has not been ordained."

"Why not?"

"No doubt so he can marry. It is his blood that makes him dangerous. He is a Plantagenet. His brothers are here in this kingdom under our eye. But Reginald is abroad and we are afraid he is plotting with the Emperor."

"Send one to kill him. I will go."

"No, Christophe, I need you to stop the rain spoiling my hats."

"As you wish." Christophe shrugs. "But I will kill a Pole when you require it, it will be my pleasure."

The manor at Ampthill, once fortified, has airy towers and a splendid gatehouse. It stands on a hill with views over wooded countryside; it is a pleasant seat, the kind of house you'd visit after an illness to get your strength back. It was built with money gained in the French wars, in the days when the English used to win them.

To accord with Katherine's new status as Dowager Princess of Wales, Henry has trimmed her household, but still she is surrounded by chaplains and confessors, by household officers each with their own train of menials, by butlers and carvers, physicians, cooks, scullions, maltsters, harpers, lutenists, poultry keepers, gardeners, laundresses, apothecaries, and an entourage of wardrobe ladies, bedchamber ladies and their maids. But when he is ushered in she nods to her attendants to withdraw. No one had told her to expect him, but she must have spies on the road. Hence her nonchalant parade of occupation: a prayer book in her lap, and some sewing. He kneels to her, nods toward these encumbrances. "Surely, madam, one or the other?"

"So, English today? Get up, Cromwell. We will not waste our time, as at our last interview, selecting which language to use. Because nowadays you are such a busy man."

Formalities over, she says, "First thing. I shall not attend your court at Dunstable. That is what you have come to find out, is it not? I do not recognize this court. My case is at Rome, awaiting the attention of the Holy Father."

"Slow, isn't he?" He gives her a puzzled smile.

"I will wait."

"But the king wishes to settle his affairs."

"He has a man who will do it. I do not call him an archbishop."

"Clement issued the bulls."

"Clement was misled. Dr. Cranmer is a heretic."

"Perhaps you think the king is a heretic?"

"No. Only a schismatic."

"If a general council of the church were called, His Majesty would submit to its judgment."

"It will be too late, if he is excommunicated, and put outside the church."

"We all hope—I am sure you do, madam—that day will never come."

"*Nulla salus extra ecclesiam.* Outside the church there is no salvation. Even kings come to judgment. Henry knows it, and is afraid."

"Madam, give way to him. For the present. Tomorrow, who knows? Do not cut off every chance of rapprochement."

"I hear Thomas Boleyn's daughter is having a child."

"Indeed, but . . ."

Katherine, above anyone, should know that guarantees nothing. She takes his meaning; thinks about it; nods. "I see circumstances in which he might turn back to me. I have had much opportunity to study that lady's character, and she is neither patient nor kind."

It doesn't matter; she only has to be lucky. "In the event they have no children, you should think of your daughter Lady Mary. Conciliate him, madam. He may confirm her as his heir. And if you will give way, he will offer you every honor, and a great estate."

"A great estate!" Katherine stands up. Her sewing slides from her skirts, the prayer book hits the floor with a fat leathery thump, and her silver thimble goes skittering across the boards and rolls into a corner. "Before you make me any more preposterous offers, Master Cromwell, let me offer you a chapter from my history. After my lord Arthur died, I passed five years in poverty. I could not pay my servants. We bought in the cheapest food we could find, coarse food, stale food, yesterday's fish—any small merchant kept a better table than the daughter of Spain. The late King Henry would not let me go back to my father because he said he was owed money—he haggled over me like one of the doorstep women who sold us bad eggs. I put my faith in God, I did not despair, but I tasted the depth of humiliation."

"So why would you want to taste it again?"

Face-to-face. They glare at each other. "Assuming," he says, "humiliation is all the king intends."

"Say it plainly."

"If you are found out in treason the law will take its course with you, as if you were any other subject. Your nephew is threatening to invade us in your name."

"That will not happen. Not in my name."

"That is what I say, madam." He softens his tone. "I say the Emperor is busy with the Turks, he is not so fond of his aunt—saving your presence—that he will raise another army. But others say, oh, be quiet, Cromwell, what do you know? They say we must fortify our harbors, we must raise troops, we must put the country in a state of alert. Chapuys, as you know, continually agitates with Charles to blockade our ports and impound our goods and our merchant ships abroad. He urges war in every dispatch."

"I have no knowledge of what Chapuys puts in his dispatches."

It is a lie so staggering that he has to admire it. Having delivered it, Katherine seems weakened; she sinks down again into her chair, and before he can do it for her she wearily bends from the waist to pick up her sewing; her fingers are swollen, and bending seems to leave her breathless. She sits for a moment, recovering herself, and when she speaks again she is calm, deliberate. "Master Cromwell, I know I have failed you. That is to say, I have failed your country, which by now is my country too. The king was a good husband to me, but I could not do that which is most necessary for a wife to do. Nevertheless, I was, I am, a wife—you see, do you, that it is impossible for me to believe that for twenty years I was a harlot? Now the truth is, I have brought England little good, but I would be loath to bring her any harm."

"But you do, madam. You may not will it, but the harm is done."

"England is not served by a lie."

"That is what Dr. Cranmer thinks. So he will annul your marriage, whether you come to the court or not."

"Dr. Cranmer will be excommunicated too. Does it not cause him a qualm? Is he so lost to everything?"

"This archbishop is the best guardian of the church, madam, that we have seen in many centuries." He thinks of what Bainham said, before they burned him; in England there have been eight hundred years of mystification, just six years of truth and light; six years, since the gospel in English began to come into the kingdom. "Cranmer is no heretic. He believes as the king believes. He will reform what needs reformation, that is all."

"I know where this will end. You will take the church's lands and give them to the king." She laughs. "Oh, you are silent? You will. You mean to do it." She sounds almost lighthearted, as people do sometimes when they're told they're dying. "Master Cromwell, you may assure the king I will not bring an army against him. Tell him I pray for him daily. Some people, those who do not know him as I do, they say, 'Oh, he will work his will, he will have his desire at any price.' But I know that he needs to be on the side of the light. He is not a man like you, who just packs up his sins in his saddlebags and carries them from country to country, and when they grow too heavy whistles up a mule or two, and soon commands a train of them and a troop of muleteers. Henry may err, but he needs to be forgiven. I therefore believe, and will continue to believe, that he will turn out of this path of error, in order to be at peace with himself. And peace is what we all wish for, I am sure."

"What a placid end you make, madam. 'Peace is what we all wish for.' Like an abbess. You are quite sure by the way that you would not think of becoming an abbess?"

A smile. Quite a broad smile. "I shall be sorry if I don't see you again. You are so much quicker in conversation than the dukes."

"The dukes will be back."

"I am braced. Is there news of my lady Suffolk?"

"The king says she is dying. Brandon has no heart for anything."

"I can well believe it," she murmurs. "Her income as Dowager Queen of France dies with her, and that is the greater part of his revenue. Still, no doubt you will arrange him a loan, at some iniquitous rate of interest." She looks up. "My daughter will be curious to know I have seen you. She believes you were kind to her."

He only remembers giving her a stool to sit on. Her life must be bleak, if she remembers that.

"Properly, she should have remained standing, awaiting a sign from me."

Her own pain-racked little daughter. She may smile, but she doesn't yield an inch. Julius Caesar would have had more compunction. Hannibal.

"Tell me," she says, testing the ground. "The king would read a letter from me?"

Henry has taken to tearing her letters up unread, or burning them. He says they disgust him with their expressions of love. He does not have it in him to tell her this. "Then rest for an hour," she says, "while I write it. Unless you will stay a night with us? I should be glad of company at supper."

"Thank you, but I must start back, the council meets tomorrow. Besides, if I stayed, where would I put my mules? Not to mention my team of drivers."

"Oh, the stables are half empty. The king makes sure I am kept short of mounts. He thinks that I will give my household the slip and ride to the coast and escape on a ship to Flanders."

"And will you?"

He has retrieved her thimble; he hands it back; she bounces it in her hand as if it were a die and she were ready to cast it.

"No. I shall stay here. Or go where I am sent. As the king wills. As a wife should."

Until the excommunication, he thinks. That will free you from all bonds, as wife, as subject. "This is yours too," he says. He opens his palm; in it a needle, tip toward her.

❖

The word is about town that Thomas More has fallen into poverty. He laughs about it with Master Secretary Gardiner. "Alice was a rich widow when he married her," Gardiner says. "And he has land of his own; how can he be poor? And the daughters, he's married them well."

"And he still has his pension from the king." He is sifting through paperwork for Stephen, who is preparing to appear as leading counsel for Henry at Dunstable. He has filed away all the depositions from the Blackfriars hearings, which seem to have happened in another era.

"Angels defend us," Gardiner says, "is there anything you don't file?"

"If we keep on to the bottom of this chest I'll find your father's love letters to your mother." He blows dust off the last batch. "There you are." The papers hit the table. "Stephen, what can we do for John Frith? He was your pupil at Cambridge. Don't abandon him."

But Gardiner shakes his head and busies himself with the documents, leafing through them, humming under his breath, exclaiming, "Well, who'd have known!" and "Here's a nice point!"

He gets a boat down to Chelsea. The ex-Chancellor is at ease in his parlor, daughter Margaret translating from the Greek in a drone barely audible; as he approaches, he hears him pick her up on some error. "Leave us, daughter," More says, when he sees him. "I won't have you in this devil's company." But Margaret looks up and smiles, and More rises from his chair, a little stiff, as if his back is bad, and offers a hand.

It is Reginald Pole, lying in Italy, who says he is a devil. The point is, he means it; it's not an image with him, as in a fable, but something he takes to be true, as he takes the gospel to be true.

"Well," he says. "We hear you can't come to the coronation because you can't afford a new coat. The Bishop of Winchester will buy you one himself if you'll show your face on the day."

"Stephen? Will he?"

"I swear it." He relishes the thought of going back to London and asking Gardiner for ten pounds. "Or the guildsmen will make a collection, if you like, for a new hat and a doublet as well."

"And how are you to appear?" Margaret speaks gently, as if she has been asked to mind two children for the afternoon.

"They are making something for me. I leave it to others. If I only avoid exciting mirth, it will be enough."

Anne has said, you shall not dress like a lawyer on my coronation day. She has called out to Jane Rochford, taking notes like a clerk: Thomas must go into crimson. "Mistress Roper," he says, "are you not yourself curious to see the queen crowned?"

Her father cuts in, talking over her: "It is a day of shame for the women of England. One can hear them say on the streets—when the Emperor comes, wives shall have their rights again."

"Father, I am sure they take care not to say that in Master Cromwell's hearing."

He sighs. It's not much, to know that all the merry young whores are on your side. All the kept women, and the runaway daughters. Though now Anne is married, she sets herself up for an example. Already she has slapped Mary Shelton, Lady Carey tells him, for writing a riddle in her prayer book, and it was not even an indecent one. The queen sits very erect these days, child stirring in her belly, needlework in hand, and when Norris and Weston and their gentlemen friends come swarming into her apartments, she looks at them, when they lay compliments at her feet, as if they were strewing her hem with spiders. Unless you approach her with a Bible text in your mouth, better not approach her at all.

He says, "Has the Maid been up to see you again? The prophetess?"

"She has," Meg says, "but we would not receive her."

"I believe she has been to see Lady Exeter. At her invitation."

"Lady Exeter is a foolish and ambitious woman," More says.

"I understand the Maid told her that she would be Queen of England."

"I repeat my comment."

"Do you believe in her visions? Their holy nature, that is?"

"No. I think she is an impostor. She does it for attention."

"Just that?"

"You don't know what young women will do. I have a houseful of daughters."

He pauses. "You are blessed."

Meg glances up; she recalls his losses, though she never heard Anne Cromwell demand, why should Mistress More have the preeminence? She says, "There were holy maids before this. One at Ipswich. Only a little girl of twelve. She was of good family, and they say she did miracles, and she got nothing out of it, no personal profit, and she died young."

"But then there was the Maid of Leominster," More says, with gloomy relish. "They say she is a whore at Calais now, and laughs with her clients after supper at all the tricks she worked on the believing people."

So he does not like holy maids. But Bishop Fisher does. He has seen her often. He has dealings with her. As if taking the words out of his mouth, More says, "Of course, Fisher, he has his own views."

"Fisher believes she has raised the dead." More lifts an eyebrow. "But only for so long as it took for the corpse to make his confession and get absolution. And then he fell down and died again."

More smiles. "That sort of miracle."

"Perhaps she is a witch," Meg says. "Do you think so? There are witches in the scriptures. I could cite you."

Please don't. More says, "Meg, did I show you where I put the letter?" She rises, marking with a thread her place in the Greek text. "I have written to this maid, Barton . . . Dame Elizabeth, we must call her, now she is a professed nun. I have advised her to leave the realm in tranquillity, to cease to trouble the king with her prophecies, to avoid the company of great men and women, to listen to her spiritual advisers, and, in short, to stay at home and say her prayers."

"As we all should, Sir Thomas. Following your example." He nods, vigorously. "Amen. And I suppose you kept a copy?"

"Get it, Meg. Otherwise he may never leave."

More gives his daughter some rapid instructions. But he is satisfied that he is not ordering her to fabricate such a letter on the spot. "I would leave," he says, "in time. I'm not going to miss the coronation. I've got my new clothes to wear. Will you not come and bear us company?"

"You'll be company for each other, in Hell."

This is what you forget, this vehemence; his ability to make his twisted jokes, but not take them.

"The queen looks well," he says. "Your queen, I mean, not mine. She seems very comfortable at Ampthill. But you know that, of course."

More says, unblinking, I have no correspondence with the, with the Princess Dowager. Good, he says, because I am watching two friars who have been carrying her letters abroad—I am beginning to think that whole order of the Franciscans is working against the king. If I take them and if I cannot persuade them, and you know I am very persuasive, into confirming my suspicion, I may have to hang them up by their wrists, and start a sort of contest between them, as to which one will emerge first into better sense. Of course, my own inclination would be to take them home, feed them and ply them with strong drink, but then, Sir Thomas, I have always looked up to you, and you have been my master in these proceedings.

He has to say it all before Margaret Roper comes back. He raps his fingers on the table, to make More sit up and pay attention. John Frith, he says. Ask to see Henry. He will welcome you like a lost child. Talk to him and ask him to meet Frith face-to-face. I'm not asking you to agree with John—you think he's a heretic, perhaps he is a heretic—I'm asking you to concede just this, and to tell it to the king, that Frith is a pure soul, he is a fine scholar, so let him live. If his doctrine is false and yours is true you can talk him back to you, you are an eloquent man, you are the great persuader of our age, not me—talk him back to Rome, if you can. But if he dies you will never know, will you, if you could have won his soul?

Margaret's footstep. "Is this it, Father?"

"Give it to him."

"There are copies of the copy, I suppose?"

"You would expect us," the girl says, "to take all reasonable care."

"Your father and I were discussing monks and friars. How can they be good subjects of the king, if they owe their allegiance to the heads of their orders, who are abroad in other countries, and who are themselves perhaps subjects of the King of France, or the Emperor?"

"I suppose they are still Englishmen."

"I meet few who behave as such. Your father will enlarge on what I say." He bows to her. He takes More's hand, holding its shifting sinews in his own palm; scars vanish, it is surprising how they do, and now his own hand is white, a gentleman's hand, flesh running easily over the joints, though once he thought the burn marks, the stripes that any smith picks up in the course of business, would never fade.

He goes home. Helen Barre meets him. "I've been fishing," he says. "At Chelsea."

"Catch More?"

"Not today."

"Your robes came."

"Yes?"

"Crimson."

"Dear God." He laughs. "Helen—" She looks at him; she seems to be waiting. "I haven't found your husband."

Her hands are plunged into the pocket of her apron. She shifts them, as if she were holding something; he sees that one of her hands is clutching the other. "So you suppose he is dead?"

"It would be reasonable to think so. I have spoken with the man who saw him go into the river. He seems a good witness."

"So I could marry again. If anybody wanted me."

Helen's eyes rest on his face. She says nothing. Just stands. The moment seems to last a long time. Then: "What happened to our picture? The one with the man holding his heart shaped like a book? Or do I mean his book shaped like a heart?"

"I gave it to a Genovese."

"Why?"

"I needed to pay for an archbishop."

She moves, reluctant, slow. She drags her eyes from his face. "Hans is here. He has been waiting for you. He is angry. He says time is money."

"I'll make it up to him."

Hans is taking time off from his preparations for the coronation. He is building a living model of Mount Parnassus on Gracechurch Street, and today he has to put the Nine Muses through their paces, so he doesn't like being kept waiting by Thomas Cromwell. He is banging around in the next room. It seems he is moving the furniture.

❖

They take Frith to the archbishop's palace at Croydon, to be examined by Cranmer. The new archbishop could have seen him at Lambeth;

but the way to Croydon is longer, and lies through the woods. In the depth of these woods, they say to him, it would be a bad day for us if you were to give us the slip. For see how thick the trees are on the Wandsworth side. You could hide an army in there. We could spend two days searching there, more—and if you'd gone east, to Kent and the river, you'd be clear away before we got around to that side.

But Frith knows his road; he is going toward his death. They stand on the path, whistling, talking about the weather. One pisses, leisurely, against a tree. One follows the flight of a jay through the branches. But when they turn back, Frith is waiting, placid, for his journey to resume.

❖

Four days. Fifty barges in procession, furnished by the city livery companies; two hours from the city to Blackwall, their rigging hung with bells and flags; a light but brisk breeze, as ordered from God in his prayers. Reverse order, anchor at the steps of Greenwich Palace, collect incoming queen in her own barge—Katherine's old one, rebadged, twenty-four oars: next her women, her guard, all the ornaments of the king's court, all those proud and noble souls who swore they'd sabotage the event. Boats packed with musicians; three hundred craft afloat, banners and pennants flying, the music ringing bank to bank, and each bank lined with Londoners. Downstream with the tide, led by an aquatic dragon spitting fire, and accompanied by wild men throwing fireworks. Seagoing ships discharge their ordnance in salute.

By the time they reach the Tower the sun is out. It looks as if the Thames is ablaze. Henry is waiting to greet Anne as she lands. He kisses her without formality, scooping back her gown, pinning it at her sides to show her belly to England.

Next, Henry makes knights: a shoal of Howards and Boleyns, their friends and followers. Anne rests.

Uncle Norfolk is missing the show. Henry has sent him to King Francis, to reaffirm the most cordial alliance between our two kingdoms. He is Earl Marshal and should be in charge of the coronation, but there is another Howard to step in as his deputy, and besides, he, Thomas Cromwell, is running everything, including the weather.

He has conferred with Arthur Lord Lisle, who will preside at the coronation banquet: Arthur Plantagenet, a gentle relic of a former age. He is to go to Calais, directly this is over, to replace Lord Berners as Governor, and he, Cromwell, must brief him before he goes. Lisle has a long bony Plantagenet face, and he is tall like his father King Edward, who no doubt had many bastards, but none so distinguished as this elderly man, bending his creaky knee in obeisance before Boleyn's daughter. His wife, Honor, his second wife, is twenty years his junior, small and delicate, a toy wife. She wears tawny silk, coral bracelets with gold hearts, and an expression of vigilant dissatisfaction, bordering on the peevish. She looks him up and down. "I suppose you are Cromwell?" If a man spoke to you in that tone, you'd invite him to step outside and ask someone to hold your coat.

Day Two: bringing Anne to Westminster. He is up before first light, watching from the battlements as thin clouds disperse over the Bermondsey bank, and an early chill as clear as water is replaced by a steady, golden heat.

Her procession is led by the retinue of the French ambassador. The judges in scarlet follow, the Knights of the Bath in blue-violet of antique cut, then the bishops, Lord Chancellor Audley and his retinue, the great lords in crimson velvet. Sixteen knights carry Anne in a white litter hung with silver bells which ring at each step, at each breath; the queen is in white, her body shimmering in its strange skin, her face held in a conscious solemn smile, her hair loose beneath a circle of gems. After her, ladies on palfreys trapped with white velvet; and ancient dowagers in their chariots, their faces acidulated.

At every turn on the route there are pageants and living statues, recitations of her virtue and gifts of gold from city coffers, her white falcon emblem crowned and entwined with roses, and blossoms mashed and minced under the treading feet of the stout sixteen, so scent rises like smoke. The route is hung with tapestries and banners, and at his orders the ground beneath the horses' hooves is graveled to prevent slipping, and the crowds restrained behind rails in case of riots and crush; every law officer London can muster is among the crowd, because he is determined that in time to come, when this is remembered and told to those who were not here, no one is going to say, oh, Queen Anne's coronation, that was the day I got my pocket picked. Fenchurch Street, Leadenhall, Cheap, Paul's Churchyard, Fleet, Temple Bar, Westminster Hall. So many fountains flowing with wine that it's hard to find one flowing with water. And looking down on them, the other Londoners, those monsters who live in the air, the city's uncounted population of stone men and women and beasts, and things that are neither human nor beasts, fanged rabbits and flying hares, four-legged birds and pinioned snakes, imps with bulging eyes and ducks' bills, men who are wreathed in leaves or have the heads of goats or rams; creatures with knotted coils and leather wings, with hairy ears and cloven feet, horned and roaring, feathered and scaled, some laughing, some singing, some pulling back their lips to show their teeth; lions and friars, donkeys and geese, devils with children crammed into their maws, all chewed up except for their helpless paddling feet; limestone or leaden, metaled or marbled, shrieking and sniggering above the populace, hooting and gurning and dry-heaving from buttresses, walls and roofs.

That night, the king permitting, he goes back to Austin Friars. He visits his neighbor Chapuys, who has secluded himself from the events of the day, bolting his shutters and stuffing his ears against the fanfares, the ceremonial cannon fire. He goes in a small satirical procession led by Thurston, taking the ambassador sweetmeats to ease his sulks, and some fine Italian wine sent to him by the Duke of Suffolk.

Chapuys greets him without a smile. "Well, you have succeeded where the cardinal failed, Henry has what he wants at last. I say to my master, who is capable of looking at these things impartially, it is a pity from Henry's point of view that he did not take up Cromwell years ago. His affairs would have gone on much better." He is about to say, the cardinal taught me everything, but Chapuys talks over him. "When the cardinal came to a closed door he would flatter it—oh beautiful yielding door! Then he would try tricking it open. And you are just the same, just the same." He pours himself some of the duke's present. "But in the last resort, you just kick it in."

The wine is one of those big, noble wines that Brandon favors, and Chapuys drinks appreciatively and says, I don't understand it, nothing do I understand in this benighted country. Is Cranmer Pope now? Or is Henry Pope? Perhaps you are Pope? My men who were among the press today say they heard few voices raised for the concubine, and plenty who called upon God to bless Katherine, the rightful queen.

Did they? I don't know what city they were in.

Chapuys sniffs: they may well wonder. These days it is nothing but Frenchmen about the king, and she, Boleyn, she is half French herself, and wholly bought by them; her entire family are in the pocket of Francis. But you, Thomas, you are not taken in by these Frenchmen, are you?

He reassures him: my dear friend, not for one instant.

Chapuys weeps; it's unlike him: all credit to the noble wine. "I have failed my master the Emperor. I have failed Katherine."

"Never mind." He thinks, tomorrow is another battle, tomorrow is another world.

❖

He is at the abbey by dawn. The procession is forming up by six. Henry will watch the coronation from a box screened by a lattice, sequestered in the painted stonework. When he puts his head in about eight o'clock the king is already sitting expectantly on a velvet cushion, and a kneeling servant is unpacking his breakfast. "The French ambassador will be joining me," Henry says; and he meets that gentleman as he is hurrying away.

"One hears you have been painted, Maître Cremuel. I too have been painted. You have seen the result?"

"Not yet. Hans is so occupied." Even on this fine morning, here beneath fan vaulting the ambassador looks blue-tinged. "Well," he says, "it appears that with the coronation of this queen, our two nations have reached a state of perfect amity. How to improve on perfection? I ask you, monsieur."

The ambassador bows. "Downhill from here?"

"Let's try, you know. To maintain a state of mutual usefulness. When our sovereigns are once again snapping at each other."

"Another Calais meeting?"

"Perhaps in a year."

"No sooner?"

"I will not put my king on the high seas for no cause."

"We'll talk, Cremuel." Flat-palmed, the ambassador taps him on the chest, over the heart.

Anne's procession forms up at nine. She is mantled in purple velvet, edged in ermine. She has seven hundred yards to walk, on the blue cloth that stretches to the altar, and her face is entranced. Far behind her, the Dowager Duchess of Norfolk, supporting her train; nearer, holding up the hem of her long robe, the Bishop of Winchester at one side, the Bishop of London at the other. Both of them, Gardiner and Stokesley, were king's men in the matter of the divorce; but now they look as if they wish they were far distant from the living object of his remarriage, who has a fine sheen of sweat on her high forehead, and whose compressed lips—by the time she reaches the altar—seem to have vanished into her face. Who says two bishops should hold up her hem? It's all written down in a great book, so old that one hardly dare touch it, breathe on it; Lisle seems to know it by heart. Perhaps it should be copied and printed, he thinks.

He makes a mental note, and then concentrates his will on Anne: Anne not to stumble, as she folds herself toward the ground to lie face-down in prayer before the altar, her attendants stepping forward to support her for the crucial twelve inches before belly hits sacred pavement. He finds himself praying: this child, his half-formed heart now beating against the stone floor, let him be sanctified by this moment, and let him be like his father's father, like his Tudor uncles; let him be hard, alert, watchful of opportunity, wringing use from the smallest turn of fortune. If Henry lives twenty years, Henry who is Wolsey's creation, and then leaves this child to succeed him, I can build my own prince: to the glorification of God and the commonwealth of England. Because I will not be too old. Look at Norfolk, already he is sixty, his father was seventy when he fought at Flodden. And I shall not be like Henry Wyatt and say, now I am retiring from affairs. Because what is there, but affairs?

Anne, shaky, is back on her feet. Cranmer, in a dense cloud of incense, is pressing into her hand the scepter, the rod of ivory, and resting the crown of St. Edward briefly on her head, before changing for a lighter and more bearable crown: a prestidigitation, his hands as supple as if he'd been shuffling crowns all his life. The prelate looks mildly excited, as if someone had offered him a cup of warm milk.

Anointed, Anna withdraws, incense billowing around her, swallowed into its murk: Anna Regina, to a bedchamber provided for her, to prepare for the feast in Westminster Hall. He pushes unceremoniously through the dignitaries—all you, all you who said you would not be here—and catches sight of Charles Brandon, Constable of England, mounted on his white horse and ready to ride into the hall among them. He is a huge, blazing presence, from which he withdraws his sight; Charles, he thinks, will not outlive me either. Back into the dimness, toward Henry. Only one thing checks him, the sight, whisking around a corner, of the hem of a scarlet robe; no doubt it is one of the judges, escaped from his procession.

The Venetian ambassador is blocking the entrance to Henry's box, but the king waves him aside, and says, "Cromwell, did not my wife look well, did she not look beautiful? Will you go and see her, and give her . . ." he looks around, for some likely present, then wrenches a diamond from his knuckle, "will you give her this?" He kisses the ring. "And this too?"

"I shall hope to convey the sentiment," he says, and sighs, as if he were Cranmer.

The king laughs. His face is alight. "This is my best," he says. "This is my best day."

"Until the birth, Majesty," says the Venetian, bowing.

❖

It is Mary Howard, Norfolk's little daughter, who opens the door to him.

"No, you most certainly cannot come in," she says. "Utterly not. The queen is undressed."

Richmond is right, he thinks; she has no breasts at all. Still. For fourteen. I'll charm this small Howard, he thinks, so he stands spinning words around her, complimenting her gown and her jewels, till he hears a voice from within, muffled like a voice from a tomb; and Mary Howard jumps and says, oh, all right, if she says so you can see her.

The bed curtains are drawn close. He pulls them back. Anne is lying in her shift. She looks flat as a ghost, except for the shocking mound of her six-month child. In her ceremonial robes, her condition had hardly showed, and only that sacred instant, as she lay belly-down to stone, had connected him to her body, which now lies stretched out like a sacrifice: her breasts puffy beneath the linen, her swollen feet bare.

"Mother of God," she says. "Can you not leave Howard women alone? For an ugly man, you are very sure of yourself. Let me look at you." She bobs her head up. "Is that crimson? It's a very black crimson. Did you go against my orders?"

"Your cousin Francis Bryan says I look like a traveling bruise."

"A contusion on the body politic." Jane Rochford laughs.

"Can you do this?" he asks: almost doubting, almost tender. "You are exhausted."

"Oh, I think she will bear up." There is no sisterly pride in Mary's voice. "She was born for this, was she not?"

Jane Seymour: "Is the king watching?"

"He is proud of her." He speaks to Anne, stretched out on her catafalque. "He says you have never looked more beautiful. He sends you this."

Anne makes a little sound, a moan, poised between gratitude and boredom: oh, what, another diamond?

"And a kiss, which I said he had better bring in person."

She shows no sign of taking the ring from him. It is almost irresistible, to place it on her belly and walk away. Instead he hands it to her sister. He says, "The feast will wait for you, Highness. Come only when you feel ready."

She levers herself upright, with a gasp. "I am coming now." Mary

Howard leans forward and rubs her lower back, with an unpracticed hand, a fluttering virginal motion as if she were stroking a bird. "Oh, get away," the anointed queen snaps. She looks sick. "Where were you last evening? I wanted you. The streets cheered for me. I heard them. They say the people love Katherine, but really, it is just the women, they pity her. We will show them something better. They will love me, when this creature is out of me."

Jane Rochford: "Oh, but madam, they love Katherine because she is the daughter of two anointed sovereigns. Make your mind up to it, madam—they will never love you, any more than they love . . . Cromwell here. It is nothing to do with your merits. It is a point of fact. There is no use trying to evade it."

"Perhaps enough," Jane Seymour says. He turns to her and sees something surprising; she has grown up.

"Lady Carey," Jane Rochford says, "we must get your sister on her feet now and back in her robes, so see Master Cromwell out and enjoy your usual confabulation. This is not a day to break with tradition."

At the door: "Mary?" he says. Notices the dark stains under her eyes.

"Yes?" She speaks in a tone of "yes, and what is it now?"

"I am sorry the marriage with my nephew did not come off."

"Not that I was ever asked, of course." She smiles tightly. "I shall never see your house. And one hears so much of it."

"What do you hear?"

"Oh . . . of chests bursting with gold pieces."

"We would never allow that. We would get bigger chests."

"They say it is the king's money."

"It's all the king's money. His image is on it. Mary, look," he takes her hand, "I could not dissuade him from his liking for you. He—"

"How hard did you try?"

"I wish you were safe with us. Though of course it was not the great match you might expect, as the queen's sister."

"I doubt there are many sisters who expect what I receive, nightly."

She will get another child by Henry, he thinks. Anne will have it strangled in the cradle. "Your friend William Stafford is at court. At least, I think he is still your friend?"

"Imagine how he likes my situation. Still, at least I get a kind word from my father. Monseigneur finds he needs me again. God forbid the king should ride a mare from any other stable."

"This will end. He will free you. He will give you a settlement. A pension. I'll speak for you."

"Does a dirty dishcloth get a pension?" Mary sways on the spot; she seems dazed with misery and fatigue; great tears swell in her eyes. He stands catching them, dabbing them away, whispering to her and soothing her, and wanting to be elsewhere. When he breaks free he gives her a backward glance, as she stands in the doorway, desolate. Something must be done for her, he thinks. She's losing her looks.

❖

Henry watches from a gallery, high above Westminster Hall, as his queen takes her seat in the place of honor, her ladies around her, the flower of the court and the nobility of England. The king has fortified himself earlier, and is picking at a spice plate, dipping thin slices of apple into cinnamon. In the gallery with him, *encore les ambassadeurs,* Jean de Dinteville furred against the June chill, and his friend the Bishop of Lavaur, wrapped in a fine brocade gown.

"This has all been most impressive, Cremuel," de Selve says; astute brown eyes study him, taking everything in. He takes in everything too: stitching and padding, studding and dyeing; he admires the deep mulberry of the bishop's brocade. They say these two Frenchmen favor the gospel, but favor at François's court extends no further than a small circle of scholars that the king, for his own vanity, wishes to patronize; he has never quite been able to grow his own Thomas More, his own Erasmus, which naturally piques his pride.

"Look at my wife the queen." Henry leans over the gallery. He might as well be down there. "She is worth the show, is she not?"

"I have had all the windows reglazed," he says. "The better to see her."

"*Fiat lux,*" de Selve murmurs.

"She has done very well," de Dinteville says. "She must have been six hours on her feet today. One must congratulate Your Majesty on obtaining a queen who is as strong as a peasant woman. I mean no disrespect, of course."

In Paris they are burning Lutherans. He would like to take it up with the envoys, but he cannot while the odor of roast swan and peacock drifts up from below.

"Messieurs," he asks (music rising around them like a shallow tide, silver ripples of sound), "do you know of the man Guilio Camillo? I hear he is at your master's court."

De Selve and his friend exchange glances. This has thrown them. "The man who builds the wooden box," Jean murmurs. "Oh yes."

"It is a theater," he says.

De Selve nods. "In which you yourself are the play."

"Erasmus has written to us about it," Henry says, over his shoulder. "He is having the cabinetmakers create him little wooden shelves and drawers, one inside another. It is a memory system for the speeches of Cicero."

"With your permission, he intends it as more than that. It is a theater on the ancient Vitruvian plan. But it is not to put on plays. As my lord the bishop says, you as the owner of the theater are to stand in the center of it, and look up. Around you there is arrayed a system of human knowledge. Like a library, but as if—can you imagine a library in which each book contains another book, and a smaller book inside that? Yet it is more than that."

The king slips into his mouth an aniseed comfit, and snaps down on it. "Already there are too many books in the world. There are more every day. One man cannot hope to read them all."

"I do not see how you understand so much about it," de Selve says. "All credit to you, Maître Cremuel. Guilio will only speak his own Italian dialect, and even in that he stammers."

"If it pleases your master to spend his money," Henry says. "He is not a sorcerer, is he, this Guilio? I should not like Francis to fall into the hands of a sorcerer. By the way, Cromwell, I am sending Stephen back to France."

Stephen Gardiner. So the French do not like doing business with Norferk. Not surprising. "His mission will be of some duration?"

De Selve catches his eye. "But who will do Master Secretary's job?"

"Oh, Cromwell will do it. Won't you?" Henry smiles.

❖

He is hardly down into the body of the hall before Master Wriothesley intercepts him. This is a big day for the heralds and their officers, their children and their friends; fat fees coming their way. He says so, and Call-Me says, fat fees coming your way. He edges back against the screens, voice low; one could foresee this, he says, because Henry is tired of it, Winchester's grinding opposition to him every step of the way. He is tired of arguing; now he is a married man he looks for a little more *douceur*. With Anne? he says and Call-Me laughs: you know her better than me, if as they say she is a lady with a sharp tongue, then all the more he needs ministers who are kind to him. So devote yourself to keeping Stephen abroad, and in time he will confirm you in the post.

Christophe, dressed up for the afternoon, is hovering nearby and making signals to him. You will excuse me, he says, but Wriothesley touches his gown of crimson, as if for luck, and says, you are the master of the house and the master of the revels, you are the origin of the king's happiness, you have done what the cardinal could not, and much more besides. Even this—he gestures around him, to where the nobility of England, having already eaten their words, are working through twenty-three dishes—even this feast has been superbly managed. No one need call for anything, it is all at his hand before he thinks of it.

He inclines his head, Wriothesley walks away, and he beckons the boy. Christophe says, one tells me to impart nothing of confidence in the hearing of Call-Me, as Rafe says he go trit-trot to Gardineur with anything he can get. Now sir, I have a message, you must go quick to the archbishop. When the feast is done. He glances up to the dais where the archbishop sits beside Anne, under her canopy of state. Neither of them is eating, though Anne is pretending to, both of them are scanning the hall.

"I go trit-trot," he says. He is taken with the phrase. "Where?"

"His old lodging which he says you know. He wishes you to be secret. He says not to bring any person."

"Well, you can come, Christophe. You're not a person."

The boy grins.

He is apprehensive; does not quite like the thought of the abbey precincts, the drunken crowds at dusk, without somebody to watch his back. Unfortunately, a man cannot have two fronts.

❖

They have almost reached Cranmer's lodging when fatigue enwraps his shoulders, an iron cloak. "Pause for a moment," he says to Christophe. He has hardly slept these last nights. He takes a breath, in shadow; here it is cold, and as he passes into the cloisters he is dipped in night. The rooms around are shuttered, empty, no sound from within. From behind him, an inchoate shouting from the Westminster streets, like the cries of those lost after a battle.

Cranmer looks up; he is already at his desk. "These are days we will never forget," he says. "No one who has missed it would believe it. The king spoke warm words in your praise today. I think it was intended I should convey them."

"I wonder why I ever gave any thought to the cost of brick-making for the Tower. It seems such a small item now. And tomorrow the jousts. Will you be there? My boy Richard is listed for the bouts on foot, fighting in single combat."

"He will prevail," Christophe declares. "Biff, and one is flat, never to rise again."

"Hush," Cranmer says. "You are not here, child. Cromwell, please."

He opens a low door at the back of the chamber. He dips his head, and framed by the doorway in the half-light he sees a table, a stool, and on the stool a woman sitting, young, tranquil, her head bowed over a book. She looks up. *"Ich bitte Sie, ich brauch eine Kerze."*

"Christophe, a candle for her."

The book before her he recognizes; it is a tract of Luther's. "May I?" he says, and picks it up.

He finds himself reading. His mind leaps along the lines. Is she some fugitive Cranmer is sheltering? Does he know the cost if she is taken? He has time to read half a page, before the archbishop trickles in, like a late apology. "This woman is . . . ?"

Cranmer says, "Margarete. My wife."

"Dear God." He slams Luther down on the table. "What have you done? Where did you find her? Germany, evidently. This is why you were slow to return. I see it now. Why?"

Cranmer says meekly, "I could not help it."

"Do you know what the king will do to you when he finds you out? The master executioner of Paris has devised a machine, with a counterweighted beam—shall I draw it for you?—which when a heretic is burned dips him into the fire and lifts him out again, so that the people can see the stages of his agony. Now Henry will be wanting one. Or he will get some device to tease your head off your shoulders, over a period of forty days."

The young woman looks up. *"Mein Onkel—"*

"Who is that?"

She names a theologian, Andreas Osiander: a Nuremberger, a Lutheran. Her uncle and his friends, she says, and the learned men of her town, they believe—

"It may be the belief in your country, madam, that a pastor should have a wife, but not here. Did Dr. Cranmer not warn you of this?"

"Please," Cranmer begs, "tell me what she is saying. Does she blame me? Is she wishing herself at home?"

"No. No, she says you are kind. What took hold of you, man?"

"I told you I had a secret."

So you did. Down the side of the page. "But to keep her here, under the king's nose?"

"I have kept her in the country. But I could not refuse her wish to see the celebrations."

"She has been out on the streets?"

"Why not? No one knows her."

True. The protection of the stranger in the city; one young woman in a cheerful cap and gown, one pair of eyes among the thousands of eyes: you can hide a tree in a forest. Cranmer approaches him. He holds out his hands, so lately smeared with the sacred oil; fine hands, long fingers, the pale rectangles of his palms crossed and recrossed by news of sea voyages and alliances. "I asked you here as my friend. For I count you my chief friend, Cromwell, in this world."

So there is nothing to do, in friendship, but to take these bony digits in his own. "Very well. We will find a way. We will keep your lady secret. I only wonder that you did not leave her with her own family, till we can turn the king our way."

Margarete is watching them, blue eyes flitting from face to face. She stands up. She pushes the table away from her; he watches her do it, and his heart lurches. Because he has seen a woman do this before, his own wife, and he has seen how she puts her palms down on the surface, to haul herself up. Margarete is tall, and the bulge of her belly juts above the tabletop.

"Jesus," he says.

"I hope for a daughter," the archbishop says.

"About when?" he asks Margarete.

Instead of answering, she takes his hand. She places it on her belly, pressing it down with her own. At one with the celebrations, the child is dancing: spanoletta, Estampie Royal. This is a perhaps a foot; this is a fist. "You need a friend," he says. "A woman with you."

Cranmer follows him as he pounds out of the room. "About John Frith . . ." he says.

"What?"

"Since he was brought to Croydon, I have seen him three times in private conversation. A worthy young man, a most gentle creature. I have spent hours, I regret not a second of it, but I cannot turn him from his path."

"He should have run into the woods. That was his path."

"We do not all . . ." Cranmer drops his gaze. "Forgive me, but we do not all see as many paths as you."

"So you must hand him to Stokesley now, because he was taken in Stokesley's diocese."

"I never thought, when the king gave me this dignity, when he insisted I occupy this seat, that among my first actions would be to come against a young man like John Frith, and to try to argue him out of his faith."

Welcome to this world below. "I cannot much longer delay," Cranmer says.

"Nor can your wife."

❖

The streets around Austin Friars are almost deserted. Bonfires are starting up across the city, and the stars are obscured by smoke. His guards are on the gate: sober, he is pleased to note. He stops for a word; there is an art to being in a hurry but not showing it. Then he walks in and says, "I want Mistress Barre."

Most of his household have gone to see the bonfires, and they will be out till midnight, dancing. They have permission to do this; who should celebrate the new queen, if they do not? John Page comes out: something want doing, sir? William Brabazon, pen in hand, one of Wolsey's old crew: the king's business never stops. Thomas Avery, fresh from his accounts: there's always money flowing in, money flowing out. When Wolsey fell, his household deserted him, but Thomas Cromwell's servants stayed to see him through.

A door bangs overhead. Rafe comes down, boots clattering, hair sticking up. He looks flushed and confused. "Sir?"

"I don't want you. Is Helen here, do you know?"

"Why?"

At that moment Helen appears. She is fastening up her hair under a clean cap. "I need you to pack a bag and come with me."

"For how long, sir?"

"I cannot say."

"To go out of London?"

He thinks, I'll make some arrangement, the wives and daughters of men in the city, discreet women, they will find her servants, and a midwife, some competent woman who will put Cranmer's child into his hands. "Perhaps for a short time."

"The children—"

"We will take care of your children."

She nods. Speeds away. You wish you had men in your service as swift as she. Rafe calls after her. "Helen . . ." He looks irate. "Where is she going, sir? You can't just drag her off into the night."

"Oh, I can," he says mildly.

"I need to know."

"Believe me, you don't." He relents. "Or if you do, this is not the time—Rafe, I'm tired. I'm not going to argue."

He could perhaps leave it to Christophe, and some of the more unquestioning members of his household, to take Helen from the warmth of Austin Friars to the chill of the abbey precincts; or he could leave it till the morning. But his mind is alive to the loneliness of Cranmer's wife, the strangeness of the city *en fête*, the deserted aspect of Cannon Row, where even in the shadow of the abbey robbers are bound to lurk. Even in the time of King Richard the district was home to gangs of thieves, who issued out by night at their pleasure, and when the dawn came swarmed back to claim the privilege of sanctuary, and no doubt to share the spoils with the clergy. I shall clean out that lot, he thinks. My men will be after them like ferrets down a hole.

Midnight: stone exhales a mossy breath, flagstones are slippery with the city's exhalations. Helen puts her hand into his. A servant admits them, eyes downcast; he slips him a coin to raise his eyes no higher. No sign of the archbishop: good. A lamp is lit. A door pushed ajar. Cranmer's wife is lying in a little cot. He says to Helen, "Here is a lady who needs your compassion. You see her situation. She does not speak English. In any case, you need not ask her name."

"Here is Helen," he says. "She has two children of her own. She will help you."

Mistress Cranmer, her eyes closed, merely nods and smiles. But when Helen places a gentle hand on her, she reaches out and strokes it.

"Where is your husband?"

"Er betet."

"I hope he is praying for me."

❖

The day of Frith's burning he is hunting with the king over the country outside Guildford. It is raining before dawn, a gusty, tugging wind bending the treetops: raining all over England, soaking the crops in the fields. Henry's mood is not to be dented. He sits down to write to Anne, left back at Windsor. After he has twirled his quill in his fingers, turned his paper about and about, he loses the will: you write it for me, Cromwell. I'll tell you what to put.

A tailor's apprentice is going to the stake with Frith: Andrew Hewitt.

Katherine used to have relics brought to her, Henry says, for when she was in labor with her children. A girdle of the Blessed Virgin. I hired it.

I don't think the queen will want that.

And special prayers to St. Margaret. These are women's things.

Best left to them, sir.

Later he will hear that Frith and the boy suffered, the wind blowing the flames away from them repeatedly. Death is a japester; call him and he will not come. He is a joker and he lurks in the dark, a black cloth over his face.

There are cases of the sweat in London. The king, who embodies all his people, has all the symptoms every day.

Now Henry stares at the rain falling. Cheering himself up, he says, it may abate, Jupiter is rising. Now, tell her, tell the queen . . .

He waits, his pen poised.

No, that's enough. Give it to me, Thomas, I will sign it.

He waits to see if the king will draw a heart. But the frivolities of courtship are over. Marriage is a serious business. *Henricus Rex.*

I think I have a stomach cramp, the king says. I think I have a headache. I feel queasy, and there are black spots before my eyes, that's a sign, isn't it?

If Your Majesty will rest a little, he says. And take courage.

You know what they say about the sweat. Merry at breakfast, dead by dinner. But do you know it can kill you in two hours?

He says, I have heard that some people die of fear.

By afternoon the sun is struggling out. Henry, laughing, spurs away his hunter under the dripping trees. At Smithfield Frith is being shoveled up, his youth, his grace, his learning and his beauty: a compaction of mud, grease, charred bone.

The king has two bodies. The first exists within the limits of his physical being; you can measure it, and often Henry does, his waist, his calf, his other parts. The second is his princely double, free-floating, untethered, weightless, which may be in more than one place at a time. Henry may be hunting in the forest, while his princely double makes laws. One fights, one prays for peace. One is wreathed in the mystery of his kingship: one is eating a duckling with sweet green peas.

The Pope now says his marriage to Anne is void. He will excommunicate him if he does not return to Katherine. Christendom will slough him off, body and soul, and his subjects will rise up and eject him, into ignominy, exile; no Christian hearth will shelter him, and when he dies his corpse will be dug with animal bones into a common pit.

He has taught Henry to call the Pope "the Bishop of Rome." To laugh when his name is mentioned. If it is uncertain laughter, it is better than his former genuflection.

Cranmer has invited the prophetess, Elizabeth Barton, to a meeting at his house in Kent. She has seen a vision of Mary, the former princess, as queen? Yes. Of Gertrude, Lady Exeter, as queen? Yes. He says gently, both cannot be true. The Maid says, I only report what I see. He writes that she is bouncing and full of confidence; she is used to dealing with archbishops, and she takes him for another Warham, hanging on her every word.

She is a mouse under the cat's paw.

Queen Katherine is on the move, her household much reduced, to the Bishop of Lincoln's palace at Buckden, an old redbrick house with a great hall and gardens that run out into copses and fields and so into the fenland landscape. September will bring her the first fruits of autumn, as October will bring the mists.

The king demands that Katherine give up for his coming child the robes in which the child Mary was christened. When he hears Katherine's answer, he, Thomas Cromwell, laughs. Nature wronged Katherine, he says, in not making her a man; she would have surpassed all the heroes of antiquity. A paper is put before her, in which she is addressed as "Princess Dowager"; shocked, they show him how her pen has ripped through it, as she scores out the new title.

Rumors crop up in the short summer nights. Dawn finds them like mushrooms in the damp grass. Members of Thomas Cromwell's household have been seeking a midwife in the small hours of the morning. He is hiding a woman at some country house of his, a foreign woman who has given him a daughter. Whatever you do, he says to Rafe, don't defend my honor. I have women like that all over the place.

They will believe it, Rafe says. The word in the city is that Thomas Cromwell has a prodigious . . .

Memory, he says. I have a very large ledger. A huge filing system, in which are recorded (under their name, and also under their offense) the details of people who have cut across me.

All the astrologers say that the king will have a son. But you are better not to deal with these people. A man came to him, months ago, offering to make the king a philosopher's stone, and when he was told to make himself scarce he turned rude and contrary, as these alchemists do, and now gives it out that the king will die this year. Waiting in Saxony, he says, is the eldest son of the late King Edward. You thought him a rattling skeleton beneath the pavements of the Tower, only his murderers know where: you are deceived, for he is a man grown, and ready to claim his kingdom.

He counts it up: King Edward V, were he living, would be sixty-four this November coming. He's a bit late to the fight, he says.

He puts the alchemist in the Tower, to rethink his position.

No more from Paris. Whatever Maître Guilio's up to, he's very quiet about it.

Hans Holbein says, Thomas, I've got your hands done but I haven't paid much attention to your face. I promise this autumn I'll finish you off.

Suppose within every book there is another book, and within every letter on every page another volume constantly unfolding; but these volumes take no space on the desk. Suppose knowledge could be reduced to a quintessence, held within a picture, a sign, held within a place which is no place. Suppose the human skull were to become capacious, spaces opening inside it, humming chambers like beehives.

Lord Mountjoy, Katherine's Chamberlain, has sent him a list of all the necessities for the confinement of a Queen of England. It amuses him, the smooth and civil handover; the court and its ceremonies roll on, whoever the personnel, but it is clear Lord Mountjoy takes him as the man in charge of everything now.

He goes down to Greenwich and refurbishes the apartments, ready for Anne. Proclamations (undated) are prepared, to go out to the people of England and the rulers of Europe, announcing the birth of a prince. Just leave a little gap, he suggests, at the end of "prince," so if need be you can squash in . . . But they look at him as if he's a traitor, so he leaves off.

When a woman withdraws to give birth the sun may be shining but the shutters of her room are closed so she can make her own weather. She is kept in the dark so she can dream. Her dreams drift her far away, from terra firma to a marshy tract of land, to a landing stage, to a river where a mist closes over the farther bank, and earth and sky are inseparate; there she must embark toward life and death, a muffled figure in the stern directing the oars. In this vessel prayers are said that men never hear. Bargains are struck between a woman and her God. The river is tidal, and between one feather-stroke and the next, her tide may turn.

On August 26, 1533, a procession escorts the queen to her sealed rooms at Greenwich. Her husband kisses her, adieu and bon voyage, and she neither smiles nor speaks. She is very pale, very grand, a tiny jeweled head balanced on the swaying tent of her body, her steps small and circumspect, a prayer book in her hands. On the quay she turns her head: one lingering glance. She sees him; she sees the archbishop. One last look and then, her women steadying her elbows, she puts her foot into the boat.

II

Devil's Spit

t is magnificent. At the moment of impact, the king's eyes are open, his body braced for the *atteint;* he takes the blow perfectly, its force absorbed by a body securely armored, moving in the right direction, moving at the right speed. His color does not alter. His voice does not shake.

"Healthy?" he says. "Then I thank God for his favor to us. As I thank you, my lords, for this comfortable intelligence."

He thinks, Henry has been rehearsing. I suppose we all have.

The king walks away toward his own rooms. Says over his shoulder, "Call her Elizabeth. Cancel the jousts."

A bleat from a Boleyn: "The other ceremonies as planned?"

No reply. Cranmer says, all as planned, till we hear different. I am to stand godfather to the . . . the princess. He falters. He can hardly believe it. For himself, he ordered a daughter, and he got a daughter. His eyes follow Henry's retreating back. "He did not ask after the queen. He did not ask how she does."

"It hardly matters, does it?" Edward Seymour, saying brutally what everyone is thinking.

Then Henry, on his long solitary walk, stops, turns back. "My lord archbishop. Cromwell. But you only."

In Henry's closet: "Had you imagined this?"

Some would smile. He does not. The king drops into a chair. The urge arises to put a hand on his shoulder, as one does for any inconsolable being. He resists it; simply folds his fingers, protectively, into the fist which holds the king's heart. "One day we will make a great marriage for her."

"Poor scrap. Her own mother will wish her away."

"Your Majesty is young enough," Cranmer says. "The queen is strong and her family are fertile. You can get another child soon. And perhaps God intends some peculiar blessing by this princess."

"My dear friend, I am sure you are right." Henry sounds dubious, but he looks around to take strength from his surroundings, as if God might have left some friendly message written on the wall: though there is only precedent for the hostile kind. He takes a breath and stands up and shakes out his sleeves. He smiles: and one can catch in flight, as if it were a bird with a strong-beating heart, the act of will that transforms a desolate wretch into the beacon of his nation.

He whispers to Cranmer later, "It was like watching Lazarus get up."

Soon Henry is striding about the palace at Greenwich, putting the celebrations under way. We are young enough, he says, and next time it will be a boy. One day we will make a great marriage for her. Believe me, God intends some peculiar blessing by this princess.

Boleyn faces brighten. It's Sunday, four in the afternoon. He goes and laughs a bit at the clerks who have "prince" written on their proclamations, and who now have to squeeze extra letters in, then he goes back to working out the expenses for the new princess's household. He has advised that Gertrude, Lady Exeter, be among the child's godparents. Why should only the Maid have a vision of her? It will do her good to be seen by the whole court, smiling a forced smile and holding Anne's baby at the font.

❖

The Maid herself, brought to London, is kept in a private house, where the beds are soft and the voices around her, the voices of Cromwell women, hardly disturb her prayers; where the key is turned in the oiled lock with a click as small as the snap of a bird's bone. "Does she eat?" he asks Mercy, and she says, she eats as heartily as you: well, no, Thomas, perhaps not quite so heartily as you.

"I wonder what happened to her project of living on the Communion host?"

"They can't see her dining now, can they? Those priests and monks who set her on this course."

Away from their scrutiny, the nun has started to act like an ordinary woman, acknowledging the simple claims of her body, like anyone who wants to live; but it may be too late. He likes it that Mercy doesn't say, ahh, the poor harmless soul. That she is not harmless by nature is clear when they have her over to Lambeth Palace to question her. You would think Lord Chancellor Audley, his chain of office hung about his splendid person, would be enough to subdue any country girl. Throw in the Archbishop of Canterbury, and you would imagine a young nun might feel some awe. Not a bit of it. The Maid treats Cranmer with condescension—as if he were a novice in the religious life. When he challenges her on any point and says, "How do you know that?" she smiles pityingly and says, "An angel told me."

Audley brings Richard Riche with him to their second session, to take notes for them, and put any points that occur to him. He is Sir Richard now, knighted and promoted to Solicitor General. In his student days he was known for a sharp slanderous tongue, for irreverence to his seniors, for drinking and gaming for high stakes. But who would hold up his head, if people judged us by what we were like at twenty? Riche turns out to have a talent for drafting legislation which is second only to his own. His features, beneath his soft fair hair, are pinched with concentration; the boys call him Sir Purse. You'd never think, to see him precisely laying out his papers, that he was once the great disgrace of the Inner Temple. He says so, in an undertone, teasing him, while they wait for the girl to be brought in. Well, Master Cromwell! Riche says; what about you and that abbess in Halifax?

He knows better than to deny it: or any of those stories the cardinal told about him. "Oh, that," he says. "It was nothing—they expect it in Yorkshire."

He is afraid the girl may have caught the tail end of the exchange, because today, as she takes the chair they have placed for her, she gives him a particularly hard stare. She arranges her skirts, folds her arms and waits for them to entertain her. His niece Alice Wellyfed sits on a stool by the door: just there in case of fainting, or other upset. Though a glance at the Maid tells you she is no more likely to faint than Audley is.

"Shall I?" Riche says. "Start?"

"Oh, why not?" Audley says. "You are young and hearty."

"These prophecies of yours—you are always changing the timing of the disaster you foresee, but I understood you said that the king would not reign one month after he married Lady Anne. Well, the months have passed, Lady Anne is crowned queen, and has given the king a fine daughter. So what do you say now?"

"I say in the eyes of the world he seems to be king. But in the eyes of God," she shrugs, "not anymore. He is no more the real king than he," she nods toward Cranmer, "is really archbishop."

Riche is not to be sidetracked. "So it would be justified to raise rebellion against him? To depose him? To assassinate him? To put another in his place?"

"Well, what do you think?"

"And among the claimants your choice has fallen on the Courtenay family, not the Poles. Henry, Marquis of Exeter. Not Henry, Lord Montague."

"Or," he says sympathetically, "do you get them mixed up?"

"Of course not." She flushes. "I have met both those gentlemen."

Riche makes a note.

Audley says, "Now Courtenay, that is Lord Exeter, descends from a daughter of King Edward. Lord Montague descends from King Edward's brother, the Duke of Clarence. How do you weigh their claims? Because if we are talking of true kings and false kings, some say Edward was a bastard his mother got by an archer. I wonder if you can cast any light?"

"Why would she?" Riche says.

Audley rolls his eyes. "Because she talks to the saints on high. They'd know."

He looks at Riche and it is as if he can read his thoughts: Niccolò's book says, the wise prince exterminates the envious, and if I, Riche, were king, those claimants and their families would be dead. The girl is braced for the next question: how is it she has seen two queens in her vision? "I suppose it will sort itself out," he says, "in the fighting? It's good to have a few kings and queens in reserve, if you're going to start a war in a country."

"It is not necessary to have a war," the nun says. Oh? Sir Purse sits up: this is new. "God is sending a plague on England instead. Henry will be dead in six months. So will she, Thomas Boleyn's daughter."

"And me?"

"You too."

"And all in this room? Except you, of course? All including Alice Wellyfed, who never did you harm?"

"All the women of your house are heretics, and the plague will rot them body and soul."

"And what about the princess Elizabeth?"

She turns in her seat, to aim her words at Cranmer. "They say when you christened her you warmed the water to spare her a shock. You should have poured it boiling."

Oh, Christ in Heaven, Riche says. He throws his pen down. He is a tender young father, with a daughter in the cradle.

He drops a consoling hand on his, the Solicitor General's. You would think Alice would need consoling; but when the Maid condemned her to death, he had looked down the room at his niece to note that her face was the perfect picture of derision. He says to Riche, "She didn't think it up herself, the boiling water. It is a thing they are saying on the streets."

Cranmer huddles into himself; the Maid has bruised him, she has scored a point. He, Cromwell, says, "I saw the princess yesterday. She is thriving, in spite of her ill-wishers." His voice suggests calm: we must get the archbishop back in the saddle. He turns to the Maid: "Tell me: did you locate the cardinal?"

"What?" Audley says.

"Dame Elizabeth said she would look out for my old master, on one of her excursions to Heaven, Hell and Purgatory, and I offered to pay her traveling expenses on the occasion. I gave her people a down payment—I hope we see some progress?"

"Wolsey would have had another fifteen years of life," the girl says. He nods: he has said the same himself. "But then God cut him off, as an example. I have seen devils disputing for his soul."

"You know the result?" he asks.

"There is no result. I searched for him all over. I thought God had extinguished him. Then one night I saw him." A long, tactical hesitation. "I saw his soul seated among the unborn."

There is a silence. Cranmer shrinks in his seat. Riche gently nibbles the end of his pen. Audley twists a button on his sleeve, round and round till the thread tightens.

"If you like I can pray for him," the Maid says. "God usually answers my requests."

"Formerly, when you had your advisers about you, Father Bocking and Father Gold and Father Risby and the rest, you would start bargaining at this point. I would propose a further sum for your goodwill, and your spiritual directors would drive it up."

"Wait." Cranmer lays a hand over his rib cage. "Can we go back? Lord Chancellor?"

"We can go in any direction you choose, my lord archbishop. Three times round the mulberry bush . . ."

"You see devils?"

She nods.

"They appear how?"

"Birds."

"A relief," Audley says drily.

"No, sir. Lucifer stinks. His claws are deformed. He comes as a cockerel smeared in blood and shit."

He looks up at Alice. He is ready to send her out. He thinks, what has been done to this woman?

Cranmer says, "That must be disagreeable for you. But it is a characteristic of devils, I understand, to show themselves in more than one way."

"Yes. They do it to deceive you. He comes as a young man."

"Indeed?"

"Once he brought a woman. To my cell at night." She pauses. "Pawing her."

Riche: "He is known to have no shame."

"No more than you."

"And what then, Dame Elizabeth? After the pawing?"

"Pulled up her skirts."

"And she didn't resist?" Riche says. "You surprise me."

Audley says, "Prince Lucifer, I don't doubt he has a way with him."

"Before my eyes, he had to do with her, on my bed."

Riche makes a note. "This woman, did you know her?" No answer. "And the devil did not try the same with you? You can speak freely. It will not be held against you."

"He came to sweet-talk me. Swaggering in his blue silk coat, it's the best he has. And new hose with diamonds down his legs."

"Diamonds down his legs," he says. "Now that must have been a temptation?"

She shakes her head.

"But you are a fine young woman—good enough for any man, I'd say."

She looks up; a flicker of a smile. "I am not for Master Lucifer."

"What did he say when you refused him?"

"He asked me to marry him." Audley puts his head in his hands. "I said I was vowed to chastity."

"Was he not angry when you would not consent?"

"Oh yes. He spat in my face."

"I would expect no better of him," Riche says.

"I wiped his spit off with a napkin. It's black. It has the stench of Hell."

"What is that like?"

"Like something rotting."

"Where is it now, the napkin? I suppose you didn't send it to the laundry?"

"Dom Edward has it."

"Does he show it to people? For money?"

"For offerings."

"For money."

Cranmer takes his face from his hands. "Shall we pause?"

"A quarter hour?" Riche says.

Audley: "I told you he was young and hearty."

"Perhaps we will meet tomorrow," Cranmer says. "I need to pray. And a quarter of an hour will not do it."

"But tomorrow is Sunday," the nun says. "There was a man who went out hunting on a Sunday and he fell down a bottomless pit into Hell. Imagine that."

"How was it bottomless," Riche asks, "if Hell was there to receive him?"

"I wish I were going hunting," Audley says. "Christ knows, I'd take a chance on it."

Alice rises from her stool and signals for her escort. The Maid gets to her feet. She is smiling broadly. She has made the archbishop flinch, and himself grow cold, and the Solicitor General all but weep with her talk of scalded babies. She thinks she is winning; but she is losing, losing, losing all the time. Alice puts a gentle hand on her arm, but the Maid shakes it off.

Outside, Richard Riche says, "We should burn her."

Cranmer says, "Much as we may mislike her talk of the late cardinal appearing to her, and devils in her bedchamber, she speaks in this way because she has been taught to ape the claims of certain nuns who have gone before her, nuns whom Rome is pleased to recognize as saints. I cannot convict them of heresy, retrospectively. Nor have I evidence to try her for heresy."

"Burned for treason, I meant."

It is the woman's penalty; where a man is half-hanged and castrated, then slowly gutted by the executioner.

He says, "There is no overt action. She has only expressed an intent."

"Intent to raise rebellion, to depose the king, should that not be treason? Words have been construed as treasons, there are precedents, you know them."

"I should be astonished," Audley says, "if they have escaped Cromwell's attention."

It is as if they can smell the devil's spit; they are almost jostling each other to get into the air, which is mild, damp: a faint scent of leaves, a green-gold, rustling light. He can see that, in the years ahead, treason will take new and various forms. When the last treason act was made, no one could circulate their words in a printed book or bill, because printed books were not thought of. He feels a moment of jealousy toward the dead, to those who served kings in slower times than these; nowadays the products of some bought or poisoned brain can be disseminated through Europe in a month.

"I think new laws are needed," Riche says.

"I have it in hand."

"And I think this woman is too leniently kept. We are too soft. We are just playing with her."

Cranmer walks away, shoulders stooped, his trailing habit brushing up the leaves. Audley turns to him, bright and resolute, a man keen to change the subject. "So, the princess, you say she was well?"

❖

The princess, unswaddled, had been placed on cushions at Anne's feet: an ugly, purple, grizzling knot of womankind, with an upstanding ruff of pale hair and a habit of kicking up her gown as if to display her most unfortunate feature. It seems stories have been put about that Anne's child was born with teeth, has six fingers on each hand, and is furred all over like a monkey, so her father has shown her off naked to the ambassadors, and her mother is keeping her on display in the hope of countering the rumors. The king has chosen Hatfield for her seat, and Anne says, "It seems to me waste might be saved, and the proper order of things asserted, if Spanish Mary's household were broken up and she were to become a member of the household of the princess Elizabeth my daughter."

"In the capacity of . . . ?" The child is quiet; only, he notes, because she has crammed a fist into her maw, and is cannibalizing herself.

"In the capacity of my daughter's servant. What else should she be? There can be no pretense at equality. Mary is a bastard."

The brief respite is over; the princess sets up a screech that would bring out the dead. Anne's glance slides away sideways, and a sideways grin of infatuation takes over her whole face, and she leans down toward her daughter, but at once women swoop, flapping and bustling; the screaming creature is plucked up, wrapped up, swept away, and the queen's eyes follow pitifully as the fruit of her womb exits, in procession. He says gently, "I think she was hungry."

❖

Saturday evening: supper at Austin Friars for Stephen Vaughan, so often in transit: William Butts, Hans, Kratzer, Call-Me-Risley. Conversation is in various tongues and Rafe Sadler translates adroitly, smoothly, his head turning from side to side: high topics and low, statecraft and gossip, Zwingli's theology, Cranmer's wife. About the latter, it has not been possible to suppress the talk at the Steelyard and in the city; Vaughan says, "Can Henry know and not know?"

"That is perfectly possible. He is a prince of very large capacities."

Larger by the day, Wriothesley says, laughing; Dr. Butts says, he is one of those men who must be active, and recently his leg is troubling him, that old injury; but think, is it likely that a man who has not spared himself on the hunting field and in the tilt yard should not get some injury by the time he is the king's age? He is forty-three this year, you know, and I should be glad, Kratzer, to have your view on what the planets suggest, for the later years of a man whose chart is so dominated by air and fire; by the by, did I not always warn of his moon in Aries (rash and hasty planet) in the house of marriage?

He says, impatient, we heard very little about the Aries moon when he was settled with Katherine for twenty years. It is not the stars that make us, Dr. Butts, it is circumstance and *necessità*, the choices we make under pressure; our virtues make us, but virtues are not enough, we must deploy our vices at times. Or don't you agree?

He beckons to Christophe to fill their glasses. They talk about the Mint, where Vaughan is to have a position; about Calais, where Honor Lisle seems more busy in affairs than her husband, the Governor. He thinks about Guilio Camillo in Paris, pacing and fretting between the wooden walls of his memory machine, while knowledge grows unseen and of itself in its cavities and concealed inner spaces. He thinks of the Holy Maid—by now established as not holy, and not a maid—no doubt at this moment sitting down to supper with his nieces. He thinks of his fellow interrogators: Cranmer on his knees in prayer, Sir Purse frowning over the day's transcripts, Audley—what will the Lord Chancellor be doing? Polishing his chain of office, he decides. He thinks of saying to Vaughan, below the conversation, was there not a girl in your house called Jenneke? What happened to her? But Wriothesley breaks in on his train of thought. "When shall we see my master's portrait? You have been at work on it a while, Hans, it is time it came home. We are keen to see what you have made of him."

"He is still busy with the French envoys," Kratzer says. "De Dinteville wants to take his picture home with him when he gets his recall . . ."

There is some laughter at the expense of the French ambassador, always doing his packing and having to undo it again, as his master commands him to stay where he is. "Anyway, I hope he does not take it too quick," Hans says, "because I mean to show it and get commissions off it. I want the king to see it, indeed I want to paint the king, do you think I can?"

"I will ask him," he says easily. "Let me choose the time." He looks down the table to see Vaughan glow with pride, like Jupiter on a painted ceiling.

After they get up from the table his guests eat ginger comfits and candied fruits, and Kratzer makes some drawings. He draws the sun and the planets moving in their orbits according to the plan he has heard of from Father Copernicus. He shows how the world is turning on its axis, and nobody in the room denies it. Under your feet you can feel the tug and heft of it, the rocks groaning to tear away from their beds, the oceans tilting and slapping at their shores, the giddy lurch of

Alpine passes, the forests of Germany ripping at their roots to be free. The world is not what it was when he and Vaughan were young, it is not what it was even in the cardinal's day.

The company has left when his niece Alice comes in, past his watchmen, wrapped up in a cloak; she is escorted by Thomas Rotherham, one of his wards who lives in the house. "Never fear, sir," she says, "Jo is sitting up with Dame Elizabeth, and nothing gets by Jo."

Does it not? That child perpetually in tears over her spoiled sewing? That grubby little girl sometimes found rolling under a table with a wet dog, or chasing a peddler down the street? "I would like to talk to you," Alice says, "if you have time for me?" Of course, he says, taking her arm, folding her hand in his; Thomas Rotherham turns pale—which puzzles him—and slides away.

Alice sits down in his office. She yawns. "Excuse me—but she is hard work and the hours are long." She tucks a strand of hair into her hood. "She is ready to break," she says. "She is brave to your faces, but she cries at night, because she knows she is a fraud. And even while she is crying, she peeps under her eyelids to see what effect she is making."

"I want it over with now," he says. "For all the trouble she has caused, we do not find ourselves an edifying spectacle, three or four of us learned in the law and the scriptures, convening day after day to try to trip one chit of a girl."

"Why did you not bring her in before?"

"I didn't want her to shut the prophecy shop. I wanted to see who would come to her whistle. And Lady Exeter has, and Bishop Fisher. And a score of monks and foolish priests whose names I know, and a hundred perhaps whose names I don't know yet."

"And will the king kill them all?"

"Very few, I hope."

"You incline him to mercy?"

"I incline him to patience."

"What will happen to her? Dame Eliza?"

"We will frame charges."

"She will not go in a dungeon?"

"No, I shall move the king to treat her with consideration, he is always—he is usually—respectful of any person in the religious life. But Alice," he sees that she is dissolving into tears, "I think this has all been too much for you."

"No, not at all. We are soldiers in your army."

"She has not been frightening you, talking about the devil's wicked offers?"

"No, it's Thomas Rotherham's offers . . . he wants to marry me."

"So that's what's wrong with him!" He is amused. "Could he not ask himself?"

"He thought you would look at him in that way you have . . . as if you were weighing him."

Like a clipped coin? "Alice, he owns a fat slice of Bedfordshire, and his manors prosper very nicely since I have been looking after them. And if you like each other, how could I object? You are a clever girl, Alice. Your mother," he says softly, "and your father, they would be very pleased with you, if they were able to see."

This is why Alice is crying. She must ask her uncle's permission because this last year has left her orphaned. The day his sister Bet died, he was up-country with the king. Henry was receiving no messengers from London for fear of contagion, so she was dead and buried before he knew she was ill. When the news crept through at last, the king spoke to him with tenderness, a hand on his arm; he spoke of his own sister, the silver-haired lady like a princess in a book, removed from this life to gardens of Paradise, he had claimed, reserved for royal dead; for it is impossible, he had said, to think of that lady in any low place, any place of darkness, the barred charnel house of Purgatory with its flying cinders and sulfur reek, its boiling tar and roiling clouds of sleet.

"Alice," he says, "dry your tears, find Thomas Rotherham, and end his pain. You need not come to Lambeth tomorrow. Jo can come, if she is as formidable as you say."

Alice turns in the doorway. "I will see her again, though? Eliza Barton? I should like to see her before . . ."

Before they kill her. Alice is no innocent in this world. Just as well.

Look how the innocent end; used by the sin-sodden and the cynical, pulped to their purpose and ground under their heels.

He hears Alice running upstairs. He hears her calling, Thomas, Thomas . . . It is a name that will bring half the house out, tumbling from their bedside prayers, from their very beds: yes, are you looking for me? He pulls his furred gown around him and goes outside to look at the stars. The precincts of his house are kept well lit; the gardens by torchlight are the site of excavations, trenches dug out for foundations, earth banked up into barrows and mounds. The vast timber frame of a new wing juts against the sky; in the middle distance, his new planting, a city orchard where Gregory, one day, will pick the fruit, and Alice, and Alice's sons. He has fruit trees already, but he wants cherries and plums like the ones he has eaten abroad, and late pears to use in the Tuscan fashion, to match their crisp metallic flesh with winter's salt cod. Then next year he means to make another garden at the hunting lodge he has at Canonbury, make it a retreat from the city, a summer-house in the fields. He has work in hand at Stepney too, expansion; John Williamson is looking after the builders for him. Strange, but like a miracle the family's prosperity seems to have cured him of his killing cough. I like John Williamson, he thinks, why ever did I, with his wife . . . Beyond the gate, cries and shouts, London never still or quiet; so many in the graveyards, but the living parading in the streets, drunken fighters pitching from London Bridge, sanctuary men steal-ing out to thieve, Southwark whores bawling out their prices like butchers selling dead flesh.

He goes inside. His desk draws him back. In a small chest he keeps his wife's book, her book of hours. Inside it are prayers on loose papers which she has inserted. Say the name of Christ a thousand times and it keeps fever away. But it doesn't, does it? The fever comes anyway and kills you. Beside the name of her first husband, Thomas Williams, she has written his own name, but she never, he notices, crossed Tom Wil-liams out. She has recorded the births of her children, and he has writ-ten in beside them the dates of his daughters' deaths. He finds a space where he will note the marriages of his sisters' children: Richard to Frances Murfyn, Alice to his ward.

He thinks, perhaps I have got over Liz. It didn't seem possible that weight would ever shift from inside his chest, but it has lightened enough to let him get on with his life. I could marry again, he thinks, but is this not what people are always telling me? He says to himself, I never think of Johane Williamson now: not Johane as she was for me. Her body once had special meaning, but that meaning is now un-made; the flesh created beneath his fingertips, hallowed by desire, be-comes just the ordinary substance of a city wife, a fading woman with no particular looks. He says to himself, I never think of Anselma now; she is just the woman in the tapestry, the woman in the weave.

He reaches for his pen. I have got over Liz, he says to himself. Surely? He hesitates, the quill in his hand, weighted by ink. He holds the pages down flat, and strikes out the name of her first husband. He thinks, I've meant to do that for years.

It is late. Upstairs he closes the shutter, where the moon gapes in hollow-eyed, like a drunk lost in the street. Christophe, folding gar-ments, says, "Is there *loups*? In this kingdom?"

"I think the wolves all died when the great forests were cut down. That howling you hear is only the Londoners."

❖

Sunday: in rose-tinted light they set out from Austin Friars, his men in their new livery of gray marbled cloth collecting the party from the city house where the nun has been held. It would be convenient, he thinks, if I had Master Secretary's barge, instead of making ad hoc ar-rangements when we have to cross the river. He has already heard Mass; Cranmer insists they all hear another. He watches the girl and sees her tears flow. Alice is right; she is at the end of her invention.

By nine o'clock she is unwinding the threads she has spent years rav-eling up. She confesses in style, so hard and fast that Riche can hardly keep track, and she appeals to them as men of the world, as people with their way to make: "You know how it is. You mention something and people are at you, what do you mean, what do you mean? You say you've had a vision and they won't leave you alone."

"You can't disappoint people?" he says; she agrees, that's it, you can't. Once you start you have to keep going. If you try to go back they'll slaughter you.

She confesses that her visions are inventions. She never spoke to heavenly persons. Or raised the dead; that was all a fraud. She never had a hand in miracles. The letter from Mary Magdalene, Father Bocking wrote it, and a monk put gilding on the letters, in a minute she'll think of his name. The angels came out of her own invention, she seemed to see them but she knows now that they were just flashes of light against the wall. The voices she heard were not their voices, they were not distinct voices at all, just the sounds of her sisters singing in the chapel, or a woman in the road crying because she has been beaten and robbed, or perhaps the meaningless clatter of dishes from the kitchen; and those groans and cries, that seemed to come from the throats of the damned, it was someone above scraping a trestle across the floor, it was the whimper of a lost dog. "I know now, sirs, that those saints were not real. Not in the way you are real."

Something has broken inside her, and he wonders what that thing is.

She says, "Is there any chance I could go home again to Kent?"

"I'll see what can be arranged."

Hugh Latimer is sitting with them, and he gives him a hard look, as if he's making false promises. No, really, he says. Leave it with me.

Cranmer tells her gently, "Before you can go anywhere, it will be necessary for you to make public acknowledgment of your imposture. Public confession."

"She's not shy of crowds, are you?" These many years she's been on the road, a traveling show, and will be again, though now the nature of the show has changed; he means to display her, repentant, at Paul's Cross, and perhaps outside London too. He feels that she will take to the role of fraud with the same relish with which she took to her role as saint.

He says to Riche, Niccolò tells us unarmed prophets always fail. He smiles and says, I mention this, Ricardo, because I know you like to have it by the book.

Cranmer leans forward and says to the Maid, these men about you, Edward Bocking and the rest, which of them were your lovers?

She is shocked: perhaps because the question has come from him, the sweetest of her interrogators. She just stares at him, as if one of them were stupid.

He says, murmuring, she may think *lovers* is not the word.

Enough. To Audley, to Latimer, to Riche, he says, "I shall begin bringing in her followers, and her leaders. She has ruined many, if we care to press for their ruin. Fisher certainly, Margaret Pole perhaps, Gertrude and her husband for sure. Lady Mary the king's daughter, quite possibly. Thomas More no, Katherine no, but a fat haul of Franciscans."

The court rises, if court is what you call it. Jo stands up. She has been sewing—or rather, unsewing, teasing out the pomegranate border from a crewelwork panel—these remnants of Katherine, of the dusty kingdom of Granada, linger in England still. She folds her work, dropping her scissors into her pocket, pinching up her sleeve and feeding her needle into the fabric for later use. She walks up to the prisoner and puts a hand on her arm. "We must say adieu."

"William Hawkhurst," the girl says, "I remember the name now. The monk who gilded the letter from Mary Magdalene."

Richard Riche makes a note.

"Do not say any more today," Jo advises.

"Will you come with me, mistress? Where I am going?"

"Nobody will come with you," Jo says. "I do not think you have the sense of it, Dame Eliza. You are going to the Tower, and I am going home to my dinner."

❖

This summer of 1533 has been a summer of cloudless days, of strawberry feasts in London gardens, the drone of fumbling bees, warm evenings to stroll under rose arbors and hear from the allées the sound of young gentlemen quarreling over their bowls. The grain harvest is abundant even in the north. The trees are bowed under the weight of ripening fruit. As if he has decreed that the heat must continue, the king's court burns bright through the autumn. Monseigneur, the queen's father, shines like the sun, and around him spins a smaller but still blazing noonday planet, his son George Rochford. But it is Brandon who leads the dancing, galloping through the halls towing his new bride, whose age is fourteen. She is an heiress, and was betrothed to his son, but Charles thought an experienced man like him could turn her to better use.

The Seymours have put their family scandal behind them, and their fortunes are mending. Jane Seymour says to him, looking at her feet, "Master Cromwell, my brother Edward smiled last week."

"That was rash of him, what made him do so?"

"He heard his wife is sick. The wife he used to have. The one that my father, you know."

"Is she likely to die?"

"Oh, very likely. Then he will get a new one. But he will keep her at his house in Elvetham, and never let her come within a mile of Wolf Hall. And when my father visits Elvetham, she will be locked in the linen room till he has gone again."

Jane's sister Lizzie is at court with her husband, the Governor of Jersey, who is some connection of the new queen's. Lizzie comes packaged into her velvet and lace, her outlines as firm as her sister's are indefinite and blurred, her eyes bold and hazel and eloquent. Jane whispers in her wake; her eyes are the color of water, where her thoughts slip past, like gilded fishes too small for hook or net.

It is Jane Rochford—whose mind, in his view, is underoccupied—who sees him watching the sisters. "Lizzie Seymour must have a lover," she says, "it cannot be her husband who puts that glow in her cheeks, he is an old man. He was old when he was in the Scots wars." The two sisters are just a little alike, she points out; they have the same habit of dipping their head and drawing in their underlip. "Otherwise," she says, smirking, "you would think their mother had been up to the same tricks as her husband. She was a beauty in her day, you know, Margery Wentworth. And nobody knows what goes on down in Wiltshire."

"I'm surprised you don't, Lady Rochford. You seem to know everyone's business."

"You and me, we keep our eyes open." She lowers her head, and says, as if directing the words inward, to her own body, "I could keep my eyes open, if you like, in places you cannot go."

Dear God, what does she want? It can't be money, surely? The question comes out colder than he means: "Upon what possible inducement?"

She lifts her eyes to his. "I should like your friendship."

"No conditions attach to that."

"I thought I might help you. Because your ally Lady Carey has gone down to Hever now to see her daughter. She is no longer wanted since Anne is back on duty in the bedchamber. Poor Mary." She laughs. "God dealt her a good enough hand but she never knew how to play it. Tell me, what will you do if the queen does not have another child?"

"There is no reason to fear it. Her mother had a child a year. Boleyn used to complain it kept him poor."

"Have you ever observed that when a man gets a son he takes all the credit, and when he gets a daughter he blames his wife? And if they do not breed at all, we say it is because her womb is barren. We do not say it is because his seed is bad."

"It's the same in the gospels. The stony ground gets the blame."

The stony places, the thorny unprofitable waste. Jane Rochford is childless after seven years of marriage. "I believe my husband wishes I would die." She says it lightly. He does not know how to answer. He has not asked for her confidence. "If I do die," she says, in the same bright tone, "have my body opened. I ask you this in friendship. I am afraid of poison. My husband and his sister are closeted together for hours, and Anne knows all manner of poisons. She has boasted that she will give Mary a breakfast she will not recover from." He waits. "Mary the king's daughter, I mean. Though I am sure if it pleased Anne she would not scruple to make away with her own sister." She glances up again. "In your heart, if you are honest, you would like to know the things I know."

She is lonely, he thinks, and breeding a savage heart, like Leontina in her cage. She imagines everything is about her, every glance or secret conversation. She is afraid the other women pity her, and she hates to be pitied. He says, "What do you know of my heart?"

"I know where you have disposed it."

"It is more than I know myself."

"That is not uncommon among men. I can tell you who you love. Why do you not ask for her, if you want her? The Seymours are not rich. They will sell you Jane, and be glad of the bargain."

"You are mistaken in the nature of my interest. I have young gentlemen in my house, I have wards, their marriages are my business."

"Oh, fa-la-la," she says. "Sing another song. Tell it to infants in the nursery. Tell it to the House of Commons, you do most usually lie to them. But do not think you can deceive me."

"For a lady who offers friendship, you have rough manners."

"Get used to them, if you want my information. You go into Anne's rooms now, and what do you see? The queen at her prie-dieu. The queen sewing a smock for a beggar woman, wearing pearls the size of chickpeas."

It is hard not to smile. The portrait is exact. Anne has Cranmer entranced. He thinks her the pattern of pious womanhood.

"So do you imagine that is what is really going on? Do you imagine she has given up communing with nimble young gentlemen? Riddles and verses and songs in praise of her, do you suppose she has given them up?"

"She has the king to praise her."

"Not a good word will she hear from that quarter till her belly is big again."

"And what will hinder that?"

"Nothing. If he is up to it."

"Be careful." He smiles.

"I never knew it was treason to say what passes in a prince's bed. All Europe talked about Katherine, what body part was put where, was she penetrated, and if she was did she know?" She sniggers. "Harry's leg pains him at night. He is afraid the queen will kick him in the throes of her passion." She puts her hand before her mouth, but the words creep out, narrow between her fingers. "But if she lies still under him he says, what, madam, are you so little interested in making my heir?"

"I do not see what she is to do."

"She says she gets no pleasure with him. And he—as he fought seven years to get her, he can hardly admit it has staled so soon. It was stale before they came from Calais, that is what I think."

It's possible; maybe they were battle-weary, exhausted. Yet he gives her such magnificent presents. And they quarrel so much. Would they quarrel so much, if they were indifferent?

"So," she goes on, "between the kicking and the sore leg, and his lack of prowess, and her lack of desire, it will be a wonder if we ever have a Prince of Wales. Oh, he is a good man enough, if he had a new woman each week. If he craves novelty, who is to say she does not? Her own brother is in her service."

He turns to look at her. "God help you, Lady Rochford," he says.

"To fetch his friends her way, I mean. What did you think I meant?" A little, grating laugh.

"Do you know what you mean yourself? You have been at court long enough, you know what games are played. It is no matter if any lady receives verses and compliments, even though she is married. She knows her husband writes verses elsewhere."

"Oh, she knows that. At least, I know. There is not a minx within thirty miles who has not had a set of Rochford's verses. But if you think the gallantry stops at the bedchamber's door, you are more innocent than I took you for. You may be in love with Seymour's daughter, but you need not emulate her in having the wit of a sheep."

He smiles. "Sheep are maligned in that way. Shepherds say they can recognize each other. They answer to their names. They make friends for life."

"And I will tell you who is in and out of everyone's bedchamber, it is that sneaking little boy Mark. He is the go-between for them all. My husband pays him in pearl buttons and comfit boxes and feathers for his hat."

"Why, is Lord Rochford short of ready money?"

"You see an opportunity for usury?"

"How not?" At least, he thinks, there is one point on which we concur: pointless dislike of Mark. In Wolsey's house he had duties, teaching the choir children. Here he does nothing but stand about, wherever the court is, in greater or lesser proximity to the queen's apartments. "Well, I can see no harm in the boy," he says.

"He sticks like a burr to his betters. He does not know his place. He is a jumped-up nobody, taking his chance because the times are disordered."

"I suppose you could say the same of me, Lady Rochford. And I am sure you do."

❖

Thomas Wyatt brings him baskets of cobnuts and filberts, bushels of Kentish apples, jolting up himself to Austin Friars on the carrier's cart. "The venison follows," he says, jumping down. "I come with the fresh fruit, not the carcasses." His hair smells of apples, his clothes are dusty from the road. "Now you will have words with me," he says, "for risking a doublet worth—"

"The carrier's yearly earnings."

Wyatt looks chastened. "I forget you are my father."

"I have rebuked you, so now we can fall to idle boyish talk." Standing in a wash of chary autumn sun, he holds an apple in his hand. He pares it with a thin blade, and the peel whispers away from the flesh and lies among his papers, like the shadow of an apple, green on white paper and black ink. "Did you see Lady Carey when you were in the country?"

"Mary Boleyn in the country. What dew-fresh pleasures spring to mind. I expect she's rutting in some hayloft."

"Just that I want to keep hold of her, for the next time her sister is *hors de combat.*"

Wyatt sits down amid the files, an apple in his hand. "Cromwell, suppose you'd been away from England for seven years? If you'd been like a knight in a story, lying under an enchantment? You would look around you and wonder, who are they, these people?"

This summer, Wyatt vowed, he would stay down in Kent. He would read and write on wet days, hunt when it is fine. But the fall comes, and the nights deepen, and Anne draws him back and back.

His heart is true, he believes: and if she is false, it is difficult to pick where the falsehood lies. You cannot joke with Anne these days. You cannot laugh. You must think her perfect, or she will find some way to punish you.

"My old father talks about King Edward's days. He says, you see now why it's not good for the king to marry a subject, an Englishwoman?"

The trouble is, though Anne has remade the court, there are still people who knew her before, in the days when she came from France, when she set herself to seduce Harry Percy. They compete to tell stories of how she is not worthy. Or not human. How she is a snake. Or a swan. *Una candida cerva.* One single white doe, concealed in leaves of silver-gray; shivering, she hides in the trees, waiting for the lover who will turn her back from animal to goddess. "Send me back to Italy," Wyatt says. Her dark, her lustrous, her slanting eyes: she haunts me. She comes to me in my solitary bed at night.

"Solitary? I don't think so."

Wyatt laughs. "You're right. I take it where I can."

"You drink too much. Water your wine."

"It could have been different."

"Everything could."

"You never think about the past."

"I never talk about it."

Wyatt pleads, "Send me away somewhere."

"I will. When the king needs an ambassador."

"Is it true that the Medici have offered for the Princess Mary's hand?"

"Not Princess Mary, you mean the Lady Mary. I have asked the king to think about it. But they are not grand enough for him. You know, if Gregory showed any interest in banking, I would look for a bride for him in Florence. It would be pleasant to have an Italian girl in the house."

"Send me back there. Deploy me where I can be useful, to you or the king, as here I am useless and worse than useless to myself, and necessary to no one's pleasure."

He says, "Oh, by the bleached bones of Becket. Stop feeling sorry for yourself."

Norfolk has his own view of the queen's friends. He rattles a little while he expresses it, his relics clinking, his gray disordered eyebrows working over wide-open eyes. These men, he says, these men who hang around with women! Norris, I thought better of him! And Henry Wyatt's son! Writing verse. Singing. Talk-talk-talking. "What's the use of talking to women?" he asks earnestly. "Cromwell, you don't talk to women, do you? I mean, what would be the topic? What would you find to say?"

I'll speak to Norfolk, he decides, when he comes back from France; ask him to incline Anne to caution. The French are meeting the Pope in Marseilles, and in default of his own attendance Henry must be represented by his most senior peer. Gardiner is already there. For me every day is like a holiday, he says to Tom Wyatt, when those two are away.

Wyatt says, "I think Henry may have a new interest by then."

In the days following he follows Henry's eyes, as they rest on various ladies of the court. Nothing in them, perhaps, except the speculative interest of any man; it's only Cranmer who thinks that if you look twice at a woman you have to marry her. He watches the king dancing with Lizzie Seymour, his hand lingering on her waist. He sees Anne watching, her expression cold, pinched.

Next day, he lends Edward Seymour some money on very favorable terms.

❖

In the damp autumn mornings, when it is still half light, his household are out early, in the damp and dripping woods. You don't get *torta di funghi* unless you pick the raw ingredients.

Richard Riche arrives at eight o'clock, his face astonished and alarmed. "They stopped me at your gate, sir, and said, where's your bag of mushrooms? No one comes in here without mushrooms." Riche's dignity is affronted. "I don't think they would have asked the Lord Chancellor for mushrooms."

"Oh, they would, Richard. But in an hour you will eat them with eggs baked in cream, and the Lord Chancellor will not. Shall we get down to work?"

Through September he has been rounding up the priests and monks who have been close to the Maid. He and Sir Purse sift the papers and conduct the interrogations. The clerics are no sooner under lock and key than they begin to deny her, and deny each other: I never believed in her, it was Father So-and-So who convinced me, I never wanted any trouble. As for their contacts with Exeter's wife, with Katherine, with Mary—each disclaims his own involvement and rushes to implicate his brother-in-Christ. The Maid's people have been in constant contact with the Exeter household. She herself has been at many of the chief monastic houses of the realm—Syon Abbey, the Charterhouse at Sheen, the Franciscan house at Richmond. He knows this because he has many contacts among disaffected monks. In every house there are a few, and he seeks out the most intelligent. Katherine herself has not met the nun. Why should she? She has Fisher to act as a go-between, and Gertrude, Lord Exeter's wife.

The king says, "It is hard for me to believe Henry Courtenay would betray me. A Garter knight, a great man in the lists, my friend since I was a boy. Wolsey tried to part us, but I wouldn't have it." He laughs. "Brandon, do you remember Greenwich, that Christmas, which year was it? Remember the snowball fight?"

This is the whole difficulty of dealing with them, men who are always talking about ancient pedigrees, and boyhood friendships, and things that happened when you were still trading wool on the Antwerp exchange. You put the evidence under their noses, and they start getting teary over snowball fights. "Look," Henry says, "it is Courtenay's wife that is to blame. When he knows the whole of her practices he will want to be rid of her. She is fickle and weak like all her sex, easily led into scheming."

"So forgive her," he says. "Write her a pardon. Put these people under a debt of gratitude to you, if you want them to leave off their foolish sentiment toward Katherine."

"You think you can buy hearts?" Charles Brandon says. He sounds as if he would be sad if the answer were yes.

He thinks, the heart is like any other organ, you can weigh it on a scale. "It is not a price in money we are offering. I have enough to put the Courtenay family on trial, all Exeter's people. If we forbear to do it, we are offering their freedom and their lands. We are giving them a chance to recoup the honor of their name."

Henry says, "His grandfather left Crookback for my father's service."

"If we forgive them they will play us for fools," Charles says.

"I think not, my lord. Everything they do from now on, they do under my eye."

"And the Poles, Lord Montague: what do you propose there?"

"He should not assume he will be pardoned."

"Make him sweat, eh?" Charles says. "I am not sure I like your way of dealing with noblemen."

"They get their deserts," the king says. "Hush, my lord, I need to think."

A pause. Brandon's position is too complicated for him to sustain. He wants to say, pay them out as traitors, Cromwell: but mind you butcher them respectfully. Suddenly his face clears. "Ah, now I re- member Greenwich. The snow was knee-deep that year. Ah, we were young then, Harry. You don't get snow anymore, like you did when we were young."

He gathers up his papers and begs to be excused. Reminiscence is setting in for the afternoon and there is work to be done. "Rafe, ride over to West Horsley. Tell Exeter's wife the king thinks all women fickle and weak—though I should have thought he has plenty of evi- dence to the contrary. Tell her to set down in writing that she has not the wit of a flea. Tell her to claim she is exceptionally easy to mislead, even for a woman. Tell her to grovel. Advise her on the wording. You know how to do it. Nothing can be too humble for Henry."

This is the season for humility. The word from the talks in Mar- seilles is that King Francis has fallen at the Pope's feet and kissed his slippers. When the news comes, Henry bellows an obscenity and shreds the dispatch in his hands.

He collects up the pieces, lays it out on a table and reads it. "Francis has kept faith with you after all," he says. "Surprisingly." He has persuaded the Pope to suspend his bull of excommunication. England has a breathing space.

"I wish Pope Clement in his grave," Henry says. "God knows he is a man of filthy life, and he is always ailing, so he ought to die. Sometimes," he says, "I pray that Katherine might be translated into glory. Is that wrong?"

"If you snap your fingers, Majesty, a hundred priests will come running to tell you right from wrong."

"It seems I prefer to hear it from you." Henry broods, in a sulky twitching silence. "If Clement dies, who will be the next rogue in office?"

"I've put my money on Alessandro Farnese."

"Really?" Henry sits up. "One lays bets?"

"But the odds are short. He has thrown about such bribes to the Roman mob all these years, that they will put the cardinals in terror when the time comes."

"Remind me how many children has he."

"Four I know of."

The king is looking into the tapestry on the near wall, where white-shouldered women walk barefoot on a carpet of spring flowers. "I may have another child soon."

"The queen has spoken to you?"

"Not yet." But he sees, we all do, the flare of color in Anne's cheeks, the silk sleekness of her person, the tone of command ringing in her voice as she hands out favors and rewards to the people around her. This last week, there are more rewards than black looks, and Stephen Vaughan's wife, who is in the Bedchamber, says she has missed her courses. The king says, "She has missed her . . ." and then he stops, blushing like a schoolboy. He crosses the room, flings open his arms and embraces him, shining like a star, his great hands with their blazing rings seizing handfuls of the black velvet of his jacket. "This time for sure. England is ours."

Archaic, that cry from his heart: as if he were standing on the battlefield between the bloodied banners, the crown in a thornbush, his enemies dead at his feet.

He disengages himself gently, smiling. He uncrumples the memorandum he had clenched in his fist when the king seized him; because is that not how men embrace, they knead each other with big fists, as if to knock each other down? Henry squeezes his arm and says, "Thomas, it is like hugging a seawall. What are you made of?" He takes the paper. He gapes. "Is this what we must do this morning? This list?"

"Not more than fifty items. We shall soon work through."

For the rest of the day he cannot stop smiling. Who cares for Clement and his bulls? He might as well stand on Cheap and let the populace pelt him. He might as well stand under the Christmas garlands—which we dust with flour in years when there is no snow—and sing, "Hey nonny no, Fa-la-la, Under the trees so green-o."

❖

On a cold day toward the end of November the Maid and half a dozen of her principal supporters do penance at Paul's Cross. They stand shackled and barefoot in a whipping wind. The crowd is large and boisterous, the sermon lively, telling what the Maid did on her night walks when her sisters in religion were sleeping, and what lurid tales of devils she told to keep her followers in awe. Her confession is read out, at the end of which she asks the Londoners to pray for her, and begs for the king's mercy.

You wouldn't know her now, for the bonny girl they had at Lambeth. She looks haggard and ten years older. Not that she has been hurt, he would not countenance that for a woman, and in fact they have all talked without duress; the hard thing has been to stop them complicating the story by rumors and fantasies, so that half England is dragged into it. The one priest who had persistently lied, he had simply locked up with an informer; the man was detained for murder, and in no time at all Father Rich had set about saving his soul and interpreting to him the Maid's prophecies and impressing him with the names of important people he knew at court. Pitiful, really. But it has been necessary to put on this show, and next he will take it to Canterbury, so Dame Elizabeth can confess on her home ground. It is necessary to break the hold of these people who talk of the end times and threaten us with plagues and damnation. It is necessary to dispel the terror they create.

Thomas More is there, jostled among the city dignitaries; he is making toward him now, as the preachers step down and the prisoners are being led from the platform. More rubs his cold hands. He blows on them. "Her crime is, she was made use of."

He thinks, why did Alice let you out without your gloves? "For all the testimony I have got," he says, "I still cannot understand how she arrived here, from the edge of the marshes to a public scaffold at Paul's. For sure she made no money out of it."

"How will you frame the charges?" His tone is neutral, interested, lawyer-to-lawyer.

"The common law does not deal with women who say they can fly, or raise the dead. I shall put an act of attainder into Parliament. Treason charges for the principals. The accessories, life imprisonment, confiscation, fines. The king will be circumspect, I think. Even merciful. I am more interested in unraveling the plans of these people than in exacting penalties. I don't want a trial with scores of defendants and hundreds of witnesses, tying the courts up for years."

More hesitates.

"Come on," he says, "you would have seen them off that way yourself, when you were Chancellor."

"You may be right. I am clear anyway." A pause. More says, "Thomas. *In the name of Christ, you know that.*"

"As long as the king knows it. We must keep it firmly in his mind. A letter from you perhaps, inquiring after the princess Elizabeth."

"I can do that."

"Making it plain you accept her rights and title."

"That is not a difficulty. The new marriage is made and must be accepted."

"You don't think you could bring yourself to praise it?"

"Why does the king want other men to praise his wife?"

"Suppose you were to write an open letter. To say that you have seen the light in the matter of the king's natural jurisdiction over the church." He looks across to where the prisoners are being loaded into the waiting carts. "They are taking them back to the Tower now." He pauses. "You mustn't stand about. Come home with me to dinner."

"No." More shakes his head. "I would rather be blown around on the river and go home hungry. If I could trust you only to put food in my mouth—but you will put words into it."

He watches him melt into the crowd of home-going aldermen. He thinks, More is too proud to retreat from his position. He is afraid to lose his credibility with the scholars in Europe. We must find some way for him to do it, that doesn't depend on abjection. The sky has cleared now, to a flawless lapis blue. The London gardens are bright with berries. There is an obdurate winter ahead. But he feels a force ready to break, as spring breaks from the dead tree. As the word of God spreads, the people's eyes are opened to new truths. Until now, like Helen Barre, they knew Noah and the Flood, but not St. Paul. They could count over the sorrows of our Blessed Mother, and say how the damned are carried down to Hell. But they did not know the manifold miracles and sayings of Christ, nor the words and deeds of the apostles, simple men who, like the poor of London, pursued simple wordless trades. The story is much bigger than they ever thought it was. He says to his nephew Richard, you cannot tell people just part of the tale and then stop, or just tell them the parts you choose. They have seen their religion painted on the walls of churches, or carved in stone, but now God's pen is poised, and he is ready to write his words in the books of their hearts.

But in these same streets Chapuys sees the stirrings of sedition, a city ready to open its gates to the Emperor. He was not at the sack of Rome but there are nights when he dreams of it as if he had been there: the black guts spilled on antique pavements, the half-dead draped in the fountains, the chiming of bells through the marsh fog, and the flames of arsonists' torches leaping along the walls. Rome has fallen and everything within it; it was not invaders but Pope Julius himself who knocked down old St. Peter's, which had stood for twelve hundred years, the site where the Emperor Constantine himself had dug the first trench, twelve scoops of soil, one for each of the apostles;

where the Christian martyrs, sewn into the skins of wild beasts, had been torn apart by dogs. Twenty-five feet he dug down to lay his new foundations, through a necropolis, through twelve centuries of fish bones and ash, his workmen's shovels powdering the skulls of saints. In the place where martyrs had bled, ghost-white boulders stood: marble, waiting for Michelangelo.

In the street he sees a priest carrying the host, no doubt to a dying Londoner; the passersby uncover their heads and kneel, but a boy leans out of an upper window and jeers, "Show us your Christ-is-Risen. Show us your Jack-in-the-Box." He glances up; the boy's face, before it vanishes, is vivid with rage.

He says to Cranmer, these people want a good authority, one they can properly obey. For centuries Rome has asked them to believe what only children could believe. Surely they will find it more natural to obey an English king, who will exercise his powers under Parliament and under God.

Two days after he sees More shivering at the sermon, he conveys a pardon to Lady Exeter. It comes with some blistering words from the king, directed to her husband. It is St. Catherine's Day: in honor of the saint who was threatened with martyrdom on a wheel, we all walk in circles to our destination. At least, that's the theory. He has never seen anyone over the age of twelve actually doing it.

There's a feeling of power in reserve, a power that drives right through the bone, like the shiver you sense in the shaft of an ax when you take it into your hand. You can strike, or you can not strike, and if you choose to hold back the blow, you can still feel inside you the resonance of the omitted thing.

❖

Next day, at Hampton Court, the king's son the Duke of Richmond marries Norfolk's daughter Mary. Anne has arranged this marriage for the glorification of the Howards; also, to stop Henry marrying his bastard, to the boy's advantage, to some princess abroad. She has persuaded the king to waive the magnificent dower payment he would have expected and, triumphant in all her designs, she joins the dancing, her thin face flushed, her shining hair braided with dagger-tips of diamonds. Henry cannot take his eyes off her, and nor can he.

Richmond draws to him all other eyes, gamboling like a colt, showing off his wedding finery, turning, leaping, bouncing and strutting. Look at him, the older ladies say, and you will see how his father was once: that perfect glow, skin as thin as a girl's. "Master Cromwell," he demands, "tell the king my father that I want to live with my wife. He says that I am to go back to my household and Mary is to stay with the queen."

"He has a care for your health, my lord."

"I am fifteen next."

"It wants half a year till your birthday."

The boy's blithe expression vanishes; a stony look takes over his face. "Half a year is nothing. A man of fifteen is competent."

"So we hear," Lady Rochford says, standing idly by. "The king your father brought witnesses to court to say his brother could do the deed at fifteen, and more than once a night."

"It is also your bride's health that we need to think of."

"Brandon's wife is younger than mine, and he has her."

"Every time he sees her," Lady Rochford says, "if I judge by the startled expression on her face."

Richmond is digging himself in for a long argument, entrenching himself behind precedent: it is his father's way of arguing.

"Did not my great-grandmother Lady Margaret Beaufort give birth at thirteen years, to the prince who would be Henry Tudor?"

Bosworth, the tattered standards, the bloody field; the stained sheet of maternity. Where do we all come from, he thinks, but this same hole-and-corner dealing: sweetheart, yield to me. "I never heard it improved her health," he says, "or her temper. She had no children after." Suddenly he is tired of the argument; he cuts it short, his voice tired and flat. "Be reasonable, my lord. Once you've done it, you'll want to do it all the time. For about three years. That's the way it goes. And your father has other work in mind for you. He may send you to hold court in Dublin."

Jane Rochford says, "Be easy, my lamb. There are ways that can be contrived. A man may always meet a woman, if she is willing."

"May I speak as your friend, Lady Rochford? You risk the king's displeasure if you meddle in this."

"Oh," she says easily, "Henry will forgive anything to a pretty woman. They only seek to do what is natural."

The boy says, "Why should I live like a monk?"

"A monk? They go to it like goats. Master Cromwell here will tell you."

"Perhaps," Richmond says, "it is madam the queen who wants to keep us apart. She doesn't mean the king to have a grandson in the cradle, before he has a son of his own."

"But do you not know?" Jane Rochford turns to him. "Has it not reached your ears that La Ana is *enceinte*?"

She gives her the name Chapuys gives her. He sees the boy's face open in blank dismay. Jane says, "I fear by summer you will have lost your place, sweetheart. Once he has a son born in wedlock, you may tup to your heart's content. You will never reign, and your offspring will never inherit."

It isn't often that you see a princeling's hopes destroyed, in the instant it takes to pinch out a candle flame: and with the same calculated movement, as if born of the neatness of habit. She has not even licked her fingers.

Richmond says, his face crumpling, "It may be another girl."

"It is almost treason to hope so," Lady Rochford says. "And if it is, she will have a third child, and a fourth. I thought she would not conceive again but I was wrong, Master Cromwell. She has proved herself now."

❖

Cranmer is in Canterbury, walking on a path of sand barefoot to his enthronement as primate of England. The ceremony done, he is sweeping out the priory of Christ Church, whose members gave so much encouragement to the false prophetess. It could be a long job, interviewing each monk, picking their stories apart. Rowland Lee storms into town to put some brawn into the business, and Gregory is in his train; so he sits in London reading a letter from his son, no longer nor more informative than his schoolboy letters: and now no more for lack of time.

He writes to Cranmer, be merciful to the community there, as nothing worse than misled. Spare the monk who gilded the Magdalene's letter. I suggest they give a present in cash to the king, three hundred pounds will please him. Clean out Christ Church and the whole diocese; Warham was archbishop for thirty years, his family are entrenched, his bastard son is archdeacon, take a new broom to them. Put in people from home: your sad east Midlands clerks, formed under sober skies.

There is something beneath his desk, under his foot, the nature of which he has avoided thinking about. He pushes his chair back; it is half a shrew, a gift from Marlinspike. He picks it up and thinks of Henry Wyatt, eating vermin in his cell. He thinks of the cardinal, resplendent at Cardinal College. He throws the shrew on the fire. The corpse fizzes and shrivels, bones gone with an empty little pop. He picks up his pen and writes to Cranmer, shake out those Oxford men from your diocese, and put in Cambridge men we know.

He writes to his son, come home and spend the new year with us.

❖

December: in her frozen angularity, a blue light behind her cast up from the snow, Margaret Pole looks as if she has stepped from a church window, slivers of glass shaking from her gown; in fact, those splinters are diamonds. He has made her come to him, the countess, and now she looks at him from beneath her heavy lids, she looks at him down her long Plantagenet nose, and her greeting, ice-bright, flies out into the room. "Cromwell." Just that.

She comes to business. "The Princess Mary. Why must she quit the house in Essex?"

"My lord Rochford wants it for his use. It's good hunting country, you see. Mary is to join her royal sister's household, at Hatfield. She will not need her own attendants there."

"I offer to support my place in her household at my own expense. You cannot prevent me from serving her."

Try me. "I am only the minister of the king's wishes, and you, I suppose, are as anxious as I am to carry them out."

"These are the wishes of the concubine. We do not believe, the princess and I, that they are the king's own wishes."

"You must stretch your credulity, madam."

She looks down at him from her plinth: she is Clarence's daughter, old King Edward's niece. In her time, men like him knelt down to speak to women like her. "I was in Katherine the queen's suite on the day she was married. To the princess, I stand as a second mother."

"Blood of Christ, madam, you think she needs a second? The one she has will kill her."

They stare at each other, across an abyss. "Lady Margaret, if I may advise you . . . your family's loyalty is suspect."

"So you say. This is why you are parting me from Mary, as punishment. If you have matter enough to indict me, then send me to the Tower with Elizabeth Barton."

"That would be much against the king's wishes. He reveres you, madam. Your ancestry, your great age."

"He has no evidence."

"In June last year, just after the queen was crowned, your son Lord Montague and your son Geoffrey Pole dined with Lady Mary. Then a scant two weeks later, Montague dined with her again. I wonder what they discussed?"

"Do you really?"

"No," he says, smiling. "The boy who carried in the dish of asparagus, that was my boy. The boy who sliced the apricots was mine too. They talked about the Emperor, about the invasion, how he might be brought to it. So you see, Lady Margaret, all your family owes much to my forbearance. I trust they will repay the king with future loyalty."

He does not say, I mean to use your sons against their troublemaking brother abroad. He does not say, I have your son Geoffrey on my pay- roll. Geoffrey Pole is a violent, unstable man. You do not know how he will turn. He has paid him forty pounds this year to turn the Crom- well way.

The countess curls her lip. "The princess will not leave her home quietly."

"My lord of Norfolk intends to ride to Beaulieu, to tell her of the change in her circumstances. She may defy him, of course."

He had advised the king, leave Mary in possession of her style as princess, do not diminish anything. Do not give her cousin the Em- peror a reason to make war.

Henry had shouted, "Will you go to the queen, and suggest to her that Mary keep her title? For I tell you, Master Cromwell, I am not go- ing to do it. And if you put her in a great passion, as you will, and she falls ill and miscarries her child, you will be responsible! And I shall not incline to mercy!"

Outside the door of the presence chamber, he leans on the wall. He rolls his eyes and says to Rafe, "God in Heaven, no wonder the cardi- nal was old before his time. If he thinks her pique will dislodge it, it cannot be stuck very fast. Last week I was his brother-in-arms, this week he is threatening me with a bloody end."

Rafe says, "It is a good thing you are not like the cardinal."

Indeed. The cardinal expected the gratitude of his prince, in which matter he was bound to be disappointed. For all his capacities he was a man whose emotions would master him and wear him out. He, Crom- well, is no longer subject to vagaries of temperament, and he is almost never tired. Obstacles will be removed, tempers will be soothed, knots unknotted. Here at the close of the year 1533, his spirit is sturdy, his will strong, his front imperturbable. The courtiers see that he can shape events, mold them. He can contain the fears of other men, and give them a sense of solidity in a quaking world: this people, this dynasty, this miserable rainy island at the edge of the world.

By way of recreation at the end of the day, he is looking into Kather- ine's land holdings and judging what he can redistribute. Sir Nicholas Carew, who does not like him and does not like Anne, is amazed to receive from him a package of grants, including two fat Surrey manors to adjoin his existing holdings in the county. He seeks an interview to express his thanks; he has to ask Richard, who keeps the Cromwell diary now, and Richard fits him in after two days. As the cardinal used to say, deference means making people wait.

When Carew comes in he is arranging his face. Chilly, self-absorbed, the complete courtier, he works at turning up the corners of his mouth. The result is a maidenly simper, incongruous above a luxuriant beard.

"Oh, I am sure you are deserving," he says, shrugging it off. "You are a boyhood friend of His Majesty and nothing gives him greater pleasure than to reward his old friends. Your wife is in touch with the Lady Mary, is she not? They are close? Ask her," he says gently, "to give the young woman good advice. Warn her to be conformable to the king in all things. His temper is short these days and I cannot answer for the consequences of defiance."

Deuteronomy tells us, gifts blind the eyes of the wise. Carew is not particularly wise, in his opinion, but the principle holds good; and if not exactly blinded, at least he looks dazed. "Call it an early Christmas present," he tells him, smiling. He pushes the papers across his desk.

At Austin Friars they are cleaning out storerooms and building strong rooms. They will keep the feast at Stepney. The angel's wings are moved there; he wants to keep them, till there is another child in the house of the right size. He sees them going, shivering in their shroud of fine linen, and watches the Christmas star loaded onto a cart. Christophe asks, "How would one work it, that savage machine that is all over points?"

He draws off one of the canvas sleeves, shows him the gilding. "Jesus Maria," the boy says. "The star that guides us to Bethlehem. I thought it was an engine for torture."

Norfolk goes down to Beaulieu to tell Lady Mary she must move to the manor at Hatfield, and be an attendant to the little princess, and live under the governance of Lady Anne Shelton, aunt to the queen. What ensues, he reports back in aggrieved tones.

"Aunt to the queen?" says Mary. "There is but one queen, and that is my mother."

"Lady Mary . . ." Norfolk says, and the words make her burst into tears, and run to her room and lock herself in.

Suffolk goes up the country to Buckden, to convince Katherine to move to another house. She has heard that they mean to send her somewhere even damper than Buckden, and she says the damp will kill her, so she too shuts herself up, rattling the bolts into place and shouting at Suffolk in three languages to go away. She will go nowhere, she says, unless he is prepared to break down the door and bind her with ropes and carry her. Which Charles thinks is a little extreme.

Brandon sounds so sorry for himself when he writes back to London for instructions: a man with a bride of fourteen awaiting his attentions, to spend the holiday like this! When his letter is read out to the council, he, Cromwell, bursts out laughing. The sheer joy of it carries him into the new year.

There is a young woman walking the roads of the kingdom, saying she is the princess Mary, and that her father has turned her out to beg. She has been seen as far north as York and as far east as Lincoln, and simple people in these shires are lodging and feeding her and giving her money to see her on her way. He has people keeping an eye out for her, but they haven't caught her yet. He doesn't know what he would do with her if he did catch her. It is punishment enough, to take on the burden of a prophecy, and to be out unprotected on the winter roads. He pictures her, a dun-colored, dwindling figure, tramping away toward the horizon over the flat muddy fields.

III

A Painter's Eye

1534

hen Hans brings the finished portrait to Austin Friars he feels shy of it. He remembers when Walter would say, look me in the face, boy, when you tell me a lie. He looks at the picture's lower edge, and allows his gaze to creep upward. A quill, scissors, papers, his seal in a little bag, and a heavy volume, bound in blackish green: the leather tooled in gold, the pages gilt-edged. Hans had asked to see his Bible, rejected it as too plain, too thumbed. He had scoured the house and found the finest volume he owned on the desk of Thomas Avery. It is the monk Pacioli's work, the book on how to keep your books, sent to him by his kind friends in Venice.

He sees his painted hand, resting on the desk before him, holding a paper in a loose fist. It is uncanny, as if he had been pulled apart, to look at himself in sections, digit by digit. Hans has made his skin smooth as the skin of a courtesan, but the motion he has captured, that folding of the fingers, is as sure as that of a slaughterman's when he picks up the killing knife. He is wearing the cardinal's turquoise.

He had a turquoise ring of his own, one time, which Liz gave to him when Gregory was born. It was a ring in the shape of a heart.

He raises his eyes, to his own face. It does not much improve on the Easter egg which Jo painted. Hans had penned him in a little space, pushing a heavy table to fasten him in. He had time to think, while Hans drew him, and his thoughts took him far off, to another country. You cannot trace those thoughts behind his eyes.

He had asked to be painted in his garden. Hans said, the very notion makes me sweat. Can we keep it simple, yes?

He wears his winter clothes. Inside them, he seems made of a more impermeable substance than most men, more compacted. He could well be wearing armor. He foresees the day when he might have to. There are men in this realm and abroad (not only in Yorkshire now) who would stab him as soon as look at him.

I doubt, he thinks, they can hack through to the heart. The king had said, what are you made of?

He smiles. There is no trace of a smile on the face of his painted self.

"Right." He sweeps into the next room. "You can come and see it."

They crowd in, jostling. There is a short, appraising silence. It lengthens. Alice says, "He has made you look rather stout, Uncle. More than he need."

Richard says, "As Leonardo has demonstrated to us, a curved surface better deflects the impact of cannonballs."

"I don't think you look like that," Helen Barre says. "I see that your features are true enough. But that is not the expression on your face."

Rafe says, "No, Helen, he saves it for men."

Thomas Avery says, "The Emperor's man is here, can he come in and have a look?"

"He is welcome, as always."

Chapuys prances in. He positions himself before the painting; he skips forward; he leaps back. He is wearing marten furs over silks. "Dear God," Johane says behind her hand, "he looks like a dancing monkey."

"Oh no, I fear not," Eustache says. "Oh, no, no, no, no, no. Your Protestant painter has missed the mark this time. For one never thinks of you alone, Cremuel, but in company, studying the faces of other people, as if you yourself mean to paint them. You make other men think, not 'what does he look like?' but 'what do I look like?'" He whisks away, then swings around, as if to catch the likeness in the act of moving. "Still. Looking at that, one would be loath to cross you. To that extent, I think Hans has achieved his aim."

When Gregory comes home from Canterbury, he takes him in alone to see the painting, still in his riding coat, muddy from the road; he wants to hear his son's opinion, before the rest of the household get to him. He says, "Your lady mother always said she didn't pick me for my looks. I was surprised, when the picture came, to find I was vain. I thought of myself as I was when I left Italy, twenty years ago. Before you were born."

Gregory stands at his shoulder. His eyes rest on the portrait. He doesn't speak.

He is conscious that his son is taller than he is: not that it takes much. He steps sideways, though only in his mind, to see his boy with a painter's eye: a boy with fine white skin and hazel eyes, a slender angel of the second rank in a fresco dappled with damp, in some hill town far from here. He thinks of him as a page in a forest riding across vellum, dark curls crisp under a narrow band of gold; whereas the young men about him every day, the young men of Austin Friars, are muscled like fighting dogs, hair cropped to stubble, eyes sharp as sword points. He thinks, Gregory is all he should be. He is everything I have a right to hope for: his openness, his gentleness, the reserve and consideration with which he holds back his thoughts till he has framed them. He feels such tenderness for him he thinks he might cry.

He turns to the painting. "I fear Mark was right."

"Who is Mark?"

"A silly little boy who runs after George Boleyn. I once heard him say I looked like a murderer."

Gregory says, "Did you not know?"

PART SIX

I

Supremacy

1534

n the convivial days between Christmas and New
Year's, while the court is feasting and Charles Bran-
don is in the fens shouting at a door, he is rereading
Marsiglio of Padua. In the year 1324 Marsiglio put
to us forty-two propositions. When the feast of the
Epiphany is past, he ambles along to put a few of
them to Henry.

Some of these propositions the king knows, some are strange to
him. Some are congenial, in his present situation; some have been
denounced to him as heresy. It's a morning of brilliant, bone-chilling
cold, the wind off the river like a knife in the face. We are breezing in
to push our luck.

Marsiglio tells us that when Christ came into this world he came
not as a ruler or a judge, but as a subject: subject to the state as he found
it. He did not seek to rule, nor pass on to his disciples a mission to rule.
He did not give power to one of his followers more than another; if you
think he did, read again those verses about Peter. Christ did not make
Popes. He did not give his followers the power to make laws or levy
taxes, both of which churchmen have claimed as their right.

Henry says, "I never remember the cardinal spoke of this."

"Would you, if you were a cardinal?"

Since Christ did not induce his followers into earthly power, how
can it be maintained that the princes of today derive their power from
the Pope? In fact, all priests are subjects, as Christ left them. It is for
the prince to govern the bodies of his citizens, to say who is married
and who can marry, who is a bastard and who legitimate.

Where does the prince get this power, and his power to enforce the law? He gets it through a legislative body, which acts on behalf of the citizens. It is from the will of the people, expressed in Parliament, that a king derives his kingship.

When he says this, Henry seems to be straining his ears, as if he might catch the sound of the people coming down the road to turn him out of his palace. He reassures him on the point: Marsiglio gives no legitimacy to rebels. Citizens may indeed band together to overthrow a despot, but he, Henry, is not a despot; he is a monarch who rules within the law. Henry likes the people to cheer him as he rides through London, but the wise prince is not always the most popular prince; he knows this.

He has other propositions to put to him. Christ did not bestow on his followers grants of land, or monopolies, offices, promotions. All these things are the business of the secular power. A man who has taken vows of poverty, how can he have property rights? How can monks be landlords?

The king says, "Cromwell, with your facility for large numbers . . ." He stares into the distance. His fingers pick at the silver lacing of his cuff.

"The legislative body," he says, "should provide for the maintenance of priests and bishops. After that, it should be able to use the church's wealth for the public good."

"But how to free it," Henry says. "I suppose shrines can be broken." Gem-studded himself, he thinks of the kind of wealth you can weigh. "If there were any who dared."

It is a characteristic of Henry, to run before you to where you were not quite going. He had meant to gentle him toward an intricate legal process of dispossession, repossession: the assertion of ancient sovereign rights, the taking back of what was always yours. He will remember that it was Henry who first suggested picking up a chisel and gouging the sapphire eyes out of saints. But he is willing to follow the king's thought. "Christ taught us how to remember him. He left us bread and wine, body and blood. What more do we need? I cannot see where he asked for shrines to be set up, or instituted a trade in body parts, in hair and nails, or asked us to make plaster images and worship them."

"Would you be able to estimate," Henry says, "even . . . no, I suppose you wouldn't." He gets to his feet. "Well, the sun shines, so . . ."

Better make hay. He sweeps the day's papers together. "I can finish up." Henry goes off to get into his double-padded riding coat. He thinks, we don't want our king to be the poor man of Europe. Spain and Portugal have treasure flowing in every year from the Americas. Where is our treasure?

Look around you.

His guess is, the clergy own a third of England. One day soon, Henry will ask him how the Crown can own it instead. It's like dealing with a child; one day you bring in a box, and the child asks, what is in there? Then it goes to sleep and forgets, but next day, it asks again. It doesn't rest until the box is open and the treats given out.

Parliament is about to reconvene. He says to the king, no parliament in history has worked as hard as I mean to work this one.

Henry says, "Do what you have to do. I will back you."

It's like hearing words you've waited all your life to hear. It's like hearing a perfect line of poetry, in a language you knew before you were born.

He goes home happy, but the cardinal is waiting for him in a corner. He is plump as a cushion in his scarlet robes and his face wears a martial and mutinous expression. Wolsey says, you know he will take the credit for your good ideas, and you the blame for his bad ones? When fortune turns against you, you will feel her lash: you always, he never.

He says, my dear Wolsey. (For now that cardinals are finished in this realm, he addresses him as a colleague, not a master.) My dear Wolsey, not entirely so—he didn't blame Charles Brandon for splintering a lance inside his helmet, he blamed himself for not putting his visor down.

The cardinal says, do you think this is a tilting ground? Do you think there are rules, protocols, judges to see fair play? One day, when you are still adjusting your harness, you will look up and see him thundering at you downhill.

The cardinal vanishes, with a chortle.

Even before the Commons convenes, his opponents meet to work out their tactics. Their meetings are not secret. Servants go in and out, and his method with the Pole conclaves bears repeating: there are young men in the Cromwell household not too proud to put on an apron and bring in a platter of halibut or a joint of beef. The gentlemen of England apply for places in his household now, for their sons and nephews and wards, thinking they will learn statecraft with him, how to write a secretary's hand and deal with translation from abroad, and what books one ought to read to be a courtier. He takes it seriously, the trust placed in him; he takes gently from the hands of these noisy young persons their daggers, their pens, and he talks to them, finding out behind the passion and pride of young men of fifteen or twenty what they are really worth, what they value and would value under duress. You learn nothing about men by snubbing them and crushing their pride. You must ask them what it is they can do in this world, that they alone can do.

The boys are astonished by the question, their souls pour out. Perhaps no one has talked to them before. Certainly not their fathers.

You introduce these boys, violent or unscholarly as they are, to humble occupations. They learn the psalms. They learn the use of a filleting blade and a paring knife; only then, for self-defense and in no formal lesson, they learn the *estoc,* the killing jerk under the ribs, the simple twist of the wrist that makes you sure. Christophe offers himself as instructor. These messieurs, he says, be sure they are dainty. They are cutting off the head of the stag or the tail of the rat, I know not what, to send home to their dear papa. Only you and me, master, and Richard Cremuel, we know how to stop some little fuckeur in his tracks, so that's the end of him, and he doesn't even squeak.

Before spring comes, some of the poor men who stand at his gate find their way inside it. The eyes and ears of the unlettered are as sharp as those of the gentry, and you need not be a scholar to have a good wit. Horseboys and kennelmen overhear the confidences of earls. A boy with kindling and bellows hears the sleepy secrets of early morning, when he goes in to light a fire.

On a day of strong sunlight, sudden and deceptive warmth, Call-Me-Risley strides into Austin Friars. He barks, "Give you good morning, sir," throws off his jacket, sits down to his desk and scrapes forward his stool. He picks up his quill and looks at the tip of it. "Right, what do you have for me?" His eyes are glittering and the tips of his ears are pink.

"I think Gardiner must be back," he says.

"How did you know?" Call-Me throws down his pen. He jumps up. He strides about. "Why is he like he is? All this wrangling and jangling and throwing out questions when he doesn't care about the answers?"

"You liked it well enough when you were at Cambridge."

"Oh, then," Wriothesley says, with contempt for his young self. "It's supposed to train our minds. I don't know."

"My son claims it wore him out, the practice of scholarly disputation. He calls it the practice of futile argument."

"Perhaps Gregory's not completely stupid."

"I would be glad to think not."

Call-Me blushes a deep red. "I mean no offense, sir. You know Gregory's not like us. As the world goes, he is too good. But you don't have to be like Gardiner, either."

"When the cardinal's advisers met, we would propose plans, there would perhaps be some dispute, but we would talk it through; then we would refine our plans, and implement them. The king's council doesn't work like that."

"How could it? Norfolk? Charles Brandon? They'll fight you because of who you are. Even if they agree with you, they'll fight you. Even if they know you're right."

"I suppose Gardiner has been threatening you."

"With ruin." He folds one fist into the other. "I don't regard it."

"But you should. Winchester is a powerful man and if he says he will ruin you that is what he means to do."

"He calls me disloyal. He says while I was abroad I should have minded his interests, instead of yours."

"My understanding is, you serve Master Secretary, whoever is acting in that capacity. If I," he hesitates, "if—Wriothesley, I make you this offer, if I am confirmed in the post, I will put you in charge at the Signet."

"I will be chief clerk?" He sees Call-Me adding up the fees.

"So now, go to Gardiner, apologize, and get him to make you a better offer. Hedge your bets."

His face alarmed, Call-Me hovers. "Run, boy." He scoops up his jacket and thrusts it at him. "He's still Secretary. He can have his seals back. Only tell him, he has to come here and collect them in person."

Call-Me laughs. He rubs his forehead, dazed, as if he's been in a fight. He throws on his coat. "We're hopeless, aren't we?"

Inveterate scrappers. Wolves snapping over a carcass. Lions fighting over Christians.

❖

The king calls him in, with Gardiner, to look through the bill he proposes to put into Parliament to secure the succession of Anne's children. The queen is with them; many private gentlemen see less of their wives, he thinks, than the king does. He rides, Anne rides. He hunts, Anne hunts. She takes his friends, and makes them into hers.

She has a habit of reading over Henry's shoulder; she does it now, her exploring hand sliding across his silky bulk, through the layers of his clothing, so that a tiny fingernail hooks itself beneath the embroidered collar of his shirt, and she raises the fabric just a breath, just a fraction, from pale royal skin; Henry's vast hand reaches to caress hers, an absent, dreamy motion, as if they were alone. The draft refers, time and again, and correctly it would seem, to *"your most dear and entirely beloved wife Queen Anne."*

The Bishop of Winchester is gaping. As a man, he cannot unglue himself from the spectacle, yet as a bishop, it makes him clear his throat. Anne takes no notice; she carries on doing what she's doing, and reading out the bill, until she looks up, shocked: it mentions my death! *"If it should happen your said dear and entirely beloved wife Queen Anne to decease . . ."*

"I can't exclude the event," he says. "Parliament can do anything, madam, except what is against nature."

She flushes. "I shall not die of the child. I am strong."

He doesn't remember that Liz lost her wits when she was carrying a child. If anything, she was ever more sober and frugal, and spent time making store-cupboard inventories. Anne the queen takes the draft out of Henry's hand. She shakes it in a passion. She is angry with the paper, jealous of the ink. She says, "This bill provides that if I die, say I die now, say I die of a fever and I die undelivered, then he can put another queen in my place."

"Sweetheart," the king says, "I cannot imagine another in your place. It is only notional. He must make provision for it."

"Madam," Gardiner says, "if I may defend Cromwell, he envisages only the customary situation. You would not condemn His Majesty to a life as perpetual widower? And we know not the hour, do we?"

Anne takes no notice, it's as if Winchester had not spoken. "And if she has a son, it says, that son will inherit. It says, *heirs male lawfully begotten.* Then what happens to my daughter and her claim?"

"Well," Henry says, "she is still a princess of England. If you look further down the paper, it says that . . ." He closes his eyes. God give me strength.

Gardiner springs to supply some: "If the king never had a son, not in lawful matrimony with any woman, then your daughter would be queen. That is what Cromwell proposes."

"But why must it be written like this? And where does it say that Spanish Mary is a bastard?"

"Lady Mary is out of the line of succession," he says, "so the inference is clear. We don't need to say more. You must forgive any coldness of expression. We try to write laws sparingly. And so that they are not personal."

"By God," Gardiner says with relish, "if this isn't personal, what is?"

The king seems to have invited Stephen to this conference in order to snub him. Tomorrow, of course, it could go the other way; he could arrive to see Henry arm in arm with Winchester and strolling among the snowdrops. He says, "We mean to seal this act with an oath. His Majesty's subjects to swear to uphold the succession to the throne, as laid out in this paper and ratified by Parliament."

"An oath?" Gardiner says. "What sort of legislation needs to be confirmed by an oath?"

"You will always find those who will say a parliament is misled, or bought, or in some way incapable of representing the commonwealth. Again, you will find those who will deny Parliament's competence to legislate in certain matters, saying they must be left to some other jurisdiction—to Rome, in effect. But I think that is a mistake. Rome has no legitimate voice in England. In my bill I mean to state a position. It is a modest one. I draft it, it may please Parliament to pass it, it may please the king to sign it. I shall then ask the country to endorse it."

"So what will you do?" Stephen says, jeering. "Have your boys from Austin Friars up and down the land, swearing every man Jack you dig out of an alehouse? Every man Jack and every Jill?"

"Why should I not swear them? Do you think because they are not bishops they are brutes? One Christian's oath is as good as another's. Look at any part of this kingdom, my lord bishop, and you will find dereliction, destitution. There are men and women on the roads. The sheep farmers are grown so great that the little man is knocked off his acres and the plowboy is out of house and home. In a generation these people can learn to read. The plowman can take up a book. Believe me, Gardiner, England can be otherwise."

"I have made you angry," Gardiner observes. "Provoked, you mistake the question. I asked you not if their word is good, but how many of them you propose to swear. But of course, in the Commons you have brought in a bill against sheep—"

"Against the runners of sheep," he says, smiling.

The king says, "Gardiner, it is to help the common people—no grazier to run more than two thousand animals—"

The bishop cuts his king off as if he were a child. "Two thousand, yes, so while your commissioners are rampaging through the shires counting sheep, perhaps they can swear the shepherds at the same time, eh?

And these plowboys of yours, in their preliterate condition? And any drabs they find in a ditch?"

He has to laugh. The bishop is so vehement. "My lord, I will swear whoever is necessary to make the succession safe, and unite the country behind us. The king has his officers, his justices of the peace—and the lords of the council will be put on their honor to make this work, or I will know why."

Henry says, "The bishops will take the oath. I hope they will be conformable."

"We want some new bishops," Anne says. She names her friend Hugh Latimer. His friend Rowland Lee. It seems after all she does have a list, which she carries in her head. Liz made preserves. Anne makes pastors.

"Latimer?" Stephen shakes his head, but he cannot accuse the queen, to her face, of loving heretics. "Rowland Lee, to my certain knowledge, has never stood in a pulpit in his life. Some men come into the religious life only for ambition."

"And have barely the grace to disguise it," he says.

"I make the best of my road," Stephen says. "I was set upon it. By God, Cromwell, I walk it."

He looks up at Anne. Her eyes sparkle with glee. Not a word is lost on her.

Henry says, "My lord Winchester, you have been out of the country a great while, on your embassy."

"I hope Your Majesty thinks it has been to his profit."

"Indeed, but you have not been able to avoid neglecting your diocese."

"As a pastor, you should mind your flock," Anne says. "Count them, perhaps."

He bows. "My flock is safe in fold."

Short of kicking the bishop downstairs himself, or having him hauled out by the guards, the king can't do much more. "All the same, feel free to attend to it," Henry murmurs.

There is a feral stink that rises from the hide of a dog about to

fight. It rises now into the room, and he sees Anne turn aside, fastidious, and Stephen put his hand to his chest, as if to ruffle up his fur, to
warn of his size before he bares his teeth. "I shall be back with Your
Majesty within a week," he says. His dulcet sentiment comes out as a
snarl from the depth of his guts.

Henry bursts into laughter. "Meanwhile we like Cromwell. Cromwell treats us very well."

Once Winchester has gone, Anne hangs over the king again; her
eyes flick sideways, as if she were drawing him into conspiracy. Anne's
bodice is still tight-laced, only a slight fullness of her breasts indicating her condition. There has been no announcement; announcements
are never made, women's bodies are uncertain things and mistakes
can occur. But the whole court is sure she is carrying the heir, and she
says so herself; apples are not mentioned this time, and all the foods
she craved when she was carrying the princess revolt her, so the signs
are good it will be a boy. This bill he will bring into the Commons is
not, as she thinks, some anticipation of disaster, but a confirmation of
her place in the world. She must be thirty-three this year. For how
many years did he laugh at her flat chest and yellow skin? Even he can
see her beauty, now she is queen. Her face seems sculpted in the purity
of its lines, her skull small like a cat's; her throat has a mineral glitter,
as if it were powdered with fool's gold.

Henry says, "Stephen is a resolute ambassador, no doubt, but I
cannot keep him near me. I have trusted him with my innermost
councils, and now he turns." He shakes his head. "I hate ingratitude. I
hate disloyalty. That is why I value a man like you. You were good to
your old master in his trouble. Nothing could commend you more to
me than that." He speaks as if he, personally, hadn't caused the trouble; as if Wolsey's fall were caused by a thunderbolt. "Another who has
disappointed me is Thomas More."

Anne says, "When you write your bill against the false prophetess
Barton, put More in it, beside Fisher."

He shakes his head. "It won't run. Parliament won't have it. There
is plenty of evidence against Fisher, and the Commons don't like him,
he talks to them as if they were Turks. But More came to me even

before Barton was arrested and showed me how he was clear in the matter."

"But it will frighten him," Anne says. "I want him frightened. Fright may unmake a man. I have seen it occur."

❖

Three in the afternoon: candles brought in. He consults Richard's daybook: John Fisher is waiting. It is time to be enraged. He tries thinking about Gardiner, but he keeps laughing. "Arrange your face," Richard says.

"You'd never imagine that Stephen owed me money. I paid for his installation at Winchester."

"Call it in, sir."

"But I have already taken his house for the queen. He is still grieving. I had better not drive him to an extremity. I ought to leave him a way back."

Bishop Fisher is seated, his skeletal hands resting on an ebony cane. "Good evening, my lord," he says. "Why are you so gullible?"

The bishop seems surprised that they are not to start off with a prayer. Nevertheless, he murmurs a blessing.

"You had better ask the king's pardon. Beg the favor of it. Plead with him to consider your age and infirmities."

"I do not know my offense. And, whatever you think, I am not in my second childhood."

"But I believe you are. How else would you have given credence to this woman Barton? If you came across a puppet show in the street, would you not stand there cheering, and shout, 'Look at their little wooden legs walking, look how they wave their arms? Hear them blow their trumpets.' Would you not?"

"I don't think I ever saw a puppet show," Fisher says sadly. "At least, not one of the kind of which you speak."

"But you're in one, my lord bishop! Look around you. It's all one great puppet show."

"And yet so many did believe in her," Fisher says mildly. "Warham himself, Canterbury that was. A score, a hundred of devout and learned men. They attested her miracles. And why should she not voice her knowledge, being inspired? We know that before the Lord goes to work, he gives warning of himself through his servants, for it is stated by the prophet Amos . . ."

"Don't 'prophet Amos' me, man. She threatened the king. Foresaw his death."

"Foreseeing it is not the same as desiring it, still less plotting it."

"Ah, but she never foresaw anything that she didn't hope would happen. She sat down with the king's enemies and told them how it would be."

"If you mean Lord Exeter," the bishop says, "he is already pardoned, of course, and so is Lady Gertrude. If they were guilty, the king would have proceeded."

"That does not follow. Henry wishes for reconciliation. He finds it in him to be merciful. As he may be to you even yet, but you must admit your faults. Exeter has not been writing against the king, but you have."

"Where? Show me."

"Your hand is disguised, my lord, but not from me. Now you will publish no more." Fisher's glance shoots upward. Delicately, his bones move beneath his skin; his fist grips his cane, the handle of which is a gilded dolphin. "Your printers abroad are working for me now. My friend Stephen Vaughan has offered them a better rate."

"It is about the divorce you are hounding me," Fisher says. "It is not about Elizabeth Barton. It is because Queen Katherine asked my counsel and I gave it."

"You say I am hounding you, when I ask you to keep within the law? Do not try to lead me away from your prophetess, or I will lead you where she is and lock you up next door to her. Would you have been so keen to believe her, if in one of her visions she had seen Anne crowned queen a year before it occurred, and Heaven smiling down on the event? In that case, I put it to you, you would have called her a witch."

Fisher shakes his head; he retreats into bafflement. "I always wondered, you know, it has puzzled me many a year, if in the gospels Mary Magdalene was the same Mary who was Martha's sister. Elizabeth

Barton told me for a certainty she was. In the whole matter, she didn't hesitate."

He laughs. "Oh, she's familiar with these people. She's in and out of their houses. She's shared a bowl of pottage many a time with our Blessed Lady. Look now, my lord, holy simplicity was well enough in its day, but its day is over. We're at war. Just because the Emperor's soldiers aren't running down the street, don't deceive yourself—this is a war and you are in the enemy camp."

The bishop is silent. He sways a little on his stool. Sniffs. "I see why Wolsey retained you. You are a ruffian and so was he. I have been a priest forty years, and I have never seen such ungodly men as those who flourish today. Such evil councillors."

"Fall ill," he says. "Take to your bed. That's what I recommend."

❖

The bill of attainder against the Maid and her allies is laid before the House of Lords on a Saturday morning, February 21. Fisher's name is in it and so, at Henry's command, is More's. He goes to the Tower to see the woman Barton, to see if she has anything else to get off her conscience before her death is scheduled.

She has survived the winter, trailed across country to her outdoor confessions, standing exposed on scaffolds in the cutting wind. He brings a candle in with him, and finds her slumped on her stool like a badly tied bundle of rags; the air is both cold and stale. She looks up and says, as if they were resuming a conversation, "Mary Magdalene told me I should die."

Perhaps, he thinks, she has been talking to me in her head. "Did she give you a date?"

"You'd find that helpful?" she asks. He wonders if she knows that Parliament, indignant over More's inclusion, could delay the bill against her till spring. "I'm glad you've come, Master Cromwell. Nothing happens here."

Not even his most prolonged, his most subtle interrogations had frightened her. To get Katherine pulled into it, he had tried every trick he knew: with no result. He says, "You are fed properly, are you?"

"Oh yes. And my laundry done. But I miss it, when I used to go to Lambeth, see the archbishop, I liked that. Seeing the river. All the people bustling along, and the boats unloading. Do you know if I shall be burned? Lord Audley said I would be burned." She speaks as if Audley were an old friend.

"I hope you can be spared that. It is for the king to say."

"I go to Hell these nights," she says. "Master Lucifer shows me a chair. It is carved of human bones and padded with cushions of flame."

"Is it for me?"

"Bless you, no. For the king."

"Any sightings of Wolsey?"

"The cardinal's where I left him." Seated among the unborn. She pauses; a long drifting pause. "They say it can take an hour for the body to burn. Mother Mary will exalt me. I shall bathe in the flames, as one bathes in a fountain. To me, they will be cool." She looks into his face but at his expression she turns away. "Sometimes they pack gunpowder in the wood, don't they? Makes it quick then. How many will be going with me?"

Six. He names them. "It could have been sixty. Do you know that? Your vanity brought them here."

As he says it he thinks, it is also true that their vanity brought her: and he sees that she would have preferred sixty to die, to see Exeter and the Pole family pulled down to disgrace; it would have sealed her fame. That being so, why would she not name Katherine as party to the plot? What a triumph that would be for a prophet, to ruin a queen. There, he thinks, I shouldn't have been so subtle after all; I should have played on her greed to be infamous. "Shall I not see you again?" she says. "Or will you be there, when I suffer?"

"This throne," he says. "This chair of bones. It would be as well to keep it to yourself. Not to let the king hear of it."

"I think he ought. He should have warning of what is waiting for him after death. And what can he do to me, worse than he already plans?"

"You don't want to plead your belly?"

She blushes. "I'm not with child. You're laughing at me."

"I would advise anyone to get a few more weeks of life, by any means they can. Say you have been ill-used on the road. Say your guards have dishonored you."

"But then I would have to say who did it, and they would be taken before a judge."

He shakes his head, pitying her. "When a guard despoils a prisoner, he doesn't leave her his name."

Anyway, she doesn't like his idea, that's plain. He leaves her. The Tower is like a small town and its morning routine clatters on around him, the guards and the men from the Mint greet him, and the keeper of the king's beasts trots up to say it's dinnertime—they eat early, the beasts—and does he want to see them fed? I take it very kindly, he says, waiving the pleasure; unbreakfasted himself, slightly nauseous, he can smell stale blood and from the direction of their cages hear their truffling grunts and smothered roars. High up on the walls above the river, out of sight, a man is whistling an old tune, and at the refrain breaks into song; he is a jolly forester, he sings. Which is most certainly untrue.

He looks around for his boatmen. He wonders whether the Maid is ill, and whether she will live to be killed. She was never harmed in his custody, only harassed; kept awake a night or two, but no longer than the king's business keeps him awake, and you don't, he thinks, find me confessing to anything. It's nine o'clock; by ten o'clock dinner, he has to be with Norfolk and Audley, who he hopes will not scream and smell, like the beasts. There is a tentative, icy sun; loops of vapor coil across the river, a scribble of mist.

At Westminster, the duke chases out the servants. "If I want a drink I'll get it for myself. Go on, out, out you go. And shut the door! Any lurking at the keyhole, I'll skin you alive and salt you!" He turns, swearing under his breath, and takes his chair with a grunt. "What if I begged him?" he says. "What if I went down on my knees, said, Henry for the Lord's sake, take Thomas More out of the attainder?"

"What if we all begged him," Audley says, "on our knees?"

"Oh, and Cranmer too," he says. "We'll have him in. He's not to escape this delectable interlude."

"The king swears," Audley says, "that if the bill is opposed, he will come before Parliament himself, both houses if need be, and insist."

"He may have a fall," the duke says. "And in public. For God's sake, Cromwell, don't let him do it. He knew More was against him and he let him creep off to Chelsea to coddle his conscience. But it's my niece, I suppose, who wants him brought to book. She takes it personally. Women do."

"I think the king takes it personally."

"Which is weak," Norfolk says, "in my view. Why should he care how More judges him?"

Audley smiles uncertainly. "You call the king weak?"

"Call the king weak?" The duke lurches forward and squawks into Audley's face, as if he were a talking magpie. "What's this, Lord Chancellor, speaking up for yourself? You do usually wait till Cromwell speaks, and then it's chirrup-chirrup, yes-sir-no-sir, whatever you say, Tom Cromwell."

The door opens and Call-Me-Risley appears, in part. "By God," says the duke, "if I had a crossbow, I'd shoot your very head off. I said nobody was to come in here."

"Will Roper is here. He has letters from his father-in-law. More wants to know what you will do for him, sir, as you have admitted that in law he has no case to answer."

"Tell Will we are just now rehearsing how to beg the king to take More's name out of the bill."

The duke knocks back his drink, the one he has poured himself. He bounces his goblet back on the table. "Your cardinal used to say, Henry will give half his realm rather than be balked, he will not be cheated of any part of his will."

"But I reason . . . do not you, Lord Chancellor . . ."

"Oh, he does," the duke says. "Whatever you reason, Tom, he reasons. Squawk, squawk."

Wriothesley looks startled. "Could I bring Will in?"

"So we are united? On our knees to beg?"

"I won't do it unless Cranmer will," the duke says. "Why should a layman wear out his joints?"

"Shall we send for my lord Suffolk too?" Audley suggests.

"No. His boy is dying. His heir." The duke scrubs his hand across his mouth. "He wants just a month of his eighteenth birthday." His fingers fidget for his holy medals, his relics. "Brandon's got the one boy. So have I. So have you, Cromwell. And Thomas More. Just the one boy. God help Charles, he'll have to start breeding again with his new wife; that'll be a hardship to him, I'm sure." He gives a bark of laughter. "If I could pension my lady wife off, I could get a juicy fifteen-year-old too. But she won't go."

It is too much for Audley. His face flushes. "My lord, you have been married, and well married, these twenty years."

"Do I not know it? It's like placing your person in a grizzled leather bag." The duke's bony hand descends; he squeezes his shoulder. "Get me a divorce, Cromwell, will you? You and my lord archbishop, come up with some grounds. I promise there'll be no murder done over it."

"Where is murder done?" Wriothesley says.

"We're preparing to murder Thomas More, aren't we? Old Fisher, we're whetting the knife for him, eh?"

"God forbid." The Lord Chancellor rises, sweeping his gown around him. "These are not capital charges. More and the Bishop of Rochester, they are only accessories."

"Which," Wriothesley says, "in all conscience is grave enough."

Norfolk shrugs. "Kill them now or later. More won't take your oath. Fisher won't."

"I am quite sure they will," Audley says. "We shall use efficacious persuasions. No reasonable man will refuse to swear to the succession, for the safety of this realm."

"So is Katherine to be sworn," the duke says, "to uphold the succession of my niece's infant? What about Mary—is she to be sworn? And if they will not, what do you propose? Draw them to Tyburn on a hurdle and hang them up kicking, for their relative the Emperor to see?"

He and Audley exchange a glance. Audley says, "My lord, you shouldn't drink so much wine before noon."

"Oh, *tweet, tweet,*" the duke says.

❖

A week ago he had been up to Hatfield, to see the two royal ladies: the princess Elizabeth, and Lady Mary the king's daughter. "Make sure you get the titles right," he had said to Gregory as they rode.

Gregory had said, "Already you are wishing you had brought Richard."

He had not wanted to leave London during such a busy Parliament, but the king persuaded him: two days and you can be back, I want your eye on things. The route out of the city was running with thaw water, and in copses shielded from the sun the standing pools were still iced. A weak sun blinked at them as they crossed into Hertfordshire, and here and there a ragged blackthorn blossomed, waving at him a petition against the length of winter.

"I used to come here years ago. It was Cardinal Morton's place, you know, and he would leave town when the law term was over and the weather was getting warm, and when I was nine or ten my uncle John used to pack me in a provisions cart with the best cheeses and the pies, in case anybody tried to steal them when we stopped."

"Did you not have guards?"

"It was the guards he was afraid of."

"*Quis custodiet ipsos custodes?*"

"Me, evidently."

"What would you have done?"

"I don't know. Bitten them?"

The mellow brick frontage is smaller than he remembers, but that is what memory does. These pages and gentlemen running out, these grooms to lead away the horses, the warmed wine that awaits them, the noise and the fuss, it is a different sort of arrival from those of long ago. The portage of wood and water, the firing up the ranges, these tasks were beyond the strength or skill of a child, but he was unwilling to concede them, and worked alongside the men, grubby and hungry, till someone saw that he was about to fall over: or until he actually did.

Sir John Shelton is head of this strange household, but he has chosen a time when Sir John is away from home; talk to the women, is his idea, rather than listen to Shelton after supper on the subjects of horses, dogs and his youthful exploits. But on the threshold, he almost changes his mind; coming downstairs at a rapid, creaking scuttle is Lady Bryan, mother of one-eyed Francis, who is in charge of the tiny princess. She is a woman of nearly seventy, well bedded into grandmaternity, and he can see her mouth moving before she is within range of his hearing: Her Grace slept till eleven, squalled till midnight, exhausted herself, poor little chicken! fell asleep an hour, woke up grizzling, cheeks scarlet, suspicion of fever, Lady Shelton woken, physician aroused, teething already, a treacherous time! soothing draft, settled by sun-up, woke at nine, took a feed . . . "Oh, Master Cromwell," Lady Bryan says, "this is never your son! Bless him! What a lovely tall young man! What a pretty face he has, he must get it from his mother. What age would he be now?"

"Of an age to talk, I believe."

Lady Bryan turns to Gregory, her face aglow as if at the prospect of sharing a nursery rhyme with him. Lady Shelton sweeps in. "Give you good day, masters." A small hesitation: does the queen's aunt bow to the Master of the Jewel House? On the whole she thinks not. "I expect Lady Bryan has given you a full account of her charge?"

"Indeed, and perhaps we could have an account of yours?"

"You will not see Lady Mary for yourself?"

"Yes, but forewarned . . ."

"Indeed. I do not go armed, though my niece the queen recommends I use my fists on her." Her eyes sweep over him, assessing; the air crackles with tension. How do women do that? One could learn it, perhaps; he feels, rather than sees, his son back off, till his regress is checked by the cupboard displaying the princess Elizabeth's already extensive collection of gold and silver plate. Lady Shelton says, "I am charged that, if the Lady Mary does not obey me, I should, and here I quote you my niece's words, beat her and buffet her like the bastard she is."

"Oh, Mother of God!" Lady Bryan moans. "I was Mary's nurse too, and she was stubborn as an infant, so she'll not change now, buffet her as you may. You'd like to see the baby first, would you not? Come with me . . ." She takes Gregory into custody, hand squeezing his elbow. On she rattles: you see, with a child of that age, a fever could be anything. It could be the start of the measles, God forbid. It could be the start of the smallpox. With a child of six months, you don't know what it could be the start of . . . A pulse is beating in Lady Bryan's throat. As she chatters she licks her dry lips, and swallows.

He understands now why Henry wanted him here. The things that are happening cannot be put in a letter. He says to Lady Shelton, "Do you mean the queen has written to you about Lady Mary, using these terms?"

"No. She has passed on a verbal instruction." She sweeps ahead of him. "Do you think I should implement it?"

"We will perhaps speak in private," he murmurs.

"Yes, why not?" she says: a turn of her head, a little murmur back.

The child Elizabeth is wrapped tightly in layers, her fists hidden: just as well, she looks as if she would strike you. Ginger bristles poke from beneath her cap, and her eyes are vigilant; he has never seen an infant in the crib look so ready to take offense. Lady Bryan says, "Do you think she looks like the king?"

He hesitates, trying to be fair to both parties. "As much as a little maid ought."

"Let us hope she doesn't share his girth," Lady Shelton says. "He fleshes out, does he not?"

"Only George Rochford says not." Lady Bryan leans over the cradle. "He says, she's every bit a Boleyn."

"We know my niece lived some thirty years in chastity," Lady Shelton says, "but not even Anne could manage a virgin birth."

"But the hair!" he says.

"I know," Lady Bryan sighs. "Saving Her Grace's dignity, and with all respect to His Majesty, you could show her at a fair as a pig-baby." She pinches up the child's cap at the hairline, and her fingers work busily, trying to stuff the bristles out of sight. The child screws up her face and hiccups in protest.

Gregory frowns down at her: "She could be anybody's."

Lady Shelton raises a hand to hide her smile. "You mean to say, Gregory, all babies look the same. Come, Master Cromwell."

She takes him by the sleeve to lead him away. Lady Bryan is left re-knotting the princess, who seems to have become loose in some particular. Over his shoulder, he says, "For God's sake, Gregory." People have gone to the Tower for saying less. He says to Lady Shelton, "I don't see how Mary can be a bastard. Her parents were in good faith when they got her."

She stops, an eyebrow raised. "Would you say that to my niece the queen? To her face, I mean?"

"I already have."

"And how did she take it?"

"Well, I tell you, Lady Shelton, if she had had an ax to hand, she would have essayed to cut off my head."

"I tell you something in return, and you can carry it to my niece if you will. If Mary were indeed a bastard, and the bastard of the poorest landless gentleman that is in England, she should receive nothing but gentle treatment at my hands, for she is a good young woman, and you would need a heart of stone not to pity her situation."

She is walking fast, her train sweeping over stone floors, into the body of the house. Mary's old servants are about, faces he has seen before; there are clean patches on their jackets where Mary's livery badge has been unpicked and replaced by the king's badge. He looks about and recognizes everything. He stops at the foot of the great staircase. Never was he allowed to run up it; there was a back staircase for boys like him, carrying wood or coals. Once he broke the rules; and when he reached the top, a fist came out of the darkness and punched the side of his head. Cardinal Morton himself, lurking?

He touches the stone, cold as a tomb: vine leaves intertwined with some nameless flower. Lady Shelton looks at him smiling, quizzical: why does he hesitate? "Perhaps we should change out of our riding clothes before we meet Lady Mary. She might feel slighted . . ."

"So she might if you delay. She will make something of it, in either case. I say I pity her, but oh, she is not easy! She graces neither our dinner table nor supper table, because she will not sit below the little princess. And my niece the queen has laid down that food must not be carried to her own room, except the little bread for breakfast we all take."

She has led him to a closed door. "Do they still call this the blue chamber?"

"Ah, your father has been here before," she says to Gregory.

"He's been everywhere," Gregory says.

She turns. "See how you get on, gentlemen. By the way, she will not answer to 'Lady Mary.'"

It is a long room, it is almost empty of furniture, and the chill, like a ghost's ambassador, meets them on the threshold. The blue tapestries have been taken down and the plaster walls are naked. By an almost dead fire, Mary is sitting: huddled, tiny and pitifully young. Gregory whispers, "She looks like Malekin."

Poor Malekin, she is a spirit girl; she eats at night, lives on crumbs and apple peel. Sometimes, if you come down early and are quiet on the stairs, you find her sitting in the ashes.

Mary glances up; surprisingly, her little face brightens. "Master Cromwell." She gets to her feet, takes a step toward him and almost stumbles, her feet entangled in the hem of her dress. "How long is it since I saw you at Windsor?"

"I hardly know," he says gravely. "The years have been good to you, madam."

She giggles; she is now eighteen. She casts around her as if bewildered for the stool on which she was sitting. "Gregory," he says, and his son dives to catch the ex-princess, before she sits down on empty air. Gregory does it as if it were a dance step; he has his uses.

"I am sorry to keep you standing. You might," she waves vaguely, "sit down on that chest."

"I think we are strong enough to stand. Though I do not think you are." He sees Gregory glance at him, as if he has never heard this softened tone. "They do not make you sit alone, and by this miserable fire, surely?"

"The man who brings the wood will not give me my title of princess."

"Do you have to speak to him?"

"No. But it would be an evasion if I did not."

That's right, he thinks: make life as hard as possible for yourself. "Lady Shelton has told me about the difficulty in . . . the dinner difficulty. Suppose I were to send you a physician?"

"We have one here. Or rather, the child has."

"I could send a more useful one. He might give you a regimen for your health, and lay it down that you were to take a large breakfast, in your own room."

"Meat?" Mary says.

"In quantity."

"But who would you send?"

"Dr. Butts?"

Her face softens. "I knew him at my court at Ludlow. When I was Princess of Wales. Which I still am. How is it I am put out of the succession, Master Cromwell? How is it lawful?"

"It is lawful if Parliament makes it so."

"There is a law above Parliament. It is the law of God. Ask Bishop Fisher."

"I find God's purposes obscure, and God knows I find Fisher no fit elucidator. By contrast, I find the will of Parliament plain."

She bites her lip; now she will not look at him. "I have heard Dr. Butts is a heretic these days."

"He believes as your father the king believes."

He waits. She turns, her gray eyes fixed on his face. "I will not call my lord father a heretic."

"Good. It is better that these traps are tested, first, by your friends."

"I do not see how you can be my friend, if you are also friend to the person, I mean the Marquess of Pembroke." She will not give Anne her royal title.

"That lady stands in a place where she has no need of friends, only of servants."

"Pole says you are Satan. My cousin Reginald Pole. Who lies abroad at Genoa. He says that when you were born, you were like any Christian soul, but that at some date the devil entered into you."

"Did you know, Lady Mary, I came here when I was a boy, nine or ten? My uncle was a cook to Morton, and I was a poor sniveling lad who bundled the hawthorn twigs at dawn to light the ovens, and killed the chickens for the boiling house before the sun was up." He speaks gravely. "Would you suppose the devil had entered me by that date? Or was it earlier, around the time when other people are baptized? You understand it is of interest to me."

Mary watches him, and she does it sideways; she still wears an old-style gable hood, and she seems to blink around it, like a horse whose headcloth has slipped. He says softly, "I am not Satan. Your lord father is not a heretic."

"And I am not a bastard, I suppose."

"Indeed no." He repeats what he told Anne Shelton: "You were conceived in good faith. Your parents thought they were married. That does not mean their marriage was good. You can see the difference, I think?"

She rubs her forefinger under her nose. "Yes, I can see the difference. But in fact the marriage was good."

"The queen will be coming to visit her daughter soon. If you would simply greet her respectfully in the way you should greet your father's wife—"

"—except she is his concubine—"

"—then your father would take you back to court, you would have everything you lack now, and the warmth and comfort of society. Listen to me, I intend this for your good. The queen does not expect your friendship, only an outward show. Bite your tongue and bob her a curtsy. It will be done in a heartbeat, and it will change everything. Make terms with her before her new child is born. If she has a son, she will have no reason afterward to conciliate you."

"She is frightened of me," Mary says, "and she will still be frightened, even if she has a son. She is afraid I will make a marriage, and my own sons will threaten her."

"Does anyone talk to you of marriage?"

A dry little laugh, incredulous. "I was a baby at the breast when I was married into France. Then to the Emperor, into France again, to the king, to his first son, to his second son, to his sons I have lost count of, and once again to the Emperor, or one of his cousins. I have been contracted in marriage till I am exhausted. One day I shall really do it."

"But you will not marry Pole."

She flinches, and he knows that it has been put to her: perhaps by her old governess Margaret Pole, perhaps by Chapuys, who stays up till dawn studying the tables of descent of the English aristocracy: strengthen her claim, put her beyond reproach, marry the half-Spanish Tudor back into the old Plantagenet line. He says, "I have seen Pole. I knew him before he went out of the kingdom. He is not the man for you. Whatever husband you get, he will need a strong sword arm. Pole is like an old wife sitting by the fire, starting at Hob in the Corner and the Boneless Man. He has nothing but a little holy water in his veins, and they say he weeps copiously if his servant swats a fly."

She smiles: but she slaps a hand over her mouth like a gag. "That's right," he says. "You say nothing to anybody."

She says, from behind her fingers, "I can't see to read."

"What, they keep you short of candles?"

"No, I mean my sight is failing. All the time my head aches."

"You cry a good deal?" She nods. "Dr. Butts will bring a remedy. Till then, have someone read to you."

"They do. They read me Tyndale's gospel. Do you know that Bishop Tunstall and Thomas More between them have identified two thousand errors in his so-called Testament? It is more heretical than the holy book of the Moslems."

Fighting talk. But he sees that tears are welling up. "All this can be put right." She stumbles toward him and for a moment he thinks she will forget herself and lurch and sob against his riding coat. "The doctor will be here in a day. Now you shall have a proper fire, and your supper. Wherever you like it served."

"Let me see my mother."

"Just now the king cannot permit it. But that may change."

"My father loves me. It is only she, it is only that wretch of a woman, who poisons his mind."

"Lady Shelton would be kind, if you would let her."

"What is she, to be kind or not kind? I shall survive Anne Shelton, believe me. And her niece. And anyone else who sets themselves up against my title. Let them do their worst. I am young. I will wait them out."

He takes his leave. Gregory follows him, his fascinated gaze trailing back to the girl who resumes her seat by the almost dead fire: who folds her hands, and begins the waiting, her expression set.

"All that rabbit fur she is bundled up in," Gregory says. "It looks as if it has been nibbled."

"She's Henry's daughter for sure."

"Why, does someone say she is not?"

He laughs. "I didn't mean that. Imagine . . . if the old queen had been persuaded into adultery, it would have been easy to be rid of her, but how do you fault a woman who has never known but the one man?" He checks himself: it is hard even for the king's closest supporters to remember that Katherine is supposed to have been Prince Arthur's wife. "Known two men, I should say." He sweeps his eyes over his son. "Mary never looked at you, Gregory."

"Did you think she would?"

"Lady Bryan thinks you such a darling. Wouldn't it be in a young woman's nature?"

"I don't think she has a nature."

"Get somebody to mend the fire. I'll order the supper. The king can't mean her to starve."

"She likes you," Gregory says. "That's strange."

He sees that his son is in earnest. "Is it impossible? My daughters liked me, I think. Poor little Grace, I am never sure if she knew who I was."

"She liked you when you made her the angel's wings. She said she was always going to keep them." His son turns away; speaks as if he is afraid of him. "Rafe says you will be the second man in the kingdom soon. He says you already are, except in title. He says the king will put you over the Lord Chancellor, and everybody. Over Norfolk, even."

"Rafe is running ahead of himself. Listen, son, don't talk about Mary to anyone. Not even to Rafe."

"Did I hear more than I should?"

"What do you think would happen if the king died tomorrow?"

"We should all be very sorry."

"But who would rule?"

Gregory nods toward Lady Bryan, toward the infant in her cradle. "Parliament says so. Or the queen's child that is not born yet."

"But would that happen? In practice? An unborn child? Or a daughter not a year old? Anne as regent? It would suit the Boleyns, I grant you."

"Then Fitzroy."

"There is a Tudor who is better placed."

Gregory's eyes turn back toward Lady Mary. "Exactly," he says. "And look, Gregory, it's all very well planning what you will do in six months, what you will do in a year, but it's no good at all if you don't have a plan for tomorrow."

❖

After supper he sits talking to Lady Shelton. Lady Bryan has gone to bed, then come down again to chivvy them along. "You'll be tired in the morning!"

"Yes," Anne Shelton agrees, waving her away. "In the morning there'll be no doing anything with us. We'll throw our breakfasts on the floor."

They sit till the servants yawn off to another room, and the candles burn down, and they retreat into the house, to smaller and warmer rooms, to talk some more. You have given Mary good advice, she says, I hope she heeds it, I fear there are hard times ahead for her. She talks about her brother Thomas Boleyn, the most selfish man I ever knew, it is no wonder Anne is so grasping, all she has ever heard from him is talk of money, and how to gain a mean advantage over people, he would have sold those girls naked at a Barbary slave market if he had thought he would get a good price.

He imagines himself surrounded by his scimitared retainers, placing a bid for Mary Boleyn; he smiles, and returns his attention to her aunt. She tells him Boleyn secrets; he tells her no secrets, though she thinks he has.

Gregory is asleep when he comes in, but he turns over and says, "Dear father, where have you been, to bed with Lady Shelton?"

These things happen: but not with Boleyns. "What strange dreams you must have. Lady Shelton has been thirty years married."

"I thought I could have sat with Mary after supper," Gregory murmurs. "If I didn't say the wrong thing. But then she is so sneery. I couldn't sit with such a sneery girl." He flounces over in the feather bed, and falls asleep again.

❖

When Fisher comes to his senses and asks pardon, the old bishop begs the king to consider that he is ill and infirm. The king indicates that the bill of attainder must take its course: but it is his habit, he says, to grant mercy to those who admit their fault.

The Maid is to be hanged. He says nothing of the chair of human bones. He tells Henry she has stopped prophesying, and hopes that at Tyburn, with the noose around her neck, she will not make a liar out of him.

When his councillors kneel before the king, and beg that Thomas More's name be taken out of the bill, Henry yields the point. Perhaps he has been waiting for this: to be persuaded. Anne is not present, or it might have gone otherwise.

They get up and go out, dusting themselves. He thinks he hears the cardinal laughing at them, from some invisible part of the room. Audley's dignity has not suffered, but the duke looks agitated; when he tried to get up, elderly knees had failed him, and he and Audley had lifted him by the elbows and set him on his feet. "I thought I might be fixed there another hour," he says. "Entreating and entreating him."

"The joke is," he says to Audley, "More's still being paid a pension from the treasury. I suppose that had better stop."

"He has a breathing space now. I pray to God he'll see sense. Has he arranged his affairs?"

"Made over what he can to the children. So Roper tells me."

"Oh, you lawyers!" the duke says. "On the day I go down, who will look after me?"

Norfolk is sweating; he eases his pace, and Audley checks too, so they are dawdling along, and Cranmer comes behind like an afterthought. He turns back and takes his arm. He has been at every sitting of Parliament: the bench of bishops, otherwise, conspicuously underpopulated.

The Pope chooses this month, while he is rolling his great bills through Parliament, to give his judgment at last on Queen Katherine's marriage—a judgment so long delayed that he thought Clement meant to die in his indecision. The original dispensations, Clements finds, are sound; therefore the marriage is sound. The supporters of the Emperor let off fireworks in the streets of Rome. Henry is contemptuous, sardonic. He expresses these feelings by dancing. Anne can dance still, though her belly shows; she must take the summer quietly. He remembers the king's hand on Lizzie Seymour's waist. Nothing came of that, the young woman is no fool. Now it is little Mary Shelton he is whirling around, lifting her off her feet and tickling her and squeezing her and making her breathless with compliments. These things mean nothing; he sees Anne lift up her chin and avert her gaze and lean back in her chair, making some murmured comment, her expression arch; her veil brushing, for the briefest moment, against the jacket of that grinning cur Francis Weston. It is clear Anne thinks Mary Shelton must be tolerated, kept sweet even. It's safest to keep the king among cousins, if no sister is on hand. Where is Mary Boleyn? Down in the country, perhaps longing like him for warmer weather.

And the summer arrives, with no intermission for spring, promptly on a Monday morning, like a new servant with a shining face: April 13. They are at Lambeth—Audley, himself, the archbishop—the sun shining strongly through the windows. He stands looking down at the palace gardens. This is how the book *Utopia* begins: friends, talking in a garden. On the paths below, Hugh Latimer and some of the king's chaplains are play-fighting, pulling each other around like schoolboys, Hugh hanging around the necks of two of his clerical fellows so his feet swing off the floor. All they need is a football to make a proper holiday of it. "Master More," he says, "why don't you go out and enjoy the sunshine? And we'll call for you again in half an hour, and put the oath to you again: and you'll give us a different answer, yes?"

He hears More's joints snap as he stands. "Thomas Howard went on his knees for you!" he says. That seems like weeks ago. Late-night sittings and a fresh row every day have tired him, but sharpened his senses too, so he is aware that in the room behind him Cranmer is working himself into a terrible anxiety, and he wants More out of the room before the dam breaks.

"I don't know what you think a half hour will do for me," More says. His tone is easy, bantering. "Of course, it might do something for you."

More had asked to see a copy of the Act of Succession. Now Audley unrolls it; pointedly, he bends his head and begins reading, though he has read it a dozen times. "Very well," More says. "But I trust I have made myself clear. I cannot swear, but I will not speak against your oath, and I will not try to dissuade anyone else from it."

"That is not enough. And you know it is not."

More nods. He meanders toward the door, careering first into the corner of the table, making Cranmer flinch, his arm darting out to steady the ink. The door closes after him.

"So?"

Audley rolls up the statute. Gently he taps it on the table, looking at the place where More had stood. Cranmer says, "Look, this is my idea. What if we let him swear in secret? He swears, but we offer not to tell anybody? Or if he cannot take this oath, we ask him what oath he can take?"

He laughs.

"That would hardly meet the king's purpose," Audley sighs. Tap, tap, tap. "After all we did for him, and for Fisher. His name taken out of the attainder, Fisher fined instead of locked up for life, what more could they ask for? Our efforts flung back at us."

"Oh well. Blessed are the peacemakers," he says. He wants to strangle somebody.

Cranmer says, "We will try again with More. At least, if he refuses, he should give his reasons."

He swears under his breath, turns from the window. "We know his reasons. All Europe knows them. He is against the divorce. He does not believe the king can be head of the church. But will he say that? Not he. I know him. Do you know what I hate? I hate to be part of this play, which is entirely devised by him. I hate the time it will take that could be better spent, I hate it that minds could be better employed, I hate to see our lives going by, because depend upon it, we will all be feeling our age before this pageant is played out. And what I hate most of all is that Master More sits in the audience and sniggers when I trip over my lines, for he has written all the parts. And written them these many years."

Cranmer, like a waiting-boy, pours him a cup of wine, edges toward him. "Here."

In the archbishop's hand, the cup cannot help a sacramental character: not watered wine, but some equivocal mixture, this is my blood, this is like my blood, this is more or less somewhat like my blood, do this in commemoration of me. He hands the cup back. The north Germans make a strong liquor, aquavitae: a shot of that would be more use. "Get More back," he says.

A moment, and More stands in the doorway, sneezing gently. "Come now," Audley says, smiling, "that's not how a hero arrives."

"I assure you, I intend in no wise to be a hero," More says. "They have been cutting the grass." He pinches his nose on another sneeze, and shambles toward them, hitching his gown onto his shoulder; he takes the chair placed for him. Before, he had refused to sit down.

"That's better," Audley says. "I knew the air would do you good." He glances up, in invitation; but he, Cromwell, signals he will stay where he is, leaning by the window. "I don't know," Audley says, good-humored. "First one won't sit. Then t'other won't sit. Look," he pushes a piece of paper toward More, "these are the names of the priests we have seen today, who have sworn to the act, and set you an example. And you know all the members of Parliament are conformable. So why not you?"

More glances up, from under his eyebrows. "This is not a comfortable place for any of us."

"More comfortable than where you're going," he says.

"Not Hell," More says, smiling. "I trust not."

"So if taking the oath would damn you, what about all these?" He launches himself forward from the wall. He snatches the list of names from Audley, rolls it up and slaps it onto More's shoulder. "Are they all damned?"

"I cannot speak for their consciences, only for my own. I know that, if I took your oath, I should be damned."

"There are those who would envy your insight," he says, "into the workings of grace. But then, you and God have always been on familiar terms, not so? I wonder how you dare. You talk about your maker as if he were some neighbor you went fishing with on a Sunday afternoon."

Audley leans forward. "Let us be clear. You will not take the oath because your conscience advises you against it?"

"Yes."

"Could you be a little more comprehensive in your answers?"

"No."

"You object but you won't say why?"

"Yes."

"Is it the matter of the statute you object to, or the form of the oath, or the business of oath-taking in itself?"

"I would rather not say."

Cranmer ventures, "Where it is a question of conscience, there must always be some doubt . . ."

"Oh, but this is no whim. I have made long and diligent consultation with myself. And in this matter I hear the voice of my conscience clearly." He puts his head on one side, smiling. "It is not so with you, my lord?"

"Nonetheless, there must be some perplexity? For you must ask yourself, as you are a scholar and accustomed to controversy, to debate, how can so many learned men think on the one side, and I on the other? But one thing is certain, and it is that you owe a natural obedience to your king, as every subject does. Also, when you entered the king's council, long ago, you took a most particular oath, to obey him. So will not you do so?" Cranmer blinks. "Set your doubts against that certainty, and swear."

Audley sits back in his chair. Eyes closed. As if to say, we're not going to do better than that.

More says, "When you were consecrated archbishop, appointed by the Pope, you swore your oath to Rome, but all day in your fist, they say, all through the ceremonies, you kept a little paper folded up, saying that you took the oath under protest. Is that not true? They say the paper was written by Master Cromwell here."

Audley's eyes snap open: he thinks More has shown himself the way out. But More's face, smiling, is a mask of malice. "I would not be such a juggler," he says softly. "I would not treat the Lord my God to such a puppet show, let alone the faithful of England. You say you have the majority. I say I have it. You say Parliament is behind you, and I say all the angels and saints are behind me, and all the company of the Christian dead, for as many generations as there have been since the church of Christ was founded, one body, undivided—"

"Oh, for Christ's sake!" he says. "A lie is no less a lie because it is a thousand years old. Your undivided church has liked nothing better than persecuting its own members, burning them and hacking them apart when they stood by their own conscience, slashing their bellies open and feeding their guts to dogs. You call history to your aid, but what is history to you? It is a mirror that flatters Thomas More. But I have another mirror, I hold it up and it shows a vain and dangerous man, and when I turn it about it shows a killer, for you will drag down with you God knows how many, who will only have the suffering, and not your martyr's gratification. You are not a simple soul, so don't try to make this simple. You know I have respected you? You know I have respected you since I was a child? I would rather see my only son dead, I would rather see them cut off his head, than see you refuse this oath, and give comfort to every enemy of England."

More looks up. For a fraction of a second, he meets his gaze, then turns away, coy. His low, amused murmur: he could kill him for that alone. "Gregory is a goodly young man. Don't wish him away. If he has done badly, he will do better. I say the same of my own boy. What's the use of him? But he is worth more than a debating point."

Cranmer, distressed, shakes his head. "This is no debating point."

"You speak of your son," he says. "What will happen to him? To your daughters?"

"I shall advise them to take the oath. I do not suppose them to share my scruples."

"That is not what I mean, and you know it. It is the next generation you are betraying. You want the Emperor's foot on their neck? You are no Englishman."

"You are barely that yourself," More says. "Fight for the French, eh, bank for the Italians? You were scarcely grown up in this realm before your boyhood transgressions drove you out of it, you ran away to escape jail or a noose. No, I tell you what you are, Cromwell, you are an Italian through and through, and you have all their vices, all their passions." He sits back in his chair: one mirthless grunt of laughter. "This relentless bonhomie of yours. I knew it would wear out in the end. It is a coin that has changed hands so often. And now the small silver is worn out, and we see the base metal."

Audley smirks. "You seem not to have noted Master Cromwell's efforts at the Mint. His coinage is sound, or it is nothing."

The Chancellor cannot help it, that he is a smirking sort of man; someone must keep calm. Cranmer is pale and sweating, and he can see the pulse galloping at More's temple. He says, "We cannot let you go home. Still, it seems to me that you are not yourself today, so rather than commit you to the Tower, we could perhaps place you in the custody of the Abbot of Westminster . . . Would that seem suitable to you, my lord of Canterbury?"

Cranmer nods. More says, "Master Cromwell, I should not mock you, should I? You have shown yourself my most especial and tender friend."

Audley nods to the guard at the door. More rises smoothly, as if the thought of custody has put a spring in his step; the effect is spoiled only by his usual grab at his garments, the scuffle as he shrugs himself together; and even then he seems to step backward, and tread on his own feet. He thinks of Mary at Hatfield, rising from her stool and forgetting where she'd left it. After some fashion, More is bundled out of the room. "Now he's got exactly what he wants," he says.

He puts his palm against the glass of the window. He sees the smudge it makes, against the old flawed glass. A bank of cloud has come up over the river; the best of the day is behind them. Audley crosses the room to him. Hesitant, he stands at his shoulder. "If only More would indicate which part of the oath he finds objectionable, it is possible something might be written to meet his objection."

"You can forget that. If he indicates anything, he is done for. Silence is his only hope, and it is not much of a hope at that."

"The king might accept some compromise," Cranmer says. "But I fear the queen will not. And indeed," he says faintly, "why should she?"

Audley puts a hand on his arm. "My dear Cromwell. Who can understand More? His friend Erasmus told him to keep away from government, he told him he had not the stomach for it and he was right. He should never have accepted the office I now hold. He only did it to spite Wolsey, whom he hated."

Cranmer says, "He told him to keep away from theology too. Unless I am wrong?"

"How could you be? More publishes all his letters from his friends. Even when they reprove him, he makes a fine show of his humility and so turns it to his profit. He has lived in public. Every thought that passes through his mind he has committed to paper. He never kept anything private, till now."

Audley reaches past him, opens the window. A torrent of birdsong crests on the edge of the sill and spills into the room, the liquid, fluent notes of the storm-thrush.

"I suppose he's writing an account of today," he says. "And sending it out of the kingdom to be printed. Depend upon it, in the eyes of Europe we will be the fools and the oppressors, and he will be the poor victim with the better turn of phrase."

Audley pats his arm. He wants to console him. But who can begin to do it? He is the inconsolable Master Cromwell: the unknowable, the inconstruable, the probably indefeasible Master Cromwell.

❖

Next day the king sends for him. He supposes it is to berate him for failing to get More to take the oath. "Who will accompany me to this fiesta?" he inquires. "Master Sadler?"

As soon as he enters the king's presence, Henry gestures with a peremptory sweep of his arm for his attendants to clear a space, and leave him alone in it. His face is like thunder. "Cromwell, have I not been a good lord to you?"

He begins to talk . . . gracious, and more than gracious . . . own sad unworthiness . . . if fallen short in any particular begs most gracious pardon . . .

He can do this all day. He learned it from Wolsey.

Henry says, "Because my lord archbishop thinks I have not done well by you. But," he says, in the tone of one misunderstood, "I am a prince known for my munificence."

The whole thing seems to puzzle him. "You are to be Master Secretary. Rewards shall follow. I do not understand why I have not done this long ago. But tell me: when it was put to you, about the lords Cromwell that once were in England, you said you were nothing to them. Have you thought further?"

"To be honest, I never gave it another thought. I wouldn't wear another man's coat, or bear his arms. He might rise up from his grave and take issue with me."

"My lord Norfolk says you enjoy being low-born. He says you have devised it so, to torment him." Henry takes his arm. "It would seem convenient to me," he says, "that wherever we go—though we shall not go far this summer, considering the queen's condition—you should have rooms provided for you next to mine, so we can speak whenever I need you; and where it is possible, rooms that communicate directly, so that I need no go-between." He smiles toward the courtiers; they wash back, like a tide. "God strike me," Henry says, "if I meant to neglect you. I know when I have a friend."

Outside, Rafe says, "God strike him . . . What terrible oaths he swears." He hugs his master. "This has been too long in coming. But listen, I have something to tell you when we get home."

"Tell me now. Is it something good?"

A gentleman comes forward and says, "Master Secretary, your barge is waiting to take you back to the city."

"I should have a house on the river," he says. "Like More."

"Oh, but leave Austin Friars? Think of the tennis court," Rafe says. "The gardens."

The king has made his preparations in secret. Gardiner's arms have been burned off the paintwork. A flag with his coat of arms is raised beside the Tudor flag. He steps into his barge for the first time, and on the river, Rafe tells his news. The rocking of the boat beneath them is imperceptible. The flags are limp; it is a still morning, misty and dappled, and where the light touches flesh or linen or fresh leaves, there is a sheen like the sheen on an eggshell: the whole world luminous, its angles softened, its scent watery and green.

"I have been married half a year," Rafe says, "and no one knows, but you know now. I have married Helen Barre."

"Oh, blood of Christ," he says. "Beneath my own roof. What did you do that for?"

Rafe sits mute while he says it all: she is a lovely nobody, a poor woman with no advantage to bring to you, you could have married an heiress. Wait till you tell your father! He will be outraged, he will say I have not looked after your interests. "And suppose one day her husband turns up?"

"You told her she was free," Rafe says. He is trembling.

"Which of us is free?"

He remembers what Helen had said: "So I could marry again? If anybody wanted me?" He remembers how she had looked at him, a long look and full of meaning, only he did not read it. She might as well have turned somersaults, he would not have noticed, his mind had moved elsewhere; that conversation was over for him and he was on to something else. If I had wanted her for myself, and taken her, who could have reproached me for marrying a penniless laundress, even a beggar off the street? People would have said, so that was what Cromwell wanted, a beauty with supple flesh; no wonder he disdained the widows of the city. He doesn't need money, he doesn't need connections, he can afford to follow his appetites: he is Master Secretary now, and what next?

He stares down into the water, now brown, now clear as the light catches it, but always moving; the fish in its depths, the weeds, the drowned men with bony hands swimming. On the mud and shingle there are cast up belt buckles, fragments of glass, small warped coins with the kings' faces washed away. Once when he was a boy he found a horseshoe. A horse in the river? It seemed to him a very lucky find. But his father said, if horseshoes were lucky, boy, I would be the King of Cockaigne.

❖

First he goes out to the kitchens to tell Thurston the news. "Well," the cook says easily, "as you're doing the job anyway." A chuckle. "Bishop Gardiner will be burning up inside. His giblets will be sizzling in his own grease." He whisks a bloodied cloth from a tray. "See these quails? You get more meat on a wasp."

"Malmsey?" he suggests. "Seethe them?"

"What, three dozen? Waste of good wine. I'll do some for you, if you like. Come from Lord Lisle at Calais. When you write, tell him if he sends another batch, we want them fatter or not at all. Will you remember?"

"I'll make a note," he says gravely. "From now on I thought we might have the council meet here sometimes, when the king isn't sitting with us. We can give them dinner before."

"Right." Thurston titters. "Norfolk could do with some flesh on his twiggy little legs."

"Thurston, you needn't dirty your hands—you have enough staff. You could put on a gold chain, and strut about."

"Is that what you'll be doing?" A wet poultry slap; then Thurston looks up at him, wiping pluck from his fingers. "I think I'd rather keep my hand in. In case things take a downturn. Not that I say they will. Remember the cardinal, though."

He remembers Norfolk: tell him to go north, or I will come where he is and tear him with my teeth.

May I substitute the word "bite"?

The saying comes to him, *homo homini lupus,* man is wolf to man.

❖

"So," he says to Rafe after supper, "you've made your name, Master Sadler. You'll be held up as a prime example of how to waste your connections. Fathers will point you out to their sons."

"I couldn't help it, sir."

"How, not help it?"

Rafe says, as dry as he can manage, "I am violently in love with her."

"How does that feel? Is it like being violently angry?"

"I suppose. Maybe. In that you feel more alive."

"I do not think I could feel any more alive than I am."

He wonders if the cardinal was ever in love. But of course, why did he doubt? The all-consuming passion of Wolsey for Wolsey was hot enough to scorch all England. "Tell me, that evening after the queen was crowned . . ." He shakes his head, turns over some papers on his desk: letters from the mayor of Hull.

"I will tell you anything you ask," Rafe says. "I cannot imagine how I was not frank with you. But Helen, my wife, she thought it was better to be secret."

"But now she is carrying a child, I suppose, so you must declare yourselves?"

Rafe blushes.

"That evening, when I came into Austin Friars looking for her, to take her to Cranmer's wife . . . and she came down," his eyes move as if he were seeing it, "she came down without her cap, and you after, with your hair sticking up, and you were angry with me for taking her away . . ."

"Well, yes," Rafe says. His hand creeps up and he flattens his hair with his palm, as if that would help matters now. "They were all gone out to the feasts. That was the first time I took her to bed, but it was no blame. By then she had promised herself to me."

He thinks, I am glad I have not brought up in my house a young man without feeling, who only studies his advancement. If you are without impulses, you are, to a degree, without joy; under my protection, impulses are a thing Rafe can afford. "Look, Rafe, this is a—well, God knows, a folly but not a disaster. Tell your father my promotion in the world will ensure yours. Of course, he will stamp and roar. It is what fathers are for. He will shout, I rue the day I parted with my boy to the debauched house of Cromwell. But we will bring him around. A little and a little."

Till now the boy has been standing; he subsides onto a stool, hands on his head, head flung back; relief washes through his whole body. Was he so afraid? Of me? "Look, when your father sets eyes on Helen, he'll understand, unless he's . . ." Unless he's what? You'd have to be dead and entombed not to notice: her bold and beautiful body, her mild eyes. "We just need to get her out of that canvas apron she goes around in, and dress her up as Mistress Sadler. And of course you will want a house of your own. I will help you there. I shall miss the little children, I have grown fond of them, and Mercy too, we are all fond of them. If you want this new one to be the first child in your house, we can keep them here."

"It is good of you. But Helen would never part with them. It is understood between us."

So I shall never have any more children at Austin Friars, he thinks. Well, not unless I take time out of the king's business and go wooing: not unless, when a woman speaks to me, I actually listen. "What will reconcile your father, and you can tell him this, is that from now on, when I am not with the king, you will be with him. Master Wriothesley will tease the diplomats and keep the ciphers, for it is sly work which will suit him, and Richard will be here to head the household when I am absent and drive my work forward, and you and I will attend on Henry, as sweet as two nursemaids, and cater to his whims." He laughs. "You are a gentleman born. He may promote you close to his person, to the privy chamber. Which would be useful to me."

"I did not look for this to happen. I did not plan it." Rafe drops his eyes. "I know I can never take Helen with me to court."

"Not as the world is now. And I do not think it will change in our lifetimes. But look, you have made your choice. You must never repent it."

Rafe says, passionate, "How could I think to keep a secret from you? You see everything, sir."

"Ah. Only up to a point."

When Rafe has gone he takes out his evening's work and begins on it, methodical, tapping the papers into place. His bills are passed but there is always another bill. When you are writing laws you are testing words to find their utmost power. Like spells, they have to make things happen in the real world, and like spells, they only work if people believe in them. If your law exacts a penalty, you must be able to enforce it—on the rich as well as the poor, the people on the Scottish borders and the Welsh marches, the men of Cornwall as well as the men of Sussex and Kent. He has written this oath, a test of loyalty to Henry, and he means to swear the men of every burgh and village, and all women of any consequence: widows with inheritances, landowners. His people will be tramping the wold and heathland, pledging those who have barely heard of Anne Boleyn to uphold the succession of the child in her womb. If a man knows the king is called Henry, swear him; never mind if he confuses this king with his father or some Henry who came before. For princes like other men fade from the memory of common people; their features, on those coins he used to sift from the river silt, were no more than a slight irregularity under his fingertips, and even when he had taken the coins home and scrubbed them he could not say who they might be; is this, he asked, Prince Caesar? Walter had said, let's see; then he had flipped the coin away from him in disgust, saying, it's but a tinny farthing from one of those kings who fought the French wars. Get out there and earn, he'd said, never mind Prince Caesar; Caesar was old when Adam was a lad.

He would chant, "When Adam delved and Eve span, Who was then the gentleman?" Walter would chase him and hit him if he could catch him: there's a bloody rebel song for you, we know what to do with rebels here. They are dug into shallow graves, the Cornishmen who came up the country when he was a boy; but there are always more Cornishmen. And beneath Cornwall, beyond and beneath this whole realm of England, beneath the sodden marches of Wales and the rough territory of the Scots border, there is another landscape; there is a buried empire, where he fears his commissioners cannot reach. Who will swear the hobs and bogarts who live in the hedges and in hollow trees, and the wild men who hide in the woods? Who will swear the saints in their niches, and the spirits that cluster at holy wells rustling like fallen leaves, and the miscarried infants dug into unconsecrated ground: all those unseen dead who hover in winter around forges and village hearths, trying to warm their bare bones? For they too are his countrymen: the generations of the uncounted dead, breathing through the living, stealing their light from them, the bloodless ghosts of lord and knave, nun and whore, the ghosts of priest and friar who feed on living England, and suck the substance from the future.

He stares down at the papers on his desk, but his thoughts are far from here. My daughter Anne said, "I choose Rafe." He lowers his head into his hands and closes his eyes; Anne Cromwell stands before him, ten or eleven years old, broad and resolute like a man at arms, her small eyes unblinking, sure of her power to make her fate.

He rubs his eyes. Sifts his papers. What is this? A list. A meticulous clerk's hand, legible but making scant sense.

Two carpets. One cut in pieces.
7 sheets. 2 pillows. 1 bolster.
2 platters, 4 dishes, 2 saucers.
One small basin, weight 12lbs @ 4d the pound; my Lady Prioress
has it, paid 4 shillings.

He turns the paper over, trying to find its origin. He sees that he is looking at the inventory of Elizabeth Barton's goods, left behind at her nunnery. All this is forfeit to the king, the personal property of a traitor: a piece of plank which serves as a table, three pillowcases, two candlesticks, a coat valued at five shillings. An old mantle has been given in charity to the youngest nun in her convent. Another nun, a Dame Alice, has received a bedcover.

He had said to More, prophecy didn't make her rich. He makes a memorandum to himself: "Dame Elizabeth Barton to have money to fee the hangman." She has five days to live. The last person she will see as she climbs the ladder is her executioner, holding out his paw. If she cannot pay her way at the last, she may suffer longer than she needs. She had imagined how long it takes to burn, but not how long it takes to choke at the end of a rope. In England there is no mercy for the poor. You pay for everything, even a broken neck.

Thomas More's family has taken the oath. He has seen them himself, and Alice has left him in no doubt that she holds him personally responsible for failing to talk her husband into conformity. "Ask him what in the name of God he's about. Ask him, is it clever, does he think it is, to leave his wife without company, his son without advice, his daughters without protection, and all of us at the mercy of a man like Thomas Cromwell?"

"That's you told," Meg had murmured, with half a smile. Head bowed, she had taken his hand between her own. "My father has spoken very warmly of you. Of how you have been courteous to him and how you have been vehement—which he accounts no less a favor. He says he believes you understand him. As he understands you."

"Meg? Surely you can look at me?"

Another face bowed under the weight of a gable hood: Meg twitches her veils about her, as if she were out in a gale and they would provide protection.

"I can hold the king off for a day or two. I don't believe he wishes to see your father in the Tower, every moment he looks for some sign of . . ."

"Surrender?"

"Support. And then . . . no honor would be too high."

"I doubt the king can offer the sort of honor he cares for," Will Roper says. "Unfortunately. Come on, Meg, let's go home. We need to get your mother on the river before she starts a brawl." Roper holds out his hand. "We know you are not vengeful, sir. Though God knows, he has never been a friend to your friends."

"There was a time you were a Bible man yourself."

"Men may change opinions."

"I agree entirely. Tell your father-in-law that."

It was a sour note to part on. I shall not indulge More, he thinks, or his family, in any illusion that they *understand me*. How could that be, when my workings are hidden from myself?

He makes a note: Richard Cromwell to present himself to the Abbot of Westminster, to escort Sir Thomas More, prisoner, to the Tower. Why do I hesitate?

Let's give him one more day.

It is April 15, 1534. He calls in a clerk to tidy and file his papers, ready for tomorrow, and lingers by the fire, chatting; it is midnight, and the candles are burned down. He takes one and goes upstairs; Christophe, snoring, sprawls across the foot of his wide and lonely bed. Dear God, he thinks, my life is ridiculous. "Wake up," he says, but in a whisper; when Christophe does not respond, he lays hands on him and rolls him up and down, as if he were the lid for a pie, till the boy wakes up, expostulating in gutter French. "Oh by the hairy balls of Jesus." He blinks violently. "My good master, I didn't know it was you, I was dreaming I was a pastry. Forgive me, I am completely drunk, we have been celebrating the conjunction of the beautiful Helen with the fortunate Rafe." He raises a forearm, curls up his fist, makes a gesture of the utmost lewdness; his arm falls limp across his body, his eyelids slide ineluctably toward his cheeks, and with a final hiccup he subsides into sleep.

He hauls the boy to his pallet. Christophe is heavy now, a rotund bulldog pup; he grunts, he mutters, but he does not wake again.

He lays aside his clothes and says his prayers. He puts his head on the pillow: *7 sheets 2 pillows 1 bolster.* He sleeps as soon as the candle is out. But his daughter Anne comes to him in a dream. She holds up her left hand, sorrowful, to show him she wears no wedding ring. She twists up her long hair and wraps it around her neck like a noose.

❖

Midsummer: women hurry to the queen's apartments with clean linen folded over their arms. Their faces are blank and shocked and they walk so quickly you know not to stop them. Fires are lit within the queen's apartments to burn what has bled away. If there is anything to bury, the women keep it a secret between themselves.

That night, huddled in a window embrasure, the sky lit by stars like daggers, Henry will tell him, it is Katherine I blame. I believe she ill-wishes me. The truth is her womb is diseased. All those years she deceived me—she couldn't carry a son, and she and her doctors knew it. She claims she still loves me, but she is destroying me. She comes in the night with her cold hands and her cold heart, and lies between me and the woman I love. She puts her hand on my member and her hand smells of the tomb.

The lords and ladies give the maids and midwives money, to say what sex the child was, but the women give different answers each time. Indeed, what would be worse: for Anne to have conceived another girl, or to have conceived and miscarried a boy?

Midsummer: bonfires are lit all over London, burning through the short nights. Dragons stalk the streets, puffing out smoke and clattering their mechanical wings.

II

The Map of Christendom

1534–1535

D o you want Audley's post?" Henry asks him. "It's yours if you say so."

The summer is over. The Emperor has not come. Pope Clement is dead, and his judgments with him; the game is to play again, and he has left the door open, just a chink, for the next Bishop of Rome to hold a conversation with England. Personally, he would slam it shut; but these are not personal matters.

Now he thinks carefully: would it suit him to be Chancellor? It would be good to have a post in the legal hierarchy, so why not at the top? "I have no wish to disturb Audley. If Your Majesty is satisfied with him, I am too."

He remembers how the post tied Wolsey to London, when the king was elsewhere. The cardinal was active in the law courts; but we have lawyers enough.

Henry says, only tell me what you deem best. Abased, like a lover, he cannot think of the best presents. He says, Cranmer bids me listen to Cromwell, and if he needs a post, a tax, an impost, a measure in Parliament or a royal proclamation, give it to him.

The post of Master of the Rolls is vacant. It is an ancient judicial office, it commands one of the kingdom's great secretariats. His predecessors will be those men, bishops for the most part, eminent in learning: those who lie down on their tombs, with their virtues in Latin engraved beneath. He is never more alive than when he twists the stem of this ripe fruit and snaps it from the tree.

"You were also right about Cardinal Farnese," Henry says. "Now we have a new Pope—Bishop of Rome, I should say—I have collected on my bets."

"You see," he says, smiling. "Cranmer is right. Be advised by me."

The court is amused to hear how the Romans have celebrated Pope Clement's death. They have broken into his tomb, and dragged his naked body through the streets.

❖

The Master's house in Chancery Lane is the most curious house he has ever entered. It smells of must, mold and tallow, and behind its crooked facade it meanders back, a warren of little spaces with low doorways; were our forebears all dwarves, or were they not perfectly certain how to prop up a ceiling?

This house was founded three hundred years ago, by the Henry that was then; he built it as a refuge for Jews who wished to convert. If they took this step—advisable if they wished to be preserved from violence—they would forfeit all their possessions to the Crown. This being so, it was just that the Crown should house and feed them for their natural lives.

Christophe runs ahead of him, into the depths of the house. "Look!" He trails his finger through a vast spider's web.

"You've broken up her home, you heartless boy." He examines Ariane's crumbling prey: a leg, a wing. "Let's be gone, before she comes back."

Some fifty years after Henry had endowed the house, all Jews were expelled from the realm. Yet the refuge was never quite empty; even today two women live here. I shall call on them, he says.

Christophe is tapping the walls and beams, for all the world as if he knew what he was looking for. "Wouldn't you run," he says with relish, "if someone tapped back?"

"Oh, Jesus!" Christophe crosses himself. "I expect a hundred men have died here, Jews and Christians both."

Behind this wainscot, it is true, he can sense the tiny bones of mice: a hundred generations, their articulated forefeet folded in eternal rest. Their descendants, thriving, he can smell in the air. This is a job for Marlinspike, he says, if we can catch him. The cardinal's cat is feral now, ranging at will through London gardens, lured by the scent of carp from the ponds of city monasteries, tempted—for all he knows—across the river, to be snuggled to the bosoms of whores, slack breasts rubbed with rose petals and ambergris; he imagines Marlinspike lolling, purring, declining to come home again. He says to Christophe, "I wonder how I can be Master of the Rolls, if I am not master of a cat."

"The Rolls have not paws to go walking." Christophe is kicking a skirting. "My foot go through it," he says, demonstrating.

Will he leave the comforts of Austin Friars, for the tiny windows with their warped panes, the creaking passages, the ancient drafts? "It will be a shorter journey to Westminster," he says. His aim is bent there—Whitehall, Westminster and the river, Master Secretary's barge down to Greenwich or up to Hampton Court. I shall be back at Austin Friars often, he says to himself, almost every day. He is building a treasure room, a repository secure for any gold plate the king entrusts to him; whatever he deposits can quickly be turned into ready money. His treasure comes through the street on ordinary carts, to attract no attention, though there are vigilant outriders. The chalices are fitted into soft leather cases made for them. The bowls and dishes travel in canvas bags, interleaved with white woolen cloth at seven pence the yard. The jewels are swaddled in silk and packed into chests with new and shiny locks: and he has the keys. There are great pearls which gleam wet from the ocean, sapphires hot as India. There are jewels like the fruit you pick on a country afternoon: garnets like sloes, pink diamonds like rose hips. Alice says, "For a handful of these I would, myself, overthrow any queen in Christendom."

"What a good thing the king hasn't met you, Alice."

Jo says, "I would as soon have it in export licenses. Or army contracts. Someone will make a fortune in the Irish wars. Beans, flour, malt, horseflesh . . ."

"I shall see what I can do for you," he says.

At Austin Friars he holds the lease for ninety-nine years. His great-grandchildren will have it: some unknown Londoners. When they look at the documents his name will be there. His arms will be carved over the doorways. He rests his hand on the banister of the great staircase, looks up into the dust-mote glitter from a high window. When did I do this? At Hatfield, early in the year: looking up, listening for the sounds of Morton's household, long ago. If he himself went to Hatfield, must not Thomas More have gone up too? Perhaps it was his light footstep he expected, overhead?

He starts to think again, about that fist that came out of nowhere.

His first idea had been, move clerks and papers to the Rolls, then Austin Friars will become a home again. But for whom? He has taken out Liz's book of hours, and on the page where she kept the family listed he has made alterations, additions. Rafe will be moving out soon, to his new house in Hackney; and Richard is building in the same neighborhood, with his wife, Frances. Alice is marrying his ward Thomas Rotherham. Her brother Christopher is ordained and beneficed. Jo's wedding clothes are ordered; she is snapped up by his friend John ap Rice, a lawyer, a scholar, a man he admires and on whose loyalty he counts. I have done well for my folk, he thinks: not one of them poor, or unhappy, or uncertain of their place in this uncertain world. He hesitates, looking up into the light: now gold, now blue as a cloud passes. Whoever will come downstairs and claim him, must do it now. His daughter Anne with her thundering feet: Anne, he would say to her, couldn't we have felt mufflers over those hooves of yours? Grace skimming down like dust, drawn into a spiral, a lively swirl . . . going nowhere, dispersing, gone.

Liz, come down.

But Liz keeps her silence; she neither stays nor goes. She is always with him and not with him. He turns away. So this house will become a place of business. As all his houses will become places of business. My home will be where my clerks and files are; otherwise, my home will be with the king, where he is.

Christophe says, "Now we are removed to the Rolls House, I can tell you, *cher maître,* how I am happy that you did not leave me behind. For in your absence they would call me snail brain and turnip head."

"Alors . . ." he takes a view of Christophe, "your head is indeed like a turnip. Thank you for attracting my attention to it."

Installed at the Rolls, he takes a view of his situation: satisfactory. He has sold off his two Kent manors, but the king has given him one in Monmouthshire and he is buying another in Essex. He has his eye on plots in Hackney and Shoreditch, and is taking in leases on the properties around Austin Friars, which he intends to enfold in his building plans; and then, build a big wall around the lot. He has surveys to hand of a manor in Bedfordshire, one in Lincolnshire, and two Essex properties he intends to put in trust for Gregory. All this is small stuff. It's nothing to what he intends to have, or to what Henry will owe him.

Meanwhile, his outgoings would frighten a lesser man. If the king wants something done, you have to be able to staff the enterprise and fund it. It is hard to keep up with the spending of his noble councillors, and yet there are a crew of them who live at the pawnshop and come to him month by month to patch the holes in their accounts. He knows when to let these debts run; there is more than one kind of currency in England. What he senses is a great net is spreading about him, a web of favors done and favors received. Those who want access to the king expect to pay for it, and no one has better access than he. And at the same time, the word is out: help Cromwell and he will help you. Be loyal, be diligent, be intelligent on his behalf; you will come into a reward. Those who commit their service to him will be promoted and protected. He is a good friend and master; this is said of him everywhere. Otherwise, it is the usual abuse. His father was a blacksmith, a crooked brewer, he was an Irishman, he was a criminal, he was a Jew, and he himself was just a wool-trader, he was a shearsman, and now he is a sorcerer: how else but by being a sorcerer would he get the reins of power in his hand? Chapuys writes to the Emperor about him; his early life remains a mystery, but he is excellent company, and he keeps his household and retainers in magnificent style. He is a master of language, Chapuys writes, a man of most eloquent address; though his French, he adds, is only *assez bien.*

He thinks, it's good enough for you. A nod and a wink will do for you.

These last months, the council has never been out of harness. A hard summer of negotiating has brought a treaty with the Scots. But Ireland is in revolt. Only Dublin Castle itself and the town of Waterford hold out for the king, while the rebel lords are offering their services and their harbors to the Emperor's troops. Among these isles it is the most wretched of territories, which does not pay the king what it costs him to garrison it; but he cannot turn his back on it, for fear of who else might come in. Law is barely respected there, for the Irish think you can buy off murder with money, and like the Welsh they cost out a man's life in cattle. The people are kept poor by imposts and seizures, by forfeitures and plain daylight robbery; the pious English abstain from meat on Wednesdays and Fridays, but the joke runs that the Irish are so godly they abstain every other day as well. Their great lords are brutal and imperious men, treacherous and fickle, inveterate feuders, extortionists and hostage takers, and their allegiance to England they hold cheap, for they are loyal to nothing and prefer force of arms to law. As for the native chiefs, they recognize no natural limit to their claims. They say that on their land they own every ferny slope and lake, they own the heather, the meadow grass and the winds that riffle it; they own every beast and every man, and in times of scarcity they take the bread to feed their hunting dogs.

No wonder they don't want to be English. It would interrupt their status as slave owners. The Duke of Norfolk still has serfs on his land, and even if the law courts move to free them the duke expects a fee from it. The king proposes to send Norfolk to Ireland, but he says he's spent enough futile months over there and the only way he'll go back is if they build a bridge so he can get home at the end of the week without getting his feet wet.

He and Norfolk fight in the council chamber. The duke rants, and he sits back and folds his arms and watches him ranting. You should have sent young Fitzroy to Dublin, he tells the council. An apprentice king—make a show, stage a spectacle, throw some money about.

Richard says to him, "Perhaps we should go to Ireland, sir."

"I think my campaigning days are over."

"I would like to be in arms. Every man should be a soldier once in his life."

"That is your grandfather speaking through you. Ap Evan the archer. Concentrate for now on making a show in the tournaments."

Richard has proved a formidable man in the lists. It is more or less as Christophe says: biff, and they are flat. You would think the sport was in his nephew's blood, as it is in the blood of the lords who compete. He carries the Cromwell colors, and the king loves him for it, as he loves any man with flair and courage and physical strength. Increasingly, his bad leg forces him to sit with the spectators. When he is in pain he is panicked, you can see it in his eyes, and when he is recovering he is restless. Uncertainty about his own state of health makes him less inclined for the expense and trouble of organizing a large tournament. When he does run a course, with his experience, his weight and height, his superb horses and the steel of his temperament, he is likely to win. But to avoid accidents, he prefers to run against opponents he knows.

Henry says, "The Emperor, two or three years back when he was in Germany, did he not have an evil humor in his thigh? They say the weather didn't suit him. But then his dominions offer a change of climate. Whereas from one part of my kingdom to the next there is no change to be found."

"Oh, I expect it's worse in Dublin."

Henry looks out, hopeless, at the teeming rain. "And when I ride out the people shout at me. They rise up out of ditches, and shout about Katherine, how I should take her back. How would they like it if I told them how to order their houses and wives and children?"

Even when the weather clears the king's fears do not diminish. "She will escape and raise an army against me," he says. "Katherine. You do not know what she would do."

"She told me she would not run."

"And you think she never lies? I know she lies. I have proof of it. She lied about her own virginity."

Oh, that, he thinks tiredly.

It seems Henry doesn't believe in the power of armed guards, in locks and keys. He thinks an angel recruited by the Emperor Charles will make them fall away. When he travels, he takes with him a great iron lock, which is affixed to his chamber door by a servant who goes with him for the purpose. His food is tasted for poison and his bed examined, last thing at night, for concealed weapons, such as needles; but even so, he is afraid he will be murdered as he sleeps.

❖

Autumn: Thomas More is losing weight, a wiry little man emerging from what was never a superfluity of flesh. He lets Antonio Bonvisi send him food in. "Not that you Lucchese know how to eat. I'd send it myself, but if he took ill, you know what people would say."

"He likes dishes of eggs. I don't know if he likes much else."

A sigh. "Milk puddings."

He smiles. These are carnivorous days. "No wonder he doesn't thrive."

"I've known him for forty years," Bonvisi says. "A lifetime, Tommaso. You wouldn't hurt him, would you? Please assure me, if you can, that no one will hurt him."

"Why do you think I'm no better than he is? Look, I have no need to put him under pressure. His family and friends will do it. Won't they?"

"Can't you just leave him there? Forget him?"

"Of course. If the king allows."

He arranges for Meg Roper to visit. Father and daughter walk in the gardens, arm in arm. Sometimes he watches them from a window in the Lord Lieutenant's lodgings.

By November, this policy has failed. Turned back, really, and bitten his hand, like a dog that out of kindness you pick up in the street. Meg says, "He has told me, and he has asked me to tell his friends, that he will have no more to do with oaths of any kind, and that if we hear he has sworn, we are to take it that he has been forced, by ill-usage and rough handling. And if a paper is shown to the council, with his signature on it, we are to understand it is not his hand."

More is now required to swear to the Act of Supremacy, an act which draws together all the powers and dignities assumed by the king in the last two years. It doesn't, as some say, make the king head of the church. It states that he is head of the church, and always has been. If people don't like new ideas, let them have old ones. If they want precedents, he has precedents. A second enactment, which will come into force in the new year, defines the scope of treason. It will be a treasonable offense to deny Henry's titles or jurisdiction, to speak or write maliciously against him, to call him a heretic or a schismatic. This law will catch the friars who spread panic and say the Spanish are landing with the next tide to seize the throne for the Lady Mary. It will catch the priests who in their sermons rant against the king's authority and say he is dragging his subjects after him to Hell. Is it much for a monarch to ask, that a subject keep a civil tongue in his head?

This is new, people say to him, this treason by words, and he says, no, be assured, it is old. It casts into statute law what the judges in their wisdom have already defined as common law. It is a measure for clarification. I am all for clarity.

Upon More's refusal of this second oath, a bill is brought in against him, forfeiting his goods to the Crown. He now has no hope of release; or rather, the hope lies in himself. It is his duty to visit him, tell him he will no longer be allowed visitors, or strolls in the gardens.

"Nothing to see, this time of year." More casts a glance at the sky, a narrow strip of gray through the high window. "I can still have my books? Write letters?"

"For now."

"And John Wood, he stays with me?"

His servant. "Yes, of course."

"He brings me a little news from time to time. They say the sweating sickness has broken out among the king's troops in Ireland. So late in the year, too."

Plague has also broken out; he's not going to tell More that, or that the whole Irish campaign is a debacle and a money sink and that he wishes he had done as Richard said and gone out there himself.

"The sweat takes off so many," More says, "and so swiftly, and in their prime too. And if you survive it, you are in no condition to fight the wild Irish, that's for sure. I remember when Meg took it, she nearly died. Have you had it? No, you're never ill, are you?" He is chattering pointlessly, then he looks up. "Tell me, what do you hear from Antwerp? They say Tyndale is there. They say he lives straitly. He dare not stray beyond the English merchants' house. They say he is in prison, almost as I am."

It is true, or partly true. Tyndale has labored in poverty and obscurity, and now his world has shrunk to a little room; while outside in the city, under the Emperor's laws, printers are branded and have their eyes put out, and brothers and sisters are killed for their faith, the men beheaded, the women buried alive. More has a sticky web in Europe still, a web made of money; it is his belief that his men have followed Tyndale these many months, but all his ingenuity, and Stephen Vaughan's on the spot, have not been able to find out which of the Englishmen who pass through that busy town are More's agents. "Tyndale would be safer in London," More says. "Under yourself, the protector of error. Now, look at Germany today. You see, Thomas, where heresy leads us. It leads us to Münster, does it not?"

Sectaries, anabaptists, have taken over the city of Münster. Your worst nightmares—when you wake, paralyzed, and think you have died—are bliss compared with this. The burgomasters have been ejected from the council, and thieves and lunatics have taken their places, proclaiming that the end times have come and all must be rebaptized. Citizens who dissent have been driven beyond the walls, naked, to perish in the snow. Now the city is under siege from its own prince-bishop, who intends to starve it out. The defenders, they say, are for the most part the women and children left behind; they are held in dread by a tailor called Bockelson, who has crowned himself King of Jerusalem. It is rumored that Bockelson's friends have instituted polygamy, as recommended in the Old Testament, and that some of the women have been hanged or drowned rather than submit to rape under cover of Abraham's law. These prophets engage in daylight robbery, in the name of holding goods in common. It is said they have seized the houses of the rich, burned their letters, slashed their pictures, mopped the floors with fine embroidery, and shredded the records of who owns what, so former times can never come back.

"Utopia," he says. "Is it not?"

"I hear they are burning the books from the city libraries. Erasmus has gone into the flames. What kind of devils would burn the gentle Erasmus? But no doubt, no doubt," More nods, "Münster will be restored to order. Philip the prince of Hesse, Luther's friend, I have no doubt he will lend the good bishop his cannon and his cannoneers, and one heretic will put down another. The brethren fall to scrapping, do you see? Like rabid dogs drooling in the streets, who tear out each other's entrails when they meet."

"I tell you how Münster will end. Someone inside the city will surrender it."

"You think so? You look as if you would offer me odds. But there, I was never much of a gambler. And now the king has all my money."

"A man like that, a tailor, jumps up for a month or two—"

"A wool merchant, a blacksmith's son, he jumps up for a year or two . . ."

He stands, picks up his cape: black wool, lambskin lining. More's eyes gleam, ah, look, I have you on the run. Now he murmurs, as if it were a supper party, must you go? Stay a little, can't you? He lifts his chin. "So I shall not see Meg again?"

The man's tone, the emptiness, the loss: it goes straight to his heart. He turns away, to keep his reply calm and trite. "You have to say some words. That's all."

"Ahh. Just words."

"And if you don't want to say them I can put them to you in writing. Sign your name and the king will be happy. I will send my barge to row you back to Chelsea, and tie up at the wharf at the end of your own garden—not much to see, as you say, at this time of year, but think of the warm welcome within. Dame Alice is waiting—Alice's cooking, well, that alone would restore you; she is standing by your side watching you chew and the minute you wipe your mouth she picks you up in her arms and kisses away the mutton fat, why husband

I have missed you! She bears you off to her bedchamber, locks the door and drops the key in her pocket and pulls off your clothes till there you are in your shirt and nothing but your little white legs sticking out—well, admit it, the woman is within her rights. Then next day—think of it—you rise before dawn, shuffle to your familiar cell and flog yourself, call for your bread and water, and by eight o'clock back in your hair shirt, and over it your old woolen gown, that blood-colored one with the rent in . . . feet up on a stool, and your only son bringing in your letters . . . snapping the seal on your darling Erasmus . . . Then when you have read your letters, you can hobble out—let's say it's a sunny day—and look at your caged birds, and your little fox in its pen, and you can say, I was a prisoner too, but no more, because Cromwell showed me I could be free . . . Don't you want it? Don't you want to come out of this place?"

"You should write a play," More says wonderingly.

He laughs. "Perhaps I shall."

"It's better than Chaucer. Words. Words. Just words."

He turns. He stares at More. It's as if the light has changed. A window has opened on a strange country, where a cold wind from childhood blows. "That book . . . Was it a dictionary?"

More frowns. "I'm sorry?"

"I came up the stairs at Lambeth—give me a moment . . . I came running up the stairs, carrying your measure of small beer and your wheaten loaf, to keep you from being hungry if you woke in the night. It was seven in the evening. You were reading, and when you looked up you held your hands over the book," he makes the shape of wings, "as if you were protecting it. I asked you, Master More, what is in that great book? You said, words, words, just words."

More tilts his head. "This was when?"

"I believe I was seven."

"Oh, nonsense," More says genially. "I didn't know you when you were seven. Why, you were . . ." He frowns. "You must have been . . . and I was . . ."

"About to go to Oxford. You don't remember. But why would you?" He shrugs. "I thought you were laughing at me."

"Oh, very probably I was," More says. "If indeed such a meeting took place. Now witness these present days, when you come here and laugh at me. Talking about Alice. And my little white legs."

"I think it must have been a dictionary. You are sure you don't remember? Well . . . my barge is waiting, and I don't want to keep the oars out in the cold."

"The days are very long in here," More says. "The nights are longer. My chest is bad. My breathing is tight."

"Back to Chelsea then, Dr. Butts will visit, tut-tut Thomas More, what have you been doing to yourself? Hold your nose and drink off this foul mixture . . ."

"Sometimes I think I shall not see morning."

He opens the door. "Martin?"

Martin is thirty, wiry, his fair hair under his cap already sparse: pleasant face with a crinkly smile. His native town is Colchester, his father a tailor, and he learned to read on Wycliffe's gospel, which his father hid in their roof under the thatch. This is a new England; an England where Martin can dust the old text down, and show it to his neighbors. He has brothers, all of them Bible men. His wife is just now confined with her third child, "crawled into the straw," as he puts it.

"Any news?"

"Not yet. But will you stand godfather? Thomas if it's a boy, or if it's a girl you name her, sir."

A touch of palms and a smile. "Grace," he says. A money gift is understood; the child's start in life. He turns back to the sick man, who now slumps over his table. "Sir Thomas says at night his breath comes short. Bring him some bolsters, cushions, whatever you can find, prop him up to ease him. I want him to have every opportunity to live to rethink his position, show loyalty to our king, and go home. And now, bid you both good afternoon."

More looks up. "I want to write a letter."

"Of course. You shall have ink and paper."

"I want to write to Meg."

"Then send her a human word."

More's letters are beyond the human. They may be addressed to his daughter, but they are written for his friends in Europe to read.

"Cromwell . . . ?" More's voice calls him back. "How is the queen?"

More is always correct, not like those who slip up and say, "Queen Katherine." How is Anne? he means. But what could he tell him? He is on his way. He is out of the door. In the narrow window a blue dusk has replaced the gray.

❖

He had heard her voice, from the next room: low, relentless. Henry yelping in indignation. "Not me! Not me."

In the antechamber, Thomas Boleyn, Monseigneur, his narrow face rigid. Some Boleyn hangers-on, exchanging glances: Francis Weston, Francis Bryan. In a corner, trying to make himself inconspicuous, the lutenist Mark Smeaton; what's he doing here? Not quite a family conclave: George Boleyn is in Paris, holding talks. An idea has been floated that the infant Elizabeth should marry a son of France; the Boleyns really think this is going to happen.

"Whatever can have occurred," he says, "to upset the queen?" His tone is astonished: as if she were the most placid of women.

Weston says, "It's Lady Carey, she is—that is to say she finds herself—"

Bryan snorts. "With a bellyful of bastard."

"Ah. Didn't you know?" The shock around him is gratifying. He shrugs. "I thought it a family matter."

Bryan's eyepatch winks at him, today a jaundiced yellow. "You must watch her very closely, Cromwell."

"A matter in which I have failed," Boleyn says. "Evidently. She claims the child's father is William Stafford, and she has married him. You know this Stafford, do you?"

"Just about. Well," he says cheerfully, "shall we go in? Mark, we are not setting this affair to music, so take yourself off to where you can be useful."

Only Henry Norris is attending the king: Jane Rochford, the

queen. Henry's big face is white. "You blame me, madam, for what I did before I even knew you."

They have crowded in behind him. Henry says, "My lord Wiltshire, can you not control either of your daughters?"

"Cromwell knew," Bryan says. He snorts with laughter.

Monseigneur begins to talk, stumbling—he, Thomas Boleyn, diplomat famed for his silver-tongued finesse. Anne cuts him off: "Why should she get a child by Stafford? I don't believe it's his. Why would he agree to marry her, unless for ambition—well, he has made a false move there, for he will never come to court again, nor will she. She can crawl on her knees to me. I care not. She can starve."

If Anne were my wife, he thinks, I'd go out for the afternoon. She looks haggard, and she cannot stay still; you wouldn't trust her near a sharp knife. "What to do?" Norris whispers. Jane Rochford is standing back against the tapestries, where nymphs entwine themselves in trees; the hem of her skirt is dipped in some fabulous stream, and her veil brushes a cloud, from which a goddess peeps. She lifts her face; her look is one of sober triumph.

I could have the archbishop fetched, he thinks. Anne wouldn't rage and stamp under his eyes. Now she has Norris by the sleeve; what is she doing? "My sister has done this to spite me. She thinks she will sail about the court with her great belly, and pity me and laugh at me, because I have lost my own child."

"I feel sure that, if the matter were to be viewed—" her father begins.

"Get out!" she says. "Leave me, and tell her—Mistress Stafford—that she has forfeited any claim on my family. I don't know her. She is no longer a Boleyn."

"Wiltshire, go." Henry adds, in the tone in which a schoolboy is promised a whipping, "I shall speak to you later."

He says to the king, innocent, "Majesty, shall we do no business today?" Henry laughs.

❖

Lady Rochford runs beside him. He does not slow his pace so she has to pick up her skirts. "Did you really know, Master Secretary? Or did you say that just to see their faces?"

"You are too good for me. You see through all my ploys."

"Lucky I see through Lady Carey's."

"It was you who detected her?" Who else, he thinks? With her husband, George, away she has no one to spy on.

Mary's bed is strewn with silks—flame, orange, carnation—as if a fire has broken out in the mattress. Across stools and a window seat trail lawn smocks, entangled ribbons and unpaired gloves. Are those the same green stockings she once revealed to the knee, running full-tilt toward him on the day she proposed marriage?

He stands in the doorway. "William Stafford, eh?"

She straightens up, her cheeks flushed, a velvet slipper in her hand. Now the secret is out, she has loosened her bodice. Her eyes slide past him. "Good girl, Jane, bring that here."

"Excuse me, Master." It is Jane Seymour, tiptoeing past him with an armful of folded laundry. Then a boy after her, bumping a yellow leather chest. "Just here, Mark."

"Behold me, Master Secretary," Smeaton says. "I'm making myself useful."

Jane kneels before the chest and swings it open. "Cambric to line it?"

"Never mind cambric. Where's my other shoe?"

"Best be gone," Lady Rochford warns. "If Uncle Norfolk sees you he'll take a stick to you. Your royal sister thinks the king has fathered your child. She says, why would it be William Stafford?"

Mary snorts. "So much does she know. What would Anne know of taking a man for himself? You can tell her he loves me. You can tell her he cares for me and no one else does. No one else in this world."

He leans down and whispers, "Mistress Seymour, I did not think you were a friend of Lady Carey."

"No one else will help her." She keeps her head down; the nape of her neck flushes pink.

"Those bed hangings are mine," Mary says. "Pull them down."

Embroidered on them, he sees, are the arms of her husband, Will Carey, dead what—seven years now? "I can unpick the badges." Of course: what use are a dead man and his devices? "Where's my gilt basin, Rochford, have you got it?" She gives the yellow chest a kick; it is stamped all over with Anne's falcon badge. "If they see me with this, they'll take it off me and tip my stuff in the road."

"If you can wait an hour," he says, "I'll send someone with a chest for you."

"Will it be stamped Thomas Cromwell? God save me, I haven't an hour. I know what!" She begins to haul the sheets off the bed. "Make bundles!"

"For shame," Jane Rochford says. "And run off like a servant who's stolen the silver? Besides, you won't need these things down in Kent. Stafford has a farm or something, hasn't he? Some little manor? Still, you can sell them. You'll have to, I suppose."

"My sweet brother will help me when he returns from France. He will not see me cut off."

"I beg to differ. Lord Rochford will be sensible, as I am, that you have disgraced all your kin."

Mary turns on her, arm sweeping out like a cat flashing claws. "This is better than your wedding day, Rochford. It's like getting a houseful of presents. You can't love, you don't know what love is, and all you can do is envy those who do know, and rejoice in their troubles. You are a wretched unhappy woman whose husband loathes her, and I pity you, and I pity my sister Anne, I would not change places with her, I had rather be in the bed of an honest poor gentleman who cares only for me than be like the queen and only able to keep her man with old whore's tricks—yes, I know it is so, he has told Norris what she offers him, and it doesn't conduce to getting a child, I can tell you. And now she is afraid of every woman at court—have you looked at her, have you looked at her lately? Seven years she schemed to be queen, and God protect us from answered prayers. She thought it would be like her coronation every day." Mary, breathless, reaches into the mill of her possessions and throws Jane Seymour a pair of sleeves. "Take these, sweetheart, with my blessing. You have the only kind heart at court."

Jane Rochford, in departing, slams the door.

"Let her go," Jane Seymour murmurs. "Forget her."

"Good riddance!" Mary snaps. "I must be glad she didn't pick my things over, and offer me a price." In the silence, her words go crash, flap, rattling around the room like trapped birds who panic and shit down the walls: he has told Norris what she offers him. By night, her ingenious proceedings. He is rephrasing it: as, surely, one must? I'll bet Norris is all ears. Christ alive, these people! The boy Mark is standing, gapey-faced, behind the door. "Mark, if you stand there like a landed fish I shall have you filleted and fried." The boy flees.

When Mistress Seymour has tied the bundles they look like birds with broken wings. He takes them from her and reties them, not with silk tags but serviceable string. "Do you always carry string, Master Secretary?"

Mary says, "Oh, my book of love poems! Shelton has it." She pitches from the room.

"She'll need that," he says. "No poems down in Kent."

"Lady Rochford would tell her that sonnets don't keep you warm. Not," Jane says, "that I've ever had a sonnet. So I wouldn't really know."

Liz, he thinks, take your dead hand off me. Do you grudge me this one little girl, so small, so thin, so plain? He turns. "Jane—"

"Master Secretary?" She dips her knees and rolls sideways onto the mattress; she sits up, drags her skirts from under her, finds her footing: gripping the bedpost, she scrambles up, reaches above her head, and begins to unhook the hangings.

"Come down! I'll do that. I'll send a wagon after Mistress Stafford. She can't carry all she owns."

"I can do it. Master Secretary doesn't deal with bed hangings."

"Master Secretary deals with everything. I'm surprised I don't make the king's shirts."

Jane sways gently above him. Her feet sink into the feathers. "Queen Katherine does. Still."

"The Dowager Katherine. Come down."

She hops down to the rushes, giving her skirts a shake. "Even now after all that has passed between them. She sent a new parcel last week."

"I thought the king had forbidden her."

"Anne says they should be torn up and used for, well, you know what for, in a jakes. He was angry. Possibly because he doesn't like the word *jakes*."

"No more does he." The king deprecates coarse language, and not a few courtiers have been frozen out for telling some dirty story. "Is it true what Mary says? That the queen is afraid?"

"For now he is sighing over Mistress Shelton. Well, you know that. You have observed."

"But surely that is harmless? A king is obliged to be gallant, till he reaches the age when he puts on his long gown and sits by the fire with his chaplains."

"Explain it to Anne, she doesn't see it. She wanted to send Shelton away. But her father and her brother would not have it. Because the Sheltons are their cousins, so if Henry is going to look elsewhere, they want it to be close to home. Incest is so popular these days! Uncle Norfolk said—I mean, His Grace—"

"It's all right," he says, distracted, "I call him that too."

Jane puts a hand over her mouth. It is a child's hand, with tiny gleaming nails. "I shall think of that when I am in the country and have nothing to amuse me. And then does he say, dear nephew Cromwell?"

"You are leaving court?" No doubt she has a husband in view: some country husband.

"I hope that when I have served another season I might be released."

Mary rips into the room, snarling. She juggles two embroidered cushions above the bulk of her child, a bulk which now seems evident; she has a hand free for her gilt basin, in which is her poetry book. She throws down the cushions, opens her fist and scatters a handful of silver buttons, which rattle into the basin like dice. "Shelton had these. Curse her for a magpie."

"It is not as if the queen likes me," Jane says. "And it is a long time since I saw Wolf Hall."

❖

For the king's New Year's gift he has commissioned from Hans a miniature on vellum, which shows Solomon on his throne receiving Sheba. It is to be an allegory, he explains, of the king receiving the fruits of the church and the homage of his people. Hans gives him a withering look. "I grasp the point."

Hans prepares sketches. Solomon is seated in majesty. Sheba stands before him, unseen face raised, her back to the onlooker. "In your own mind," he says, "can you see her face, even though it's hidden?"

"You pay for the back of her head, that's what you get!" Hans rubs his forehead. He relents. "Not true. I can see her."

"See her like a woman you meet in the street?"

"Not quite like that. More like someone you remember. Like some woman you used to know when you were a child."

They are seated in front of the tapestry the king gave him. The painter's eyes stray to it. "This woman on the wall. Wolsey had her, Henry had her, now you."

"I assure you, she has no counterpart in real life." Well, not unless Westminster has some very discreet and versatile whore.

"I know who she is." Hans nods emphatically, lips pressed together, eyes bright and taunting, like a dog who steals a handkerchief so you will chase it. "They talk about it in Antwerp. Why don't you go over and claim her?"

"She is married." He is taken aback, to think that his private business is common talk.

"You think she would not come away with you?"

"It's years. I have changed."

"*Ja*. Now you are rich."

"But what would be said of me, if I enticed away a woman from her husband?"

Hans shrugs. They are so matter-of-fact, the Germans. More says the Lutherans fornicate in church. "Besides," Hans says, "there is the matter of the—"

"The what?"

Hans shrugs: nothing. "Nothing! You are going to hang me up by my hands till I confess?"

"I don't do that. I only threaten to do it."

"I meant only," Hans says soothingly, "there is the matter of all the other women who want to marry you. The wives of England, they all keep secret books of whom they are going to have next when they have poisoned their husbands. And you are the top of everyone's list."

In his idle moments—in the week there are two or three—he has been picking through the records of the Rolls House. Though the Jews are forbidden the realm, you cannot know what human flotsam will be washed up by the tide of fortune, and only once, for a single month in these three hundred years, has the house been empty. He runs his eye over the accounts of the successive wardens, and he handles, curious, the receipts for their relief given by the dead inhabitants, written in Hebrew characters. Some of them spent fifty years within these walls, flinching from the Londoners outside. When he walks the crooked passages, he feels their footsteps under his.

He goes to see the two who remain. They are silent and vigilant women of indeterminate age, and the names they go by are Katherine Wheteley and Mary Cook.

"What do you do?" With your time, he means.

"We say our prayers."

They watch him for evidence of his intentions, good or ill. Their faces say, we are two women with nothing left but our life stories. Why should we part with them to you?

He sends them presents of fowl but he wonders if they eat flesh from gentile hands. Toward Christmas, the prior of Christchurch in Canterbury sends him twelve Kentish apples, each one wrapped in gray linen, of a special kind that is good with wine. He takes these apples to the converts, with wine he has picked out. "In the year 1353," he says, "there was only one person in the house. I am sorry to think she lived here without company. Her last domicile was the city of Exeter, but I wonder where before that? Her name was Claricia."

"We know nothing of her," says Katherine, or possibly Mary. "It would be surprising if we did." Her fingertip tests the apples. Possibly she does not recognize their rarity, or that they are the best present the prior could find. If you don't like them, he says, or if you do, I have stewing pears. Somebody sent me five hundred.

"A man who meant to get himself noticed," says Katherine or Mary, and the other says, "Five hundred pounds would have been better."

The women laugh, but their laughter is cold. He sees he will never be on terms with them. He likes the name Claricia and he wishes he had suggested it for the jailer's daughter. It is a name for a woman you might dream of: one you could see straight through.

When the king's New Year's present is done Hans says, "It is the first time I have made his portrait."

"You shall make another soon, I hope."

Hans knows he has an English Bible, a translation almost ready. He puts a finger to his lips; too soon to talk about it, next year maybe. "If you were to dedicate it to Henry," Hans says, "could he now refuse it? I will put him on the title page, displayed in glory, head of the church." Hans paces, growls out a few figures. He is thinking of paper and printer's costs, estimating his profits. Lucas Cranach draws title pages for Luther. "Those pictures of Martin and his wife, he has sold prints by the basketful. And Cranach makes everybody look like a pig."

True. Even those silvery nudes he paints have sweet pig-faces, and laborer's feet, and gristly ears. "But if I paint Henry, I must flatter, I suppose. Show him how he was five years ago. Or ten."

"Stick to five. He will think you are mocking him."

Hans draws his finger across his throat, buckles at the knees, thrusts out his tongue like a man hanged; it seems he envisages every method of execution.

"An easy majesty would be called for," he says.

Hans beams. "I can do it by the yard."

❖

The end of the year brings cold and a green aqueous light, washing across the Thames and the city. Letters fall to his desk with a soft shuffle like great snowflakes: doctors of theology from Germany, ambassadors from France, Mary Boleyn from her exile in Kent.

He breaks the seal. "Listen to this," he says to Richard. "Mary wants money. She says, she knows she should not have been so hasty. She says, love overcame reason."

"Love, was it?"

He reads. She does not regret for a minute she has taken on William Stafford. She could have had, she says, other husbands, with titles and wealth. But *"if I were at liberty and might choose, I ensure you, Master Secretary, I have tried so much honesty to be in him, that I had rather beg my bread with him than to be the greatest Queen christened."*

She dare not write to her sister the queen. Or her father or her uncle or her brother. They are all so cruel. So she is writing to him . . . He wonders, did Stafford lean over her shoulder, while she was writing? Did she giggle and say, Thomas Cromwell, I once raised his hopes.

Richard says, "I hardly remember how Mary and I were to be married."

"That was in other days than these." And Richard is happy; see how it has worked out; we can thrive without the Boleyns. But Christendom was overturned for the Boleyn marriage, to put the ginger pig in the cradle; what if it is true, what if Henry is sated, what if the enterprise is cursed? "Get Wiltshire in."

"Here to the Rolls?"

"He will come to the whistle."

He will humiliate him—in his genial fashion—and make him give Mary an annuity. The girl worked for him, on her back, and now he must pension her. Richard will sit in the shadows and take notes. It will remind Boleyn of the old days: the old days now being approximately six, seven years back. Last week Chapuys said to him, in this kingdom now you are all the cardinal was, and more.

❖

It is Christmas Eve when Alice More comes to see him. There is a thin sharp light, like the edge of an old knife, and in this light Alice looks old.

He greets her like a princess, and leads her into one of the chambers he has had repaneled and painted, where a great fire leaps up a rebuilt chimney. The air smells of pine boughs. "You keep the feast here?" Alice has made an effort for him; pinned her hair back fiercely, under a bonnet sewn with seed pearls. "Well! When I came here before it was a musty old place. My husband used to say," and he notes the past tense, "my husband used to say, lock Cromwell in a deep dungeon in the morning, and when you come back that night he'll be sitting on a plush cushion eating larks' tongues, and all the jailers will owe him money."

"Did he talk a lot about locking me in dungeons?"

"It was only talk." She is uneasy. "I thought you might take me to see the king. I know he's always courteous to women, and kind."

He shakes his head. If he takes Alice to the king she will talk about when he used to come to Chelsea and walk in the gardens. She will upset him: agitate his mind, make him think about More, which at present he doesn't. "He is very busy with the French envoys. He means to keep a large court this season. You will have to trust my judgment."

"You have been good to us," she says, reluctant. "I ask myself why. You always have some trick."

"Born tricky," he says. "Can't help it. Alice, why is your husband so stubborn?"

"I no more comprehend him than I do the Blessed Trinity."

"Then what are we to do?"

"I think he'd give the king his reasons. In his private ear. If the king said beforehand that he would take away all penalties from him."

"You mean, license him for treason? The king can't do it."

"Holy Agnes! Thomas Cromwell, to tell the king what he can't do!

I've seen a cock swagger in a barnyard, master, till a girl comes one day and wrings his neck."

"It's the law of the land. The custom of the country."

"I thought Henry was set over the law."

"We don't live at Constantinople, Dame Alice. Though I say nothing against the Turk. We cheer on the infidels, these days. As long as they keep the Emperor's hands tied."

"I don't have much money left," she says. "I have to find fifteen shillings every week for his keep. I worry he'll be cold." She sniffs. "Still, he could tell me so himself. He doesn't write to me. It's all her, her, his darling Meg. She's not my child. I wish his first wife were here, to tell me if she was born the way she is now. She's close, you know. Keeps her own counsel, and his. She tells me now he gave her his shirts to wash the blood out, that he wore a shirt of hair beneath his linen. He did so when we were married and I begged him to leave it off and I thought he had. But how would I know? He slept alone and drew the bolt on his door. If he had an itch I never knew it, he was perforce to scratch it himself. Well, whatever, it was between the two of them, and me no part of it."

"Alice—"

"Don't think I have no tenderness for him. He didn't marry me to live like a eunuch. We have had dealings, one time or another." She blushes, more angry than shy. "And when that is true, you cannot help feeling it, if a man might be cold, if he might be hungry, his flesh being one with yours. You feel to him as you might a child."

"Fetch him out, Alice, if it is within your power."

"More in yours than mine." She smiles sadly. "Is your little man Gregory home for the season? I have sometimes said to my husband, I wish Gregory Cromwell were my boy. I could bake him in a sugar crust and eat him all up."

❖

Gregory comes home for Christmas, with a letter from Rowland Lee saying he is a treasure and can come back to his household anytime. "So must I go back," Gregory says, "or am I finished being educated now?"

"I have a scheme for the new year to improve your French."

"Rafe says I am being brought up like a prince."

"For now, you are all I have to practice on."

"My sweet father . . ." Gregory picks up his little dog. He hugs her, and nuzzles the fur at the back of her neck. He waits. "Rafe and Richard say that when my education is sufficient you mean to marry me to some old dowager with a great settlement and black teeth, and she will wear me out with lechery and rule me with her whims, and she will leave her estate away from the children she has and they will hate me and scheme against my life and one morning I shall be dead in my bed."

The spaniel swivels in his son's arms, turns on him her mild, round, wondering eyes. "They are making sport of you, Gregory. If I knew such a woman, I would marry her myself."

Gregory nods. "She would never rule you, sir. And I dare say she would have a good deer park, which would be convenient to hunt. And the children would be in fear of you, even if they were men grown." He appears half-consoled. "What's that map? Is it the Indies?"

"This is the Scots border," he says gently. "Harry Percy's country. Look, let me show you. These are parcels of his estates he has given away to his creditors. We cannot let it continue, because we can't leave our borders to chance."

"They say he is sick."

"Sick, or mad." His tone is indifferent. "He has no heir, and he and his wife never come together, so it is not likely he will. He has fallen out with his brothers, and he owes a deal of money to the king. So it would make sense to name the king his heir, would it not? He will be brought to see it."

Gregory looks stricken. "Take his earldom?"

"He can keep the style. We'll give him something to live on."

"Is this because of the cardinal?"

Harry Percy stopped Wolsey at Cawood, as he was riding south. He came in, keys in his hand, spattered with mud from the road: my lord, I arrest you for high treason. Look at my face, the cardinal said: I am not afraid of any man alive.

He shrugs. "Gregory, go and play. Take Bella and practice your French with her; she came to me from Lady Lisle in Calais. I won't be long. I have to settle the kingdom's bills."

For Ireland at the next dispatch, brass cannon and iron shot, rammers and charging ladles, serpentine powder and four hundredweight of brimstone, five hundred yew bows and two barrels of bowstrings, two hundred each of spades, shovels, crowbars, pickaxes, horsehides, one hundred felling axes, one thousand horseshoes, eight thousand nails. The goldsmith Cornelys has not been paid for the cradle he made for the king's last child, the one that never saw the light; he claims for twenty shillings disbursed to Hans for painting Adam and Eve on the cradle, and he is owed for white satin, gold tassels and fringes, and the silver for modeling the apples in the Garden of Eden.

He is talking to people in Florence about hiring a hundred arquebusiers for the Irish campaign. They don't down tools, like Englishmen do, if they have to fight in the woods or on rocky terrain.

The king says, a lucky New Year to you, Cromwell. And more to follow. He thinks, luck has nothing to do with it. Of all his presents, Henry is most pleased with the Queen of Sheba, and with a unicorn's horn, and a device to squeeze oranges with a great gold "H" on it.

❖

Early in the new year the king gives him a title no one has ever held before: Vicegerent in Spirituals, his deputy in church affairs. Rumors that the religious houses will be put down have been running about the kingdom for three years and more. Now he has the power to visit, inspect and reform monasteries; to close them, if need be. There is hardly an abbey whose affairs he does not know, by virtue of his training under the cardinal and the letters that arrive day by day—some monks complaining of abuses and scandals and their superiors' disloyalty, others seeking offices within their communities, assuring him that a word in the right quarter will leave them forever in his debt.

He says to Chapuys, "Were you ever at the cathedral in Chartres? You walk the labyrinth," he says, "set into the pavement, and it seems there is no sense in it. But if you follow it faithfully it leads you straight to the center. Straight to where you should be."

Officially, he and the ambassador are barely on speaking terms. Unofficially, Chapuys sends him a vat of good olive oil. He retaliates with capons. The ambassador himself arrives, followed by a retainer carrying a parmesan cheese.

Chapuys looks doleful and chilly. "Your poor queen keeps the season meagerly at Kimbolton. She is so afraid of the heretic councillors about her husband that she has all her food cooked over the fire in her own room. And Kimbolton is more like a stable than a house."

"Nonsense," he says briskly. He hands the ambassador a warming glass of spiced wine. "We only moved her from Buckden because she complained it was damp. Kimbolton is a very good house."

"Ah, you say that because it has thick walls and a wide moat." The scent of honey and cinnamon wafts into the room, logs crackle in the hearth, the green boughs decorating his hall diffuse their own resinous scent. "And the Princess Mary is ill."

"Oh, the Lady Mary is always ill."

"The more cause to care for her!" But Chapuys softens his tone. "If her mother could see her, it would be much comfort to them both."

"Much comfort to their escape plans."

"You are a heartless man." Chapuys sips his wine. "You know, the Emperor is ready to stand your friend." A pause, heavy with significance; into which, the ambassador sighs. "There are rumors that La Ana is distraught. That Henry is looking at another lady."

He takes a breath and begins to talk. Henry has no time for other women. He is too busy counting his money. He is growing very close, he doesn't want Parliament to know his income. I have difficulty getting him to part with anything for the universities, or to pay his builders, or even for the poor. He only thinks of ordnance. Munitions. Shipbuilding. Beacons. Forts.

Chapuys turns down his mouth. He knows when he's being spun a line; if he didn't, where would be the pleasure in it? "So I am to tell my master, am I, that the King of England is so set on war he has no time for love?"

"There will be no war unless your master makes it. Which, with the Turks at his heels, he scarcely has time to do. Oh, I know his coffers are bottomless. The Emperor could ruin us all if he liked." He smiles. "But what good would that do the Emperor?"

The fate of peoples is made like this, two men in small rooms. Forget the coronations, the conclaves of cardinals, the pomp and processions. This is how the world changes: a counter pushed across a table, a pen stroke that alters the force of a phrase, a woman's sigh as she passes and leaves on the air a trail of orange flower or rose water; her hand pulling close the bed curtain, the discreet sigh of flesh against flesh. The king—lord of generalities—must now learn to labor over detail, led on by intelligent greed. As his prudent father's son, he knows all the families of England and what they have. He has registered their holdings in his head, down to the last watercourse and copse. Now the church's assets are to come under his control, he needs to know their worth. The law of who owns what—the law generally—has accreted a parasitic complexity: it is like a barnacled hull, a roof slimy with moss. But there are lawyers enough, and how much ability does it require, to scrape away as you are directed? Englishmen may be superstitious, they may be afraid of the future, they may not know what England is; but the skills of adding and subtraction are not scarce. Westminster has a thousand scratching pens, but Henry will need, he thinks, new men, new structures, new thinking. Meanwhile he, Cromwell, puts his commissioners on the road. *Valor ecclesiasticus*. I will do it in six months, he says. Such an exercise has never been attempted before, it is true, but he has already done much that no one else has even dreamed of.

One day at the beginning of spring he comes back from Westminster chilled. His face aches, as if his bones lie open to the weather, and nagging at his memory is that day when his father mashed him into the cobblestones: his sideways view of Walter's boot. He wants to get back to Austin Friars, because he has had stoves installed and the whole house is warm; the Chancery Lane house is only warm in patches. Besides, he wants to be behind his wall.

Richard says, "Your eighteen-hour days, sir, can't continue forever."

"The cardinal did them."

That night in his sleep he goes down to Kent. He is looking over the accounts of Bayham Abbey, which is to be closed by Wolsey's command. The hostile faces of the monks, hovering over him, cause him to swear and say to Rafe, pack these ledgers and get them on the mule, we'll examine them over our supper and a glass of white burgundy. It is high summer. On horseback, the mule plodding after them, they pick a route through the monastery's neglected vineyards, dipping with the track into a sylvan dimness, into the bowl of broadleaved green at the valley bottom. He says to Rafe, we are like two caterpillars sliding through a salad. They ride out again into a flood of sunlight, and before them is the tower of Scotney Castle: its sandstone walls, gold stippled with gray, shimmer above its moat.

He wakes. He has dreamed of Kent, or been there? The ripple of the sunshine is still on his skin. He calls for Christophe.

Nothing happens. He lies still. No one comes. It is early: no sound from the house below. The shutters are closed, and the stars are struggling to get in, working themselves with steel points into the splinters of the wood. It occurs to him that he has not really called for Christophe, only dreamed he has.

Gregory's many tutors have presented him with a sheaf of bills. The cardinal stands at the foot of his bed, wearing his full pontificals. The cardinal becomes Christophe, opening the shutter, moving against the light. "You have a fever, master?"

Surely he knows, one way or the other? Have I to do everything, know everything? "Oh, it is the Italian one," he says, as if that discounts it.

"So must we fetch an Italian doctor?" Christophe sounds dubious.

Rafe is here. The whole household is here. Charles Brandon is here, who he thinks is real, till Morgan Williams comes in, who is dead, and William Tyndale, who is in the English House at Antwerp and dare not venture. On the stairs he can hear the efficient, deathly clip of his father's steel-tipped boots.

Richard Cromwell roars, can we have quiet in here? When he roars, he sounds Welsh; he thinks, on an ordinary day I would never have noticed that. He closes his eyes. Ladies move behind his lids: transparent like little lizards, lashing their tails. The serpent queens of England, black-fanged and haughty, dragging their blood-soaked linen and their crackling skirts. They kill and eat their own children; this is well-known. They suck their marrow before they are even born.

Someone asks him if he wants to confess.

"Must I?"

"Yes, sir, or you will be thought a sectary."

But my sins are my strength, he thinks; the sins I have done, that others have not even found the opportunity of committing. I hug them close; they're mine. Besides, when I come to judgment I mean to come with a memorandum in my hand: I shall say to my Maker, I have fifty items here, possibly more.

"If I must confess, I'll have Rowland."

Bishop Lee is in Wales, they tell him. It might take days.

Dr. Butts comes, with other doctors, a swarm of them sent by the king. "It is a fever I got in Italy," he explains.

"Let's say it is." Butts frowns down at him.

"If I am dying, get Gregory. I have things to tell him. But if I am not, don't interrupt his studies."

"Cromwell," Butts says, "I couldn't kill you if I shot you through with cannon. The sea would refuse you. A shipwreck would wash you up."

They talk about his heart; he overhears them. He feels they should not: the book of my heart is a private book, it is not an order book left on the counter for any passing clerk to scrawl in. They give him a draft to swallow. Shortly afterward he returns to his ledgers. The lines keep slipping and the figures intermingling and as soon as he has totaled up one column the total unmakes itself and all sense is subtracted. But he keeps trying and trying and adding and adding, until the poison or the healing draft loosens its grip on him and he wakes. The pages of the ledgers are still before his eyes. Butts thinks he is resting as ordered, but in the privacy of his mind little stick figures with arms and legs of ink climb out of the ledgers and walk about. They are carrying firewood in for the kitchen range, but the venison that is

trussed to butcher turns back into deer, who rub themselves in innocence on the bark of the trees. The songbirds for the fricassee refeather
themselves, hopping back onto the branches not yet cut for firewood,
and the honey for basting has gone back to the bee, and the bee has
gone back to the hive. He can hear the noises of the house below, but it
is some other house, in another country: the chink of coins changing
hands, and the scrape of wooden chests over a stone floor. He can hear
his own voice, telling some story in Tuscan, in Putney, in the French
of the camp and the Latin of a barbarian. Perhaps this is Utopia? At
the center of that place, which is an island, there is a place called Am-
aurotum, the City of Dreams.

He is tired out from the effort of deciphering the world. Tired from
the effort of smiling at the foe.

Thomas Avery comes up from the countinghouse. He sits by him
and holds his hand. Hugh Latimer comes and says psalms. Cranmer
comes and looks at him dubiously. Perhaps he is afraid that he will
ask, in his fever, how is your wife, Grete, these days?

Christophe says to him, "I wish your old master the cardinal were
here to comfort you, sir. He was a comfortable man."

"What do you know of him?"

"I robbed him, sir. Did you not know? I robbed his gold plate."

He struggles to sit up. "Christophe? You were the boy at Compiègne?"

"Certainly it was me. Up and down the stairs with buckets of hot
water for the bath, and each time a gold cup in the empty bucket. I
was sorry to rob him, for he was so *gentil*. 'What, you again with your
pail, Fabrice?' You must understand, Fabrice was my name in Compiègne. 'Give this poor child his dinner,' he said. I tasted apricots,
which I never had before."

"But did they not catch you?"

"My master was caught, a very great thief. They branded him. There
was a hue and cry. But you see, master, I was meant for greater fortune."

I remember, he says, I remember Calais, the alchemists, the memory machine. "Guilio Camillo is making it for François so he will be
the wisest king in the world, but the dolt will never learn how to use it."

This is fantasy, Butts says, the fever rising, but Christophe says, no, I assure you, there is a man in Paris who has built a soul. It is a building but it is alive. The whole of it is lined with little shelves. On these shelves you find certain parchments, fragments of writing, they are in the nature of keys, which lead to a box which contains a key which contains another key, but these keys are not made of metal, or these enfolded boxes of wood.

Then what, frog-boy? someone says.

They are made of spirit. They are what we shall have left, if all the books are burned. They will enable us to remember not only the past, but the future, and to see all the forms and customs that will one day inhabit the earth.

Butts says, he is burning up. He thinks of Little Bilney, how he put a hand in the candle flame the night before he died, testing out the pain. It seared his shrinking flesh; in the night he whimpered like a child and sucked his raw hand, and in the morning the city councillors of Norwich dragged him to the pit where their forefathers had burned Lollards. Even when his face was burned away, they were still pushing into it the emblems and banners of popery: their fabric singed and fringes alight, their blank-eyed virgins cured like herring and curling in the smoke.

He asks, politely and in several languages, for water. Not too much, Butts says, a little and a little. He has heard of an island called Ormuz, the driest kingdom in the world, where there are no trees and no crop but salt. Stand at its center, and you look over thirty miles in all directions of ashy plain: beyond which lies the seashore, encrusted with pearls.

His daughter Grace comes by night. She makes her own light, wrapped within her shining hair. She watches him, steady, unblinking, till it is morning, and when they open the shutter the stars are fading and the sun and moon hang together in a pale sky.

A week passes. He is better and he wants work brought in but the doctors forbid it. How will it go forward, he asks, and Richard says, sir, you have trained us all and we are your disciples, you have made a thinking machine that marches forward as if it were alive, you don't need to be tending it every minute of every day.

Still, Christophe says, they say *le roi Henri* is groaning as if he were in pain himself: oh, where is Cremuel?

A message is brought. Henry has said, I am coming to visit. It's an Italian fever, so I am sure not to take it.

He can hardly believe it. Henry ran away from Anne when she had the sweat: even at the height of his love for her.

He says, send Thurston up. They have been keeping him on a low diet, invalid food like turkey. Now, he says, we are going to plan—what?—a piglet, stuffed and roasted in the way I once saw it done at a papal banquet. You will need chopped chicken, lardo, and a goat's liver, minced fine. You will need fennel seeds, marjoram, mint, ginger, butter, sugar, walnuts, hen's eggs and some saffron. Some people put in cheese but we don't make the right kind here in London, besides I myself think it is unnecessary. If you're in trouble about any of this send out to Bonvisi's cook, he'll see you right.

He says, "Send next door to prior George, tell him to keep his friars off the streets when the king comes, lest he reform them too soon." It's his feeling that the whole process should go slowly, slowly, so people will see the justice of it; no need to spill the religious out onto the streets. The friars who live at his gates are a disgrace to their order, but they are good neighbors to him. They have given up their refectory, and from their chamber windows at night drifts the sound of merry supper parties. Any day you can join a crowd of them drinking at the Well with Two Buckets, just outside his gates. The abbey church is more like a market, and a fleshmarket too. The district is full of young bachelors from the Italian merchant houses, who are serving their London year; he often entertains them, and when they leave his table (drained of market information) he knows they make a dash for the friars' precincts, where enterprising London girls are sheltering from the rain and waiting to make amiable terms.

❖

It is April 17 when the king makes his visit. At dawn there are showers. By ten o'clock the air is mild as buttermilk. He is up and in a chair, from which he rises. My dear Cromwell: Henry kisses him firmly on both cheeks, takes him by the arms and (in case he thinks he is the only strong man in the kingdom) he sits him back, decisively, in his chair. "You sit and give me no argument," Henry says. "Give me no argument for once, Master Secretary."

The ladies of the house, Mercy and his sister-in-law Johane, are decked out like Walsingham madonnas on a feast day. They curtsy low, and Henry sways above them, informally attired, jacket of silver brocade, vast gold chain across his chest, his fists flashing with Indian emeralds. He has not wholly mastered the family relationships, for which no one can blame him. "Master Secretary's sister?" he says to Johane. "No, forgive me. I remember now that you lost your sister Bet at the same time my own lovely sister died."

It is such a simple, human sentence, coming from a king; at the mention of their most recent loss, tears well into the eyes of the two women, and Henry, turning to one, then the other, with a careful forefinger dots them from their cheeks, and makes them smile. The little brides Alice and Jo he whirls up into the air as if they were butterflies, and kisses them on the mouth, saying he wishes he had known them when he was a boy. The sad truth is, do you not notice, Master Secretary, the older one gets, the lovelier the girls?

Then eighty will have its advantages, he says: every drab will be a pearl. Mercy says to the king, as if talking to a neighbor, give over, sir: you're no age. Henry stretches out his arms and displays himself before the company: "Forty-five in July."

He notes the incredulous hush. It does the job. Henry is gratified.

Henry walks around and looks at all his paintings and asks who the people are. He looks at Anselma, the Queen of Sheba, on the wall. He makes them laugh by picking up Bella and talking to her in Honor Lisle's atrocious French. "Lady Lisle sent the queen a little creature even smaller. He tips his head to one side and his ears prick up, as if to say, why are you speaking to me? So she calls him Pourquoi." When he speaks of Anne his voice drips uxorious sentiment: like clear honey. The women smile, pleased to see their king set such an example. "You know him, Cromwell, you have seen him on her arm. She takes him everywhere. Sometimes," and now he nods judiciously, "I think she loves him better than me. Yes, I am second to the dog."

He sits smiling, no appetite, watching as Henry eats from the silver dishes Hans has designed.

Henry speaks kindly to Richard, calling him cousin. He signals for him to stand by while he talks to his councillor, and for others to retreat a little way. What if King Francis this and Francis that, should I cross the sea myself to patch together some sort of deal, would you cross over yourself when you are on your feet again? What if the Irish, what if the Scots, what if it all gets out of hand and we have wars like in Germany and peasants crowning themselves, what if these false prophets, what if Charles overruns me and Katherine takes the field, she is of mettlesome temper and the people love her, God knows why for I do not.

If that happens, he says, I will be out of this chair and take the field, my own sword in my hand.

When the king has enjoyed his dinner he sits by him and talks softly about himself. The April day, fresh and showery, puts him in mind of the day his father died. He talks of his childhood: I lived at the palace at Eltham, I had a fool called Goose. When I was seven the Cornish rebels came up, led by a giant, do you remember that? My father sent me to the Tower to keep me safe. I said, let me out, I want to fight! I wasn't frightened of a giant from the west, but I was frightened of my grandmother Margaret Beaufort, because her face was like a death's head, and her grip on my wrist was like a skeleton's grip.

When we were young, he says, we were always told, your grandmother gave birth to your lord father the king when she was a little creature of thirteen years. Her past was like a sword she held over us. What, Harry, are you laughing in Lent? When I, at little more years than you, gave birth to the Tudor? What, Harry, are you dancing, what, Harry, are you playing at ball? Her life was all duty. She kept twelve paupers in her house at Woking and once she made me kneel down with a basin and wash their yellow feet, she's lucky I didn't throw up on them. She used to start praying every morning at five.

When she knelt down at her prie-dieu she cried out from the pain in her knees. And whenever there was a celebration, a wedding or a birth, a pastime or an occasion of mirth, do you know what she did? Every time? Without failing? She wept.

And with her, it was all Prince Arthur. Her shining light and her creeping saint. "When I became king instead, she lay down and died out of spite. And on her deathbed, do you know what she told me?" Henry snorts. "Obey Bishop Fisher in all things! Pity she didn't tell Fisher to obey me!"

When the king has left with his gentlemen, Johane comes to sit with him. They talk quietly; though everything they say is fit to be overheard. "Well, it came off sweetly."

"We must give the kitchen a present."

"The whole household did well. I am glad to have seen him."

"Is he what you hoped?"

"I had not thought him so tender. I see why Katherine has fought so hard for him. I mean, not just to be queen, which she thinks is her right, but to have him for a husband. I would say he is a man very apt to be loved."

Alice bursts in. "Forty-five! I thought he was past that."

"You would have bedded him for a handful of garnets," Jo sneers. "You said so."

"Well, you for export licenses!"

"Stop!" he says. "You girls! If your husbands should hear you."

"Our husbands know what we are," Jo says. "We are full of ourselves, aren't we? You don't come to Austin Friars to look for shy little maids. I wonder our uncle doesn't arm us."

"Custom constrains me. Or I'd send you to Ireland."

Johane watches them rampage away. When they are out of earshot, she checks over her shoulder and murmurs, you will not credit what I am going to say next.

"Try me."

"Henry is frightened of you."

He shakes his head. Who frightens the Lion of England?

"Yes, I swear to you. You should have seen his face, when you said you would take your sword in your hand."

❖

The Duke of Norfolk comes to visit him, clattering up from the yard where his servants hold his plumed horse. "Liver, is it? My liver's shot to pieces. And these five years my muscles have been wasting. Look at that!" He sticks out a claw. "I've tried every physician in the realm, but they don't know what ails me. Yet they never fail to send in their accounts."

Norfolk, he knows it for a fact, would never pay anything so mere as a doctor's bill.

"And the colics and the gripes," the duke says, "they make my mortal life a Purgatory. Sometimes I'm at stool all night."

"Your Grace should take life more easily," Rafe says. Not bolt your food, he means. Not race about in a lather like a post horse.

"I intend to, believe me. My niece makes it clear she wants none of my company and none of my counsel. I'm for my house at Kenninghall, and Henry can find me there if he wants me. God restore you, Master Secretary. St. Walter is good, I hear, if a job's getting too much for you. And St. Ubald against the headache, he does the trick for me." He gropes inside his jacket. "Brought you a medal. Pope blessed it. Bishop of Rome, sorry." He drops it on the table. "Thought you might not have one."

He is out of the door. Rafe picks up the medal. "It's probably cursed."

On the stairs they can hear the duke, his voice raised, plaintive: "I thought he was nearly dead! They told me he was nearly dead . . ."

He says to Rafe, "Seen him off."

Rafe grins. "Suffolk too."

Henry has never remitted the fine of thirty thousand pounds he imposed when Suffolk married his sister. From time to time he remembers it, and this is one of those times; Brandon has had to give up his lands in Oxfordshire and Berkshire to pay his debts, and now he keeps small state down in the country.

He closes his eyes. It is bliss to think of: two dukes on the run from him.

His neighbor Chapuys comes in. "I told my master in dispatches that the king has visited you. My master is amazed that the king would go to a private house, to one not even a lord. But I told him, you should see the work he gets out of Cromwell."

"He should have such a servant," he says. "But Eustache, you are an old hypocrite, you know. You would dance on my grave."

"My dear Thomas, you are always the only opponent."

Thomas Avery smuggles in to him Luca Pacioli's book of chess puzzles. He has soon done all the puzzles, and drawn out some of his own on blank pages at the back. His letters are brought and he reviews the latest round of disasters. They say that the tailor at Münster, the King of Jerusalem with sixteen wives, has had a row with one of them and cut her head off in the marketplace.

He reemerges into the world. Knock him down and he will get up. Death has called to inspect him, she has measured him, breathed into his face: walked away again. He is a little leaner, his clothes tell him; for a while he feels light, no longer grounded in the world, each day buoyant with possibilities. The Boleyns congratulate him heartily on his return to health, and so they should, for without him how would they be what they are now? Cranmer, when they meet, keeps leaning forward to pat his shoulder and squeeze his hand.

While he has been recovering, the king has cropped his hair. He has done this to disguise his increasing baldness, though it doesn't, not at all. His loyal councillors have done the same, and soon it becomes a mark of fellowship between them. "By God, sir," Master Wriothesley says, "if I wasn't frightened of you before, I would be now."

"But Call-Me," he says, "you were frightened of me before."

There is no change in Richard's aspect; committed to the tilting ground, he keeps his hair cropped to fit under a helmet. The shorn Master Wriothesley looks more intelligent, if that were possible, and Rafe more determined and alert. Richard Riche has lost the vestiges of the boy he was. Suffolk's huge face has acquired a strange innocence. Monseigneur looks deceptively ascetic. As for Norfolk, no one notices the change. "What sort of hair did he have before?" Rafe asks. Strips of iron-gray fortify his scalp, as if laid out by a military engineer.

The fashion spreads into the country. When Rowland Lee next pitches into the Rolls House, he thinks a cannonball is coming at him. His son's eyes look large and calm, a still golden color. Your mother would have wept over your baby curls, he says, rubbing his head affectionately. Gregory says, "Would she? I hardly remember her."

❖

As April goes out, four treacherous monks are put on trial. The oath has been offered them repeatedly, and refused. It is a year since the Maid was put to death. The king showed mercy to her followers; he is not now so disposed. It is the Charterhouse of London where the mischief originates, that austere house of men who sleep on straw; it is where Thomas More tried his vocation, before it was revealed to him that the world needed his talents. He, Cromwell, has visited the house, as he has visited the recalcitrant community at Syon. He has spoken gently, he has spoken bluntly, he has threatened and cajoled; he has sent enlightened clerics to argue the king's case, and he has interviewed the disaffected members of the community and set them to work against their brethren. It is all to no avail. Their response is, go away, go away and leave me to my sanctified death.

If they think that they will maintain to the end the equanimity of their prayer-lives, they are wrong, because the law demands the full traitor's penalty, the short spin in the wind and the conscious public disemboweling, a brazier alight for human entrails. It is the most horrible of all deaths, pain and rage and humiliation swallowed to the dregs, the fear so great that the strongest rebel is unmanned before the executioner with his knife can do the job; before each one dies he watches his fellows and, cut down from the rope, he crawls like an animal round and round on the bloody boards.

Wiltshire and George Boleyn are to represent the king at the spectacle, and Norfolk, who, grumbling, has been dragged up from the country and told to prepare for an embassy to France. Henry thinks of going himself to see the monks die, for the court will wear masks, edging on their high-stepping horses among the city officials and the ragged populace, who turn out by the hundred to see any such show. But the king's build makes it difficult to disguise him, and he fears there may be demonstrations for Katherine, still a favorite with the more verminous portion of every crowd. Young Richmond shall stand in for me, his father decides; one day he may have to defend, in battle, his half sister's title, so it becomes him to learn the sights and sounds of slaughter.

The boy comes to him at night, as the deaths are scheduled next day: "Good Master Secretary, take my place."

"Will you take mine, at my morning meeting with the king? Think of it like this," he says, firm and pleasant. "If you plead sickness, or fall off your horse tomorrow or vomit in front of your father-in-law, he'll never let you forget it. If you want him to let you into your bride's bed, prove yourself a man. Keep your eyes on the duke, and pattern your conduct on his."

But Norfolk himself comes to him, when it is over, and says, Cromwell, I swear upon my life that one of the monks spoke when his heart was out. Jesus, he called, Jesus save us, poor Englishmen.

"No, my lord. It is not possible he should do so."

"Do you know that for a fact?"

"I know it from experience."

The duke quails. Let him think it, that his past deeds have included the pulling out of hearts. "I dare say you're right." Norfolk crosses himself. "It must have been a voice from the crowd."

❖

The night before the monks met their end, he had signed a pass for Margaret Roper, the first in months. Surely, he thinks, for Meg to be with her father when traitors are being led out to their deaths; surely she will turn from her resolve, she will say to her father, come now, the king is in his killing vein, you must take the oath as I have done. Make a mental reservation, cross your fingers behind your back; only ask for Cromwell or any officer of the king, say the words, come home.

But his tactic fails. She and her father stood dry-eyed at a window as the traitors were brought out, still in their habits, and launched on their journey to Tyburn. I always forget, he thinks, how More neither pities himself nor takes pity on others. Because I would have protected my own girls from such a sight, I think he would too. But he uses Meg to harden his resolve. If she will not give way, he cannot; and she will not give way.

The following day he goes in to see More himself. The rain splashes and hisses from the stones underfoot; walls and water are indistinguishable, and around small corners a wind moans like a winter wind. When he has struggled out of his wet outer layers he stands chatting to the turnkey Martin, getting the news of his wife and new baby. How shall I find him, he asks at last and Martin says, have you ever noticed how he has one shoulder up and the other down?

It comes from overmuch writing, he says. One elbow on the desk, the other shoulder dropped. Well, whatever, Martin says: he looks like a little carved hunchback on a bench end.

More has grown his beard; he looks as one imagines the prophets of Münster to look, though he would abhor the comparison. "Master Secretary, how does the king take the news from abroad? They say the Emperor's troops are on the move."

"Yes, but to Tunis, I think." He casts a glance at the rain. "If you were the Emperor, wouldn't you pick Tunis, rather than London? Look, I haven't come to quarrel with you. Just to see if you are comfortable."

More says, "I hear you have sworn my fool, Henry Pattinson." He laughs.

"Whereas the men who died yesterday had followed your example, and refused to swear."

"Let me be clear. I am no example. I am just myself, alone. I say nothing against the act. I say nothing against the men that made it. I say nothing against the oath, or against any man that swears it."

"Ah, yes," he sits down on the chest where More keeps his possessions, "but all this saying nothing, it won't do for a jury, you know. Should it come to a jury."

"You have come to threaten me."

"The Emperor's feats of arms shorten the king's temper. He means to send you a commission, who will want a straight answer as to his title."

"Oh, I'm sure your friends will be too good for me. Lord Audley? And Richard Riche? Listen. Ever since I came here I have been preparing for my death, at your hands—yes, yours—or at the hands of nature. All I require is peace and silence for my prayers."

"You want to be a martyr."

"No, what I want is to go home. I am weak, Thomas. I am weak as we all are. I want the king to take me as his servant, his loving subject, as I have never ceased to be."

"I have never understood where the line is drawn, between sacrifice and self-slaughter."

"Christ drew it."

"You don't see anything wrong with the comparison?"

Silence. The loud, contentious quality of More's silence. It's bouncing off the walls. More says he loves England, and he fears all England will be damned. He is offering some kind of bargain to his God, his God who loves slaughter: "It is expedient that one man shall die for the people." Well, I tell you, he says to himself. Bargain all you like. Consign yourself to the hangman if you must. The people don't give a fourpenny fuck. Today is May 5. In two days' time the commission will visit you. We will ask you to sit, you will decline. You will stand before us looking like a desert father, and we snugly wrapped against the summer chill. I will say what I say. You will say what you say. And maybe I will concede you have won. I will walk away and leave you, the king's good subject if you say so, till your beard grows down to your knees and the spiders weave webs across your eyes.

❖

Well, that's his plan. Events overtake it. He says to Richard, has any damnable bishop of Rome in the history of his pox-ridden jurisdiction ever done anything so stupidly ill-timed as this? Farnese has announced England is to have a new cardinal: Bishop Fisher. Henry is enraged. He swears he will send Fisher's head across the sea to meet his hat.

The third of June: himself to the Tower, with Wiltshire for the Boleyn interest, and Charles Brandon, looking as if he would as soon be fishing. Riche to make notes; Audley to make jokes. It's wet again, and Brandon says, this must be the worst summer ever, eh? Yes, he says, good thing His Majesty isn't superstitious. They laugh: Suffolk, a little uncertainly.

Some said the world would end in 1533. Last year had its adherents too. Why not this year? There is always somebody ready to claim that these are the end times, and nominate his neighbor as the Antichrist. The news from Münster is that the skies are falling fast. The besiegers are demanding unconditional surrender; the besieged are threatening mass suicide.

He leads the way. "Christ, what a place," Brandon says. Drips are spoiling his hat. "Doesn't it oppress you?"

"Oh, we're always here." Riche shrugs. "One thing or another. Master Secretary is wanted at the Mint or the Jewel House."

Martin lets them in. More's head jerks up as they enter.

"It's yes or no today," he says.

"Not even good day and how do you." Somebody has given More a comb for his beard. "Well, what do I hear from Antwerp? Do I hear Tyndale is taken?"

"That is not to the point," the Lord Chancellor says. "Answer to the oath. Answer to the statute. Is it a lawfully made statute?"

"They say he strayed outside and the Emperor's soldiers have seized him."

He says coldly, "Had you prior knowledge?"

Tyndale has been, not just taken, but betrayed. Someone tempted him out of his haven, and More knows who. He sees himself, a second self, enacting another rainy morning just like this: in which he crosses the room, hauls the prisoner to his feet, beats out of him the name of his agent. "Now, Your Grace," he says to Suffolk, "you are wearing a violent expression, pray be calm."

Me? Brandon says. Audley laughs. More says, "Tyndale's devil will desert him now. The Emperor will burn him. And the king will not lift a finger to save him, because Tyndale would not support his new marriage."

"Perhaps you think he showed sense there?" Riche says.

"You must speak," Audley says, gently enough.

More is agitated, words tumbling over each other. He is ignoring Audley, speaking to him, Cromwell. "You cannot compel me to put myself in hazard. For if I had an opinion against your Act of Suprem-acy, which I do not concede, then your oath would be a two-edged sword. I must put my body in peril if I say no to it, my soul if I say yes to it. Therefore I say nothing."

"When you interrogated men you called heretics, you did not al-low evasion. You compelled them to speak and racked them if they would not. If they were made to answer, why not you?"

"The cases are not the same. When I compel an answer from a heretic, I have the whole body of law behind me, the whole might of Christendom. What I am threatened with here is one particular law, one singular dispensation of recent make, recognized here but in no other country—"

He sees Riche make a note. He turns away. "The end is the same. Fire for them. Ax for you."

"If the king grants you that mercy," Brandon says.

More quails; he curls up his fingers on the tabletop. He notices this, detached. So that's a way in. Put him in fear of the more lingering death. Even as he thinks it, he knows he will not do it; the notion is contaminating. "On numbers I suppose you have me beat. But have you looked at a map lately? Christendom is not what it was."

Riche says, "Master Secretary, Fisher is more a man than this pris-oner before us, for Fisher dissents and takes the consequences. Sir Thomas, I think you would be an overt traitor, if you dared."

More says softly, "Not so. It is not for me to thrust myself on God. It is for God to draw me to him."

"We take note of your obstinacy," Audley says. "We spare you the

methods you have used on others." He stands up. "It is the king's pleasure that we move to indictment and trial."

"In the name of God! What ill can I effect from this place? I do
nobody harm. I say none harm. I think none harm. If this be not
enough to keep a man alive—"

He cuts in on him, incredulous. "You do nobody harm? What about
Bainham, you remember Bainham? You forfeited his goods, committed
his poor wife to prison, saw him racked with your own eyes, you locked
him in Bishop Stokesley's cellar, you had him back at your own house
two days chained upright to a post, you sent him again to Stokesley, saw
him beaten and abused for a week, and still your spite was not exhausted: you sent him back to the Tower and had him racked again, so
that finally his body was so broken that they had to carry him in a chair
when they took him to Smithfield to be burned alive. And you say,
Thomas More, that you do no harm?"

Riche begins to gather More's papers from the table. It is suspected
he has been passing letters to Fisher upstairs: which is not a bad thing,
if collusion in Fisher's treason can be shown. More drops his hand on
them, fingers spread; then shrugs, and yields them. "Have them if you
must. You read all I write."

He says, "Unless we hear soon of a change of heart, we must take
away your pen and papers. And your books. I will send someone."

More seems to shrink. He bites his lip. "If you must take them,
take them now."

"For shame," Suffolk says. "Do you take us for porters, Master More?"

❖

Anne says, "It is all about me." He bows. "When finally you have out
of More what troubles his singular conscience, you will find that what
is at the root of it is that he will not bend his knee to my queenship."

She is small and white and angry. Long fingers tip to tip, bending
each other back; eyes bright.

Before they go further, he has to recall to Henry last year's disaster;
remind him that he cannot always have his own way, just by asking

for it. Last summer Lord Dacre, who is one of the northern lords, was indicted for treason, accused of collusion with the Scots. Behind the accusation were the Clifford family, Dacre's hereditary enemies and rivals; behind them the Boleyns, for Dacre had been outspoken in support of the former queen. The stage was set in Westminster Hall, Norfolk presiding over the court, as High Steward of the kingdom: and Dacre to be judged, as was his right, by twenty fellow lords. And then . . . mistakes were made. Possibly the whole thing was a miscalculation, an affair driven too fast and hard by the Boleyns. Possibly he had erred in not taking charge of the prosecution himself; he had thought it was best to stay in the background, as many titled men have a spite against him for being who he is, and will take a risk to work him displeasure. Or else Norfolk was the problem, losing control of the court . . . Whatever the reason, the charges were thrown out, to an outpouring by the king of astonishment and rage. Dacre was taken straight back to the Tower by the king's guard, and he was sent in to strike some deal, which must, he knew, end with Dacre broken. At his trial Dacre had talked for seven hours, in his own defense; but he, Cromwell, can talk for a week. Dacre had admitted to misprision of treason, a lesser offense. He bought a royal pardon for £10,000. He was released to go north again, a pauper.

But the queen was sick with frustration; she wanted an example made. And affairs in France are not going her way; some say that at the mention of her name, François sniggers. She suspects, and she is right, that her man Cromwell is more interested in the friendship of the German princes than in an alliance with France; but she has to pick her time for that quarrel, and she says she will have no peace till Fisher is dead, till More is dead. So now she circles the room, agitated, less than regal, and she keeps veering toward Henry, touching his sleeve, touching his hand, and he brushes her away, each time, as if she were a fly. He, Cromwell, watches. They are not the same couple from day to day: sometimes doting, sometimes chilly and distanced. The billing and cooing, on the whole, is the more painful to watch.

"Fisher gives me no anxiety," he says, "his offense is clear. In More's case . . . morally, our cause is unimpeachable. No one is in doubt of his loyalty to Rome and his hatred of Your Majesty's title as head of the church. Legally, however, our case is slender, and More will use every legal, every procedural device open to him. This is not going to be easy."

Henry stirs into life. "Do I retain you for what is easy? Jesus pity my simplicity, I have promoted you to a place in this kingdom that no one, no one of your breeding has ever held in the whole of the history of this realm." He drops his voice. "Do you think it is for your personal beauty? The charm of your presence? I keep you, Master Cromwell, because you are as cunning as a bag of serpents. But do not be a viper in my bosom. You know my decision. Execute it."

As he leaves, he is conscious of the silence falling behind him. Anne walking to the window. Henry staring at his feet.

❖

So when Riche comes in, quivering with undisclosed secrets, he is inclined to swat him like a fly; but then he takes hold of himself, rubs his palms together instead: the merriest man in London. "Well, Sir Purse, did you pack up the books? And how was he?"

"He drew the blind down. I asked him why, and he said, the goods are taken away, so now I am closing the shop."

He can hardly bear it, to think of More sitting in the dark.

"Look, sir." Riche has a folded paper. "We had some conversation. I wrote it down."

"Talk me through it." He sits down. "I am More. You are Riche." Riche stares at him. "Shall I close the shutter? Is this better played out in the dark?"

"I could not," Riche says, hesitant, "leave him without trying once again—"

"Quite. You have your way to make. But why would he talk to you, if he would not talk to me?"

"Because he has no time for me. He thinks I don't matter."

"And you Solicitor General," he says, mocking.

"So we were putting cases."

"What, as if you were at Lincoln's Inn after supper?"

"To tell the truth I pitied him, sir. He craves conversation and you know he rattles away. I said to him, suppose Parliament were to pass an act saying that I, Richard Riche, were to be king. Would you not take me for king? And he laughed."

"Well, you admit it is not likely."

"So I pressed him on it; he said, yes, majestic Richard, I so take you, for Parliament can do it, and considering what they have done already I should hardly be surprised if I woke up in the reign of King Cromwell, for if a tailor can be King of Jerusalem I suppose a lad from the smithy can be King of England."

Riche pauses: has he given offense? He beams at him. "When I am King Cromwell, you shall be a duke. So, to the point, Purse . . . or isn't there one?"

"More said, well, you have put a case, I shall put you a higher case. Suppose Parliament were to pass an act saying God should not be God? I said, it would have no effect, for Parliament has no power to do it. Then he said, aye, well, young man, at least you recognize an absurdity. And there he stopped, and gave me a look, as if to say, let us deal in the real world now. I said to him, I will put you a middle case. You know our lord the king has been named by Parliament head of the church. Why will you not go with the vote, as you go with it when it makes me monarch? And he said—as if he were instructing some child—the cases are not alike. For one is a temporal jurisdiction, and Parliament can do it. The other is a spiritual jurisdiction, and is what Parliament cannot exercise, for the jurisdiction is out of this realm."

He stares at Riche. "Hang him for a papist," he says.

"Yes, sir."

"We know he thinks it. He has never stated it."

"He said that a higher law governed this and all realms, and if Parliament trespassed on God's law . . ."

"On the Pope's law, he means—for he holds them the same, he couldn't deny that, could he? Why is he always examining his conscience, if not to check day and night that it is in accord with the church of Rome? That is his comfort, that is his guide. It seems to me, if he plainly denies Parliament its capacity, he denies the king his title.

Which is treason. Still," he shrugs, "how far does it take us? Can we show the denial was malicious? He will say, I suppose, that it was just talk, to pass the time. That you were putting cases, and that anything said in that wise cannot be held against a man."

"A jury won't understand that. They'll take him to mean what he said. After all, sir, he knew it wasn't some students' debate."

"True. You don't hold those at the Tower."

Riche offers the memorandum. "I have written it down faithfully to the best of my recollection."

"You don't have a witness?"

"They were in and out, packing up the books in a crate, he had a lot of books. You cannot blame me for carelessness, sir, for how was I to know he would talk to me at all?"

"I don't blame you." He sighs. "In fact, Purse, you are the apple of my eye. You'll stand behind this in court?"

Doubtful, Riche nods. "Tell me you will, Richard. Or tell me you won't. Let's have it straight. Have the grace to say so now, if you think your courage might fail. If we lose another trial, we can kiss goodbye to our livelihoods. And all our work will be for nothing."

"You see, he couldn't resist it, the chance to put me right," Riche says. "He will never let it drop, what I did as a boy. He uses me to make his sermon on. Well, let him make his next sermon on the block."

❖

The evening before Fisher is to die, he visits More. He takes a strong guard with him, but he leaves them in the outer chamber and goes in alone. "I've got used to the blind drawn," More says, almost cheerfully. "You don't mind sitting in the twilight?"

"You need not be afraid of the sun. There is none."

"Wolsey used to boast that he could change the weather." He chuckles. "It's good of you to visit me, Thomas, now that we have no more to say. Or have we?"

"The guards will come for Bishop Fisher early tomorrow. I am afraid they will wake you."

"I should be a poor Christian if I could not keep vigil with him."

His smile has seeped away. "I hear the king has granted him mercy as to the manner of his death."

"He being a very old man, and frail."

More says, with tart pleasantness, "I'm doing my best, you know. A man can only shrivel at his own rate."

"Listen." He reaches across the table, takes his hand, wrings it: harder than he meant. My blacksmith's grip, he thinks: he sees More flinch, feels his fingers, the skin dry as paper over the bones. "Listen. When you come before the court, throw yourself at that instant on the king's mercy."

More says, wonderingly, "What good will that do me?"

"He is not a cruel man. You know that."

"Do I? He used not to be. He had a sweet disposition. But then he changed the company he kept."

"He is susceptible always to a plea for mercy. I do not say he will let you live, the oath unsworn. But he may grant you the same mercy as Fisher."

"It is not so important, what happens to the body. I have led in some ways a blessed life. God has been good and not tested me. Now he does I cannot fail him. I have been vigilant over my heart, and I have not always liked what I have found there. If it comes into the hands of the hangman at the last, so be it. It will be in God's hands soon enough."

"Will you think me sentimental, if I say I do not want to see you butchered?" No reply. "Are you not afraid of the pain?"

"Oh yes, I am very much afraid, I am not a bold and robust man such as yourself, I cannot help but rehearse it in my mind. But I will only feel it for a moment, and God will not let me remember it afterward."

"I am glad I am not like you."

"Undoubtedly. Or you would be sitting here."

"I mean, my mind fixed on the next world. I realize you see no prospect of improving this one."

"And you do?"

Almost a flippant question. A handful of hail smacks itself against the window. It startles them both; he gets up, restless. He would rather know what's outside, see the summer in its sad blowing wreckage, than cower behind the blind and wonder what the damage is. "I once had every hope," he says. "The world corrupts me, I think. Or perhaps it's just the weather. It pulls me down and makes me think like you, that one should shrink inside, down and down to a little point of light, preserving one's solitary soul like a flame under a glass. The spectacles of pain and disgrace I see around me, the ignorance, the unthinking vice, the poverty and the lack of hope, and oh, the rain—the rain that falls on England and rots the grain, puts out the light in a man's eye and the light of learning too, for who can reason if Oxford is a giant puddle and Cambridge is washing away downstream, and who will enforce the laws if the judges are swimming for their lives? Last week the people were rioting in York. Why would they not, with wheat so scarce, and twice the price of last year? I must stir up the justices to make examples, I suppose, otherwise the whole of the north will be out with billhooks and pikes, and who will they slaughter but each other? I truly believe I should be a better man if the weather were better. I should be a better man if I lived in a commonwealth where the sun shone and the citizens were rich and free. If only that were true, Master More, you wouldn't have to pray for me nearly as hard as you do."

"How you can talk," More says. Words, words, just words. "I do, of course, pray for you. I pray with all my heart that you will see that you are misled. When we meet in Heaven, as I hope we will, all our differences will be forgot. But for now, we cannot wish them away. Your task is to kill me. Mine is to keep alive. It is my role and my duty. All I own is the ground I stand on, and that ground is Thomas More. If you want it you will have to take it from me. You cannot reasonably believe I will yield it."

"You will want pen and paper to write out your defense. I will grant you that."

"You never give up trying, do you? No, Master Secretary, my defense is up here," he taps his forehead, "where it will stay safe from you."

How strange the room is, how empty, without More's books: it is filling with shadows. "Martin, a candle," he calls.

"Will you be here tomorrow? For the bishop?"

He nods. Though he will not witness the moment of Fisher's death. The protocol is that the spectators bow their knee and doff their hats to mark the passing of the soul.

Martin brings a pricket candle. "Anything else?" They pause while he sets it down. When he is gone, they still pause: the prisoner sits hunched over, looking into the flame. How does he know if More has begun on a silence, or on preparation for speech? There is a silence which precedes speech, there is a silence which is instead of speech. One need not break it with a statement, one can break it with a hesitation: if . . . as it may be . . . if it were possible . . . He says, "I would have left you, you know. To live out your life. To repent of your butcheries. If I were king."

The light fades. It is as if the prisoner has withdrawn himself from the room, leaving barely a shape where he should be. A draft pulls at the candle flame. The bare table between them, clear now of More's driven scribblings, has taken on the aspect of an altar; and what is an altar for, but a sacrifice? More breaks his silence at last: "If, at the end and after I am tried, if the king does not grant, if the full rigor of the penalty . . . Thomas, how is it done? You would think when a man's belly were slashed open he would die, with a great effusion of blood, but it seems it is not so . . . Do they have some special implement, that they use to pith him while he is alive?"

"I am sorry you should think me expert."

But had he not told Norfolk, as good as told him, that he had pulled out a man's heart?

He says, "It is the executioner's mystery. It is kept secret, to keep us in awe."

"Let me be killed cleanly. I ask nothing, but I ask that." Swaying on his stool, he is seized, between one heartbeat and the next, in the grip of bodily agitation; he cries out, shudders from head to foot. His hand beats, weakly, at the clean tabletop; and when he leaves him—"Martin, go in, give him some wine"—he is still crying out, shuddering, beating the table.

The next time he sees him will be in Westminster Hall.

❖

On the day of the trial, rivers breach their banks; the Thames itself rises, bubbling like some river in Hell, and washes its flotsam over the quays.

It's England against Rome, he says. The living against the dead.

Norfolk will preside. He tells him how it will be. The early counts in the indictment will be thrown out: they concern sundry words spoken, at sundry times, about the act and the oath, and More's treasonable conspiracy with Fisher—letters went between the two of them, but it seems those letters are now destroyed. "Then on the fourth count, we will hear the evidence of the Solicitor General. Now, Your Grace, this will divert More, because he cannot see young Riche without working himself into a fit about his derelictions when he was a boy—" The duke raises an eyebrow. "Drinking. Fighting. Women. Dice."

Norfolk rubs his bristly chin. "I have noticed, a soft-looking lad like that, he always does fight. To make a point, you see. Whereas we damned slab-faced old bruisers who are born with our armor on, there's no point we need to make."

"Quite," he says. "We are the most pacific of men. My lord, please attend now. We don't want another mistake like Dacre. We would hardly survive it. The early counts will be thrown out. At the next, the jury will look alert. And I have given you a handsome jury."

More will face his peers, Londoners, the merchants of the livery companies. They are experienced men, with all the city's prejudices. They have seen enough, as all Londoners have, of the church's rapacity and arrogance, and they do not take kindly to being told they are unfit to read the scriptures in their own tongue. They are men who know More and have known him these twenty years. They know how he widowed Lucy Petyt. They know how he wrecked Humphrey Monmouth's business, because Tyndale had been a guest at his house.

They know how he has set spies in their households, among their apprentices whom they treat as sons, among the servants so familiar and homely that they hear every night their master's bedside prayers.

One name makes Audley hesitate: "John Parnell? It might be taken wrong. You know he has been after More since he gave judgment against him in Chancery—"

"I know the case. More botched it, he didn't read the papers, too busy writing a billet-doux to Erasmus, or locking some poor Christian soul in his stocks at Chelsea. What do you want, Audley, do you want me to go to Wales for a jury, or up to Cumberland, or somewhere they think better of More? I must make do with London men, and unless I swear in a jury of newborns, I cannot wipe their memories clear."

Audley shakes his head. "I don't know, Cromwell."

"Oh, he's a sharp fellow," the duke says. "When Wolsey came down, I said, mark him, he's a sharp fellow. You'd have to get up early in the morning to be ahead of him."

❖

The night before the trial, as he is going through his papers at the Austin Friars, a head appears around the door: a little, narrow London head with a close-shaved skull and a raw young face. "Dick Purser. Come in."

Dick Purser looks around the room. He keeps the snarling bandogs who guard the house by night, and he has not been in here before. "Come here and sit. Don't be afraid." He pours him some wine, into a thin Venetian glass that was the cardinal's. "Try this. Wiltshire sent it to me, I don't make much of it myself."

Dick takes the glass and juggles it dangerously. The liquid is pale as straw or summer light. He takes a gulp. "Sir, can I come in your train to the trial?"

"It still smarts, does it?" Dick Purser was the boy whom More had whipped before the household at Chelsea, for saying the host was a piece of bread. He was a child then, he is not much more now; when he first came to Austin Friars, they say he cried in his sleep. "Get yourself a livery coat," he says. "And remember to wash your hands and face in the morning. I don't want you to disgrace me."

It is the word "disgrace" that works on the child. "I hardly minded the pain," he says. "We have all had, saving you, sir, as much if not worse from our fathers."

"True," he says. "My father beat me as if I were a sheet of metal."

"It was that he laid my flesh bare. And the women looking on. Dame Alice. The young girls. I thought one of them might speak up for me, but when they saw me unbreached, I only disgusted them. It made them laugh. While the fellow was whipping me, they were laughing."

In stories it is always the young girls, innocent girls, who stay the hand of the man with the rod or the ax. But we seem to have strayed into a different story: a child's thin buttocks dimpling against the cold, his skinny little balls, his shy prick shrinking to a button, while the ladies of the house giggle and the menservants jeer, and the thin weals spring out against his skin and bleed.

"It's done and forgotten now. Don't cry." He comes from behind his desk. Dick Purser drops his shorn head against his shoulder and bawls, in shame, in relief, in triumph that soon he will have outlived his tormentor. More did John Purser to death, he harassed him for owning German books; he holds the boy, feeling the jump of his pulses, his stiff sinews, the ropes of his muscles, and makes sounds of comfort, as he did to his children when they were small, or as he does to a spaniel whose tail has been trodden on. Comfort is often, he finds, imparted at the cost of a flea or two.

"I will follow you to the death," the boy declares. His arms, fists clenched, grip his master: knuckles knead his spine. He sniffs. "I think I will look well in a livery coat. What time do we start?"

❖

Early. With his staff he is at Westminster Hall before anybody else, vigilant for last-minute hitches. The court convenes around him, and when More is brought in, the hall is visibly shocked at his appearance. The Tower was never known to do a man good, but he startles them, with his lean person and his ragged white beard, looking more like a man of seventy than what he is. Audley whispers, "He looks as if he has been badly handled."

"And he says I never miss a trick."

"Well, my conscience is clear," the Lord Chancellor says breezily. "He has had every consideration."

John Parnell gives him a nod. Richard Riche, both court official and witness, gives him a smile. Audley asks for a seat for the prisoner, but More twitches to the edge of it: keyed up, combative.

He glances around to check that someone is taking notes for him.

Words, words, just words.

He thinks, I remembered you, Thomas More, but you didn't remember me. You never even saw me coming.

III

To Wolf Hall

JULY 1535

n the evening of More's death the weather clears, and he walks in the garden with Rafe and Richard. The sun shows itself, a silver haze between rags of cloud. The beaten-down herb beds are scentless, and a skittish wind pulls at their clothes, hitting the backs of their necks and then veering round to slap their faces. Rafe says, it's like being at sea. They walk at either side of him, and close, as if there were danger from whales, pirates and mermaids.

It is five days since the trial. Since then, much business has supervened, but they cannot help rehearse its events, trading with each other the pictures in their heads: the Attorney General jotting a last note on the indictment; More sniggering when some clerk made a slip in his Latin; the cold smooth faces of the Boleyns, father and son, on the judges' bench. More had never raised his voice; he sat in the chair Audley had provided for him, attentive, head tipped a little to the left, picking away at his sleeve.

So Riche's surprise, when More turned on him, was visible; he had taken a step backward, and steadied himself against a table. "I know you of old, Riche, why would I open my mind to you?" More on his feet, his voice dripping contempt. "I have known you since your youth, a gamer and a dicer, of no commendable fame even in your own house . . ."

"By St. Julian!" Justice Fitzjames had exclaimed; it was ever his oath. Under his breath, to him, Cromwell: "Will he gain by this?"

The jury had not liked it: you never know what a jury will like. They took More's sudden animation to be shock and guilt, at being confronted with his own words. For sure, they all knew Riche's reputation. But are not drinking, dice and fighting more natural in a young man, on the whole, than fasting, beads and self-flagellation? It was Norfolk who had cut in on More's tirade, his voice dry: "Leave aside the man's character. What do you say to the matter in hand? Did you speak those words?"

Was it then that Master More played a trick too many? He had pulled himself together, hauling his slipping gown onto his shoulder; the gown secured, he paused, he calmed himself, he fitted one fist into the other. "I did not say what Riche alleges. Or if I did say it, I did not mean it with malice, therefore I am clear under the statute."

He had watched an expression of derision cross Parnell's face. There's nothing harder than a London burgess who thinks he's being played for a fool. Audley or any of the lawyers could have put the jury right: it's just how we lawyers argue. But they don't want a lawyer's argument, they want the truth: did you say it, or didn't you? George Boleyn leans forward: can the prisoner let us have his own version of the conversation?

More turns, smiling, as if to say, a good point there, young master George. "I made no note of it. I had no writing materials, you see. They had already taken them away. For if you remember, my lord Rochford, that was the very reason Riche came to me, to remove from me the means of recording."

And he had paused again, and looked at the jury as if expecting applause; they looked back, faces like stones.

Was that the turning point? They might have trusted More, being, as he was, Lord Chancellor at one time, and Purse, as everybody knows, such a waster. You never know what a jury will think: though when he had convened them, of course he had been persuasive. He had spoken with them that morning: I do not know what his defense is, but I don't hold out hope we will be finished by noon; I hope you all had a good breakfast? When you retire, you must take your time, of course, but if you are gone more than twenty minutes by my reckoning, I will come in to see how you do. To put you out of doubt, on any points of law.

Fifteen minutes was all they needed.

Now, this evening in the garden, July 6, the feast day of St. Godelva (a blameless young wife of Bruges, whose evil husband drowned her in a pond), he looks up at the sky, feeling a change in the air, a damp drift like autumn. The interlude of feeble sun is over. Clouds drift and mass in towers and battlements, blowing in from Essex, stacking up over the city, driven by the wind across the broad soaked fields, across the sodden pastureland and swollen rivers, across the dripping forests of the west and out over the sea to Ireland. Richard retrieves his hat from a lavender bed and knocks droplets from it, swearing softly. A spatter of rain hits their faces. "Time to go in. I have letters to write."

"You'll not work till all hours tonight."

"No, grandfather Rafe. I shall get my bread and milk and say my Ave and so to bed. Can I take my dog up with me?"

"Indeed no! And have you scampering overhead till all hours?"

It's true he didn't sleep much last night. It had come to him, the wrong side of midnight, that More was no doubt asleep himself, not knowing that it was his last night on earth. It is not usual, till the morning, to prepare the condemned man; so, he had thought, any vigil I keep for him, I keep alone.

They hurry in; the wind bangs a door behind them. Rafe takes his arm. He says, this silence of More's, it was never really silence, was it? It was loud with his treason; it was quibbling as far as quibbles would serve him, it was demurs and cavils, suave ambiguities. It was fear of plain words, or the assertion that plain words pervert themselves; More's dictionary, against our dictionary. You can have a silence full of words. A lute retains, in its bowl, the notes it has played. The viol, in its strings, holds a concord. A shriveled petal can hold its scent, a prayer can rattle with curses; an empty house, when the owners have gone out, can still be loud with ghosts.

❖

Someone—probably not Christophe—has put on his desk a shining silver pot of cornflowers. The dusky blueness at the base of the crinkled petals reminds him of this morning's light; a late dawn for July, a sullen sky. By five, the Lieutenant of the Tower would have gone in to More.

Down below, he can hear a stream of messengers coming into the courtyard. There is much to do, tidying up after the dead man; after all, he thinks, I did it when I was a child, picking up after Morton's young gentlemen, and this is the last time I will have to do it; he pictures himself in the dawn, slopping into a leather jug the dregs of small beer, squeezing up the candle ends to take to the chandlery for remelting.

He can hear voices in the hall; never mind them: he returns to his letters. The Abbot of Rewley solicits a vacant post for his friend. The Mayor of York writes to him about weirs and fish traps; the Humber is running clean and sweet, he reads, so is the Ouse. A letter from Lord Lisle in Calais, relating some muddled tale of self-justification: he said, then I said, so he said.

Thomas More stands before him, more solid in death than he was in life. Perhaps he will always be here now: so agile of mind and so adamant, as he appeared in his final hour before the court. Audley was so happy with the guilty verdict that he began to pass sentence without asking the prisoner if he had anything to say; Fitzjames had to reach out and slap his arm, and More himself rose from his chair to halt him. He had much to say, and his voice was lively, his tone biting, and his eyes, his gestures, hardly those of a condemned man, in law already dead.

But there was nothing new in it: not new anyway to him. I follow my conscience, More said, you must follow yours. My conscience satisfies me—and now I will speech plainly—that your statute is faulty (and Norfolk roars at him) and that your authority is baseless (Norfolk roars again: "Now we see your malice plain"). Parnell had laughed, and the jury exchanged glances, nodding to each other; and while the whole of Westminster Hall murmured, More proffered again, speaking against the noise, his treasonable method of counting. My conscience holds with the majority, which makes me know it does not speak false. "Against Henry's kingdom, I have all the kingdoms of Christendom. Against each one of your bishops, I have a hundred saints. Against your one parliament, I have all the general councils of the church, stretching back for a thousand years."

Norfolk said, take him out. It is finished.

Now it is Tuesday, it is eight o'clock. The rain drums against the window. He breaks the seal of a letter from the Duke of Richmond. The boy complains that in Yorkshire where he is seated, he has no deer park, so can show his friends no sport. Oh, you poor tiny duke, he thinks, how can I relieve your pain? Gregory's dowager with the black teeth, the one he is going to marry; she has a deer park, so perhaps the princeling should divorce Norfolk's daughter and marry her instead? He flips aside Richmond's letter, tempted to file it on the floor; he passes on. The Emperor has left Sardinia with his fleet, sailing to Sicily. A priest at St. Mary Woolchurch says Cromwell is a sectary and he is not frightened of him: fool. Harry Lord Morley sends him a greyhound. There is news of refugees pouring out of the Münster area, some of them heading for England.

Audley had said, "Prisoner, the court will ask the king to make grace upon you, as to the manner of your death." Audley had leaned across: Master Secretary, did you promise him anything? On my life, no: but surely the king will be good to him? Norfolk says, Cromwell, will you move him in that regard? He will take it from you; but if he will not, I myself will come and plead with him. What a marvel: Norfolk, asking for mercy? He had glanced up, to see More taken out, but he had vanished already, the tall halberdiers closing rank behind him: the boat for the Tower is waiting at the steps. It must feel like going home: the familiar room with the narrow window, the table empty of papers, the pricket candle, the drawn blind.

The window rattles; it startles him, and he thinks, I shall bolt the shutter. He is rising to do it when Rafe comes in with a book in his hand. "It is his prayer book, that More had with him at the last."

He examines it. Mercifully, no blood specks. He holds it up by the spine and lets the leaves fan out. "I already did that," Rafe says.

More has written his name in it. There are underlinings in the text: *Remember not the sins of my youth.* "What a pity he remembered Richard Riche's."

"Shall I have it sent to Dame Alice?"

"No. She might think she is one of the sins." The woman has put up with enough. In his last letter, he didn't even say goodbye to her. He shuts the book. "Send it to Meg. He probably meant it for her anyway."

The whole house is rocking about him; wind in the eaves, wind in the chimneys, a piercing draft under every door. It's cold enough for a fire, Rafe says, shall I see to it? He shakes his head. "Tell Richard, tomorrow morning, go to London Bridge and see the bridge-master. Mistress Roper will come to him and beg her father's head to bury it. The man should take what Meg offers and see she is not impeded. And keep his mouth shut."

Once in Italy, when he was young, he had joined a burial party. It isn't something you volunteer for; you're just told. They had bound cloth across their mouths, and shoveled their comrades into unhallowed ground; walked away with the smell of putrefaction on their boots.

Which is worse, he thinks, to have your daughters dead before you, or to leave them to tidy away your remains?

"There's something . . ." He frowns down at his papers. "What have I forgotten, Rafe?"

"Your supper?"

"Later."

"Lord Lisle?"

"I've dealt with Lord Lisle." Dealt with the river Humber. With the slanderous priest from Mary Woolchurch; well, not dealt with him, but put him in the pending pile. He laughs. "You know what I need? I need the memory machine."

Guilio has quit Paris, they say. He has scuttled back to Italy and left the device half built. They say that before his flight for some weeks he had neither spoken nor eaten. His well-wishers say he has gone mad, awed by the capacities of his own creature: fallen into the abyss of the divine. His ill-wishers maintain that demons crawled out of the crannies and crevices of the device, and panicked him so that he ran off by night in his shirt with not even a crust and a lump of cheese for the journey, leaving all his books behind him and his magus's robes.

It is not impossible that Guilio has left writings behind in France. For a fee they might be obtained. It is not impossible to have him followed to Italy; but would there be any point? It is likely, he thinks, that we shall never know what his invention really was. A printing press that can write its own books? A mind that thinks about itself? If I don't have it, at least the King of France doesn't either.

He reaches for his pen. He yawns and puts it down and picks it up again. I shall be found dead at my desk, he thinks, like the poet Petrarch. The poet wrote many unsent letters: he wrote to Cicero, who died twelve hundred years before he was born. He wrote to Homer, who possibly never even existed; but I, I have enough to do with Lord Lisle, and the fish traps, and the Emperor's galleons tossing on the Middle Sea. Between one dip of the pen, Petrarch writes, "between one dip of the pen and the next, the time passes: and I hurry, I drive myself, and I speed toward death. We are always dying—I while I write, you while you read, and others while they listen or block their ears; they are all dying."

He picks up the next batch of letters. A man called Batcock wants a license to import one hundred tuns of woad. Harry Percy is sick again. The authorities in Yorkshire have rounded up their rioters, and divided them into those to be charged with affray and manslaughter, and those to be indicted for murder and rape. Rape? Since when do food riots involve rape? But I forget, this is Yorkshire.

"Rafe, bring me the king's itinerary. I'll check that and then I'm finished here. I think we might have some music before we go to bed."

The court is riding west this summer, as far as Bristol. The king is ready to leave, despite the rain. They will depart from Windsor, then to Reading, Missenden, Abingdon, moving across Oxfordshire, their spirits lifting, we hope, with the distance from London; he says to Rafe, if the country air goes to work, the queen will return with a big belly. Rafe says, I wonder the king can stand the hope each time. It would wear out a lesser man.

"If we ourselves leave London on the eighteenth, we can aim to catch up with them at Sudely. Will that work?"

"Better leave a day earlier. Consider the state of the roads."

"There won't be any shortcuts, will there?" He will use no fords but bridges, and against his inclination he will stick to the main roads; better maps would help. Even in the cardinal's day he was asking himself, might this be a project we could undertake? There are maps, of a kind; castles stud their fields, their battlements prettily inked, their chases and parks marked by lines of bushy trees, with drawings of harts and bristling boar. It is no wonder Gregory mistook Northumbria for the Indies, for these maps are deficient in all practical respects; they do not, for example, tell you which way is north. It would be useful to know where the bridges are, and to have a note of the distance between them. It would be useful to know how far you are from the sea. But the trouble is, maps are always last year's. England is always remaking herself, her cliffs eroding, her sandbanks drifting, springs bubbling up in dead ground. They regroup themselves while we sleep, the landscapes through which we move, and even the histories that trail us; the faces of the dead fade into other faces, as a spine of hills into the mist.

When he was a small child, six years old or about that, his father's apprentice had been making nails from the scrap pile: just common old flat-heads, he'd said, for fastening coffin lids. The nail rods glowed in the fire, a lively orange. "What for do we nail down the dead?"

The boy barely paused, tapping out each head with two neat strokes. "It's so the horrible old buggers don't spring out and chase us."

He knows different now. It's the living that turn and chase the dead. The long bones and skulls are tumbled from their shrouds, and words like stones thrust into their rattling mouths: we edit their writings, we rewrite their lives. Thomas More had spread the rumor that Little Bilney, chained to the stake, had recanted as the fire was set. It wasn't enough for him to take Bilney's life away; he had to take his death too.

Today, More was escorted to the scaffold by Humphrey Monmouth, serving his turn as Sheriff of London. Monmouth is too good a man to rejoice in the reversal of fortune. But perhaps we can rejoice for him?

More is at the block, he can see him now. He is wrapped in a rough gray cape that he remembers as belonging to his servant John Wood. He is speaking to the headsman, apparently making some quip to him, wiping the drizzle from his face and beard. He is shedding the cape, the hem of which is sodden with rainwater. He kneels at the block, his lips moving in his final prayer.

Like all the other witnesses, he swirls his own cloak about him and kneels. At the sickening sound of the ax on flesh he darts one glance upward. The corpse seems to have leapt back from the stroke and folded itself like a stack of old clothes—inside which, he knows, its pulses are still beating. He makes the sign of the cross. The past moves heavily inside him, a shifting of ground.

"So, the king," he says. "From Gloucester, he strikes out to Thornbury. Then Nicholas Poynz's house at Iron Acton: does Poynz know what he's letting himself in for? From there to Bromham . . ."

Just this last year a scholar, a foreigner, has written a chronicle of Britain, which omits King Arthur on the ground that he never existed. A good ground, if he can sustain it; but Gregory says, no, he is wrong. Because if he is right, what will happen to Avalon? What will happen to the sword in the stone?

He looks up. "Rafe, are you happy?"

"With Helen?" Rafe blushes. "Yes, sir. No man was ever happier."

"I knew your father would come round, once he had seen her."

"It is only thanks to you, sir."

From Bromham—we are now in early September—toward Winchester. Then Bishop's Waltham, Alton, Alton to Farnham. He plots it out, across country. The object is to get the king back to Windsor for early October. He has his sketch map across the page, England in a drizzle of ink; his calendar, quickly jotted, running down it. "I seem to have four, five days in hand. Ah well. Who says I never get a holiday?"

Before "Bromham," he makes a dot in the margin, and draws a long arrow across the page. "Now here, before we go to Winchester, we have time to spare, and what I think is, Rafe, we shall visit the Seymours."

He writes it down.

Early September. Five days. Wolf Hall.

AUTHOR'S NOTE

In parts of medieval Europe, the official new year began on March 25, Lady Day, which was believed to be the date when an angel announced to Mary that she was carrying the child Jesus. As early as 1522, Venice adopted January 1 as the start of the new year, and other European countries followed at intervals, though England did not catch up till 1752. In this book, as in most histories, the years are dated from January 1, which was celebrated as one of the twelve days of Christmas and was the day on which gifts were exchanged.

The gentleman usher George Cavendish, after the death of Wolsey, retired to the country, and in 1554, when Mary came to the throne, began a book, *Thomas Wolsey, Late Cardinal, His Life and Death*. It has been published in many editions, and can be found online in an edition with original spelling. It is not always accurate, but it is a very touching, immediate and readable account of Wolsey's career and Thomas Cromwell's part in it. Its influence on Shakespeare is clear. Cavendish took four years to complete his book, and died just as Elizabeth came to the throne.

ACKNOWLEDGMENTS

I should like to thank Delyth Neil for the Welsh, Leslie Wilson for the German, and a Norfolk lady for the Flemish. Guada Abale for lending me a song. Judith Flanders for helping me when I couldn't get to the British Library. Dr. Christopher Haigh for inviting me to a splendid dinner in Wolsey's hall at Christ Church. Jan Rogers for sharing a pilgrimage to Canterbury and a drink at the Cranmer Arms at Aslockton. Gerald McEwen for driving me around and putting up with my preoccupations. My agent, Bill Hamilton, and my publishers for their support and encouragement. Above all, Dr. Mary Robertson; her business as a scholar has been with the facts of Cromwell's life, but she has encouraged me and lent me her expertise through the production of this fiction, put up with my fumbling speculations and been kind enough to recognize the portrait I have produced. This book is dedicated to her, with my thanks and love.